GREAT SHORT STORIES BY GREAT AMERICAN WRITERS

Also by Thomas Fasano

Selected Early Poems by Robert Frost

The Dead

A Concise Guide to MLA Style and Documentation

GREAT SHORT STORIES BY GREAT AMERICAN WRITERS

Selected and Edited by
Thomas Fasano

Coyote Canyon Press
CLAREMONT, CALFORNIA

Coyote Canyon Press

GREAT SHORT STORIES BY GREAT AMERICAN WRITERS
Published in the United States of America
For information:
Email: info@coyotecanyonpress.com
Internet: www.coyotecanyonpress.com

FIRST COYOTE CANYON PRESS EDITION PUBLISHED 2011

Library of Congress Cataloging-in-Publication Data
Great short stories by great American writers / edited by Thomas Fasano.
p. cm.
ISBN 978-0-9821298-7-6 (pbk.)
1. Short stories, American. I. Fasano, Thomas, 1956- II. Title.

PS648.S5G75 2011
813'.0108--dc22

2010031207

A Note on the Making of this Book

The short story is to a remarkable degree an American creation. After its introduction to the New World in the early eighteenth century, the short story flourished as it had nowhere else. In England, then as now, it remained a subordinate form to the novel, which has dominated the English literary landscape for centuries. By the mid-nineteenth century in America, however, short fiction had become a major literary genre. The first important writers in the genre were Americans, and the critic who first formulated a theoretical framework for the short story, and who gained international recognition for his own short stories, was the American Edgar Allan Poe.

American writers have commanded respect and attention for their short stories for almost two centuries, or as long as the short story has been a recognizable literary genre. American stories are, in a very important sense, an examination of a diverse and complex culture, a record of ideas, trends, conflicts, politics, and social history, a powerful record of a nation.

This present collection attempts to give the reader a representative view of the ways in which the American short story evolved from the time of Washington Irving and William Austin to Sherwood Anderson and F. Scott Fitzgerald. The thirty stories that compose this book reflect the development of not only the American short story but also American literature and an undeniably American imagination. Such familiar stories as Nathaniel Hawthorne's "Rappaccini's Daughter," Bret Harte's "The Luck of Roaring Camp," Stephen Crane's "The Blue Hotel," and Jack London's "To Build a Fire" are included because each uniquely showcases its author's creative universe. On the other hand, I have chosen stories that are rarely anthologized today. Among them are Rebecca Harding Davis' "Marcia," Joel Chandler Harris' "Free Joe and the Rest of the World," Mary Wilkins Freeman's "The Revolt of 'Mother,'" and Charles W. Chesnutt's "The Wife of His Youth."

Like every collection of short stories, this book is wholly a reflection of one editor's likes and dislikes. Nonetheless, I strove to make this anthology a representation of the best short stories by American writers during the one hundred years of its rise as a major literary art form, with the hope of maintaining a balance between works familiar and unfamiliar.

Of course this anthology is not a complete offering but rather a sampling of the enormous wealth of the American short story. Because the aim of this collection is to give the reader a sense of the development of the American short story, I focused on authors whose work played the greatest role in shaping the genre. The stories I selected not only engaged me when I first read them years ago but retain a richness after several readings many years later.

THOMAS FASANO
DECEMBER 2010

CONTENTS

WASHINGTON IRVING (1783-1859) 1
Rip Van Winkle

WILLIAM AUSTIN (1778-1841) 14
Peter Rugg, the Missing Man

NATHANIEL HAWTHORNE (1804-1864) 36
Rappaccini's Daughter

EDGAR ALLAN POE (1809-1849) 56
The Fall of the House of Usher

HARRIET BEECHER STOWE (1811-1896) 70
The Ghost in the Mill

HERMAN MELVILLE (1819-1891) 79
Bartleby, The Scrivener: A Story of Wall Street

REBECCA HARDING DAVIS (1831-1910) 106
Marcia

MARK TWAIN (1835-1910) 112
The Man That Corrupted Hadleyburg

BRET HARTE (1836-1902) 147
The Luck of Roaring Camp

WILLIAM DEAN HOWELLS (1837-1920) 155
Editha

AMBROSE BIERCE (1842-1913?) 166
Chickamauga

HENRY JAMES (1843-1916) 171
The Middle Years

JOEL CHANDLER HARRIS (1845-1908) 186
Free Joe and the Rest of the World

SARAH ORNE JEWETT (1849-1909) 195
A White Heron

KATE CHOPIN (1851-1904) 203
Desirée's Baby

MARY ELEANOR WILKINS FREEMAN (1852-1930) 208
The Revolt of "Mother"

CHARLES W. CHESNUTT (1858-1932) 220
The Wife of His Youth

HAMLIN GARLAND (1860-1940) 229
Up the Coolly

CHARLOTTE PERKINS GILMAN (1860-1935) 259
The Yellow Wallpaper

EDITH WHARTON (1862-1937) 272
A Journey

O. HENRY (1862-1910) 280
The Trimmed Lamp

FRANK NORRIS (1870-1902) 289
A Deal in Wheat

THEODORE DREISER (1871-1945) 297
The Lost Phoebe

STEPHEN CRANE (1871-1900) 309
The Blue Hotel

PAUL LAURENCE DUNBAR (1872-1906) 330
The Lynching of Jube Benson

WILLA CATHER (1873-1947) 336
Paul's Case

JACK LONDON (1876-1916) 351
To Build a Fire

SHERWOOD ANDERSON (1876-1941) 363
I Want To Know Why

RING LARDNER (1885-1933) 370
The Golden Honeymoon

F. SCOTT FITZGERALD (1896-1940) 382
Winter Dreams

RIP VAN WINKLE

Washington Irving (1783-1859)

By Woden, God of Saxons,
From whence comes Wensday, that is Wodensday,
Truth is a thing that ever I will keep
Unto thylke day in which I creep into
My sepulchre——

CARTWRIGHT.

[The following Tale was found among the papers of the late Diedrich Knickerbocker, an old gentleman of New York, who was very curious in the Dutch history of the province, and the manners of the descendants from its primitive settlers. His historical researches, however, did not lie so much among books as among men; for the former are lamentably scanty on his favorite topics; whereas he found the old burghers, and still more their wives, rich in that legendary lore, so invaluable to true history. Whenever, therefore, he happened upon a genuine Dutch family, snugly shut up in its low-roofed farmhouse, under a spreading sycamore, he looked upon it as a little clasped volume of black-letter, and studied it with the zeal of a book-worm.

The result of all these researches was a history of the province during the reign of the Dutch governors, which he published some years since. There have been various opinions as to the literary character of his work, and, to tell the truth, it is not a whit better than it should be. Its chief merit is its scrupulous accuracy, which indeed was a little questioned on its first appearance, but has since been completely established; and it is now admitted into all historical collections, as a book of unquestionable authority.

The old gentleman died shortly after the publication of his work, and now that he is dead and gone, it cannot do much harm to his memory to say that his time might have been better employed in weightier labors. He, however, was apt to ride his hobby his own way; and though it did now and then kick up the dust a little in the eyes of his neighbors, and grieve the spirit of some friends, for whom he felt the truest deference and affection; yet his errors and follies are remembered "more in sorrow than in anger," and it begins to be suspected, that he never intended to injure or offend. But however his memory may be appreciated by critics, it is still held dear by many folks, whose good opinion is well worth having; particularly by certain biscuit-bakers, who have gone so far as to imprint his likeness on their new-year cakes; and have thus given him a chance for immortality, almost equal to the being stamped on a Waterloo Medal, or a Queen Anne's Farthing.]

WHOEVER has made a voyage up the Hudson must remember the Kaatskill mountains. They are a dismembered branch of the great Appalachian family, and are seen away to the west of the river, swelling up to a noble height, and lording it over the surrounding country. Every change of season, every change of weather, indeed, every hour of the day, produces some change in the magical hues and shapes of these mountains, and they are regarded by all the good wives, far and near, as perfect barometers. When the weather is fair and settled, they are clothed in blue and purple, and print their bold outlines on the clear evening sky, but, sometimes, when the rest of the landscape is cloudless, they will gather a hood of gray vapors about their summits, which, in the last rays of the setting sun, will glow and light up like a crown of glory.

At the foot of these fairy mountains, the voyager may have descried the light smoke curling up from a village, whose shingle-roofs gleam among the trees, just where the blue tints of the upland melt away into the fresh green of the nearer landscape. It is a little village of great antiquity, having been founded by some of the Dutch colonists, in the early times of the province, just about the beginning of the government of the good Peter Stuyvesant, (may he rest in peace!) and there were some of the houses of the original settlers standing within a few years, built of small yellow bricks brought from Holland, having latticed windows and gable fronts, surmounted with weather-cocks.

In that same village, and in one of these very houses (which, to tell the precise truth, was sadly time-worn and weather-beaten), there lived many years since, while the country was yet a province of Great Britain, a simple good-natured fellow of the name of Rip Van Winkle. He was a descendant of the Van Winkles who figured so gallantly in the chivalrous days of Peter Stuyvesant, and accompanied him to the siege of Fort Christina. He inherited, however, but little of the martial character of his ancestors. I have observed that he was a simple good-natured man; he was, moreover, a kind neighbor, and an obedient henpecked husband. Indeed, to the latter circumstance might be owing that meekness of spirit which gained him such universal popularity; for those men are most apt to be obsequious and conciliating abroad, who are under the discipline of shrews at home. Their tempers, doubtless, are rendered pliant and malleable in the fiery furnace of domestic tribulation; and a curtain lecture is worth all the sermons in the world for teaching the virtues of patience and long-suffering. A termagant wife may, therefore, in some respects, be considered a tolerable blessing; and if so, Rip Van Winkle was thrice blessed.

Certain it is, that he was a great favorite among all the good wives of the village, who, as usual, with the amiable sex, took his part in all family squabbles; and never failed, whenever they talked those matters over in their evening gossipings, to lay all the blame on Dame Van Winkle. The children of the village, too, would shout with joy whenever he approached. He assisted at their sports, made their playthings, taught them to fly kites and shoot marbles, and told them long stories of ghosts, witches, and Indians. Whenever he went dodging about the village, he was surrounded by a troop of them, hanging on his skirts, clambering on his back, and playing a thousand tricks on him with impunity; and not a dog would bark at him throughout the neighborhood.

The great error in Rip's composition was an insuperable aversion to all kinds of profitable labor. It could not be from the want of assiduity or perseverance; for he would sit on a wet rock, with a rod as long and heavy as a Tartar's lance, and fish all day without a murmur, even though he should not be encouraged by a single nibble. He would carry a fowling-piece on his shoulder for hours together, trudging through woods and swamps, and up hill and down dale, to shoot a few squirrels or wild pigeons. He would never refuse to assist a neighbor even in the roughest toil, and was a foremost man at all country frolics for husking Indian corn, or building stone-fences; the women of the village, too, used to employ him to run their errands, and to do such little odd jobs as their less obliging husbands would not do for them. In a word Rip was ready to attend to anybody's business but his own; but as to doing family duty, and keeping his farm in order, he found it impossible.

In fact, he declared it was of no use to work on his farm; it was the most pestilent little piece of ground in the whole country; every thing about it went wrong, and would go wrong, in spite of him. His fences were continually falling to pieces; his cow would either go astray, or get among the cabbages; weeds were sure to grow quicker in his fields than anywhere else; the rain always made a point of setting in just as he had some out-door work to do; so that though his patrimonial estate had dwindled away under his management, acre by acre, until there was little more left than a mere patch of Indian corn and potatoes, yet it was the worst conditioned farm in the neighborhood.

His children, too, were as ragged and wild as if they belonged to nobody. His son Rip, an urchin begotten in his own likeness, promised to inherit the habits, with the old clothes of his father. He was generally seen trooping like a colt at his mother's heels, equipped in a pair of his father's cast-off galligaskins, which he had much ado to hold up with one hand, as a fine lady does her train in bad weather

Rip Van Winkle, however, was one of those happy mortals, of foolish, well-oiled dispositions, who take the world easy, eat white bread or brown, whichever can be got with least thought or trouble, and would rather starve on a penny than work for a pound. If left to himself, he would have whistled life away in perfect contentment; but his wife kept continually dinning in his ears about his idleness, his carelessness, and the ruin he was bringing on his family. Morning, noon, and night, her tongue was incessantly going, and everything he said or did was sure to produce a torrent of household eloquence. Rip had but one way of replying to all lectures of the kind, and that, by frequent use, had grown into a habit. He shrugged his shoulders, shook his head, cast up his eyes, but said nothing. This, however, always provoked a fresh volley from his wife; so that he was fain to draw off his forces, and take to the outside of the house — the only side which, in truth, belongs to a hen-pecked husband.

Rip's sole domestic adherent was his dog Wolf, who was as much hen-pecked as his master; for Dame Van Winkle regarded them as companions in idleness, and even looked upon Wolf with an evil eye, as the cause of his master's going so often astray. True it is, in all points of spirit befitting an honorable dog, he was as courageous an animal as ever scoured the woods — but what courage can withstand the ever-during and all-besetting terrors of a woman's tongue? The moment Wolf entered the house his crest fell, his tail drooped to the ground, or curled between his legs, he sneaked about with a gallows air, casting many a sidelong glance at Dame Van Winkle, and at the least flourish of a broom-stick or ladle, he would fly to the door with yelping precipitation.

Times grew worse and worse with Rip Van Winkle as years of matrimony rolled on; a tart temper never mellows with age, and a sharp tongue is the only edged tool that grows keener with constant use. For a long while he used to console himself, when driven from home, by frequenting a kind of perpetual club of the sages, philosophers, and other idle personages of the village; which held its sessions on a bench before a small inn, designated by a rubicund portrait of His Majesty George the Third. Here they used to sit in the shade through a long lazy summer's day, talking listlessly over village gossip, or telling endless sleepy stories about nothing. But it would have been worth any statesman's money to have heard the profound discussions that sometimes took place, when by chance an old newspaper fell into their hands from some passing traveller. How solemnly they would listen to the contents, as drawled out by Derrick Van Bummel, the schoolmaster, a dapper learned little man, who was not to be daunted by the most gigantic word in the dictionary; and how sagely they would deliberate upon public events some months after they had taken place.

The opinions of this junto were completely controlled by Nicholas Vedder, a patriarch of the village, and landlord of the inn, at the door of which he took his seat from morning till night, just moving sufficiently to avoid the sun and keep in the shade of a large tree; so that the neighbors could tell the hour by his movements as accurately as by a sundial. It is true he was rarely heard to speak, but smoked his pipe incessantly. His adherents, however (for every great man has his adherents), perfectly understood him, and knew how to gather his opinions. When anything that was read or related displeased him, he was observed to smoke his pipe vehemently, and to send forth short, frequent and angry puffs; but when pleased, he would inhale the smoke slowly and tranquilly, and emit it in light and placid clouds;

and sometimes, taking the pipe from his mouth, and letting the fragrant vapor curl about his nose, would gravely nod his head in token of perfect approbation.

From even this stronghold the unlucky Rip was at length routed by his termagant wife, who would suddenly break in upon the tranquillity of the assemblage and call the members all to naught; nor was that august personage, Nicholas Vedder himself, sacred from the daring tongue of this terrible virago, who charged him outright with encouraging her husband in habits of idleness.

Poor Rip was at last reduced almost to despair; and his only alternative, to escape from the labor of the farm and clamor of his wife, was to take gun in hand and stroll away into the woods. Here he would sometimes seat himself at the foot of a tree, and share the contents of his wallet with Wolf, with whom he sympathized as a fellow-sufferer in persecution. "Poor Wolf," he would say, "thy mistress leads thee a dog's life of it; but never mind, my lad, whilst I live thou shalt never want a friend to stand by thee!" Wolf would wag his tail, look wistfuly in his master's face, and if dogs can feel pity I verily believe he reciprocated the sentiment with all his heart.

In a long ramble of the kind on a fine autumnal day, Rip had unconsciously scrambled to one of the highest parts of the Kaatskill mountains. He was after his favorite sport of squirrel shooting, and the still solitudes had echoed and re-echoed with the reports of his gun. Panting and fatigued, he threw himself, late in the afternoon, on a green knoll, covered with mountain herbage, that crowned the brow of a precipice. From an opening between the trees he could overlook all the lower country for many a mile of rich woodland. He saw at a distance the lordly Hudson, far, far below him, moving on its silent but majestic course, with the reflection of a purple cloud, or the sail of a lagging bark, here and there sleeping on its glassy bosom, and at last losing itself in the blue highlands.

On the other side he looked down into a deep mountain glen, wild, lonely, and shagged, the bottom filled with fragments from the impending cliffs, and scarcely lighted by the reflected rays of the setting sun. For some time Rip lay musing on this scene; evening was gradually advancing; the mountains began to throw their long blue shadows over the valleys; he saw that it would be dark long before he could reach the village, and he heaved a heavy sigh when he thought of encountering the terrors of Dame Van Winkle.

As he was about to descend, he heard a voice from a distance, hallooing, "Rip Van Winkle! Rip Van Winkle!" He looked round, but could see nothing but a crow winging its solitary flight across the mountain. He thought his fancy must have deceived him, and turned again to descend, when he heard the same cry ring through the still evening air: "Rip Van Winkle! Rip Van Winkle!" — at the same time Wolf bristled up his back, and giving a low growl, skulked to his master's side, looking fearfully down into the glen. Rip now felt a vague apprehension stealing over him; he looked anxiously in the same direction, and perceived a strange figure slowly toiling up the rocks, and bending under the weight of something he carried on his back. He was surprised to see any human being in this lonely and unfrequented place, but supposing it to be some one of the neighborhood in need of his assistance, he hastened down to yield it.

On nearer approach he was still more surprised at the singularity of the stranger's appearance. He was a short square-built old fellow, with thick bushy hair, and a grizzled beard. His dress was of the antique Dutch fashion — a cloth jerkin strapped round the waist — several pair of breeches, the outer one of ample volume, decorated with rows of buttons down the sides, and bunches at the knees. He bore on his shoulder a stout keg, that seemed full of liquor, and made signs for Rip to approach and assist him with the load. Though rather shy and distrustful of this new acquaintance, Rip complied with his usual alacrity; and mutually relieving one another, they clambered up a narrow gully, apparently the dry bed of a mountain torrent. As they ascended, Rip every now and then heard long rolling peals, like distant thunder, that seemed to issue out of a deep ravine, or rather cleft, between lofty rocks, toward which their rugged path conducted. He paused for an instant, but supposing it to be the muttering of one of those transient thunder-showers which often take place in mountain heights, he proceeded. Passing through the ravine, they came to a hollow, like a small amphitheatre, surrounded by perpendicular precipices, over the brinks of which impending trees shot their branches, so that you only caught glimpses of the azure sky and the bright evening cloud. During the whole time Rip and his companion had labored on in silence; for though the former marvelled greatly what could be the object of carrying a keg of liquor up this wild mountain, yet there was something strange and incomprehensible about the unknown, that inspired awe and checked familiarity.

On entering the amphitheatre, new objects of wonder presented themselves. On a level spot in the center was a company of odd-looking personages playing at nine-pins. They were dressed in a quaint outlandish fashion; some wore short doublets, others jerkins, with long knives in their belts, and most of them had enormous breeches, of similar style with that of the guide's. Their visages, too, were peculiar: one had a large beard, broad face, and small piggish eyes: the face of another seemed to consist entirely of nose, and was surmounted by a white sugar-loaf hat set off with a little red cock's tail. They all had beards, of various shapes and colors. There was one who seemed to be the commander. He was a stout old gentleman, with a weather-beaten countenance; he wore a laced doublet, broad belt and hanger, high-crowned hat and feather, red stockings, and high-heeled shoes, with roses in them. The whole group reminded Rip of the figures in an old Flemish painting, in the parlor of Dominie Van Shaick, the village parson, and which had been brought over from Holland at the time of the settlement.

What seemed particularly odd to Rip was, that though these folks were evidently amusing themselves, yet they maintained the gravest faces, the most mysterious silence, and were, withal, the most melancholy party of pleasure he had ever witnessed. Nothing interrupted the stillness of the scene but the noise of the balls, which, whenever they were rolled, echoed along the mountains like rumbling peals of thunder

As Rip and his companion approached them, they suddenly desisted from their play, and stared at him with such fixed statue-like gaze, and such strange, uncouth, lack-lustre countenances, that his heart turned within him, and his knees smote together. His companion now emptied the contents of the keg into large flagons, and made signs to him to wait upon the company. He obeyed with fear and trembling; they quaffed the liquor in profound silence, and then returned to their game.

By degrees Rip's awe and apprehension subsided. He even ventured, when no eye was fixed upon him, to taste the beverage, which he found had much of the flavor of excellent Hollands. He was naturally a thirsty soul, and was soon tempted to repeat the draught. One taste provoked another; and he reiterated his visits to the flagon so often that at length his senses were overpowered, his eyes swam in his head, his head gradually declined, and he fell into a deep sleep.

On waking, he found himself on the green knoll whence he had first seen the old man of the glen. He rubbed his eyes — it was a bright sunny morning. The birds were hopping and twittering among the bushes, and the eagle was wheeling aloft, and breasting the pure mountain breeze. "Surely," thought Rip, "I have not slept here all night." He recalled the occurrences before he fell asleep. The strange man with a keg of liquor — the mountain ravine — the wild retreat among the rocks — the woe-begone party at ninepins — the flagon — "Oh! that flagon! that wicked flagon!" thought Rip — "what excuse shall I make to Dame Van Winkle!"

He looked round for his gun, but in place of the clean well-oiled fowling-piece, he found an old firelock lying by him, the barrel incrusted with rust, the lock falling off, and the stock worm-eaten. He now suspected that the grave roysterers of the mountain had put a trick upon him, and having dosed him with liquor, had robbed him of his gun. Wolf, too, had disappeared, but he might have strayed away after a squirrel or partridge. He whistled after him and shouted his name, but all in vain; the echoes repeated his whistle and shout, but no dog was to be seen.

He determined to revisit the scene of the last evening's gambol, and if he met with any of the party, to demand his dog and gun. As he rose to walk, he found himself stiff in the joints, and wanting in his usual activity. "These mountain beds do not agree with me," thought Rip; "and if this frolic should lay me up with a fit of the rheumatism, I shall have a blessed time with Dame Van Winkle." With some difficulty he got down into the glen: he found the gully up which he and his companion had ascended the preceding evening; but to his astonishment a mountain stream was now foaming down it, leaping from rock to rock, and filling the glen with babbling murmurs. He, however, made shift to scramble up its sides, working his toilsome way through thickets of birch, sassafras, and witch-hazel, and sometimes tripped up or entangled by the wild grapevines that twisted their coils or tendrils from tree to tree, and spread a kind of network in his path.

At length he reached to where the ravine had opened through the cliffs to the amphitheatre; but no traces of such opening remained. The rocks presented a high impenetrable wall over which the torrent came tumbling in a sheet of feathery foam, and fell into a broad deep basin, black from the shadows of the surrounding forest. Here, then, poor Rip was brought to a stand. He again called and whistled after his dog; he was only answered by the cawing of a flock of idle crows, sporting high in air about a dry tree that overhung a sunny precipice; and who, secure in their elevation, seemed to look down and scoff at the poor man's perplexities. What was to be done? the morning was passing away, and Rip felt famished for want of his breakfast. He grieved to give up his dog and gun; he dreaded to meet his wife; but it would not do to starve among the mountains. He shook his head, shouldered the rusty firelock, and, with a heart full of trouble and anxiety, turned his steps homeward.

As he approached the village he met a number of people, but none whom he knew, which somewhat surprised him, for he had thought himself acquainted with every one in the country round. Their dress, too, was of a different fashion from that to which he was accustomed. They all stared at him with equal marks of surprise, and whenever they cast their eyes upon him, invariably stroked their chins. The constant recurrence of this gesture induced Rip, involuntarily, to do the same, when to his astonishment, he found his beard had grown a foot long!

He had now entered the skirts of the village. A troop of strange children ran at his heels, hooting after him, and pointing at his gray beard. The dogs, too, not one of which he recognized for an old acquaintance, barked at him as he passed. The very village was altered; it was larger and more populous. There were rows of houses which he had never seen before, and those which had been his familiar haunts had disappeared. Strange names were over the doors — strange faces at the windows — every thing was strange. His mind now misgave him; he began to doubt whether both he and the world around him were not bewitched. Surely this was his native village, which he had left but the day before. There stood the Kaatskill mountains — there ran the silver Hudson at a distance — there was every hill and dale precisely as it had always been — Rip was sorely perplexed — "That flagon last night," thought he, "has addled my poor head sadly!"

It was with some difficulty that he found the way to his own house, which he approached with silent awe, expecting every moment to hear the shrill voice of Dame Van Winkle. He found the house gone to decay — the roof fallen in, the windows shattered, and the doors off the hinges. A half-starved dog that looked like Wolf was skulking about it. Rip called him by name, but the cur snarled, showed his teeth, and passed on. This was an unkind cut indeed — "My very dog," sighed poor Rip, "has forgotten me!"

He entered the house, which, to tell the truth, Dame Van Winkle had always kept in neat order. It was empty, forlorn, and apparently abandoned. This desolateness overcame all his connubial fears — he called loudly for his wife and children — the lonely chambers rang for a moment with his voice, and then all again was silence.

He now hurried forth, and hastened to his old resort, the village inn — but it too was gone. A large rickety wooden building stood in its place, with great gaping windows, some of them broken and mended with old hats and petticoats, and over the door was painted, "the Union Hotel, by Jonathan Doolittle." Instead of the great tree that used to shelter the quiet little Dutch inn of yore, there now was reared a tall naked pole, with something on the top that looked like a red night-cap, and from it was fluttering a flag, on which was a singular assemblage of stars and stripes — all this was strange and incomprehensible. He recognized on the sign, however, the ruby face of King George, under which he had smoked so many a peaceful pipe; but even this was singularly metamorphosed. The red coat was changed for one of blue and buff, a sword was held in the hand instead of a sceptre, the head was decorated with a cocked hat, and underneath was painted in large characters, GENERAL WASHINGTON.

There was, as usual, a crowd of folk about the door, but none that Rip recollected. The very character of the people seemed changed. There was a busy, bustling, disputatious tone about it, instead of the accustomed phlegm and drowsy tranquillity. He looked in vain for the sage Nicholas Vedder, with his broad face, double chin, and fair long pipe, uttering clouds of tobacco-smoke instead of idle speeches; or Van Bummel, the schoolmaster, doling forth the contents of an ancient newspaper. In place of these, a lean, bilious-looking fellow, with his pockets full of handbills, was haranguing vehemently about rights of citizens — elections — members of congress — liberty — Bunker's Hill — heroes of seventy-six — and other words, which were a perfect Babylonish jargon to the bewildered Van Winkle.

The appearance of Rip, with his long grizzled beard, his rusty fowling-piece, his uncouth dress, and an army of women and children at his heels, soon attracted the attention of the tavern politicians. They crowded round him, eyeing him from head to foot with great curiosity. The orator bustled up to him, and, drawing him partly aside, inquired "on which side he voted?" Rip stared in vacant stupidity. Another short but busy little fellow pulled him by the arm, and, rising on tiptoe, inquired in his ear, "Whether he was Federal or Democrat?" Rip was equally at a loss to comprehend the question; when a knowing, self-important old gentleman, in a sharp cocked hat, made his way through the crowd, putting them to the right and left with his elbows as he passed, and planting himself before Van Winkle, with one arm akimbo, the other resting on his cane, his keen eyes and sharp hat penetrating, as it were, into his very soul, demanded in an austere tone, "what brought him to the election with a gun on his shoulder, and a mob at his heels, and whether he meant to breed a riot in the village?" — "Alas! gentlemen," cried Rip, somewhat dismayed, "I am a poor quiet man, a native of the place, and a loyal subject of the king, God bless him!"

Here a general shout burst from the by-standers — "A tory! a tory! a spy! a refugee! hustle him! away with him!" It was with great difficulty that the self-important man in the cocked hat restored order; and, having assumed a tenfold austerity of brow, demanded again of the unknown culprit, what he came there for, and whom he was seeking? The poor man humbly assured him that he meant no harm, but merely came there in search of some of his neighbors, who used to keep about the tavern.

"Well — who are they? — name them."

Rip bethought himself a moment, and inquired, "Where's Nicholas Vedder?"

There was a silence for a little while, when an old man replied, in a thin piping voice, "Nicholas Vedder! why, he is dead and gone these eighteen years! There was a wooden tombstone in the church-yard that used to tell all about him, but that's rotten and gone too."

"Where's Brom Dutcher?"

"Oh, he went off to the army in the beginning of the war; some say he was killed at the storming of Stony Point — others say he was drowned in a squall at the foot of Antony's Nose. I don't know — he never came back again."

"Where's Van Bummel, the schoolmaster?"

"He went off to the wars too, was a great militia general, and is now in congress."

Rip's heart died away at hearing of these sad changes in his home and friends, and finding himself thus alone in the world. Every answer puzzled him too, by treating of such enormous lapses of time, and of matters which he could not understand: war — congress — Stony Point; — he had no courage to ask after any more friends, but cried out in despair, "Does nobody here know Rip Van Winkle?"

"Oh, Rip Van Winkle!" exclaimed two or three, "Oh, to be sure! that's Rip Van Winkle yonder, leaning against the tree."

Rip looked, and beheld a precise counterpart of himself, as he went up the mountain: apparently as lazy, and certainly as ragged. The poor fellow was now completely confounded. He doubted his own identity, and whether he was himself or another man. In the midst of his bewilderment, the man in the cocked hat demanded who he was, and what was his name?

"God knows," exclaimed he, at his wit's end; "I'm not myself — I'm somebody else — that's me yonder — no — that's somebody else got into my shoes — I was myself last night, but I fell asleep on the mountain, and they've changed my gun, and every thing's changed, and I'm changed, and I can't tell what's my name, or who I am!"

The by-standers began now to look at each other, nod, wink significantly, and tap their fingers against their foreheads. There was a whisper also, about securing the gun, and keeping the old fellow from doing mischief, at the very suggestion of which the self-important man in the cocked hat retired with some precipitation. At this critical moment a fresh comely woman pressed through the throng to get a peep at the gray-bearded man. She had a chubby child in her arms, which, frightened at his looks, began to cry. "Hush, Rip," cried she, "hush, you little fool; the old man won't hurt you." The name of the child, the air of the mother, the tone of her voice, all awakened a train of recollections in his mind. "What is your name, my good woman?" asked he.

"Judith Gardenier."

"And your father's name?"

"Ah, poor man, Rip Van Winkle was his name, but it's twenty years since he went away from home with his gun, and never has been heard of since — his dog came home without him; but whether he shot himself, or was carried away by the Indians, nobody can tell. I was then but a little girl."

Rip had but one question more to ask; but he put it with a faltering voice:

"Where's your mother?"

"Oh, she too had died but a short time since; she broke a blood-vessel in a fit of passion at a New-England peddler."

There was a drop of comfort, at least, in this intelligence. The honest man could contain himself no longer. He caught his daughter and her child in his arms. "I am your father!" cried he — "Young Rip Van Winkle once — old Rip Van Winkle now! — Does nobody know poor Rip Van Winkle?"

All stood amazed, until an old woman, tottering out from among the crowd, put her hand to her brow, and peering under it in his face for a moment, exclaimed, "Sure enough! it is Rip Van Winkle — it is himself! Welcome home again, old neighbor — Why, where have you been these twenty long years?"

Rip's story was soon told, for the whole twenty years had been to him but as one night. The neighbors stared when they heard it; some were seen to wink at each other, and put their tongues in their cheeks: and the self-important man in the cocked hat, who, when the alarm was over, had returned to the field, screwed down the corners of his mouth, and shook his head — upon which there was a general shaking of the head throughout the assemblage.

It was determined, however, to take the opinion of old Peter Vanderdonk, who was seen slowly advancing up the road. He was a descendant of the historian of that name, who wrote one of the earliest accounts of the province. Peter was the most ancient inhabitant of the village, and well versed in all the wonderful events and traditions of the neighborhood. He recollected Rip at once, and corroborated his story in the most satisfactory manner. He assured the company that it was a fact, handed down from his ancestor the historian, that the Kaatskill mountains had always been haunted by strange beings. That it was affirmed that the great Hendrick Hudson, the first discoverer of the river and country, kept a kind of vigil there every twenty years, with his crew of the *Half-Moon*; being permitted in this way to revisit the scenes of his enterprise, and keep a guardian eye upon the river, and the great city called by his name. That his father had once seen them in their old Dutch dresses playing at nine-pins in a hollow of the mountain; and that he himself had heard, one summer afternoon, the sound of their balls, like distant peals of thunder.

To make a long story short, the company broke up, and returned to the more important concerns of the election. Rip's daughter took him home to live with her; she had a snug, well-furnished house, and a stout cheery farmer for a husband, whom Rip recollected for one of the urchins that used to climb upon his back. As to Rip's son and heir, who was the ditto of himself, seen leaning against the tree, he was employed to work on the farm; but evinced an hereditary disposition to attend to anything else but his business.

Rip now resumed his old walks and habits; he soon found many of his former cronies, though all rather the worse for the wear and tear of time; and preferred making friends among the rising generation, with whom he soon grew into great favor.

Having nothing to do at home, and being arrived at that happy age when a man can be idle with impunity, he took his place once more on the bench at the inn door, and was reverenced as one of the patriarchs of the village, and a chronicle of the old times "before the war." It was some time before he could get into the regular track of gossip, or could be made to comprehend the strange events that had taken place during his torpor. How that there had been a revolutionary war — that the country had thrown off the yoke of old England — and that, instead of being a subject of his Majesty George the Third, he was now a free citizen of the United States. Rip, in fact, was no politician; the changes of states and empires made but little impression on him; but there was one species of despotism under which he had long groaned, and that was — petticoat government. Happily that was at an end; he had got his neck out of the yoke of matrimony, and could go in and out whenever he pleased, without dreading the tyranny of Dame Van Winkle. Whenever her name was mentioned, however, he shook his head, shrugged his shoulders, and cast up his eyes; which might pass either for an expression of resignation to his fate, or joy at his deliverance.

He used to tell his story to every stranger that arrived at Mr. Doolittle's hotel. He was observed, at first, to vary on some points every time he told it, which was, doubtless, owing to his having so recently awaked. It at last settled down precisely to the tale I have related, and not a man, woman, or child in the neighborhood, but knew it by heart. Some always pretended to doubt the reality of it, and insisted that Rip had been out of his head, and that this was one point on which he always remained flighty. The old Dutch inhabitants, however, almost universally gave it full credit. Even to this day they never hear a thunderstorm of a summer afternoon about the Kaatskill, but they say Hendrick Hudson and his crew are at their game of nine-pins; and it is a common wish of all hen-pecked husbands in the neighborhood, when life hangs heavy on their hands, that they might have a quieting draught out of Rip Van Winkle's flagon.

NOTE. — The foregoing tale, one would suspect, had been suggested to Mr. Knickerbocker by a little German superstition about the Emperor Frederick *der Rothbart*, and the Kyffhaüser mountain: the subjoined note, however, which he had appended to the tale, shows that it is an absolute fact, narrated with his usual fidelity:

"The story of Rip Van Winkle may seem incredible to many, but nevertheless I give it my full belief, for I know the vicinity of our old Dutch settlements to have been very subject to marvellous events and appearances. Indeed, I have heard many stranger stories than this, in the villages along the Hudson; all of which were too well authenticated to admit of a doubt. I have even talked with Rip Van Winkle myself who, when last I saw him, was a very venerable old man, and so perfectly rational and consistent on every other point, that I think no conscientious person could refuse to take this into the bargain; nay, I have seen a certificate on the subject taken before a country justice and signed with a cross, in the justice's own handwriting. The story, therefore, is beyond the possibility of doubt.

"D.K."

POSTSCRIPT. — The following are travelling notes from a memorandum-book of Mr. Knickerbocker:

The Kaatsberg, or Catskill mountains, have always been a region full of fable. The Indians considered them the abode of spirits, who influenced the weather, spreading sunshine or clouds over the landscape, and sending good or bad hunting seasons. They were ruled by an old squaw spirit, said to be their mother. She dwelt on the highest peak of the Catskills, and had charge of the doors of day and night to open and shut them at the proper hour. She hung up the new moons in the skies, and cut up the old ones into stars. In times of drought, if properly propitiated, she would spin light summer clouds out of cobwebs and morning dew, and send them off from the crest of the mountain, flake after flake, like flakes of carded cotton, to float in the air; until, dissolved by the heat of the sun, they would fall in gentle showers, causing the grass to spring, the fruits to ripen, and the corn to grow an inch an hour. If displeased, however, she would brew up clouds black as ink, sitting in the midst of them like a bottle-bellied spider in the midst of its web; and when these clouds broke, woe betide the valleys!

In old times, say the Indian traditions, there was a kind of Manitou or Spirit, who kept about the wildest recesses of the Catskill Mountains, and took a mischievous pleasure in wreaking all kinds of evils and vexations upon the red men. Sometimes he would assume the form of a bear, a panther, or a deer, lead the bewildered hunter a weary chase through tangled forests and among ragged rocks; and then spring off with a loud ho! ho! leaving him aghast on the brink of a beetling precipice or raging torrent.

The favorite abode of this Manitou is still shown. It is a great rock or cliff on the loneliest part of the mountains, and, from the flowering vines which clamber about it, and the wild flowers which abound in its neighborhood, is known by the name of the Garden Rock. Near the foot of it is a small lake, the haunt of the solitary bittern, with water-snakes basking in the sun on the leaves of the pond-lilies which lie on the surface. This place was held in great awe by the Indians, insomuch that the boldest hunter would not pursue his game within its precincts. Once upon a time, however, a hunter who had lost his way, penetrated to the garden rock, where he beheld a number of gourds placed in the crotches of trees. One of these he seized and made off with it, but in the hurry of his retreat he let it fall among the rocks, when a great stream gushed forth, which washed him away and swept him down precipices, where he was dashed to pieces, and the stream made its way to the Hudson, and continues to flow to the present day; being the identical stream known by the name of the Kaaters-kill.

PETER RUGG, THE MISSING MAN

William Austin (1778-1841)

From Jonathan Dunwell of New York to Mr. Herman Krauff

Sir, — Agreeably to my promise, I now relate to you all the particulars of the lost man and child which I have been able to collect. It is entirely owing to the humane interest you seemed to take in the report, that I have pursued the inquiry to the following result.

You may remember that business called me to Boston in the summer of 1820. I sailed in the packet to Providence, and when I arrived there I learned that every seat in the stage was engaged. I was thus obliged either to wait a few hours or accept a seat with the driver, who civilly offered me that accommodation. Accordingly, I took my seat by his side, and soon found him intelligent and communicative. When we had travelled about ten miles, the horses suddenly threw their ears on their necks, as flat as a hare's. Said the driver, "Have you a surtout with you?"

"No," said I; "why do you ask?"

"You will want one soon," said he. "Do you observe the ears of all the horses?"

"Yes; and was just about to ask the reason."

"They see the storm-breeder, and we shall see him soon."

At this moment there was not a cloud visible in the firmament. Soon after, a small speck appeared in the road.

"There," said my companion, "comes the storm-breeder. He always leaves a Scotch mist behind him. By many a wet jacket do I remember him. I suppose the poor fellow suffers much himself — much more than is known to the world."

Presently a man with a child beside him, with a large black horse, and a weather-beaten chair, once built for a chaise-body, passed in great haste, apparently at the rate of twelve miles an hour. He seemed to grasp the reins of his horse with firmness, and appeared to anticipate his speed. He seemed dejected, and looked anxiously at the passengers particularly at the stage-driver and myself. In a moment after he passed us, the horses' ears were up, and bent themselves forward so that they nearly met.

"Who is that man?" said I. "He seems in great trouble."

"Nobody knows who he is, but his person and the child are familiar to me. I have met him more than a hundred times, and have been so often asked the way to Boston by that man, even when he was travelling directly from that town, that of late I have refused any communication with him; and that is the reason he gave me such a fixed look."

"But does he never stop anywhere?"

"I have never known him to stop anywhere longer than to inquire the way to Boston; and let him be where he may, he will tell you he cannot stay a moment, for he must reach Boston that night."

We were now ascending a high hill in Walpole; and as we had a fair view of the heavens, I was rather disposed to jeer the driver for thinking of his surtout, as not a cloud as big as a marble could be discerned.

"Do you look," said he, "in the direction whence the man came; that is the place to look. The storm never meets him; it follows him."

We presently approached another hill; and when at the height, the driver pointed out in an eastern direction a little black speck about as big as a hat. "There," said he, "is the seed-storm. We may possibly reach Polley's before it reaches us, but the wanderer and his child will go to Providence through rain, thunder, and lightning."

And now the horses, as though taught by instinct, hastened with increased speed. The little black cloud came on rolling over the turnpike, and doubled and trebled itself in all directions. The appearance of this cloud attracted the notice of all the passengers, for after it had spread itself to a great bulk it suddenly became more limited in circumference, grew more compact, dark, and consolidated. And now the successive flashes of chain lightning caused the whole cloud to appear like a sort of irregular network, and displayed a thousand fantastic images. The driver bespoke my attention to a remarkable configuration in the cloud. He said every flash of lightning near its center discovered to him, distinctly, the form of a man sitting in an open carriage drawn by a black horse. But in truth I saw no such thing; the man's fancy was doubtless at fault. It is a very common thing for the imagination to paint for the senses, both in the visible and invisible world.

In the meantime the distant thunder gave notice of a shower at hand; and just as we reached Polley's tavern the rain poured down in torrents. It was soon over, the cloud passing in the direction of the turnpike toward Providence. In a few moments after, a respectable-looking man in a chaise stopped at the door. The man and child in the chair having excited some little sympathy among the passengers, the gentleman was asked if he had observed them. He said he had met them; that the man seemed bewildered, and inquired the way to Boston; that he was driving at great speed, as though he expected to outstrip the tempest; that the moment he had passed him, a thunderclap broke directly over the man's head, and seemed to envelop both man and child, horse and carriage. "I stopped," said the gentleman, "supposing the lightning had struck him; but the horse only seemed to loom up and increase his speed; and as well as I could judge, he travelled just as fast as the thunder-cloud."

While this man was speaking, a pedlar with a cart of tin merchandise came up, all dripping; and on being questioned, he said he had met that man and carriage, within a fortnight, in four different states; that at each time he had inquired the way to Boston; and that a thunder-shower like the present had each time deluged his wagon and his wares, setting his tin pots, etc., afloat, so that he had determined to get a marine insurance for the future. But that which excited his surprise most was the strange conduct of his horse, for long before he could distinguish the man in the chair his own horse stood still in the road, and flung back his ears. "In short," said the Pedlar, "I wish never to see that man and horse again; they do not look to me as though they belonged to this world."

This was all I could learn at that time; and the occurrence soon after would have become with me "like one of those things which had never happened," had I not, as I stood recently on the door-step of Bennett's hotel in Hartford, heard a man say, "There goes Peter Rugg and his child! He looks wet and weary, and farther from Boston than ever." I was satisfied it was the same man I had seen more than three years before; for whoever has once seen Peter Rugg can never after be deceived as to his identity.

"Peter Rugg!" said I. "And who is Peter Rugg?"

"That," said the stranger, "is more than anyone can tell exactly. He is a famous traveller, held in light esteem by all innholders, for he never stops to eat, drink, or sleep. I wonder why the government does not employ him to carry the mail."

"Aye," said a bystander, "that is a thought bright only on one side; how long would it take in that case to send a letter to Boston? for Peter has already, to my knowledge, been more than twenty years travelling to that place."

"But," said I, "does the man never stop anywhere; does he never converse with anyone? I saw the same man more than three years since, near Providence, and I heard a strange story about him. Pray, sir, give me some account of this man."

"Sir," said the stranger, "those who know the most respecting that man say the least. I have heard it asserted that Heaven sometimes sets a mark on a man, either for judgment or a trial. Under which Peter Rugg now labours, I cannot say; therefore I am rather inclined to pity than to judge."

"You speak like a humane man," said I; "and if you have known him so long, I pray you will give me some account of him. Has his appearance much altered in that time?"

"Why, yes. He looks as though he never ate, drank, or slept; and his child looks older than himself, and he looks like time broken off from eternity, and anxious to gain a resting-place."

"And how does his horse look?" said I.

"As for his horse, he looks fatter and gayer, and shows more animation and courage than he did twenty years ago. The last time Rugg spoke to me he inquired how far it was to Boston. I told him just one hundred miles.

"'Why,' said he, 'how can you deceive me so? It is cruel to mislead a traveller. I have lost my way; pray direct me the nearest way to Boston.'

"I repeated, it was one hundred miles.

"'How can you say so?' said he. 'I was told last evening it was but fifty, and I have travelled all night.'

"'But,' said I, 'you are now travelling from Boston. You must turn back.'

"'Alas,' said he, 'it is all turn back! Boston shifts with the wind, and plays all around the compass. One man tells me it is to the east, another to the west; and the guide-posts too, they all point the wrong way.'

"'But will you not stop and rest?' said I. 'You seem wet and weary.'

"'Yes,' said he, 'it has been foul weather since I left home.'

"'Stop, then, and refresh yourself.'

"'I must not stop; I must reach home tonight, if possible: though I think you must be mistaken in the distance to Boston.'

"He then gave the reins to his horse, which he restrained with difficulty, and disappeared in a moment. A few days afterward I met the man a little this side of Claremont, winding around the hills in Unity, at the rate, I believe, of twelve miles an hour."

"Is Peter Rugg his real name, or has he accidentally gained that name?"

"I know not, but presume he will not deny his name; you can ask him — for see, he has turned his horse, and is passing this way."

In a moment a dark-coloured, high-spirited horse approached, and would have passed without stopping, but I had resolved to speak to Peter Rugg, or whoever the man might be. Accordingly I stepped into the street; and as the horse approached, I made a feint of stopping him. The man immediately reined in his horse. "Sir," said I, "may I be so bold as to inquire if you are not Mr. Rugg? For I think I have seen you before."

"My name is Peter Rugg," said he. "I have unfortunately lost my way; I am wet and weary, and will take it kindly of you to direct me to Boston."

"You live in Boston, do you; and in what street?"

"In Middle Street."

"When did you leave Boston?"

"I cannot tell precisely; it seems a considerable time."

"But how did you and your child become so wet? It has not rained, here today."

"It has just rained a heavy shower up the river. But I shall not reach Boston tonight if I tarry. Would you advise me to take the old road or the turnpike?"

"Why, the old road is one hundred and seventeen miles, and the turnpike is ninety-seven."

"How can you say so? You impose on me; it is wrong to trifle with a traveller; you know it is but forty miles from Newburyport to Boston."

"But this is not Newburyport; this is Hartford."

"Do not deceive me, sir. Is not this town Newburyport, and the river that I have been following the Merrimack?"

"No, sir; this is Hartford, and the river, the Connecticut."

He wrung his hands and looked incredulous. "Have the rivers, too, changed their courses, as the cities have changed places? But see! The clouds are gathering in the south, and we shall have a rainy night. Ah, that fatal oath!"

He would tarry no longer; his impatient horse leaped off, his hind flanks rising like wings; he seemed to devour all before him, and to scorn all behind.

I had now, as I thought, discovered a clue to the history of Peter Rugg; and I determined, the next time my business called me to Boston, to make a further inquiry. Soon after, I was enabled to collect the following particulars from Mrs. Croft, an aged lady in Middle Street, who has resided in Boston during the last twenty years. Her narration is this:

Just at twilight last summer a person stopped at the door of the late Mrs. Rugg. Mrs. Croft on coming to the door perceived a stranger, with a child by his side, in an old weather-beaten carriage, with a black horse. The stranger asked for Mrs. Rugg, and was informed that Mrs. Rugg had died at a good old age, more than twenty years before that time.

The stranger replied, "How can you deceive me so? Do ask Mrs. Rugg to step to the door."

"Sir, I assure you Mrs. Rugg has not lived here these twenty years; no one lives here but myself, and my name is Betsy Croft."

The stranger paused, looked up and down the street, and said, "Though the paint is rather faded, this looks like my house."

"Yes," said the child, "that is the stone before the door that I used to sit on to eat my bread-and-milk."

"But," said the stranger, "it seems to be on the wrong side of the street. Indeed, everything here seems to be misplaced. The streets are all changed, the people are all changed, the town seems changed, and what is strangest of all, Catherine Rugg has deserted her husband and child. Pray," continued the stranger, "has John Foy come home from sea? He went a long voyage; he is my kinsman. If I could see him, he could give me some account of Mrs. Rugg."

"Sir," said Mrs. Croft, "I never heard of John Foy. Where did he live?"

"Just above here, in Orange-tree Lane."

"There is no such place in this neighbourhood."

"What do you tell me! Are the streets gone? Orange-tree Lane is at the head of Hanover Street, near Pemberton's Hill."

"There is no such lane now."

"Madam, you cannot be serious! But you doubtless know my brother, William Rugg. He lives in Royal Exchange Lane, near King Street."

"I know of no such lane; and I am sure there is no such street as King Street in this town."

"No such street as King Street! Why, woman, you mock me! You may as well tell me there is no King George. However, madam, you see I am wet and weary, I must find a resting-place. I will go to Hart's tavern, near the market."

"Which market, sir? for you seem perplexed; we have several markets."

"You know there is but one market near the town dock."

"Oh, the old market; but no such person has kept there these twenty years."

Here the stranger seemed disconcerted, and uttered to himself quite audibly, "Strange mistake; how much this looks like the town of Boston! It certainly has a great resemblance to it; but I perceive my mistake now. Some other Mrs. Rugg, some other Middle Street. Then," said he, "madam, can you direct me to Boston?"

"Why, this is Boston, the city of Boston; I know of no other Boston."

"City of Boston it may be; but it is not the Boston where I live. I recollect now, I came over a bridge instead of a ferry. Pray, what bridge is that I just came over?"

"It is Charles River bridge."

"I perceive my mistake; there is a ferry between Boston and Charlestown; there is no bridge. Ah, I perceive my mistake. If I were in Boston my horse would carry me directly to my own door. But my horse shows by his impatience that he is in a strange place. Absurd, that I should have mistaken this place for the old town of Boston! It is a much finer city than the town of Boston. It has been built long since Boston. I fancy Boston must lie at a distance from this city, as the good woman seems ignorant of it."

At these words his horse began to chafe, and strike the pavement with his forefeet. The stranger seemed a little bewildered, and said, "No home tonight"; and giving the reins to his horse, passed up the street, and she saw no more of him.

It was evident that the generation to which Peter Rugg belonged had passed away.

This was all the account of Peter Rugg I could obtain from Mrs. Croft; but she directed me to an elderly man, Mr. James Felt, who lived near her, and who had kept a record of the principal occurrences for the last fifty years. At my request she sent for him; and after I had related to him the object of my inquiry, Mr. Felt told me he had known Rugg in his youth, and that his disappearance had caused some surprise; but as it sometimes happens that men run away — sometimes to be rid of others, and sometimes to be rid of themselves — and Rugg took his child with him, and his own horse and chair, and as it did not appear that any creditors made a stir, the occurrence soon mingled itself in the stream of oblivion; and Rugg and his child, horse, and chair were soon forgotten.

"It is true," said Mr. Felt, "sundry stories grew out of Rugg's affair, whether true or false I cannot tell; but stranger things have happened in my day, without even a newspaper notice."

"Sir," said I, "Peter Rugg is now living. I have lately seen Peter Rugg and his child, horse, and chair; therefore I pray you to relate to me all you know or ever heard of him."

"Why, my friend," said James Felt, "that Peter Rugg is now a living man, I will not deny; but that you have seen Peter Rugg and his child, is impossible, if you mean a small child; for Jenny Rugg, if living, must be at least — let me see — Boston massacre, 1770 — Jenny Rugg, was about ten years old. Why, sir, Jenny Rugg, if living, must be more than sixty years of age. That Peter Rugg is living, is highly probable, as he was only ten years older than myself, and I was only eighty last March; and I am as likely to live twenty years longer as any man."

Here I perceived that Mr. Felt was in his dotage, and I despaired of gaining any intelligence from him on which I could depend.

I took my leave of Mrs. Croft, and proceeded to my lodgings at the Marlborough Hotel.

"If Peter Rugg," thought I, "has been travelling since the Boston massacre, there is no reason why he should not travel to the end of time. If the present generation know little of him, the next will know less, and Peter and his child will have no hold on this world."

In the course of the evening, I related my adventure in Middle Street.

"Ha," said one of the company, smiling, "do you really think you have seen Peter Rugg? I have heard my grandfather speak of him, as though he seriously believed his own story."

"Sir," said I, "pray let us compare your grandfather's story of Mr. Rugg with my own."

"Peter Rugg, sir — if my grandfather was worthy of credit — once lived in Middle Street, in this city. He was a man in comfortable circumstances, had a wife and one daughter, and was generally esteemed for his sober life and manners. But unhappily, his temper, at times, was altogether ungovernable, and then his language was terrible. In these fits of passion, if a door stood in his way, he would never do less than kick a panel through. He would sometimes throw his heels over his head, and come down on his feet, uttering oaths in a circle; and thus in a rage, he was the first who performed a somersault, and did what others have since learned to do for merriment and money. Once Rugg was seen to bite a tenpenny nail in halves. In those days everybody, both men and boys, wore wigs; and Peter, at these moments of violent passion, would become so profane that his wig would rise up from his head. Some said it was on account of his terrible language; others accounted for it in a more philosophical way, and said it was caused by the expansion of his scalp, as violent passion, we know, will swell the veins and expand the head. While these fits were on him, Rugg had no respect for heaven or earth. Except this infirmity, all agreed that Rugg was a good sort of a man; for when his fits were over nobody was so ready to commend a placid temper as Peter.

"One morning, late in autumn, Rugg, in his own chair, with a fine large bay horse, took his daughter and proceeded to Concord. On his return a violent storm overtook him. At dark he stopped in Menotomy, now West Cambridge, at the door of a Mr. Cutter, a friend of his, who urged him to tarry the night. On Rugg's declining to stop, Mr. Cutter urged him vehemently. 'Why, Mr. Rugg,' said Cutter, 'the storm is overwhelming you. The night is exceedingly dark. Your little daughter will perish. You are in an open chair, and the tempest is increasing.'

'*Let the storm increase,*' said Rugg, with a fearful oath, '*I will see home tonight, in spite of the last tempest, or may I never see home!*' At these words he gave his whip to his high-spirited horse and disappeared in a moment. But Peter Rugg did not reach home that night, nor the next; nor, when he became a missing man, could he ever be traced beyond Mr. Cutter's, in Menotomy.

"For a long time after, on every dark and stormy night the wife of Peter Rugg would fancy she heard the crack of a whip, and the fleet tread of a horse, and the rattling of a carriage passing her door. The neighbours, too, heard the same noises, and some said they knew it was Rugg's horse; the tread on the pavement was perfectly familiar to them. This occurred so repeatedly that at length the neighbours watched lanterns, and saw the real Peter Rugg, with his own horse and chair and the child sitting beside him, pass directly before his own door, his head turned towards his house, and himself making every effort to stop his horse, but in vain.

"The next day the friends of Mrs. Rugg exerted themselves to find her husband and child. They inquired at every public-house and stable town; but it did not appear that Rugg made any stay in Boston. No one, after Rugg, had passed his own door, could give any account of him, though it was asserted by some that the clatter of Rugg's horse and carriage over the pavements shook the houses on both sides of the streets. And this is credible, if indeed Rugg's horse and carriage did pass on that night; for at this day, in many of the streets, a loaded truck or team in passing will shake the houses like an earthquake. However, Rugg's neighbours never afterward watched. Some of them treated it all as a delusion, and thought no more of it. Others of a different opinion shook their heads and said nothing.

"Thus Rugg and his child, horse, and chair were soon forgotten; and probably many in the neighbourhood never heard a word on the subject.

"There was indeed a rumour that Rugg was seen afterward in Connecticut, between Suffield and Hartford, passing through the country at headlong speed. This gave occasion to Rugg's friends to make further inquiry; but the more they inquired, the more they were baffled. If they heard of Rugg one day in Connecticut, the next they heard of him winding round the hills in New Hampshire; and soon after a man in a chair, with a small child, exactly answering the description of Peter Rugg, would be seen in Rhode Island inquiring the way to Boston.

"But that which chiefly gave a colour of mystery to the story of Peter Rugg was the affair at Charlestown bridge. The toll-gatherer asserted that sometimes, on the darkest and most stormy nights, when no object could be discerned, about the time Rugg was missing, a horse and wheel-carriage, with a noise equal to a troop, would at midnight, in utter contempt of the rates of toll, pass over the bridge. This occurred so frequently that the toll-gatherer resolved to attempt a discovery. Soon after, at the usual time, apparently the same horse and carriage approached the bridge from Charlestown Square. The toll-gatherer, prepared, took his stand as near the middle of the bridge as he dared, with a large three-legged stool in his hand; as the appearance passed, he threw the stool at the horse, but heard nothing except the noise of the stool skipping across the bridge. The toll-gatherer on the next day asserted that the stool went directly through the body of the horse, and he persisted in that belief ever after. Whether Rugg, or whoever the person was, ever passed the bridge again, the toll-gatherer would never tell; and when questioned, seemed anxious to waive the subject. And thus Peter Rugg and his child, horse, and carriage, remain a mystery to this day."

This, sir, is all that I could learn of Peter Rugg in Boston.

Further Account Of Peter Rugg
by Jonathan Dunwell

In the autumn of 1825 I attended the races at Richmond in Virginia. As two new horses of great promise were run, the race-ground was never better attended, nor was expectation ever more deeply excited. The partisans of Dart and Lightning, the two racehorses, were equally anxious and equally dubious of the result. To an indifferent spectator, it was impossible to perceive any difference. They were equally beautiful to behold, alike in colour and height, and as they stood side by side they measured from heel to forefeet within half an inch of each other. The eyes of each were full, prominent, and resolute; and when at times they regarded each other, they assumed a lofty demeanour, seemed to shorten their necks, project their eyes, and rest their bodies equally on their four hoofs. They certainly showed signs of intelligence, and displayed a courtesy to each other unusual even with statesmen.

It was now nearly twelve o'clock, the hour of expectation, doubt, and anxiety. The riders mounted their horses; and so trim, light, and airy they sat on the animals as to seem a part of them. The spectators, many deep in a solid column, had taken their places, and as many thousand breathing statues were there as spectators. All eyes were turned to Dart and Lightning and their two fairy riders. There was nothing to disturb this calm except a busy woodpecker on a neighbouring tree. The signal was given, and Dart and Lightning answered it with ready intelligence. At first they proceed at a slow trot, then they quicken to a canter, and then a gallop; presently they sweep the plain. Both horses lay themselves flat on the ground, their riders bending forward and resting their chins between their horses' ears. Had not the ground been perfectly level, had there been any undulation, the least rise and fall, the spectator would now and then have lost sight of both horses and riders.

While these horses, side by side, thus appeared, flying without wings, flat as a hare, and neither gaining on the other, all eyes were diverted to a new spectacle. Directly in the rear of Dart and Lightning, a majestic black horse of unusual size, drawing an old weather-beaten chair, strode over the plain; and although he appeared to make no effort, for he maintained a steady trot, before Dart and Lightning approached the goal the black horse and chair had overtaken the racers, who, on perceiving this new competitor pass them, threw back their ears, and suddenly stopped in their course. Thus neither Dart nor Lightning carried away the purse.

The spectators now were exceedingly curious to learn whence came the black horse and chair. With many it was the opinion that nobody was in the vehicle. Indeed, this began to be the prevalent opinion; for those at a short distance, so fleet was the black horse, could not easily discern who, if anybody, was in the carriage. But both the riders, very near to whom the black horse passed, agreed in this particular — that a sad-looking man and a little girl were in the chair. When they stated this I was satisfied that the man was Peter Rugg. But what caused no little surprise, John Spring, one of the riders (he who rode Lightning), asserted that no earthly horse without breaking his trot could, in a carriage, outstrip his racehorse, and he persisted, with some passion, that it was not a horse — or, he was sure it was not a horse, but a large black ox. "What a great black ox can do," said John, "I cannot pretend to say; but no racehorse, not even flying Childers, could out-trot Lightning in a fair race."

This opinion of John Spring excited no little merriment, for it was obvious to everyone that it was a powerful black horse that interrupted the race; but John Spring, jealous of Lightning's reputation as a horse, would rather have it thought that any other beast, even an ox, had been the victor. However, the "horse-laugh" at John Spring's expense was soon suppressed; for as soon as Dart and Lightning began to breathe more freely, it was observed that both of them walked deliberately to the track of the race-ground, and putting their heads to the earth, suddenly raised them again and began to snort. They repeated this till John Spring said, "These horses have discovered something strange; they suspect foul play. Let me go and talk with Lightning."

He went up to Lightning and took hold of his mane; and Lightning put his nose toward the ground and smelt of the earth without touching it, then reared his head very high, and snorted so loudly that the sound echoed from the next hill. Dart did the same. John Spring stooped down to examine the spot where Lightning had smelled. In a moment he raised himself up, and the countenance of the man was, changed. His strength failed him, and he sidled against Lightning.

At length John Spring recovered from his stupor, and exclaimed, "It was an ox! I told you it was an ox. No real horse ever yet beat Lightning."

And, now, on a close inspection of the black horse's tracks in the path, it was evident to everyone that the forefeet of the black horse were cloven. Notwithstanding these appearances, to me it was evident, that the strange horse was in reality a horse. Yet when the people left the race-ground, I presume one-half of all those present would have testified that a large black ox had distanced two of the fleetest coursers that ever trod the Virginia turf. So uncertain are all things called historical facts.

While I was proceeding to my lodgings, pondering on the events of the day, a stranger rode up to me, and accosted me thus, "I think your name is Dunwell, sir."

"Yes, sir," I replied.

"Did I not see you a year or two since in Boston, at the Marlborough Hotel?"

"Very likely, sir, for I was there."

"And you heard a story about one Peter Rugg?"

"I recollect it all," said I.

"The account you heard in Boston must be true, for here he was to-day. The man has found his way to Virginia, and for aught that appears, has been to Cape Horn. I have seen him before today, but never saw him travel with such fearful velocity. Pray, sir, where does Peter Rugg spend his winters, for I have seen him only in summer, and always in foul weather except this time?"

I replied, "No one knows where Peter Rugg spends his winters; where or when he eats, drinks, sleeps, or lodges. He seems to have an indistinct idea of day and night, time and space, storm and sunshine. His only object is Boston. It appears to me that Rugg's horse has some control of the chair; and that Rugg himself is, in some sort, under the control of his horse."

I then inquired of the stranger where he first saw the man and horse.

"Why, sir," said he, "in the summer of 1824, I travelled to the North for my health; and soon after I saw you at the Marlborough Hotel I returned homeward to Virginia, and, if my memory is correct, I saw this man and horse in every state between here and Massachusetts. Sometimes he would meet me, but oftener overtake me. He never spoke but once, and that once was in Delaware. On his approach he checked his horse with some difficulty. A more beautiful horse I never saw; his hide was as fair and rotund and glossy as the skin of a Congo beauty. When Rugg's horse approached mine he reined in his neck, bent his ears forward until they met, and looked my horse full in the face. My horse immediately withered into half a horse, his hide curling up like a piece of burnt leather; spellbound, he was fixed to the earth as though a nail had been driven through each hoof.

" 'Sir,' said Rugg, 'perhaps you are travelling to Boston; and if so, I should be happy to accompany you, for I have lost my way, and I must reach home tonight. See how sleepy this little girl looks; poor thing, she is a picture of patience.'

" 'Sir,' said I, 'it is impossible for you to reach home tonight, for you are in Concord, in the county of Sussex, in the state of Delaware.'

" 'What do you mean,' said he, 'by state of Delaware? If I were in Concord, that is only twenty miles from Boston, and my horse Lightfoot could carry me to Charlestown ferry in less than two hours. You mistake, sir; you are a stranger here; this town is nothing like Concord. I am well acquainted with Concord. I went to Concord when I left Boston.'

" 'But,' said I, 'you are in Concord, in the state of Delaware.'

" 'What do you mean by state?' said Rugg.

" 'Why, one of the United States.'

" 'States!' said he, in a low voice; 'the man is a wag, and would persuade me I am in Holland.' Then, raising his voice, he said, 'You seem, sir, to be a gentleman, and I entreat you to mislead me not; tell me, quickly, for pity's sake, the right road to Boston, for you see my horse will swallow his bits; he has eaten nothing since I left Concord.'

" 'Sir,' said I, 'this town is Concord — Concord in Delaware, not Concord in Massachusetts; and you are now five hundred miles from Boston.'

"Rugg looked at me for a moment, more in sorrow than resentment, and then repeated, 'Five hundred miles! Unhappy man, who would have thought him deranged; but nothing in this world is so deceitful as appearances. Five hundred miles! This beats Connecticut River.'

"What he meant by Connecticut River, I know not; his horse broke away, and Rugg disappeared in a moment."

I explained to the stranger the meaning of Rugg's expression, "Connecticut River," and the incident respecting him that occurred at Hartford, as I stood on the door-stone of Mr. Bennett's excellent hotel. We both agreed that the man we had seen that day was the true Peter Rugg.

Soon after, I saw Rugg again, at the toll-gate on the turnpike between Alexandria and Middleburgh. While I was paying the toll, I observed to the toll-gatherer that the drought was more severe in his vicinity than farther south.

"Yes," said he, "the drought is excessive; but if I had not heard yesterday, by a traveller, that the man with the black horse was seen in Kentucky a day or two since, I should be sure of a shower in a few minutes."

I looked all around the horizon, and could not discern a cloud that could hold a pint of water.

"Look, sir," said the toll-gatherer, "you perceive to the eastward, just above that hill, a small black cloud not bigger than a blackberry, and while I am speaking it is doubling and trebling itself, and rolling up the turn steadily, as if its sole design was to deluge some object."

"True," said I, "I do perceive it; but what connexion is there between a thunder-cloud and a man and horse?"

"More than you imagine, or I can tell you; but stop a moment, sir, I may need your assistance. I know that cloud; I have seen it several times before, and can testify to its identity. You will soon see a man and black horse under it."

While he was speaking, true enough, we began to hear the distant thunder, and soon the chain lightning performed all the figures of a country-dance. About a mile distant we saw the man and black horse under the cloud; but before he arrived at the toll-gate, the thunder-cloud had spent itself, and not even a sprinkle fell near us.

As the man, whom I instantly knew to be Rugg, attempted to pass, the toll-gatherer swung the gate across the road, seized Rugg's horse by the reins, and demanded two dollars.

Feeling some little regard for Rugg, I interfered, and began to question the toll-gatherer, and requested him not to be wroth with the man. The toll-gatherer replied that he had just cause, for the man had run his toll ten times, and moreover that the horse had discharged a cannon-ball at him, to the great danger of his life; that the man had always before approached so rapidly that he was too quick for the rusty hinges of the toll-gate; "but now I will have full satisfaction."

Rugg looked wistfully at me, and said, "I entreat you, sir, to delay me not; I have found at length the direct road to Boston, and shall not reach home before night if you detain me. You see I am dripping wet, and ought to change my clothes."

The toll-gatherer then demanded why he had run his toll so many times.

"Toll! Why," said Rugg, "do you demand toll? There is no toll to pay on the king's highway."

"King's highway! Do you not perceive this is a turnpike?"

"Turnpike! There are no turnpikes in Massachusetts."

"That may be, but we have several in Virginia."

"Virginia! Do you pretend I am in Virginia?"

Rugg then, appealing to me, asked how far it was to Boston.

Said I, "Mr. Rugg, I perceive you are bewildered, and am sorry to see you so far from home; you are, indeed, in Virginia."

"You know me, then, sir, it seems; and you say I am in Virginia. Give me leave to tell you, sir, you are the most impudent man alive; for I was never forty miles from Boston, and I never saw a Virginian in my life. This beats Delaware!"

"Your toll, sir, your toll!"

"I will not pay you a penny," said Rugg; "you are both of you highway robbers. There are no turnpikes in this country. Take toll on the king's highway! Robbers take toll on the king's highway!" Then in a low tone he said, "Here is evidently a conspiracy against me; alas, I shall never see Boston! The highways refuse me a passage, the rivers change their courses, and there is no faith in the compass."

But Rugg's horse had no idea of stopping more than one minute; for in the midst of this altercation, the horse, whose nose was resting on the upper bar of the turnpike-gate, seized it between his teeth, lifted it gently off its staples, and trotted off with it. The toll-gatherer, confounded, strained his eyes after his gate.

"Let him go," said I, "the horse will soon drop your gate, and you will get it again."

I then questioned the toll-gatherer respecting his knowledge of this man; and he related the following particulars:

"The first time," said he, "that man ever passed this toll-gate was in the year 1806, at the moment of the great eclipse. I thought the horse was frightened at the sudden darkness, and concluded he had run away with the man. But within a few days after, the same man and horse repassed with equal speed, without the least respect to the tollgate or to me, except by a vacant stare. Some few years afterward, during the late war, I saw the same man approaching again, and I resolved to check his career. Accordingly I stepped into the middle of the road, and stretched wide both my arms, and cried, 'Stop, sir, on your peril!' At this the man said, 'Now, Lightfoot, confound the robber!' At the same time he gave the whip liberally to the flank of his horse, which bounded off with such force that it appeared to me two such horses, give them a place to stand, would overcome any check man could devise. An ammunition wagon which had just passed on to Baltimore had dropped an eighteen-pounder in the road; this unlucky ball lay in the way of the horse's heels, and the beast, with the sagacity of a demon, clinched it with of his heels and hurled it behind him. I feel dizzy in relating the fact, but so nearly did the ball pass my head, that the wind thereof blew off my hat; and the ball embedded itself in that gate-post, as you may see if you will cast your eye on the post. I have permitted it to remain there in memory of the occurrence — as the people of Boston, I am told, preserve the eighteen-pounder which is now to be seen half embedded in Brattle Street church."

I then took leave of the toll-gatherer, and promised him if I saw or heard of his gate I would send him notice.

A strong inclination had possessed me to arrest Rugg and search his pockets, thinking great discoveries might be made in the examination; but what I saw and heard that day convinced me that no human force could detain Peter Rugg against his consent. I therefore determined if I ever saw Rugg again to treat him in the gentlest manner.

In pursuing my way to New York, I entered on the turnpike in Trenton; and when I arrived at New Brunswick, I perceived the road was newly macadamized. The small stones had just been laid thereon. As I passed this piece of road, I observed that, at regular distances of about eight feet, the stones were entirely displaced from spots as large as the circumference of a half-bushel measure. This singular appearance induced me to inquire the cause of it at the turnpike-gate.

"Sir," said the toll-gatherer, "I wonder not at the question, but, I am unable to give you a satisfactory answer. Indeed, sir, I believe I am bewitched, and that the turnpike is under a spell of enchantment; for what appeared to me last night cannot be a real transaction, otherwise a turnpike is a useless thing."

"I do not believe in witchcraft or enchantment," said I; "and if you will relate circumstantially what happened last night, I will endeavour to account for it by natural means."

"You may recollect the night was uncommonly dark. Well, sir, just after I had closed the gate for the night, down the turnpike, as far as my eye could reach, I beheld what at first appeared to be two armies engaged. The report of the musketry, and the flashes of their firelocks, were incessant and continuous. As this strange spectacle approached me with the fury of a tornado, the noise increased; and the appearance rolled on in one compact body over the surface of the ground. The most splendid fireworks rose out of the earth and encircled this moving spectacle. The divers tints of the rainbow, the most brilliant dyes that the sun lays in the lap of spring, added to the whole family of gems, could not display a more beautiful, radiant, and dazzling spectacle than accompanied the black horse. You would have thought all the stars of heaven had met in merriment on the turnpike. In the midst of this luminous configuration sat a man, distinctly to be seen, in a miserable-looking chair, drawn by a black horse. The turnpike-gate ought, by the laws of nature and the laws of the state, to have made a wreck of the whole, and have dissolved the enchantment; but no, the horse without an effort passed over the gate, and drew the man and chair horizontally after him without touching the bar. This was what I call enchantment. What think you, sir?"

"My friend," said I, "you have grossly magnified a natural occurrence. The man was Peter Rugg, on his way to Boston. It is true, his horse travelled with unequalled speed, but as he reared high his forefeet, he could not help displacing the thousand small stones on which he trod, which flying in all directions struck one another, and resounded and scintillated. The top bar of your gate is not more than two feet from the ground, and Rugg's horse at every vault could easily lift the carriage over that gate."

This satisfied Mr. McDoubt, and I was pleased at that occurrence; for otherwise Mr. McDoubt, who is a worthy man, late from the Highlands, might have added to his calendar of superstitions. Having thus disenchanted the macadamized road and the turnpike-gate, and also Mr. McDoubt, I pursued my journey homeward to New York.

Little did I expect to see or hear anything further of Mr. Rugg, for he was now more than twelve hours in advance of me. I could hear nothing of him on my way to Elizabethtown, and therefore concluded that during the past night he had turned off from the turnpike and pursued a westerly direction; but just before I arrived at Powles's Hook, I observed a considerable collection of passengers in the ferry-boat, all standing motionless, and steadily looking at the same object. One of the ferry-men, Mr. Hardy, who knew me well, observing my approach delayed a minute, in order to afford me a passage, and coming up, said, "Mr. Dunwell, we have a curiosity on board that would puzzle Dr. Mitchell."

"Some strange fish, I suppose, has found its way into the Hudson?"

"No," said he, "it is a man who looks as if he had lain hidden in the ark, and had just now ventured out. He has a little girl with him, the counterpart of himself, and the finest horse you ever saw, harnessed to the queerest carriage that ever was made."

"Ah, Mr. Hardy," said I, "you have, indeed, hooked a prize; no one before you could ever detain Peter Rugg long enough to examine him."

"Do you know the man?" said Mr. Hardy.

"No, nobody knows him, but everybody has seen him. Detain him as long as possible; delay the boat under any pretence, cut the gear of the horse, do anything to detain him."

As I entered the ferry-boat, I was struck at the spectacle before me. There, indeed, sat Peter Rugg and Jenny Rugg in the chair, and there stood the black horse, all as quiet as lambs, surrounded by more than fifty men and women, who seemed to have lost all their senses but one. Not a motion, not a breath, not a rustle. They were all eye. Rugg appeared to them to be a man not of this world; and they appeared to Rugg a strange generation of men. Rugg spoke not, and they spoke, not; nor was I disposed to disturb the calm, satisfied to reconnoitre Rugg in a state of rest. Presently, Rugg observed in a low voice, addressed to nobody, "A new contrivance, horses instead of oars; Boston folks are full of notions."

It was plain that Rugg was of Dutch extraction. He had on three pairs of small clothes, called in former days of simplicity breeches, not much the worse for wear; but time had proved the fabric, and shrunk one more than another, so that they showed at the knees their different qualities and colours. His several waistcoats, the flaps of which rested on his knees, made him appear rather corpulent. His capacious drab, coat would supply the stuff for half a dozen modern ones; the sleeves were like meal bags, in the cuffs of which you might nurse a child to sleep. His hat, probably once black, now of a tan colour, was neither round nor crooked, but in shape much like the one President Monroe, wore on his late tour. This dress gave the rotund face of Rugg an antiquated dignity. The man, though deeply sunburned, did not appear to be more than thirty years of age. He had lost his sad and anxious look, was quite composed, and seemed happy. The chair in which Rugg sat was very capacious, evidently made for service, and calculated to last for ages; the timber would supply material for three modern carriages. This chair, like a Nantucket coach, would answer for everything that ever went on wheels. The horse, too, was an object of curiosity; his majestic height, his natural mane and tail, gave him a commanding appearance, and his large open nostrils indicated inexhaustible wind. It was apparent that the hoofs of his forefeet had been split, probably on some newly macadamized road, and were now growing together, again; so that John Spring was not altogether in the wrong.

How long this dumb scene would otherwise have continued I cannot tell. Rugg discovered no sign of impatience. But Rugg's horse having been quiet more than five minutes, had no idea of standing idle; he began to whinny, and in a moment after, with his right forefoot he started a plank. Said Rugg, "My horse is impatient, he sees the North End. You must be quick, or he will be ungovernable."

At these words, the horse raised his left forefoot; and when he laid it down every inch of the ferry-boat trembled. Two men immediately seized Rugg's horse by the nostrils. The horse nodded, and both of them were in the Hudson. While we were fishing up the men, the horse was perfectly quiet.

"Fret not the horse," said Rugg, "and he will do no harm. He is only anxious, like myself, to arrive at yonder beautiful shore; he sees the North Church, and smells his own stable."

"Sir," said I to Rugg, practising a little deception, "pray tell me, for I am a stranger here, what river is this, and what city is that opposite, for you seem to be an inhabitant of it?"

"This river sir is called Mystic River, and this is Winnisimmet ferry — we have retained the Indian names — and that town is Boston. You must, indeed, be a stranger in these parts, not to know that yonder is Boston, the capital of the New England provinces."

"Pray, sir, how long have you been absent from Boston?"

"Why, that I cannot exactly tell. I lately went with this little girl of mine to Concord, to see my friends; and I am ashamed to tell you, in returning lost the way, and have been travelling ever since. No one would direct me right. It is cruel to mislead a traveller. My horse, Lightfoot, has boxed the compass; and it seems to me he has boxed it back again. But, sir, you perceive my horse is uneasy; Lightfoot, as yet, has only given a hint and a nod. I cannot be answerable for his heels."

At these words Lightfoot reared his long tail, and snapped it as you would a whiplash. The Hudson reverberated with the sound. Instantly the six horses began to move the boat. The Hudson was a sea of glass, smooth as oil, not a ripple. The horses, from a smart trot, soon passed to a gallop; water now ran over the gunwale; the ferry-boat was soon buried in an ocean of foam, and the noise of the spray was like the roaring of many waters. When we arrived at New York, you might see the beautiful white wake of the ferry-boat across the Hudson.

Though Rugg refused to pay toll at turnpikes, when Mr. Hardy reached his hand for the ferriage, Rugg readily put his hand into one of his many pockets, took out a piece of silver, and handed it to Hardy.

"What is this?" said Mr. Hardy.

"It is thirty shillings," said Rugg.

"It might once have been thirty shillings, old tenor," said Mr. Hardy, "but it is not at present."

"The money is good English coin," said Rugg; "my grandfather brought a bag of them from England, and had them hot from the mint."

Hearing this, I approached near to Rugg, and asked permission see the coin. It was a half-crown, coined by the English Parliament dated in the year 1649. On one side, "The Commonwealth of England," and St. George's cross encircled with a wreath of laurel wreath. On the other, "God with us," and a harp and St. George's cross united. I winked at Mr. Hardy, and pronounced it good current money; and said loudly, "I will not permit the gentleman to be imposed on, for I will exchange the money myself."

On this, Rugg spoke. "Please to give me your name, sir."

"My name, is Dunwell, sir," I replied.

"Mr. Dunwell," said Rugg, "you are the only honest man I have seen since I left Boston. As you are a stranger here, my house is your home; Dame Rugg will be happy to see her husband's friend. Step into my chair, sir, there is room enough; move a little, Jenny, for the gentleman, and we will be in Middle Street in a minute."

Accordingly I took a seat by Peter Rugg.

"Were you never in Boston before?" said Rugg.

"No," said I.

"Well, you will now see the queen of New England, a town second only to Philadelphia, in all North America."

"You forget New York," said I.

"Poh, New York is nothing; though I never was there. I am told you might put all New York in our mill-pond. No, sir, New York, I assure you, is but a sorry affair; no more to be compared with Boston than a wigwam with a palace."

As Rugg's horse turned into Pearl Street, I looked Rugg as fully in the face as good manners would allow, and said, "Sir, if this is Boston, I acknowledge New York is not worthy to be one of its suburbs."

Before we had proceeded far in Pearl Street, Rugg's countenance changed: his nerves began to twitch; his eyes trembled in their sockets; he was evidently bewildered. "What is the matter, Mr. Rugg? You seem disturbed."

"This surpasses all human comprehension; if you know, sir, where we are, I beseech you to tell me."

"If this place," I replied, "is not Boston, it must be New York."

"No, sir, it is not Boston; nor can it be New York. How could I be in New York, which is nearly two hundred miles from Boston?"

By this time we had passed into Broadway, and then Rugg, in truth, discovered a chaotic mind. "There is no such place as this in North America. This is all the effect of enchantment; this is a grand delusion, nothing real. Here is seemingly a great city, magnificent houses, shops and goods, men and women innumerable, and as busy as in real life, all sprung up in one night from the wilderness; or what is more probable, some tremendous convulsion of nature has thrown London or Amsterdam on the shores of New England. Or, possibly, I may be dreaming, though the night seems rather long; but before now I have sailed in one night to Amsterdam, bought goods of Vandogger, and returned to Boston before morning."

At this moment a hue and cry was heard: "Stop the madmen, they will endanger the lives of thousands!" In vain hundreds attempted to stop Rugg's horse. Lightfoot interfered with nothing; his course was straight as a shooting-star. But on my part, fearful that before night I should find myself behind the Alleghenies, I addressed Mr. Rugg in a tone of entreaty, and requested him to restrain the horse and permit me to alight.

"My friend," said he, "we shall be in Boston before dark, and Dame Rugg will be most exceedingly glad to see us."

"Mr. Rugg," said I, "you must excuse me. Pray look to the west; see that thunder-cloud swelling with rage, as if in pursuit of us."

"Ah!" said Rugg, "it is in vain to attempt to escape. I know that cloud; it is collecting new wrath to spend on my head." Then checking his horse, he permitted me to descend, saying, "Farewell, Mr. Dunwell, I shall be happy to see you in Boston; I live in Middle Street."

It is uncertain in what direction Mr. Rugg pursued his course, after he disappeared in Broadway; but one thing is sufficiently known to everybody — that in the course of two months after he was seen in New York, he found his way most opportunely to Boston.

It seems the estate of Peter Rugg had recently fallen to the Commonwealth of Massachusetts for want of heirs; and the Legislature had ordered the solicitor-general to advertise and sell it at public auction. Happening to be in Boston at the time, and observing his advertisement, which described a considerable extent of land, I felt a kindly curiosity to see the spot where Rugg once lived. Taking the advertisement in my hand, I wandered a little way down Middle Street, and without asking a question of anyone, when I came to a certain spot I said to myself, "This is Rugg's estate; I will proceed no farther. This must be the spot; it is a counterpart of Peter Rugg." The premises, indeed, looked as if they had fulfilled a sad prophecy. Fronting on Middle Street, they extended in the rear to Ann Street, and embraced about half an acre of land. It was not uncommon in former times to have half an acre for a house-lot; for an acre of land then, in many parts of Boston, was not more valuable than a foot in some places at present. The old mansion-house had become a powder-post, and been blown away. One other building, uninhabited, stood ominous, courting dilapidation. The street had been so much raised that the bedchamber had descended to the kitchen and was level with the street. The house seemed conscious of its fate; and as though tired of standing there, the front was fast retreating from the rear, and waiting the next south wind to project itself into the street. If the most wary animals had sought a place of refuge, here they would have rendezvoused. Here, under the ridge-pole, the crow would have perched in security; and in the recesses below, you might have caught the fox and the weasel asleep. "The hand of destiny," said I, "has pressed heavy on this spot; still heavier on the former owners. Strange that so large a lot of land as this should want an heir! Yet Peter Rugg, at this day, might pass by his own door-stone, and ask, 'Who once lived here?'"

The auctioneer, appointed by the solicitor to sell this estate, was a man of eloquence, as many of the auctioneers of Boston are. The occasion seemed to warrant, and his duty urged, him to make a display. He addressed his audience as follows:

"The estate, gentlemen, which we offer you this day, was once the property of a family now extinct. For that reason it has escheated to the Commonwealth. Lest any one of you should be deterred from bidding on so large an estate as this for fear of a disputed title, I am authorized by the solicitor-general to proclaim that the purchaser shall have the best of all titles — a warranty — deed from the Commonwealth. I state this, gentlemen, because I know there is an idle rumour in this vicinity that one Peter Rugg, the original owner of this estate, is still living. This rumour, gentlemen, has no foundation, and can have no foundation in the nature of things. It originated about two years since, from the incredible story of one Jonathan Dunwell, of New York. Mrs. Croft, indeed, whose husband I see present, and whose mouth waters for this estate, has countenanced this fiction. But, gentlemen, was it ever known that any estate, especially an estate of this value, lay unclaimed for nearly half a century, if any heir, ever so remote, were existing? For, gentlemen, all agree that old Peter Rugg, if living, would be at least one hundred years of age. It is said that he and his daughter, with a horse and chaise, were missed more than half a century ago; and because they never returned home, forsooth, they must be now living, and will some day come and claim this great estate. Such logic, gentlemen, never led to a good investment. Let not this idle story cross the noble purpose of consigning these ruins to the genius of architecture. If such a contingency could check the spirit of enterprise, farewell to all mercantile excitement. Your surplus money, instead of refreshing your sleep with the golden dreams of new sources of speculation, would turn to the nightmare. A man's money, if not employed, serves only to disturb his rest. Look, then, to the prospect before you. Here is half an acre of land — more than twenty thousand square feet — a corner lot, with wonderful capabilities; none of your contracted lots of forty feet by fifty, where, in dog-days, you can breathe only through your scuttles. On the contrary, an architect cannot contemplate this lot of land without rapture, for here is room enough for his genius to shame the temple of Solomon. Then the prospect — how commanding! To the cast, so near to the Atlantic that Neptune, freighted with the select treasures of the whole earth, can knock at your door with his trident. From the west, the produce of the river of Paradise — the Connecticut — will soon, by the blessings of steam, railways, and canals, pass under your windows; and thus, on this spot, Neptune shall marry Ceres, and Pomona from Roxbury, and Flora from Cambridge, shall dance at the wedding.

"Gentlemen of science, men of taste, ye of the literary emporium — for I perceive many of you present — to you this is holy ground. If the spot on which in times past a hero left only the print of a footstep is now sacred, of what price is the birthplace of one who all the world knows was born in Middle Street, directly opposite to this lot; and who, if his birthplace were not well known, would now be claimed by more than seven cities! To you, then, the value of these premises must be inestimable. For ere long there will arise in full view of the edifice to be erected here, a monument, the wonder and veneration of the world. A column shall spring to the clouds; and on that column will be engraven one word which will convey all that is wise in intellect, useful in science, good in morals, prudent in counsel, and benevolent in principle — a name of one who, when living, was the patron of the poor, the delight of the cottage, and the admiration of kings; now dead, worth the whole seven wise men of Greece. Need I tell you his name? He fixed the thunder and guided the lightning.

"Men of the North End! Need I appeal to your patriotism, in order to enhance the value of this lot? The earth affords no such scenery as this; there, around that corner, lived James Otis; here, Samuel Adams; there, Joseph Warren; and around that other corner, Josiah Quincy. Here was the birthplace of Freedom; here Liberty was born, and nursed, and grew to manhood. Here man was newly created. Here is the nursery of American Independence — I am too modest — here began the emancipation of the world; a thousand generations hence, millions of men will cross the Atlantic just to look at the North End of Boston. Your fathers — what do I say! — yourselves — yes, this moment, I behold several attending this auction who lent a hand to rock the cradle of Indpendence.

"Men of speculation — ye who are deaf to everything except the sound of money — you, I know, will give me both of your ears when I tell you the city of Boston must have a piece of this estate in order to widen Ann Street. Do you hear me — do you all hear me? I say the city must have a large piece of this land in order to widen Ann Street. What a chance! The city scorns to take a man's land for nothing. If it seizes your property, it is generous beyond the dreams of avarice. The only oppression is, you are in danger of being smothered under a load of wealth. Witness the old lady who lately died of a broken heart when the mayor paid her for a piece of her kitchen-garden. All the faculty agreed that the sight of the treasure, which the mayor incautiously paid her in dazzling dollars, warm from the mint, sped joyfully all the blood of her body into her heart, and rent it with raptures. Therefore, let him who purchases this estate fear his good fortune, and not Peter Rugg. Bid, then, liberally, and do not let the name of Rugg damp your ardour. How much will you give per foot for this estate?"

Thus spoke the auctioneer, and gracefully waved his ivory hammer. From fifty to seventy-five cents per foot were offered in a few moments. The bidding laboured from seventy-five to ninety. At length one dollar was offered. The auctioneer seemed satisfied; and looking at his watch, said he would knock off the estate in five minutes, if no one offered more.

There was a deep silence during this short period. While the hammer was suspended, a strange rumbling noise was heard, which arrested the attention of everyone. Presently, it was like the sound of many shipwrights driving home the bolts of a seventy-four. As the sound approached nearer, some exclaimed, "The buildings in the new market are falling in promiscuous ruins." Others said, "No, it is an earthquake; we perceive the earth tremble." Others said, "Not so; the sound proceeds from Hanover Street, and approaches nearer"; and this proved true, for presently Peter Rugg was in the midst of us.

"Alas, Jenny," said Peter, "I am ruined; our house has been burned, and here are all our neighbours around the ruins. Heaven grant your mother, Dame Rugg, is safe."

"They don't look like our neighbours," said Jenny; "but sure enough our house is burned, and nothing left but the door-stone and an old cedar post. Do ask where mother is."

In the meantime more than a thousand men had surrounded Rugg and his horse and chair. Yet neither Rugg personally, nor his horse and carriage, attracted more attention than the auctioneer. The look and searching eyes of Rugg carried more conviction to everyone present that the estate was his than could any parchment or paper with signature and seal. The impression which the auctioneer had just made on the company was effaced in a moment; and although the latter words of the auctioneer were, "Fear not Peter Rugg," the moment the auctioneer met the eye of Rugg his occupation was gone; his arm fell down to his hips, his late lively hammer hung heavy in his hand, and the auction was forgotten. The black horse, too, gave his evidence. He knew his journey was ended; for he stretched himself into a horse and a half, rested his head over the cedar post, and whinnied thrice, causing his harness to tremble from headstall to crupper.

Rugg then stood upright in his chair, and asked with some authority, "Who has demolished my house in my absence, for I see no signs of a conflagration? I demand by what accident this has happened, and wherefore this collection of strange people has assembled before my door-step. I thought I knew every man in Boston, but you appear to me a new generation of men. Yet I am familiar with many of the countenances here present, and I can call some of you by name; but in truth I do not recollect that before this moment I ever saw any one of you. There, I am certain, is a Winslow, and here a Sargent; there stands a Sewall, and next to him a Dudley. Will none of you speak to me — or is this all a delusion? I see, indeed, many forms of men, and no want of eyes, but of motion, speech, and hearing, you seem to be destitute. Strange! Will no one inform me who has demolished my house?"

Then spake a voice from the crowd, but whence it came I could not discern. "There is nothing strange here but yourself, Mr. Rugg. Time, which destroys and renews all things, has dilapidated your house, and placed us here. You have suffered many years under an illusion. The tempest which you profanely defied at Menotomy has at length subsided; but you will never see home, for your house and wife and neighbours have all disappeared. Your estate, indeed, remains, but no home. You were cut off from the last age, and you can never be fitted to the present. Your home is gone, and you can never have another home in this world."

RAPPACCINI'S DAUGHTER

Nathaniel Hawthorne (1804-1864)

A Young Man, named Giovanni Guasconti, came, very long ago, from the more southern region of Italy, to pursue his studies at the University of Padua. Giovanni, who had but a scanty supply of gold ducats in his pocket, took lodgings in a high and gloomy chamber of an old edifice, which looked not unworthy to have been the palace of a Paduan noble, and which, in fact, exhibited over its entrance the armorial bearings of a family long since extinct. The young stranger, who was not unstudied in the great poem of his country, recollected that one of the ancestors of this family, and perhaps an occupant of this very mansion, had been pictured by Dante as a partaker of the immortal agonies of his Inferno. These reminiscences and associations, together with the tendency to heart-break natural to a young man for the first time out of his native sphere, caused Giovanni to sigh heavily, as he looked around the desolate and ill-furnished apartment.

"Holy Virgin, signor," cried old dame Lisabetta, who, won by the youth's remarkable beauty of person, was kindly endeavoring to give the chamber a habitable air, "what a sigh was that to come out of a young man's heart! Do you find this old mansion gloomy? For the love of heaven, then, put your head out of the window, and you will see as bright sunshine as you have left in Naples."

Guasconti mechanically did as the old woman advised, but could not quite agree with her that the Lombard sunshine was as cheerful as that of southern Italy. Such as it was, however, it fell upon a garden beneath the window, and expended its fostering influences on a variety of plants, which seemed to have been cultivated with exceeding care.

"Does this garden belong to the house?" asked Giovanni.

"Heaven forbid, signor! — unless it were fruitful of better pot-herbs than any that grow there now," answered old Lisabetta. "No; that garden is cultivated by the own hands of Signor Giacomo Rappaccini, the famous Doctor, who, I warrant him, has been heard of as far as Naples. It is said he distils these plants into medicines that are as potent as a charm. Oftentimes you may see the Signor Doctor at work, and perchance the Signora his daughter, too, gathering the strange flowers that grow in the garden."

The old woman had now done what she could for the aspect of the chamber, and, commending the young man to the protection of the saints, took her departure.

Giovanni still found no better occupation than to look down into the garden beneath his window. From its appearance, he judged it to be one of those botanic gardens, which were of earlier date in Padua than elsewhere in Italy, or in the world. Or, not improbably, it might once have been the pleasure-place of an opulent family; for there was the ruin of a marble fountain in the center, sculptured with rare art, but so wofully shattered that it was impossible to trace the original design from the chaos of remaining fragments. The water, however, continued to gush and sparkle into the sunbeams as cheerfully as ever. A little gurgling sound ascended to the young man's window, and made him feel as if a fountain were an immortal spirit, that sung its song unceasingly, and without heeding the vicissitudes around it; while one century embodied it in marble, and another scattered the perishable garniture on the soil. All about the pool into which the water subsided, grew various plants, that seemed to require a plentiful supply of moisture for the nourishment of gigantic leaves, and, in some instances, flowers gorgeously magnificent. There was one shrub in particular, set in a marble vase in the midst of the pool, that bore a profusion of purple blossoms, each of which had the lustre and richness of a gem; and the whole together made a show so resplendent that it seemed enough to illuminate the garden, even had there been no sunshine. Every portion of the soil was peopled with plants and herbs, which, if less beautiful, still bore tokens of assiduous care; as if all had their individual virtues, known to the scientific mind that fostered them. Some were placed in urns, rich with old carving, and others in common garden-pots; some crept serpent-like along the ground, or climbed on high, using whatever means of ascent was offered them. One plant had wreathed itself round a statue of Vertumnus, which was thus quite veiled and shrouded in a drapery of hanging foliage, so happily arranged that it might have served a sculptor for a study.

While Giovanni stood at the window, he heard a rustling behind a screen of leaves, and became aware that a person was at work in the garden. His figure soon emerged into view, and showed itself to be that of no common laborer, but a tall, emaciated, sallow, and sickly looking man, dressed in a scholar's garb of black. He was beyond the middle term of life, with gray hair, a thin gray beard, and a face singularly marked with intellect and cultivation, but which could never, even in his more youthful days, have expressed much warmth of heart.

Nothing could exceed the intentness with which this scientific gardener examined every shrub which grew in his path; it seemed as if he was looking into their inmost nature, making observations in regard to their creative essence, and discovering why one leaf grew in this shape, and another in that, and wherefore such and such flowers differed among themselves in hue and perfume. Nevertheless, in spite of the deep intelligence on his part, there was no approach to intimacy between himself and these vegetable existences. On the contrary, he avoided their actual touch, or the direct inhaling of their odors, with a caution that impressed Giovanni most disagreeably; for the man's demeanor was that of one walking among malignant influences, such as savage beasts, or deadly snakes, or evil spirits, which, should he allow them one moment of license, would wreak upon him some terrible fatality. It was strangely frightful to the young man's imagination, to see this air of insecurity in a person cultivating a garden, that most simple and innocent of human toils, and which had been alike the joy and labor of the unfallen parents of the race. Was this garden, then, the Eden of the present world? — and this man, with such a perception of harm in what his own hands caused to grow, was he the Adam?

The distrustful gardener, while plucking away the dead leaves or pruning the too luxuriant growth of the shrubs, defended his hands with a pair of thick gloves. Nor were these his only armor. When, in his walk through the garden, he came to the magnificent plant that hung its purple gems beside the marble fountain, he placed a kind of mask over his mouth and nostrils, as if all this beauty did but conceal a deadlier malice. But finding his task still too dangerous, he drew back, removed the mask, and called loudly, but in the infirm voice of a person affected with inward disease:

"Beatrice! — Beatrice!"

"Here am I, my father! What would you?" cried a rich and youthful voice from the window of the opposite house; a voice as rich as a tropical sunset, and which made Giovanni, though he knew not why, think of deep hues of purple or crimson, and of perfumes heavily delectable. — "Are you in the garden?"

"Yes, Beatrice," answered the gardener, "and I need your help."

Soon there emerged from under a sculptured portal the figure of a young girl, arrayed with as much richness of taste as the most splendid of the flowers, beautiful as the day, and with a bloom so deep and vivid that one shade more would have been too much. She looked redundant with life, health, and energy; all of which attributes were bound down and compressed, as it were, and girdled tensely, in their luxuriance, by her virgin zone. Yet Giovanni's fancy must have grown morbid, while he looked down into the garden; for the impression which the fair stranger made upon him was as if here were another flower, the human sister of those vegetable ones, as beautiful as they — more beautiful than the richest of them — but still to be touched only with a glove, nor to be approached without a mask. As Beatrice came down the garden-path, it was observable that she handled and inhaled the odor of several of the plants, which her father had most sedulously avoided.

"Here, Beatrice," said the latter, — "see how many needful offices require to be done to our chief treasure. Yet, shattered as I am, my life might pay the penalty of approaching it so closely as circumstances demand. Henceforth, I fear, this plant must be consigned to your sole charge."

"And gladly will I undertake it," cried again the rich tones of the young lady, as she bent towards the magnificent plant, and opened her arms as if to embrace it. "Yes, my sister, my splendor, it shall be Beatrice's task to nurse and serve thee; and thou shalt reward her with thy kisses and perfume breath, which to her is as the breath of life!"

Then, with all the tenderness in her manner that was so strikingly expressed in her words, she busied herself with such attentions as the plant seemed to require; and Giovanni, at his lofty window, rubbed his eyes, and almost doubted whether it were a girl tending her favorite flower, or one sister performing the duties of affection to another. The scene soon terminated. Whether Doctor Rappaccini had finished his labors in the garden, or that his watchful eye had caught the stranger's face, he now took his daughter's arm and retired. Night was already closing in; oppressive exhalations seemed to proceed from the plants, and steal upward past the open window; and Giovanni, closing the lattice, went to his couch, and dreamed of a rich flower and beautiful girl. Flower and maiden were different and yet the same, and fraught with some strange peril in either shape.

But there is an influence in the light of morning that tends to rectify whatever errors of fancy, or even of judgment, we may have incurred during the sun's decline, or among the shadows of the night, or in the less wholesome glow of moonshine. Giovanni's first movement on starting from sleep, was to throw open the window, and gaze down into the garden which his dreams had made so fertile of mysteries. He was surprised, and a little ashamed, to find how real and matter-of-fact an affair it proved to be, in the first rays of the sun, which gilded the dew-drops that hung upon leaf and blossom, and, while giving a brighter beauty to each rare flower, brought everything within the limits of ordinary experience. The young man rejoiced, that, in the heart of the barren city, he had the privilege of overlooking this spot of lovely and luxuriant vegetation. It would serve, he said to himself, as a symbolic language, to keep him in communion with Nature. Neither the sickly and thought-worn Doctor Giacomo Rappaccini, it is true, nor his brilliant daughter, were now visible; so that Giovanni could not determine how much of the singularity which he attributed to both, was due to their own qualities, and how much to his wonder-working fancy. But he was inclined to take a most rational view of the whole matter.

In the course of the day, he paid his respects to Signor Pietro Baglioni, Professor of Medicine in the University, a physician of eminent repute, to whom Giovanni had brought a letter of introduction. The Professor was an elderly personage, apparently of genial nature, and habits that might almost be called jovial; he kept the young man to dinner, and made himself very agreeable by the freedom and liveliness of his conversation, especially when warmed by a flask or two of Tuscan wine. Giovanni, conceiving that men of science, inhabitants of the same city, must needs be on familiar terms with one another, took an opportunity to mention the name of Doctor Rappaccini. But the Professor did not respond with so much cordiality as he had anticipated.

"Ill would it become a teacher of the divine art of medicine," said Professor Pietro Baglioni, in answer to a question of Giovanni, "to withhold due and well-considered praise of a physician so eminently skilled as Rappaccini. But, on the other hand, I should answer it but scantily to my conscience, were I to permit a worthy youth like yourself, Signor Giovanni, the son of an ancient friend, to imbibe erroneous ideas respecting a man who might hereafter chance to hold your life and death in his hands. The truth is, our worshipful Doctor Rappaccini has as much science as any member of the faculty — with perhaps one single exception — in Padua, or all Italy. But there are certain grave objections to his professional character."

"And what are they?" asked the young man.

"Has my friend Giovanni any disease of body or heart, that he is so inquisitive about physicians?" said the Professor, with a smile. "But as for Rappaccini, it is said of him — and I, who know the man well, can answer for its truth — that he cares infinitely more for science than for mankind. His patients are interesting to him only as subjects for some new experiment. He would sacrifice human life, his own among the rest, or whatever else was dearest to him, for the sake of adding so much as a grain of mustard-seed to the great heap of his accumulated knowledge."

"Methinks he is an awful man, indeed," remarked Guasconti, mentally recalling the cold and purely intellectual aspect of Rappaccini. "And yet, worshipful Professor, is it not a noble spirit? Are there many men capable of so spiritual a love of science?"

"God forbid," answered the Professor, somewhat testily — "at least, unless they take sounder views of the healing art than those adopted by Rappaccini. It is his theory, that all medicinal virtues are comprised within those substances which we term vegetable poisons. These he cultivates with his own hands, and is said even to have produced new varieties of poison, more horribly deleterious than Nature, without the assistance of this learned person, would ever have plagued the world withal. That the Signor Doctor does less mischief than might be expected, with such dangerous substances, is undeniable. Now and then, it must be owned, he has effected — or seemed to effect — a marvellous cure. But, to tell you my private mind, Signor Giovanni, he should receive little credit for such instances of success — they being probably the work of chance — but should be held strictly accountable for his failures, which may justly be considered his own work."

The youth might have taken Baglioni's opinions with many grains of allowance, had he known that there was a professional warfare of long continuance between him and Doctor Rappaccini, in which the latter was generally thought to have gained the advantage. If the reader be inclined to judge for himself, we refer him to certain black-letter tracts on both sides, preserved in the medical department of the University of Padua.

"I know not, most learned Professor," returned Giovanni, after musing on what had been said of Rappaccini's exclusive zeal for science — "I know not how dearly this physician may love his art; but surely there is one object more dear to him. He has a daughter."

"Aha!" cried the Professor with a laugh. "So now our friend Giovanni's secret is out. You have heard of this daughter, whom all the young men in Padua are wild about, though not half a dozen have ever had the good hap to see her face. I know little of the Signora Beatrice, save that Rappaccini is said to have instructed her deeply in his science, and that, young and beautiful as fame reports her, she is already qualified to fill a professor's chair. Perchance her father destines her for mine! Other absurd rumors there be, not worth talking about, or listening to. So now, Signor Giovanni, drink off your glass of Lacryma."

Guasconti returned to his lodgings somewhat heated with the wine he had quaffed, and which caused his brain to swim with strange fantasies in reference to Doctor Rappaccini and the beautiful Beatrice. On his way, happening to pass by a florist's, he bought a fresh bouquet of flowers.

Ascending to his chamber, he seated himself near the window, but within the shadow thrown by the depth of the wall, so that he could look down into the garden with little risk of being discovered. All beneath his eye was a solitude. The strange plants were basking in the sunshine, and now and then nodding gently to one another, as if in acknowledgment of sympathy and kindred. In the midst, by the shattered fountain, grew the magnificent shrub, with its purple gems clustering all over it; they glowed in the air, and gleamed back again out of the depths of the pool, which thus seemed to overflow with colored radiance from the rich reflection that was steeped in it. At first, as we have said, the garden was a solitude. Soon, however, — as Giovanni had half hoped, half feared, would be the case, — a figure appeared beneath the antique sculptured portal, and came down between the rows of plants, inhaling their various perfumes, as if she were one of those beings of old classic fable, that lived upon sweet odors. On again beholding Beatrice, the young man was even startled to perceive how much her beauty exceeded his recollection of it; so brilliant, so vivid in its character, that she glowed amid the sunlight, and, as Giovanni whispered to himself, positively illuminated the more shadowy intervals of the garden path. Her face being now more revealed than on the former occasion, he was struck by its expression of simplicity and sweetness; qualities that had not entered into his idea of her character, and which made him ask anew, what manner of mortal she might be. Nor did he fail again to observe, or imagine, an analogy between the beautiful girl and the gorgeous shrub that hung its gem-like flowers over the fountain; a resemblance which Beatrice seemed to have indulged a fantastic humor in heightening, both by the arrangement of her dress and the selection of its hues.

Approaching the shrub, she threw open her arms, as with a passionate ardor, and drew its branches into an intimate embrace; so intimate, that her features were hidden in its leafy bosom, and her glistening ringlets all intermingled with the flowers.

"Give me thy breath, my sister," exclaimed Beatrice; "for I am faint with common air! And give me this flower of thine, which I separate with gentlest fingers from the stem, and place it close beside my heart."

With these words, the beautiful daughter of Rappaccini plucked one of the richest blossoms of the shrub, and was about to fasten it in her bosom. But now, unless Giovanni's draughts of wine had bewildered his senses, a singular incident occurred. A small orange colored reptile, of the lizard or chameleon species, chanced to be creeping along the path, just at the feet of Beatrice. It appeared to Giovanni — but, at the distance from which he gazed, he could scarcely have seen anything so minute — it appeared to him, however, that a drop or two of moisture from the broken stem of the flower descended upon the lizard's head. For an instant, the reptile contorted itself violently, and then lay motionless in the sunshine. Beatrice observed this remarkable phenomenon, and crossed herself, sadly, but without surprise; nor did she therefore hesitate to arrange the fatal flower in her bosom. There it blushed, and almost glimmered with the dazzling effect of a precious stone, adding to her dress and aspect the one appropriate charm, which nothing else in the world could have supplied. But Giovanni, out of the shadow of his window, bent forward and shrank back, and murmured and trembled.

"Am I awake? Have I my senses?" said he to himself. "What is this being? — beautiful, shall I call her? — or inexpressibly terrible?"

Beatrice now strayed carelessly through the garden, approaching closer beneath Giovanni's window, so that he was compelled to thrust his head quite out of its concealment, in order to gratify the intense and painful curiosity which she excited. At this moment, there came a beautiful insect over the garden wall; it had perhaps wandered through the city and found no flowers nor verdure among those antique haunts of men, until the heavy perfumes of Doctor Rappaccini's shrubs had lured it from afar. Without alighting on the flowers, this winged brightness seemed to be attracted by Beatrice, and lingered in the air and fluttered about her head. Now here it could not be but that Giovanni Guasconti's eyes deceived him. Be that as it might, he fancied that while Beatrice was gazing at the insect with childish delight, it grew faint and fell at her feet; — its bright wings shivered; it was dead — from no cause that he could discern, unless it were the atmosphere of her breath. Again Beatrice crossed herself and sighed heavily, as she bent over the dead insect.

An impulsive movement of Giovanni drew her eyes to the window. There she beheld the beautiful head of the young man — rather a Grecian than an Italian head, with fair, regular features, and a glistening of gold among his ringlets — gazing down upon her like a being that hovered in mid-air. Scarcely knowing what he did, Giovanni threw down the bouquet which he had hitherto held in his hand.

"Signora," said he, "there are pure and healthful flowers. Wear them for the sake of Giovanni Guasconti!"

"Thanks, Signor," replied Beatrice, with her rich voice that came forth as it were like a gush of music; and with a mirthful expression half childish and half woman-like. "I accept your gift, and would fain recompense it with this precious purple flower; but if I toss it into the air, it will not reach you. So Signor Guasconti must even content himself with my thanks."

She lifted the bouquet from the ground, and then as if inwardly ashamed at having stepped aside from her maidenly reserve to respond to a stranger's greeting, passed swiftly homeward through the garden. But, few as the moments were, it seemed to Giovanni when she was on the point of vanishing beneath the sculptured portal, that his beautiful bouquet was already beginning to wither in her grasp. It was an idle thought; there could be no possibility of distinguishing a faded flower from a fresh one, at so great a distance.

For many days after this incident, the young man avoided the window that looked into Doctor Rappaccini's garden, as if something ugly and monstrous would have blasted his eye-sight, had he been betrayed into a glance. He felt conscious of having put himself, to a certain extent, within the influence of an unintelligible power, by the communication which he had opened with Beatrice. The wisest course would have been, if his heart were in any real danger, to quit his lodgings and Padua itself, at once; the next wiser, to have accustomed himself, as far as possible, to the familiar and day-light view of Beatrice; thus bringing her rigidly and systematically within the limits of ordinary experience. Least of all, while avoiding her sight, should Giovanni have remained so near this extraordinary being, that the proximity and possibility even of intercourse, should give a kind of substance and reality to the wild vagaries which his imagination ran riot continually in producing. Guasconti had not a deep heart — or at all events, its depths were not sounded now — but he had a quick fancy, and an ardent southern temperament, which rose every instant to a higher fever-pitch. Whether or no Beatrice possessed those terrible attributes — that fatal breath — the affinity with those so beautiful and deadly flowers — which were indicated by what Giovanni had witnessed, she had at least instilled a fierce and subtle poison into his system. It was not love, although her rich beauty was a madness to him; nor horror, even while he fancied her spirit to be imbued with the same baneful essence that seemed to pervade her physical frame; but a wild offspring of both love and horror that had each parent in it, and burned like one and shivered like the other. Giovanni knew not what to dread; still less did he know what to hope; yet hope and dread kept a continual warfare in his breast, alternately vanquishing one another and starting up afresh to renew the contest. Blessed are all simple emotions, be they dark or bright! It is the lurid intermixture of the two that produces the illuminating blaze of the infernal regions.

Sometimes he endeavored to assuage the fever of his spirit by a rapid walk through the streets of Padua, or beyond its gates; his footsteps kept time with the throbbings of his brain, so that the walk was apt to accelerate itself to a race. One day, he found himself arrested; his arm was seized by a portly personage who had turned back on recognizing the young man, and expended much breath in overtaking him.

"Signor Giovanni! — stay, my young friend!" — cried he. "Have you forgotten me? That might well be the case, if I were as much altered as yourself."

It was Baglioni, whom Giovanni had avoided, ever since their first meeting, from a doubt that the Professor's sagacity would look too deeply into his secrets. Endeavoring to recover himself, he stared forth wildly from his inner world into the outer one, and spoke like a man in a dream.

"Yes; I am Giovanni Guasconti. You are Professor Pietro Baglioni. Now let me pass!"

"Not yet — not yet, Signor Giovanni Guasconti," said the Professor, smiling, but at the same time scrutinizing the youth with an earnest glance. "What, did I grow up side by side with your father, and shall his son pass me like a stranger, in these old streets of Padua? Stand still, Signor Giovanni; for we must have a word or two before we part."

"Speedily, then, most worshipful Professor, speedily!" said Giovanni, with feverish impatience. "Does not your worship see that I am in haste?"

Now, while he was speaking, there came a man in black along the street, stooping and moving feebly, like a person in inferior health. His face was all overspread with a most sickly and sallow hue, but yet so pervaded with an expression of piercing and active intellect, that an observer might easily have overlooked the merely physical attributes, and have seen only this wonderful energy. As he passed, this person exchanged a cold and distant salutation with Baglioni, but fixed his eyes upon Giovanni with an intentness that seemed to bring out whatever was within him worthy of notice. Nevertheless, there was a peculiar quietness in the look, as if taking merely a speculative, not a human interest, in the young man.

"It is Doctor Rappaccini!" whispered the Professor, when the stranger had passed. — "Has he ever seen your face before?"

"Not that I know," answered Giovanni, starting at the name.

"He *has* seen you! — he must have seen you!" said Baglioni, hastily. "For some purpose or other, this man of science is making a study of you. I know that look of his! It is the same that coldly illuminates his face, as he bends over a bird, a mouse, or a butterfly, which, in pursuance of some experiment, he has killed by the perfume of a flower; — a look as deep as Nature itself, but without Nature's warmth of love. Signor Giovanni, I will stake my life upon it, you are the subject of one of Rappaccini's experiments!"

"Will you make a fool of me?" cried Giovanni, passionately. "That, Signor Professor, were an untoward experiment."

"Patience, patience!" replied the imperturbable Professor. "I tell thee, my poor Giovanni, that Rappaccini has a scientific interest in thee. Thou hast fallen into fearful hands! And the Signora Beatrice? What part does she act in this mystery?"

But Guasconti, finding Baglioni's pertinacity intolerable, here broke away, and was gone before the Professor could again seize his arm. He looked after the young man intently, and shook his head.

"This must not be," said Baglioni to himself. "The youth is the son of my old friend, and shall not come to any harm from which the arcana of medical science can preserve him. Besides, it is too insufferable an impertinence in Rappaccini thus to snatch the lad out of my own hands, as I may say, and make use of him for his infernal experiments. This daughter of his! It shall be looked to. Perchance, most learned Rappaccini, I may foil you where you little dream of it!"

Meanwhile, Giovanni had pursued a circuitous route, and at length found himself at the door of his lodgings. As he crossed the threshold, he was met by old Lisabetta, who smirked and smiled, and was evidently desirous to attract his attention; vainly, however, as the ebullition of his feelings had momentarily subsided into a cold and dull vacuity. He turned his eyes full upon the withered face that was puckering itself into a smile, but seemed to behold it not. The old dame, therefore, laid her grasp upon his cloak.

"Signor! — Signor!" whispered she, still with a smile over the whole breadth of her visage, so that it looked not unlike a grotesque carving in wood, darkened by centuries — "Listen, Signor! There is a private entrance into the garden!"

"What do you say?" exclaimed Giovanni, turning quickly about, as if an inanimate thing should start into feverish life. — "A private entrance into Doctor Rappaccini's garden!"

"Hush! hush! — not so loud!" whispered Lisabetta, putting her hand over his mouth. "Yes; into the worshipful Doctor's garden, where you may see all his fine shrubbery. Many a young man in Padua would give gold to be admitted among those flowers."

Giovanni put a piece of gold into her hand.

"Show me the way," said he.

A surmise, probably excited by his conversation with Baglioni, crossed his mind, that this interposition of old Lisabetta might perchance be connected with the intrigue, whatever were its nature, in which the Professor seemed to suppose that Doctor Rappaccini was involving him. But such a suspicion, though it disturbed Giovanni, was inadequate to restrain him. The instant he was aware of the possibility of approaching Beatrice, it seemed an absolute necessity of his existence to do so. It mattered not whether she were angel or demon; he was irrevocably within her sphere, and must obey the law that whirled him onward, in ever lessening circles, towards a result which he did not attempt to foreshadow. And yet, strange to say, there came across him a sudden doubt, whether this intense interest on his part were not delusory — whether it were really of so deep and positive a nature as to justify him in now thrusting himself into an incalculable position — whether it were not merely the fantasy of a young man's brain, only slightly, or not at all, connected with his heart!

He paused — hesitated — turned half about — but again went on. His withered guide led him along several obscure passages, and finally undid a door, through which, as it was opened, there came the sight and sound of rustling leaves, with the broken sunshine glimmering among them. Giovanni stepped forth, and forcing himself through the entanglement of a shrub that wreathed its tendrils over the hidden entrance, he stood beneath his own window, in the open area of Doctor Rappaccini's garden.

How often is it the case, that, when impossibilities have come to pass, and dreams have condensed their misty substance into tangible realities, we find ourselves calm, and even coldly self-possessed, amid circumstances which it would have been a delirium of joy or agony to anticipate! Fate delights to thwart us thus. Passion will choose his own time to rush upon the scene, and lingers sluggishly behind, when an appropriate adjustment of events would seem to summon his appearance. So was it now with Giovanni. Day after day, his pulses had throbbed with feverish blood, at the improbable idea of an interview with Beatrice, and of standing with her, face to face, in this very garden, basking in the oriental sunshine of her beauty, and snatching from her full gaze the mystery which he deemed the riddle of his own existence. But now there was a singular and untimely equanimity within his breast. He threw a glance around the garden to discover if Beatrice or her father were present, and perceiving that he was alone, began a critical observation of the plants.

The aspect of one and all of them dissatisfied him; their gorgeousness seemed fierce, passionate, and even unnatural. There was hardly an individual shrub which a wanderer, straying by himself through a forest, would not have been startled to find growing wild, as if an unearthly face had glared at him out of the thicket. Several, also, would have shocked a delicate instinct by an appearance of artificialness, indicating that there had been such commixture, and, as it were, adultery of various vegetable species, that the production was no longer of God's making, but the monstrous offspring of man's depraved fancy, glowing with only an evil mockery of beauty. They were probably the result of experiment, which, in one or two cases, had succeeded in mingling plants individually lovely into a compound possessing the questionable and ominous character that distinguished the whole growth of the garden. In fine, Giovanni recognized but two or three plants in the collection, and those of a kind that he well knew to be poisonous. While busy with these contemplations, he heard the rustling of a silken garment, and turning, beheld Beatrice emerging from beneath the sculptured portal.

Giovanni had not considered with himself what should be his deportment; whether he should apologize for his intrusion into the garden, or assume that he was there with the privity, at least, if not by the desire, of Doctor Rappaccini or his daughter. But Beatrice's manner placed him at his ease, though leaving him still in doubt by what agency he had gained admittance. She came lightly along the path, and met him near the broken fountain. There was surprise in her face, but brightened by a simple and kind expression of pleasure.

"You are a connoisseur in flowers, Signor," said Beatrice with a smile, alluding to the bouquet which he had flung her from the window. "It is no marvel, therefore, if the sight of my father's rare collection has tempted you to take a nearer view. If he were here, he could tell you many strange and interesting facts as to the nature and habits of these shrubs, for he has spent a life-time in such studies, and this garden is his world."

"And yourself, lady" — observed Giovanni — "if fame says true — you, likewise, are deeply skilled in the virtues indicated by these rich blossoms, and these spicy perfumes. Would you deign to be my instructress, I should prove an apter scholar than under Signor Rappaccini himself."

"Are there such idle rumors?" asked Beatrice, with the music of a pleasant laugh. "Do people say that I am skilled in my father's science of plants? What a jest is there! No; though I have grown up among these flowers, I know no more of them than their hues and perfume; and sometimes, methinks I would fain rid myself of even that small knowledge. There are many flowers here, and those not the least brilliant, that shock and offend me, when they meet my eye. But, pray, Signor, do not believe these stories about my science. Believe nothing of me save what you see with your own eyes."

"And must I believe all that I have seen with my own eyes?" asked Giovanni pointedly, while the recollection of former scenes made him shrink. "No, Signora, you demand too little of me. Bid me believe nothing, save what comes from your own lips."

It would appear that Beatrice understood him. There came a deep flush to her cheek; but she looked full into Giovanni's eyes, and responded to his gaze of uneasy suspicion with a queen-like haughtiness.

"I do so bid you, Signor!" she replied. "Forget whatever you may have fancied in regard to me. If true to the outward senses, still it may be false in its essence. But the words of Beatrice Rappaccini's lips are true from the heart outward. Those you may believe!"

A fervor glowed in her whole aspect, and beamed upon Giovanni's consciousness like the light of truth itself. But while she spoke, there was a fragrance in the atmosphere around her rich and delightful, though evanescent, yet which the young man, from an indefinable reluctance, scarcely dared to draw into his lungs. It might be the odor of the flowers. Could it be Beatrice's breath, which thus embalmed her words with a strange richness, as if by steeping them in her heart? A faintness passed like a shadow over Giovanni, and flitted away; he seemed to gaze through the beautiful girl's eyes into her transparent soul, and felt no more doubt or fear.

The tinge of passion that had colored Beatrice's manner vanished; she became gay, and appeared to derive a pure delight from her communion with the youth, not unlike what the maiden of a lonely island might have felt, conversing with a voyager from the civilized world. Evidently her experience of life had been confined within the limits of that garden. She talked now about matters as simple as the day-light or summer-clouds, and now asked questions in reference to the city, or Giovanni's distant home, his friends, his mother, and his sisters; questions indicating such seclusion, and such lack of familiarity with modes and forms, that Giovanni responded as if to an infant. Her spirit gushed out before him like a fresh rill, that was just catching its first glimpse of the sunlight, and wondering, at the reflections of earth and sky which were flung into its bosom. There came thoughts, too, from a deep source, and fantasies of a gem-like brilliancy, as if diamonds and rubies sparkled upward among the bubbles of the fountain. Ever and anon, there gleamed across the young man's mind a sense of wonder, that he should be walking side by side with the being who had so wrought upon his imagination — whom he had idealized in such hues of terror — in whom he had positively witnessed such manifestations of dreadful attributes — that he should be conversing with Beatrice like a brother, and should find her so human and so maiden-like. But such reflections were only momentary; the effect of her character was too real, not to make itself familiar at once.

In this free intercourse, they had strayed through the garden, and now, after many turns among its avenues, were come to the shattered fountain, beside which grew the magnificent shrub with its treasury of glowing blossoms. A fragrance was diffused from it, which Giovanni recognized as identical with that which he had attributed to Beatrice's breath, but incomparably more powerful. As her eyes fell upon it, Giovanni beheld her press her hand to her bosom, as if her heart were throbbing suddenly and painfully.

"For the first time in my life," murmured she, addressing the shrub, "I had forgotten thee!"

"I remember, Signora," said Giovanni, "that you once promised to reward me with one of these living gems for the bouquet, which I had the happy boldness to fling to your feet. Permit me now to pluck it as a memorial of this interview."

He made a step towards the shrub, with extended hand. But Beatrice darted forward, uttering a shriek that went through his heart like a dagger. She caught his hand, and drew it back with the whole force of her slender figure. Giovanni felt her touch thrilling through his fibres.

"Touch it not!" exclaimed she, in a voice of agony. "Not for thy life! It is fatal!"

Then, hiding her face, she fled from him, and vanished beneath the sculptured portal. As Giovanni followed her with his eyes, he beheld the emaciated figure and pale intelligence of Doctor Rappaccini, who had been watching the scene, he knew not how long, within the shadow of the entrance.

No sooner was Guasconti alone in his chamber, than the image of Beatrice came back to his passionate musings, invested with all the witchery that had been gathering around it ever since his first glimpse of her, and now likewise imbued with a tender warmth of girlish womanhood. She was human: her nature was endowed with all gentle and feminine qualities; she was worthiest to be worshipped; she was capable, surely, on her part, of the height and heroism of love. Those tokens, which he had hitherto considered as proofs of a frightful peculiarity in her physical and moral system, were now either forgotten, or, by the subtle sophistry of passion, transmuted into a golden crown of enchantment, rendering Beatrice the more admirable, by so much as she was the more unique. Whatever had looked ugly, was now beautiful; or, if incapable of such a change, it stole away and hid itself among those shapeless half-ideas, which throng the dim region beyond the daylight of our perfect consciousness. Thus did Giovanni spend the night, nor fell asleep, until the dawn had begun to awake the slumbering flowers in Doctor Rappaccini's garden, whither his dreams doubtless led him. Up rose the sun in his due season, and flinging his beams upon the young man's eyelids, awoke him to a sense of pain. When thoroughly aroused, he became sensible of a burning and tingling agony in his hand — in his right hand — the very hand which Beatrice had grasped in her own, when he was on the point of plucking one of the gem-like flowers. On the back of that hand there was now a purple print, like that of four small fingers, and the likeness of a slender thumb upon his wrist.

Oh, how stubbornly does love — or even that cunning semblance of love which flourishes in the imagination, but strikes no depth of root into the heart — how stubbornly does it hold its faith, until the moment come, when it is doomed to vanish into thin mist! Giovanni wrapt a handkerchief about his hand, and wondered what evil thing had stung him, and soon forgot his pain in a reverie of Beatrice.

After the first interview, a second was in the inevitable course of what we call fate. A third; a fourth; and a meeting with Beatrice in the garden was no longer an incident in Giovanni's daily life, but the whole space in which he might be said to live; for the anticipation and memory of that ecstatic hour made up the remainder. Nor was it otherwise with the daughter of Rappaccini. She watched for the youth's appearance, and flew to his side with confidence as unreserved as if they had been playmates from early infancy — as if they were such playmates still. If, by any unwonted chance, he failed to come at the appointed moment, she stood beneath the window, and sent up the rich sweetness of her tones to float around him in his chamber, and echo and reverberate throughout his heart — "Giovanni! Giovanni! Why tarriest thou? Come down!" And down he hastened into that Eden of poisonous flowers.

But, with all this intimate familiarity, there was still a reserve in Beatrice's demeanor, so rigidly and invariably sustained, that the idea of infringing it scarcely occurred to his imagination. By all appreciable signs, they loved; they had looked love, with eyes that conveyed the holy secret from the depths of one soul into the depths of the other, as if it were too sacred to be whispered by the way; they had even spoken love, in those gushes of passion when their spirits darted forth in articulated breath, like tongues of long-hidden flame; and yet there had been no seal of lips, no clasp of hands, nor any slightest caress, such as love claims and hallows. He had never touched one of the gleaming ringlets of her hair; her garment — so marked was the physical barrier between them — had never been waved against him by a breeze. On the few occasions when Giovanni had seemed tempted to overstep the limit, Beatrice grew so sad, so stern, and withal wore such a look of desolate separation, shuddering at itself, that not a spoken word was requisite to repel him. At such times, he was startled at the horrible suspicions that rose, monster-like, out of the caverns of his heart, and stared him in the face; his love grew thin and faint as the morning-mist; his doubts alone had substance. But when Beatrice's face brightened again, after the momentary shadow, she was transformed at once from the mysterious, questionable being, whom he had watched with so much awe and horror; she was now the beautiful and unsophisticated girl, whom he felt that his spirit knew with a certainty beyond all other knowledge.

A considerable time had now passed since Giovanni's last meeting with Baglioni. One morning, however, he was disagreeably surprised by a visit from the Professor, whom he had scarcely thought of for whole weeks, and would willingly have forgotten still longer. Given up, as he had long been, to a pervading excitement, he could tolerate no companions, except upon condition of their perfect sympathy with his present state of feeling. Such sympathy was not to be expected from Professor Baglioni.

The visitor chatted carelessly, for a few moments, about the gossip of the city and the University, and then took up another topic.

"I have been reading an old classic author lately," said he, "and met with a story that strangely interested me. Possibly you may remember it. It is of an Indian prince, who sent a beautiful woman as a present to Alexander the Great. She was as lovely as the dawn, and gorgeous as the sunset; but what especially distinguished her was a certain rich perfume in her breath — richer than a garden of Persian roses. Alexander, as was natural to a youthful conqueror, fell in love at first sight with this magnificent stranger. But a certain sage physician, happening to be present, discovered a terrible secret in regard to her."

"And what was that?" asked Giovanni, turning his eyes downward to avoid those of the Professor.

"That this lovely woman," continued Baglioni, with emphasis, "had been nourished with poisons from her birth upward, until her whole nature was so imbued with them, that she herself had become the deadliest poison in existence. Poison was her element of life. With that rich perfume of her breath, she blasted the very air. Her love would have been poison! — her embrace death! Is not this a marvellous tale?"

"A childish fable," answered Giovanni, nervously starting from his chair. "I marvel how your worship finds time to read such nonsense, among your graver studies."

"By the bye," said the Professor, looking uneasily about him, "what singular fragrance is this in your apartment? Is it the perfume of your gloves? It is faint, but delicious, and yet, after all, by no means agreeable. Were I to breathe it long, methinks it would make me ill. It is like the breath of a flower — but I see no flowers in the chamber."

"Nor are there any," replied Giovanni, who had turned pale as the Professor spoke; "nor, I think, is there any fragrance, except in your worship's imagination. Odors, being a sort of element combined of the sensual and the spiritual, are apt to deceive us in this manner. The recollection of a perfume — the bare idea of it — may easily be mistaken for a present reality."

"Aye; but my sober imagination does not often play such tricks," said Baglioni; "and were I to fancy any kind of odor, it would be that of some vile apothecary drug, wherewith my fingers are likely enough to be imbued. Our worshipful friend Rappaccini, as I have heard, tinctures his medicaments with odors richer than those of Araby. Doubtless, likewise, the fair and learned Signora Beatrice would minister to her patients with draughts as sweet as a maiden's breath. But wo to him that sips them!"

Giovanni's face evinced many contending emotions. The tone in which the Professor alluded to the pure and lovely daughter of Rappaccini was a torture to his soul; and yet, the intimation of a view of her character, opposite to his own, gave instantaneous distinctness to a thousand dim suspicions, which now grinned at him like so many demons. But he strove hard to quell them, and to respond to Baglioni with a true lover's perfect faith.

"Signor Professor," said he, "you were my father's friend — perchance, too, it is your purpose to act a friendly part towards his son. I would fain feel nothing towards you save respect and deference. But I pray you to observe, Signor, that there is one subject on which we must not speak. You know not the Signora Beatrice. You cannot, therefore, estimate the wrong — the blasphemy, I may even say — that is offered to her character by a light or injurious word."

"Giovanni! — my poor Giovanni!" answered the Professor, with a calm expression of pity, "I know this wretched girl far better than yourself. You shall hear the truth in respect to the poisoner Rappaccini, and his poisonous daughter. Yes; poisonous as she is beautiful! Listen; for even should you do violence to my gray hairs, it shall not silence me. That old fable of the Indian woman has become a truth, by the deep and deadly science of Rappaccini, and in the person of the lovely Beatrice!"

Giovanni groaned and hid his face.

"Her father," continued Baglioni, "was not restrained by natural affection from offering up his child, in this horrible manner, as the victim of his insane zeal for science. For — let us do him justice — he is as true a man of science as ever distilled his own heart in an alembic. What, then, will be your fate? Beyond a doubt, you are selected as the material of some new experiment. Perhaps the result is to be death — perhaps a fate more awful still! Rappaccini, with what he calls the interest of science before his eyes, will hesitate at nothing."

"It is a dream!" muttered Giovanni to himself, "surely it is a dream!"

"But," resumed the Professor, "be of good cheer, son of my friend! It is not yet too late for the rescue. Possibly, we may even succeed in bringing back this miserable child within the limits of ordinary nature, from which her father's madness has estranged her. Behold this little silver vase! It was wrought by the hands of the renowned Benvenuto Cellini, and is well worthy to be a love-gift to the fairest dame in Italy. But its contents are invaluable. One little sip of this antidote would have rendered the most virulent poisons of the Borgias innocuous. Doubt not that it will be as efficacious against those of Rappaccini. Bestow the vase, and the precious liquid within it, on your Beatrice, and hopefully await the result."

Baglioni laid a small, exquisitely wrought silver phial on the table, and withdrew, leaving what he had said to produce its effect upon the young man's mind.

"We will thwart Rappaccini yet!" thought he, chuckling to himself, as he descended the stairs. "But, let us confess the truth of him, he is a wonderful man! — a wonderful man indeed! A vile empiric, however, in his practice, and therefore not to be tolerated by those who respect the good old rules of the medical profession!"

Throughout Giovanni's whole acquaintance with Beatrice, he had occasionally, as we have said, been haunted by dark surmises as to her character. Yet, so thoroughly had she made herself felt by him as a simple, natural, most affectionate and guileless creature, that the image now held up by Professor Baglioni, looked as strange and incredible, as if it were not in accordance with his own original conception. True, there were ugly recollections connected with his first glimpses of the beautiful girl; he could not quite forget the bouquet that withered in her grasp, and the insect that perished amid the sunny air, by no ostensible agency save the fragrance of her breath. These incidents, however, dissolving in the pure light of her character, had no longer the efficacy of facts, but were acknowledged as mistaken fantasies, by whatever testimony of the senses they might appear to be substantiated. There is something truer and more real, than what we can see with the eyes, and touch with the finger. On such better evidence, had Giovanni founded his confidence in Beatrice, though rather by the necessary force of her high attributes, than by any deep and generous faith on his part. But, now, his spirit was incapable of sustaining itself at the height to which the early enthusiasm of passion had exalted it; he fell down, grovelling among earthly doubts, and defiled therewith the pure whiteness of Beatrice's image. Not that he gave her up; he did but distrust. He resolved to institute some decisive test that should satisfy him, once for all, whether there were those dreadful peculiarities in her physical nature, which could not be supposed to exist without some corresponding monstrosity of soul. His eyes, gazing down afar, might have deceived him as to the lizard, the insect, and the flowers. But if he could witness, at the distance of a few paces, the sudden blight of one fresh and healthful flower in Beatrice's hand, there would be room for no further question. With this idea, he hastened to the florist's, and purchased a bouquet that was still gemmed with the morning dew-drops.

It was now the customary hour of his daily interview with Beatrice. Before descending into the garden, Giovanni failed not to look at his figure in the mirror; a vanity to be expected in a beautiful young man, yet, as displaying itself at that troubled and feverish moment, the token of a certain shallowness of feeling and insincerity of character. He did gaze, however, and said to himself, that his features had never before possessed so rich a grace, nor his eyes such vivacity, nor his cheeks so warm a hue of superabundant life.

"At least," thought he, "her poison has not yet insinuated itself into my system. I am no flower to perish in her grasp!"

With that thought, he turned his eyes on the bouquet, which he had never once laid aside from his hand. A thrill of indefinable horror shot through his frame, on perceiving that those dewy flowers were already beginning to droop; they wore the aspect of things that had been fresh and lovely, yesterday. Giovanni grew white as marble, and stood motionless before the mirror, staring at his own reflection there, as at the likeness of something frightful. He remembered Baglioni's remark about the fragrance that seemed to pervade the chamber. It must have been the poison in his breath! Then he shuddered — shuddered at himself! Recovering from his stupor, he began to watch, with curious eye, a spider that was busily at work, hanging its web from the antique cornice of the apartment, crossing and re-crossing the artful system of interwoven lines, as vigorous and active a spider as ever dangled from an old ceiling. Giovanni bent towards the insect, and emitted a deep, long breath. The spider suddenly ceased its toil; the web vibrated with a tremor originating in the body of the small artizan. Again Giovanni sent forth a breath, deeper, longer, and imbued with a venomous feeling out of his heart; he knew not whether he were wicked or only desperate. The spider made a convulsive gripe with his limbs, and hung dead across the window.

"Accursed! Accursed!" muttered Giovanni, addressing himself. "Hast thou grown so poisonous, that this deadly insect perishes by thy breath?"

At that moment, a rich, sweet voice came floating up from the garden: "Giovanni! Giovanni! It is past the hour! Why tarriest thou! Come down!"

"Yes," muttered Giovanni again. "She is the only being whom my breath may not slay! Would that it might!"

He rushed down, and in an instant, was standing before the bright and loving eyes of Beatrice. A moment ago, his wrath and despair had been so fierce that he could have desired nothing so much as to wither her by a glance. But, with her actual presence, there came influences which had too real an existence to be at once shaken off; recollections of the delicate and benign power of her feminine nature, which had so often enveloped him in a religious calm; recollections of many a holy and passionate outgush of her heart, when the pure fountain had been unsealed from its depths, and made visible in its transparency to his mental eye; recollections which, had Giovanni known how to estimate them, would have assured him that all this ugly mystery was but an earthly illusion, and that, whatever mist of evil might seem to have gathered over her, the real Beatrice was a heavenly angel. Incapable as he was of such high faith, still her presence had not utterly lost its magic. Giovanni's rage was quelled into an aspect of sullen insensibility. Beatrice, with a quick spiritual sense, immediately felt that there was a gulf of blackness between them, which neither he nor she could pass. They walked on together, sad and silent, and came thus to the marble fountain, and to its pool of water on the ground, in the midst of which grew the shrub that bore gem-like blossoms. Giovanni was affrighted at the eager enjoyment — the appetite, as it were — with which he found himself inhaling the fragrance of the flowers.

"Beatrice," asked he abruptly, "whence came this shrub!"

"My father created it," answered she, with simplicity.

"Created it! created it!" repeated Giovanni. "What mean you, Beatrice?"

"He is a man fearfully acquainted with the secrets of nature," replied Beatrice; "and, at the hour when I first drew breath, this plant sprang from the soil, the offspring of his science, of his intellect, while I was but his earthly child. Approach it not!" continued she, observing with terror that Giovanni was drawing nearer to the shrub. "It has qualities that you little dream of. But I, dearest Giovanni — I grew up and blossomed with the plant, and was nourished with its breath. It was my sister, and I loved it with a human affection: for — alas! hast thou not suspected it? there was an awful doom."

Here Giovanni frowned so darkly upon her that Beatrice paused and trembled. But her faith in his tenderness reassured her, and made her blush that she had doubted for an instant.

"There was an awful doom," she continued, — "the effect of my father's fatal love of science — which estranged me from all society of my kind. Until Heaven sent thee, dearest Giovanni, Oh! how lonely was thy poor Beatrice!"

"Was it a hard doom?" asked Giovanni, fixing his eyes upon her.

"Only of late have I known how hard it was," answered she tenderly. "Oh, yes; but my heart was torpid, and therefore quiet."

Giovanni's rage broke forth from his sullen gloom like a lightning-flash out of a dark cloud.

"Accursed one!" cried he, with venomous scorn and anger. "And finding thy solitude wearisome, thou hast severed me, likewise, from all the warmth of life, and enticed me into thy region of unspeakable horror!"

"Giovanni!" exclaimed Beatrice, turning her large bright eyes upon his face. The force of his words had not found its way into her mind; she was merely thunder-struck.

"Yes, poisonous thing!" repeated Giovanni, beside himself with passion. "Thou hast done it! Thou hast blasted me! Thou hast filled my veins with poison! Thou hast made me as hateful, as ugly, as loathsome and deadly a creature as thyself — a world's wonder of hideous monstrosity! Now — if our breath be happily as fatal to ourselves as to all others — let us join our lips in one kiss of unutterable hatred, and so die!"

"What has befallen me?" murmured Beatrice, with a low moan out of her heart. "Holy Virgin pity me, a poor heartbroken child!"

"Thou! Dost thou pray?" cried Giovanni, still with the same fiendish scorn. "Thy very prayers, as they come from thy lips, taint the atmosphere with death. Yes, yes; let us pray! Let us to church, and dip our fingers in the holy water at the portal! They that come after us will perish as by a pestilence. Let us sign crosses in the air! It will be scattering curses abroad in the likeness of holy symbols!"

"Giovanni," said Beatrice calmly, for her grief was beyond passion, "Why dost thou join thyself with me thus in those terrible words? I, it is true, am the horrible thing thou namest me. But thou! — what hast thou to do, save with one other shudder at my hideous misery, to go forth out of the garden and mingle with thy race, and forget that there ever crawled on earth such a monster as poor Beatrice?"

"Dost thou pretend ignorance?" asked Giovanni, scowling upon her. "Behold! This power have I gained from the pure daughter of Rappaccini!"

There was a swarm of summer-insects flitting through the air, in search of the food promised by the flower-odors of the fatal garden. They circled round Giovanni's head, and were evidently attracted towards him by the same influence which had drawn them, for an instant, within the sphere of several of the shrubs. He sent forth a breath among them, and smiled bitterly at Beatrice, as at least a score of the insects fell dead upon the ground.

"I see it! I see it!" shrieked Beatrice. "It is my father's fatal science? No, no, Giovanni; it was not I! Never, never! I dreamed only to love thee, and be with thee a little time, and so to let thee pass away, leaving but thine image in mine heart. For, Giovanni — believe it — though my body be nourished with poison, my spirit is God's creature, and craves love as its daily food. But my father! — he has united us in this fearful sympathy. Yes; spurn me! — tread upon me! — kill me! Oh, what is death, after such words as thine? But it was not I! Not for a world of bliss would I have done it!"

Giovanni's passion had exhausted itself in its outburst from his lips. There now came across him a sense, mournful, and not without tenderness, of the intimate and peculiar relationship between Beatrice and himself. They stood, as it were, in an utter solitude, which would be made none the less solitary by the densest throng of human life. Ought not, then, the desert of humanity around them to press this insulated pair closer together? If they should be cruel to one another, who was there to be kind to them? Besides, thought Giovanni, might there not still be a hope of his returning within the limits of ordinary nature, and leading Beatrice — the redeemed Beatrice — by the hand? Oh, weak, and selfish, and unworthy spirit, that could dream of an earthly union and earthly happiness as possible, after such deep love had been so bitterly wronged as was Beatrice's love by Giovanni's blighting words! No, no; there could be no such hope. She must pass heavily, with that broken heart, across the borders of Time — she must bathe her hurts in some fount of Paradise, and forget her grief in the light of immortality — and *there* be well!

But Giovanni did not know it.

"Dear Beatrice," said he, approaching her, while she shrank away, as always at his approach, but now with a different impulse — "dearest Beatrice, our fate is not yet so desperate. Behold! There is a medicine, potent, as a wise physician has assured me, and almost divine in its efficacy. It is composed of ingredients the most opposite to those by which thy awful father has brought this calamity upon thee and me. It is distilled of blessed herbs. Shall we not quaff it together, and thus be purified from evil?"

"Give it me!" said Beatrice, extending her hand to receive the little silver phial which Giovanni took from his bosom. She added, with a peculiar emphasis: "I will drink — but do thou await the result."

She put Baglioni's antidote to her lips; and, at the same moment, the figure of Rappaccini emerged from the portal, and came slowly towards the marble fountain. As he drew near, the pale man of science seemed to gaze with a triumphant expression at the beautiful youth and maiden, as might an artist who should spend his life in achieving a picture or a group of statuary, and finally be satisfied with his success. He paused — his bent form grew erect with conscious power, he spread out his hand over them, in the attitude of a father imploring a blessing upon his children. But those were the same hands that had thrown poison into the stream of their lives! Giovanni trembled. Beatrice shuddered very nervously, and pressed her hand upon her heart.

"My daughter," said Rappaccini, "thou art no longer lonely in the world! Pluck one of those precious gems from thy sister shrub, and bid thy bridegroom wear it in his bosom. It will not harm him now! My science, and the sympathy between thee and him, have so wrought within his system, that he now stands apart from common men, as thou dost, daughter of my pride and triumph, from ordinary women. Pass on, then, through the world, most dear to one another, and dreadful to all besides!"

"My father," said Beatrice, feebly — and still, as she spoke, she kept her hand upon her heart — "wherefore didst thou inflict this miserable doom upon thy child?"

"Miserable!" exclaimed Rappaccini. "What mean you, foolish girl? Dost thou deem it misery to be endowed with marvellous gifts, against which no power nor strength could avail an enemy? Misery, to be able to quell the mightiest with a breath? Misery, to be as terrible as thou art beautiful? Wouldst thou, then, have preferred the condition of a weak woman, exposed to all evil, and capable of none?"

"I would fain have been loved, not feared," murmured Beatrice, sinking down upon the ground. — "But now it matters not; I am going, father, where the evil, which thou hast striven to mingle with my being, will pass away like a dream — like the fragrance of these poisonous flowers, which will no longer taint my breath among the flowers of Eden. Farewell, Giovanni! Thy words of hatred are like lead within my heart — but they, too, will fall away as I ascend. Oh, was there not, from the first, more poison in thy nature than in mine?"

To Beatrice — so radically had her earthly part been wrought upon by Rappaccini's skill — as poison had been life, so the powerful antidote was death. And thus the poor victim of man's ingenuity and of thwarted nature, and of the fatality that attends all such efforts of perverted wisdom, perished there, at the feet of her father and Giovanni. Just at that moment, Professor Pietro Baglioni looked forth from the window, and called loudly, in a tone of triumph mixed with horror, to the thunder-stricken man of science: "Rappaccini! Rappaccini! And is *this* the upshot of your experiment?"

THE FALL OF THE HOUSE OF USHER

Edgar Allan Poe (1809-1849)

During the whole of a dull, dark, and soundless day in the autumn of the year, when the clouds hung oppressively low in the heavens, I had been passing alone, on horseback, through a singularly dreary tract of country; and at length found myself, as the shades of the evening drew on, within view of the melancholy House of Usher. I know not how it was — but, with the first glimpse of the building, a sense of insufferable gloom pervaded my spirit. I say insufferable; for the feeling was unrelieved by any of that half-pleasurable, because poetic, sentiment, with which the mind usually receives even the sternest natural images of the desolate or terrible. I looked upon the scene before me — upon the mere house, and the simple landscape features of the domain — upon the bleak walls — upon the vacant eye-like windows — upon a few rank sedges — and upon a few white trunks of decayed trees — with an utter depression of soul which I can compare to no earthly sensation more properly than to the after-dream of the reveller upon opium — the bitter lapse into every-day life — the hideous dropping off of the veil. There was an iciness, a sinking, a sickening of the heart — an unredeemed dreariness of thought which no goading of the imagination could torture into aught of the sublime. What was it — I paused to think — what was it that so unnerved me in the contemplation of the House of Usher? It was a mystery all insoluble; nor could I grapple with the shadowy fancies that crowded upon me as I pondered. I was forced to fall back upon the unsatisfactory conclusion, that while, beyond doubt, there are combinations of very simple natural objects which have the power of thus affecting us, still the analysis of this power lies among considerations beyond our depth. It was possible, I reflected, that a mere different arrangement of the particulars of the scene, of the details of the picture, would be sufficient to modify, or perhaps to annihilate its capacity for sorrowful impression; and, acting upon this idea, I reined my horse to the precipitous brink of a black and lurid tarn that lay in unruffled lustre by the dwelling, and gazed down — but with a shudder even more thrilling than before — upon the re-modelled and inverted images of the gray sedge, and the ghastly tree-stems, and the vacant and eye-like windows.

Nevertheless, in this mansion of gloom I now proposed to myself a sojourn of some weeks. Its proprietor, Roderick Usher, had been one of my boon companions in boyhood; but many years had elapsed since our last meeting. A letter, however, had lately reached me in a distant part of the country — a letter from him — which, in its wildly importunate nature, had admitted of no other than a personal reply. The MS. gave evidence of nervous agitation. The writer spoke of acute bodily illness — of a mental disorder which oppressed him — and of an earnest desire to see me, as his best, and indeed his only personal friend, with a view of attempting, by the cheerfulness of my society, some alleviation of his malady. It was the manner in which all this, and much more, was said — it was the apparent *heart* that went with his request — which allowed me no room for hesitation; and I accordingly obeyed forthwith what I still considered a very singular summons.

Although, as boys, we had been even intimate associates, yet I really knew little of my friend. His reserve had been always excessive and habitual. I was aware, however, that his very ancient family had been noted, time out of mind, for a peculiar sensibility of temperament, displaying itself, through long ages, in many works of exalted art, and manifested, of late, in repeated deeds of munificent yet unobtrusive charity, as well as in a passionate devotion to the intricacies, perhaps even more than to the orthodox and easily recognizable beauties, of musical science. I had learned, too, the very remarkable fact, that the stem of the Usher race, all time-honored as it was, had put forth, at no period, any enduring branch; in other words, that the entire family lay in the direct line of descent, and had always, with very trifling and very temporary variation, so lain. It was this deficiency, I considered, while running over in thought the perfect keeping of the character of the premises with the accredited character of the people, and while speculating upon the possible influence which the one, in the long lapse of centuries, might have exercised upon the other — it was this deficiency, perhaps, of collateral issue, and the consequent undeviating transmission, from sire to son, of the patrimony with the name, which had, at length, so identified the two as to merge the original title of the estate in the quaint and equivocal appellation of the "House of Usher" — an appellation which seemed to include, in the minds of the peasantry who used it, both the family and the family mansion.

I have said that the sole effect of my somewhat childish experiment — that of looking down within the tarn — had been to deepen the first singular impression. There can be no doubt that the consciousness of the rapid increase of my superstition — for why should I not so term it? — served mainly to accelerate the increase itself. Such, I have long known, is the paradoxical law of all sentiments having terror as a basis. And it might have been for this reason only, that, when I again uplifted my eyes to the house itself, from its image in the pool, there grew in my mind a strange fancy — a fancy so ridiculous, indeed, that I but mention it to show the vivid force of the sensations which oppressed me. I had so worked upon my imagination as really to believe that about the whole mansion and domain there hung an atmosphere peculiar to themselves and their immediate vicinity — an atmosphere which had no affinity with the air of heaven, but which had reeked up from the decayed trees, and the gray wall, and the silent tarn — a pestilent and mystic vapor, dull, sluggish, faintly discernible, and leaden-hued.

Shaking off from my spirit what *must* have been a dream, I scanned more narrowly the real aspect of the building. Its principal feature seemed to be that of an excessive antiquity. The discoloration of ages had been great. Minute fungi overspread the whole exterior, hanging in a fine tangled web-work from the eaves. Yet all this was apart from any extraordinary dilapidation. No portion of the masonry had fallen; and there appeared to be a wild inconsistency between its still perfect adaptation of parts, and the crumbling condition of the individual stones. In this there was much that reminded me of the specious totality of old wood-work which has rotted for long years in some neglected vault, with no disturbance from the breath of the external air. Beyond this indication of extensive decay, however, the fabric gave little token of instability. Perhaps the eye of a scrutinizing observer might have discovered a barely perceptible fissure, which, extending from the roof of the building in front, made its way down the wall in a zigzag direction, until it became lost in the sullen waters of the tarn.

Noticing these things, I rode over a short causeway to the house. A servant in waiting took my horse, and I entered the Gothic archway of the hall. A valet, of stealthy step, thence conducted me, in silence, through many dark and intricate passages in my progress to the studio of his master. Much that I encountered on the way contributed, I know not how, to heighten the vague sentiments of which I have already spoken. While the objects around me — while the carvings of the ceilings, the sombre tapestries of the walls, the ebon blackness of the floors, and the phantasmagoric armorial trophies which rattled as I strode, were but matters to which, or to such as which, I had been accustomed from my infancy — while I hesitated not to acknowledge how familiar was all this — I still wondered to find how unfamiliar were the fancies which ordinary images were stirring up. On one of the staircases, I met the physician of the family. His countenance, I thought, wore a mingled expression of low cunning and perplexity. He accosted me with trepidation and passed on. The valet now threw open a door and ushered me into the presence of his master.

The room in which I found myself was very large and lofty. The windows were long, narrow, and pointed, and at so vast a distance from the black oaken floor as to be altogether inaccessible from within. Feeble gleams of encrimsoned light made their way through the trellised panes, and served to render sufficiently distinct the more prominent objects around; the eye, however, struggled in vain to reach the remoter angles of the chamber, or the recesses of the vaulted and fretted ceiling. Dark draperies hung upon the walls. The general furniture was profuse, comfortless, antique, and tattered. Many books and musical instruments lay scattered about, but failed to give any vitality to the scene. I felt that I breathed an atmosphere of sorrow. An air of stern, deep, and irredeemable gloom hung over and pervaded all.

Upon my entrance, Usher arose from a sofa on which he had been lying at full length, and greeted me with a vivacious warmth which had much in it, I at first thought, of an overdone cordiality — of the constrained effort of the ennuyé man of the world. A glance, however, at his countenance, convinced me of his perfect sincerity. We sat down; and for some moments, while he spoke not, I gazed upon him with a feeling half of pity, half of awe. Surely, man had never before so terribly altered, in so brief a period, as had Roderick Usher! It was with difficulty that I could bring myself to admit the identity of the wan being before me with the companion of my early boyhood. Yet the character of his face had been at all times remarkable. A cadaverousness of complexion; an eye large, liquid, and luminous beyond comparison; lips somewhat thin and very pallid, but of a surpassingly beautiful curve; a nose of a delicate Hebrew model, but with a breadth of nostril unusual in similar formations; a finely moulded chin, speaking, in its want of prominence, of a want of moral energy; hair of a more than web-like softness and tenuity; these features, with an inordinate expansion above the regions of the temple, made up altogether a countenance not easily to be forgotten. And now in the mere exaggeration of the prevailing character of these features, and of the expression they were wont to convey, lay so much of change that I doubted to whom I spoke. The now ghastly pallor of the skin, and the now miraculous lustre of the eye, above all things startled and even awed me. The silken hair, too, had been suffered to grow all unheeded, and as, in its wild gossamer texture, it floated rather than fell about the face, I could not, even with effort, connect its Arabesque expression with any idea of simple humanity.

In the manner of my friend I was at once struck with an incoherence — an inconsistency; and I soon found this to arise from a series of feeble and futile struggles to overcome an habitual trepidancy — an excessive nervous agitation. For something of this nature I had indeed been prepared, no less by his letter, than by reminiscences of certain boyish traits, and by conclusions deduced from his peculiar physical conformation and temperament. His action was alternately vivacious and sullen. His voice varied rapidly from a tremulous indecision (when the animal spirits seemed utterly in abeyance) to that species of energetic concision — that abrupt, weighty, unhurried, and hollow-sounding enunciation — that leaden, self-balanced and perfectly modulated guttural utterance, which may be observed in the lost drunkard, or the irreclaimable eater of opium, during the periods of his most intense excitement.

It was thus that he spoke of the object of my visit, of his earnest desire to see me, and of the solace he expected me to afford him. He entered, at some length, into what he conceived to be the nature of his malady. It was, he said, a constitutional and a family evil, and one for which he despaired to find a remedy — a mere nervous affection, he immediately added, which would undoubtedly soon pass off. It displayed itself in a host of unnatural sensations. Some of these, as he detailed them, interested and bewildered me; although, perhaps, the terms, and the general manner of the narration had their weight. He suffered much from a morbid acuteness of the senses; the most insipid food was alone endurable; he could wear only garments of certain texture; the odors of all flowers were oppressive; his eyes were tortured by even a faint light; and there were but peculiar sounds, and these from stringed instruments, which did not inspire him with horror.

To an anomalous species of terror I found him a bounden slave. "I shall perish," said he, "I *must* perish in this deplorable folly. Thus, thus, and not otherwise, shall I be lost. I dread the events of the future, not in themselves, but in their results. I shudder at the thought of any, even the most trivial, incident, which may operate upon this intolerable agitation of soul. I have, indeed, no abhorrence of danger, except in its absolute effect — in terror. In this unnerved — in this pitiable condition — I feel that the period will sooner or later arrive when I must abandon life and reason together, in some struggle with the grim phantasm, *fear*."

I learned, moreover, at intervals, and through broken and equivocal hints, another singular feature of his mental condition. He was enchained by certain superstitious impressions in regard to the dwelling which he tenanted, and whence, for many years, he had never ventured forth — in regard to an influence whose supposititious force was conveyed in terms too shadowy here to be re-stated — an influence which some peculiarities in the mere form and substance of his family mansion, had, by dint of long sufferance, he said, obtained over his spirit — an effect which the *physique* of the gray walls and turrets, and of the dim tarn into which they all looked down, had, at length, brought about upon the morale of his existence.

He admitted, however, although with hesitation, that much of the peculiar gloom which thus afflicted him could be traced to a more natural and far more palpable origin — to the severe and long-continued illness — indeed to the evidently approaching dissolution — of a tenderly beloved sister — his sole companion for long years — his last and only relative on earth. "Her decease," he said, with a bitterness which I can never forget, "would leave him (him the hopeless and the frail) the last of the ancient race of the Ushers." While he spoke, the lady Madeline (for so was she called) passed slowly through a remote portion of the apartment, and, without having noticed my presence, disappeared. I regarded her with an utter astonishment not unmingled with dread — and yet I found it impossible to account for such feelings. A sensation of stupor oppressed me, as my eyes followed her retreating steps. When a door, at length, closed upon her, my glance sought instinctively and eagerly the countenance of the brother — but he had buried his face in his hands, and I could only perceive that a far more than ordinary wanness had overspread the emaciated fingers through which trickled many passionate tears.

The disease of the lady Madeline had long baffled the skill of her physicians. A settled apathy, a gradual wasting away of the person, and frequent although transient affections of a partially cataleptical character, were the unusual diagnosis. Hitherto she had steadily borne up against the pressure of her malady, and had not betaken herself finally to bed; but, on the closing in of the evening of my arrival at the house, she succumbed (as her brother told me at night with inexpressible agitation) to the prostrating power of the destroyer; and I learned that the glimpse I had obtained of her person would thus probably be the last I should obtain — that the lady, at least while living, would be seen by me no more.

For several days ensuing, her name was unmentioned by either Usher or myself: and during this period I was busied in earnest endeavors to alleviate the melancholy of my friend. We painted and read together; or I listened, as if in a dream, to the wild improvisations of his speaking guitar. And thus, as a closer and still closer intimacy admitted me more unreservedly into the recesses of his spirit, the more bitterly did I perceive the futility of all attempt at cheering a mind from which darkness, as if an inherent positive quality, poured forth upon all objects of the moral and physical universe, in one unceasing radiation of gloom.

I shall ever bear about me a memory of the many solemn hours I thus spent alone with the master of the House of Usher. Yet I should fail in any attempt to convey an idea of the exact character of the studies, or of the occupations, in which he involved me, or led me the way. An excited and highly distempered ideality threw a sulphurous lustre over all. His long improvised dirges will ring forever in my ears. Among other things, I hold painfully in mind a certain singular perversion and amplification of the wild air of the last waltz of Von Weber. From the paintings over which his elaborate fancy brooded, and which grew, touch by touch, into vagueness at which I shuddered the more thrillingly, because I shuddered knowing not why; — from these paintings (vivid as their images now are before me) I would in vain endeavor to educe more than a small portion which should lie within the compass of merely written words. By the utter simplicity, by the nakedness of his designs, he arrested and overawed attention. If ever mortal painted an idea, that mortal was Roderick Usher. For me at least — in the circumstances then surrounding me — there arose out of the pure abstractions which the hypochondriac contrived to throw upon his canvass, an intensity of intolerable awe, no shadow of which felt I ever yet in the contemplation of the certainly glowing yet too concrete reveries of Fuseli.

One of the phantasmagoric conceptions of my friend, partaking not so rigidly of the spirit of abstraction, may be shadowed forth, although feebly, in words. A small picture presented the interior of an immensely long and rectangular vault or tunnel, with low walls, smooth, white, and without interruption or device. Certain accessory points of the design served well to convey the idea that this excavation lay at an exceeding depth below the surface of the earth. No outlet was observed in any portion of its vast extent, and no torch, or other artificial source of light was discernible; yet a flood of intense rays rolled throughout, and bathed the whole in a ghastly and inappropriate splendor.

I have just spoken of that morbid condition of the auditory nerve which rendered all music intolerable to the sufferer, with the exception of certain effects of stringed instruments. It was, perhaps, the narrow limits to which he thus confined himself upon the guitar, which gave birth, in great measure, to the fantastic character of his performances. But the fervid *facility* of his impromptus could not be so accounted for. They must have been, and were, in the notes, as well as in the words of his wild fantasias (for he not unfrequently accompanied himself with rhymed verbal improvisations), the result of that intense mental collectedness and concentration to which I have previously alluded as observable only in particular moments of the highest artificial excitement. The words of one of these rhapsodies I have easily remembered. I was, perhaps, the more forcibly impressed with it, as he gave it, because, in the under or mystic current of its meaning, I fancied that I perceived, and for the first time, a full consciousness on the part of Usher, of the tottering of his lofty reason upon her throne. The verses, which were entitled "The Haunted Palace," ran very nearly, if not accurately, thus:

I.

In the greenest of our valleys,
By good angels tenanted,
Once a fair and stately palace —
Radiant palace — reared its head.
In the monarch Thought's dominion —
It stood there!
Never seraph spread a pinion
Over fabric half so fair.

II.

Banners yellow, glorious, golden,
On its roof did float and flow;
(This — all this — was in the olden
Time long ago)
And every gentle air that dallied,
In that sweet day,
Along the ramparts plumed and pallid,
A winged odor went away.

III.

Wanderers in that happy valley
Through two luminous windows saw
Spirits moving musically
To a lute's well-tunéd law,
Round about a throne, where sitting
(Porphyrogene!)
In state his glory well befitting,
The ruler of the realm was seen.

IV.

And all with pearl and ruby glowing
Was the fair palace door,
Through which came flowing, flowing, flowing,
And sparkling evermore,
A troop of Echoes whose sweet duty
Was but to sing,
In voices of surpassing beauty,
The wit and wisdom of their king.

V.

But evil things, in robes of sorrow,
   Assailed the monarch's high estate;
(Ah, let us mourn, for never morrow
   Shall dawn upon him, desolate!)
And, round about his home, the glory
   That blushed and bloomed
Is but a dim-remembered story
   Of the old time entombed.

VI.

And travellers now within that valley,
   Through the red-litten windows, see
Vast forms that move fantastically
   To a discordant melody;
While, like a rapid ghastly river,
   Through the pale door,
A hideous throng rush out forever,
   And laugh — but smile no more.

I well remember that suggestions arising from this ballad, led us into a train of thought wherein there became manifest an opinion of Usher's which I mention not so much on account of its novelty, (for other men have thought thus,) as on account of the pertinacity with which he maintained it. This opinion, in its general form, was that of the sentience of all vegetable things. But, in his disordered fancy, the idea had assumed a more daring character, and trespassed, under certain conditions, upon the kingdom of inorganization. I lack words to express the full extent, or the earnest *abandon* of his persuasion. The belief, however, was connected (as I have previously hinted) with the gray stones of the home of his forefathers. The conditions of the sentience had been here, he imagined, fulfilled in the method of collocation of these stones — in the order of their arrangement, as well as in that of the many fungi which overspread them, and of the decayed trees which stood around — above all, in the long undisturbed endurance of this arrangement, and in its reduplication in the still waters of the tarn. Its evidence — the evidence of the sentience — was to be seen, he said, (and I here started as he spoke,) in *the gradual yet certain condensation of an atmosphere of their own about the waters and the walls*. The result was discoverable, he added, in that silent, yet importunate and terrible influence which for centuries had moulded the destinies of his family, and which made him what I now saw *him* — what he was. Such opinions need no comment, and I will make none.

Our books — the books which, for years, had formed no small portion of the mental existence of the invalid — were, as might be supposed, in strict keeping with this character of phantasm. We pored together over such works as the Ververt et Chartreuse of Gresset; the Belphegor of Machiavelli; the Heaven and Hell of Swedenborg; the Subterranean Voyage of Nicholas Klimm by Holberg;

the Chiromancy of Robert Flud, of Jean D'Indaginé, and of De la Chambre; the Journey into the Blue Distance of Tieck; and the City of the Sun of Campanella. One favorite volume was a small octavo edition of the *Directorium Inquisitorum*, by the Dominican Eymeric de Gironne; and there were passages in Pomponius Mela, about the old African Satyrs and Œgipans, over which Usher would sit dreaming for hours. His chief delight, however, was found in the perusal of an exceedingly rare and curious book in quarto Gothic — the manual of a forgotten church — the *Vigiliae Mortuorum secundum Chorum Ecclesiae Maguntinae.*

I could not help thinking of the wild ritual of this work, and of its probable influence upon the hypochondriac, when, one evening, having informed me abruptly that the lady Madeline was no more, he stated his intention of preserving her corpse for a fortnight, (previously to its final interment,) in one of the numerous vaults within the main walls of the building. The worldly reason, however, assigned for this singular proceeding, was one which I did not feel at liberty to dispute. The brother had been led to his resolution (so he told me) by consideration of the unusual character of the malady of the deceased, of certain obtrusive and eager inquiries on the part of her medical men, and of the remote and exposed situation of the burial-ground of the family. I will not deny that when I called to mind the sinister countenance of the person whom I met upon the staircase, on the day of my arrival at the house, I had no desire to oppose what I regarded as at best but a harmless, and by no means an unnatural, precaution.

At the request of Usher, I personally aided him in the arrangements for the temporary entombment. The body having been encoffined, we two alone bore it to its rest. The vault in which we placed it (and which had been so long unopened that our torches, half smothered in its oppressive atmosphere, gave us little opportunity for investigation) was small, damp, and entirely without means of admission for light; lying, at great depth, immediately beneath that portion of the building in which was my own sleeping apartment. It had been used, apparently, in remote feudal times, for the worst purposes of a donjon-keep, and, in later days, as a place of deposit for powder, or some other highly combustible substance, as a portion of its floor, and the whole interior of a long archway through which we reached it, were carefully sheathed with copper. The door, of massive iron, had been, also, similarly protected. Its immense weight caused an unusually sharp grating sound, as it moved upon its hinges.

Having deposited our mournful burden upon tressels within this region of horror, we partially turned aside the yet unscrewed lid of the coffin, and looked upon the face of the tenant. A striking similitude between the brother and sister now first arrested my attention; and Usher, divining, perhaps, my thoughts, murmured out some few words from which I learned that the deceased and himself had been twins, and that sympathies of a scarcely intelligible nature had always existed between them. Our glances, however, rested not long upon the dead — for we could not regard her unawed. The disease which had thus entombed the lady in the maturity of youth, had left, as usual in all maladies of a strictly cataleptical character, the mockery of a faint blush upon the bosom and the face, and that suspiciously lingering smile upon the lip which is so terrible in death. We replaced and screwed down the lid, and, having secured the door of iron, made our way, with toil, into the scarcely less gloomy apartments of the upper portion of the house.

And now, some days of bitter grief having elapsed, an observable change came over the features of the mental disorder of my friend. His ordinary manner had vanished. His ordinary occupations were neglected or forgotten. He roamed from chamber to chamber with hurried, unequal, and objectless step. The pallor of his countenance had assumed, if possible, a more ghastly hue — but the luminousness of his eye had utterly gone out. The once occasional huskiness of his tone was heard no more; and a tremulous quaver, as if of extreme terror, habitually characterized his utterance. There were times, indeed, when I thought his unceasingly agitated mind was laboring with some oppressive secret, to divulge which he struggled for the necessary courage. At times, again, I was obliged to resolve all into the mere inexplicable vagaries of madness, for I beheld him gazing upon vacancy for long hours, in an attitude of the profoundest attention, as if listening to some imaginary sound. It was no wonder that his condition terrified — that it infected me. I felt creeping upon me, by slow yet certain degrees, the wild influences of his own fantastic yet impressive superstitions.

It was, especially, upon retiring to bed late in the night of the seventh or eighth day after the placing of the lady Madeline within the donjon, that I experienced the full power of such feelings. Sleep came not near my couch — while the hours waned and waned away. I struggled to reason off the nervousness which had dominion over me. I endeavored to believe that much, if not all of what I felt, was due to the bewildering influence of the gloomy furniture of the room — of the dark and tattered draperies, which, tortured into motion by the breath of a rising tempest, swayed fitfully to and fro upon the walls, and rustled uneasily about the decorations of the bed. But my efforts were fruitless. An irrepressible tremor gradually pervaded my frame; and, at length, there sat upon my very heart an incubus of utterly causeless alarm. Shaking this off with a gasp and a struggle, I uplifted myself upon the pillows, and, peering earnestly within the intense darkness of the chamber, harkened — I know not why, except that an instinctive spirit prompted me — to certain low and indefinite sounds which came, through the pauses of the storm, at long intervals, I knew not whence. Overpowered by an intense sentiment of horror, unaccountable yet unendurable, I threw on my clothes with haste (for I felt that I should sleep no more during the night), and endeavored to arouse myself from the pitiable condition into which I had fallen, by pacing rapidly to and fro through the apartment.

I had taken but few turns in this manner, when a light step on an adjoining staircase arrested my attention. I presently recognized it as that of Usher. In an instant afterward he rapped, with a gentle touch, at my door, and entered, bearing a lamp. His countenance was, as usual, cadaverously wan — but, moreover, there was a species of mad hilarity in his eyes — an evidently restrained *hysteria* in his whole demeanor. His air appalled me — but anything was preferable to the solitude which I had so long endured, and I even welcomed his presence as a relief.

"And you have not seen it?" he said abruptly, after having stared about him for some moments in silence — "you have not then seen it? — but, stay! you shall." Thus speaking, and having carefully shaded his lamp, he hurried to one of the casements, and threw it freely open to the storm.

The impetuous fury of the entering gust nearly lifted us from our feet. It was, indeed, a tempestuous yet sternly beautiful night, and one wildly singular in its terror and its beauty. A whirlwind had apparently collected its force in our vicinity; for there were frequent and violent alterations in the direction of the wind; and the exceeding density of the clouds (which hung so low as to press upon the turrets of the house) did not prevent our perceiving the life-like velocity with which they flew careering from all points against each other, without passing away into the distance. I say that even their exceeding density did not prevent our perceiving this — yet we had no glimpse of the moon or stars — nor was there any flashing forth of the lightning. But the under surfaces of the huge masses of agitated vapor, as well as all terrestrial objects immediately around us, were glowing in the unnatural light of a faintly luminous and distinctly visible gaseous exhalation which hung about and enshrouded the mansion.

"You must not — you shall not behold this!" said I, shudderingly, to Usher, as I led him, with a gentle violence, from the window to a seat. "These appearances, which bewilder you, are merely electrical phenomena not uncommon — or it may be that they have their ghastly origin in the rank miasma of the tarn. Let us close this casement; — the air is chilling and dangerous to your frame. Here is one of your favorite romances. I will read, and you shall listen; — and so we will pass away this terrible night together."

The antique volume which I had taken up was the "Mad Trist" of Sir Launcelot Canning; but I had called it a favorite of Usher's more in sad jest than in earnest; for, in truth, there is little in its uncouth and unimaginative prolixity which could have had interest for the lofty and spiritual ideality of my friend. It was, however, the only book immediately at hand; and I indulged a vague hope that the excitement which now agitated the hypochondriac, might find relief (for the history of mental disorder is full of similar anomalies) even in the extremeness of the folly which I should read. Could I have judged, indeed, by the wild overstrained air of vivacity with which he harkened, or apparently harkened, to the words of the tale, I might well have congratulated myself upon the success of my design.

I had arrived at that well-known portion of the story where Ethelred, the hero of the Trist, having sought in vain for peaceable admission into the dwelling of the hermit, proceeds to make good an entrance by force. Here, it will be remembered, the words of the narrative run thus:

"And Ethelred, who was by nature of a doughty heart, and who was now mighty withal, on account of the powerfulness of the wine which he had drunken, waited no longer to hold parley with the hermit, who, in sooth, was of an obstinate and maliceful turn, but, feeling the rain upon his shoulders, and fearing the rising of the tempest, uplifted his mace outright, and, with blows, made quickly room in the plankings of the door for his gauntleted hand; and now pulling therewith sturdily, he so cracked, and ripped, and tore all asunder, that the noise of the dry and hollow-sounding wood alarummed and reverberated throughout the forest."

At the termination of this sentence I started, and for a moment, paused; for it appeared to me (although I at once concluded that my excited fancy had deceived me) — it appeared to me that, from some very remote portion of the mansion, there came, indistinctly, to my ears, what might have been, in its exact similarity of character, the echo (but a stifled and dull one certainly) of the very cracking and ripping sound which Sir Launcelot had so particularly described. It was, beyond doubt, the coincidence alone which had arrested my attention; for, amid the rattling of the sashes of the casements, and the ordinary commingled noises of the still increasing storm, the sound, in itself, had nothing, surely, which should have interested or disturbed me. I continued the story:

"But the good champion Ethelred, now entering within the door, was sore enraged and amazed to perceive no signal of the maliceful hermit; but, in the stead thereof, a dragon of a scaly and prodigious demeanor, and of a fiery tongue, which sate in guard before a palace of gold, with a floor of silver; and upon the wall there hung a shield of shining brass with this legend enwritten —

Who entereth herein, a conqueror hath bin;
Who slayeth the dragon, the shield he shall win;

And Ethelred uplifted his mace, and struck upon the head of the dragon, which fell before him, and gave up his pesty breath, with a shriek so horrid and harsh, and withal so piercing, that Ethelred had fain to close his ears with his hands against the dreadful noise of it, the like whereof was never before heard."

Here again I paused abruptly, and now with a feeling of wild amazement — for there could be no doubt whatever that, in this instance, I did actually hear (although from what direction it proceeded I found it impossible to say) a low and apparently distant, but harsh, protracted, and most unusual screaming or grating sound — the exact counterpart of what my fancy had already conjured up for the dragon's unnatural shriek as described by the romancer.

Oppressed, as I certainly was, upon the occurrence of this second and most extraordinary coincidence, by a thousand conflicting sensations, in which wonder and extreme terror were predominant, I still retained sufficient presence of mind to avoid exciting, by any observation, the sensitive nervousness of my companion. I was by no means certain that he had noticed the sounds in question; although, assuredly, a strange alteration had, during the last few minutes, taken place in his demeanor. From a position fronting my own, he had gradually brought round his chair, so as to sit with his face to the door of the chamber; and thus I could but partially perceive his features, although I saw that his lips trembled as if he were murmuring inaudibly. His head had dropped upon his breast — yet I knew that he was not asleep, from the wide and rigid opening of the eye as I caught a glance of it in profile. The motion of his body, too, was at variance with this idea — for he rocked from side to side with a gentle yet constant and uniform sway. Having rapidly taken notice of all this, I resumed the narrative of Sir Launcelot, which thus proceeded:

"And now, the champion, having escaped from the terrible fury of the dragon, bethinking himself of the brazen shield, and of the breaking up of the enchantment which was upon it, removed the carcass from out of the way before him, and approached valorously over the silver pavement of the castle to where the shield was upon the wall; which in sooth tarried not for his full coming, but fell down at his feet upon the silver floor, with a mighty great and terrible ringing sound."

No sooner had these syllables passed my lips, than — as if a shield of brass had indeed, at the moment, fallen heavily upon a floor of silver — I became aware of a distinct, hollow, metallic, and clangorous, yet apparently muffled reverberation. Completely unnerved, I leaped to my feet; but the measured rocking movement of Usher was undisturbed. I rushed to the chair in which he sat. His eyes were bent fixedly before him, and throughout his whole countenance there reigned a stony rigidity. But, as I placed my hand upon his shoulder, there came a strong shudder over his whole person; a sickly smile quivered about his lips; and I saw that he spoke in a low, hurried, and gibbering murmur, as if unconscious of my presence. Bending closely over him, I at length drank in the hideous import of his words.

"Not hear it? — yes, I hear it, and *have* heard it. Long — long — long — many minutes, many hours, many days, have I heard it — yet I dared not — oh, pity me, miserable wretch that I am! — I *dared* not — I dared not speak! *We have put her living in the tomb!* Said I not that my senses were acute? I *now* tell you that I heard her first feeble movements in the hollow coffin. I heard them — many, many days ago — yet I dared not — I *dared not speak!* And now — to-night — Ethelred — ha! ha! — the breaking of the hermit's door, and the death-cry of the dragon, and the clangor of the shield! — say, rather, the rending of her coffin, and the grating of the iron hinges of her prison, and her struggles within the coppered archway of the vault! Oh whither shall I fly? Will she not be here anon? Is she not hurrying to upbraid me for my haste? Have I not heard her footstep on the stair? Do I not distinguish that heavy and horrible beating of her heart? Madman!" — here he sprang furiously to his feet, and shrieked out his syllables, as if in the effort he were giving up his soul — "MADMAN! I TELL YOU THAT SHE NOW STANDS WITHOUT THE DOOR!"

As if in the superhuman energy of his utterance there had been found the potency of a spell — the huge antique pannels to which the speaker pointed, threw slowly back, upon the instant, their ponderous and ebony jaws. It was the work of the rushing gust — but then without those doors there *did* stand the lofty and enshrouded figure of the lady Madeline of Usher. There was blood upon her white robes, and the evidence of some bitter struggle upon every portion of her emaciated frame. For a moment she remained trembling and reeling to and fro upon the threshold — then, with a low moaning cry, fell heavily inward upon the person of her brother, and in her violent and now final death-agonies, bore him to the floor a corpse, and a victim to the terrors he had anticipated.

From that chamber, and from that mansion, I fled aghast. The storm was still abroad in all its wrath as I found myself crossing the old causeway. Suddenly there shot along the path a wild light, and I turned to see whence a gleam so unusual could have issued; for the vast house and its shadows were alone behind me. The radiance was that of the full, setting, and blood-red moon, which now shone vividly through that once barely-discernible fissure, of which I have before spoken as extending from the roof of the building, in a zigzag direction, to the base. While I gazed, this fissure rapidly widened — there came a fierce breath of the whirlwind — the entire orb of the satellite burst at once upon my sight — my brain reeled as I saw the mighty walls rushing asunder — there was a long tumultuous shouting sound like the voice of a thousand waters — and the deep and dank tarn at my feet closed sullenly and silently over the fragments of the *"House of Usher."*

THE GHOST IN THE MILL

Harriet Beecher Stowe (1811-1896)

"Come, Sam, tell us a story," said I, as Harry and I crept to his knees, in the glow of the bright evening firelight; while Aunt Lois was busily rattling the tea-things, and grandmamma, at the other end of the fireplace, was quietly setting the heel of a blue-mixed yarn stocking.

In those days we had no magazines and daily papers, each reeling off a serial story. Once a week, "The Columbian Sentinel" came from Boston with its slender stock of news and editorial; but all the multiform devices — pictorial, narrative, and poetical — which keep the mind of the present generation ablaze with excitement, had not then even an existence. There was no theatre, no opera; there were in Oldtown no parties or balls, except, perhaps, the annual election, or Thanksgiving festival; and when winter came, and the sun went down at half-past four o'clock, and left the long, dark hours of evening to be provided for, the necessity of amusement became urgent. Hence, in those days, chimney-corner story-telling became an art and an accomplishment. Society then was full of traditions and narratives which had all the uncertain glow and shifting mystery of the firelit hearth upon them. They were told to sympathetic audiences, by the rising and falling light of the solemn embers, with the hearth-crickets filling up every pause. Then the aged told their stories, to the young, — tales of early life; tales of war and adventure, of forest-days, of Indian captivities and escapes, of bears and wild-cats and panthers, of rattlesnakes, of witches and wizards, and strange and wonderful dreams and appearances and providences.

In those days of early Massachusetts, faith and credence were in the very air. Two-thirds of New England was then dark, unbroken forests, through whose tangled paths the mysterious winter wind groaned and shrieked and howled with weird noises and unaccountable clamours. Along the iron-bound shore, the stormful Atlantic raved and thundered, and dashed its moaning waters, as if to deaden and deafen any voice that might tell of the settled life of the old civilized world, and shut us forever into the wilderness. A good story-teller, in those days, was always sure of a warm seat at the hearth-stone, and the delighted homage of children; and in all Oldtown there was no better story-teller than Sam Lawson.

"Do, do, tell us a story," said Harry, pressing upon him, and opening very wide blue eyes, in which undoubting faith shone as in a mirror; "and let it be something strange, and different from common."

"Wal, I know lots o' strange things," said Sam, looking mysteriously into the fire. "Why, I know things, that ef I should tell, — why, people might say they wa'n't so; but then they *is* so for all that."

"Oh, *do*, do, tell us!"

"Why, I should scare ye to death, mebbe," said Sam doubtingly.

"Oh, pooh! no, you wouldn't," we both burst out at once.

But Sam was possessed by a reticent spirit, and loved dearly to be wooed and importuned; and so he only took up the great kitchen-tongs, and smote on the hickory forestick, when it flew apart in the middle, and scattered a shower of clear bright coals all over the hearth.

"Mercy on us, Sam Lawson!" said Aunt Lois in an indignant voice, spinning round from her dishwashing.

"Don't you worry a grain, Miss Lois," said Sam composedly. "I see that are stick was e'en a'most in two, and I thought I'd jest settle it. I'll sweep up the coals now," he added, vigorously applying a turkey-wing to the purpose, as he knelt on the hearth, his spare, lean figure glowing in the blaze of the firelight, and getting quite flushed with exertion.

"There, now!" he said, when he had brushed over and under and between the fire-irons, and pursued the retreating ashes so far into the red, fiery citadel, that his finger-ends were burning and tingling, "that are's done now as well as Hepsy herself could a' done it. I allers sweeps up the haarth: I think it's part o' the man's bisness when he makes the fire. But Hepsy's so used to seein' me a-doin' on't, that she don't see no kind o' merit in't. It's just as Parson Lothrop said in his sermon, — folks allers overlook their common marcies" —

"But come, Sam, that story," said Harry and I coaxingly, pressing upon him, and pulling him down into his seat in the corner.

"Lordy massy, these 'ere young uns!" said Sam. "There's never no contentin' on 'em: ye tell 'em one story, and they jest swallows it as a dog does a gob o' meat; and they're all ready for another. What do ye want to hear now?"

Now, the fact was, that Sam's stories had been told us so often, that they were all arranged and ticketed in our minds. We knew every word in them, and could set him right if he varied a hair from the usual track; and still the interest in them was unabated. Still we shivered, and clung to his knee, at the mysterious parts, and felt gentle, cold chills run down our spines at appropriate places. We were always in the most receptive and sympathetic condition. Tonight, in particular, was one of those thundering stormy ones, when the winds appeared to be holding a perfect mad carnival over my grandfather's house. They yelled and squealed round the corners; they collected in troops, and came tumbling and roaring down chimney; they shook and rattled the buttery-door and the sinkroom-door and the cellar-door and the chamber-door, with a constant undertone of squeak and clatter, as if at every door were a cold, discontented spirit, tired of the chill outside, and longing for the warmth and comfort within.

"Wal, boys," said Sam confidentially, "what'll ye have?"

"Tell us 'Come down, come down!' " we both shouted with one voice. This was, in our mind, an "A No. 1" among Sam's stories.

"Ye mus'n't be frightened now," said Sam Paternally.

"Oh, no! we ar'n't frightened *ever* ," said we both in one breath.

"Not when ye go down the cellar arter cider?" said Sam with severe scrutiny. "Ef ye should be down cellar, and the candle should go out, now?"

"I ain't," said I: "I ain't afraid of any thing. I never knew what it was to be afraid in my life."

"Wal, then," said Sam, "I'll tell ye. This 'ere's what Cap'n Eb Sawin told me when I was a boy about your bigness, I reckon.

"Cap'n Eb Sawin was a most respectable man. Your gran'ther knew him very well; and he was a deacon in the church in Dedham afore he died. He was at Lexington when the fust gun was fired agin the British. He was a dreffle smart man, Cap'n Eb was, and driv team a good many years atween here and Boston. He married Lois Peabody, that was cousin to your gran'ther then. Lois was a real sensible woman; and I've heard her tell the story as he told her, and it was jest as he told it to me, — jest exactly; and I shall never forget it if I live to be nine hundred years old, like Mathuselah.

"Ye see, along back in them times, there used to be a fellow come round these 'ere parts, spring and fall, a-peddlin' goods, with his pack on his back; and his name was Jehiel Lommedieu. Nobody rightly knew where he come from. He wasn't much of a talker; but the women rather liked him, and kind o' liked to have him round. Women will like some fellows, when men can't see no sort o' reason why they should; and they liked this 'ere Lommedieu, though he was kind o' mournful and thin and shadbellied, and hadn't nothin' to say for himself. But it got to be so, that the women would count and calculate so many weeks afore 'twas time for Lommedieu to be along; and they'd make up gingersnaps and preserves and pies, and make him stay to tea at the houses, and feed him up on the best there was: and the story went round, that he was a-courtin' Phebe Ann Parker, or Phebe Ann was a-courtin' him, — folks didn't rightly know which. Wal, all of a sudden, Lommedieu stopped comin' round; and nobody knew why, — only jest he didn't come. It turned out that Phebe Ann Parker had got a letter from him, sayin' he'd be along afore Thanksgiving; but he didn't come, neither afore nor at Thanksgiving time, nor arter, nor next spring: and finally the women they gin up lookin' for him. Some said he was dead; some said he was gone to Canada; and some said he hed gone over to the Old Country.

"Wal, as to Phebe Ann, she acted like a gal o' sense, and married 'Bijah Moss, and thought no more 'bout it. She took the right view on't, and said she was sartin that all things was ordered out for the best; and it was jest as well folks couldn't always have their own way. And so, in time, Lommedieu was gone out o' folks's minds, much as a last year's apple-blossom.

"It's relly affectin' to think how little these 'ere folks is missed that's so much sot by. There ain't nobody, ef they's ever so important, but what the world gets to goin' on without 'em, pretty much as it did with 'em, though there's some little flurry at fust. Wal, the last thing that was in anybody's mind was, that they ever should hear from Lommedieu agin. But there ain't nothin' but what has its time o' turnin' up; and it seems his turn was to come.

"Wal, ye see, 'twas the 19th o' March, when Cap'n Eb Sawin started with a team for Boston. That day, there come on about the biggest snow-storm that there'd been in them parts sence the oldest man could remember. 'Twas this 'ere fine, siftin' snow, that drives in your face like needles, with a wind to cut your nose off: it made teamin' pretty tedious work. Cap'n Eb was about the toughest man in them parts. He'd spent days in the woods a-loggin', and he'd been up to the deestrict o' Maine a-lumberin', and was about up to any sort o' thing a man gen'ally could be up to; but these 'ere March winds sometimes does set on a fellow so, that neither natur' nor grace can stan' 'em. The cap'n used to say he could stan' any wind that blew one way't time for five minutes; but come to winds that blew all four p'ints at the same minit, — why, they flustered him.

"Wal, that was the sort o' weather it was all day: and by sundown Cap'n Eb he got clean bewildered, so that he lost his road; and, when night came on, he didn't know nothin' where he was. Ye see the country was all under drift, and the air so thick with snow, that he couldn't see a foot afore him; and the fact was, he got off the Boston road without knowin' it, and came out at a pair o' bars nigh upon Sherburn, where old Cack Sparrock's mill is.

"Your gran'ther used to know old Cack, boys. He was a drefful drinkin' old crittur, that lived there all alone in the woods by himself a-tendin' saw and grist mill. He wa'n't allers jest what he was then. Time was that Cack was a pretty consid'ably likely young man, and his wife was a very respectable woman, — Deacon Amos Petengall's dater from Sherburn.

"But ye see, the year arter his wife died, Cack he gin up goin' to meetin' Sundays, and, all the tithing-men and selectmen could do, they couldn't get him out to meetin'; and, when a man neglects means o' grace and sanctuary privileges, there ain't no sayin' *what* he'll do next. Why, boys, jist think on't! — an immortal crittur lyin' round loose all day Sunday, and not puttin' on so much as a clean shirt, when all 'spectable folks has on their best close, and is to meetin' worshippin' the Lord! What can you spect to come' of it, when he lies idlin' round in his old week-day close, fishing, or some sich, but what the Devil should be arter him at last, as he was arter old Cack?"

Here Sam winked impressively to my grandfather in the opposite corner, to call his attention to the moral which he was interweaving with his narrative.

"Wal, ye see, Cap'n Eb he told me, that when he come to them bars and looked up, and saw the dark a-comin' down, and the storm a-thickenin' up, he felt that things was gettin' pretty consid'able serious. There was a dark piece o' woods on ahead of him inside the bars; and he knew, come to get in there, the light would give out clean. So he jest thought he'd take the hoss out o' the team, and go ahead a little, and see where he was. So he driv his oxen up ag'in the fence, and took out the hoss, and got on him, and pushed along through the woods, not rightly knowin' where he was goin'.

"Wal, afore long he see a light through the trees; and, sure enough, he come out to Cack Sparrock's old mill.

"It was a pretty consid'able gloomy sort of a place, that are old mill was. There was a great fall of water that come rushin' down the rocks, and fell in a deep pool; and it sounded sort o' wild and lonesome: but Cap'n Eb he knocked on the door with his whiphandle, and got in.

"There, to be sure, sot old Cack beside a great blazin' fire, with his rum-jug at his elbow. He was a drefful fellow to drink, Cack was! For all that, there was some good in him, for he was pleasant-spoken and 'bliging; and he made the cap'n welcome.

" 'Ye see, Cack,' said Cap'n Eb, 'I'm off my road, and got snowed up down by your bars,' says he.

" 'Want ter know!' says Cack. 'Calculate you'll jest have to camp down here till mornin',' says he.

"Wal, so old Cack he got out his tin lantern, and went with Cap'n Eb back to the bars to help him fetch along his critturs. He told him he could put 'em under the mill-shed. So they got the critturs up to the shed, and got the cart under; and by that time the storm was awful.

"But Cack he made a great roarin' fire, 'cause, ye see, Cack allers had slab-wood a plenty from his mill; and a roarin' fire is jest so much company. It sort o' keeps a fellow's spirits up, a good fire does. So Cack he sot on his old teakettle, and made a swingeing lot o' toddy; and he and Cap'n Eb were havin' a tol'able comfortable time there. Cack was a pretty good hand to tell stories; and Cap'n Eb warn't no way backward in that line, and kep' up his end pretty well: and pretty soon they was a-roarin' and haw-hawin' inside about as loud as the storm outside; when all of a sudden, 'bout midnight, there come a loud rap on the door.

" 'Lordy massy! what's that?' says Cack. Folks is rather startled allers to be checked up sudden when they are a-carryin' on and laughin'; and it was such an awful blowy night, it was a little scary to have a rap on the door.

"Wal, they waited a minit, and didn't hear nothin' but the wind a-screechin' round the chimbley; and old Cack was jest goin' on with his story, when the rap come ag'in, harder'n ever, as if it'd shook the door open.

" 'Wal,' says old Cack, 'if 'tis the Devil, we'd jest as good's open, and have it out with him to onst,' says he; and so he got up and opened the door and, sure enough, there was old Ketury there. Expect you've heard your grandma tell about old Ketury. She used to come to meetin's sometimes, and her husband was one o' the prayin' Indians; but Ketury was one of the real wild sort, and you couldn't no more convert *her* than you could convert a wild-cat or a panth'a. Lordy massy! Ketury used to come to meetin', and sit there on them Indian benches; and when the second bell was a-tollin', and when Parson Lothrop and his wife was comin' up the broad aisle, and everybody in the house ris' up and stood, Ketury would sit there, and look at 'em out o' the corner o' her eyes; and folks used to say she rattled them necklaces o' rattlesnakes' tails and wild-cat teeth, and sich like heathen trumpery, and looked for all the world as if the spirit of the old Sarpent himself was in her. I've seen her sit and look at Lady Lothrop out o' the corner o' her eyes; and her old brown baggy neck would kind o' twist and work; and her eyes they looked so, that 'twas enough to scare a body. For all the world, she looked jest as if she was a-workin' up to spring at her. Lady Lothrop was jest as kind to Ketury as she always was to every poor crittur. She'd bow and smile as gracious to her when meetin' was over, and she come down the aisle, passin' out o' meetin'; but Ketury never took no notice. Ye see, Ketury's father was one o' them great powwows down to Martha's Vineyard; and people used to say she was set apart, when she was a child, to the sarvice o' the Devil: any way, she never could be made nothin' of in a Christian way. She come down to Parson Lothrop's study once or twice to be catechised; but he couldn't get a word out o' her, and she kind o' seemed to sit scornful while he was a-talkin'. Folks said, if it was in old times, Ketury wouldn't have been allowed to go on so; but Parson Lothrop's so sort o' mild, he let her take pretty much her own way. Everybody thought that Ketury was a witch: at least, she knew consid'able more'n she ought to know, and so they was kind o' 'fraid on her. Cap'n Eb says he never see a fellow seem scareder than Cack did when he see Ketury a-standin' there.

"Why, ye see, boys, she was as withered and wrinkled and brown as an old frosted punkin-vine; and her little snaky eyes sparkled and snapped, and it made yer head kind o' dizzy to look at 'em; and folks used to say that anybody that Ketury got mad at was sure to get the worst of it fust or last. And so, no matter what day or hour Ketury had a mind to rap at anybody's door, folks gen'lly thought it was best to let her in; but then, they never thought her coming was for any good, for she was just like the wind, — she came when the fit was on her, she staid jest so long as it pleased her, and went when she got ready, and not before. Ketury understood English, and could talk it well enough, but always seemed to scorn it, and was allers mowin' and mutterin' to herself in Indian, and winkin' and blinkin' as if she saw more folks round than you did, so that she wa'n't no way pleasant company; and yet everybody took good care to be polite to her.

So old Cack asked her to come in, and didn't make no question where she come from, or what she come on; but he knew it was twelve good miles from where she lived to his hut, and the snow was drifted above her middle: and Cap'n Eb declared that there wa'n't no track, nor sign o' a track, of anybody's coming through that snow next morning."

"How did she get there, then?" said I.

"Didn't ye never see brown leaves a-ridin' on the wind? Well, Cap'n Eb he says, 'she came on the wind,' and I'm sure it was strong enough to fetch her. But Cack he got her down into the warm corner, and he poured her out a mug o' hot toddy, and give her: but ye see her bein' there sort o' stopped the conversation; for she sot there a-rockin' back'ards and for'ards, a-sippin her toddy, and a-mutterin', and lookin' up chimbley.

"Cap'n Eb says in all his born days he never hearn such screeches and yells as the wind give over that chimbley; and old Cack got so frightened, you could fairly hear his teeth chatter.

"But Cap'n Eb he was a putty brave man, and he wa'n't goin' to have conversation stopped by no woman, witch or no witch; and so, when he see her mutterin', and lookin' up chimbley, he spoke up, and says he, 'Well, Ketury, what do you see?' says he. 'Come, out with it; don't keep it to yourself.' Ye see Cap'n Eb was a hearty fellow, and then he was a leetle warmed up with the toddy.

"Then he said he see an evil kind o' smile on Ketury's face, and she rattled her necklace o' bones and snakes' tails; and her eyes seemed to snap; and she looked up the chimbley, and called out, 'Come down, come down! let's see who ye be.'

"Then there was a scratchin' and a rumblin' and a groan; and a pair of feet come down the chimbley, and stood right in the middle of the haarth, the toes pi'ntin' out'rds, with shoes and silver buckles a-shin-in' in the firelight. Cap'n Eb says he never come so near bein' scared in his life; and, as to old Cack, he jest wilted right down in his chair.

"Then old Ketury got up, and reached her stick up chimbley, and called out louder, 'Come down, come down! let's see who ye be.' And, sure enough, down came a pair o' legs, and j'ined right on to the feet: good fair legs they was, with ribbed stockings and leather breeches.

"'Wal, we're in for it now,' says Cap'n Eb. 'Go it, Ketury, and let's have the rest on him.'

"Ketury didn't seem to mind him: she stood there as stiff as a stake, and kep' callin' out, 'Come down, come down! let's see who ye be.' And then come down the body of a man with a brown coat and yellow vest, and j'ined right on to the legs; but there wa'n't no arms to it. Then Ketury shook her stick up chimbley, and called, '*Come down, come down!*' And there came down a pair o' arms, and went on each side o' the body; and there stood a man all finished, only there wa'n't no head on him.

"'Wal, Ketury,' says Cap'n Eb, 'this 'ere's getting serious. I 'spec' you must finish him up, and let's see what he wants of us.'

"Then Ketury called out once more, louder'n ever, 'Come down, come down! let's see who ye be.' And, sure enough, down comes a man's head, and settled on the shoulders straight enough; and Cap'n Eb, the minit he sot eyes on him, knew he was Jehiel Lommedieu.

"Old Cack knew him too; and he fell flat on his face, and prayed the Lord to have mercy on his soul: but Cap'n Eb he was for gettin' to the bottom of matters, and not have his scare for nothin'; so he says to him, 'What do you want, now you hev come?'

"The man he didn't speak; he only sort o' moaned, and p'inted to the chimbley. He seemed to try to speak, but couldn't; for ye see it isn't often that his sort o' folks is permitted to speak: but just then there came a screechin' blast o' wind, and blowed the door open, and blowed the smoke and fire all out into the room, and there seemed to be a whirlwind and darkness and moans and screeches; and, when it all cleared up, Ketury and the man was both gone, and only old Cack lay on the ground, rolling and moaning as if he'd die.

"Wal, Cap'n Eb he picked him up, and built up the fire, and sort o' comforted him up, 'cause the crittur was in distress o' mind that was drefful. The awful Providence, ye see, had awakened him, and his sin had been set home to his soul; and he was under such conviction, that it all had to come out, — how old Cack's father had murdered poor Lommedieu for his money, and Cack had been privy to it, and helped his father build the body up in that very chimbley; and he said that he hadn't had neither peace nor rest since then, and that was what had driv' him away from ordinances; for ye know sinnin' will always make a man leave prayin'. Wal, Cack didn't live but a day or two. Cap'n Eb he got the minister o' Sherburn and one o' the selectmen down to see him; and they took his deposition. He seemed railly quite penitent; and Parson Carryl he prayed with him, and was faithful in settin' home the providence to his soul: and so, at the eleventh hour, poor old Cack might have got in; at least it looks a leetle like it. He was distressed to think he couldn't live to be hung. He sort o' seemed to think, that if he was fairly tried, and hung, it would make it all square. He made Parson Carryl promise to have the old mill pulled down, and bury the body; and, after he was dead, they did it.

"Cap'n Eb he was one of a party o' eight that pulled down the chimbley; and there, sure enough, was the skeleton of poor Lommedieu.

"So there you see, boys, there can't be no iniquity so hid but what it'll come out. The wild Indians of the forest, and the stormy winds and tempests, j'ined together to bring out this 'ere."

"For my part," said Aunt Lois sharply, "I never believed that story."

"Why, Lois," said my grandmother, "Cap'n Eb Sawin was a regular church-member, and a most respectable man."

"Law, mother! I don't doubt he thought so. I suppose he and Cack got drinking toddy together, till he got asleep, and dreamed it. I wouldn't believe such a thing if it did happen right before my face and eyes. I should only think I was crazy, that's all."

"Come, Lois, if I was you, I wouldn't talk so like a Sadducee," said my grandmother. "What would become of all the accounts in Dr. Cotton Mather's 'Magnilly' if folks were like you?"

"Wal," said Sam Lawson, drooping contemplatively over the coals, and gazing into the fire, "there's a putty consid'able sight o' things in this world that's true; and then ag'in there's a sight o' things that ain't true. Now, my old gran'ther used to say, 'Boys,' says he, 'if ye want to lead a pleasant and prosperous life, ye must contrive allers to keep jest the *happy medium* between truth and falsehood.' Now, that are's my doctrine."

Aunt Lois knit severely.

"Boys," said Sam, "don't you want ter go down with me and get a mug o' cider?"

Of course we did, and took down a basket to bring up some apples to roast.

"Boys," says Sam mysteriously, while he was drawing the cider, "you jest ask your Aunt Lois to tell you what she knows 'bout Ruth Sullivan."

"Why, what is it?"

"Oh! you must ask *her*. These 'ere folks that's so kind o' toppin' about sperits and sich, come sift 'em down, you gen'lly find they knows one story that kind o' puzzles 'em. Now you mind, and jist ask your Aunt Lois about Ruth Sullivan."

BARTLEBY, THE SCRIVENER: A STORY OF WALL STREET

Herman Melville (1819-1891)

I am a rather elderly man. The nature of my avocations for the last thirty years has brought me into more than ordinary contact with what would seem an interesting and somewhat singular set of men, of whom as yet nothing that I know of has ever been written: — I mean the law-copyists or scriveners. I have known very many of them, professionally and privately, and if I pleased, could relate divers histories, at which good-natured gentlemen might smile, and sentimental souls might weep. But I waive the biographies of all other scriveners for a few passages in the life of Bartleby, who was a scrivener of the strangest I ever saw or heard of. While of other law-copyists I might write the complete life, of Bartleby nothing of that sort can be done. I believe that no materials exist for a full and satisfactory biography of this man. It is an irreparable loss to literature. Bartleby was one of those beings of whom nothing is ascertainable, except from the original sources, and in his case those are very small. What my own astonished eyes saw of Bartleby, *that* is all I know of him, except, indeed, one vague report which will appear in the sequel.

Ere introducing the scrivener, as he first appeared to me, it is fit I make some mention of myself, my employees, my business, my chambers, and general surroundings; because some such description is indispensable to an adequate understanding of the chief character about to be presented. *Imprimis*: I am a man who, from his youth upwards, has been filled with a profound conviction that the easiest way of life is the best. Hence, though I belong to a profession proverbially energetic and nervous, even to turbulence, at times, yet nothing of that sort have I ever suffered to invade my peace. I am one of those unambitious lawyers who never addresses a jury, or in any way draws down public applause; but in the cool tranquility of a snug retreat, do a snug business among rich men's bonds and mortgages and title-deeds. All who know me, consider me an eminently *safe* man. The late John Jacob Astor, a personage little given to poetic enthusiasm, had no hesitation in pronouncing my first grand point to be prudence; my next, method. I do not speak it in vanity, but simply record the fact, that I was not unemployed in my profession by the late John Jacob Astor; a name which, I admit, I love to repeat, for it hath a rounded and orbicular sound to it, and rings like unto bullion. I will freely add, that I was not insensible to the late John Jacob Astor's good opinion.

Some time prior to the period at which this little history begins, my avocations had been largely increased. The good old office, now extinct in the State of New York, of a Master in Chancery, had been conferred upon me. It was not a very arduous office, but very pleasantly remunerative. I seldom lose my temper; much more seldom indulge in dangerous indignation at wrongs and outrages; but I must be permitted to be rash here and declare, that I consider the sudden and violent abrogation of the office of Master in Chancery, by the new Constitution, as a —— premature act; inasmuch as I had counted upon a life-lease of the profits, whereas I only received those of a few short years. But this is by the way.

My chambers were upstairs at No. —— Wall-street. At one end they looked upon the white wall of the interior of a spacious sky-light shaft, penetrating the building from top to bottom. This view might have been considered rather tame than otherwise, deficient in what landscape painters call "life." But if so, the view from the other end of my chambers offered, at least, a contrast, if nothing more. In that direction my windows commanded an unobstructed view of a lofty brick wall, black by age and everlasting shade; which wall required no spy-glass to bring out its lurking beauties, but for the benefit of all near-sighted spectators, was pushed up to within ten feet of my window panes. Owing to the great height of the surrounding buildings, and my chambers being on the second floor, the interval between this wall and mine not a little resembled a huge square cistern.

At the period just preceding the advent of Bartleby, I had two persons as copyists in my employment, and a promising lad as an office-boy. First, Turkey; second, Nippers; third, Ginger Nut. These may seem names, the like of which are not usually found in the Directory. In truth they were nicknames, mutually conferred upon each other by my three clerks, and were deemed expressive of their respective persons or characters. Turkey was a short, pursy Englishman of about my own age, that is, somewhere not far from sixty. In the morning, one might say, his face was of a fine florid hue, but after twelve o'clock, meridian — his dinner hour — it blazed like a grate full of Christmas coals; and continued blazing — but, as it were, with a gradual wane — till 6 o'clock, P.M. or thereabouts, after which I saw no more of the proprietor of the face, which gaining its meridian with the sun, seemed to set with it, to rise, culminate, and decline the following day, with the like regularity and undiminished glory. There are many singular coincidences I have known in the course of my life, not the least among which was the fact, that exactly when Turkey displayed his fullest beams from his red and radiant countenance, just then, too, at that critical moment, began the daily period when I considered his business capacities as seriously disturbed for the remainder of the twenty-four hours. Not that he was absolutely idle, or averse to business then; far from it. The difficulty was, he was apt to be altogether too energetic. There was a strange, inflamed, flurried, flighty recklessness of activity about him. He would be incautious in dipping his pen into his inkstand. All his blots upon my documents, were dropped there after twelve o'clock, meridian. Indeed, not only would he be reckless and sadly given to making blots in the afternoon, but some days he went further, and was rather noisy. At such times, too, his face flamed with augmented blazonry, as if cannel coal had been heaped on anthracite. He made an unpleasant racket with his chair; spilled his sand-box; in mending his pens, impatiently split them all to pieces, and threw them on the floor in a sudden passion; stood up and leaned over his table, boxing his papers about in a most indecorous manner, very sad to behold in an elderly man like him. Nevertheless, as he was in many ways a most valuable person to me, and all the time before twelve o'clock, meridian, was the quickest, steadiest creature too, accomplishing a great deal of work in a style not easy to be matched — for these reasons, I was willing to overlook his eccentricities, though indeed, occasionally, I remonstrated with him. I did this very gently, however, because, though the civilest, nay, the blandest and most reverential of men in the morning, yet in the afternoon he was disposed, upon provocation, to be slightly rash with his tongue, in fact, insolent. Now, valuing his morning services as I did, and resolved not to lose them; yet, at the same time made uncomfortable by his inflamed ways after twelve o'clock; and being a man of peace, unwilling by my admonitions to call forth unseemly retorts from him; I took upon me, one Saturday noon (he was always worse on Saturdays), to hint to him, very kindly, that perhaps now that he was growing old, it might be well to abridge his labors; in short, he need not come to my chambers after twelve o'clock, but, dinner over, had best go home to his lodgings and rest himself till teatime. But no; he insisted upon his afternoon devotions. His countenance became intolerably fervid, as he oratorically assured me — gesticulating with a long ruler at the other end of the room — that if his services in the morning were useful, how indispensable, then, in the afternoon?

"With submission, sir," said Turkey on his occasion, "I consider myself your right-hand man. In the morning I but marshal and deploy my columns; but in the afternoon I put myself at their head, and gallantly charge the foe, thus!" — and he made a violent thrust with the ruler.

"But the blots, Turkey," intimated I.

"True, — but, with submission, sir, behold these hairs! I am getting old. Surely, sir, a blot or two of a warm afternoon is not to be severely urged against gray hairs. Old age — even if it blot the page — is honorable. With submission, sir, we *both* are getting old."

This appeal to my fellow-feeling was hardly to be resisted. At all events, I saw that go he would not. So I made up my mind to let him stay, resolving, nevertheless, to see to it, that during the afternoon he had to do with my less important papers.

Nippers, the second on my list, was a whiskered, sallow, and, upon the whole, rather piratical-looking young man of about five and twenty. I always deemed him the victim of two evil powers — ambition and indigestion. The ambition was evinced by a certain impatience of the duties of a mere copyist, an unwarrantable usurpation of strictly professional affairs, such as the original drawing up of legal documents. The indigestion seemed betokened in an occasional nervous testiness and grinning irritability, causing the teeth to audibly grind together over mistakes committed in copying; unnecessary maledictions, hissed, rather than spoken, in the heat of business; and especially by a continual discontent with the height of the table where he worked. Though of a very ingenious mechanical turn, Nippers could never get this table to suit him. He put chips under it, blocks of various sorts, bits of pasteboard, and at last went so far as to attempt an exquisite adjustment by final pieces of folded blotting paper. But no invention would answer. If, for the sake of easing his back, he brought the table lid at a sharp angle well up towards his chin, and wrote there like a man using the steep roof of a Dutch house for his desk: — then he declared that it stopped the circulation in his arms. If now he lowered the table to his waistbands, and stooped over it in writing, then there was a sore aching in his back. In short, the truth of the matter was, Nippers knew not what he wanted. Or, if he wanted any thing, it was to be rid of a scrivener's table altogether. Among the manifestations of his diseased ambition was a fondness he had for receiving visits from certain ambiguous-looking fellows in seedy coats, whom he called his clients. Indeed I was aware that not only was he, at times, considerable of a ward-politician, but he occasionally did a little business at the Justices' courts, and was not unknown on the steps of the Tombs. I have good reason to believe, however, that one individual who called upon him at my chambers, and who, with a grand air, he insisted was his client, was no other than a dun, and the alleged title-deed, a bill. But with all his failings, and the annoyances he caused me, Nippers, like his compatriot Turkey, was a very useful man to me; wrote a neat, swift hand; and, when he chose, was not deficient in a gentlemanly sort of deportment. Added to this, he always dressed in a gentlemanly sort of way; and so, incidentally, reflected credit upon my chambers. Whereas with respect to Turkey, I had much ado to keep him from being a reproach to me. His clothes were apt to look oily and smell of eating-houses. He wore his pantaloons very loose and baggy in summer. His coats were execrable; his hat not to be handled. But while the hat was a thing of indifference to me, inasmuch as his natural civility and deference, as a dependent Englishman, always led him to doff it the moment he entered the room, yet his coat was another matter. Concerning his coats, I reasoned with him; but with no effect. The truth was, I suppose, that a man of so small an income, could not afford to sport such a lustrous face and a lustrous coat at one and the same time. As Nippers once observed, Turkey's money went chiefly for red ink. One winter day I presented Turkey with a highly-respectable looking coat of my own, a padded gray coat, of a most comfortable warmth, and which buttoned straight up from the knee to the neck. I thought Turkey would appreciate the favor, and abate his rashness and obstreperousness of afternoons. But no. I verily believe that buttoning himself up in so downy and blanket-like a coat had a pernicious effect upon him; upon the same principle that too much oats are bad for horses. In fact, precisely as a rash, restive horse is said to feel his oats, so Turkey felt his coat. It made him insolent. He was a man whom prosperity harmed.

Though concerning the self-indulgent habits of Turkey I had my own private surmises, yet touching Nippers I was well persuaded that whatever might be his faults in other respects, he was, at least, a temperate young man. But indeed, nature herself seemed to have been his vintner, and at his birth charged him so thoroughly with an irritable, brandy-like disposition, that all subsequent potations were needless. When I consider how, amid the stillness of my chambers, Nippers would sometimes impatiently rise from his seat, and stooping over his table, spread his arms wide apart, seize the whole desk, and move it, and jerk it, with a grim, grinding motion on the floor, as if the table were a perverse voluntary agent, intent on thwarting and vexing him; I plainly perceive that for Nippers, brandy and water were altogether superfluous.

It was fortunate for me that, owing to its peculiar cause — indigestion — the irritability and consequent nervousness of Nippers were mainly observable in the morning, while in the afternoon he was comparatively mild. So that Turkey's paroxysms only coming on about twelve o'clock, I never had to do with their eccentricities at one time. Their fits relieved each other like guards. When Nippers' was on, Turkey's was off; and vice versa. This was a good natural arrangement under the circumstances.

Ginger Nut, the third on my list, was a lad some twelve years old. His father was a carman, ambitious of seeing his son on the bench instead of a cart, before he died. So he sent him to my office as student at law, errand boy, and cleaner and sweeper, at the rate of one dollar a week. He had a little desk to himself, but he did not use it much. Upon inspection, the drawer exhibited a great array of the shells of various sorts of nuts. Indeed, to this quick-witted youth the whole noble science of the law was contained in a nut-shell. Not the least among the employments of Ginger Nut, as well as one which he discharged with the most alacrity, was his duty as cake and apple purveyor for Turkey and Nippers. Copying law papers being proverbially a dry, husky sort of business, my two scriveners were fain to moisten their mouths very often with Spitzenbergs, to be had at the numerous stalls nigh the Custom House and Post Office. Also, they sent Ginger Nut very frequently for that peculiar cake — small, flat, round, and very spicy — after which he had been named by them. Of a cold morning when business was but dull, Turkey would gobble up scores of these cakes, as if they were mere wafers — indeed they sell them at the rate of six or eight for a penny — the scrape of his pen blending with the crunching of the crisp particles in his mouth. Of all the fiery afternoon blunders and flurried rashnesses of Turkey was his once moistening a ginger-cake between his lips and clapping it on to a mortgage for a seal. I came within an ace of dismissing him then. But he mollified me by making an oriental bow, and saying: — "With submission, sir, it was generous of me to find you in stationery on my own account."

Now my original business — that of a conveyancer and title hunter, and drawer-up of recondite documents of all sorts — was considerably increased by receiving the master's office. There was now great work for scriveners. Not only must I push the clerks already with me, but I must have additional help. In answer to my advertisement, a motionless young man one morning stood upon my office threshold, the door being open, for it was summer. I can see that figure now — pallidly neat, pitiably respectable, incurably forlorn! It was Bartleby.

After a few words touching his qualifications, I engaged him, glad to have among my corps of copyists a man of so singularly sedate an aspect, which I thought might operate beneficially upon the flighty temper of Turkey, and the fiery one of Nippers.

I should have stated before that ground glass folding-doors divided my premises into two parts, one of which was occupied by my scriveners, the other by myself. According to my humor I threw open these doors, or closed them. I resolved to assign Bartleby a corner by the folding-doors, but on my side of them, so as to have this quiet man within easy call, in case any trifling thing was to be done. I placed his desk close up to a small side-window in that part of the room, a window which originally had afforded a lateral view of certain grimy back-yards and bricks, but which, owing to subsequent erections, commanded at present no view at all, though it gave some light. Within three feet of the panes was a wall, and the light came down from far above, between two lofty buildings, as from a very small opening in a dome. Still further to a satisfactory arrangement, I procured a high green folding screen, which might entirely isolate Bartleby from my sight, though not remove him from my voice. And thus, in a manner, privacy and society were conjoined.

At first Bartleby did an extraordinary quantity of writing. As if long famishing for something to copy, he seemed to gorge himself on my documents. There was no pause for digestion. He ran a day and night line, copying by sunlight and by candle-light. I should have been quite delighted with his application, had he been cheerfully industrious. But he wrote on silently, palely, mechanically.

It is, of course, an indispensable part of a scrivener's business to verify the accuracy of his copy, word by word. Where there are two or more scriveners in an office, they assist each other in this examination, one reading from the copy, the other holding the original. It is a very dull, wearisome, and lethargic affair. I can readily imagine that to some sanguine temperaments it would be altogether intolerable. For example, I cannot credit that the mettlesome poet Byron would have contentedly sat down with Bartleby to examine a law document of, say five hundred pages, closely written in a crimpy hand.

Now and then, in the haste of business, it had been my habit to assist in comparing some brief document myself, calling Turkey or Nippers for this purpose. One object I had in placing Bartleby so handy to me behind the screen, was to avail myself of his services on such trivial occasions. It was on the third day, I think, of his being with me, and before any necessity had arisen for having his own writing examined, that, being much hurried to complete a small affair I had in hand, I abruptly called to Bartleby. In my haste and natural expectancy of instant compliance, I sat with my head bent over the original on my desk, and my right hand sideways, and somewhat nervously extended with the copy, so that immediately upon emerging from his retreat, Bartleby might snatch it and proceed to business without the least delay.

In this very attitude did I sit when I called to him, rapidly stating what it was I wanted him to do — namely, to examine a small paper with me. Imagine my surprise, nay, my consternation, when without moving from his privacy, Bartleby in a singularly mild, firm voice, replied, "I would prefer not to."

I sat awhile in perfect silence, rallying my stunned faculties. Immediately it occurred to me that my ears had deceived me, or Bartleby had entirely misunderstood my meaning. I repeated my request in the clearest tone I could assume. But in quite as clear a one came the previous reply, "I would prefer not to."

"Prefer not to," echoed I, rising in high excitement, and crossing the room with a stride. "What do you mean? Are you moon-struck? I want you to help me compare this sheet here — take it," and I thrust it towards him.

"I would prefer not to," said he.

I looked at him steadfastly. His face was leanly composed; his gray eye dimly calm. Not a wrinkle of agitation rippled him. Had there been the least uneasiness, anger, impatience or impertinence in his manner; in other words, had there been any thing ordinarily human about him, doubtless I should have violently dismissed him from the premises. But as it was, I should have as soon thought of turning my pale plaster-of-paris bust of Cicero out of doors. I stood gazing at him awhile, as he went on with his own writing, and then reseated myself at my desk. This is very strange, thought I. What had one best do? But my business hurried me. I concluded to forget the matter for the present, reserving it for my future leisure. So calling Nippers from the other room, the paper was speedily examined.

A few days after this, Bartleby concluded four lengthy documents, being quadruplicates of a week's testimony taken before me in my High Court of Chancery. It became necessary to examine them. It was an important suit, and great accuracy was imperative. Having all things arranged I called Turkey, Nippers and Ginger Nut from the next room, meaning to place the four copies in the hands of my four clerks, while I should read from the original. Accordingly Turkey, Nippers and Ginger Nut had taken their seats in a row, each with his document in hand, when I called to Bartleby to join this interesting group.

"Bartleby! quick, I am waiting."

I heard a slow scrape of his chair legs on the uncarpeted floor, and soon he appeared standing at the entrance of his hermitage.

"What is wanted?" said he mildly.

"The copies, the copies," said I hurriedly. "We are going to examine them. There" — and I held towards him the fourth quadruplicate.

"I would prefer not to," he said, and gently disappeared behind the screen.

For a few moments I was turned into a pillar of salt, standing at the head of my seated column of clerks. Recovering myself, I advanced towards the screen, and demanded the reason for such extraordinary conduct.

"*Why* do you refuse?"

"I would prefer not to."

With any other man I should have flown outright into a dreadful passion, scorned all further words, and thrust him ignominiously from my presence. But there was something about Bartleby that not only strangely disarmed me, but in a wonderful manner touched and disconcerted me. I began to reason with him.

"These are your own copies we are about to examine. It is labor saving to you, because one examination will answer for your four papers. It is common usage. Every copyist is bound to help examine his copy. Is it not so? Will you not speak? Answer!"

"I prefer not to," he replied in a flute-like tone. It seemed to me that while I had been addressing him, he carefully revolved every statement that I made; fully comprehended the meaning; could not gainsay the irresistible conclusions; but, at the same time, some paramount consideration prevailed with him to reply as he did.

"You are decided, then, not to comply with my request — a request made according to common usage and common sense?"

He briefly gave me to understand that on that point my judgment was sound. Yes: his decision was irreversible.

It is not seldom the case that when a man is browbeaten in some unprecedented and violently unreasonable way, he begins to stagger in his own plainest faith. He begins, as it were, vaguely to surmise that, wonderful as it may be, all the justice and all the reason is on the other side. Accordingly, if any disinterested persons are present, he turns to them for some reinforcement for his own faltering mind.

"Turkey," said I, "what do you think of this? Am I not right?"

"With submission, sir," said Turkey, with his blandest tone, "I think that you are."

"Nippers," said I, "what do *you* think of it?"

"I think I should kick him out of the office."

(The reader of nice perceptions will here perceive that, it being morning, Turkey's answer is couched in polite and tranquil terms, but Nippers replies in ill-tempered ones. Or, to repeat a previous sentence, Nippers' ugly mood was on duty and Turkey's off.)

"Ginger Nut," said I, willing to enlist the smallest suffrage in my behalf, "what do *you* think of it?"

"I think, sir, he's a little *luny*," replied Ginger Nut with a grin.

"You hear what they say," said I, turning towards the screen, "come forth and do your duty."

But he vouchsafed no reply. I pondered a moment in sore perplexity. But once more business hurried me. I determined again to postpone the consideration of this dilemma to my future leisure. With a little trouble we made out to examine the papers without Bartleby, though at every page or two, Turkey deferentially dropped his opinion that this proceeding was quite out of the common; while Nippers, twitching in his chair with a dyspeptic nervousness, ground out between his set teeth occasional hissing maledictions against the stubborn oaf behind the screen. And for his (Nippers') part, this was the first and the last time he would do another man's business without pay.

Meanwhile Bartleby sat in his hermitage, oblivious to every thing but his own peculiar business there.

Some days passed, the scrivener being employed upon another lengthy work. His late remarkable conduct led me to regard his ways narrowly. I observed that he never went to dinner; indeed that he never went anywhere. As yet I had never of my personal knowledge known him to be outside of my office. He was a perpetual sentry in the corner. At about eleven o'clock though, in the morning, I noticed that Ginger Nut would advance toward the opening in Bartleby's screen, as if silently beckoned thither by a gesture invisible to me where I sat. The boy would then leave the office jingling a few pence, and reappear with a handful of ginger-nuts which he delivered in the hermitage, receiving two of the cakes for his trouble.

He lives, then, on ginger-nuts, thought I; never eats a dinner, properly speaking; he must be a vegetarian then; but no; he never eats even vegetables, he eats nothing but ginger-nuts. My mind then ran on in reveries concerning the probable effects upon the human constitution of living entirely on ginger-nuts. Ginger-nuts are so called because they contain ginger as one of their peculiar constituents, and the final flavoring one. Now what was ginger? A hot, spicy thing. Was Bartleby hot and spicy? Not at all. Ginger, then, had no effect upon Bartleby. Probably he preferred it should have none.

Nothing so aggravates an earnest person as a passive resistance. If the individual so resisted be of a not inhumane temper, and the resisting one perfectly harmless in his passivity, then, in the better moods of the former, he will endeavor charitably to construe to his imagination what proves impossible to be solved by his judgment. Even so, for the most part, I regarded Bartleby and his ways. Poor fellow! thought I, he means no mischief; it is plain he intends no insolence; his aspect sufficiently evinces that his eccentricities are involuntary. He is useful to me. I can get along with him. If I turn him away, the chances are he will fall in with some less indulgent employer, and then he will be rudely treated, and perhaps driven forth miserably to starve. Yes. Here I can cheaply purchase a delicious self-approval. To befriend Bartleby, to humor him in his strange willfulness, will cost me little or nothing, while I lay up in my soul what will eventually prove a sweet morsel for my conscience. But this mood was not invariable with me. The passiveness of Bartleby sometimes irritated me. I felt strangely goaded on to encounter him in new opposition, to elicit some angry spark from him answerable to my own. But indeed I might as well have essayed to strike fire with my knuckles against a bit of Windsor soap. But one afternoon the evil impulse in me mastered me, and the following little scene ensued:

"Bartleby," said I, "when those papers are all copied, I will compare them with you."

"I would prefer not to."

"How? Surely you do not mean to persist in that mulish vagary?"

No answer.

I threw open the folding-doors near by, and turning upon Turkey and Nippers, exclaimed in an excited manner:

"He says, a second time, he won't examine his papers. What do you think of it, Turkey?"

It was afternoon, be it remembered. Turkey sat glowing like a brass boiler, his bald head steaming, his hands reeling among his blotted papers.

"Think of it?" roared Turkey; "I think I'll just step behind his screen, and black his eyes for him!"

So saying, Turkey rose to his feet and threw his arms into a pugilistic position. He was hurrying away to make good his promise, when I detained him, alarmed at the effect of incautiously rousing Turkey's combativeness after dinner.

"Sit down, Turkey," said I, "and hear what Nippers has to say. What do you think of it, Nippers? Would I not be justified in immediately dismissing Bartleby?"

"Excuse me, that is for you to decide, sir. I think his conduct quite unusual, and indeed unjust, as regards Turkey and myself. But it may only be a passing whim."

"Ah," exclaimed I, "you have strangely changed your mind then — you speak very gently of him now."

"All beer," cried Turkey; "gentleness is effects of beer — Nippers and I dined together to-day. You see how gentle *I* am, sir. Shall I go and black his eyes?"

"You refer to Bartleby, I suppose. No, not to-day, Turkey," I replied; "pray, put up your fists."

I closed the doors, and again advanced towards Bartleby. I felt additional incentives tempting me to my fate. I burned to be rebelled against again. I remembered that Bartleby never left the office.

"Bartleby," said I, "Ginger Nut is away; just step round to the Post Office, won't you? (it was but a three minute walk,) and see if there is any thing for me."

"I would prefer not to."

"You *will* not?"

"I *prefer* not."

I staggered to my desk, and sat there in a deep study. My blind inveteracy returned. Was there any other thing in which I could procure myself to be ignominiously repulsed by this lean, penniless wight? — my hired clerk? What added thing is there, perfectly reasonable, that he will be sure to refuse to do?

"Bartleby!"

No answer.

"Bartleby," in a louder tone.

No answer.

"Bartleby," I roared.

Like a very ghost, agreeably to the laws of magical invocation, at the third summons, he appeared at the entrance of his hermitage.

"Go to the next room, and tell Nippers to come to me."

"I prefer not to," he respectfully and slowly said, and mildly disappeared.

"Very good, Bartleby," said I, in a quiet sort of serenely severe self-possessed tone, intimating the unalterable purpose of some terrible retribution very close at hand. At the moment I half intended something of the kind. But upon the whole, as it was drawing towards my dinner-hour, I thought it best to put on my hat and walk home for the day, suffering much from perplexity and distress of mind.

Shall I acknowledge it? The conclusion of this whole business was that it soon became a fixed fact of my chambers that a pale young scrivener, by the name of Bartleby, had a desk there; that he copied for me at the usual rate of four cents a folio (one hundred words); but he was permanently exempt from examining the work done by him, that duty being transferred to Turkey and Nippers, out of compliment, doubtless, to their superior acuteness; moreover, said Bartleby was never on any account to be dispatched on the most trivial errand of any sort; and that even if entreated to take upon him such a matter, it was generally understood that he would "prefer not to" — in other words, that he would refuse pointblank.

As days passed on, I became considerably reconciled to Bartleby. His steadiness, his freedom from all dissipation, his incessant industry (except when he chose to throw himself into a standing revery behind his screen), his great stillness, his unalterableness of demeanor under all circumstances, made him a valuable acquisition. One prime thing was this — *he was always there* — first in the morning, continually through the day, and the last at night. I had a singular confidence in his honesty. I felt my most precious papers perfectly safe in his hands. Sometimes to be sure I could not, for the very soul of me, avoid falling into sudden spasmodic passions with him. For it was exceeding difficult to bear in mind all the time those strange peculiarities, privileges, and unheard-of exemptions, forming the tacit stipulations on Bartleby's part under which he remained in my office. Now and then, in the eagerness of dispatching pressing business, I would inadvertently summon Bartleby, in a short, rapid tone, to put his finger, say, on the incipient tie of a bit of red tape with which I was about compressing some papers. Of course, from behind the screen the usual answer, "I prefer not to," was sure to come; and then, how could a human creature with the common infirmities of our nature, refrain from bitterly exclaiming upon such perverseness — such unreasonableness. However, every added repulse of this sort which I received only tended to lessen the probability of my repeating the inadvertence.

Here it must be said, that according to the custom of most legal gentlemen occupying chambers in densely-populated law buildings, there were several keys to my door. One was kept by a woman residing in the attic, which person weekly scrubbed and daily swept and dusted my apartments. Another was kept by Turkey for convenience sake. The third I sometimes carried in my own pocket. The fourth I knew not who had.

Now, one Sunday morning I happened to go to Trinity Church, to hear a celebrated preacher, and finding myself rather early on the ground, I thought I would walk around to my chambers for a while. Luckily I had my key with me; but upon applying it to the lock, I found it resisted by something inserted from the inside.

Quite surprised, I called out; when to my consternation a key was turned from within; and thrusting his lean visage at me, and holding the door ajar, the apparition of Bartleby appeared, in his shirt sleeves, and otherwise in a strangely tattered *déshabillé*, saying quietly that he was sorry, but he was deeply engaged just then, and — preferred not admitting me at present. In a brief word or two, he moreover added, that perhaps I had better walk round the block two or three times, and by that time he would probably have concluded his affairs.

Now, the utterly unsurmised appearance of Bartleby, tenanting my law-chambers of a Sunday morning, with his cadaverously gentlemanly *nonchalance*, yet withal firm and self-possessed, had such a strange effect upon me, that incontinently I slunk away from my own door, and did as desired. But not without sundry twinges of impotent rebellion against the mild effrontery of this unaccountable scrivener. Indeed, it was his wonderful mildness chiefly, which not only disarmed me, but unmanned me, as it were. For I consider that one, for the time, is sort of unmanned when he tranquilly permits his hired clerk to dictate to him, and order him away from his own premises. Furthermore, I was full of uneasiness as to what Bartleby could possibly be doing in my office in his shirt sleeves, and in an otherwise dismantled condition of a Sunday morning. Was any thing amiss going on? Nay, that was out of the question. It was not to be thought of for a moment that Bartleby was an immoral person. But what could he be doing there? — copying? Nay again, whatever might be his eccentricities, Bartleby was an eminently decorous person. He would be the last man to sit down to his desk in any state approaching to nudity. Besides, it was Sunday; and there was something about Bartleby that forbade the supposition that he would by any secular occupation violate the proprieties of the day.

Nevertheless, my mind was not pacified; and full of a restless curiosity, at last I returned to the door. Without hindrance I inserted my key, opened it, and entered. Bartleby was not to be seen. I looked round anxiously, peeped behind his screen; but it was very plain that he was gone. Upon more closely examining the place, I surmised that for an indefinite period Bartleby must have ate, dressed, and slept in my office, and that too without plate, mirror, or bed. The cushioned seat of a rickety old sofa in one corner bore the faint impress of a lean, reclining form. Rolled away under his desk, I found a blanket; under the empty grate, a blacking box and brush; on a chair, a tin basin, with soap and a ragged towel; in a newspaper a few crumbs of ginger-nuts and a morsel of cheese. Yes, thought I, it is evident enough that Bartleby has been making his home here, keeping bachelor's hall all by himself. Immediately then the thought came sweeping across me, What miserable friendlessness and loneliness are here revealed! His poverty is great; but his solitude, how horrible! Think of it. Of a Sunday, Wall Street is deserted as Petra; and every night of every day it is an emptiness. This building too, which of weekdays hums with industry and life, at nightfall echoes with sheer vacancy, and all through Sunday is forlorn. And here Bartleby makes his home; sole spectator of a solitude which he has seen all populous — a sort of innocent and transformed Marius brooding among the ruins of Carthage!

For the first time in my life a feeling of overpowering stinging melancholy seized me. Before, I had never experienced aught but a not unpleasing sadness. The bond of a common humanity now drew me irresistibly to gloom. A fraternal melancholy! For both I and Bartleby were sons of Adam. I remembered the bright silks and sparkling faces I had seen that day, in gala trim, swan-like sailing down the Mississippi of Broadway; and I contrasted them with the pallid copyist, and thought to myself, Ah, happiness courts the light, so we deem the world is gay; but misery hides aloof, so we deem that misery there is none. These sad fancyings — chimeras, doubtless, of a sick and silly brain — led on to other and more special thoughts, concerning the eccentricities of Bartleby. Presentiments of strange discoveries hovered round me. The scrivener's pale form appeared to me laid out, among uncaring strangers, in its shivering winding sheet.

Suddenly I was attracted by Bartleby's closed desk, the key in open sight left in the lock.

I mean no mischief, seek the gratification of no heartless curiosity, thought I; besides, the desk is mine, and its contents too, so I will make bold to look within. Everything was methodically arranged, the papers smoothly placed. The pigeonholes were deep, and removing the files of documents, I groped into their recesses. Presently I felt something there, and dragged it out. It was an old bandanna handkerchief, heavy and knotted. I opened it, and saw it was a savings' bank.

I now recalled all the quiet mysteries which I had noted in the man. I remembered that he never spoke but to answer; that though at intervals he had considerable time to himself, yet I had never seen him reading — no, not even a newspaper; that for long periods he would stand looking out, at his pale window behind the screen, upon the dead brick wall; I was quite sure he never visited any refectory or eating house; while his pale face clearly indicated that he never drank beer like Turkey, or tea and coffee even, like other men; that he never went anywhere in particular that I could learn' never went out for a walk, unless indeed that was the case at present; that he had declined telling who he was, or whence he came, or whether he had any relatives in the world; that though so thin and pale, he never complained of ill health. And more than all, I remembered a certain unconscious air of pallid — how shall I call it? — of pallid haughtiness, say, or rather an austere reserve about him, which had positively awed me into my tame compliance with his eccentricities, when I had feared to ask him to do the slightest incidental thing for me, even though I might know, from his long-continued motionlessness, that behind his screen he must be standing in one of those dead-wall reveries of his.

Revolving all these things, and coupling them with the recently discovered fact that he made my office his constant abiding place and home, and not forgetful of his morbid moodiness; revolving all these things, a prudential feeling began to steal over me. My first emotions had been those of pure melancholy and sincerest pity; but just in proportion as the forlornness of Bartleby grew and grew to my imagination, did that same melancholy merge into fear, that pity into repulsion. So true it is, and so terrible too, that up to a certain point the thought or sight of misery enlists our best affections; but, in certain special cases, beyond that point it does not. They err who would assert that invariably this is owing to the inherent selfishness of the human heart. It rather proceeds from a certain hopelessness of remedying excessive and organic ill. To a sensitive being, pity is not seldom pain. And when at last it is perceived that such pity cannot lead to effectual succor, common sense bids the soul rid of it. What I saw that morning persuaded me that the scrivener was the victim of innate and incurable disorder. I might give alms to his body; but his body did not pain him; it was his soul that suffered, and his soul I could not reach.

I did not accomplish the purpose of going to Trinity Church that morning. Somehow, the things I had seen disqualified me for the time from church-going. I walked homeward, thinking what I would do with Bartleby. Finally, I resolved upon this — I would put certain calm questions to him the next morning, touching his history, etc., and if he declined to answer them openly and unreservedly (and I supposed he would prefer not), then to give him a twenty dollar bill over and above whatever I might owe him, and tell him his services were no longer required; but that if in any other way I could assist him, I would be happy to do so, especially if he desired to return to his native place, wherever that might be, I would willingly help to defray the expenses. Moreover, if, after reaching home, he found himself at any time in want of aid, a letter from him would be sure of a reply.

The next morning came.

"Bartleby," said I, gently calling to him behind his screen.

No reply.

"Bartleby," said I, in a still gentler tone, "come here; I am not going to ask you to do anything you would prefer not to do — I simply wish to speak to you."

Upon this he noiselessly slid into view.

"Will you tell me, Bartleby, where you were born?"

"I would prefer not to."

"Will you tell me anything about yourself?"

"I would prefer not to."

"But what reasonable objection can you have to speak to me? I feel friendly towards you."

He did not look at me while I spoke, but kept his glance fixed upon my bust of Cicero, which as I then sat, was directly behind me, some six inches above my head.

"What is your answer, Bartleby?" said I, after waiting a considerable time for a reply, during which his countenance remained immovable, only there was the faintest conceivable tremor of the white attenuated mouth.

"At present I prefer to give no answer," he said, and retired into his hermitage.

It was rather weak in me I confess, but his manner on this occasion nettled me. Not only did there seem to lurk in it a certain calm disdain, but his perverseness seemed ungrateful, considering the undeniable good usage and indulgence he had received from me.

Again I sat ruminating what I should do. Mortified as I was at his behavior, and resolved as I had been to dismiss him when I entered my offices, nevertheless I strangely felt something superstitious knocking at my heart, and forbidding me to carry out my purpose, and denouncing me for a villain if I dared to breathe one bitter word against this forlornest of mankind. At last, familiarly drawing my chair behind his screen, I sat down and said: "Bartleby, never mind then about revealing your history; but let me entreat you, as a friend, to comply as far as may be with the usages of this office. Say now you will help to examine papers tomorrow or next day: in short, say now that in a day or two you will begin to be a little reasonable: — say so, Bartleby."

"At present I would prefer not to be a little reasonable," was his mildly cadaverous reply.

Just then the folding-doors opened, and Nippers approached. He seemed suffering from an unusually bad night's rest, induced by severer indigestion then common. He overheard those final words of Bartleby.

"*Prefer not, eh?*" gritted Nippers — "I'd *prefer* him, if I were you, sir," addressing me — "I'd *prefer* him; I'd give him preferences, the stubborn mule! What is it, sir, pray, that he *prefers* not to do now?"

Bartleby moved not a limb.

"Mr. Nippers," said I, "I'd prefer that you would withdraw for the present."

Somehow, of late I had got into the way of involuntarily using this word "prefer" upon all sorts of not exactly suitable occasions. And I trembled to think that my contact with the scrivener had already and seriously affected me in a mental way. And what further and deeper aberration might it not yet produce? This apprehension had not been without efficacy in determining me to summary means.

As Nippers, looking very sour and sulky, was departing, Turkey blandly and deferentially approached.

"With submission, sir," said he, "yesterday I was thinking about Bartleby here, and I think that if he would but prefer to take a quart of good ale every day, it would do much towards mending him, and enabling him to assist in examining his papers."

"So you have got the word too," said I, slightly excited.

"With submission, what word, sir," asked Turkey, respectfully crowding himself into the contracted space behind the screen, and by so doing, making me jostle the scrivener. "What word, sir?"

"I would prefer to be left alone here," said Bartleby, as if offended at being mobbed in his privacy.

"*That's* the word, Turkey," said I — "that's it."

"Oh, *prefer*? oh yes — queer word. I never use it myself. But, sir, as I was saying, if he would but prefer — "

"Turkey," interrupted I, "you will please withdraw."

"Oh certainly, sir, if you prefer that I should."

As he opened the folding-door to retire, Nippers at his desk caught a glimpse of me, and asked whether I would prefer to have a certain paper copied on blue paper or white. He did not in the least roguishly accent the word prefer. It was plain that it involuntarily rolled form his tongue. I thought to myself, surely I must get rid of a demented man, who already has in some degree turned the tongues, if not the heads of myself and clerks. But I thought it prudent not to break the dismission at once.

The next day I noticed that Bartleby did nothing but stand at his window in his dead-wall revery. Upon asking him why he did not write, he said that he had decided upon doing no more writing.

"Why, how now? what next?" exclaimed I, "do no more writing?"

"No more."

"And what is the reason?"

"Do you not see the reason for yourself," he indifferently replied.

I looked steadfastly at him, and perceived that his eyes looked dull and glazed. Instantly it occurred to me, that his unexampled diligence in copying by his dim window for the first few weeks of his stay with me might have temporarily impaired his vision.

I was touched. I said something in condolence with him. I hinted that of course he did wisely in abstaining from writing for a while; and urged him to embrace that opportunity of taking wholesome exercise in the open air. This, however, he did not do. A few days after this, my other clerks being absent, and being in a great hurry to dispatch certain letters by the mail, I thought that, having nothing else earthly to do, Bartleby would surely be less inflexible than usual, and carry these letters to the post-office. But he blankly declined. So, much to my inconvenience, I went myself.

Still added days went by. Whether Bartleby's eyes improved or not, I could not say. To all appearance, I thought they did. But when I asked him if they did, he vouchsafed no answer. At all events, he would do no copying. At last, in reply to my urgings, he informed me that he had permanently given up copying.

"What!" exclaimed I; "suppose your eyes should get entirely well — better than ever before — would you not copy then?"

"I have given up copying," he answered, and slid aside.

He remained as ever, a fixture in my chamber. Nay — if that were possible — he became still more of a fixture than before. What was to be done? He would do nothing in the office: why should he stay there? In plain fact, he had now become a millstone to me, not only useless as a necklace, but afflictive to bear. Yet I was sorry for him. I speak less than truth when I say that, on his own account, he occasioned me uneasiness. If he would but have named a single relative or friend, I would instantly have written, and urged their taking the poor fellow away to some convenient retreat. But he seemed alone, absolutely alone in the universe. A bit of wreck in the mid Atlantic. At length, necessities connected with my business tyrannized over all other considerations. Decently as I could, I told Bartleby that in six days' time he must unconditionally leave the office. I warned him to take measures, in the interval, for procuring some other abode. I offered to assist him in this endeavor, if he himself would but take the first step towards a removal. "And when you finally quit me, Bartleby," added I, "I shall see that you go not away entirely unprovided. Six days from this hour, remember."

At the expiration of that period, I peeped behind the screen, and lo! Bartleby was there.

I buttoned up my coat, balanced myself; advanced slowly towards him, touched his shoulder, and said, "The time has come; you must quit this place; I am sorry for you; here is money; but you must go."

"I would prefer not," he replied, with his back still towards me.

"You *must*."

He remained silent.

Now I had an unbounded confidence in this man's common honesty. He had frequently restored to me sixpences and shillings carelessly dropped upon the floor, for I am apt to be very reckless in such shirt-button affairs. The proceeding then which followed will not be deemed extraordinary.

"Bartleby," said I, "I owe you twelve dollars on account; here are thirty-two; the odd twenty are yours. — Will you take it?" and I handed the bills towards him.

But he made no motion.

"I will leave them here then," putting them under a weight on the table. Then taking my hat and cane and going to the door I tranquilly turned and added — "After you have removed your things from these offices, Bartleby, you will of course lock the door — since every one is now gone for the day but you — and if you please, slip your key underneath the mat, so that I may have it in the morning. I shall not see you again; so good-bye to you. If hereafter in your new place of abode I can be of any service to you, do not fail to advise me by letter. Good-bye, Bartleby, and fare you well."

But he answered not a word; like the last column of some ruined temple, he remained standing mute and solitary in the middle of the otherwise deserted room.

As I walked home in a pensive mood, my vanity got the better of my pity. I could not but highly plume myself on my masterly management in getting rid of Bartleby. Masterly I call it, and such it must appear to any dispassionate thinker. The beauty of my procedure seemed to consist in its perfect quietness. There was no vulgar bullying, no bravado of any sort, no choleric hectoring, and striding to and fro across the apartment, jerking out vehement commands for Bartleby to bundle himself off with his beggarly traps. Nothing of the kind. Without loudly bidding Bartleby depart — as an inferior genius might have done — I *assumed* the ground that depart he must; and upon that assumption built all I had to say. The more I thought over my procedure, the more I was charmed with it. Nevertheless, next morning, upon awakening, I had my doubts, — I had somehow slept off the fumes of vanity. One of the coolest and wisest hours a man has, is just after he awakes in the morning. My procedure seemed as sagacious as ever — but only in theory. How it would prove in practice — there was the rub. It was truly a beautiful thought to have assumed Bartleby's departure; but, after all, that assumption was simply my own, and none of Bartleby's. The great point was, not whether I had assumed that he would quit me, but whether he would prefer so to do. He was more a man of preferences than assumptions.

After breakfast, I walked down town, arguing the probabilities pro and con. One moment I thought it would prove a miserable failure, and Bartleby would be found all alive at my office as usual; the next moment it seemed certain that I should see his chair empty. And so I kept veering about. At the corner of Broadway and Canal Street, I saw quite an excited group of people standing in earnest conversation.

"I'll take odds he doesn't," said a voice as I passed.

"Doesn't go? — done!" said I, "put up your money."

I was instinctively putting my hand in my pocket to produce my own, when I remembered that this was an election day. The words I had overheard bore no reference to Bartleby, but to the success or nonsuccess of some candidate for the mayoralty. In my intent frame of mind, I had, as it were, imagined that all Broadway shared in my excitement, and were debating the same question with me. I passed on, very thankful that the uproar of the street screened my momentary absent-mindedness.

As I had intended, I was earlier than usual at my office door. I stood listening for a moment. All was still. He must be gone. I tried the knob. The door was locked. Yes, my procedure had worked to a charm; he indeed must be vanished. Yet a certain melancholy mixed with this: I was almost sorry for my brilliant success. I was fumbling under the door mat for the key, which Bartleby was to have left there for me, when accidentally my knee knocked against a panel, producing a summoning sound, and in response a voice came to me from within — "Not yet; I am occupied."

It was Bartleby.

I was thunderstruck. For an instant I stood like the man who, pipe in mouth, was killed one cloudless afternoon long ago in Virginia, by a summer lightning; at his own warm open window he was killed, and remained leaning out there upon the dreamy afternoon, till someone touched him, when he fell.

"Not gone!" I murmured at last. But again obeying that wondrous ascendancy which the inscrutable scrivener had over me, and from which ascendancy, for all my chafling, I could not completely escape, I slowly went downstairs and out into the street, and while walking round the block, considered what I should next do in this unheard-of perplexity. Turn the man out by an actual thrusting I could not; to drive him away by calling him hard names would not do; calling in the police was an unpleasant idea; and yet, permit him to enjoy his cadaverous triumph over me — this too I could not think of. What was to be done? or, if nothing could be done, was there anything further that I could *assume* in the matter? Yes, as before I had prospectively assumed that Bartleby would depart, so now I might retrospectively assume that departed he was. In the legitimate carrying out of this assumption, I might enter my office in a great hurry, and pretending not to see Bartleby at all, walk straight against him as if he were air. Such a proceeding would in a singular degree have the appearance of a home-thrust. It was hardly possible that Bartleby could withstand such an application of the doctrine of assumptions. But upon second thoughts the success of the plan seemed rather dubious. I resolved to argue the matter over with him again.

"Bartleby," said I, entering the office, with a quietly severe expression, "I am seriously displeased. I am pained, Bartleby. I had thought better of you. I had imagined you of such a gentlemanly organization, that in any delicate dilemma a slight hint would suffice — in short, an assumption. But it appears I am deceived. Why," I added, unaffectedly starting, "you have not even touched that money yet," pointing to it, just where I had left it the evening previous.

He answered nothing.

"Will you, or will you not, quit me?" I now demanded in a sudden passion, advancing close to him.

"I would prefer *not* to quit you," he replied, gently emphasizing the *not*.

"What earthly right have you to stay here? Do you pay any rent? Do you pay my taxes? Or is this property yours?"

He answered nothing.

"Are you ready to go on and write now? Are your eyes recovered? Could you copy a small paper for me this morning? or help examine a few lines? or step round to the Post Office? In a word, will you do anything at all, to give a coloring to your refusal to depart the premises?"

He silently retired into his hermitage.

I was now in such a state of nervous resentment that I thought it but prudent to check myself at present from further demonstrations. Bartleby and I were alone. I remembered the tragedy of the unfortunate Adams and the still more unfortunate Colt in the solitary office of the latter; and how poor Colt, being dreadfully incensed by Adams, and imprudently permitting himself to get wildly excited, was at unawares hurried into his fatal act — an act which certainly no man could possibly deplore more than the actor himself. Often it had occurred to me in my ponderings upon the subject, that had that altercation taken place in the public street, or at a private residence, it would not have terminated as it did. It was the circumstance of being alone in a solitary office, upstairs, of a building entirely unhallowed by humanizing domestic associations — an uncarpeted office, doubtless, of a dusty, haggard sort of appearance — this it must have been, which greatly helped to enhance the irritable desperation of the hapless Colt.

But when this old Adam of resentment rose in me and tempted me concerning Bartleby, I grappled him and threw him. How? Why, simply by recalling the divine injunction: "A new commandment give I unto you, that ye love one another." Yes, this it was that saved me. Aside from higher considerations, charity often operates as a vastly wise and prudent principle — a great safeguard to its possessor. Men have committed murder for jealousy's sake, and anger's sake, and hatred's sake, and selfishness' sake, and spiritual pride's sake; but no man that ever I heard of ever committed a diabolical murder for sweet charity's sake. Mere self-interest, then, if no better motive can be enlisted, should, especially with high-tempered men, prompt all beings to charity and philanthropy. At any rate, upon the occasion in question, I strove to drown my exasperated feelings towards the scrivener by benevolently construing his conduct. Poor fellow, poor fellow! thought I, he don't mean anything; and besides, he has seen hard times, and ought to be indulged.

I endeavored also immediately to occupy myself, and at the same time to comfort my despondency. I tried to fancy that in the course of the morning, at such time as might prove agreeable to him. Bartleby, of his own free accord, would emerge from his hermitage, and take up some decided line of march in the direction of the door. But no. Half-past twelve o'clock came; Turkey began to glow in the face, overturn his inkstand, and become generally obstreperous; Nippers abated down into quietude and courtesy; Ginger Nut munched his noon apple; and Bartleby remained standing at his window in one of his profoundest dead-wall reveries. Will it be credited? Ought I to acknowledge it? That afternoon I left the office without saying one further word to him.

Some days now passed, during which, at leisure intervals I looked a little into "Edwards on the Will," and "Priestly on Necessity." Under the circumstances, those books induced a salutary feeling. Gradually I slid into the persuasion that these troubles of mine touching the scrivener had been all predestinated from eternity, and Bartleby was billeted upon me for some mysterious purpose of an all-wise Providence, which it was not for a mere mortal like me to fathom. Yes, Bartleby, stay there behind your screen, thought I; I shall persecute you no more; you are harmless and noiseless as any of these old chairs; in short, I never feel so private as when I know you are here. At least I see it, I feel it; I penetrate to the predestinated purpose of my life. I am content. Others may have loftier parts to enact; but my mission in this world, Bartleby, is to furnish you with office-room for such period as you may see fit to remain.

I believe that this wise and blessed frame of mind would have continued with me, had it not been for the unsolicited and uncharitable remarks obtruded upon me by me professional friends who visited the rooms. But thus it often is, that the constant friction of illiberal minds wears out at last the best resolves of the more generous. Though to be sure, when I reflected upon it, it was not strange that people entering my office should be struck by the peculiar aspect of the unaccountable Bartleby, and so be tempted to throw out some sinister observations concerning him. Sometimes an attorney having business with me, and calling at my office and finding no one but the scrivener there, would undertake to obtain some sort of precise information from him touching my whereabouts; but without heeding his idle talk, Bartleby would remain standing immovable in the middle of the room. So after contemplating him in that position for a time, the attorney would depart, no wiser than he came.

Also, when a reference was going on, and the room full of lawyers and witnesses, and business was driving fast, some deeply occupied legal gentleman present, seeing Bartleby wholly unemployed, would request him to run round to his (the legal gentleman's) office and fetch some papers for him. Thereupon, Bartleby would tranquilly decline, and yet remain idle as before. Then the lawyer would give a great stare, and turn to me. And what could I say? At last I was made aware that all through the circle of my professional acquaintance, a whisper of wonder was running round, having reference to the strange creature I kept at my office. This worried me very much. And as the idea came upon me of his possibly turning out a long-lived man, and keep occupying my chambers, and denying my authority; and perplexing my visitors; and scandalizing my professional reputation; and casting a general gloom over the premises; keeping soul and body together to the last upon his savings (for doubtless he spent but half a dime a day), and in the end perhaps outlive me, and claim possession of my office by right of his perpetual occupancy: as all these dark anticipations crowded upon me more and more, and my friends continually intruded their relentless remarks upon the apparition in my room; a great change was wrought in me. I resolved to gather all my faculties together, and forever rid me of this intolerable incubus.

Ere revolving any complicated project, however, adapted to this end, I first simply suggested to Bartleby the propriety of his permanent departure. In a calm and serious tone, I commended the idea to his careful and mature consideration. But having taken three days to meditate upon it, he apprised me that his original determination remained the same; in short, that he still preferred to abide with me.

What shall I do? I now said to myself, buttoning up my coat to the last button. What shall I do? what ought I to do? what does conscience say I *should* do with this man, or, rather, ghost. Rid myself of him, I must; go, he shall. But how? You will not thrust him, the poor, pale, passive mortal — you will not thrust such a helpless creature out of your door? you will not dishonor yourself by such cruelty? No, I will not, I cannot do that. Rather would I let him live and die here, and then mason up his remains in the wall. What then will you do? For all your coaxing, he will not budge. Bribes he leaves under your own paperweight on your table; in short, it is quite plain that he prefers to cling to you.

Then something severe, something unusual must be done. What! surely you will not have him collared by a constable, and commit his innocent pallor to the common jail? And upon what ground could you procure such a thing to be done? — a vagrant, is he? What! he a vagrant, a wanderer, who refuses to budge? It is because he will not be a vagrant, then, that you seek to count him as a vagrant. That is too absurd. No visible means of support: there I have him. Wrong again: for indubitably he *does* support himself, and that is the only unanswerable proof that any man can show of his possessing the means so to do. No more, then. Since he will not quit me, I must quit him. I will change my offices; I will move elsewhere; and give him fair notice, that if I find him on my new premises I will then proceed against him as a common trespasser.

Acting accordingly, next day I thus addressed him: "I find these chambers too far from the City Hall; the air is unwholesome. In a word, I propose to remove my offices next week, and shall no longer require your services. I tell you this now, in order that you may seek another place."

He made no reply, and nothing more was said.

On the appointed day I engaged carts and men, proceeded to my chambers, and having but little furniture, everything was removed in a few hours. Throughout, the scrivener remained standing behind the screen, which I directed to be removed the last thing. It was withdrawn; and being folded up like a huge folio, left him the motionless occupant of a naked room. I stood in the entry watching him a moment, while something from within me upbraided me.

I re-entered, with my hand in my pocket — and — and my heart in my mouth.

"Good-bye, Bartleby; I am going — good-bye, and God some way bless you; and take that," slipping something in his hand. But it dropped upon the floor, and then — strange to say — I tore myself from him whom I had so longed to be rid of.

Established in my new quarters, for a day or two I kept the door locked, and started at every footfall in the passages. When I returned to my rooms after any little absence, I would pause at the threshold for an instant, and attentively listen ere applying my key. But these fears were needless. Bartleby never came nigh me.

I thought all was going well, when a perturbed looking stranger visited me, inquiring whether I was the person who had recently occupied rooms at No. —— Wall Street.

Full of forebodings, I replied that I was.

"Then sir," said the stranger, who proved a lawyer, "you are responsible for the man you left there. He refuses to do any copying; he refuses to do anything; he says he prefers not to; and he refuses to quit the premises."

"I am very sorry, sir," said I, with assumed tranquility, but an inward tremor, "but, really, the man you allude to is nothing to me — he is no relation or apprentice of mine, that you should hold me responsible for him."

"In mercy's name, who is he?"

"I certainly cannot inform you. I know nothing about him. Formerly I employed him as a copyist; but he has done nothing for me now for some time past."

"I shall settle him then — good morning, sir."

Several days passed, and I heard nothing more; and though I often felt a charitable prompting to call at the place and see poor Bartleby, yet a certain squeamishness of I know not what withheld me.

All is over with him, by this time, thought I at last, when through another week no further intelligence reached me. But coming to my room the day after, I found several persons waiting at my door in a high state of nervous excitement.

"That's the man — here he comes," cried the foremost one, whom I recognized as the lawyer who had previously called upon me alone.

"You must take him away, sir, at once," cried a portly person among them, advancing upon me, and whom I knew to be the landlord of No. —— Wall Street. "These gentlemen, my tenants, cannot stand it any longer; Mr. B —— " pointing to the lawyer, "has turned him out of his room, and he now persists in haunting the building generally, sitting upon the banisters of the stairs by day, and sleeping in the entry by night. Everybody is concerned; clients are leaving the offices; some fears are entertained of a mob; something you must do, and that without delay."

Aghast at this torrent, I fell back before it, and would fain have locked myself in my new quarters. In vain I persisted that Bartleby was nothing to me — no more than to anyone else. In vain — I was the last person known to have any thing to do with him, and they held me to the terrible account. Fearful then of being exposed in the papers (as one person present obscurely threatened) I considered the matter, and at length said that if the lawyer would give me a confidential interview with the scrivener, in his (the lawyer's) own room, I would that afternoon strive my best to rid them of the nuisance they complained of.

Going up stairs to my old haunt, there was Bartleby silently sitting upon the banister at the landing.

"What are you doing here, Bartleby?" said I.

"Sitting upon the banister," he mildly replied.

I motioned him into the lawyer's room, who then left us.

"Bartleby," said I, "are you aware that you are the cause of great tribulation to me, by persisting in occupying the entry after being dismissed from the office?"

No answer.

"Now one of two things must take place. Either you must do something, or something must be done to you. Now what sort of business would you like to engage in? Would you like to re-engage in copying for someone?"

"No; I would prefer not to make any change."

"Would you like a clerkship in a dry-goods store?"

"There is too much confinement about that. No, I would not like a clerkship; but I am not particular."

"Too much confinement," I cried, "why you keep yourself confined all the time!"

"I would prefer not to take a clerkship," he rejoined, as if to settle that little item at once.

"How would a bartender's business suit you? There is no trying of the eyesight in that."

"I would not like it at all; though, as I said before, I am not particular."

His unwonted wordiness inspirited me. I returned to the charge.

"Well then, would you like to travel through the country collecting bills for the merchants? That would improve your health."

"No, I would prefer to be doing something else."

"How then would going as a companion to Europe, to entertain some young gentleman with your conversation — how would that suit you?"

"Not at all. It does not strike me that there is anything definite about that. I like to be stationary. But I am not particular."

"Stationary you shall be then," I cried, now losing all patience, and for the first time in all my exasperating connection with him fairly flying into a passion. "If you do not go away from these premises before night, I shall feel bound — indeed I *am* bound — to — to — to quit the premises myself!" I rather absurdly concluded, knowing not with what possible threat to try to frighten his immobility into compliance. Despairing of all further efforts, I was precipitately leaving him, when a final thought occurred to me — one which had not been wholly unindulged before.

"Bartleby," said I, in the kindest tone I could assume under such exciting circumstances, "will you go home with me now — not to my office, but my dwelling — and remain there till we can conclude upon some convenient arrangement for you at our leisure? Come, let us start now, right away."

"No: at present I would prefer not to make any change at all."

I answered nothing; but effectually dodging every one by the suddenness and rapidity of my flight, rushed from the building, ran up Wall Street towards Broadway, and jumping into the first omnibus was soon removed from pursuit. As soon as tranquility returned I distinctly perceived that I had now done all that I possibly could, both in respect to the demands of the landlord and his tenants, and with regard to my own desire and sense of duty, to benefit Bartleby, and shield him from rude persecution. I now strove to be entirely carefree and quiescent; and my conscience justified me in the attempt; though indeed it was not so successful as I could have wished. So fearful was I of being again hunted out by the incensed landlord and his exasperated tenants, that, surrendering my business to Nippers, for a few days I drove about the upper part of the town and through the suburbs, in my rockaway; crossed over to Jersey City and Hoboken, and paid fugitive visits to Manhattanville and Astoria. In fact I almost lived in my rockaway for the time.

When again I entered my office, lo, a note from the landlord lay upon the desk. I opened it with trembling hands. It informed me that the writer had sent to the police, and had Bartleby removed to the Tombs as a vagrant. Moreover, since I knew more about him than any one else, he wished me to appear at that place, and make a suitable statement of the facts. These tidings had a conflicting effect upon me. At first I was indignant; but at last almost approved. The landlord's energetic, summary disposition had led him to adopt a procedure which I do not think I would have decided upon myself; and yet as a last resort, under such peculiar circumstances, it seemed the only plan.

As I afterwards learned, the poor scrivener, when told that he must be conducted to the Tombs, offered not the slightest obstacle, but in his pale unmoving way, silently acquiesced.

Some of the compassionate and curious bystanders joined the party; and headed by one of the constables arm in arm with Bartleby, the silent procession filed its way through all the noise, and heat, and joy of the roaring thoroughfares at noon.

The same day I received the note I went to the Tombs, or to speak more properly, the Halls of Justice. Seeking the right officer, I stated the purpose of my call, and was informed that the individual I described was indeed within. I then assured the functionary that Bartleby was a perfectly honest man, and greatly to be compassionated, however unaccountably eccentric. I narrated all I knew, and closed by suggesting the idea of letting him remain in as indulgent confinement as possible till something less harsh might be done — though indeed I hardly knew what. At all events, if nothing else could be decided upon, the almshouse must receive him. I then begged to have an interview.

Being under no disgraceful charge, and quite serene and harmless in all his ways, they had permitted him freely to wander about the prison, and especially in the inclosed grass-platted yard thereof. And so I found him there, standing all alone in the quietest of the yards, his face towards a high wall, while all around, from the narrow slits of the jail windows, I thought I saw peering out upon him the eyes of murderers and thieves.

"Bartleby!"

"I know you," he said, without looking round — "and I want nothing to say to you."

"It was not I that brought you here, Bartleby," said I, keenly pained at his implied suspicion. "And to you, this should not be so vile a place. Nothing reproachful attaches to you by being here. And see, it is not so sad a place as one might think. Look, there is the sky, and here is the grass."

"I know where I am," he replied, but would say nothing more, and so I left him.

As I entered the corridor again, a broad meatlike man, in an apron, accosted me, and jerking his thumb over his shoulder said — "Is that your friend?"

"Yes."

"Does he want to starve? If he does, let him live on the prison fare, that's all."

"Who are you?" asked I, not knowing what to make of such an unofficially speaking person in such a place.

"I am the grub-man. Such gentlemen as have friends here, hire me to provide them with something good to eat."

"Is this so?" said I, turning to the turnkey.

He said it was.

"Well then," said I, slipping some silver into the grubman's hands (for so they called him). "I want you to give particular attention to my friend there; let him have the best dinner you can get. And you must be as polite to him as possible."

"Introduce me, will you?" said the grubman, looking at me with an expression which seemed to say he was all impatience for an opportunity to give a specimen of his breeding.

Thinking it would prove of benefit to the scrivener, I acquiesced; and asking the grubman his name, went up with him to Bartleby.

"Bartleby, this is Mr. Cutlets; you will find him very useful to you."

"Your sarvant, sir, your sarvant," said the grubman, making a low salutation behind his apron. "Hope you find it pleasant here, sir — spacious grounds — cool apartments, sir — hope you'll stay with us some time — try to make it agreeable. May Mrs. Cutlets and I have the pleasure of your company to dinner, sir, in Mrs. Cutlets' private room?"

"I prefer not to dine today," said Bartleby, turning away. "It would disagree with me; I am unused to dinners." So saying he slowly moved to the other side of the inclosure, and took up a position fronting the dead-wall.

"How's this?" said the grubman, addressing me with a stare of astonishment. "He's odd, aint he?"

"I think he is a little deranged," said I, sadly.

"Deranged? deranged is it? Well now, upon my word, I thought that friend of yourn was a gentleman forger; they are always pale and genteel-like, them forgers.

I can't pity 'em — can't help it, sir. Did you know Monroe Edwards?" he added touchingly, and paused. Then, laying his hand pityingly on my shoulder, sighed, "he died of consumption at Sing-Sing. So you weren't acquainted with Monroe?"

"No, I was never socially acquainted with any forgers. But I cannot stop longer. Look to my friend yonder. You will not lose by it. I will see you again."

Some few days after this, I again obtained admission to the Tombs, and went through the corridors in quest of Bartleby; but without finding him.

"I saw him coming from his cell not long ago," said a turnkey, "maybe he's gone to loiter in the yards."

So I went in that direction.

"Are you looking for the silent man?" said another turnkey passing me. "Yonder he lies — sleeping in the yard there. 'Tis not twenty minutes since I saw him lie down."

The yard was entirely quiet. It was not accessible to the common prisoners. The surrounding walls, of amazing thickness, kept off all sounds behind them. The Egyptian character of the masonry weighed upon me with its gloom. But a soft imprisoned turf grew underfoot. The heart of the eternal pyramids, it seemed, wherein, by some strange magic, through the clefts, grass-seed, dropped by birds, had sprung.

Strangely huddled at the base of the wall, his knees drawn up, and lying on his side, his head touching the cold stones, I saw the wasted Bartleby. But nothing stirred. I paused; then went close up to him; stooped over, and saw that his dim eyes were open; otherwise he seemed profoundly sleeping. Something prompted me to touch him. I felt his hand, when a tingling shiver ran up my arm and down my spine to my feet.

The round face of the grubman peered upon me now. "His dinner is ready. Won't he dine today, either? Or does he live without dining?"

"Lives without dining," said I, and closed his eyes.

"Eh! — He's asleep, aint he?"

"With kings and counselors," murmured I.

There would seem little need for proceeding further in this history. Imagination will readily supply the meager recital of poor Bartleby's interment. But ere parting with the reader, let me say, that if this little narrative has sufficiently interested him, to awaken curiosity as to who Bartleby was, and what manner of life he led prior to the present narrator's making his acquaintance, I can only reply, that in such curiosity I fully share, but am wholly unable to gratify it. Yet here I hardly know whether I should divulge one little item of rumor, which came to my ear a few months after the scrivener's decease. Upon what basis it rested, I could never ascertain; and hence, how true it is I cannot now tell. But inasmuch as this vague report has not been without certain strange suggestive interest to me, however sad, it may prove the same with some others; and so I will briefly mention it. The report was this: that Bartleby had been a subordinate clerk in the Dead Letter Office at Washington, from which he had been suddenly removed by a change in the administration. When I think over this rumor, I cannot adequately express the emotions which seize me. Dead letters! does it not sound like dead men? Conceive a man by nature and misfortune prone to a pallid hopelessness, can any business seem more fitted to heighten it than that of continually handling these dead letters, and assorting them for the flames? For by the cartload they are annually burned. Sometimes from out the folded paper the pale clerk takes a ring — the finger it was meant for, perhaps, moulders in the grave; a bank-note sent in swiftest charity — he whom it would relieve nor eats nor hungers any more; pardon for those who died despairing; hope for those who died unhoping; good tidings for those who died stifled by unrelieved calamities. On errands of life, these letters speed to death.

Ah Bartleby! Ah humanity!

MARCIA

Rebecca Harding Davis (1831-1910)

One winter morning a few years ago the mail brought me a roll of MS. (with one stamp too many, as if to bribe the post to care for so precious a thing) and a letter. Every publisher, editor, or even the obscurest of writers receives such packages so often as to know them at a glance. Half a dozen poems or a story — a blur of sunsets, duchesses, violets, bad French, and worse English; not a solid grain of common-sense, not a hint of reality or even of possibility, in the whole of it. The letter — truth in every word: formal, hard, practical, and the meaning of it a woman's cry for bread for her hungry children.

Each woman who writes such a letter fancies that she is the first, that its pathos will move hard-hearted editors, and that the extent of her need will supply the lack of wit, wisdom, or even grammar in her verses or story. Such appeals pour in literally by the thousand every year to every publishing office. The sickly daughter of a poor family; the wife of a drunken husband; a widow; children that must be fed and clothed. What is the critic's honest opinion of her work? How much will it bring in dollars and cents? etc., etc.

I did not open the letter that day. When we reach middle age we have learned, through rough experiences, how many tragedies there are in our street or under our own roof which will be none the better for our handling, and are apt, selfishly, to try to escape the hearing of them.

This letter, however, when I opened it next morning, proved to be not of a tragical sort. The writer was "not dependent on her pen for support"; she "had vowed herself to literature"; she was "resolved to assist in the Progress of humanity." Scarcely had I laid down the letter when I was told that she waited below to see me. The card she sent up was a bit of the fly-leaf of a book, cut oblong with scissors, and the name — Miss Barr — written in imitation of engraving. Her back was toward me when I came down, and I had time to read the same sham stylishness written all over her thin little person. The sleazy black silk was looped in the prevailing fashion, a sweeping white plume drooped from the cheap hat, and on her hands were washed cotton gloves.

Instead of the wizened features of the "dead beat" which I expected, she turned on me a child's face: an ugly face, I believe other women called it, but one of the most innocent and honest in the world. Her brown eyes met mine eagerly, full of a joyous goodfellowship for everything and everybody alive. She poured out her story, too, in a light-hearted way, and in the lowest, friendliest of voices. To see the girl was to be her ally. "People will do anything for me — but publish my manuscripts," she said.

She came from Mississippi; had been the only white child on a poor plantation on the, banks of the Yazoo. "I have only had such teaching as my mother could give: she had but two years with a governess. We had no books nor newspapers, except an occasional copy of a magazine sent to us by friends in the North." Her mother was the one central figure in the world to her then. In our after-intercourse she talked of her continually. "She is a little woman — less than I; but she has one of the finest minds in the world," she would cry. "The sight of anything beautiful or the sound of music sways her as the wind does a reed. But she never was twenty miles from the plantation; she has read nothing, knows nothing. My father thinks women are like mares — only useful to bring forth children. My mother's children all died in babyhood but me. There she has lived all her life, with the swamp on one side and the forest of live-oak on the other: nothing to do, nothing to think of. Oh, it was frightful! With a mind like hers, any woman would go mad, with that eternal forest and swamp, and the graves of her dead babies just in sight! She rubbed snuff a good deal to quiet herself, but of late years she has taken opium."

"And you?"

"I left her. I hoped to do something for us both. My mind is not of as high order as hers, but it is very different from that of most women. I shall succeed some day," in the most matter-of-fact tones. "As soon as I knew that I was a poet I determined to come to Philadelphia and go straight to real publishers and real editors. In my country nobody had ever seen a man who had written a book. Ever since I came here I find how hard it is to find out anything about the business of authorship. Medicine, or law, or blacksmithing — everybody knows the workings of those trades, but people with pens in their hands keep the secret of their craft like Freemasons," laughing.

"You came alone?"

"Quite alone. I hired a little room over a baker's shop in Pine Street. They are a very decent couple, the baker and his wife. I board myself, and send out my manuscripts. They always come back to me."

"Where do you send them?"

"Oh, everywhere. I can show you printed forms of rejection from every magazine and literary newspaper in the country," opening and shutting again a black satchel on her lap. "I have written three novels, and sent them to the —— s' and —— s'. They sent them back as unavailable. But they never read them. I trick them this a-way: I put a loose blue thread between the third and fourth pages of the manuscript, and it is always there when it comes back." Her voice broke a little, but she winked her brown eyes and laughed bravely.

"How long have you been here?"

"Three years."

"Impossible! You are but a child."

"I am twenty. I had an article published once in a Sunday paper," producing a slip about two inches long.

Three years, and only that little grain of success! She had supported herself meanwhile, as I learned afterward, by sewing men's socks for a firm in German town.

"You are ready to give up now?"

"No; not if it were ten years instead of three."

Yet I can swear there was not a drop of New England blood in her little body. One was certain, against all reason, that she would succeed. When even such puny ceatures as this take the world by the throat in that fashion, they are sure to conquer it.

Her books and poems must, I think, have seemed unique to any editor. The spelling was atrocious; the errors of grammar in every line beyond remedy. The lowest pupil in our public schools would have detected her ignorance on the first page. There was, too, in all that she said or wrote an occasional gross indecency, such as a child might show: her life on the plantation explained it. Like Juliet she spoke the language of her nurse. But even Shakspeare's nurse and Juliet would not be allowed nowadays to chatter at will in the pages of a family magazine.

But in all her ignorance, mistakes, and weaknesses there was no trace of imitation. She plagiarized nobody. There was none of the usual talk of countesses, heather, larks, or emotions of which she knew nothing. She painted over and over again her own home on the Yazoo: the hot still sunshine, the silence of noon, the swamp, the slimy living things in the stagnant ponds, the semi-tropical forest, the house and negro quarters, with all their dirt and dreary monotony. It was a picture which remained in the mind strong and vivid as one of Gerome's deserts or Hardy's moors.

There could be but one kind of advice to give her — to put away pen and ink, and for three years at least devote herself to hard study. She would, of course, have none of such counsel. The popular belief in the wings of genius, which can carry it over hard work and all such obstacles as ignorance of grammar or even the spelling-book, found in her a marked example. Work was for commonplace talent, not for those whose veins were full of the divine ichor.

Meanwhile she went on sewing socks, and sending off her great yellow envelopes, with stamps to bring them back.

"Stamps and paper count up so fast!" she said, with a laugh, into which had grown a pitiful quaver. She would take not a penny of aid. "I shall not starve. When the time has come for me to know that I have failed, I can go back to my own country and live like the other women there."

Meanwhile her case very nearly reached starvation. I remember few things more pathetic than the damp, forlorn little figure in a shabby water-proof, black satchel in hand, which used to come to our door through the snows and drenching rains that winter. Her shoes were broken, and her hands shrivelled blue with cold. But a plated gilt chain or a scarlet ribbon used to flaunt somewhere over the meagre, scant pov'erty. Sometimes she brought news with her. She had work given her — to collect a column of jokes for a Sunday paper, by which she made three dollars a week. But she lost it from trying to insert her own matter, which could not well be reckoned as funny sayings. One day she came flushed with excitement. Somebody had taken her through the Academy of Design and a private gallery of engravings then on exhibition. She had a keen, just eye for form and color, and the feeling of a true artist for both.

"That is what I could hare done," she said, after keeping silence a long while. "But what chance had I? I never even saw a picture at home, except those which were cut out of illustrated papers. There seemed to be no way for me but to write."

It was suggested to her that she might find the other way even now. Painting, designing, woodengraving, were expressions for a woman's mind, even though, like her own, it was "one of the finest in the world."

She did not smile. "It is too late," she said. "I will go on as I have begun. But it is a pity my mother and I had not known of such things."

After that her light-hearted courage seemed to give way. She persevered, but it was with dogged, indomitable resolution, and little hope.

One day in the spring I was summoned to see a visitor on business. I found a tall, lank young man stalking up and down the room, the most noticeable point about him the shock of red hair and whisker falling over his neck and greasy coat collar. The face was that of an ignorant, small-minded man. But it was candid and not sensual.

He came straight toward me. "Is Marcia Barr here?"

"No; she has been gone for an hour."

He damned his luck in a white heat of rage, which must, I thought, have required some time to kindle. Indeed, I found he had been pacing up and down the street half the morning, having seen her come in. She had gone out by a side door.

"I caught a glimpse of her half a mile off. I have come to Philadelphia three times this year to find her. Good God! how rank poor she is! Where does she live?"

I could not tell him, as Marcia had long ago left the baker's, and changed her quarters every month.

"And I reckon I'll have to wait until she comes hyah again. Tell her it's Zack Biron, the overseer's son, on — on business."

He was not long in unveiling his business, which any woman would soon have guessed. He had come to bring Marcia home and marry her. He had always "wanted her," and the old colonel, her father, had promised he should marry her provided he could bring her back from her mad flight. The colonel was dead, and he was now "runnin' the plantation for ole madam. She's no better than a walkin' corpse, with that damned drug she chews. She can't keep still now: walks, walks incessant about the place, with her eyes set an' the skin clingin' to her bones. I couldn't 'a borne it, I ashuah you, but for the sake of findm' Marcia."

Two months passed, in which he haunted the house. But Marcia did not come. She had begun to frequent newspaper offices, and occasionally was given a trifling bit of work by the managers of the reporting corps — a description of the dresses at a Mannerchor ball to write, or a puff of some coming play, etc. She came at last to tell me of what she had done.

"It is miserable work. I would rather sew the heels of stockings; but the stocking looms have stopped, and I must live a little longer, at any rate. I think I have something to say, if people only would hear it."

I told her of Biron and his chase for her.

"I saw him outside the window the last time I was here. That was the reason I went out by the side street. I knew he was looking for me. You will not tell him I have been here?"

"But, Marcia, the man seems honest and kindly — "

"If he found me," in the same quiet tone, "he would marry me and take me back to the plantation."

"And you are not ready to give up?"

"No, I will not give up. I shall get into the right groove at last," with the infectious little laugh which nobody could resist.

The water-proof cloak was worn down quite into the cotton by this time, and the straw hat had been darned around the ragged edge. But there was a cheap red rose in it. Her cheek-bones showed high, and her eyes shone out of black hollows.

"No, I have no cough, and I don't need medicine," she said, irritably, when questioned. "I have had plenty of offers of help. But I'd rather steal than take alms." She rose hastily and buttoned her cloak.

"This man Biron waits only a word to come to you. He is faithful as a dog."

She nodded carelessly. Biron, or a return to her old home, held no part in her world, it was plain to see.

I was out of the city for several months. A few weeks after my return I saw in the evening paper one day, in the usual list of crimes and casualties, an item headed "*Pitiable Case* — A young woman named Burr was arrested yesterday on charge of theft, and taken to the Central Station. About eleven o'clock the other women in the cell where she was confined perceiving that she lay on a bench breathing in a stertorous manner, summoned Lieutenant Pardy, who found life to be almost extinct. A physician was called, who discovered that the woman had swallowed some poisonous drug. With her first breath of returning consciousness she protested her innocence of the charge. She appears to have been in an extreme state of want. But little hope is entertained of her recovery. Miss Burr is favorably known, we believe, as a writer of some ability for the daily press."

In spite of the difference of name, it must be Marcia.

When we reached the Central Station we were told that her discharge was already procured. She had friends who knew what wires to work. In the outer room were half a dozen young men, reporters, a foreman of a printing-room, and one or two women, dramatic or musical critics. There is as eager an *esprit de corps* among that class of journalists as among actors. They were all talking loudly, and zealous in defence of "Little Marty," as they called her, whom they declared to be "a dunce so far as head went, but pure and guileless as a child."

"I knew she was devilishly hard up," said one, "but never suspected she was starving. She would not borrow a dollar, she had that pride in her."

Marcia was still in the cell, lying on an iron stretcher. The Mississippian, Biron, was with her, kneeling on the floor in his shirt sleeves, chafing her hand. He had taken off his coat to wrap about her.

"I've a good Quaker nurse and a room ready for her at the Continental the minute she can be moved," he whispered. "Look a-here!" turning down the poor bit of lace and red ribbon at her throat, his big hairy hand shaking. "Them bones is a'most through the skin! The doctor says it's hunger — hunger! And I was eatin' three solid meals a day — like a beast!"

Hunger had almost done its work. There was but a feeble flicker of life left in the emaciated little body; not enough to know or speak to us when at last she opened her dull eyes.

"None o' them folks need consarn themselves any furder about her," said Biron savagely. "She'll come home to her own now, thank God, and be done with rubbishy book-makers. Mrs. Biron will live like a lady."

Two or three weeks later, the most splendid of hired phaetons stopped at my door, and Mr. and Mrs. Biron sent up their cards. Mr. Biron was glowing with happiness. It asserted itself offensively somehow in the very jingling of his watch chain and tie of his cravat.

"We return immediately to the plantation," he said, grandiloquently. "I reckon largely on the effect of her native air in restorin' Mrs. Biron to health."

Marcia was magnificent in silk and plumes, the costliest that her owner's money could buy. Her little face was pale, however, and she looked nobody in the eye.

"We leave for the South to-morrow," she said, calmly, "and I shall not return to Philadelphia. I have no wish to return."

"Shall I send you books or papers, Marcia?"

"No, I thank you; nothing."

When they rose to go, her husband said, "Mrs. Biron has some — rubbish she wishes to leave with you. Hyah!" calling out of the window. "You nigger, bring that thah bag!"

It was the old black satchel. Marcia took it in her white-gloved hands, half opened it, shut it quickly, came up closer.

"These are my manuscripts," she said. "Will you burn them for me? All; do not leave a line, a word. I could not do it."

I took the satchel, and they departed. Mr. Biron was vehement in his protestations of friendship and invitations to visit the plantation.

But Marcia did not say a word, even of farewell.

THE MAN THAT CORRUPTED HADLEYBURG

Mark Twain (1835-1910)

It was many years ago. Hadleyburg was the most honest and upright town in all the region round about. It had kept that reputation unsmirched during three generations, and was prouder of it than of any other of its possessions. It was so proud of it, and so anxious to insure its perpetuation, that it began to teach the principles of honest dealing to its babies in the cradle, and made the like teachings the staple of their culture thenceforward through all the years devoted to their education. Also, throughout the formative years temptations were kept out of the way of the young people, so that their honesty could have every chance to harden and solidify, and become a part of their very bone. The neighbouring towns were jealous of this honorable supremacy, and affected to sneer at Hadleyburg's pride in it and call it vanity; but all the same they were obliged to acknowledge that Hadleyburg was in reality an incorruptible town; and if pressed they would also acknowledge that the mere fact that a young man hailed from Hadleyburg was all the recommendation he needed when he went forth from his natal town to seek for responsible employment.

But at last, in the drift of time, Hadleyburg had the ill luck to offend a passing stranger — possibly without knowing it, certainly without caring, for Hadleyburg was sufficient unto itself, and cared not a rap for strangers or their opinions. Still, it would have been well to make an exception in this one's case, for he was a bitter man, and revengeful. All through his wanderings during a whole year he kept his injury in mind, and gave all his leisure moments to trying to invent a compensating satisfaction for it. He contrived many plans, and all of them were good, but none of them was quite sweeping enough: the poorest of them would hurt a great many individuals, but what he wanted was a plan which would comprehend the entire town, and not let so much as one person escape unhurt. At last he had a fortunate idea, and when it fell into his brain it lit up his whole head with an evil joy. He began to form a plan at once, saying to himself "That is the thing to do — I will corrupt the town."

Six months later he went to Hadleyburg, and arrived in a buggy at the house of the old cashier of the bank about ten at night. He got a sack out of the buggy, shouldered it, and staggered with it through the cottage yard, and knocked at the door. A woman's voice said "Come in," and he entered, and set his sack behind the stove in the parlour, saying politely to the old lady who sat reading the "Missionary Herald" by the lamp:

"Pray keep your seat, madam, I will not disturb you. There — now it is pretty well concealed; one would hardly know it was there. Can I see your husband a moment, madam?"

No, he was gone to Brixton, and might not return before morning.

"Very well, madam, it is no matter. I merely wanted to leave that sack in his care, to be delivered to the rightful owner when he shall be found. I am a stranger; he does not know me; I am merely passing through the town to-night to discharge a matter which has been long in my mind. My errand is now completed, and I go pleased and a little proud, and you will never see me again. There is a paper attached to the sack which will explain everything. Good-night, madam."

The old lady was afraid of the mysterious big stranger, and was glad to see him go. But her curiosity was roused, and she went straight to the sack and brought away the paper. It began as follows:

"TO BE PUBLISHED;

or, the right man sought out by private inquiry — either will answer. This sack contains gold coin weighing a hundred and sixty pounds four ounces — "

"Mercy on us, and the door not locked!"

Mrs. Richards flew to it all in a tremble and locked it, then pulled down the window-shades and stood frightened, worried, and wondering if there was anything else she could do toward making herself and the money more safe. She listened awhile for burglars, then surrendered to curiosity, and went back to the lamp and finished reading the paper:

"I am a foreigner, and am presently going back to my own country, to remain there permanently. I am grateful to America for what I have received at her hands during my long stay under her flag; and to one of her citizens — a citizen of Hadleyburg — I am especially grateful for a great kindness done me a year or two ago. Two great kindnesses in fact. I will explain. I was a gambler. I say I WAS. *I was a ruined gambler. I arrived in this village at night, hungry and without a penny. I asked for help — in the dark; I was ashamed to beg in the light. I begged of the right man. He gave me twenty dollars — that is to say, he gave me*

life, as I considered it. He also gave me fortune; for out of that money I have made myself rich at the gaming-table. And finally, a remark which he made to me has remained with me to this day, and has at last conquered me; and in conquering has saved the remnant of my morals: I shall gamble no more. Now I have no idea who that man was, but I want him found, and I want him to have this money, to give away, throw away, or keep, as he pleases. It is merely my way of testifying my gratitude to him. If I could stay, I would find him myself; but no matter, he will be found. This is an honest town, an incorruptible town, and I know I can trust it without fear. This man can be identified by the remark which he made to me; I feel persuaded that he will remember it.

"And now my plan is this: If you prefer to conduct the inquiry privately, do so. Tell the contents of this present writing to any one who is likely to be the right man. If he shall answer, 'I am the man; the remark I made was so-and-so,' apply the test — to wit: open the sack, and in it you will find a sealed envelope containing that remark. If the remark mentioned by the candidate tallies with it, give him the money, and ask no further questions, for he is certainly the right man.

"But if you shall prefer a public inquiry, then publish this present writing in the local paper — with these instructions added, to wit: Thirty days from now, let the candidate appear at the town-hall at eight in the evening (Friday), and hand his remark, in a sealed envelope, to the Rev. Mr. Burgess (if he will be kind enough to act); and let Mr. Burgess there and then destroy the seals of the sack, open it, and see if the remark is correct: if correct, let the money be delivered, with my sincere gratitude, to my benefactor thus identified."

Mrs. Richards sat down, gently quivering with excitement, and was soon lost in thinkings — after this pattern: "What a strange thing it is! . . . And what a fortune for that kind man who set his bread afloat upon the waters! . . . If it had only been my husband that did it! — for we are so poor, so old and poor! . . ." Then, with a sigh — " But it was not my Edward; no, it was not he that gave a stranger twenty dollars. It is a pity too; I see it now. . . "Then, with a shudder — " But it is *gambler's* money! the wages of sin; we couldn't take it; we couldn't touch it. I don't like to be near it; it seems a defilement." She moved to a farther chair. . . "I wish Edward would come, and take it to the bank; a burglar might come at any moment; it is dreadful to be here all alone with it."

At eleven Mr. Richards arrived, and while his wife was saying "I am *so* glad you've come!" he was saying, "I am so tired — tired clear out; it is dreadful to be poor, and have to make these dismal journeys at my time of life. Always at the grind, grind, grind, on a salary — another man's slave, and he sitting at home in his slippers, rich and comfortable."

"I am so sorry for you, Edward, you know that; but be comforted; we have our livelihood; we have our good name — "

"Yes, Mary, and that is everything. Don't mind my talk — it's just a moment's irritation and doesn't mean anything. Kiss me — there, it's all gone now, and I am not complaining any more. What have you been getting? What's in the sack?"

Then his wife told him the great secret. It dazed him for a moment; then he said:

"It weighs a hundred and sixty pounds? Why, Mary, it's forty thousand dollars — think of it — a whole fortune! Not ten men in this village are worth that much. Give me the paper."

He skimmed through it and said:

"Isn't it an adventure! Why, it's a romance; it's like the impossible things one reads about in books, and never sees in life." He was well stirred up now; cheerful, even gleeful. He tapped his old wife on the cheek, and said humorously, "Why, we're rich, Mary, rich; all we've got to do is to bury the money and burn the papers. If the gambler ever comes to inquire, we'll merely look coldly upon him and say: 'What is this nonsense you are talking? We have never heard of you and your sack of gold before'; and then he would look foolish, and — "

"And in the meantime, while you are running on with your jokes, the money is still here, and it is fast getting along toward burglar-time."

"True. Very well, what shall we do — make the inquiry private? No, not that; it would spoil the romance. The public method is better. Think what a noise it will make! And it will make all the other towns jealous; for no stranger would trust such a thing to any town but Hadleyburg, and they know it. It's a great card for us. I must get to the printing-office now, or I shall be too late."

"But stop — stop — don't leave me here alone with it, Edward!"

But he was gone. For only a little while, however. Not far from his own house he met the editor — proprietor of the paper, and gave him the document, and said "Here is a good thing for you, Cox — put it in."

"It may be too late, Mr. Richards, but I'll see."

At home again, he and his wife sat down to talk the charming mystery over; they were in no condition for sleep. The first question was, Who could the citizen have been who gave the stranger the twenty dollars? It seemed a simple one; both answered it in the same breath —

"Barclay Goodson."

"Yes," said Richards, "he could have done it, and it would have been like him, but there's not another in the town."

"Everybody will grant that, Edward — grant it privately, anyway. For six months, now, the village has been its own proper self once more — honest, narrow, self-righteous, and stingy."

"It is what he always called it, to the day of his death — said it right out publicly, too."

"Yes, and he was hated for it."

"Oh, of course; but he didn't care. I reckon he was the best-hated man among us, except the Reverend Burgess."

"Well, Burgess deserves it — he will never get another congregation here. Mean as the town is, it knows how to estimate *him*. Edward, doesn't it seem odd that the stranger should appoint Burgess to deliver the money?"

"Well, yes — it does. That is — that is — "

"Why so much that-*is*-ing? Would *you* select him?"

"Mary, maybe the stranger knows him better than this village does."

"Much *that* would help Burgess!"

The husband seemed perplexed for an answer; the wife kept a steady eye upon him, and waited. Finally Richards said, with the hesitancy of one who is making a statement which is likely to encounter doubt:

"Mary, Burgess is not a bad man."

His wife was certainly surprised.

"Nonsense!" she exclaimed.

"He is not a bad man. I know. The whole of his unpopularity had its foundation in that one thing — the thing that made so much noise."

"That 'one thing,' indeed! As if that 'one thing' wasn't enough, all by itself."

"Plenty. Plenty. Only he wasn't guilty of it."

"How you talk! Not guilty of it! Everybody knows he WAS guilty."

"Mary, I give you my word — he was innocent."

"I can't believe it and I don't. How do you know?"

"It is a confession. I am ashamed, but I will make it. I was the only man who knew he was innocent. I could have saved him, and — and — well, you know how the town was wrought up — I hadn't the pluck to do it. It would have turned everybody against me. I felt mean, ever so mean; but I didn't dare; I hadn't the manliness to face that."

Mary looked troubled, and for a while was silent. Then she said stammeringly:

"I — I don't think it would have done for you to — to — One mustn't — er — public opinion — one has to be so careful — so — " It was a difficult road, and she got mired; but after a little she got started again. "It was a great pity, but — Why, we couldn't afford it, Edward — we couldn't indeed. Oh, I wouldn't have had you do it for anything!"

"It would have lost us the good-will of so many people, Mary; and then — and then — "

"What troubles me now is, what *he* thinks of us, Edward."

"He? *He* doesn't suspect that I could have saved him."

"Oh," exclaimed the wife, in a tone of relief, "I am glad of that. As long as he doesn't know that you could have saved him, he — he — well that makes it a great deal better. Why, I might have known he didn't know, because he is always trying to be friendly with us, as little encouragement as we give him. More than once people have twitted me with it. There's the Wilsons, and the Wilcoxes, and the Harknesses, they take a mean pleasure in saying '*Your friend* Burgess,' because they know it pesters me. I wish he wouldn't persist in liking us so; I can't think why he keeps it up."

"I can explain it. It's another confession. When the thing was new and hot, and the town made a plan to ride him on a rail, my conscience hurt me so that I couldn't stand it, and I went privately and gave him notice, and he got out of the town and stayed out till it was safe to come back."

"Edward! If the town had found it out — "

"*Don't!* It scares me yet, to think of it. I repented of it the minute it was done; and I was even afraid to tell you lest your face might betray it to somebody. I didn't sleep any that night, for worrying. But after a few days I saw that no one was going to suspect me, and after that I got to feeling glad I did it. And I feel glad yet, Mary — glad through and through."

"So do I, now, for it would have been a dreadful way to treat him. Yes, I'm glad; for really you did owe him that, you know. But, Edward, suppose it should come out yet, some day!"

"It won't."

"Why?"

"Because everybody thinks it was Goodson."

"Of course they would!"

"Certainly. And of course *he* didn't care. They persuaded poor old Sawlsberry to go and charge it on him, and he went blustering over there and did it. Goodson looked him over, like as if he was hunting for a place on him that he could despise the most; then he says, 'So you are the Committee of Inquiry, are you?' Sawlsberry said that was about what he was. 'H'm. Do they require particulars, or do you reckon a kind of a *general* answer will do?' 'If they require particulars, I will come back, Mr. Goodson; I will take the general answer first.' 'Very well, then, tell them to go to hell — I reckon that's general enough. And I'll give you some advice, Sawlsberry; when you come back for the particulars, fetch a basket to carry what is left of yourself home in.' "

"Just like Goodson; it's got all the marks. He had only one vanity; he thought he could give advice better than any other person."

"It settled the business, and saved us, Mary. The subject was dropped."

"Bless you, I'm not doubting *that*."

Then they took up the gold-sack mystery again, with strong interest. Soon the conversation began to suffer breaks — interruptions caused by absorbed thinkings. The breaks grew more and more frequent. At last Richards lost himself wholly in thought. He sat long, gazing vacantly at the floor, and by-and-by he began to punctuate his thoughts with little nervous movements of his hands that seemed to indicate vexation. Meantime his wife too had relapsed into a thoughtful silence, and her movements were beginning to show a troubled discomfort. Finally Richards got up and strode aimlessly about the room, ploughing his hands through his hair, much as a somnambulist might do who was having a bad dream. Then he seemed to arrive at a definite purpose; and without a word he put on his hat and passed quickly out of the house. His wife sat brooding, with a drawn face, and did not seem to be aware that she was alone. Now and then she murmured, "Lead us not into t . . . but — but — we are so poor, so poor! . . . Lead us not into . . . Ah, who would be hurt by it? — and no one would ever know . . . Lead us . . . "The voice died out in mumblings. After a little she glanced up and muttered in a half-frightened, half-glad way:

"He is gone! But, oh dear, he may be too late — too late . . . Maybe not — maybe there is still time." She rose and stood thinking, nervously clasping and unclasping her hands. A slight shudder shook her frame, and she said, out of a dry throat, "God forgive me — it's awful to think such things — but . . . Lord, how we are made — how strangely we are made!"

She turned the light low, and slipped stealthily over and knelt down by the sack and felt of its ridgy sides with her hands, and fondled them lovingly; and there was a gloating light in her poor old eyes. She fell into fits of absence; and came half out of them at times to mutter "If we had only waited! — oh, if we had only waited a little, and not been in such a hurry!"

Meantime Cox had gone home from his office and told his wife all about the strange thing that had happened, and they had talked it over eagerly, and guessed that the late Goodson was the only man in the town who could have helped a suffering stranger with so noble a sum as twenty dollars. Then there was a pause, and the two became thoughtful and silent. And by-and-by nervous and fidgety. At last the wife said, as if to herself:

"Nobody knows this secret but the Richardses . . . and us . . . nobody."

The husband came out of his thinkings with a slight start, and gazed wistfully at his wife, whose face was become very pale; then he hesitatingly rose, and glanced furtively at his hat, then at his wife — a sort of mute inquiry. Mrs. Cox swallowed once or twice, with her hand at her throat, then in place of speech she nodded her head. In a moment she was alone, and mumbling to herself.

And now Richards and Cox were hurrying through the deserted streets, from opposite directions. They met, panting, at the foot of the printing-office stairs; by the night-light there they read each other's face. Cox whispered:

"Nobody knows about this but us?"

The whispered answer was:

"Not a soul — on honor, not a soul!"

"If it isn't too late to — "

The men were starting up-stairs; at this moment they were overtaken by a boy, and Cox asked,

"Is that you, Johnny?"

"Yes, sir."

"You needn't ship the early mail — nor *any* mail; wait till I tell you."

"It's already gone, sir."

"*Gone?*" It had the sound of an unspeakable disappointment in it.

"Yes, sir. Time-table for Brixton and all the towns beyond changed to-day, sir — had to get the papers in twenty minutes earlier than common. I had to rush; if I had been two minutes later — "

The men turned and walked slowly away, not waiting to hear the rest. Neither of them spoke during ten minutes; then Cox said, in a vexed tone:

"What possessed you to be in such a hurry, *I* can't make out."

The answer was humble enough:

"I see it now, but somehow I never thought, you know, until it was too late. But the next time — "

"Next time be hanged! It won't come in a thousand years."

Then the friends separated without a good-night, and dragged themselves home with the gait of mortally stricken men. At their homes their wives sprang up with an eager "Well?" — then saw the answer with their eyes and sank down sorrowing, without waiting for it to come in words. In both houses a discussion followed of a heated sort — a new thing; there had been discussions before, but not heated ones, not ungentle ones. The discussions to-night were a sort of seeming plagiarisms of each other. Mrs. Richards said:

"If you had only waited, Edward — if you had only stopped to think; but no, you must run straight to the printing-office and spread it all over the world."

"It *said* publish it."

"That is nothing; it also said do it privately, if you liked. There, now — is that true, or not?"

"Why, yes — yes, it is true; but when I thought what a stir it would make, and what a compliment it was to Hadleyburg that a stranger should trust it so — "

"Oh, certainly, I know all that; but if you had only stopped to think, you would have seen that you *couldn't* find the right man, because he is in his grave, and hasn't left chick nor child nor relation behind him; and as long as the money went to somebody that awfully needed it, and nobody would be hurt by it, and — and — "

She broke down, crying. Her husband tried to think of some comforting thing to say, and presently came out with this:

"But after all, Mary, it must be for the best — it *must* be; we know that. And we must remember that it was so ordered — "

"Ordered! Oh, everything's *ordered*, when a person has to find some way out when he has been stupid. Just the same, it was *ordered* that the money should come to us in this special way, and it was you that must take it on yourself to go meddling with the designs of Providence — and who gave you the right? It was wicked, that is what it was — just blasphemous presumption, and no more becoming to a meek and humble professor of — "

"But, Mary, you know how we have been trained all our lives long, like the whole village, till it is absolutely second nature to us to stop not a single moment to think when there's an honest thing to be done — "

"Oh, I know it, I know it — it's been one everlasting training and training and training in honesty — honesty shielded, from the very cradle, against every possible temptation, and so it's *artificial* honesty, and weak as water when temptation comes, as we have seen this night. God knows I never had shade nor shadow of a doubt of my petrified and indestructible honesty until now — and now, under the very first big and real temptation, I — Edward, it is my belief that this town's honesty is as rotten as mine is; as rotten as yours. It is a mean town, a hard, stingy town, and hasn't a virtue in the world but this honesty it is so celebrated for and so conceited about; and so help me, I do believe that if ever the day comes that its honesty falls under great temptation, its grand reputation will go to ruin like a house of cards. There, now, I've made confession, and I feel better; I am a humbug, and I've been one all my life, without knowing it. Let no man call me honest again — I will not have it."

"I — Well, Mary, I feel a good deal as you do: I certainly do. It seems strange, too, so strange. I never could have believed it — never."

A long silence followed; both were sunk in thought. At last the wife looked up and said:

"I know what you are thinking, Edward."

Richards had the embarrassed look of a person who is caught.

"I am ashamed to confess it, Mary, but — "

"It's no matter, Edward, I was thinking the same question myself."

"I hope so. State it."

"You were thinking, if a body could only guess out *what the remark was* that Goodson made to the stranger."

"It's perfectly true. I feel guilty and ashamed. And you?"

"I'm past it. Let us make a pallet here; we've got to stand watch till the bank vault opens in the morning and admits the sack. . . Oh dear, oh dear — if we hadn't made the mistake!"

The pallet was made, and Mary said:

"The open sesame — what could it have been? I do wonder what that remark could have been. But come; we will get to bed now."

"And sleep?"

"No; think."

"Yes; think."

By this time the Coxes too had completed their spat and their reconciliation, and were turning in — to think, to think, and toss, and fret, and worry over what the remark could possibly have been which Goodson made to the stranded derelict; that golden remark; that remark worth forty thousand dollars, cash.

The reason that the village telegraph-office was open later than usual that night was this: The foreman of Cox's paper was the local representative of the Associated Press. One might say its honorary representative, for it wasn't four times a year that he could furnish thirty words that would be accepted. But this time it was different. His despatch stating what he had caught got an instant answer:

"Send the whole thing — all the details — twelve hundred words."

A colossal order! The foreman filled the bill; and he was the proudest man in the State. By breakfast-time the next morning the name of Hadleyburg the Incorruptible was on every lip in America, from Montreal to the Gulf, from the glaciers of Alaska to the orange-groves of Florida; and millions and millions of people were discussing the stranger and his money-sack, and wondering if the right man would be found, and hoping some more news about the matter would come soon — right away.

II

Hadleyburg village woke up world-celebrated — astonished — happy — vain. Vain beyond imagination. Its nineteen principal citizens and their wives went about shaking hands with each other, and beaming, and smiling, and congratulating, and saying *this* thing adds a new word to the dictionary — *Hadleyburg*, synonym for *incorruptible* — destined to live in dictionaries forever! And the minor and unimportant citizens and their wives went around acting in much the same way. Everybody ran to the bank to see the gold-sack; and before noon grieved and envious crowds began to flock in from Brixton and all neighboring towns; and that afternoon and next day reporters began to arrive from everywhere to verify the sack and its history and write the whole thing up anew, and make dashing free-hand pictures of the sack, and of Richards's house, and the bank, and the Presbyterian church, and the Baptist church, and the public square, and the town-hall where the test would be applied and the money delivered; and damnable portraits of the Richardses, and Pinkerton the banker, and Cox, and the foreman, and Reverend Burgess, and the postmaster — and even of Jack Halliday, who was the loafing, good-natured, no-account, irreverent fisherman, hunter, boys' friend, stray-dogs' friend, typical "Sam Lawson" of the town. The little mean, smirking, oily Pinkerton showed the sack to all comers, and rubbed his sleek palms together pleasantly, and enlarged upon the town's fine old reputation for honesty and upon this wonderful endorsement of it, and hoped and believed that the example would now spread far and wide over the American world, and be epoch-making in the matter of moral regeneration. And so on, and so on.

By the end of a week things had quieted down again; the wild intoxication of pride and joy had sobered to a soft, sweet, silent delight — a sort of deep, nameless, unutterable content. All faces bore a look of peaceful, holy happiness.

Then a change came. It was a gradual change; so gradual that its beginnings were hardly noticed; maybe were not noticed at all, except by Jack Halliday, who always noticed everything; and always made fun of it, too, no matter what it was. He began to throw out chaffing remarks about people not looking quite so happy as they did a day or two ago; and next he claimed that the new aspect was deepening to positive sadness; next, that it was taking on a sick look; and finally he said that everybody was become so moody, thoughtful, and absent-minded that he could rob the meanest man in town of a cent out of the bottom of his breeches pocket and not disturb his reverie.

At this stage — or at about this stage — a saying like this was dropped at bedtime — with a sigh, usually — by the head of each of the nineteen principal households:

"Ah, what *could* have been the remark that Goodson made?"

And straightway — with a shudder — came this, from the man's wife:

"Oh, *don't!* What horrible thing are you mulling in your mind? Put it away from you, for God's sake!"

But that question was wrung from those men again the next night — and got the same retort. But weaker.

And the third night the men uttered the question yet again — with anguish, and absently. This time — and the following night — the wives fidgeted feebly, and tried to say something. But didn't.

And the night after that they found their tongues and responded — longingly:

"Oh, if we *could* only guess!"

Halliday's comments grew daily more and more sparklingly disagreeable and disparaging. He went diligently about, laughing at the town, individually and in mass. But his laugh was the only one left in the village: it fell upon a hollow and mournful vacancy and emptiness. Not even a smile was findable anywhere. Halliday carried a cigar-box around on a tripod, playing that it was a camera, and halted all passers and aimed the thing and said "Ready! — now look pleasant, please," but not even this capital joke could surprise the dreary faces into any softening.

So three weeks passed — one week was left. It was Saturday evening after supper. Instead of the aforetime Saturday-evening flutter and bustle and shopping and larking, the streets were empty and desolate. Richards and his old wife sat apart in their little parlour — miserable and thinking. This was become their evening habit now: the life-long habit which had preceded it, of reading, knitting, and contented chat, or receiving or paying neighbourly calls, was dead and gone and forgotten, ages ago — two or three weeks ago; nobody talked now, nobody read, nobody visited — the whole village sat at home, sighing, worrying, silent. Trying to guess out that remark.

The postman left a letter. Richards glanced listlessly at the superscription and the post-mark — unfamiliar, both — and tossed the letter on the table and resumed his might-have-beens and his hopeless dull miseries where he had left them off. Two or three hours later his wife got wearily up and was going away to bed without a good-night — custom now — but she stopped near the letter and eyed it awhile with a dead interest, then broke it open, and began to skim it over. Richards, sitting there with his chair tilted back against the wall and his chin between his knees, heard something fall. It was his wife. He sprang to her side, but she cried out:

"Leave me alone, I am too happy. Read the letter — read it!"

He did. He devoured it, his brain reeling. The letter was from a distant State, and it said:

> *"I am a stranger to you, but no matter: I have something to tell. I have just arrived home from Mexico, and learned about that episode. Of course you do not know who made that remark, but I know, and I am the only person living who does know. It was GOODSON. I knew him well, many years ago. I passed through your village that very night, and was his guest till the midnight train came along. I overheard him make that remark to the stranger in the dark — it was in Hale Alley. He and I talked of it the rest of the way home, and while smoking in his house. He mentioned many of your villagers in the course of his talk — most of them in a very uncomplimentary way, but two or three favourably: among these latter yourself. I say 'favourably' — nothing stronger. I remember his saying he did not actually LIKE any person in the*

town — not one; but that you — I THINK *he said you — am almost sure — had done him a very great service once, possibly without knowing the full value of it, and he wished he had a fortune, he would leave it to you when he died, and a curse apiece for the rest of the citizens. Now, then, if it was you that did him that service, you are his legitimate heir, and entitled to the sack of gold. I know that I can trust to your honor and honesty, for in a citizen of Hadleyburg these virtues are an unfailing inheritance, and so I am going to reveal to you the remark, well satisfied that if you are not the right man you will seek and find the right one and see that poor Goodson's debt of gratitude for the service referred to is paid. This is the remark* 'YOU ARE FAR FROM BEING A BAD MAN: GO, AND REFORM.'

"HOWARD L. STEPHENSON."

"Oh, Edward, the money is ours, and I am so grateful, *oh,* so grateful, — kiss me, dear, it's forever since we kissed — and we needed it so — the money — and now you are free of Pinkerton and his bank, and nobody's slave any more; it seems to me I could fly for joy."

It was a happy half-hour that the couple spent there on the settee caressing each other; it was the old days come again — days that had begun with their courtship and lasted without a break till the stranger brought the deadly money. By-and-by the wife said:

"Oh, Edward, how lucky it was you did him that grand service, poor Goodson! I never liked him, but I love him now. And it was fine and beautiful of you never to mention it or brag about it." Then, with a touch of reproach, "But you ought to have told *me*, Edward, you ought to have told your wife, you know."

"Well, I — er — well, Mary, you see — "

"Now stop hemming and hawing, and tell me about it, Edward. I always loved you, and now I'm proud of you. Everybody believes there was only one good generous soul in this village, and now it turns out that you — Edward, why don't you tell me?"

"Well — er — er — Why, Mary, I can't!"

"You *can't? Why* can't you?"

"You see, he — well, he — he made me promise I wouldn't."

The wife looked him over, and said, very slowly:

"Made — you — promise? Edward, what do you tell me that for?"

"Mary, do you think I would lie?"

She was troubled and silent for a moment, then she laid her hand within his and said:

"No . . . no. We have wandered far enough from our bearings — God spare us that! In all your life you have never uttered a lie. But now — now that the foundations of things seem to be crumbling from under us, we — we — " She lost her voice for a moment, then said, brokenly, "Lead us not into temptation. . . I think you made the promise, Edward. Let it rest so. Let us keep away from that ground. Now — that is all gone by; let us be happy again; it is no time for clouds."

Edward found it something of an effort to comply, for his mind kept wandering — trying to remember what the service was that he had done Goodson.

The couple lay awake the most of the night, Mary happy and busy, Edward busy, but not so happy. Mary was planning what she would do with the money. Edward was trying to recall that service. At first his conscience was sore on account of the lie he had told Mary — if it was a lie. After much reflection — suppose it *was* a lie? What then? Was it such a great matter? Aren't we always *acting* lies? Then why not *tell* them? Look at Mary — look what she had done. While he was hurrying off on his honest errand, what was she doing? Lamenting because the papers hadn't been destroyed and the money kept. Is theft better than lying?

That point lost its sting — the lie dropped into the background and left comfort behind it. The next point came to the front: *Had* he rendered that service? Well, here was Goodson's own evidence as reported in Stephenson's letter; there could be no better evidence than that — it was even *proof* that he had rendered it. Of course. So that point was settled. . . . No, not quite. He recalled with a wince that this unknown Mr. Stephenson was just a trifle unsure as to whether the performer of it was Richards or some other — and, oh dear, he had put Richards on his honor! He must himself decide whither that money must go — and Mr. Stephenson was not doubting that if he was the wrong man he would go honorably and find the right one. Oh, it was odious to put a man in such a situation — ah, why couldn't Stephenson have left out that doubt? What did he want to intrude that for?

Further reflection. How did it happen that *Richards's* name remained in Stephenson's mind as indicating the right man, and not some other man's name? That looked good. Yes, that looked very good. In fact it went on looking better and better, straight along — until by-and-by it grew into positive *proof*. And then Richards put the matter at once out of his mind, for he had a private instinct that a proof once established is better left so.

He was feeling reasonably comfortable now, but there was still one other detail that kept pushing itself on his notice: of course he had done that service — that was settled; but what *was* that service? He must recall it — he would not go to sleep till he had recalled it; it would make his peace of mind perfect. And so he thought and thought. He thought of a dozen things — possible services, even probable services — but none of them seemed adequate, none of them seemed large enough, none of them seemed worth the money — worth the fortune Goodson had wished he could leave in his will. And besides, he couldn't remember having done them, anyway. Now, then — now, then — what *kind* of a service would it be that would make a man so inordinately grateful? Ah — the saving of his soul! That must be it. Yes, he could remember, now, how he once set himself the task of converting Goodson, and laboured at it as much as — he was going to say three months; but upon closer examination it shrunk to a month, then to a week, then to a day, then to nothing. Yes, he remembered now, and with unwelcome vividness, that Goodson had told him to go to thunder and mind his own business — *he* wasn't hankering to follow Hadleyburg to heaven!

So that solution was a failure — he hadn't saved Goodson's soul. Richards was discouraged. Then after a little came another idea: had he saved Goodson's property? No, that wouldn't do — he hadn't any. His life? That is it! Of course. Why, he might have thought of it before. This time he was on the right track, sure. His imagination-mill was hard at work in a minute, now.

Thereafter, during a stretch of two exhausting hours, he was busy saving Goodson's life. He saved it in all kinds of difficult and perilous ways. In every case he got it saved satisfactorily up to a certain point; then, just as he was beginning to get well persuaded that it had really happened, a troublesome detail would turn up which made the whole thing impossible. As in the matter of drowning, for instance. In that case he had swum out and tugged Goodson ashore in an unconscious state with a great crowd looking on and applauding, but when he had got it all thought out and was just beginning to remember all about it, a whole swarm of disqualifying details arrived on the ground: the town would have known of the circumstance, Mary would have known of it, it would glare like a limelight in his own memory instead of being an inconspicuous service which he had possibly rendered "without knowing its full value." And at this point he remembered that he couldn't swim anyway.

Ah — *there* was a point which he had been overlooking from the start: it had to be a service which he had rendered "possibly without knowing the full value of it." Why, really, that ought to be an easy hunt — much easier than those others. And sure enough, by-and-by he found it. Goodson, years and years ago, came near marrying a very sweet and pretty girl, named Nancy Hewitt, but in some way or other the match had been broken off; the girl died, Goodson remained a bachelor, and by-and-by became a soured one and a frank despiser of the human species. Soon after the girl's death the village found out, or thought it had found out, that she carried a spoonful of negro blood in her veins. Richards worked at these details a good while, and in the end he thought he remembered things concerning them which must have gotten mislaid in his memory through long neglect. He seemed to dimly remember that it was *he* that found out about the negro blood; that it was he that told the village; that the village told Goodson where they got it; that he thus saved Goodson from marrying the tainted girl; that he had done him this great service "without knowing the full value of it," in fact without knowing that he *was* doing it; but that Goodson knew the value of it, and what a narrow escape he had had, and so went to his grave grateful to his benefactor and wishing he had a fortune to leave him. It was all clear and simple, now, and the more he went over it the more luminous and certain it grew; and at last, when he nestled to sleep, satisfied and happy, he remembered the whole thing just as if it had been yesterday. In fact, he dimly remembered Goodson's *telling* him his gratitude once. Meantime Mary had spent six thousand dollars on a new house for herself and a pair of slippers for her pastor, and then had fallen peacefully to rest.

That same Saturday evening the postman had delivered a letter to each of the other principal citizens — nineteen letters in all. No two of the envelopes were alike, and no two of the superscriptions were in the same hand, but the letters inside were just like each other in every detail but one. They were exact copies of the letter received by Richards — handwriting and all — and were all signed by Stephenson, but in place of Richards's name each receiver's own name appeared.

All night long eighteen principal citizens did what their caste-brother Richards was doing at the same time — they put in their energies trying to remember what notable service it was that they had unconsciously done Barclay Goodson. In no case was it a holiday job; still they succeeded.

And while they were at this work, which was difficult, their wives put in the night spending the money, which was easy. During that one night the nineteen wives spent an average of seven thousand dollars each out of the forty thousand in the sack — a hundred and thirty-three thousand altogether.

Next day there was a surprise for Jack Halliday. He noticed that the faces of the nineteen chief citizens and their wives bore that expression of peaceful and holy happiness again. He could not understand it, neither was he able to invent any remarks about it that could damage it or disturb it. And so it was his turn to be dissatisfied with life. His private guesses at the reasons for the happiness failed in all instances, upon examination. When he met Mrs. Wilcox and noticed the placid ecstasy in her face, he said to himself, "Her cat has had kittens" — and went and asked the cook; it was not so, the cook had detected the happiness, but did not know the cause. When Halliday found the duplicate ecstasy in the face of "Shadbelly" Billson (village nickname), he was sure some neighbour of Billson's had broken his leg, but inquiry showed that this had not happened. The subdued ecstasy in Gregory Yates's face could mean but one thing — he was a mother-in-law short; it was another mistake. "And Pinkerton — Pinkerton — he has collected ten cents that he thought he was going to lose." And so on, and so on. In some cases the guesses had to remain in doubt, in the others they proved distinct errors. In the end Halliday said to himself, "Anyway it roots up that there's nineteen Hadleyburg families temporarily in heaven: I don't know how it happened; I only know Providence is off duty to-day."

An architect and builder from the next State had lately ventured to set up a small business in this unpromising village, and his sign had now been hanging out a week. Not a customer yet; he was a discouraged man, and sorry he had come. But his weather changed suddenly now. First one and then another chief citizen's wife said to him privately:

"Come to my house Monday week — but say nothing about it for the present. We think of building."

He got eleven invitations that day. That night he wrote his daughter and broke off her match with her student. He said she could marry a mile higher than that.

Pinkerton the banker and two or three other well-to-do men planned country-seats — but waited. That kind don't count their chickens until they are hatched.

The Wilsons devised a grand new thing — a fancy-dress ball. They made no actual promises, but told all their acquaintanceship in confidence that they were thinking the matter over and thought they should give it — "and if we do, you will be invited, of course." People were surprised, and said, one to another,

"Why, they are crazy, those poor Wilsons, they can't afford it." Several among the nineteen said privately to their husbands, "It is a good idea, we will keep still till their cheap thing is over, then *we* will give one that will make it sick."

The days drifted along, and the bill of future squanderings rose higher and higher, wilder and wilder, more and more foolish and reckless. It began to look as if every member of the nineteen would not only spend his whole forty thousand dollars before receiving-day, but be actually in debt by the time he got the money. In some cases light-headed people did not stop with planning to spend, they really spent — on credit. They bought land, mortgages, farms, speculative stocks, fine clothes, horses, and various other things, paid down the bonus, and made themselves liable for the rest — at ten days. Presently the sober second thought came, and Halliday noticed that a ghastly anxiety was beginning to show up in a good many faces. Again he was puzzled, and didn't know what to make of it. "The Wilcox kittens aren't dead, for they weren't born; nobody's broken a leg; there's no shrinkage in mother-in-laws; *nothing* has happened — it is an insolvable mystery."

There was another puzzled man, too — the Rev. Mr. Burgess. For days, wherever he went, people seemed to follow him or to be watching out for him; and if he ever found himself in a retired spot, a member of the nineteen would be sure to appear, thrust an envelope privately into his hand, whisper "To be opened at the town-hall Friday evening," then vanish away like a guilty thing. He was expecting that there might be one claimant for the sack — doubtful, however, Goodson being dead — but it never occurred to him that all this crowd might be claimants. When the great Friday came at last, he found that he had nineteen envelopes.

III

The town-hall had never looked finer. The platform at the end of it was backed by a showy draping of flags; at intervals along the walls were festoons of flags; the gallery fronts were clothed in flags; the supporting columns were swathed in flags; all this was to impress the stranger, for he would be there in considerable force, and in a large degree he would be connected with the press. The house was full. The 412 fixed seats were occupied; also the 68 extra chairs which had been packed into the aisles; the steps of the platform were occupied; some distinguished strangers were given seats on the platform; at the horseshoe of tables which fenced the front and sides of the platform sat a strong force of special correspondents who had come from everywhere. It was the best-dressed house the town had ever produced. There were some tolerably expensive toilets there, and in several cases the ladies who wore them had the look of being unfamiliar with that kind of clothes. At least the town thought they had that look, but the notion could have arisen from the town's knowledge of the fact that these ladies had never inhabited such clothes before.

The gold-sack stood on a little table at the front of the platform where all the house could see it. The bulk of the house gazed at it with a burning interest, a mouth-watering interest, a wistful and pathetic interest; a minority of nineteen couples gazed at it tenderly, lovingly, proprietarily, and the male half of this minority kept saying over to themselves the moving little impromptu speeches of thankfulness for the audience's applause and congratulations which they were presently going to get up and deliver. Every now and then one of these got a piece of paper out of his vest pocket and privately glanced at it to refresh his memory.

Of course there was a buzz of conversation going on — there always is; but at last, when the Rev. Mr. Burgess rose and laid his hand on the sack, he could hear his microbes gnaw, the place was so still. He related the curious history of the sack, then went on to speak in warm terms of Hadleyburg's old and well-earned reputation for spotless honesty, and of the town's just pride in this reputation. He said that this reputation was a treasure of priceless value; that under Providence its value had now become inestimably enhanced, for the recent episode had spread this fame far and wide, and thus had focussed the eyes of the American world upon this village, and made its name for all time, as he hoped and believed, a synonym for commercial incorruptibility. [*Applause.*] "And who is to be the guardian of this noble fame — the community as a whole? No! The responsibility is individual, not communal. From this day forth each and every one of you is in his own person its special guardian, and individually responsible that no harm shall come to it. Do you — does each of you — accept this great trust? [*Tumultuous assent.*] Then all is well. Transmit it to your children and to your children's children. To-day your purity is beyond reproach — see to it that it shall remain so. To-day there is not a person in your community who could be beguiled to touch a penny not his own — see to it that you abide in this grace. [*"We will! we will!"*] This is not the place to make comparisons between ourselves and other communities — some of them ungracious towards us; they have their ways, we have ours; let us be content. [*Applause.*] I am done. Under my hand, my friends, rests a stranger's eloquent recognition of what we are; through him the world will always henceforth know what we are. We do not know who he is, but in your name I utter your gratitude, and ask you to raise your voices in indorsement."

The house rose in a body and made the walls quake with the thunders of its thankfulness for the space of a long minute. Then it sat down, and Mr. Burgess took an envelope out of his pocket. The house held its breath while he slit the envelope open and took from it a slip of paper. He read its contents — slowly and impressively — the audience listening with tranced attention to this magic document, each of whose words stood for an ingot of gold:

" *'The remark which I made to the distressed stranger was this: "You are very far from being a bad man; go, and reform."* ' " Then he continued:

"We shall know in a moment now whether the remark here quoted corresponds with the one concealed in the sack; and if that shall prove to be so — and it undoubtedly will — this sack of gold belongs to a fellow-citizen who will henceforth stand before the nation as the symbol of the special virtue which has made our town famous throughout the land — Mr. Billson!"

The house had gotten itself all ready to burst into the proper tornado of applause; but instead of doing it, it seemed stricken with a paralysis; there was a deep hush for a moment or two, then a wave of whispered murmurs swept the place — of about this tenor: "*Billson!* oh, come, this is *too* thin! Twenty dollars to a stranger — or *anybody* — *Billson!* Tell it to the marines!" And now at this point the house caught its breath all of a sudden in a new access of astonishment, for it discovered that whereas in one part of the hall Deacon Billson was standing up with his head weekly bowed, in another part of it Lawyer Wilson was doing the same. There was a wondering silence now for a while. Everybody was puzzled, and nineteen couples were surprised and indignant.

Billson and Wilson turned and stared at each other. Billson asked, bitingly:

"Why do *you* rise, Mr. Wilson?"

"Because I have a right to. Perhaps you will be good enough to explain to the house why *you* rise."

"With great pleasure. Because I wrote that paper."

"It is an impudent falsity! I wrote it myself."

It was Burgess's turn to be paralysed. He stood looking vacantly at first one of the men and then the other, and did not seem to know what to do. The house was stupefied. Lawyer Wilson spoke up now, and said:

"I ask the Chair to read the name signed to that paper."

That brought the Chair to itself, and it read out the name:

"John Wharton *Billson*."

"There!" shouted Billson, "what have you got to say for yourself now? And what kind of apology are you going to make to me and to this insulted house for the imposture which you have attempted to play here?"

"No apologies are due, sir; and as for the rest of it, I publicly charge you with pilfering my note from Mr. Burgess and substituting a copy of it signed with your own name. There is no other way by which you could have gotten hold of the test-remark; I alone, of living men, possessed the secret of its wording."

There was likely to be a scandalous state of things if this went on; everybody noticed with distress that the shorthand scribes were scribbling like mad; many people were crying "Chair, chair! Order! order!" Burgess rapped with his gavel, and said:

"Let us not forget the proprieties due. There has evidently been a mistake somewhere, but surely that is all. If Mr. Wilson gave me an envelope — and I remember now that he did — I still have it."

He took one out of his pocket, opened it, glanced at it, looked surprised and worried, and stood silent a few moments. Then he waved his hand in a wandering and mechanical way, and made an effort or two to say something, then gave it up, despondently. Several voices cried out:

"Read it! read it! What is it?"

So he began, in a dazed and sleep-walker fashion:

" '*The remark which I made to the unhappy stranger was this: "You are far from being a bad man.* [The house gazed at him marvelling.] *Go, and reform.*" ' [*Murmurs:* "Amazing! what can this mean?"] "This one," said the Chair, "is signed Thurlow G. Wilson."

"There!" cried Wilson, "I reckon that settles it! I knew perfectly well my note was purloined."

"Purloined!" retorted Billson. "I'll let you know that neither you nor any man of your kidney must venture to — "

THE CHAIR: "Order, gentlemen, order! Take your seats, both of you, please."

They obeyed, shaking their heads and grumbling angrily. The house was profoundly puzzled; it did not know what to do with this curious emergency. Presently Thompson got up. Thompson was the hatter. He would have liked to be a Nineteener; but such was not for him; his stock of hats was not considerable enough for the position. He said:

"Mr. Chairman, if I may be permitted to make a suggestion, can both of these gentlemen be right? I put it to you, sir, can both have happened to say the very same words to the stranger? It seems to me — "

The tanner got up and interrupted him. The tanner was a disgruntled man; he believed himself entitled to be a Nineteener, but he couldn't get recognition. It made him a little unpleasant in his ways and speech. Said he:

"Sho, *that's* not the point! *That* could happen — twice in a hundred years — but not the other thing. *Neither* of them gave the twenty dollars!"

[*A ripple of applause.*]

BILLSON. "*I* did!"

WILSON. "*I* did!"

Then each accused the other of pilfering.

THE CHAIR. "Order! Sit down, if you please — both of you. Neither of the notes has been out of my possession at any moment."

A VOICE. "Good — that settles *that!*"

THE TANNER. "Mr. Chairman, one thing is now plain: one of these men has been eavesdropping under the other one's bed, and filching family secrets. If it is not unparliamentary to suggest it, I will remark that both are equal to it. [*The Chair.* "Order! order!"] I withdraw the remark, sir, and will confine myself to suggesting that *if* one of them has overheard the other reveal the test-remark to his wife, we shall catch him now."

A VOICE. "How?"

THE TANNER. "Easily. The two have not quoted the remark in exactly the same words. You would have noticed that, if there hadn't been a considerable stretch of time and an exciting quarrel inserted between the two readings."

A VOICE. "Name the difference."

THE TANNER. "The word *very* is in Billson's note, and not in the other."

MANY VOICES. "That's so — he's right!"

THE TANNER. "And so, if the Chair will examine the test-remark in the sack, we shall know which of these two frauds — [*The Chair.* "Order!"] — which of these two adventurers — [*The Chair.* "Order! order!"] — which of these two gentlemen — [*laughter and applause*] — is entitled to wear the belt as being the first dishonest blatherskite ever bred in this town — which he has dishonored, and which will be a sultry place for him from now out!" [*Vigorous applause.*]

MANY VOICES. "Open it! — open the sack!"

Mr. Burgess made a slit in the sack, slid his hand in, and brought out an envelope. In it were a couple of folded notes. He said:

"One of these is marked, 'Not to be examined until all written communications which have been addressed to the Chair — if any — shall have been read.' The other is marked '*The Test.*' Allow me. It is worded — to wit:

" 'I do not require that the first half of the remark which was made to me by my benefactor shall be quoted with exactness, for it was not striking, and could be forgotten; but its closing fifteen words are quite striking, and I think easily rememberable; unless *these* shall be accurately reproduced, let the applicant be regarded as an impostor. My benefactor began by saying he seldom gave advice to anyone, but that it always bore the hallmark of high value when he did give it. Then he said this — and it has never faded from my memory: "You are far from being a bad man — " ' "

FIFTY VOICES. "That settles it — the money's Wilson's! Wilson! Wilson! Speech! Speech!"

People jumped up and crowded around Wilson, wringing his hand and congratulating fervently — meantime the Chair was hammering with the gavel and shouting:

"Order, gentlemen! Order! Order! Let me finish reading, please." When quiet was restored, the reading was resumed — as follows:

" ' "*Go, and reform — or, mark my words — some day, for your sins you will die and go to hell or Hadleyburg* — TRY AND MAKE IT THE FORMER." ' "

A ghastly silence followed. First an angry cloud began to settle darkly upon the faces of the citizenship; after a pause the cloud began to rise, and a tickled expression tried to take its place; tried so hard that it was only kept under with great and painful difficulty; the reporters, the Brixtonites, and other strangers bent their heads down and shielded their faces with their hands, and managed to hold in by main strength and heroic courtesy. At this most inopportune time burst upon the stillness the roar of a solitary voice — Jack Halliday's:

"*That's* got the hall-mark on it!"

Then the house let go, strangers and all. Even Mr. Burgess's gravity broke down presently, then the audience considered itself officially absolved from all restraint, and it made the most of its privilege. It was a good long laugh, and a tempestuously wholehearted one, but it ceased at last — long enough for Mr. Burgess to try to resume, and for the people to get their eyes partially wiped; then it broke out again, and afterward yet again; then at last Burgess was able to get out these serious words:

"It is useless to try to disguise the fact — we find ourselves in the presence of a matter of grave import. It involves the honor of your town — it strikes at the town's good name. The difference of a single word between the test-remarks offered by Mr. Wilson and Mr. Billson was itself a serious thing, since it indicated that one or the other of these gentlemen had committed a theft — "

The two men were sitting limp, nerveless, crushed; but at these words both were electrified into movement, and started to get up.

"Sit down!" said the Chair, sharply, and they obeyed. "That, as I have said, was a serious thing. And it was — but for only one of them. But the matter has become graver; for the honor of *both* is now in formidable peril. Shall I go even further, and say in inextricable peril? *Both* left out the crucial fifteen words." He paused. During several moments he allowed the pervading stillness to gather and deepen its impressive effects, then added: "There would seem to be but one way whereby this could happen. I ask these gentlemen — Was there *collusion? — agreement?*"

A low murmur sifted through the house; its import was, "He's got them both."

Billson was not used to emergencies; he sat in a helpless collapse. But Wilson was a lawyer. He struggled to his feet, pale and worried, and said:

"I ask the indulgence of the house while I explain this most painful matter. I am sorry to say what I am about to say, since it must inflict irreparable injury upon Mr. Billson, whom I have always esteemed and respected until now, and in whose invulnerability to temptation I entirely believed — as did you all. But for the preservation of my own honor I must speak — and with frankness. I confess with shame — and I now beseech your pardon for it — that I said to the ruined stranger all of the words contained in the test-remark, including the disparaging fifteen. [*Sensation.*] When the late publication was made I recalled them, and I resolved to claim the sack of coin, for by every right I was entitled to it. Now I will ask you to consider this point, and weigh it well; that stranger's gratitude to me that night knew no bounds; he said himself that he could find no words for it that were adequate, and that if he should ever be able he would repay me a thousandfold. Now, then, I ask you this; could I expect — could I believe — could I even remotely imagine — that, feeling as he did, he would do so ungrateful a thing as to add those quite unnecessary fifteen words to his test? — set a trap for me? — expose me as a slanderer of my own town before my own people assembled in a public hall? It was preposterous; it was impossible. His test would contain only the kindly opening clause of my remark. Of that I had no shadow of doubt. You would have thought as I did. You would not have expected a base betrayal from one whom you had befriended and against whom you had committed no offence. And so with perfect confidence, perfect trust, I wrote on a piece of paper the opening words — ending with "Go, and reform," — and signed it. When I was about to put it in an envelope I was called into my back office, and without thinking I left the paper lying open on my desk." He stopped, turned his head slowly toward Billson, waited a moment, then added: "I ask you to note this; when I returned, a little latter, Mr. Billson was retiring by my street door." [*Sensation.*]

In a moment Billson was on his feet and shouting:

"It's a lie! It's an infamous lie!"

THE CHAIR. "Be seated, sir! Mr. Wilson has the floor."

Billson's friends pulled him into his seat and quieted him, and Wilson went on:

"Those are the simple facts. My note was now lying in a different place on the table from where I had left it. I noticed that, but attached no importance to it, thinking a draught had blown it there. That Mr. Billson would read a private paper was a thing which could not occur to me; he was an honorable man, and he would be above that. If you will allow me to say it, I think his extra word '*very*' stands explained: it is attributable to a defect of memory. I was the only man in the world who could furnish here any detail of the test-mark — by *honorable* means. I have finished."

There is nothing in the world like a persuasive speech to fuddle the mental apparatus and upset the convictions and debauch the emotions of an audience not practised in the tricks and delusions of oratory. Wilson sat down victorious. The house submerged him in tides of approving applause; friends swarmed to him and shook him by the hand and congratulated him, and Billson was shouted down and not allowed to say a word. The Chair hammered and hammered with its gavel, and kept shouting:

"But let us proceed, gentlemen, let us proceed!"

At last there was a measurable degree of quiet, and the hatter said:

"But what is there to proceed with, sir, but to deliver the money?"

VOICES. "That's it! That's it! Come forward, Wilson!"

THE HATTER. "I move three cheers for Mr. Wilson, Symbol of the special virtue which — "

The cheers burst forth before he could finish; and in the midst of them — and in the midst of the clamour of the gavel also — some enthusiasts mounted Wilson on a big friend's shoulder and were going to fetch him in triumph to the platform. The Chair's voice now rose above the noise:

"Order! To your places! You forget that there is still a document to be read." When quiet had been restored he took up the document, and was going to read it, but laid it down again saying "I forgot; this is not to be read until all written communications received by me have first been read." He took an envelope out of his pocket, removed its enclosure, glanced at it — seemed astonished — held it out and gazed at it — stared at it.

Twenty or thirty voices cried out

"What is it? Read it! read it!"

And he did — slowly, and wondering:

"*The remark which I made to the stranger* — [*Voices*. "Hello! how's this?"] — *was this: 'You are far from being a bad man.'* [*Voices*. "Great Scott!"] '*Go, and reform.*' [*Voices*. "Oh, saw my leg off!"] Signed by Mr. Pinkerton, the banker."

The pandemonium of delight which turned itself loose now was of a sort to make the judicious weep. Those whose withers were unwrung laughed till the tears ran down; the reporters, in throes of laughter, set down disordered pot-hooks which would never in the world be decipherable; and a sleeping dog jumped up scared out of its wits, and barked itself crazy at the turmoil. All manner of cries were scattered through the din: "We're getting rich — *two* Symbols of Incorruptibility! — without counting Billson!" "*Three!* — count Shadbelly in — we can't have too many!" "All right — Billson's elected!" "Alas, poor Wilson! victim of *two* thieves!"

A POWERFUL VOICE. "Silence! The Chair's fished up something more out of its pocket."

VOICES. "Hurrah! Is it something fresh? Read it! read! read!"

THE CHAIR [*reading*]. " '*The remark which I made,' etc.: 'You are far from being a bad man. "Go,"* ' etc. Signed, 'Gregory Yates.' "

TORNADO OF VOICES. "Four Symbols!" " 'Rah for Yates!" "Fish again!"

The house was in a roaring humour now, and ready to get all the fun out of the occasion that might be in it. Several Nineteeners, looking pale and distressed, got up and began to work their way towards the aisles, but a score of shouts went up:

"The doors, the doors — close the doors; no Incorruptible shall leave this place! Sit down, everybody!" The mandate was obeyed.

"Fish again! Read! read!"

The Chair fished again, and once more the familiar words began to fall from its lips — " '*You are far from being a bad man.*' "

"Name! name! What's his name?"

" 'L. Ingoldsby Sargent.' "

"Five elected! Pile up the Symbols! Go on, go on!"

" '*You are far from being a bad* — ' "

"Name! name!"

" 'Nicholas Whitworth.' "

"Hooray! hooray! it's a symbolical day!"

Somebody wailed in, and began to sing this rhyme (leaving out "it's") to the lovely "Mikado" tune of "When a man's afraid of a beautiful maid;" the audience joined in, with joy; then, just in time, somebody contributed another line —

"And don't you this forget — "

The house roared it out. A third line was at once furnished —

"Corruptibles far from Hadleyburg are — "

The house roared that one too. As the last note died, Jack Halliday's voice rose high and clear, freighted with a final line —

"But the Symbols are here, you bet!"

That was sung, with booming enthusiasm. Then the happy house started in at the beginning and sang the four lines through twice, with immense swing and dash, and finished up with a crashing three-times-three and a tiger for "Hadleyburg the Incorruptible and all Symbols of it which we shall find worthy to receive the hall-mark to-night."

Then the shoutings at the Chair began again, all over the place:

"Go on! go on! Read! read some more! Read all you've got!"

"That's it — go on! We are winning eternal celebrity!"

A dozen men got up now and began to protest. They said that this farce was the work of some abandoned joker, and was an insult to the whole community. Without a doubt these signatures were all forgeries —

"Sit down! sit down! Shut up! You are confessing. We'll find your names in the lot."

"Mr. Chairman, how many of those envelopes have you got?"

The Chair counted.

"Together with those that have been already examined, there are nineteen."

A storm of derisive applause broke out.

"Perhaps they all contain the secret. I move that you open them all and read every signature that is attached to a note of that sort — and read also the first eight words of the note."

"Second the motion!"

It was put and carried — uproariously. Then poor old Richards got up, and his wife rose and stood at his side. Her head was bent down, so that none might see that she was crying. Her husband gave her his arm, and so supporting her, he began to speak in a quavering voice:

"My friends, you have known us two — Mary and me — all our lives, and I think you have liked us and respected us — "

The Chair interrupted him:

"Allow me. It is quite true — that which you are saying, Mr. Richards; this town *does* know you two; it *does* like you; it *does* respect you; more — it honors you and *loves* you — "

Halliday's voice rang out:

"That's the hall-marked truth, too! If the Chair is right, let the house speak up and say it. Rise! Now, then — hip! hip! hip! — all together!"

The house rose in mass, faced toward the old couple eagerly, filled the air with a snow-storm of waving handkerchiefs, and delivered the cheers with all its affectionate heart.

The Chair then continued:

"What I was going to say is this: We know your good heart, Mr. Richards, but this is not a time for the exercise of charity toward offenders. [*Shouts of "Right! right!"*] I see your generous purpose in your face, but I cannot allow you to plead for these men — "

"But I was going to — "

"Please take your seat, Mr. Richards. We must examine the rest of these notes — simple fairness to the men who have already been exposed requires this. As soon as that has been done — I give you my word for this — you shall be heard."

MANY VOICES. "Right! — the Chair is right — no interruption can be permitted at this stage! Go on! — the names! the names! — according to the terms of the motion!"

The old couple sat reluctantly down, and the husband whispered to the wife, "It is pitifully hard to have to wait; the shame will be greater than ever when they find we were only going to plead for *ourselves*."

Straightway the jollity broke loose again with the reading of the names.

"'*You are far from being a bad man —*' Signature, 'Robert J. Titmarsh.'

"'*You are far from being a bad man —*' Signature, 'Eliphalet Weeks.'

"'*You are far from being a bad man —*' Signature, 'Oscar B. Wilder.'"

At this point the house lit upon the idea of taking the eight words out of the Chairman's hands. He was not unthankful for that. Thenceforward he held up each note in its turn and waited. The house droned out the eight words in a massed and measured and musical deep volume of sound (with a daringly close resemblance to a well-known church chant) — "'You are f-a-r from being a b-a-a-a-d man.'" Then the Chair said, "Signature, 'Archibald Wilcox.'" And so on, and so on, name after name, and everybody had an increasingly and gloriously good time except the wretched Nineteen. Now and then, when a particularly shining name was called, the house made the Chair wait while it chanted the whole of the test-remark from the beginning to the closing words, "And go to hell or Hadleyburg — try and make it the for-or-m-e-r!" and in these special cases they added a grand and agonised and imposing "A-a-a-a-*men*!"

The list dwindled, dwindled, dwindled, poor old Richards keeping tally of the count, wincing when a name resembling his own was pronounced, and waiting in miserable suspense for the time to come when it would be his humiliating privilege to rise with Mary and finish his plea, which he was intending to word thus: ". . . for until now we have never done any wrong thing, but have gone our humble way unreproached. We are very poor, we are old, and, have no chick nor child to help us; we were sorely tempted, and we fell. It was my purpose when I got up before to make confession and beg that my name might not be read out in this public place, for it seemed to us that we could not bear it; but I was prevented. It was just; it was our place to suffer with the rest. It has been hard for us. It is the first time we have ever heard our name fall from any one's lips — sullied. Be merciful — for the sake or the better days; make our shame as light to bear as in your charity you can." At this point in his reverie Mary nudged him, perceiving that his mind was absent. The house was chanting, "You are f-a-r," etc.

"Be ready," Mary whispered. "Your name comes now; he has read eighteen."

The chant ended.

"Next! next! next!" came volleying from all over the house.

Burgess put his hand into his pocket. The old couple, trembling, began to rise. Burgess fumbled a moment, then said:

"I find I have read them all."

Faint with joy and surprise, the couple sank into their seats, and Mary whispered:

"Oh, bless God, we are saved! — he has lost ours — I wouldn't give this for a hundred of those sacks!"

The house burst out with its "Mikado" travesty, and sang it three times with ever-increasing enthusiasm, rising to its feet when it reached for the third time the closing line —

"But the Symbols are here, you bet!"

and finishing up with cheers and a tiger for "Hadleyburg purity and our eighteen immortal representatives of it."

Then Wingate, the saddler, got up and proposed cheers "for the cleanest man in town, the one solitary important citizen in it who didn't try to steal that money — Edward Richards."

They were given with great and moving heartiness; then somebody proposed that "Richards be elected sole Guardian and Symbol of the now Sacred Hadleyburg Tradition, with power and right to stand up and look the whole sarcastic world in the face."

Passed, by acclamation; then they sang the "Mikado" again, and ended it with —

"And there's one Symbol left, you bet!"

There was a pause; then —

A VOICE. "Now, then, who's to get the sack?"

THE TANNER (*with bitter sarcasm*). "That's easy. The money has to be divided among the eighteen Incorruptibles. They gave the suffering stranger twenty dollars apiece — and that remark — each in his turn — it took twenty-two minutes for the procession to move past. Staked the stranger — total contribution, $360. All they want is just the loan back — and interest — forty thousand dollars altogether."

MANY VOICES [*derisively.*] "That's it! Divvy! divvy! Be kind to the poor — don't keep them waiting!"

THE CHAIR. "Order! I now offer the stranger's remaining document. It says: 'If no claimant shall appear [grand chorus of groans], I desire that you open the sack and count out the money to the principal citizens of your town, they to take it in trust [*Cries of "Oh! Oh! Oh!"*], and use it in such ways as to them shall seem best for the propagation and preservation of your community's noble reputation for incorruptible honesty [*more cries*] — a reputation to which their names and their efforts will add a new and far-reaching lustre." [*Enthusiastic outburst of sarcastic applause.*] That seems to be all. No — here is a postscript:

'P. S. — CITIZENS OF HADLEYBURG: *There is no test-remark — nobody made one.*

[Great sensation.] *There wasn't any pauper stranger, nor any twenty-dollar contribution, nor any accompanying benediction and compliment — these are all inventions.* [General buzz and hum of astonishment and delight.] *Allow me to tell my story — it will take but a word or two. I passed through your town at a certain time, and received a deep offence which I had not earned. Any other man would have been content to kill one or two of you and call it square, but to me that would have been a trivial revenge, and inadequate; for the dead do not suffer. Besides I could not kill you all — and, anyway, made as I am, even that would not have satisfied me. I wanted to damage every man in the place, and every woman — and not in their bodies or in their estate, but in their vanity — the place where feeble and foolish people are most vulnerable. So I disguised myself and came back and studied you. You were easy game. You had an old and lofty reputation for honesty, and naturally you were proud of it — it was your treasure of treasures, the very apple of your eye. As soon as I found out that you carefully and vigilantly kept yourselves and your children* out of temptation, *I knew how to proceed. Why, you simple creatures, the weakest of all weak things is a virtue which has not been tested in the fire. I laid a plan, and gathered a list of names. My project was to corrupt Hadleyburg the Incorruptible. My idea was to make liars and thieves of nearly half a hundred smirchless men and women who had never in their lives uttered a lie or stolen a penny. I was afraid of Goodson. He was neither born nor reared in Hadleyburg. I was afraid that if I started to operate my scheme by getting my letter laid before you, you would say to yourselves, "Goodson is the only man among us who would give away twenty dollars to a poor devil" — and then you might not bite at my bait. But heaven took Goodson; then I knew I was safe, and I set my trap and baited it. It may be that I shall not catch all the men to whom I mailed the pretended test-secret, but I shall catch the most of them, if I know Hadleyburg nature.* [Voices. *"Right — he got every last one of them."*] *I believe they will even steal ostensible* gamble-*money, rather than miss, poor, tempted, and mistrained fellows. I am hoping to eternally and everlastingly squelch your vanity and give Hadleyburg a new renown — one that will* stick — *and spread far. If I have succeeded, open the sack and summon the Committee on Propagation and Preservation of the Hadleyburg Reputation.' "*

A CYCLONE OF VOICES. "Open it! Open it! The Eighteen to the front! Committee on Propagation of the Tradition! Forward — the Incorruptibles!"

The Chair ripped the sack wide, and gathered up a handful of bright, broad, yellow coins, shook them together, then examined them.

"Friends, they are only gilded disks of lead!"

There was a crashing outbreak of delight over this news, and when the noise had subsided, the tanner called out:

"By right of apparent seniority in this business, Mr. Wilson is Chairman of the Committee on Propagation of the Tradition. I suggest that he step forward on behalf of his pals, and receive in trust the money."

A HUNDRED VOICES. "Wilson! Wilson! Wilson! Speech! Speech!"

WILSON [*in a voice trembling with anger*]. "You will allow me to say, and without apologies for my language, *damn* the money!"

A VOICE. "Oh, and him a Baptist!"

A VOICE. "Seventeen Symbols left! Step up, gentlemen, and assume your trust!"

There was a pause — no response.

THE SADDLER. "Mr. Chairman, we've got *one* clean man left, anyway, out of the late aristocracy; and he needs money, and deserves it. I move that you appoint Jack Halliday to get up there and auction off that sack of gilt twenty-dollar pieces, and give the result to the right man — the man whom Hadleyburg delights to honor — Edward Richards."

This was received with great enthusiasm, the dog taking a hand again; the saddler started the bids at a dollar, the Brixton folk and Barnum's representative fought hard for it, the people cheered every jump that the bids made, the excitement climbed moment by moment higher and higher, the bidders got on their mettle and grew steadily more and more daring, more and more determined, the jumps went from a dollar up to five, then to ten, then to twenty, then fifty, then to a hundred, then —

At the beginning of the auction Richards whispered in distress to his wife: "Oh, Mary, can we allow it? It — it — you see, it is an honor — reward, a testimonial to purity of character, and — and — can we allow it? Hadn't I better get up and — Oh, Mary, what ought we to do? — what do you think we — " [*Halliday's voice. "Fifteen I'm bid! — fifteen for the sack! — twenty! — ah, thanks! — thirty — thanks again! Thirty, thirty, thirty! — do I hear forty? — forty it is! Keep the ball rolling, gentlemen, keep it rolling! — fifty! — thanks, noble Roman! — going at fifty, fifty, fifty! — seventy! — ninety! — splendid! — a hundred! — pile it up, pile it up! — hundred and twenty — forty! — just in time! — hundred and fifty! — Two hundred! — superb! Do I hear two h — thanks! — two hundred and fifty! — "*]

"It is another temptation, Edward — I'm all in a tremble — but, oh, we've escaped one temptation, and that ought to warn us, to — [*"Six did I hear? — thanks! — six fifty, six f —* SEVEN *hundred!"*] And yet, Edward, when you think — nobody susp — [*"Eight hundred dollars! — hurrah! — make it nine! — Mr. Parsons, did I hear you say — thanks! — nine! — this noble sack of virgin lead going at only nine hundred dollars, gilding and all — come! do I hear — a thousand! — gratefully yours! — did some one say eleven? — a sack which is going to be the most celebrated in the whole Uni — "*] "Oh, Edward" (beginning to sob), "we are so poor! — but — but — do as you think best — do as you think best."

Edward fell — that is, he sat still; sat with a conscience which was not satisfied, but which was overpowered by circumstances.

Meantime a stranger, who looked like an amateur detective gotten up as an impossible English earl, had been watching the evening's proceedings with manifest interest, and with a contented expression in his face; and he had been privately commenting to himself. He was now soliloquizing somewhat like this:

'None of the Eighteen are bidding; that is not satisfactory; I must change that — the dramatic unities require it; they must buy the sack they tried to steal; they must pay a heavy price, too — some of them are rich. And another thing, when I make a mistake in Hadleyburg nature the man that puts that error upon me is entitled to a high honorarium, and some one must pay. This poor old Richards has brought my judgment to shame; he is an honest man: — I don't understand it, but I acknowledge it. Yes, he saw my deuces *and* with a straight flush, and by rights the pot is his. And it shall be a jack-pot, too, if I can manage it. He disappointed me, but let that pass."

He was watching the bidding. At a thousand, the market broke: the prices tumbled swiftly. He waited — and still watched. One competitor dropped out; then another, and another. He put in a bid or two now. When the bids had sunk to ten dollars, he added a five; some one raised him a three; he waited a moment, then flung in a fifty-dollar jump, and the sack was his — at $1,282. The house broke out in cheers — then stopped; for he was on his feet, and had lifted his hand. He began to speak.

"I desire to say a word, and ask a favour. I am a speculator in rarities, and I have dealings with persons interested in numismatics all over the world. I can make a profit on this purchase, just as it stands; but there is a way, if I can get your approval, whereby I can make every one of these leaden twenty-dollar pieces worth its face in gold, and perhaps more. Grant me that approval, and I will give part of my gains to your Mr. Richards, whose invulnerable probity you have so justly and so cordially recognized tonight; his share shall be ten thousand dollars, and I will hand him the money to-morrow. [Great applause from the house. But the "invulnerable probity" made the Richardses blush prettily; however, it went for modesty, and did no harm.] If you will pass my proposition by a good majority — I would like a two-thirds vote — I will regard that as the town's consent, and that is all I ask. Rarities are always helped by any device which will rouse curiosity and compel remark. Now if I may have your permission to stamp upon the faces of each of these ostensible coins the names of the eighteen gentlemen who — "

Nine-tenths of the audience were on their feet in a moment — dog and all — and the proposition was carried with a whirlwind of approving applause and laughter.

They sat down, and all the Symbols except "Dr." Clay Harkness got up, violently protesting against the proposed outrage, and threatening to —

"I beg you not to threaten me," said the stranger calmly. "I know my legal rights, and am not accustomed to being frightened at bluster." [*Applause.*] He sat down. "Dr." Harkness saw an opportunity here. He was one of the two very rich men of the place, and Pinkerton was the other. Harkness was proprietor of a mint; that is to say, a popular patent medicine. He was running for the Legislature on one ticket, and Pinkerton on the other. It was a close race and a hot one, and getting hotter every day. Both had strong appetites for money; each had bought a great tract of land, with a purpose; there was going to be a new railway, and each wanted to be in the Legislature and help locate the route to his own advantage; a single vote might make the decision, and with it two or three fortunes. The stake was large, and Harkness was a daring speculator. He was sitting close to the stranger. He leaned over while one or another of the other Symbols was entertaining the house with protests and appeals, and asked, in a whisper,

"What is your price for the sack?"

"Forty thousand dollars."

"I'll give you twenty."

"No."

"Twenty-five."

"No."

"Say thirty."

"The price is forty thousand dollars; not a penny less."

"All right, I'll give it. I will come to the hotel at ten in the morning. I don't want it known; will see you privately."

"Very good." Then the stranger got up and said to the house:

"I find it late. The speeches of these gentlemen are not without merit, not without interest, not without grace; yet if I may he excused I will take my leave. I thank you for the great favour which you have shown me in granting my petition. I ask the Chair to keep the sack for me until to-morrow, and to hand these three five-hundred-dollar notes to Mr. Richards." They were passed up to the Chair.

"At nine I will call for the sack, and at eleven will deliver the rest of the ten thousand to Mr. Richards in person at his home. Good-night."

Then he slipped out, and left the audience making a vast noise, which was composed of a mixture of cheers, the "Mikado" song, dog-disapproval, and the chant, "You are f-a-r from being a b-a-a-d man — a-a-a a-men!"

IV

At home the Richardses had to endure congratulations and compliments until midnight. Then they were left to themselves. They looked a little sad, and they sat silent and thinking. Finally Mary sighed and said:

"Do you think we are to blame, Edward — *much* to blame?" and her eyes wandered to the accusing triplet of big bank-notes lying on the table, where the congratulators had been gloating over them and reverently fingering them. Edward did not answer at once; then he brought out a sigh and said, hesitatingly:

"We — we couldn't help it, Mary. It — well it was ordered. *All* things are."

Mary glanced up and looked at him steadily, but he didn't return the look. Presently she said:

"I thought congratulations and praises always tasted good. But — it seems to me, now — Edward?"

"Well?"

"Are you going to stay in the bank?"

"N — no."

"Resign?"

"In the morning — by note."

"It does seem best."

Richards bowed his head in his hands and muttered:

"Before I was not afraid to let oceans of people's money pour through my hands, but — Mary, I am so tired, so tired — "

"We will go to bed."

At nine in the morning the stranger called for the sack and took it to the hotel in a cab. At ten Harkness had a talk with him privately. The stranger asked for and got five checks on a metropolitan bank — drawn to "Bearer," — four for $1,500 each, and one for $34,000. He put one of the former in his pocket-book, and the remainder, representing $38,500, he put in an envelope, and with these he added a note which he wrote after Harkness was gone. At eleven he called at the Richards' house and knocked. Mrs. Richards peeped through the shutters, then went and received the envelope, and the stranger disappeared without a word. She came back flushed and a little unsteady on her legs, and gasped out:

"I am sure I recognized him! Last night it seemed to me that maybe I had seen him somewhere before."

"He is the man that brought the sack here?"

"I am almost sure of it."

"Then he is the ostensible Stephenson too, and sold every important citizen in this town with his bogus secret. Now if he has sent checks instead of money, we are sold too, after we thought we had escaped. I was beginning to feel fairly comfortable once more, after my night's rest, but the look of that envelope makes me sick. It isn't fat enough; $8,500 in even the largest bank-notes makes more bulk than that."

"Edward, why do you object to checks?"

"Checks signed by Stephenson! I am resigned to take the $8,500 if it could come in bank-notes — for it does seem that it was so ordered, Mary — but I have never had much courage, and I have not the pluck to try to market a cheque signed with that disastrous name. It would be a trap. That man tried to catch me; we escaped somehow or other; and now he is trying a new way. If it is checks — "

"Oh, Edward, it is *too* bad!" And she held up the checks and began to cry.

"Put them in the fire! quick! we mustn't be tempted. It is a trick to make the world laugh at *us*, along with the rest, and — Give them to *me*, since you can't do it!" He snatched them and tried to hold his grip till he could get to the stove; but he was human, he was a cashier, and he stopped a moment to make sure of the signature. Then he came near to fainting.

"Fan me, Mary, fan me! They are the same as gold!"

"Oh, how lovely, Edward! Why?"

"Signed by Harkness. What can the mystery of that be, Mary?"

"Edward, do you think — "

"Look here — look at this! Fifteen — fifteen — fifteen — thirty-four. Thirty-eight thousand five hundred! Mary, the sack isn't worth twelve dollars, and Harkness — apparently — has paid about par for it."

"And does it all come to us, do you think — instead of the ten thousand?"

"Why, it looks like it. And the checks are made to 'Bearer,' too."

"Is that good, Edward? What is it for?"

"A hint to collect them at some distant bank, I reckon. Perhaps Harkness doesn't want the matter known. What is that — a note?"

"Yes. It was with the checks."

It was in the "Stephenson" handwriting, but there was no signature. It said:

"I am a disappointed man. Your honesty is beyond the reach of temptation. I had a different idea about it, but I wronged you in that, and I beg pardon, and do it sincerely. I honor you — and that is sincere too. This town is not worthy to kiss the hem of your garment. Dear sir, I made a square bet with myself that there were nineteen debauchable men in your self-righteous community. I have lost. Take the whole pot, you are entitled to it."

Richards drew a deep sigh, and said:

"It seems written with fire — it burns so. Mary — I am miserable again."

"I, too. Ah, dear, I wish — "

"To think, Mary — he *believes* in me."

"Oh, don't, Edward — I can't bear it."

"If those beautiful words were deserved, Mary — and God knows I believed I deserved them once — I think I could give the forty thousand dollars for them. And I would put that paper away, as representing more than gold and jewels, and keep it always. But now — We could not live in the shadow of its accusing presence, Mary."

He put it in the fire.

A messenger arrived and delivered an envelope. Richards took from it a note and read it; it was from Burgess:

"You saved me, in a difficult time. I saved you last night. It was at cost of a lie, but I made the sacrifice freely, and out of a grateful heart. None in this village knows so well as I know how brave and good and noble you are. At bottom you cannot respect me, knowing as you do of that matter of which I am accused, and by the general voice condemned; but I beg that you will at least believe that I am a grateful man; it will help me to bear my burden."

[Signed]
BURGESS.

"Saved, once more. And on such terms!" He put the note in the fire. "I — I wish I were dead, Mary, I wish I were out of it all!"

"Oh, these are bitter, bitter days, Edward. The stabs, through their very generosity, are so deep — and they come so fast!"

Three days before the election each of two thousand voters suddenly found himself in possession of a prized memento — one of the renowned bogus double-eagles. Around one of its faces was stamped these words: "THE REMARK I MADE TO THE POOR STRANGER WAS — " Around the other face was stamped these: "GO, AND REFORM. [SIGNED] PINKERTON." Thus the entire remaining refuse of the renowned joke was emptied upon a single head, and with calamitous effect. It revived the recent vast laugh and concentrated it upon Pinkerton; and Harkness's election was a walk-over.

Within twenty-four hours after the Richardses had received their checks their consciences were quieting down, discouraged; the old couple were learning to reconcile themselves to the sin which they had committed. But they were to learn, now, that a sin takes on new and real terrors when there seems a chance that it is going to be found out. This gives it a fresh and most substantial and important aspect. At church the morning sermon was of the usual pattern; it was the same old things said in the same old way; they had heard them a thousand times and found them innocuous, next to meaningless, and easy to sleep under; but now it was different: the sermon seemed to bristle with accusations; it seemed aimed straight and specially at people who were concealing deadly sins. After church they got away from the mob of congratulators as soon as they could, and hurried homeward, chilled to the bone at they did not know what — vague, shadowy, indefinite fears. And by chance they caught a glimpse of Mr. Burgess as he turned a corner. He paid no attention to their nod of recognition! He hadn't seen it; but they did not know that. What could his conduct mean? It might mean — it might — mean — oh, a dozen dreadful things. Was it possible that he knew that Richards could have cleared him of guilt in that bygone time, and had been silently waiting for a chance to even up accounts? At home, in their distress they got to imagining that their servant might have been in the next room listening when Richards revealed the secret to his wife that he knew of Burgess's innocence; next Richards began to imagine that he had heard the swish of a gown in there at that time; next, he was sure he *had* heard it. They would call Sarah in, on a pretext, and watch her face; if she had been betraying them to Mr. Burgess, it would show in her manner. They asked her some questions — questions which were so random and incoherent and seemingly purposeless that the girl felt sure that the old people's minds had been affected by their sudden good fortune; the sharp and watchful gaze which they bent upon her frightened her, and that completed the business. She blushed, she became nervous and confused, and to the old people these were plain signs of guilt — guilt of some fearful sort or other — without doubt she was a spy and a traitor. When they were alone again they began to piece many unrelated things together and get horrible results out of the combination. When things had got about to the worst Richards was delivered of a sudden gasp and his wife asked:

"Oh, what is it? — what is it?"

"The note — Burgess's note! Its language was sarcastic, I see it now." He quoted: " 'At bottom you cannot respect me, *knowing*, as you do, of *that matter of* which I am accused' — oh, it is perfectly plain, now, God help me! He knows that I know! You see the ingenuity of the phrasing. It was a trap — and like a fool, I walked into it. And Mary — !"

"Oh, it is dreadful — I know what you are going to say — he didn't return your transcript of the pretended test-remark."

"No — kept it to destroy us with. Mary, he has exposed us to some already. I know it — I know it well. I saw it in a dozen faces after church. Ah, he wouldn't answer our nod of recognition — *he* knew what he had been doing!"

In the night the doctor was called. The news went around in the morning that the old couple were rather seriously ill — prostrated by the exhausting excitement growing out of their great windfall, the congratulations, and the late hours, the doctor said. The town was sincerely distressed; for these old people were about all it had left to be proud of, now.

Two days later the news was worse. The old couple were delirious, and were doing strange things. By witness of the nurses, Richards had exhibited checks — for $8,500? No — for an amazing sum — $38,500! What could be the explanation of this gigantic piece of luck?

The following day the nurses had more news — and wonderful. They had concluded to hide the checks, lest harm come to them; but when they searched they were gone from under the patient's pillow — vanished away. The patient said:

"Let the pillow alone; what do you want?"

"We thought it best that the checks — "

"You will never see them again — they are destroyed. They came from Satan. I saw the hell-brand on them, and I knew they were sent to betray me to sin." Then he fell to gabbling strange and dreadful things which were not clearly understandable, and which the doctor admonished them to keep to themselves.

Richards was right; the checks were never seen again.

A nurse must have talked in her sleep, for within two days the forbidden gabblings were the property of the town; and they were of a surprising sort. They seemed to indicate that Richards had been a claimant for the sack himself, and that Burgess had concealed that fact and then maliciously betrayed it.

Burgess was taxed with this and stoutly denied it. And he said it was not fair to attach weight to the chatter of a sick old man who was out of his mind. Still, suspicion was in the air, and there was much talk.

After a day or two it was reported that Mrs. Richards's delirious deliveries were getting to be duplicates of her husband's. Suspicion flamed up into conviction, now, and the town's pride in the purity of its one undiscredited important citizen began to dim down and flicker toward extinction.

Six days passed, then came more news. The old couple were dying. Richards's mind cleared in his latest hour, and he sent for Burgess. Burgess said:

"Let the room be cleared. I think he wishes to say something in privacy."

"No!" said Richards; "I want witnesses. I want you all to hear my confession, so that I may die a man, and not a dog. I was clean — artificially — like the rest; and like the rest I fell when temptation came. I signed a lie, and claimed the miserable sack. Mr. Burgess remembered that I had done him a service, and in gratitude (and ignorance) he suppressed my claim and saved me. You know the thing that was charged against Burgess years ago. My testimony, and mine alone, could have cleared him, and I was a coward and left him to suffer disgrace — "

"No — no — Mr. Richards, you — "

"My servant betrayed my secret to him — "

"No one has betrayed anything to me — "

— "and then he did a natural and justifiable thing; he repented of the saving kindness which he had done me, and he *exposed* me — as I deserved — "

"Never! — I make oath — "

"Out of my heart I forgive him."

Burgess's impassioned protestations fell upon deaf ears; the dying man passed away without knowing that once more he had done poor Burgess a wrong. The old wife died that night.

The last of the sacred Nineteen had fallen a prey to the fiendish sack; the town was stripped of the last rag of its ancient glory. Its mourning was not showy, but it was deep.

By act of the Legislature — upon prayer and petition — Hadleyburg was allowed to change its name to (never mind what — I will not give it away), and leave one word out of the motto that for many generations had graced the town's official seal.

It is an honest town once more, and the man will have to rise early that catches it napping again.

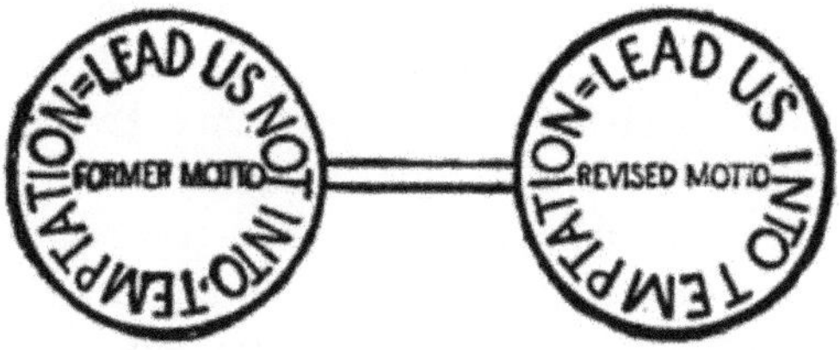

THE LUCK OF ROARING CAMP

Bret Harte (1836-1902)

There was commotion in Roaring Camp. It could not have been a fight, for in 1850 that was not novel enough to have called together the entire settlement. The ditches and claims were not only deserted, but "Tuttle's grocery" had contributed its gamblers, who, it will be remembered, calmly continued their game the day that French Pete and Kanaka Joe shot each other to death over the bar in the front room. The whole camp was collected before a rude cabin on the outer edge of the clearing. Conversation was carried on in a low tone, but the name of a woman was frequently repeated. It was a name familiar enough in the camp, — "Cherokee Sal."

Perhaps the less said of her the better. She was a coarse and, it is to be feared, a very sinful woman. But at that time she was the only woman in Roaring Camp, and was just then lying in sore extremity, when she most needed the ministration of her own sex. Dissolute, abandoned, and irreclaimable, she was yet suffering a martyrdom hard enough to bear even when veiled by sympathizing womanhood, but now terrible in her loneliness. The primal curse had come to her in that original isolation which must have made the punishment of the first transgression so dreadful. It was, perhaps, part of the expiation of her sin that, at a moment when she most lacked her sex's intuitive tenderness and care, she met only the half-contemptuous faces of her masculine associates. Yet a few of the spectators were, I think, touched by her sufferings. Sandy Tipton thought it was "rough on Sal," and, in the contemplation of her condition, for a moment rose superior to the fact that he had an ace and two bowers in his sleeve.

It will be seen also that the situation was novel. Deaths were by no means uncommon in Roaring Camp, but a birth was a new thing. People had been dismissed from the camp effectively, finally, and with no possibility of return; but this was the first time that anybody had been introduced *ab initio*. Hence the excitement.

"You go in there, Stumpy," said a prominent citizen known as "Kentuck," addressing one of the loungers. "Go in there, and see what you kin do. You've had experience in them things."

Perhaps there was a fitness in the selection. Stumpy, in other climes, had been the putative head of two families; in fact, it was owing to some legal informality in these proceedings that Roaring Camp — a city of refuge — was indebted to his company. The crowd approved the choice, and Stumpy was wise enough to bow to the majority. The door closed on the extempore surgeon and midwife, and Roaring Camp sat down outside, smoked its pipe, and awaited the issue.

The assemblage numbered about a hundred men. One or two of these were actual fugitives from justice, some were criminal, and all were reckless. Physically they exhibited no indication of their past lives and character. The greatest scamp had a Raphael face, with a profusion of blonde hair; Oakhurst, a gambler, had the melancholy air and intellectual abstraction of a Hamlet; the coolest and most courageous man was scarcely over five feet in height, with a soft voice and an embarrassed, timid manner. The term "roughs" applied to them was a distinction rather than a definition. Perhaps in the minor details of fingers, toes, ears, etc., the camp may have been deficient, but these slight omissions did not detract from their aggregate force. The strongest man had but three fingers on his right hand; the best shot had but one eye.

Such was the physical aspect of the men that were dispersed around the cabin. The camp lay in a triangular valley between two hills and a river. The only outlet was a steep trail over the summit of a hill that faced the cabin, now illuminated by the rising moon. The suffering woman might have seen it from the rude bunk whereon she lay, — seen it winding like a silver thread until it was lost in the stars above.

A fire of withered pine boughs added sociability to the gathering. By degrees the natural levity of Roaring Camp returned. Bets were freely offered and taken regarding the result. Three to five that "Sal would get through with it"; even that the child would survive; side bets as to the sex and complexion of the coming stranger. In the midst of an excited discussion an exclamation came from those nearest the door, and the camp stopped to listen. Above the swaying and moaning of the pines, the swift rush of the river, and the crackling of the fire rose a sharp, querulous cry, — a cry unlike anything heard before in the camp. The pines stopped moaning, the river ceased to rush, and the fire to crackle. It seemed as if Nature had stopped to listen too.

The camp rose to its feet as one man! It was proposed to explode a barrel of gunpowder; but in consideration of the situation of the mother, better counsels prevailed, and only a few revolvers were discharged; for whether owing to the rude surgery of the camp, or some other reason, Cherokee Sal was sinking fast. Within an hour she had climbed, as it were, that rugged road that led to the stars, and so passed out of Roaring Camp, its sin and shame, forever. I do not think that the announcement disturbed them much, except in speculation as to the fate of the child. "Can he live now?" was asked of Stumpy. The answer was doubtful. The only other being of Cherokee Sal's sex and maternal condition in the settlement was an ass. There was some conjecture as to fitness, but the experiment was tried. It was less problematical than the ancient treatment of Romulus and Remus, and apparently as successful.

When these details were completed, which exhausted another hour, the door was opened, and the anxious crowd of men, who had already formed themselves into a queue, entered in single file. Beside the low bunk or shelf, on which the figure of the mother was starkly outlined below the blankets, stood a pine table. On this a candle-box was placed, and within it, swathed in staring red flannel, lay the last arrival at Roaring Camp. Beside the candle-box was placed a hat. Its use was soon indicated. "Gentlemen," said Stumpy, with a singular mixture of authority and *ex officio* complacency, — "gentlemen will please pass in at the front door, round the table, and out at the back door. Them as wishes to contribute anything toward the orphan will find a hat handy." The first man entered with his hat on; he uncovered, however, as he looked about him, and so unconsciously set an example to the next. In such communities good and bad actions are catching. As the procession filed in comments were audible, — criticisms addressed perhaps rather to Stumpy in the character of showman: "Is that him?" "Mighty small specimen"; "Hasn't more'n got the color"; "Ain't bigger nor a derringer." The contributions were as characteristic: A silver tobacco box; a doubloon; a navy revolver, silver mounted; a gold specimen; a very beautifully embroidered lady's handkerchief (from Oakhurst the gambler); a diamond breastpin; a diamond ring (suggested by the pin, with the remark from the giver that he "saw that pin and went two diamonds better"); a slung-shot; a Bible (contributor not detected); a golden spur; a silver teaspoon (the initials, I regret to say, were not the giver's); a pair of surgeon's shears; a lancet; a Bank of England note for £5; and about $200 in loose gold and silver coin. During these proceedings Stumpy maintained a silence as impassive as the dead on his left, a gravity as inscrutable as that of the newly born on his right. Only one incident occurred to break the monotony of the curious procession. As Kentuck bent over the candle-box half curiously, the child turned, and, in a spasm of pain, caught at his groping finger, and held it fast for a moment. Kentuck looked foolish and embarrassed. Something like a blush tried to assert itself in his weather-beaten cheek. "The d — d little cuss!" he said, as he extricated his finger, with perhaps more tenderness and care than he might have been deemed capable of showing. He held that finger a little apart from its fellows as he went out, and examined it curiously. The examination provoked the same original remark in regard to the child. In fact, he seemed to enjoy repeating it. "He rastled with my finger," he remarked to Tipton, holding up the member, "the d — d little cuss!"

It was four o'clock before the camp sought repose. A light burnt in the cabin where the watchers sat, for Stumpy did not go to bed that night. Nor did Kentuck. He drank quite freely, and related with great gusto his experience, invariably ending with his characteristic condemnation of the newcomer. It seemed to relieve him of any unjust implication of sentiment, and Kentuck had the weaknesses of the nobler sex. When everybody else had gone to bed, he walked down to the river and whistled reflectingly. Then he walked up the gulch past the cabin, still whistling with demonstrative unconcern. At a large redwood-tree he paused and retraced his steps, and again passed the cabin. Halfway down to the river's bank he again paused, and then returned and knocked at the door. It was opened by Stumpy. "How goes it?" said Kentuck, looking past Stumpy toward the candle-box. "All serene!" replied Stumpy. "Anything up?" "Nothing." There was a pause — an embarrassing one — Stumpy still holding the door. Then Kentuck had recourse to his finger, which he held up to Stumpy. "Rastled with it, — the d — d little cuss," he said, and retired.

The next day Cherokee Sal had such rude sepulture as Roaring Camp afforded. After her body had been committed to the hillside, there was a formal meeting of the camp to discuss what should be done with her infant. A resolution to adopt it was unanimous and enthusiastic. But an animated discussion in regard to the manner and feasibility of providing for its wants at once sprang up. It was remarkable that the argument partook of none of those fierce personalities with which discussions were usually conducted at Roaring Camp. Tipton proposed that they should send the child to Red Dog, — a distance of forty miles, — where female attention could be procured. But the unlucky suggestion met with fierce and unanimous opposition. It was evident that no plan which entailed parting from their new acquisition would for a moment be entertained. "Besides," said Tom Ryder, "them fellows at Red Dog would swap it, and ring in somebody else on us." A disbelief in the honesty of other camps prevailed at Roaring Camp, as in other places.

The introduction of a female nurse in the camp also met with objection. It was argued that no decent woman could be prevailed to accept Roaring Camp as her home, and the speaker urged that "they didn't want any more of the other kind." This unkind allusion to the defunct mother, harsh as it may seem, was the first spasm of propriety, — the first symptom of the camp's regeneration. Stumpy advanced nothing. Perhaps he felt a certain delicacy in interfering with the selection of a possible successor in office. But when questioned, he averred stoutly that he and "Jinny" — the mammal before alluded to — could manage to rear the child. There was something original, independent, and heroic about the plan that pleased the camp. Stumpy was retained. Certain articles were sent for to Sacramento. "Mind," said the treasurer, as he pressed a bag of gold- dust into the expressman's hand, "the best that can be got, — lace, you know, and filigree-work and frills, — d — n the cost!" Strange to say, the child thrived. Perhaps the invigorating climate of the mountain camp was compensation for material deficiencies. Nature took the foundling to her broader breast. In that rare atmosphere of the Sierra foothills, — that air pungent with balsamic odor, that ethereal cordial at once bracing and exhilarating, — he may have found food and nourishment, or a subtle chemistry that transmuted ass's milk to lime and phosphorus. Stumpy inclined to the belief that it was the latter and good nursing. "Me and that ass," he would say, "has been father and mother to him! Don't you," he would add, apostrophizing the helpless bundle before him, "never go back on us."

By the time he was a month old the necessity of giving him a name became apparent. He had generally been known as "The Kid," "Stumpy's Boy," "The

Coyote" (an allusion to his vocal powers), and even by Kentuck's endearing diminutive of "The d — d little cuss." But these were felt to be vague and unsatisfactory, and were at last dismissed under another influence. Gamblers and adventurers are generally superstitious, and Oakhurst one day declared that the baby had brought "the luck" to Roaring Camp. It was certain that of late they had been successful. "Luck" was the name agreed upon, with the prefix of Tommy for greater convenience. No allusion was made to the mother, and the father was unknown. "It's better," said the philosophical Oakhurst, "to take a fresh deal all round. Call him Luck, and start him fair." A day was accordingly set apart for the christening. What was meant by this ceremony the reader may imagine who has already gathered some idea of the reckless irreverence of Roaring Camp. The master of ceremonies was one "Boston," a noted wag, and the occasion seemed to promise the greatest facetiousness. This ingenious satirist had spent two days in preparing a burlesque of the Church service, with pointed local allusions. The choir was properly trained, and Sandy Tipton was to stand godfather. But after the procession had marched to the grove with music and banners, and the child had been deposited before a mock altar, Stumpy stepped before the expectant crowd. "It ain't my style to spoil fun, boys," said the little man, stoutly eying the faces around him, "but it strikes me that this thing ain't exactly on the squar. It's playing it pretty low down on this yer baby to ring in fun on him that he ain't goin' to understand. And ef there's goin' to be any godfathers round, I'd like to see who's got any better rights than me." A silence followed Stumpy's speech. To the credit of all humorists be it said that the first man to acknowledge its justice was the satirist thus stopped of his fun. "But," said Stumpy, quickly following up his advantage, "we're here for a christening, and we'll have it. I proclaim you Thomas Luck, according to the laws of the United States and the State of California, so help me God." It was the first time that the name of the Deity had been otherwise uttered than profanely in the camp. The form of christening was perhaps even more ludicrous than the satirist had conceived; but strangely enough, nobody saw it and nobody laughed. "Tommy" was christened as seriously as he would have been under a Christian roof, and cried and was comforted in as orthodox fashion.

And so the work of regeneration began in Roaring Camp. Almost imperceptibly a change came over the settlement. The cabin assigned to "Tommy Luck" — or "The Luck," as he was more frequently called — first showed signs of improvement. It was kept scrupulously clean and whitewashed. Then it was boarded, clothed, and papered. The rosewood cradle, packed eighty miles by mule, had, in Stumpy's way of putting it, "sorter killed the rest of the furniture." So the rehabilitation of the cabin became a necessity. The men who were in the habit of lounging in at Stumpy's to see "how 'The Luck' got on" seemed to appreciate the change, and in self-defense the rival establishment of "Tuttle's grocery" bestirred itself and imported a carpet and mirrors. The reflections of the latter on the appearance of Roaring Camp tended to produce stricter habits of personal cleanliness. Again Stumpy imposed a kind of quarantine upon those who aspired to the honor and privilege of holding The Luck. It was a cruel mortification to Kentuck — who, in the carelessness of a large nature and the habits of frontier life, had begun to regard all garments as a second cuticle, which, like a snake's, only sloughed off through decay — to be debarred this privilege from certain prudential reasons. Yet such was the subtle influence of innovation that he thereafter appeared regularly every afternoon in a clean shirt and face still shining from his ablutions. Nor were moral and social sanitary laws neglected. "Tommy," who was supposed to spend his whole existence in a persistent attempt to repose, must not be disturbed by noise. The shouting and yelling, which had gained the camp its infelicitous title, were not permitted within hearing distance of Stumpy's. The men conversed in whispers or smoked with Indian gravity. Profanity was tacitly given up in these sacred precincts, and throughout the camp a popular form of expletive, known as "D — n the luck!" and "Curse the luck!" was abandoned, as having a new personal bearing. Vocal music was not interdicted, being supposed to have a soothing, tranquilizing quality; and one song, sung by "Man-o'-War Jack," an English sailor from her Majesty's Australian colonies, was quite popular as a lullaby. It was a lugubrious recital of the exploits of "the Arethusa, Seventy-four," in a muffled minor, ending with a prolonged dying fall at the burden of each verse," On b-o-o-o-ard of the Arethusa." It was a fine sight to see Jack holding The Luck, rocking from side to side as if with the motion of a ship, and crooning forth this naval ditty. Either through the peculiar rocking of Jack or the length of his song, — it contained ninety stanzas, and was continued with conscientious deliberation to the bitter end, — the lullaby generally had the desired effect. At such times the men would lie at full length under the trees in the soft summer twilight, smoking their pipes and drinking in the melodious utterances. An indistinct idea that this was pastoral happiness pervaded the camp. "This 'ere kind o' think," said the Cockney Simmons, meditatively reclining on his elbow, "is 'evingly." It reminded him of Greenwich.

On the long summer days The Luck was usually carried to the gulch from whence the golden store of Roaring Camp was taken. There, on a blanket spread over pine boughs, he would lie while the men were working in the ditches below. Latterly there was a rude attempt to decorate this bower with flowers and sweet-smelling shrubs, and generally some one would bring him a cluster of wild honeysuckles, azaleas, or the painted blossoms of Las Mariposas. The men had suddenly awakened to the fact that there were beauty and significance in these trifles, which they had so long trodden carelessly beneath their feet. A flake of glittering mica, a fragment of variegated quartz, a bright pebble from the bed of the creek, became beautiful to eyes thus cleared and strengthened, and were invariably put aside for The Luck. It was wonderful how many treasures the woods and hillsides yielded that "would do for Tommy." Surrounded by playthings such as never child out of fairyland had before, it is to be hoped that Tommy was content. He appeared to be serenely happy, albeit there was an infantine gravity about him, a contemplative light in his round gray eyes, that sometimes worried Stumpy. He was always tractable and quiet, and it is recorded that once, having crept beyond his "corral," — a hedge of tessellated pine boughs, which surrounded his bed, — he dropped over the bank on his head in the soft earth, and remained with his mottled legs in the air in that position for at least five minutes with unflinching gravity. He was extricated without a murmur. I hesitate to record the many other instances of his sagacity, which rest, unfortunately, upon the statements of prejudiced friends. Some of them were not without a tinge of superstition. "I crep' up the bank just now," said Kentuck one day, in a breathless state of excitement, "and dern my skin if he wasn't a-talking to a jaybird as was a-sittin' on his lap. There they was, just as free and sociable as anything you please, a-jawin' at each other just like two cherrybums." Howbeit, whether creeping over the pine boughs or lying lazily on his back blinking at the leaves above him, to him the birds sang, the squirrels chattered, and the flowers bloomed. Nature was his nurse and playfellow. For him she would let slip between the leaves golden shafts of sunlight that fell just within his grasp; she would send wandering breezes to visit him with the balm of bay and resinous gum; to him the tall redwoods nodded familiarly and sleepily, the bumblebees buzzed, and the rooks cawed a slumberous accompaniment.

Such was the golden summer of Roaring Camp. They were "flush times," and the luck was with them. The claims had yielded enormously. The camp was jealous of its privileges and looked suspiciously on strangers. No encouragement was given to immigration, and, to make their seclusion more perfect, the land on either side of the mountain wall that surrounded the camp they duly preempted. This, and a reputation for singular proficiency with the revolver, kept the reserve of Roaring Camp inviolate. The expressman — their only connecting link with the surrounding world — sometimes told wonderful stories of the camp. He would say, "They've a street up there in 'Roaring' that would lay over any street in Red Dog. They've got vines and flowers round their houses, and they wash themselves twice a day. But they're mighty rough on strangers, and they worship an Ingin baby."

With the prosperity of the camp came a desire for further improvement. It was proposed to build a hotel in the following spring, and to invite one or two decent families to reside there for the sake of The Luck, who might perhaps profit by female companionship. The sacrifice that this concession to the sex cost these men, who were fiercely skeptical in regard to its general virtue and usefulness, can only be accounted for by their affection for Tommy. A few still held out. But the resolve could not be carried into effect for three months, and the minority meekly yielded in the hope that something might turn up to prevent it. And it did.

The winter of 1851 will long be remembered in the foothills. The snow lay deep on the Sierras, and every mountain creek became a river, and every river a lake. Each gorge and gulch was transformed into a tumultuous watercourse that descended the hillsides, tearing down giant trees and scattering its drift and debris along the plain. Red Dog had been twice under water, and Roaring Camp had been forewarned. "Water put the gold into them gulches," said Stumpy. "It's been here once and will be here again!" And that night the North Fork suddenly leaped over its banks and swept up the triangular valley of Roaring Camp.

In the confusion of rushing water, crashing trees, and crackling timber, and the darkness which seemed to flow with the water and blot out the fair valley, but little could be done to collect the scattered camp. When the morning broke, the cabin of Stumpy, nearest the river- bank, was gone. Higher up the gulch they found the body of its unlucky owner; but the pride, the hope, the joy, The Luck, of Roaring Camp had disappeared. They were returning with sad hearts when a shout from the bank recalled them.

It was a relief-boat from down the river. They had picked up, they said, a man and an infant, nearly exhausted, about two miles below. Did anybody know them, and did they belong here?

It needed but a glance to show them Kentuck lying there, cruelly crushed and bruised, but still holding The Luck of Roaring Camp in his arms. As they bent over the strangely assorted pair, they saw that the child was cold and pulseless. "He is dead," said one. Kentuck opened his eyes. "Dead?" he repeated feebly. "Yes, my man, and you are dying too." A smile lit the eyes of the expiring Kentuck. "Dying!" he repeated; "he's a-taking me with him. Tell the boys I've got The Luck with me now"; and the strong man, clinging to the frail babe as a drowning man is said to cling to a straw, drifted away into the shadowy river that flows forever to the unknown sea.

EDITHA

William Dean Howells (1837-1920)

The air was thick with the war feeling, like the electricity of a storm which had not yet burst. Editha sat looking out into the hot spring afternoon, with her lips parted, and panting with the intensity of the question whether she could let him go. She had decided that she could not let him stay, when she saw him at the end of the still leafless avenue, making slowly up towards the house, with his head down and his figure relaxed. She ran impatiently out on the veranda, to the edge of the steps, and imperatively demanded greater haste of him with her will before she called him aloud to him: "George!"

He had quickened his pace in mystical response to her mystical urgence, before he could have heard her; now he looked up and answered, "Well?"

"Oh, how united we are!" she exulted, and then she swooped down the steps to him, "What is it?" she cried.

"It's war," he said, and he pulled her up to him and kissed her.

She kissed him back intensely, but irrelevantly, as to their passion, and uttered from deep in her throat. "How glorious!"

"It's war," he repeated, without consenting to her sense of it; and she did not know just what to think at first. She never knew what to think of him; that made his mystery, his charm. All through their courtship, which was contemporaneous with the growth of the war feeling, she had been puzzled by his want of seriousness about it. He seemed to despise it even more than he abhorred it. She could have understood his abhorring any sort of bloodshed; that would have been a survival of his old life when he thought he would be a minister, and before he changed and took up the law. But making light of a cause so high and noble seemed to show a want of earnestness at the core of his being. Not but that she felt herself able to cope with a congenital defect of that sort, and make his love for her save him from himself. Now perhaps the miracle was already wrought in him. In the presence of the tremendous fact that he announced, all triviality seemed to have gone out of him; she began to feel that. He sank down on the top step, and wiped his forehead with his handkerchief, while she poured out upon him her question of the origin and authenticity of his news.

All the while, in her duplex emotioning, she was aware that now at the very beginning she must put a guard upon herself against urging him, by any word or act, to take the part that her whole soul willed him to take, for the completion of her ideal of him. He was very nearly perfect as he was, and he must be allowed to perfect himself. But he was peculiar, and he might very well be reasoned out of his peculiarity. Before her reasoning went her emotioning: her nature pulling upon his nature, her womanhood upon his manhood, without her knowing the means she was using to the end she was willing. She had always supposed that the man who won her would have done something to win her; she did not know what, but something. George Gearson had simply asked her for her love, on the way home from a concert, and she gave her love to him, without, as it were, thinking. But now, it flashed upon her, if he could do something worthy to *have* won her — be a hero, *her* hero — it would be even better than if he had done it before asking her; it would be grander. Besides, she had believed in the war from the beginning.

"But don't you see, dearest," she said, "that it wouldn't have come to this if it hadn't been in the order of Providence? And I call any war glorious that is for the liberation of people who have been struggling for years against the cruelest oppression. Don't you think so, too?"

"I suppose so," he returned, languidly. "But war! Is it glorious to break the peace of the world?"

"That ignoble peace! It was no peace at all, with that crime and shame at our very gates." She was conscious of parroting the current phrases of the newspapers, but it was no time to pick and choose her words. She must sacrifice anything to the high ideal she had for him, and after a good deal of rapid argument she ended with the climax: "But now it doesn't matter about the how or why. Since the war has come, all that is gone. There are no two sides any more. There is nothing now but our country."

He sat with his eyes closed and his head leant back against the veranda, and he remarked, with a vague smile, as if musing aloud, "Our country — right or wrong."

"Yes, right or wrong!" she returned, fervidly. "I'll go and get you some lemonade." She rose rustling, and whisked away; when she came back with two tall glasses of clouded liquid on a tray, and the ice clucking in them, he still sat as she had left him, and she said, as if there had been no interruption: "But there is no question of wrong in this case. I call it a sacred war. A war for liberty and humanity, if ever there was one. And I know you will see it just as I do, yet."

He took half the lemonade at a gulp, and he answered as he set the glass down: "I know you always have the highest ideal. When I differ from you I ought to doubt myself."

A generous sob rose in Editha's throat for the humility of a man, so very nearly perfect, who was willing to put himself below her.

Besides, she felt, more subliminally, that he was never so near slipping through her fingers as when he took that meek way.

"You shall not say that! Only, for once I happen to be right." She seized his hand in her two hands, and poured her soul from her eyes into his. "Don't you think so?" she entreated him.

He released his hand and drank the rest of his lemonade, and she added, "Have mine, too," but he shook his head in answering, "I've no business to think so, unless I act so, too."

Her heart stopped a beat before it pulsed on with leaps that she felt in her neck. She had noticed that strange thing in men: they seemed to feel bound to do what they believed, and not think a thing was finished when they said it, as girls did. She knew what was in his mind, but she pretended not, and she said, "Oh, I am not sure," and then faltered.

He went on as if to himself, without apparently heeding her: "There's only one way of proving one's faith in a thing like this."

She could not say that she understood, but she did understand.

He went on again. "If I believed — if I felt as you do about this war — Do you wish me to feel as you do?"

Now she was really not sure; so she said: "George, I don't know what you mean."

He seemed to muse away from her as before. "There is a sort of fascination in it. I suppose that at the bottom of his heart every man would like at times to have his courage tested, to see how he would act."

"How can you talk in that ghastly way?"

"It is rather morbid. Still, that's what it comes to, unless you're swept away by ambition or driven by conviction. I haven't the conviction or the ambition, and the other thing is what it comes to with me. I ought to have been a preacher, after all; then I couldn't have asked it of myself, as I must, now I'm a lawyer. And you believe it's a holy war, Editha?" he suddenly addressed her. "Oh, I know you do! But you wish me to believe so, too?"

She hardly knew whether he was mocking or not, in the ironical way he always had with her plainer mind. But the only thing was to be outspoken with him.

"George, I wish you to believe whatever you think is true, at any and every cost. If I've tried to talk you into anything, I take it all back."

"Oh, I know that, Editha. I know how sincere you are, and how — I wish I had your undoubting spirit! I'll think it over; I'd like to believe as you do. But I don't, now; I don't, indeed. It isn't this war alone; though this seems peculiarly wanton and needless; but it's every war — so stupid; it makes me sick. Why shouldn't this thing have been settled reasonably?"

"Because," she said, very throatily again, "God meant it to be war."

"You think it was God? Yes, I suppose that is what people will say."

"Do you suppose it would have been war if God hadn't meant it?"

"I don't know. Sometimes it seems as if God had put this world into men's keeping to work it as they pleased."

"Now, George, that is blasphemy."

"Well, I won't blaspheme. I'll try to believe in your pocket Providence," he said, and then he rose to go.

"Why don't you stay to dinner?" Dinner at Balcom's Works was at one o'clock.

"I'll come back to supper, if you'll let me. Perhaps I shall bring you a convert."

"Well, you may come back, on that condition."

"All right. If I don't come, you'll understand."

He went away without kissing her, and she felt it a suspension of their engagement. It all interested her intensely; she was undergoing a tremendous experience, and she was being equal to it. While she stood looking after him, her mother came out through one of the long windows onto the veranda, with a catlike softness and vagueness.

"Why didn't he stay to dinner?"

"Because — because — war has been declared," Editha pronounced, without turning.

Her mother said, "Oh, my!" and then said nothing more until she had sat down in one of the large Shaker chairs and rocked herself for some time. Then she closed whatever tacit passage of thought there had been in her mind with the spoken words: "Well, I hope *he* won't go."

"And *I* hope he *will*," the girl said, and confronted her mother with a stormy exaltation that would have frightened any creature less unimpressionable than a cat.

Her mother rocked herself again for an interval of cogitation. What she arrived at in speech was: "Well, I guess you've done a wicked thing, Editha Balcom."

The girl said, as she passed indoors through the same window her mother had come out by: "I haven't done anything — yet."

In her room, she put together all her letters and gifts from Gearson, down to the withered petals of the first flower he had offered, with that timidity of his veiled in that irony of his. In the heart of the packet she enshrined her engagement ring which she had restored to the pretty box he had brought it her in. Then she sat down, if not calmly yet strongly, and wrote:

George: — I understood when you left me. But I think we had better emphasize your meaning that if we cannot be one in everything we had better be one in nothing. So I am sending these things for your keeping till you have made up your mind.

I shall always love you, and therefore I shall never marry any one else. But the man I marry must love his country first of all, and be able to say to me,

"I could not love thee, dear, so much,
Loved I not honor more."

There is no honor above America with me. In this great hour there is no other honor.

Your heart will make my words clear to you. I had never expected to say so much, but it has come upon me that I must say the utmost.

Editha.

She thought she had worded her letter well, worded it in a way that could not be bettered; all had been implied and nothing expressed.

She had it ready to send with the packet she had tied with red, white, and blue ribbon, when it occurred to her that she was not just to him, that she was not giving him a fair chance. He had said he would go and think it over, and she was not waiting. She was pushing, threatening, compelling. That was not a woman's part. She must leave him free, free, free. She could not accept for her country or herself a forced sacrifice.

In writing her letter she had satisfied the impulse from which it sprang; she could well afford to wait till he had thought it over. She put the packet and the letter by, and rested serene in the consciousness of having done what was laid upon her by her love itself to do, and yet used patience, mercy, justice.

She had her reward. Gearson did not come to tea, but she had given him till morning, when, late at night there came up from the village the sound of a fife and drum, with a tumult of voices, in shouting, singing, and laughing. The noise drew nearer and nearer; it reached the street end of the avenue; there it silenced itself, and one voice, the voice she knew best, rose over the silence. It fell; the air was filled with cheers; the fife and drum struck up, with the shouting, singing, and laughing again, but now retreating; and a single figure came hurrying up the avenue.

She ran down to meet her lover and clung to him. He was very gay, and he put his arm round her with a boisterous laugh. "Well, you must call me Captain now; or Cap, if you prefer; that's what the boys call me. Yes, we've had a meeting at the town-hall, and everybody has volunteered; and they selected me for captain, and I'm going to the war, the big war, the glorious war, the holy war ordained by the pocket Providence that blesses butchery. Come along; let's tell the whole family about it. Call them from their downy beds, father, mother, Aunt Hitty, and all the folks!"

But when they mounted the veranda steps he did not wait for a larger audience; he poured the story out upon Editha alone.

"There was a lot of speaking, and then some of the fools set up a shout for me. It was all going one way, and I thought it would be a good joke to sprinkle a little cold water on them. But you can't do that with a crowd that adores you. The first thing I knew I was sprinkling hell-fire on them. 'Cry havoc, and let slip the dogs of war.' That was the style. Now that it had come to the fight, there were no two parties; there was one country, and the thing was to fight to a finish as quick as possible. I suggested volunteering then and there, and I wrote my name first of all on the roster. Then they elected me — that's all. I wish I had some ice-water."

She left him walking up and down the veranda, while she ran for the ice-pitcher and a goblet, and when she came back he was still walking up and down, shouting the story he had told her to her father and mother, who had come out more sketchily dressed than they commonly were by day. He drank goblet after goblet of the ice-water without noticing who was giving it, and kept on talking, and laughing through his talk wildly. "It's astonishing," he said, "how well the worse reason looks when you try to make it appear the better. Why, I believe I was the first convert to the war in that crowd to-night! I never thought I should like to kill a man; but now I shouldn't care; and the smokeless powder lets you see the man drop that you kill. It's all for the country! What a thing it is to have a country that *can't* be wrong, but if it is, is right, anyway!"

Editha had a great, vital thought, an inspiration. She set down the ice-pitcher on the veranda floor, and ran up-stairs and got the letter she had written him. When at last he noisily bade her father and mother, "Well, good-night. I forgot I woke you up; I sha'n't want any sleep myself," she followed him down the avenue to the gate. There, after the whirling words that seemed to fly away from her thoughts and refuse to serve them, she made a last effort to solemnize the moment that seemed so crazy, and pressed the letter she had written upon him.

"What's this?" he said. "Want me to mail it?"

"No, no. It's for you. I wrote it after you went this morning. Keep it — keep it — and read it sometime — " She thought, and then her inspiration came: "Read it if ever you doubt what you've done, or fear that I regret your having done it. Read it after you've started."

They strained each other in embraces that seemed as ineffective as their words, and he kissed her face with quick, hot breaths that were so unlike him, that made her feel as if she had lost her old lover and found a stranger in his place. The stranger said: "What a gorgeous flower you are, with your red hair, and your blue eyes that look black now, and your face with the color painted out by the white moonshine! Let me hold you under the chin, to see whether I love blood, you tiger-lily!" Then he laughed Gearson's laugh, and released her, scared and giddy. Within her wilfulness she had been frightened by a sense of subtler force in him, and mystically mastered as she had never been before.

She ran all the way back to the house, and mounted the steps panting. Her mother and father were talking of the great affair. Her mother said: "Wa'n't Mr. Gearson in rather of an excited state of mind? Didn't you think he acted curious?"

"Well, not for a man who'd just been elected captain and had set 'em up for the whole of Company A," her father chuckled back.

"What in the world do you mean, Mr. Balcom? Oh! There's Editha!" She offered to follow the girl indoors.

"Don't come, mother!" Editha called, vanishing.

Mrs. Balcom remained to reproach her husband. "I don't see much of anything to laugh at."

"Well, it's catching. Caught it from Gearson. I guess it won't be much of a war, and I guess Gearson don't think so either. The other fellows will back down as soon as they see we mean it. I wouldn't lose any sleep over it. I'm going back to bed, myself."

Gearson came again next afternoon, looking pale and rather sick, but quite himself, even to his languid irony. "I guess I'd better tell you, Editha, that I consecrated myself to your god of battles last night by pouring too many libations to him down my own throat. But I'm all right now. One has to carry off the excitement, somehow."

"Promise me," she commanded, "that you'll never touch it again!"

"What! Not let the cannikin clink? Not let the soldier drink? Well, I promise."

"You don't belong to yourself now; you don't even belong to me. You belong to your country, and you have a sacred charge to keep yourself strong and well for your country's sake. I have been thinking, thinking all night and all day long."

"You look as if you had been crying a little, too," he said, with his queer smile.

"That's all past. I've been thinking, and worshipping you. Don't you suppose I know all that you've been through, to come to this? I've followed you every step from your old theories and opinions."

"Well, you've had a long row to hoe."

"And I know you've done this from the highest motives — "

"Oh, there won't be much pettifogging to do till this cruel war is — "

"And you haven't simply done it for my sake. I couldn't respect you if you had."

"Well, then we'll say I haven't. A man that hasn't got his own respect intact wants the respect of all the other people he can corner. But we won't go into that. I'm in for the thing now, and we've got to face our future. My idea is that this isn't going to be a very protracted struggle; we shall just scare the enemy to death before it comes to a fight at all. But we must provide for contingencies, Editha. If anything happens to me — "

"Oh, George!" She clung to him, sobbing.

"I don't want you to feel foolishly bound to my memory. I should hate that, wherever I happened to be."

"I am yours, for time and eternity — time and eternity." She liked the words; they satisfied her famine for phrases.

"Well, say eternity; that's all right; but time's another thing; and I'm talking about time. But there is something! My mother! If anything happens — "

She winced, and he laughed. "You're not the bold soldier-girl of yesterday!" Then he sobered. "If anything happens, I want you to help my mother out. She won't like my doing this thing. She brought me up to think war a fool thing as well as a bad thing. My father was in the Civil War; all through it; lost his arm in it." She thrilled with the sense of the arm round her; what if that should be lost? He laughed as if divining her: "Oh, it doesn't run in the family, as far as I know!" Then he added gravely: "He came home with misgivings about war, and they grew on him. I guess he and mother agreed between them that I was to be brought up in his final mind about it; but that was before my time. I only knew him from my mother's report of him and his opinions; I don't know whether they were hers first; but they were hers last. This will be a blow to her. I shall have to write and tell her — "

He stopped, and she asked: "Would you like me to write, too, George?"

"I don't believe that would do. No, I'll do the writing. She'll understand a little if I say that I thought the way to minimize it was to make war on the largest possible scale at once — that I felt I must have been helping on the war somehow if I hadn't helped keep it from coming, and I knew I hadn't; when it came, I had no right to stay out of it."

Whether his sophistries satisfied him or not, they satisfied her. She clung to his breast, and whispered, with closed eyes and quivering lips: "Yes, yes, yes!"

"But if anything should happen, you might go to her and see what you could do for her. You know? It's rather far off; she can't leave her chair — "

"Oh, I'll go, if it's the ends of the earth! But nothing will happen! Nothing *can!* I — "

She felt her lifted with his rising, and Gearson was saying, with his arm still round her, to her father: "Well, we're off at once, Mr. Balcom. We're to be formally accepted at the capital, and then bunched up with the rest somehow, and sent into camp somewhere, and got to the front as soon as possible. We all want to be in the van, of course; we're the first company to report to the Governor. I came to tell Editha, but I hadn't got round to it."

She saw him again for a moment at the capital, in the station, just before the train started southward with his regiment. He looked well, in his uniform, and very soldierly, but somehow girlish, too, with his clean-shaven face and slim figure. The manly eyes and the strong voice satisfied her, and his preoccupation with some unexpected details of duty flattered her. Other girls were weeping and bemoaning themselves, but she felt a sort of noble distinction in the abstraction, the almost unconsciousness, with which they parted. Only at the last moment he said: "Don't forget my mother. It mayn't be such a walk-over as I supposed," and he laughed at the notion.

He waved his hand to her as the train moved off — she knew it among a score of hands that were waved to other girls from the platform of the car, for it held a letter which she knew was hers. Then he went inside the car to read it, doubtless, and she did not see him again. But she felt safe for him through the strength of what she called her love. What she called her God, always speaking the name in a deep voice and with the implication of a mutual understanding, would watch over him and keep him and bring him back to her. If with an empty sleeve, then he should have three arms instead of two, for both of hers should be his for life. She did not see, though, why she should always be thinking of the arm his father had lost.

There were not many letters from him, but they were such as she could have wished, and she put her whole strength into making hers such as she imagined he could have wished, glorifying and supporting him. She wrote to his mother glorifying him as their hero, but the brief answer she got was merely to the effect that Mrs. Gearson was not well enough to write herself, and thanking her for her letter by the hand of someone who called herself "Yrs truly, Mrs. W. J. Andrews."

Editha determined not to be hurt, but to write again quite as if the answer had been all she expected. Before it seemed as if she could have written, there came news of the first skirmish, and in the list of the killed, which was telegraphed as a trifling loss on our side, was Gearson's name. There was a frantic time of trying to make out that it might be, must be, some other Gearson; but the name and the company and the regiment and the State were too definitely given.

Then there was a lapse into depths out of which it seemed as if she never could rise again; then a lift into clouds far above all grief, black clouds, that blotted out the sun, but where she soared with him, with George — George! She had the fever that she expected of herself, but she did not die in it; she was not even delirious, and it did not last long. When she was well enough to leave her bed, her one thought was of George's mother, of his strangely worded wish that she should go to her and see what she could do for her. In the exaltation of the duty laid upon her — it buoyed her up instead of burdening her — she rapidly recovered.

Her father went with her on the long railroad journey from northern New York to western Iowa; he had business out at Davenport, and he said he could just as well go then as any other time; and he went with her to the little country town where George's mother lived in a little house on the edge of the illimitable cornfields, under trees pushed to a top of the rolling prairie. George's father had settled there after the Civil War, as so many other old soldiers had done; but they were Eastern people, and Editha fancied touches of the East in the June rose overhanging the front door, and the garden with early summer flowers stretching from the gate of the paling fence.

It was very low inside the house, and so dim, with the closed blinds, that they could scarcely see one another: Editha tall and black in her crapes which filled the air with the smell of their dyes; her father standing decorously apart with his hat on his forearm, as at funerals; a woman rested in a deep arm-chair, and the woman who had let the strangers in stood behind the chair.

The seated woman turned her head round and up, and asked the woman behind her chair: "*Who* did you say?"

Editha, if she had done what she expected of herself, would have gone down on her knees at the feet of the seated figure and said, "I am George's Editha," for answer.

But instead of her own voice she heard that other woman's voice, saying: "Well, I don't know as I *did* get the name just right. I guess I'll have to make a little more light in here," and she went and pushed two of the shutters ajar.

Then Editha's father said, in his public will-now-address-a-few-remarks tone: "My name is Balcom, ma'am — Junius H. Balcom, of Balcom's Works, New York; my daughter — "

"Oh!" the seated woman broke in, with a powerful voice, the voice that always surprised Editha from Gearson's slender frame. "Let me see you. Stand round where the light can strike on your face," and Editha dumbly obeyed. "So, you're Editha Balcom," she sighed.

"Yes," Editha said, more like a culprit than a comforter.

"What did you come for?" Mrs. Gearson asked.

Editha's face quivered and her knees shook. "I came — because — because George — " She could go no further.

"Yes," the mother said, "he told me he had asked you to come if he got killed. You didn't expect that, I suppose, when you sent him."

"I would rather have died myself than done it!" Editha said, with more truth in her deep voice than she ordinarily found in it. "I tried to leave him free — "

"Yes, that letter of yours, that came back with his other things, left him free."

Editha saw now where George's irony came from.

"It was not to be read before — unless — until — I told him so," she faltered.

"Of course, he wouldn't read a letter of yours, under the circumstances, till he thought you wanted him to. Been sick?" the woman abruptly demanded.

"Very sick," Editha said, with self-pity.

"Daughter's life," her father interposed, "was almost despaired of, at one time."

Mrs. Gearson gave him no heed. "I suppose you would have been glad to die, such a brave person as you! I don't believe he was glad to die. He was always a timid boy, that way; he was afraid of a good many things; but if he was afraid he did what he made up his mind to. I suppose he made up his mind to go, but I knew what it cost him by what it cost me when I heard of it. I had been through one war before. When you sent him you didn't expect he would get killed."

The voice seemed to compassionate Editha, and it was time. "No," she huskily murmured.

"No, girls don't; women don't, when they give their men up to their country. They think they'll come marching back, somehow, just as gay as they went, or if it's an empty sleeve, or even an empty pantaloon, it's all the more glory, and they're so much the prouder of them, poor things!"

The tears began to run down Editha's face; she had not wept till then; but it was now such a relief to be understood that the tears came.

"No, you didn't expect him to get killed," Mrs. Gearson repeated, in a voice which was startlingly like George's again. "You just expected him to kill some one else, some of those foreigners, that weren't there because they had any say about it, but because they had to be there, poor wretches — conscripts, or whatever they call 'em. You thought it would be all right for my George, your George, to kill the sons of those miserable mothers and the husbands of those girls that you would never see the faces of." The woman lifted her powerful voice in a psalmlike note. "I thank my God he didn't live to do it! I thank my God they killed him first, and that he ain't livin' with their blood on his hands!" She dropped her eyes, which she had raised with her voice, and glared at Editha. "What you got that black on for?" She lifted herself by her powerful arms so high that her helpless body seemed to hang limp its full length. "Take it off, take it off, before I tear it from your back!"

The lady who was passing the summer near Balcom's Works was sketching Editha's beauty, which lent itself wonderfully to the effects of a colorist. It had come to that confidence which is rather apt to grow between artist and sitter, and Editha had told her everything.

"To think of your having such a tragedy in your life!" the lady said. She added: "I suppose there are people who feel that way about war. But when you consider the good this war has done — how much it has done for the country! I can't understand such people, for my part. And when you had come all the way out there to console her — got up out of a sick-bed! Well!"

"I think," Editha said, magnanimously, "she wasn't quite in her right mind; and so did papa."

"Yes," the lady said, looking at Editha's lips in nature and then at her lips in art, and giving an empirical touch to them in the picture. "But how dreadful of her! How perfectly — excuse me — how vulgar!"

A light broke upon Editha in the darkness which she felt had been without a gleam of brightness for weeks and months. The mystery that had bewildered her was solved by the word; and from that moment she rose from grovelling in shame and self-pity, and began to live again in the ideal.

CHICKAMAUGA

Ambrose Bierce (1842-1913?)

One sunny autumn afternoon a child strayed away from its rude home in a small field and entered a forest unobserved. It was happy in a new sense of freedom from control, happy in the opportunity of exploration and adventure; for this child's spirit, in bodies of its ancestors, had for thousands of years been trained to memorable feats of discovery and conquest — victories in battles whose critical moments were centuries, whose victors' camps were cities of hewn stone. From the cradle of its race it had conquered its way through two continents and passing a great sea had penetrated a third, there to be born to war and dominion as a heritage.

The child was a boy aged about six years, the son of a poor planter. In his younger manhood the father had been a soldier, had fought against naked savages and followed the flag of his country into the capital of a civilized race to the far South. In the peaceful life of a planter the warrior-fire survived; once kindled, it is never extinguished. The man loved military books and pictures and the boy had understood enough to make himself a wooden sword, though even the eye of his father would hardly have known it for what it was. This weapon he now bore bravely, as became the son of an heroic race, and pausing now and again in the sunny space of the forest assumed, with some exaggeration, the postures of aggression and defense that he had been taught by the engraver's art. Made reckless by the ease with which he overcame invisible foes attempting to stay his advance, he committed the common enough military error of pushing the pursuit to a dangerous extreme, until he found himself upon the margin of a wide but shallow brook, whose rapid waters barred his direct advance against the flying foe that had crossed with illogical ease. But the intrepid victor was not to be baffled; the spirit of the race which had passed the great sea burned unconquerable in that small breast and would not be denied. Finding a place where some bowlders in the bed of the stream lay but a step or a leap apart, he made his way across and fell again upon the rear-guard of his imaginary foe, putting all to the sword.

Now that the battle had been won, prudence required that he withdraw to his base of operations. Alas; like many a mightier conqueror, and like one, the mightiest, he could not

curb the lust for war,
Nor learn that tempted Fate will leave the loftiest star.

Advancing from the bank of the creek he suddenly found himself confronted with a new and more formidable enemy: in the path that he was following, sat, bolt upright, with ears erect and paws suspended before it, a rabbit! With a startled cry the child turned and fled, he knew not in what direction, calling with inarticulate cries for his mother, weeping, stumbling, his tender skin cruelly torn by brambles, his little heart beating hard with terror — breathless, blind with tears — lost in the forest! Then, for more than an hour, he wandered with erring feet through the tangled undergrowth, till at last, overcome by fatigue, he lay down in a narrow space between two rocks, within a few yards of the stream and still grasping his toy sword, no longer a weapon but a companion, sobbed himself to sleep. The wood birds sang merrily above his head; the squirrels, whisking their bravery of tail, ran barking from tree to tree, unconscious of the pity of it, and somewhere far away was a strange, muffled thunder, as if the partridges were drumming in celebration of nature's victory over the son of her immemorial enslavers. And back at the little plantation, where white men and black were hastily searching the fields and hedges in alarm, a mother's heart was breaking for her missing child.

Hours passed, and then the little sleeper rose to his feet. The chill of the evening was in his limbs, the fear of the gloom in his heart. But he had rested, and he no longer wept. With some blind instinct which impelled to action he struggled through the undergrowth about him and came to a more open ground — on his right the brook, to the left a gentle acclivity studded with infrequent trees; over all, the gathering gloom of twilight. A thin, ghostly mist rose along the water. It frightened and repelled him; instead of recrossing, in the direction whence he had come, he turned his back upon it, and went forward toward the dark inclosing wood. Suddenly he saw before him a strange moving object which he took to be some large animal — a dog, a pig — he could not name it; perhaps it was a bear. He had seen pictures of bears, but knew of nothing to their discredit and had vaguely wished to meet one. But something in form or movement of this object — something in the awkwardness of its approach — told him that it was not a bear, and curiosity was stayed by fear. He stood still and as it came slowly on gained courage every moment, for he saw that at least it had not the long, menacing ears of the rabbit. Possibly his impressionable mind was half conscious of something familiar in its shambling, awkward gait. Before it had approached near enough to resolve his doubts he saw that it was followed by another and another.

To right and to left were many more; the whole open space about him was alive with them — all moving toward the brook.

They were men. They crept upon their hands and knees. They used their hands only, dragging their legs. They used their knees only, their arms hanging idle at their sides. They strove to rise to their feet, but fell prone in the attempt. They did nothing naturally, and nothing alike, save only to advance foot by foot in the same direction. Singly, in pairs and in little groups, they came on through the gloom, some halting now and again while others crept slowly past them, then resuming their movement. They came by dozens and by hundreds; as far on either hand as one could see in the deepening gloom they extended and the black wood behind them appeared to be inexhaustible. The very ground seemed in motion toward the creek. Occasionally one who had paused did not again go on, but lay motionless. He was dead. Some, pausing, made strange gestures with their hands, erected their arms and lowered them again, clasped their heads; spread their palms upward, as men are sometimes seen to do in public prayer.

Not all of this did the child note; it is what would have been noted by an elder observer; he saw little but that these were men, yet crept like babes. Being men, they were not terrible, though unfamiliarly clad. He moved among them freely, going from one to another and peering into their faces with childish curiosity. All their faces were singularly white and many were streaked and gouted with red. Something in this — something too, perhaps, in their grotesque attitudes and movements — reminded him of the painted clown whom he had seen last summer in the circus, and he laughed as he watched them. But on and ever on they crept, these maimed and bleeding men, as heedless as he of the dramatic contrast between his laughter and their own ghastly gravity. To him it was a merry spectacle. He had seen his father's negroes creep upon their hands and knees for his amusement — had ridden them so, "making believe" they were his horses. He now approached one of these crawling figures from behind and with an agile movement mounted it astride. The man sank upon his breast, recovered, flung the small boy fiercely to the ground as an unbroken colt might have done, then turned upon him a face that lacked a lower jaw — from the upper teeth to the throat was a great red gap fringed with hanging shreds of flesh and splinters of bone. The unnatural prominence of nose, the absence of chin, the fierce eyes, gave this man the appearance of a great bird of prey crimsoned in throat and breast by the blood of its quarry. The man rose to his knees, the child to his feet. The man shook his fist at the child; the child, terrified at last, ran to a tree nearby, got upon the farther side of it and took a more serious view of the situation. And so the clumsy multitude dragged itself slowly and painfully along in hideous pantomime — moved forward down the slope like a swarm of great black beetles, with never a sound of going — in silence profound, absolute.

Instead of darkening, the haunted landscape began to brighten. Through the belt of trees beyond the brook shone a strange red light, the trunks and branches of the trees making a black lacework against it. It struck the creeping figures and gave them monstrous shadows, which caricatured their movements on the lit grass. It fell upon their faces, touching their whiteness with a ruddy tinge, accentuating the stains with which so many of them were freaked and maculated. It sparkled on buttons and bits of metal in their clothing. Instinctively the child turned toward the growing splendor and moved down the slope with his horrible companions; in a few moments had passed the foremost of the throng — not much of a feat, considering his advantages. He placed himself in the lead, his wooden sword still in hand, and solemnly directed the march, conforming his pace to theirs and occasionally turning as if to see that his forces did not straggle. Surely such a leader never before had such a following.

Scattered about upon the ground now slowly narrowing by the encroachment of this awful march to water, were certain articles to which, in the leader's mind, were coupled no significant associations: an occasional blanket, tightly rolled lengthwise, doubled and the ends bound together with a string; a heavy knapsack here, and there a broken rifle — such things, in short, as are found in the rear of retreating troops, the "spoor" of men flying from their hunters. Everywhere near the creek, which here had a margin of lowland, the earth was trodden into mud by the feet of men and horses. An observer of better experience in the use of his eyes would have noticed that these footprints pointed in both directions; the ground had been twice passed over — in advance and in retreat. A few hours before, these desperate, stricken men, with their more fortunate and now distant comrades, had penetrated the forest in thousands. Their successive battalions, breaking into swarms and re-forming in lines, had passed the child on every side — had almost trodden on him as he slept. The rustle and murmur of their march had not awakened him. Almost within a stone's throw of where he lay they had fought a battle; but all unheard by him were the roar of the musketry, the shock of the cannon, "the thunder of the captains and the shouting." He had slept through it all, grasping his little wooden sword with perhaps a tighter clutch in unconscious sympathy with his martial environment, but as heedless of the grandeur of the struggle as the dead who had died to make the glory.

The fire beyond the belt of woods on the farther side of the creek, reflected to earth from the canopy of its own smoke, was now suffusing the whole landscape. It transformed the sinuous line of mist to the vapor of gold. The water gleamed with dashes of red, and red, too, were many of the stones protruding above the surface. But that was blood; the less desperately wounded had stained them in crossing. On them, too, the child now crossed with eager steps; he was going to the fire. As he stood upon the farther bank he turned about to look at the companions of his march. The advance was arriving at the creek. The stronger had already drawn themselves to the brink and plunged their faces into the flood. Three or four who lay without motion appeared to have no heads. At this the child's eyes expanded with wonder; even his hospitable understanding could not accept a phenomenon implying such vitality as that. After slaking their thirst these men had not had the strength to back away from the water, nor to keep their heads above it. They were drowned. In rear of these, the open spaces of the forest showed the leader as many formless figures of his grim command as at first; but not nearly so many were in motion. He waved his cap for their encouragement and smilingly pointed with his weapon in the direction of the guiding light — a pillar of fire to this strange exodus.

Confident of the fidelity of his forces, he now entered the belt of woods, passed through it easily in the red illumination, climbed a fence, ran across a field, turning now and again to coquet with his responsive shadow, and so approached the blazing ruin of a dwelling. Desolation everywhere! In all the wide glare not a living thing was visible. He cared nothing for that; the spectacle pleased, and he danced with glee in imitation of the wavering flames. He ran about, collecting fuel, but every object that he found was too heavy for him to cast in from the distance to which the heat limited his approach. In despair he flung in his sword — a surrender to the superior forces of nature. His military career was at an end.

Shifting his position, his eyes fell upon some outbuildings which had an oddly familiar appearance, as if he had dreamed of them. He stood considering them with wonder, when suddenly the entire plantation, with its inclosing forest, seemed to turn as if upon a pivot. His little world swung half around; the points of the compass were reversed. He recognized the blazing building as his own home!

For a moment he stood stupefied by the power of the revelation, then ran with stumbling feet, making a half-circuit of the ruin. There, conspicuous in the light of the conflagration, lay the dead body of a woman — the white face turned upward, the hands thrown out and clutched full of grass, the clothing deranged, the long dark hair in tangles and full of clotted blood. The greater part of the forehead was torn away, and from the jagged hole the brain protruded, overflowing the temple, a frothy mass of gray, crowned with clusters of crimson bubbles — the work of a shell.

The child moved his little hands, making wild, uncertain gestures. He uttered a series of inarticulate and indescribable cries — something between the chattering of an ape and the gobbling of a turkey — a startling, soulless, unholy sound, the language of a devil. The child was a deaf mute.

Then he stood motionless, with quivering lips, looking down upon the wreck.

THE MIDDLE YEARS

Henry James (1843-1916)

The April day was soft and bright, and poor Dencombe, happy in the conceit of reasserted strength, stood in the garden of the hotel, comparing, with a deliberation in which however there was still something of languor, the attractions of easy strolls. He liked the feeling of the south so far as you could have it in the north, he liked the sandy cliffs and the clustered pines, he liked even the colourless sea. "Bournemouth as a health-resort" had sounded like a mere advertisement, but he was thankful now for the commonest conveniences. The sociable country postman, passing through the garden, had just given him a small parcel which he took out with him, leaving the hotel to the right and creeping to a bench he had already haunted, a safe recess in the cliff. It looked to the south, to the tinted walls of the Island, and was protected behind by the sloping shoulder of the down. He was tired enough when he reached it, and for a moment was disappointed; he was better of course, but better, after all, than what? He should never again, as at one or two great moments of the past, be better than himself. The infinite of life was gone, and what remained of the dose a small glass scored like a thermometer by the apothecary. He sat and stared at the sea, which appeared all surface and twinkle, far shallower than the spirit of man. It was the abyss of human illusion that was the real, the tideless deep. He held his packet, which had come by book-post, unopened on his knee, liking, in the lapse of so many joys — his illness had made him feel his age — to know it was there, but taking for granted there could be no complete renewal of the pleasure, dear to young experience, of seeing one's self "just out." Dencombe, who had a reputation, had come out too often and knew too well in advance how he should look.

His postponement associated itself vaguely, after a little, with a group of three persons, two ladies and a young man, whom, beneath him, straggling and seemingly silent, he could see move slowly together along the sands. The gentleman had his head bent over a book and was occasionally brought to a stop by the charm of this volume, which, as Dencombe could perceive even at a distance, had a cover alluringly red. Then his companions, going a little further, waited for him to come up, poking their parasols into the beach, looking around them at the sea and sky and clearly sensible of the beauty of the day. To these things the young man with the book was still more clearly indifferent; lingering, credulous, absorbed, he was an object of envy to an observer from whose connexion with literature all such artlessness had faded. One of the ladies was large and mature; the other had the spareness of comparative youth and of a social situation possibly inferior. The large lady carried back Dencombe's imagination to the age of crinoline; she wore a hat of the shape of a mushroom, decorated with a blue veil, and had the air, in her aggressive amplitude, of clinging to a vanished fashion or even a lost cause. Presently her companion produced from under the folds of a mantle a limp portable chair which she stiffened out and of which the large lady took possession. This act, and something in the movement of either party, at once characterised the performers — they performed for Dencombe's recreation — as opulent matron and humble dependent. Where moreover was the virtue of an approved novelist if one couldn't establish a relation between such figures? the clever theory for instance that the young man was the son of the opulent matron and that the humble dependent, the daughter of a clergyman or an officer, nourished a secret passion for him. Was that not visible from the way she stole behind her protectress to look back at him? — back to where he had let himself come to a full stop when his mother sat down to rest. His book was a novel, it had the catchpenny binding; so that while the romance of life stood neglected at his side he lost himself in that of the circulating library. He moved mechanically to where the sand was softer and ended by plumping down in it to finish his chapter at his ease. The humble dependent, discouraged by his remoteness, wandered with a martyred droop of the head in another direction, and the exorbitant lady, watching the waves, offered a confused resemblance to a flying-machine that had broken down.

When his drama began to fail Dencombe remembered that he had after all another pastime. Though such promptitude on the part of the publisher was rare he was already able to draw from its wrapper his "latest," perhaps his last. The cover of "The Middle Years" was duly meretricious, the smell of the fresh pages the very odour of sanctity; but for the moment he went no further — he had become conscious of a strange alienation. He had forgotten what his book was about. Had the assault of his old ailment, which he had so fallaciously come to Bournemouth to ward off, interposed utter blankness as to what had preceded it? He had finished the revision of proof before quitting London, but his subsequent fortnight in bed had passed the sponge over colour. He couldn't have chanted to himself a single sentence, couldn't have turned with curiosity or confidence to any particular page. His subject had already gone from him, leaving scarce a superstition behind. He uttered a low moan as he breathed the chill of this dark void, so desperately it seemed to represent the completion of a sinister process. The tears filled his mild eyes; something precious had passed away. This was the pang that had been sharpest during the last few years — the sense of ebbing time, of shrinking opportunity; and now he felt not so much that his last chance was going as that it was gone indeed. He had done all he should ever do, and yet hadn't done what he wanted. This was the laceration — that practically his career was over: it was as violent as a grip at his throat. He rose from his seat nervously — a creature hunted by a dread; then he fell back in his weakness and nervously opened his book. It was a single volume; he preferred single volumes and aimed at a rare compression. He began to read and, little by little, in this occupation, was pacified and reassured. Everything came back to him, but came back with a wonder, came back above all with a high and magnificent beauty. He read his own prose, he turned his own leaves, and had as he sat there with the spring sunshine on the page an emotion peculiar and intense. His career was over, no doubt, but it was over, when all was said, with *that.*

He had forgotten during his illness the work of the previous year; but what he had chiefly forgotten was that it was extraordinarily good. He dived once more into his story and was drawn down, as by a siren's hand, to where, in the dim underworld of fiction, the great glazed tank of art, strange silent subjects float. He recognized his motive and surrendered to his talent. Never probably had that talent, such as it was, been so fine. His difficulties were still there, but what was also there, to his perception, though probably, alas! to nobody's else, was the art that in most cases had surmounted them. In his surprised enjoyment of this ability he had a glimpse of a possible reprieve. Surely its force wasn't spent — there was life and service in it yet. It hadn't come to him easily, it had been backward and roundabout. It was the child of time, the nursling of delay; he had struggled and suffered for it, making sacrifices not to be counted, and now that it was really mature was it to cease to yield, to confess itself brutally beaten? There was an infinite charm for Dencombe in feeling as he had never felt before that diligence *vincit omnia.* The result produced in his little book was somehow a result beyond his conscious intention: it was as if he had planted his genius, had trusted his method, and they had grown up and flowered with this sweetness. If the achievement had been real, however, the process had been painful enough. What he saw so intensely to-day, what he felt as a nail driven in, was that only now, at the very last, had he come into possession. His development had been abnormally slow, almost grotesquely gradual. He had been hindered and retarded by experience, he had for long periods only groped his way. It had taken too much of his life to produce too little of his art. The art had come, but it had come after everything else. At such a rate a first existence was too short — long enough only to collect material; so that to fructify, to use the material, one should have a second age, an extension. This extension was what poor Dencombe sighed for. As he turned the last leaves of his volume he murmured "Ah for another go, ah for a better chance!"

The three persons drawing his attention to the sands had vanished and then reappeared; they had now wandered up a path, an artificial and easy ascent, which led to the top of the cliff. Dencombe's bench was halfway down, on a sheltered ledge, and the large lady, a massive heterogeneous person with bold black eyes and kind red cheeks, now took a few moments to rest. She wore dirty gauntlets and immense diamond ear-rings; at first she looked vulgar, but she contradicted this announcement in an agreeable off-hand tone. While her companions stood waiting for her she spread her skirts on the end of Dencombe's seat. The young man had gold spectacles, through which, with his finger still in his red-covered book, he glanced at the volume, bound in the same shade of the same colour, lying on the lap of the original occupant of the bench. After an instant Dencombe felt him struck with a resemblance; he had recognized the gilt stamp on the crimson cloth, was reading "The Middle Years" and now noted that somebody else had kept pace with him. The stranger was startled, possibly even a little ruffled, to find himself not the only person favoured with an early copy. The eyes of the two proprietors met a moment, and Dencombe borrowed amusement from the expression of those of his competitor, those, it might even be inferred, of his admirer. They confessed to some resentment — they seemed to say: "Hang it, has he got it *already?* Of course he's a brute of a reviewer!" Dencombe shuffled his copy out of sight while the opulent matron, rising from her repose, broke out: "I feel already the good of this air!"

"I can't say I do," said the angular lady. "I find myself quite let down."

"I find myself horribly hungry. At what time did you order luncheon?" her protectress pursued.

The young person put the question by. "Doctor Hugh always orders it."

"I ordered nothing to-day — I'm going to make you diet," said their comrade.

"Then I shall go home and sleep. *Qui dort dine!*"

"Can I trust you to Miss Vernham?" asked Doctor Hugh of his elder companion.

"Don't I trust *you?*" she archly enquired.

"Not too much!" Miss Vernham, with her eyes on the ground, permitted herself to declare. "You must come with us at least to the house," she went on while the personage on whom they appeared to be in attendance began to mount higher. She had got a little out of ear-shot; nevertheless Miss Vernham became, so far as Dencombe was concerned, less distinctly audible to murmur to the young man: "I don't think you realise all you owe the Countess!"

Absently, a moment, Doctor Hugh caused his gold-rimmed spectacles to shine at her. "Is that the way I strike you? I see — I see!"

"She's awfully good to us," continued Miss Vernham, compelled by the lapse of the other's motion to stand there in spite of his discussion of private matters. Of what use would it have been that Dencombe should be sensitive to shades hadn't he detected in that arrest a strange influence from the quiet old convalescent in the great tweed cape? Miss Vernham appeared suddenly to become aware of some such connexion, for she added in a moment: "If you want to sun yourself here you can come back after you've seen us home."

Doctor Hugh, at this, hesitated, and Dencombe, in spite of a desire to pass for unconscious, risked a covert glance at him. What his eyes met this time, as happened, was, on the part of the young lady, a queer stare, naturally vitreous, which made her remind him of some figure — he couldn't name it — in a play or a novel, some sinister governess or tragic old maid. She seemed to scan him, to challenge him, to say out of general spite: "What have you got to do with us?" At the same instant the rich humour of the Countess reached them from above: "Come, come, my little lambs; you should follow your old *bergere!*" Miss Vernham turned away for it, pursuing the ascent, and Doctor Hugh, after another mute appeal to Dencombe and a minute's evident demur, deposited his book on the bench as if to keep his place, or even as a gage of earnest return, and bounded without difficulty up the rougher part of the cliff.

Equally innocent and infinite are the pleasures of observation and the resources engendered by the trick of analysing life. It amused poor Dencombe, as he dawdled in his tepid air-bath, to believe himself awaiting a revelation of something at the back of a fine young mind. He looked hard at the book on the end of the bench, but wouldn't have touched it for the world. It served his purpose to have a theory that shouldn't be exposed to refutation. He already felt better of his melancholy; he had, according to his old formula, put his head at the window. A passing Countess could draw off the fancy when, like the elder of the ladies who had just retreated, she was as obvious as the giantess of a caravan. It was indeed general views that were terrible; short ones, contrary to an opinion sometimes expressed, were the refuge, were the remedy. Doctor Hugh couldn't possibly be anything but a reviewer who had understandings for early copies with publishers or with newspapers. He reappeared in a quarter of an hour with visible relief at finding Dencombe on the spot and the gleam of white teeth in an embarrassed but generous smile. He was perceptibly disappointed at the eclipse of the other copy of the book; it made a pretext the less for speaking to the quiet gentleman. But he spoke notwithstanding; he held up his own copy and broke out pleadingly: "*Do* say, if you have occasion to speak of it, that it's the best thing he has done yet!"

Dencombe responded with a laugh: "Done yet" was so amusing to him, made such a grand avenue of the future. Better still, the young man took *him* for a reviewer. He pulled out "The Middle Years" from under his cape, but instinctively concealed any telltale look of fatherhood. This was partly because a person was always a fool for insisting to others on his work. "Is that what you're going to say yourself?" he put to his visitor.

"I'm not quite sure I shall write anything. I don't, as a regular thing — I enjoy in peace. But it's awfully fine."

Dencombe just debated. If the young man had begun to abuse him he would have confessed on the spot to his identity, but there was no harm in drawing out any impulse to praise. He drew it out with such success that in a few moments his new acquaintance, seated by his side, was confessing candidly that the works of the author of the volumes before them were the only ones he could read a second time. He had come the day before from London, where a friend of his, a journalist, had lent him his copy of the last, the copy sent to the office of the journal and already the subject of a "notice" which, as was pretended there — but one had to allow for "swagger" — it had taken a full quarter of an hour to prepare. He intimated that he was ashamed for his friend, and in the case of a work demanding and repaying study, of such inferior manners; and, with his fresh appreciation and his so irregular wish to express it, he speedily became for poor Dencombe a remarkable, a delightful apparition. Chance had brought the weary man of letters face to face with the greatest admirer in the new generation of whom it was supposable he might boast. The admirer in truth was mystifying, so rare a case was it to find a bristling young doctor — he looked like a German physiologist — enamoured of literary form. It was an accident, but happier than most accidents, so that Dencombe, exhilarated as well as confounded, spent half an hour in making his visitor talk while he kept himself quiet. He explained his premature possession of "The Middle Years" by an allusion to the friendship of the publisher, who, knowing he was at Bournemouth for his health, had paid him this graceful attention. He allowed he had been ill, for Doctor Hugh would infallibly have guessed it; he even went so far as to wonder if he mightn't look for some hygienic "tip" from a personage combining so bright an enthusiasm with a presumable knowledge of the remedies now in vogue. It would shake his faith a little perhaps to have to take a doctor seriously who could take *him* so seriously, but he enjoyed this gushing modern youth and felt with an acute pang that there would still be work to do in a world in which such odd combinations were presented. It wasn't true, what he had tried for renunciation's sake to believe, that all the combinations were exhausted. They weren't by any means — they were infinite: the exhaustion was in the miserable artist.

Doctor Hugh, an ardent physiologist, was saturated with the spirit of the age — in other words he had just taken his degree; but he was independent and various, he talked like a man who would have preferred to love literature best. He would fain have made fine phrases, but nature had denied him the trick. Some of the finest in "The Middle Years" had struck him inordinately, and he took the liberty of reading them to Dencombe in support of his plea. He grew vivid, in the balmy air, to his companion, for whose deep refreshment he seemed to have been sent; and was particularly ingenuous in describing how recently he had become acquainted, and how instantly infatuated, with the only man who had put flesh between the ribs of an art that was starving on superstitions. He hadn't yet written to him — he was deterred by a strain of respect. Dencombe at this moment rejoiced more inwardly than ever that he had never answered the photographers. His visitor's attitude promised him a luxury of intercourse, though he was sure a due freedom for Doctor Hugh would depend not a little on the Countess. He learned without delay what type of Countess was involved, mastering as well the nature of the tie that united the curious trio. The large lady, an Englishwoman by birth and the daughter of a celebrated baritone, whose taste *minus* his talent she had inherited, was the widow of a French nobleman and mistress of all that remained of the handsome fortune, the fruit of her father's earnings, that had constituted her dower. Miss Vernham, an odd creature but an accomplished pianist, was attached to her person at a salary. The Countess was generous, independent, eccentric; she travelled with her minstrel and her medical man. Ignorant and passionate she had nevertheless moments in which she was almost irresistible. Dencombe saw her sit for her portrait in Doctor Hugh's free sketch, and felt the picture of his young friend's relation to her frame itself in his mind. This young friend, for a representative of the new psychology, was himself easily hypnotised, and if he became abnormally communicative it was only a sign of his real subjection. Dencombe did accordingly what he wanted with him, even without being known as Dencombe.

Taken ill on a journey in Switzerland the Countess had picked him up at an hotel, and the accident of his happening to please her had made her offer him, with her imperious liberality, terms that couldn't fail to dazzle a practitioner without patients and whose resources had been drained dry by his studies. It wasn't the way he would have proposed to spend his time, but it was time that would pass quickly, and meanwhile she was wonderfully kind. She exacted perpetual attention, but it was impossible not to like her. He gave details about his queer patient, a "type" if there ever was one, who had in connexion with her flushed obesity, and in addition to the morbid strain of a violent and aimless will, a grave organic disorder; but he came back to his loved novelist, whom he was so good as to pronounce more essentially a poet than many of those who went in for verse, with a zeal excited, as all his indiscretion had been excited, by the happy chance of Dencombe's sympathy and the coincidence of their occupation. Dencombe had confessed to a slight personal acquaintance with the author of "The Middle Years," but had not felt himself as ready as he could have wished when his companion, who had never yet encountered a being so privileged, began to be eager for particulars. He even divined in Doctor Hugh's eye at that moment a glimmer of suspicion. But the young man was too inflamed to be shrewd and repeatedly caught up the book to exclaim: "Did you notice this?" or "Weren't you immensely struck with that?" "There's a beautiful passage toward the end," he broke out; and again he laid his hand on the volume. As he turned the pages he came upon something else, while Dencombe saw him suddenly change colour. He had taken up as it lay on the bench Dencombe's copy instead of his own, and his neighbour at once guessed the reason of his start. Doctor Hugh looked grave an instant; then he said: "I see you've been altering the text!" Dencombe was a passionate corrector, a fingerer of style; the last thing he ever arrived at was a form final for himself. His ideal would have been to publish secretly, and then, on the published text, treat himself to the terrified revise, sacrificing always a first edition and beginning for posterity and even for the collectors, poor dears, with a second. This morning, in "The Middle Years," his pencil had pricked a dozen lights. He was amused at the effect of the young man's reproach; for an instant it made him change colour. He stammered at any rate ambiguously, then through a blur of ebbing consciousness saw Doctor Hugh's mystified eyes. He only had time to feel he was about to be ill again — that emotion, excitement, fatigue, the heat of the sun, the solicitation of the air, had combined to play him a trick, before, stretching out a hand to his visitor with a plaintive cry, he lost his senses altogether.

Later he knew he had fainted and that Doctor Hugh had got him home in a Bath-chair, the conductor of which, prowling within hail for custom, had happened to remember seeing him in the garden of the hotel. He had recovered his perception on the way, and had, in bed that afternoon, a vague recollection of

Doctor Hugh's young face, as they went together, bent over him in a comforting laugh and expressive of something more than a suspicion of his identity. That identity was ineffaceable now, and all the more that he was rueful and sore. He had been rash, been stupid, had gone out too soon, stayed out too long. He oughtn't to have exposed himself to strangers, he ought to have taken his servant. He felt as if he had fallen into a hole too deep to descry any little patch of heaven. He was confused about the time that had passed — he pieced the fragments together. He had seen his doctor, the real one, the one who had treated him from the first and who had again been very kind. His servant was in and out on tiptoe, looking very wise after the fact. He said more than once something about the sharp young gentleman. The rest was vagueness in so far as it wasn't despair. The vagueness, however, justified itself by dreams, dozing anxieties from which he finally emerged to the consciousness of a dark room and a shaded candle.

"You'll be all right again — I know all about you now," said a voice near him that he felt to be young. Then his meeting with Doctor Hugh came back. He was too discouraged to joke about it yet, but made out after a little that the interest was intense for his visitor. "Of course I can't attend you professionally — you've got your own man, with whom I've talked and who's excellent," Doctor Hugh went on. "But you must let me come to see you as a good friend. I've just looked in before going to bed. You're doing beautifully, but it's a good job I was with you on the cliff. I shall come in early to-morrow. I want to do something for you. I want to do everything. You've done a tremendous lot for me." The young man held his hand, hanging over him, and poor Dencombe, weakly aware of this living pressure, simply lay there and accepted his devotion. He couldn't do anything less — he needed help too much.

The idea of the help he needed was very present to him that night, which he spent in a lucid stillness, an intensity of thought that constituted a reaction from his hours of stupor. He was lost, he was lost — he was lost if he couldn't be saved. He wasn't afraid of suffering, of death, wasn't even in love with life; but he had had a deep demonstration of desire. It came over him in the long quiet hours that only with "The Middle Years" had he taken his flight; only on that day, visited by soundless processions, had he recognized his kingdom. He had had a revelation of his range. What he dreaded was the idea that his reputation should stand on the unfinished. It wasn't with his past but with his future that it should properly be concerned. Illness and age rose before him like spectres with pitiless eyes: how was he to bribe such fates to give him the second chance? He had had the one chance that all men have — he had had the chance of life. He went to sleep again very late, and when he awoke Doctor Hugh was sitting at hand. There was already by this time something beautifully familiar in him.

"Don't think I've turned out your physician," he said; "I'm acting with his consent. He has been here and seen you. Somehow he seems to trust me. I told him how we happened to come together yesterday, and he recognises that I've a peculiar right."

Dencombe felt his own face pressing. "How have you squared the Countess?"

The young man blushed a little, but turned it off. "Oh never mind the Countess!"

"You told me she was very exacting."

Doctor Hugh had a wait. "So she is."

"And Miss Vernham's an *intrigante*."

"How do you know that?"

"I know everything. One *has* to, to write decently!"

"I think she's mad," said limpid Doctor Hugh.

"Well, don't quarrel with the Countess — she's a present help to you."

"I don't quarrel," Doctor Hugh returned. "But I don't get on with silly women." Presently he added: "You seem very much alone."

"That often happens at my age. I've outlived, I've lost by the way."

Doctor Hugh faltered; then surmounting a soft scruple: "Whom have you lost?"

"Every one."

"Ah no," the young man breathed, laying a hand on his arm.

"I once had a wife — I once had a son. My wife died when my child was born, and my boy, at school, was carried off by typhoid."

"I wish I'd been there!" cried Doctor Hugh.

"Well — if you're here!" Dencombe answered with a smile that, in spite of dimness, showed how he valued being sure of his companion's whereabouts.

"You talk strangely of your age. You're not old."

"Hypocrite — so early!"

"I speak physiologically."

"That's the way I've been speaking for the last five years, and it's exactly what I've been saying to myself. It isn't till we *are* old that we begin to tell ourselves we're not."

"Yet I know I myself am young," Doctor Hugh returned.

"Not so well as I!" laughed his patient, whose visitor indeed would have established the truth in question by the honesty with which he changed the point of view, remarking that it must be one of the charms of age — at any rate in the case of high distinction — to feel that one has laboured and achieved. Doctor Hugh employed the common phrase about earning one's rest, and it made poor Dencombe for an instant almost angry. He recovered himself, however, to explain, lucidly enough, that if, ungraciously, he knew nothing of such a balm, it was doubtless because he had wasted inestimable years. He had followed literature from the first, but he had taken a lifetime to get abreast of her. Only to-day at last had he begun to *see*, so that all he had hitherto shown was a movement without a direction. He had ripened too late and was so clumsily constituted that he had had to teach himself by mistakes.

"I prefer your flowers then to other people's fruit, and your mistakes to other people's successes," said gallant Doctor Hugh. "It's for your mistakes I admire you."

"You're happy — you don't know," Dencombe answered.

Looking at his watch the young man had got up; he named the hour of the afternoon at which he would return. Dencombe warned him against committing himself too deeply, and expressed again all his dread of making him neglect the Countess — perhaps incur her displeasure.

"I want to be like you — I want to learn by mistakes!" Doctor Hugh laughed.

"Take care you don't make too grave a one! But do come back," Dencombe added with the glimmer of a new idea.

"You should have had more vanity!" His friend spoke as if he knew the exact amount required to make a man of letters normal.

"No, no — I only should have had more time. I want another go."

"Another go?"

"I want an extension."

"An extension?" Again Doctor Hugh repeated Dencombe's words, with which he seemed to have been struck.

"Don't you know? — I want to what they call 'live.' "

The young man, for good-bye, had taken his hand, which closed with a certain force. They looked at each other hard. "You *will* live," said Doctor Hugh.

"Don't be superficial. It's too serious!"

"You *shall* live!" Dencombe's visitor declared, turning pale.

"Ah that's better!" And as he retired the invalid, with a troubled laugh, sank gratefully back.

All that day and all the following night he wondered if it mightn't be arranged. His doctor came again, his servant was attentive, but it was to his confident young friend that he felt himself mentally appeal. His collapse on the cliff was plausibly explained and his liberation, on a better basis, promised for the morrow; meanwhile, however, the intensity of his meditations kept him tranquil and made him indifferent. The idea that occupied him was none the less absorbing because it was a morbid fancy. Here was a clever son of the age, ingenious and ardent, who happened to have set him up for connoisseurs to worship. This servant of his altar had all the new learning in science and all the old reverence in faith; wouldn't he therefore put his knowledge at the disposal of his sympathy, his craft at the disposal of his love? Couldn't he be trusted to invent a remedy for a poor artist to whose art he had paid a tribute? If he couldn't the alternative was hard: Dencombe would have to surrender to silence unvindicated and undivined. The rest of the day and all the next he toyed in secret with this sweet futility. Who would work the miracle for him but the young man who could combine such lucidity with such passion? He thought of the fairy-tales of science and charmed himself into forgetting that he looked for a magic that was not of this world. Doctor Hugh was an apparition, and that placed him above the law. He came and went while his patient, who now sat up, followed him with supplicating eyes. The interest of knowing the great author had made the young man begin "The Middle Years" afresh and would help him to find a richer sense between its covers. Dencombe had told him what he "tried for"; with all his intelligence, on a first perusal, Doctor Hugh had failed to guess it. The baffled celebrity wondered then who in the world *would* guess it: he was amused once more at the diffused massive weight that could be thrown into the missing of an intention. Yet he wouldn't rail at the general mind to-day — consoling as that ever had been: the revelation of his own slowness had seemed to make all stupidity sacred.

Doctor Hugh, after a little, was visibly worried, confessing, on enquiry, to a source of embarrassment at home. "Stick to the Countess — don't mind me," Dencombe said repeatedly; for his companion was frank enough about the large lady's attitude. She was so jealous that she had fallen ill — she resented such a breach of allegiance. She paid so much for his fidelity that she must have it all: she refused him the right to other sympathies, charged him with scheming to make her die alone, for it was needless to point out how little Miss Vernham was a resource in trouble. When Doctor Hugh mentioned that the Countess would already have left Bournemouth if he hadn't kept her in bed, poor Dencombe held his arm tighter and said with decision: "Take her straight away." They had gone out together, walking back to the sheltered nook in which, the other day, they had met. The young man, who had given his companion a personal support, declared with emphasis that his conscience was clear — he could ride two horses at once. Didn't he dream for his future of a time when he should have to ride five hundred? Longing equally for virtue, Dencombe replied that in that golden age no patient would pretend to have contracted with him for his whole attention. On the part of the Countess wasn't such an avidity lawful? Doctor Hugh denied it, said there was no contract, but only a free understanding, and that a sordid servitude was impossible to a generous spirit; he liked moreover to talk about art, and that was the subject on which, this time, as they sat together on the sunny bench, he tried most to engage the author of "The Middle Years." Dencombe, soaring again a little on the weak wings of convalescence and still haunted by that happy notion of an organised rescue, found another strain of eloquence to plead the cause of a certain splendid "last manner," the very citadel, as it would prove, of his reputation, the stronghold into which his real treasure would be gathered. While his listener gave up the morning and the great still sea ostensibly waited he had a wondrous explanatory hour. Even for himself he was inspired as he told what his treasure would consist of; the precious metals he would dig from the mine, the jewels rare, strings of pearls, he would hang between the columns of his temple. He was wondrous for himself, so thick his convictions crowded, but still more wondrous for Doctor Hugh, who assured him none the less that the very pages he had just published were already encrusted with gems. This admirer, however, panted for the combinations to come and, before the face of the beautiful day, renewed to Dencombe his guarantee that his profession would hold itself responsible for such a life. Then he suddenly clapped his hand upon his watch-pocket and asked leave to absent himself for half an hour. Dencombe waited there for his return, but was at last recalled to the actual by the fall of a shadow across the ground. The shadow darkened into that of Miss Vernham, the young lady in attendance on the Countess; whom Dencombe, recognising her, perceived so clearly to have come to speak to him that he rose from his bench to acknowledge the civility. Miss Vernham indeed proved not particularly civil; she looked strangely agitated, and her type was now unmistakeable.

"Excuse me if I do ask," she said, "whether it's too much to hope that you may be induced to leave Doctor Hugh alone." Then before our poor friend, greatly disconcerted, could protest: "You ought to be informed that you stand in his light — that you may do him a terrible injury."

"Do you mean by causing the Countess to dispense with his services?"

"By causing her to disinherit him." Dencombe stared at this, and Miss Vernham pursued, in the gratification of seeing she could produce an impression: "It has depended on himself to come into something very handsome. He has had a grand prospect, but I think you've succeeded in spoiling it."

"Not intentionally, I assure you. Is there no hope the accident may be repaired?" Dencombe asked.

"She was ready to do anything for him. She takes great fancies, she lets herself go — it's her way. She has no relations, she's free to dispose of her money, and she's very ill," said Miss Vernham for a climax.

"I'm very sorry to hear it," Dencombe stammered.

"Wouldn't it be possible for you to leave Bournemouth? That's what I've come to see about."

He sank to his bench. "I'm very ill myself, but I'll try!"

Miss Vernham still stood there with her colourless eyes and the brutality of her good conscience. "Before it's too late, please!" she said; and with this she turned her back, in order, quickly, as if it had been a business to which she could spare but a precious moment, to pass out of his sight.

Oh yes, after this Dencombe was certainly very ill. Miss Vernham had upset him with her rough fierce news; it was the sharpest shock to him to discover what was at stake for a penniless young man of fine parts. He sat trembling on his bench, staring at the waste of waters, feeling sick with the directness of the blow. He was indeed too weak, too unsteady, too alarmed; but he would make the effort to get away, for he couldn't accept the guilt of interference and his honor was really involved. He would hobble home, at any rate, and then think what was to be done. He made his way back to the hotel and, as he went, had a characteristic vision of Miss Vernham's great motive. The Countess hated women of course — Dencombe was lucid about that; so the hungry pianist had no personal hopes and could only console herself with the bold conception of helping Doctor Hugh in order to marry him after he should get his money or else induce him to recognise her claim for compensation and buy her off. If she had befriended him at a fruitful crisis he would really, as a man of delicacy — and she knew what to think of that point — have to reckon with her.

At the hotel Dencombe's servant insisted on his going back to bed. The invalid had talked about catching a train and had begun with orders to pack; after which his racked nerves had yielded to a sense of sickness. He consented to see his physician, who immediately was sent for, but he wished it to be understood that his door was irrevocably closed to Doctor Hugh. He had his plan, which was so fine that he rejoiced in it after getting back to bed. Doctor Hugh, suddenly finding himself snubbed without mercy, would, in natural disgust and to the joy of Miss Vernham, renew his allegiance to the Countess. When his physician arrived Dencombe learned that he was feverish and that this was very wrong: he was to cultivate calmness and try, if possible, not to think. For the rest of the day he wooed stupidity; but there was an ache that kept him sentient, the probable sacrifice of his "extension," the limit of his course. His medical adviser was anything but pleased; his successive relapses were ominous. He charged this personage to put out a strong hand and take Doctor Hugh off his mind — it would contribute so much to his being quiet. The agitating name, in his room, was not mentioned again, but his security was a smothered fear, and it was not confirmed by the receipt, at ten o'clock that evening, of a telegram which his servant opened and read him and to which, with an address in London, the signature of Miss Vernham was attached. "Beseech you to use all influence to make our friend join us here in the morning. Countess much the worse for dreadful journey, but everything may still be saved." The two ladies had gathered themselves up and had been capable in the afternoon of a spiteful revolution. They had started for the capital, and if the elder one, as Miss Vernham had announced, was very ill, she had wished to make it clear that she was proportionately reckless. Poor Dencombe, who was not reckless and who only desired that everything should indeed be "saved," sent this missive straight off to the young man's lodging and had on the morrow the pleasure of knowing that he had quitted Bournemouth by an early train.

Two days later he pressed in with a copy of a literary journal in his hand. He had returned because he was anxious and for the pleasure of flourishing the great review of "The Middle Years." Here at least was something adequate — it rose to the occasion; it was an acclamation, a reparation, a critical attempt to place the author in the niche he had fairly won. Dencombe accepted and submitted; he made neither objection nor enquiry, for old complications had returned and he had had two dismal days. He was convinced not only that he should never again leave his bed, so that his young friend might pardonably remain, but that the demand he should make on the patience of beholders would be of the most moderate. Doctor Hugh had been to town, and he tried to find in his eyes some confession that the Countess was pacified and his legacy clinched; but all he could see there was the light of his juvenile joy in two or three of the phrases of the newspaper. Dencombe couldn't read them, but when his visitor had insisted on repeating them more than once he was able to shake an unintoxicated head. "Ah no — but they would have been true of what I *could* have done!"

"What people 'could have done' is mainly what they've in fact done," Doctor Hugh contended.

"Mainly, yes; but I've been an idiot!" Dencombe said.

Doctor Hugh did remain; the end was coming fast. Two days later his patient observed to him, by way of the feeblest of jokes, that there would now be no question whatever of a second chance. At this the young man stared; then he exclaimed: "Why it has come to pass — it has come to pass! The second chance has been the public's — the chance to find the point of view, to pick up the pearl!"

"Oh the pearl!" poor Dencombe uneasily sighed. A smile as cold as a winter sunset flickered on his drawn lips as he added: "The pearl is the unwritten — the pearl is the unalloyed, the *rest*, the lost!"

From that hour he was less and less present, heedless to all appearance of what went on round him. His disease was definitely mortal, of an action as relentless, after the short arrest that had enabled him to fall in with Doctor Hugh, as a leak in a great ship. Sinking steadily, though this visitor, a man of rare resources, now cordially approved by his physician, showed endless art in guarding him from pain, poor Dencombe kept no reckoning of favour or neglect, betrayed no symptom of regret or speculation. Yet toward the last he gave a sign of having noticed how for two days Doctor Hugh hadn't been in his room, a sign that consisted of his suddenly opening his eyes to put a question. Had he spent those days with the Countess?

"The Countess is dead," said Doctor Hugh. "I knew that in a particular contingency she wouldn't resist. I went to her grave."

Dencombe's eyes opened wider. "She left you 'something handsome'?"

The young man gave a laugh almost too light for a chamber of woe. "Never a penny. She roundly cursed me."

"Cursed you?" Dencombe wailed.

"For giving her up. I gave her up for *you*. I had to choose," his companion explained.

"You chose to let a fortune go?"

"I chose to accept, whatever they might be, the consequences of my infatuation," smiled Doctor Hugh. Then as a larger pleasantry: "The fortune be hanged! It's your own fault if I can't get your things out of my head."

The immediate tribute to his humour was a long bewildered moan; after which, for many hours, many days, Dencombe lay motionless and absent. A response so absolute, such a glimpse of a definite result and such a sense of credit, worked together in his mind and, producing a strange commotion, slowly altered and transfigured his despair. The sense of cold submersion left him — he seemed to float without an effort. The incident was extraordinary as evidence, and it shed an intenser light. At the last he signed to Doctor Hugh to listen and, when he was down on his knees by the pillow, brought him very near. "You've made me think it all a delusion."

"Not your glory, my dear friend," stammered the young man.

"Not my glory — what there is of it! It *is* glory — to have been tested, to have had our little quality and cast our little spell. The thing is to have made somebody care. You happen to be crazy of course, but that doesn't affect the law."

"You're a great success!" said Doctor Hugh, putting into his young voice the ring of a marriage-bell.

Dencombe lay taking this in; then he gathered strength to speak once more. "A second chance — *that's* the delusion. There never was to be but one. We work in the dark — we do what we can — we give what we have. Our doubt is our passion and our passion is our task. The rest is the madness of art."

"If you've doubted, if you've despaired, you've always 'done' it," his visitor subtly argued.

"We've done something or other," Dencombe conceded.

"Something or other is everything. It's the feasible. It's *you!*"

"Comforter!" poor Dencombe ironically sighed.

"But it's true," insisted his friend.

"It's true. It's frustration that doesn't count."

"Frustration's only life," said Doctor Hugh.

"Yes, it's what passes." Poor Dencombe was barely audible, but he had marked with the words the virtual end of his first and only chance.

FREE JOE AND THE REST OF THE WORLD

Joel Chandler Harris (1845-1908)

The name of Free Joe strikes humorously upon the ear of memory. It is impossible to say why, for he was the humblest, the simplest, and the most serious of all God's living creatures, sadly lacking in all those elements that suggest the humorous. It is certain, moreover, that in 1850 the sober-minded citizens of the little Georgian village of Hillsborough were not inclined to take a humorous view of Free Joe, and neither his name nor his presence provoked a smile. He was a black atom, drifting hither and thither without an owner, blown about by all the winds of circumstance, and given over to shiftlessness.

The problems of one generation are the paradoxes of a succeeding one, particularly if war, or some such incident, intervenes to clarify the atmosphere and strengthen the understanding. Thus, in 1850, Free Joe represented not only a problem of large concern, but, in the watchful eyes of Hillsborough, he was the embodiment of that vague and mysterious danger that seemed to be forever lurking on the outskirts of slavery, ready to sound a shrill and ghostly signal in the impenetrable swamps, and steal forth under the midnight stars to murder, rapine, and pillage — a danger always threatening, and yet never assuming shape; intangible, and yet real; impossible, and yet not improbable. Across the serene and smiling front of safety, the pale outlines of the awful shadow of insurrection sometimes fell. With this invisible panorama as a background, it was natural that the figure of Free Joe, simple and humble as it was, should assume undue proportions. Go where he would, do what he might, he could not escape the finger of observation and the kindling eye of suspicion. His lightest words were noted, his slightest actions marked.

Under all the circumstances it was natural that his peculiar condition should reflect itself in his habits and manners. The slaves laughed loudly day by day, but Free Joe rarely laughed. The slaves sang at their work and danced at their frolics, but no one ever heard Free Joe sing or saw him dance. There was something painfully plaintive and appealing in his attitude, something touching in his anxiety to please. He was of the friendliest nature, and seemed to be delighted when he could amuse the little children who had made a playground of the public square. At times he would please them by making his little dog Dan perform all sorts of curious tricks, or he would tell them quaint stories of the beasts of the field and birds of the air; and frequently he was coaxed into relating the story of his own freedom. That story was brief, but tragical.

In the year of our Lord 1840, when a negro speculator of a sportive turn of mind reached the little village of Hillsborough on his way to the Mississippi region, with a caravan of likely negroes of both sexes, he found much to interest him. In that day and at that time there were a number of young men in the village who had not bound themselves over to repentance for the various misdeeds of the flesh. To these young men the negro speculator (Major Frampton was his name) proceeded to address himself. He was a Virginian, he declared; and, to prove the statement, he referred all the festively inclined young men of Hillsborough to a barrel of peach-brandy in one of his covered wagons. In the minds of these young men there was less doubt in regard to the age and quality of the brandy than there was in regard to the negro trader's birthplace. Major Frampton might or might not have been born in the Old Dominion — that was a matter for consideration and inquiry — but there could be no question as to the mellow pungency of the peach-brandy.

In his own estimation, Major Frampton was one of the most accomplished of men. He had summered at the Virginia Springs; he had been to Philadelphia, to Washington, to Richmond, to Lynchburg, and to Charleston, and had accumulated a great deal of experience which he found useful. Hillsborough was hid in the woods of Middle Georgia, and its general aspect of innocence impressed him. He looked on the young men who had shown their readiness to test his peach-brandy as overgrown country boys who needed to be introduced to some of the arts and sciences he had at his command. Thereupon the major pitched his tents, figuratively speaking, and became, for the time being, a part and parcel of the innocence that characterized Hillsborough. A wiser man would doubtless have made the same mistake.

The little village possessed advantages that seemed to be providentially arranged to fit the various enterprises that Major Frampton had in view. There was the auction block in front of the stuccoed court-house, if he desired to dispose of a few of his negroes; there was a quarter-track, laid out to his hand and in excellent order, if he chose to enjoy the pleasures of horse-racing; there were secluded pine thickets within easy reach, if he desired to indulge in the exciting pastime of cock-fighting; and variously lonely and unoccupied rooms in the second story of the tavern, if he cared to challenge the chances of dice or cards.

Major Frampton tried them all with varying luck, until he began his famous game of poker with Judge Alfred Wellington, a stately gentleman with a flowing white beard and mild blue eyes that gave him the appearance of a benevolent patriarch. The history of the game in which Major Frampton and Judge Alfred Wellington took part is something more than a tradition in Hillsborough, for there are still living three or four men who sat around the table and watched its progress. It is said that at various stages of the game Major Frampton would destroy the cards with which they were playing, and send for a new pack, but the result was always the same. The mild blue eyes of Judge Wellington, with few exceptions, continued to overlook "hands" that were invincible — a habit they had acquired during a long and arduous course of training from Saratoga to New Orleans. Major Frampton lost his money, his horses, his wagons, and all his negroes but one, his body-servant. When his misfortune had reached this limit, the major adjourned the game. The sun was shining brightly, and all nature was cheerful. It is said that the major also seemed to be cheerful. However this may be, he visited the court-house, and executed the papers that gave his body-servant his freedom. This being done, Major Frampton sauntered into a convenient pine thicket, and blew out his brains.

The negro thus freed came to be known as Free Joe. Compelled, under the law, to choose a guardian, he chose Judge Wellington, chiefly because his wife Lucinda was among the negroes won from Major Frampton. For several years Free Joe had what may be called a jovial time. His wife Lucinda was well provided for, and he found it a comparatively easy matter to provide for himself; so that, taking all the circumstances into consideration, it is not matter for astonishment that he became somewhat shiftless.

When Judge Wellington died, Free Joe's troubles began. The judge's negroes, including Lucinda, went to his half-brother, a man named Calderwood, who was a hard master and a rough customer generally — a man of many eccentricities of mind and character. His neighbors had a habit of alluding to him as "Old Spite"; and the name seemed to fit him so completely that he was known far and near as "Spite" Calderwood. He probably enjoyed the distinction the name gave him, at any rate he never resented it, and it was not often that he missed an opportunity to show that he deserved it. Calderwood's place was two or three miles from the village of Hillsborough, and Free Joe visited his wife twice a week, Wednesday and Saturday nights.

One Sunday he was sitting in front of Lucinda's cabin, when Calderwood happened to pass that way.

"Howdy, marster?" said Free Joe, taking off his hat.

"Who are you?" exclaimed Calderwood abruptly, halting and staring at the negro.

"I'm name' Joe, marster. I'm Lucindy's ole man."

"Who do you belong to?"

"Marse John Evans is my gyardeen, marster."

"Big name — gyardeen. Show your pass."

Free Joe produced that document, and Calderwood read it aloud slowly, as if he found it difficult to get at the meaning:

"To whom it may concern: This is to certify that the boy Joe Frampton has my permission to visit his wife Lucinda."

This was dated at Hillsborough, and signed "John W. Evans."

Calderwood read it twice, and then looked at Free Joe, elevating his eyebrows, and showing his discolored teeth.

"Some mighty big words in that there. Evans owns this place, I reckon. When's he comin' down to take hold?"

Free Joe fumbled with his hat. He was badly frightened.

"Lucindy say she speck you wouldn't min' my comin', long ez I behave, marster."

Calderwood tore the pass in pieces and flung it away.

"Don't want no free niggers 'round here," he exclaimed. "There's the big road. It'll carry you to town. Don't let me catch you here no more. Now, mind what I tell you."

Free Joe presented a shabby spectacle as he moved off with his little dog Dan slinking at his heels. It should be said in behalf of Dan, however, that his bristles were up, and that he looked back and growled. It may be that the dog had the advantage of insignificance, but it is difficult to conceive how a dog bold enough to raise his bristles under Calderwood's very eyes could be as insignificant as Free Joe. But both the negro and his little dog seemed to give a new and more dismal aspect to forlornness as they turned into the road and went toward Hillsborough.

After this incident Free Joe appeared to have clearer ideas concerning his peculiar condition. He realized the fact that though he was free he was more helpless than any slave. Having no owner, every man was his master. He knew that he was the object of suspicion, and therefore all his slender resources (ah! how pitifully slender they were!) were devoted to winning, not kindness and appreciation, but toleration; all his efforts were in the direction of mitigating the circumstances that tended to make his condition so much worse than that of the negroes around him — negroes who had friends because they had masters.

So far as his own race was concerned, Free Joe was an exile. If the slaves secretly envied him his freedom (which is to be doubted, considering his miserable condition), they openly despised him, and lost no opportunity to treat him with contumely. Perhaps this was in some measure the result of the attitude which Free Joe chose to maintain toward them. No doubt his instinct taught him that to hold himself aloof from the slaves would be to invite from the whites the toleration which he coveted, and without which even his miserable condition would be rendered more miserable still.

His greatest trouble was the fact that he was not allowed to visit his wife; but he soon found a way out of his difficulty. After he had been ordered away from the Calderwood place, he was in the habit of wandering as far in that direction as prudence would permit. Near the Calderwood place, but not on Calderwood's land, lived an old man named Micajah Staley and his sister Becky Staley. These people were old and very poor. Old Micajah had a palsied arm and hand; but, in spite of this, he managed to earn a precarious living with his turning-lathe.

When he was a slave Free Joe would have scorned these representatives of a class known as poor white trash, but now he found them sympathetic and helpful in various ways. From the back door of their cabin he could hear the Calderwood negroes singing at night, and he sometimes fancied he could distinguish Lucinda's shrill treble rising above the other voices. A large poplar grew in the woods some distance from the Staley cabin, and at the foot of this tree Free Joe would sit for hours with his face turned toward Calderwood's. His little dog Dan would curl up in the leaves near by, and the two seemed to be as comfortable as possible.

One Saturday afternoon Free Joe, sitting at the foot of this friendly poplar, fell asleep. How long he slept, he could not tell; but when he awoke little Dan was licking his face, the moon was shining brightly, and Lucinda his wife stood before him laughing. The dog, seeing that Free Joe was asleep, had grown somewhat impatient, and he concluded to make an excursion to the Calderwood place on his own account. Lucinda was inclined to give the incident a twist in the direction of superstition.

"I 'uz settn' down front er de fireplace," she said, "cookin' me some meat, w'en all of a sudden I year sumpin at de do' — scratch, scratch. I tuck'n tu'n de meat over, en make out I ain't year it. Bimeby it come dar 'gin — scratch, scratch. I up en open de do', I did, en, bless de Lord! dar wuz little Dan, en it look like ter me dat his ribs done grow terge'er. I gin 'im some bread, en den, w'en he start out, I tuck'n foller 'im, kaze, I say ter myse'f, maybe my nigger man mought be some'rs 'roun'. Dat ar little dog got sense, mon."

Free Joe laughed and dropped his hand lightly on Dan's head. For a long time after that he had no difficulty in seeing his wife. He had only to sit by the poplar tree until little Dan could run and fetch her. But after a while the other negroes discovered that Lucinda was meeting Free Joe in the woods, and information of the fact soon reached Calderwood's ears. Calderwood was what is called a man of action. He said nothing; but one day he put Lucinda in his buggy, and carried her to Macon, sixty miles away. He carried her to Macon, and came back without her; and nobody in or around Hillsborough, or in that section, ever saw her again.

For many a night after that Free Joe sat in the woods and waited. Little Dan would run merrily off and be gone a long time, but he always came back without Lucinda. This happened over and over again. The "willis-whistlers" would call and call, like fantom huntsmen wandering on a far-off shore; the screech-owl would shake and shiver in the depths of the woods; the night-hawks, sweeping by on noiseless wings, would snap their beaks as though they enjoyed the huge joke of which Free Joe and little Dan were the victims; and the whip-poor-wills would cry to each other through the gloom. Each night seemed to be lonelier than the preceding, but Free Joe's patience was proof against loneliness. There came a time, however, when little Dan refused to go after Lucinda. When Free Joe motioned him in the direction of the Calderwood place, he would simply move about uneasily and whine; then he would curl up in the leaves and make himself comfortable.

One night, instead of going to the poplar tree to wait for Lucinda, Free Joe went to the Staley cabin, and, in order to make his welcome good, as he expressed it, he carried with him an armful of fat-pine splinters. Miss Becky Staley had a great reputation in those parts as a fortune-teller, and the schoolgirls, as well as older people, often tested her powers in this direction, some in jest and some in earnest. Free Joe placed his humble offering of light-wood in the chimney corner, and then seated himself on the steps, dropping his hat on the ground outside.

"Miss Becky," he said presently, "whar in de name er gracious you reckon Lucindy is?"

"Well, the Lord he'p the nigger!" exclaimed Miss Becky, in a tone that seemed to reproduce, by some curious agreement of sight with sound, her general aspect of peakedness. "Well, the Lord he'p the nigger! hain't you been a-seein' her all this blessed time? She's over at old Spite Calderwood's, if she's anywheres, I reckon."

"No'm, dat I ain't, Miss Becky. I ain't seen Lucindy in now gwine on mighty nigh a mont'."

"Well, it hain't a-gwine to hurt you," said Miss Becky, somewhat sharply. "In my day an' time it wuz allers took to be a bad sign when niggers got to honeyin' 'roun' an' gwine on."

"Yessum," said Free Joe, cheerfully assenting to the proposition — "yessum, dat's so, but me an' my ole 'oman, we 'uz raise terge'er, en dey ain't bin many days w'en we 'uz' 'way fum one 'n'er like we is now."

"Maybe she's up an' took up wi' some un else," said Micajah Staley from the corner. "You know what the sayin' is: 'New master, new nigger.' "

"Dat's so, dat's de sayin', but tain't wid my ole 'oman like 'tis wid yuther niggers. Me en her wuz des natally raise up terge'er. Dey's lots likelier niggers dan w'at I is," said Free Joe, viewing his shabbiness with a critical eye, "but I knows Lucindy mos' good ez I does little Dan dar — dat I does."

There was no reply to this, and Free Joe continued:

"Miss Becky, I wish you please, ma'am, take en run yo' kyards en see sump'n n'er 'bout Lucindy; kaze ef she sick, I'm gwine dar. Dey ken take en take me up en gimme a stroppin', but I'm gwine dar."

Miss Becky got her cards, but first she picked up a cup, in the bottom of which were some coffee-grounds. These she whirled slowly round and round, ending finally by turning the cup upside down on the hearth and allowing it to remain in that position.

"I'll turn the cup first," said Miss Becky, "and then I'll run the cards and see what they say."

As she shuffled the cards the fire on the hearth burned low, and in its fitful light the gray-haired, thin-featured woman seemed to deserve the weird reputation which rumor and gossip had given her. She shuffled the cards for some moments, gazing intently in the dying fire; then, throwing a piece of pine on the coals, she made three divisions of the pack, disposing them about in her lap. Then she took the first pile, ran the cards slowly through her fingers, and studied them carefully. To the first she added the second pile. The study of these was evidently not satisfactory. She said nothing, but frowned heavily; and the frown deepened as she added the rest of the cards until the entire fifty-two had passed in review before her. Though she frowned, she seemed to be deeply interested. Without changing the relative position of the cards, she ran them all over again.

Then she threw a larger piece of pine on the fire, shuffled the cards afresh, divided them into three piles, and subjected them to the same careful and critical examination.

"I can't tell the day when I've seed the cards run this a-way," she said after a while. "What is an' what ain't, I'll never tell you; but I know what the cards sez."

"W'at does dey say, Miss Becky?" the negro inquired, in a tone the solemnity of which was heightened by its eagerness.

"They er runnin' quare. These here that I'm a-lookin' at," said Miss Becky, "they stan' for the past. Them there, they er the present; and the t'others, they er the future. Here's a bundle" — tapping the ace of clubs with her thumb — "an' here's a journey as plain as the nose on a man's face. Here's Lucinda — "

"Whar she, Miss Becky?"

"Here she is — the queen of spades."

Free Joe grinned. The idea seemed to please him immensely.

"Well, well, well!" he exclaimed. "Ef dat don't beat my time! De queen er spades! W'en Lucindy year dat hit'll tickle 'er, sho'!"

Miss Becky continued to run the cards back and forth through her fingers.

"Here's a bundle an' a journey, and here's Lucinda. An' here's ole Spite Calderwood."

She held the cards toward the negro and touched the king of clubs.

"De Lord he'p my soul!" exclaimed Free Joe with a chuckle. "De faver's dar. Yesser, dat's him! W'at de matter 'long wid all un um, Miss Becky?"

The old woman added the second pile of cards to the first, and then the third, still running them through her fingers slowly and critically. By this time the piece of pine in the fireplace had wrapped itself in a mantle of flame, illuminating the cabin and throwing into strange relief the figure of Miss Becky as she sat studying the cards. She frowned ominously at the cards and mumbled a few words to herself. Then she dropped her hands in her lap and gazed once more into the fire. Her shadow danced and capered on the wall and floor behind her, as if, looking over her shoulder into the future, it could behold a rare spectacle. After a while she picked up the cup that had been turned on the hearth. The coffee-grounds, shaken around, presented what seemed to be a most intricate map.

"Here's the journey," said Miss Becky, presently; "here's the big road, here's rivers to cross, here's the bundle to tote." She paused and sighed. "They hain't no names writ here, an' what it all means I'll never tell you. Cajy, I wish you'd be so good as to han' me my pipe."

"I hain't no hand wi' the kyards," said Cajy, as he handed the pipe, "but I reckon I can patch out your misinformation, Becky, bekaze the other day, whiles I was a-finishin' up Mizzers Perdue's rollin'-pin, I hearn a rattlin' in the road. I looked out, an' Spite Calderwood was a-drivin' by in his buggy, an' thar sot Lucinda by him. It'd in-about drapt out er my min'."

Free Joe sat on the door-sill and fumbled at his hat, flinging it from one hand to the other.

"You ain't see um gwine back, is you, Mars Cajy?" he asked after a while.

"Ef they went back by this road," said Mr. Staley, with the air of one who is accustomed to weigh well his words, "it must 'a' bin endurin' of the time whiles I was asleep, bekaze I hain't bin no furder from my shop than to yon bed."

"Well, sir!" exclaimed Free Joe in an awed tone, which Mr. Staley seemed to regard as a tribute to his extraordinary powers of statement.

"Ef it's my beliefs you want," continued the old man, "I'll pitch 'em at you fair and free. My beliefs is that Spite Calderwood is gone an' took Lucindy outen the county. Bless your heart and soul! when Spite Calderwood meets the Old Boy in the road they'll be a turrible scuffle. You mark what I tell you."

Free Joe, still fumbling with his hat, rose and leaned against the door-facing. He seemed to be embarrassed. Presently he said:

"I speck I better be gittin' 'long. Nex' time I see Lucindy, I'm gwine tell 'er w'at Miss Becky say 'bout de queen er spades — dat I is. Ef dat don't tickle 'er, dey ain't no nigger 'oman never bin tickle'."

He paused a moment, as though waiting for some remark or comment, some confirmation of misfortune, or, at the very least, some endorsement of his suggestion that Lucinda would be greatly pleased to know that she had figured as the queen of spades; but neither Miss Becky nor her brother said anything.

"One minnit ridin' in the buggy 'longside er Mars Spite, en de nex' highfalutin' 'roun' playin' de queen er spades. Mon, deze yer nigger gals gittin' up in de pictur's; dey sholy is."

With a brief "Good night, Miss Becky, Mars Cajy," Free Joe went out into the darkness, followed by little Dan. He made his way to the poplar, where Lucinda had been in the habit of meeting him, and sat down. He sat there a long time; he sat there until little Dan, growing restless, trotted off in the direction of the Calderwood place. Dozing against the poplar, in the gray dawn of the morning, Free Joe heard Spite Calderwood's fox-hounds in full cry a mile away.

"Shoo!" he exclaimed, scratching his head, and laughing to himself, "dem ar dogs is des a-warmin' dat old fox up."

But it was Dan the hounds were after, and the little dog came back no more. Free Joe waited and waited, until he grew tired of waiting. He went back the next night and waited, and for many nights thereafter. His waiting was in vain, and yet he never regarded it as in vain. Careless and shabby as he was, Free Joe was thoughtful enough to have his theory. He was convinced that little Dan had found Lucinda, and that some night when the moon was shining brightly through the trees, the dog would rouse him from his dreams as he sat sleeping at the foot of the poplar tree, and he would open his eyes and behold Lucinda standing over him, laughing merrily as of old; and then he thought what fun they would have about the queen of spades.

How many long nights Free Joe waited at the foot of the poplar tree for Lucinda and little Dan no one can ever know. He kept no account of them, and they were not recorded by Micajah Staley nor by Miss Becky. The season ran into summer and then into fall. One night he went to the Staley cabin, cut the two old people an armful of wood, and seated himself on the doorsteps, where he rested. He was always thankful — and proud, as it seemed — when Miss Becky gave him a cup of coffee, which she was sometimes thoughtful enough to do. He was especially thankful on this particular night.

"You er still layin' off for to strike up wi' Lucindy out thar in the woods, I reckon," said Micajah Staley, smiling grimly. The situation was not without its humorous aspects.

"Oh, dey er comin', Mars Cajy, dey er comin', sho," Free Joe replied. "I boun' you dey'll come; en w'en dey does come, I'll des take en fetch um yer, whar you kin see um wid you own eyes, you en Miss Becky."

"No," said Mr. Staley, with a quick and emphatic gesture of disapproval. "Don't! don't fetch 'em anywheres. Stay right wi' 'em as long as may be."

Free Joe chuckled, and slipped away into the night, while the two old people sat gazing in the fire. Finally Micajah spoke.

"Look at that nigger; look at 'im. He's pine-blank as happy now as a killdee by a mill-race. You can't faze 'em. I'd in-about give up my t'other hand ef I could stan' flat-footed, an' grin at trouble like that there nigger."

"Niggers is niggers," said Miss Becky, smiling grimly, "an' you can't rub it out; yit I lay I've seed a heap of white people lots meaner'n Free Joe. He grins — an' that's nigger — but I've ketched his under jaw a-tremblin' when Lucindy's name uz brung up. An' I tell you," she went on, bridling up a little, and speaking with almost fierce emphasis, "the Old Boy's done sharpened his claws for Spite Calderwood. You'll see it."

"Me, Rebecca?" said Mr. Staley, hugging his palsied arm; "me? I hope not."

"Well, you'll know it then," said Miss Becky, laughing heartily at her brother's look of alarm.

The next morning Micajah Staley had occasion to go into the woods after a piece of timber. He saw Free Joe sitting at the foot of the poplar, and the sight vexed him somewhat.

"Git up from there," he cried, "an' go an' arn your livin'. A mighty purty pass it's come to, when great big buck niggers can lie a-snorin' in the woods all day, when t'other folks is got to be up an' a-gwine. Git up from there!"

Receiving no response, Mr. Staley went to Free Joe, and shook him by the shoulder; but the negro made no response. He was dead. His hat was off, his head was bent, and a smile was on his face. It was as if he had bowed and smiled when death stood before him, humble to the last. His clothes were ragged; his hands were rough and callous; his shoes were literally tied together with strings; he was shabby in the extreme. A passer-by, glancing at him, could have no idea that such a humble creature had been summoned as a witness before the Lord God of Hosts.

A WHITE HERON

Sarah Orne Jewett (1849-1909)

I.

The woods were already filled with shadows one June evening, just before eight o'clock, though a bright sunset still glimmered faintly among the trunks of the trees. A little girl was driving home her cow, a plodding, dilatory, provoking creature in her behavior, but a valued companion for all that. They were going away from the western light, and striking deep into the dark woods, but their feet were familiar with the path, and it was no matter whether their eyes could see it or not.

There was hardly a night the summer through when the old cow could be found waiting at the pasture bars; on the contrary, it was her greatest pleasure to hide herself away among the high huckleberry bushes, and though she wore a loud bell she had made the discovery that if one stood perfectly still it would not ring. So Sylvia had to hunt for her until she found her, and call Co'! Co'! with never an answering Moo, until her childish patience was quite spent. If the creature had not given good milk and plenty of it, the case would have seemed very different to her owners. Besides, Sylvia had all the time there was, and very little use to make of it. Sometimes in pleasant weather it was a consolation to look upon the cow's pranks as an intelligent attempt to play hide and seek, and as the child had no playmates she lent herself to this amusement with a good deal of zest. Though this chase had been so long that the wary animal herself had given an unusual signal of her whereabouts, Sylvia had only laughed when she came upon Mistress Moolly at the swamp-side, and urged her affectionately homeward with a twig of birch leaves. The old cow was not inclined to wander farther, she even turned in the right direction for once as they left the pasture, and stepped along the road at a good pace. She was quite ready to be milked now, and seldom stopped to browse. Sylvia wondered what her grandmother would say because they were so late. It was a great while since she had left home at half past five o'clock, but everybody knew the difficulty of making this errand a short one. Mrs. Tilley had chased the hornéd torment too many summer evenings herself to blame any one else for lingering, and was only thankful as she waited that she had Sylvia, nowadays, to give such valuable assistance. The good woman suspected that Sylvia loitered occasionally on her own account; there never was such a child for straying about out-of-doors since the world was made! Everybody said that it was a good change for a little maid who had tried to grow for eight years in a crowded manufacturing town, but, as for Sylvia herself, it seemed as if she never had been alive at all before she came to live at the farm. She thought often with wistful compassion of a wretched dry geranium that belonged to a town neighbor.

" 'Afraid of folks,' " old Mrs. Tilley said to herself, with a smile, after she had made the unlikely choice of Sylvia from her daughter's houseful of children, and was returning to the farm. " 'Afraid of folks,' they said! I guess she won't be troubled no great with 'em up to the old place!" When they reached the door of the lonely house and stopped to unlock it, and the cat came to purr loudly, and rub against them, a deserted pussy, indeed, but fat with young robins, Sylvia whispered that this was a beautiful place to live in, and she never should wish to go home.

The companions followed the shady woodroad, the cow taking slow steps, and the child very fast ones. The cow stopped long at the brook to drink, as if the pasture were not half a swamp, and Sylvia stood still and waited, letting her bare feet cool themselves in the shoal water, while the great twilight moths struck softly against her. She waded on through the brook as the cow moved away, and listened to the thrushes with a heart that beat fast with pleasure. There was a stirring in the great boughs overhead. They were full of little birds and beasts that seemed to be wide-awake, and going about their world, or else saying good-night to each other in sleepy twitters. Sylvia herself felt sleepy as she walked along. However, it was not much farther to the house, and the air was soft and sweet. She was not often in the woods so late as this, and it made her feel as if she were a part of the gray shadows and the moving leaves. She was just thinking how long it seemed since she first came to the farm a year ago, and wondering if everything went on in the noisy town just the same as when she was there; the thought of the great red-faced boy who used to chase and frighten her made her hurry along the path to escape from the shadow of the trees.

Suddenly this little woods-girl is horror-stricken to hear a clear whistle not very far away. Not a bird's whistle, which would have a sort of friendliness, but a boy's whistle, determined, and somewhat aggressive. Sylvia left the cow to whatever sad fate might await her, and stepped discreetly aside into the bushes, but she was just too late. The enemy had discovered her, and called out in a very cheerful and persuasive tone, "Halloa, little girl, how far is it to the road?" and trembling Sylvia answered almost inaudibly, "A good ways."

She did not dare to look boldly at the tall young man, who carried a gun over his shoulder, but she came out of her bush and again followed the cow, while he walked alongside.

"I have been hunting for some birds," the stranger said kindly, "and I have lost my way, and need a friend very much. Don't be afraid," he added gallantly. "Speak up and tell me what your name is, and whether you think I can spend the night at your house, and go out gunning early in the morning."

Sylvia was more alarmed than before. Would not her grandmother consider her much to blame? But who could have foreseen such an accident as this? It did not appear to be her fault, and she hung her head as if the stem of it were broken, but managed to answer "Sylvy," with much effort when her companion again asked her name.

Mrs. Tilley was standing in the doorway when the trio came into view. The cow gave a loud moo by way of explanation.

"Yes, you'd better speak up for yourself, you old trial! Where'd she tucked herself away this time, Sylvy?" Sylvia kept an awed silence; she knew by instinct that her grandmother did not comprehend the gravity of the situation. She must be mistaking the stranger for one of the farmer-lads of the region.

The young man stood his gun beside the door, and dropped a heavy game-bag beside it; then he bade Mrs. Tilley good-evening, and repeated his wayfarer's story, and asked if he could have a night's lodging.

"Put me anywhere you like," he said. "I must be off early in the morning, before day; but I am very hungry, indeed. You can give me some milk at any rate, that's plain."

"Dear sakes, yes," responded the hostess, whose long slumbering hospitality seemed to be easily awakened. "You might fare better if you went out on the main road a mile or so, but you're welcome to what we've got. I'll milk right off, and you make yourself at home. You can sleep on husks or feathers," she proffered graciously. "I raised them all myself. There's good pasturing for geese just below here towards the ma'sh. Now step round and set a plate for the gentleman, Sylvy!" And Sylvia promptly stepped. She was glad to have something to do, and she was hungry herself.

It was a surprise to find so clean and comfortable a little dwelling in this New England wilderness. The young man had known the horrors of its most primitive housekeeping, and the dreary squalor of that level of society which does not rebel at the companionship of hens. This was the best thrift of an old-fashioned farmstead, though on such a small scale that it seemed like a hermitage. He listened eagerly to the old woman's quaint talk, he watched Sylvia's pale face and shining gray eyes with ever growing enthusiasm, and insisted that this was the best supper he had eaten for a month; then, afterward, the new-made friends sat down in the doorway together while the moon came up.

Soon it would be berry-time, and Sylvia was a great help at picking. The cow was a good milker, though a plaguy thing to keep track of, the hostess gossiped frankly, adding presently that she had buried four children, so that Sylvia's mother, and a son (who might be dead) in California were all the children she had left. "Dan, my boy, was a great hand to go gunning," she explained sadly. "I never wanted for pa'tridges or gray squer'ls while he was to home. He's been a great wand'rer, I expect, and he's no hand to write letters. There, I don't blame him, I'd ha' seen the world myself if it had been so I could.

"Sylvia takes after him," the grandmother continued affectionately, after a minute's pause. "There ain't a foot o' ground she don't know her way over, and the wild creatur's counts her one o' themselves. Squer'ls she'll tame to come an' feed right out o' her hands, and all sorts o' birds. Last winter she got the jay-birds to bangeing here, and I believe she'd 'a scanted herself of her own meals to have plenty to throw out amongst 'em, if I hadn't kep' watch. Anything but crows, I tell her, I'm willin' to help support, — though Dan he went an' tamed one o' them that did seem to have reason same as folks. It was round here a good spell after he went away. Dan an' his father they didn't hitch, — but he never held up his head ag'in after Dan had dared him an' gone off.

The guest did not notice this hint of family sorrows in his eager interest in something else.

"So Sylvy knows all about birds, does she?" he exclaimed, as he looked round at the little girl who sat, very demure but increasingly sleepy, in the moonlight. "I am making a collection of birds myself. I have been at it ever since I was a boy." (Mrs. Tilley smiled.) "There are two or three very rare ones I have been hunting for these five years. I mean to get them on my own ground if they can be found."

"Do you cage 'em up?" asked Mrs. Tilley doubtfully, in response to this enthusiastic announcement.

"Oh, no, they're stuffed and preserved, dozens and dozens of them," said the ornithologist, "and I have shot or snared every one myself. I caught a glimpse of a white heron three miles from here on Saturday, and I have followed it in this direction. They have never been found in this district at all. The little white heron, it is," and he turned again to look at Sylvia with the hope of discovering that the rare bird was one of her acquaintances.

But Sylvia was watching a hop-toad in the narrow footpath.

"You would know the heron if you saw it," the stranger continued eagerly. "A queer tall white bird with soft feathers and long thin legs. And it would have a nest perhaps in the top of a high tree, made of sticks, something like a hawk's nest."

Sylvia's heart gave a wild beat; she knew that strange white bird, and had once stolen softly near where it stood in some bright green swamp grass, away over at the other side of the woods. There was an open place where the sunshine always seemed strangely yellow and hot, where tall, nodding rushes grew, and her grandmother had warned her that she might sink in the soft black mud underneath and never be heard of more. Not far beyond were the salt marshes and beyond those was the sea, the sea which Sylvia wondered and dreamed about, but never had looked upon, though its great voice could often be heard above the noise of the woods on stormy nights.

"I can't think of anything I should like so much as to find that heron's nest," the handsome stranger was saying. "I would give ten dollars to anybody who could show it to me," he added desperately, "and I mean to spend my whole vacation hunting for it if need be. Perhaps it was only migrating, or had been chased out of its own region by some bird of prey."

Mrs. Tilley gave amazed attention to all this, but Sylvia still watched the toad, not divining, as she might have done at some calmer time, that the creature wished to get to its hole under the doorstep, and was much hindered by the unusual spectators at that hour of the evening. No amount of thought, that night, could decide how many wished-for treasures the ten dollars, so lightly spoken of, would buy.

The next day the young sportsman hovered about the woods, and Sylvia kept him company, having lost her first fear of the friendly lad, who proved to be most kind and sympathetic. He told her many things about the birds and what they knew and where they lived and what they did with themselves. And he gave her a jack-knife, which she thought as great a treasure as if she were a desert-islander. All day long he did not once make her troubled or afraid except when he brought down some unsuspecting singing creature from its bough. Sylvia would have liked him vastly better without his gun; she could not understand why he killed the very birds he seemed to like so much. But as the day waned, Sylvia still watched the young man with loving admiration. She had never seen anybody so charming and delightful; the woman's heart, asleep in the child, was vaguely thrilled by a dream of love. Some premonition of that great power stirred and swayed these young foresters who traversed the solemn woodlands with soft-footed silent care. They stopped to listen to a bird's song; they pressed forward again eagerly, parting the branches, — speaking to each other rarely and in whispers; the young man going first and Sylvia following, fascinated, a few steps behind, with her gray eyes dark with excitement.

She grieved because the longed-for white heron was elusive, but she did not lead the guest, she only followed, and there was no such thing as speaking first. The sound of her own unquestioned voice would have terrified her, — it was hard enough to answer yes or no when there was need of that. At last evening began to fall, and they drove the cow home together, and Sylvia smiled with pleasure when they came to the place where she heard the whistle and was afraid only the night before.

II.

Half a mile from home, at the farther edge of the woods, where the land was highest, a great pine-tree stood, the last of its generation. Whether it was left for a boundary mark, or for what reason, no one could say; the woodchoppers who had felled its mates were dead and gone long ago, and a whole forest of sturdy trees, pines and oaks and maples, had grown again. But the stately head of this old pine towered above them all and made a landmark for sea and shore miles and miles away. Sylvia knew it well. She had always believed that whoever climbed to the top of it could see the ocean; and the little girl had often laid her hand on the great rough trunk and looked up wistfully at those dark boughs that the wind always stirred, no matter how hot and still the air might be below. Now she thought of the tree with a new excitement, for why, if one climbed it at break of day, could not one see all the world, and easily discover whence the white heron flew, and mark the place, and find the hidden nest?

What a spirit of adventure, what wild ambition! What fancied triumph and delight and glory for the later morning when she could make known the secret! It was almost too real and too great for the childish heart to bear.

All night the door of the little house stood open, and the whippoorwills came and sang upon the very step. The young sportsman and his old hostess were sound asleep, but Sylvia's great design kept her broad awake and watching. She forgot to think of sleep. The short summer night seemed as long as the winter darkness, and at last when the whippoorwills ceased, and she was afraid the morning would after all come too soon, she stole out of the house and followed the pasture path through the woods, hastening toward the open ground beyond, listening with a sense of comfort and companionship to the drowsy twitter of a half-awakened bird, whose perch she had jarred in passing. Alas, if the great wave of human interest which flooded for the first time this dull little life should sweep away the satisfactions of an existence heart to heart with nature and the dumb life of the forest!

There was the huge tree asleep yet in the paling moonlight, and small and hopeful Sylvia began with utmost bravery to mount to the top of it, with tingling, eager blood coursing the channels of her whole frame, with her bare feet and fingers, that pinched and held like bird's claws to the monstrous ladder reaching up, up, almost to the sky itself. First she must mount the white oak tree that grew alongside, where she was almost lost among the dark branches and the green leaves heavy and wet with dew; a bird fluttered off its nest, and a red squirrel ran to and fro and scolded pettishly at the harmless housebreaker. Sylvia felt her way easily. She had often climbed there, and knew that higher still one of the oak's upper branches chafed against the pine trunk, just where its lower boughs were set close together. There, when she made the dangerous pass from one tree to the other, the great enterprise would really begin.

She crept out along the swaying oak limb at last, and took the daring step across into the old pine-tree. The way was harder than she thought; she must reach far and hold fast, the sharp dry twigs caught and held her and scratched her like angry talons, the pitch made her thin little fingers clumsy and stiff as she went round and round the tree's great stem, higher and higher upward. The sparrows and robins in the woods below were beginning to wake and twitter to the dawn, yet it seemed much lighter there aloft in the pine-tree, and the child knew that she must hurry if her project were to be of any use.

The tree seemed to lengthen itself out as she went up, and to reach farther and farther upward. It was like a great main-mast to the voyaging earth; it must truly have been amazed that morning through all its ponderous frame as it felt this determined spark of human spirit creeping and climbing from higher branch to branch. Who knows how steadily the least twigs held themselves to advantage this light, weak creature on her way! The old pine must have loved his new dependent. More than all the hawks, and bats, and moths, and even the sweet-voiced thrushes, was the brave, beating heart of the solitary gray-eyed child. And the tree stood still and held away the winds that June morning while the dawn grew bright in the east.

Sylvia's face was like a pale star, if one had seen it from the ground, when the last thorny bough was past, and she stood trembling and tired but wholly triumphant, high in the tree-top. Yes, there was the sea with the dawning sun making a golden dazzle over it, and toward that glorious east flew two hawks with slow-moving pinions. How low they looked in the air from that height when before one had only seen them far up, and dark against the blue sky. Their gray feathers were as soft as moths; they seemed only a little way from the tree, and Sylvia felt as if she too could go flying away among the clouds. Westward, the woodlands and farms reached miles and miles into the distance; here and there were church steeples, and white villages; truly it was a vast and awesome world.

The birds sang louder and louder. At last the sun came up bewilderingly bright. Sylvia could see the white sails of ships out at sea, and the clouds that were purple and rose-colored and yellow at first began to fade away. Where was the white heron's nest in the sea of green branches, and was this wonderful sight and pageant of the world the only reward for having climbed to such a giddy height? Now look down again, Sylvia, where the green marsh is set among the shining birches and dark hemlocks; there where you saw the white heron once you will see him again; look, look! a white spot of him like a single floating feather comes up from the dead hemlock and grows larger, and rises, and comes close at last, and goes by the landmark pine with steady sweep of wing and outstretched slender neck and crested head. And wait! wait! do not move a foot or a finger, little girl, do not send an arrow of light and consciousness from your two eager eyes, for the heron has perched on a pine bough not far beyond yours, and cries back to his mate on the nest, and plumes his feathers for the new day!

The child gives a long sigh a minute later when a company of shouting catbirds comes also to the tree, and vexed by their fluttering and lawlessness the solemn heron goes away. She knows his secret now, the wild, light, slender bird that floats and wavers, and goes back like an arrow presently to his home in the green world beneath. Then Sylvia, well satisfied, makes her perilous way down again, not daring to look far below the branch she stands on, ready to cry sometimes because her fingers ache and her lamed feet slip. Wondering over and over again what the stranger would say to her, and what he would think when she told him how to find his way straight to the heron's nest.

"Sylvy, Sylvy!" called the busy old grandmother again and again, but nobody answered, and the small husk bed was empty, and Sylvia had disappeared.

The guest waked from a dream, and remembering his day's pleasure hurried to dress himself that it might sooner begin. He was sure from the way the shy little girl looked once or twice yesterday that she had at least seen the white heron, and now she must really be persuaded to tell. Here she comes now, paler than ever, and her worn old frock is torn and tattered, and smeared with pine pitch. The grandmother and the sportsman stand in the door together and question her, and the splendid moment has come to speak of the dead hemlock-tree by the green marsh.

But Sylvia does not speak after all, though the old grandmother fretfully rebukes her, and the young man's kind appealing eyes are looking straight in her own. He can make them rich with money; he has promised it, and they are poor now. He is so well worth making happy, and he waits to hear the story she can tell.

No, she must keep silence! What is it that suddenly forbids her and makes her dumb? Has she been nine years growing, and now, when the great world for the first time puts out a hand to her, must she thrust it aside for a bird's sake? The murmur of the pine's green branches is in her ears, she remembers how the white heron came flying through the golden air and how they watched the sea and the morning together, and Sylvia cannot speak; she cannot tell the heron's secret and give its life away.

Dear loyalty, that suffered a sharp pang as the guest went away disappointed later in the day, that could have served and followed him and loved him as a dog loves! Many a night Sylvia heard the echo of his whistle haunting the pasture path as she came home with the loitering cow. She forgot even her sorrow at the sharp report of his gun and the piteous sight of thrushes and sparrows dropping silent to the ground, their songs hushed and their pretty feathers stained and wet with blood. Were the birds better friends than their hunter might have been, — who can tell? Whatever treasures were lost to her, woodlands and summer-time, remember! Bring your gifts and graces and tell your secrets to this lonely country child!

DÉSIRÉE'S BABY

Kate Chopin (1851-1904)

I

As the day was pleasant, Madame Valmondé drove over to L'Abri to see Désirée and the baby.

It made her laugh to think of Désirée with a baby. Why, it seemed but yesterday that Désirée was little more than a baby herself; when Monsieur in riding through the gateway of Valmondé had found her lying asleep in the shadow of the big stone pillar.

The little one awoke in his arms and began to cry for "Dada." That was as much as she could do or say. Some people thought she might have strayed there of her own accord, for she was of the toddling age. The prevailing belief was that she had been purposely left by a party of Texans, whose canvas-covered wagon, late in the day, had crossed the ferry that Coton Maïs kept, just below the plantation. In time Madame Valmondé abandoned every speculation but the one that Désirée had been sent to her by a beneficent Providence to be the child of her affection, seeing that she was without child of the flesh. For the girl grew to be beautiful and gentle, affectionate and sincere, — the idol of Valmondé.

It was no wonder, when she stood one day against the stone pillar in whose shadow she had lain asleep, eighteen years before, that Armand Aubigny riding by and seeing her there, had fallen in love with her. That was the way all the Aubignys fell in love, as if struck by a pistol shot. The wonder was that he had not loved her before; for he had known her since his father brought him home from Paris, a boy of eight, after his mother died there. The passion that awoke in him that day, when he saw her at the gate, swept along like an avalanche, or like a prairie fire, or like anything that drives headlong over all obstacles.

Monsieur Valmondé grew practical and wanted things well considered: that is, the girl's obscure origin. Armand looked into her eyes and did not care. He was reminded that she was nameless. What did it matter about a name when he could give her one of the oldest and proudest in Louisiana? He ordered the corbeille from Paris, and contained himself with what patience he could until it arrived; then they were married.

Madame Valmondé had not seen Désirée and the baby for four weeks. When she reached L'Abri she shuddered at the first sight of it, as she always did. It was a sad looking place, which for many years had not known the gentle presence of a mistress, old Monsieur Aubigny having married and buried his wife in France, and she having loved her own land too well ever to leave it. The roof came down steep and black like a cowl, reaching out beyond the wide galleries that encircled the yellow stuccoed house. Big, solemn oaks grew close to it, and their thick-leaved, far-reaching branches shadowed it like a pall. Young Aubigny's rule was a strict one, too, and under it his negroes had forgotten how to be gay, as they had been during the old master's easy-going and indulgent lifetime.

The young mother was recovering slowly, and lay full length, in her soft white muslins and laces, upon a couch. The baby was beside her, upon her arm, where he had fallen asleep, at her breast. The yellow nurse woman sat beside a window fanning herself.

Madame Valmondé bent her portly figure over Désirée and kissed her, holding her an instant tenderly in her arms. Then she turned to the child.

"This is not the baby!" she exclaimed, in startled tones. French was the language spoken at Valmondé in those days.

"I knew you would be astonished," laughed Désirée, "at the way he has grown. The little *cochon de lait!* Look at his legs, mamma, and his hands and fingernails, — real fingernails. Zandrine had to cut them this morning. Isn't it true, Zandrine?"

The woman bowed her turbaned head majestically, "Mais si, Madame."

"And the way he cries," went on Désirée, "is deafening. Armand heard him the other day as far away as La Blanche's cabin."

Madame Valmondé had never removed her eyes from the child. She lifted it and walked with it over to the window that was lightest. She scanned the baby narrowly, then looked as searchingly at Zandrine, whose face was turned to gaze across the fields.

"Yes, the child has grown, has changed," said Madame Valmondé, slowly, as she replaced it beside its mother. "What does Armand say?"

Désirée's face became suffused with a glow that was happiness itself.

"Oh, Armand is the proudest father in the parish, I believe, chiefly because it is a boy, to bear his name; though he says not, — that he would have loved a girl as well. But I know it isn't true. I know he says that to please me. And mamma," she added, drawing Madame Valmondé's head down to her, and speaking in a whisper, "he hasn't punished one of them — not one of them — since baby is born. Even Negrillon, who pretended to have burnt his leg that he might rest from work — he only laughed, and said Negrillon was a great scamp. oh, mamma, I'm so happy; it frightens me."

What Désirée said was true. Marriage, and later the birth of his son had softened Armand Aubigny's imperious and exacting nature greatly. This was what made the gentle Désirée so happy, for she loved him desperately. When he frowned she trembled, but loved him. When he smiled, she asked no greater blessing of God. But Armand's dark, handsome face had not often been disfigured by frowns since the day he fell in love with her.

When the baby was about three months old, Désirée awoke one day to the conviction that there was something in the air menacing her peace. It was at first too subtle to grasp. It had only been a disquieting suggestion; an air of mystery among the blacks; unexpected visits from far-off neighbors who could hardly account for their coming. Then a strange, an awful change in her husband's manner, which she dared not ask him to explain. When he spoke to her, it was with averted eyes, from which the old love-light seemed to have gone out. He absented himself from home; and when there, avoided her presence and that of her child, without excuse. And the very spirit of Satan seemed suddenly to take hold of him in his dealings with the slaves. Désirée was miserable enough to die.

She sat in her room, one hot afternoon, in her peignoir, listlessly drawing through her fingers the strands of her long, silky brown hair that hung about her shoulders. The baby, half naked, lay asleep upon her own great mahogany bed, that was like a sumptuous throne, with its satin-lined half-canopy. One of La Blanche's little quadroon boys — half naked too — stood fanning the child slowly with a fan of peacock feathers. Désirée's eyes had been fixed absently and sadly upon the baby, while she was striving to penetrate the threatening mist that she felt closing about her. She looked from her child to the boy who stood beside him, and back again; over and over. "Ah!" It was a cry that she could not help; which she was not conscious of having uttered. The blood turned like ice in her veins, and a clammy moisture gathered upon her face.

She tried to speak to the little quadroon boy; but no sound would come, at first. When he heard his name uttered, he looked up, and his mistress was pointing to the door. He laid aside the great, soft fan, and obediently stole away, over the polished floor, on his bare tiptoes.

She stayed motionless, with gaze riveted upon her child, and her face the picture of fright.

Presently her husband entered the room, and without noticing her, went to a table and began to search among some papers which covered it.

"Armand," she called to him, in a voice which must have stabbed him, if he was human. But he did not notice. "Armand," she said again. Then she rose and tottered towards him. "Armand," she panted once more, clutching his arm, "look at our child. What does it mean? tell me."

He coldly but gently loosened her fingers from about his arm and thrust the hand away from him. "Tell me what it means!" she cried despairingly.

"It means," he answered lightly, "that the child is not white; it means that you are not white."

A quick conception of all that this accusation meant for her nerved her with unwonted courage to deny it. "It is a lie; it is not true, I am white! Look at my hair, it is brown; and my eyes are gray, Armand, you know they are gray. And my skin is fair," seizing his wrist. "Look at my hand; whiter than yours, Armand," she laughed hysterically.

"As white as La Blanche's," he returned cruelly; and went away leaving her alone with their child.

When she could hold a pen in her hand, she sent a despairing letter to Madame Valmondé.

"My mother, they tell me I am not white. Armand has told me I am not white. For God's sake tell them it is not true. You must know it is not true. I shall die. I must die. I cannot be so unhappy, and live."

The answer that came was brief:

"My own Désirée: Come home to Valmondé; back to your mother who loves you. Come with your child."

When the letter reached Désirée she went with it to her husband's study, and laid it open upon the desk before which he sat. She was like a stone image: silent, white, motionless after she placed it there.

In silence he ran his cold eyes over the written words.

He said nothing. "Shall I go, Armand?" she asked in tones sharp with agonized suspense.

"Yes, go."

"Do you want me to go?"

"Yes, I want you to go."

He thought Almighty God had dealt cruelly and unjustly with him; and felt, somehow, that he was paying Him back in kind when he stabbed thus into his wife's soul. Moreover he no longer loved her, because of the unconscious injury she had brought upon his home and his name.

She turned away like one stunned by a blow, and walked slowly towards the door, hoping he would call her back.

"Good-by, Armand," she moaned.

He did not answer her. That was his last blow at fate.

Désirée went in search of her child. Zandrine was pacing the sombre gallery with it. She took the little one from the nurse's arms with no word of explanation, and descending the steps, walked away, under the live-oak branches.

It was an October afternoon; the sun was just sinking. Out in the still fields the negroes were picking cotton.

Désirée had not changed the thin white garment nor the slippers which she wore. Her hair was uncovered and the sun's rays brought a golden gleam from its brown meshes. She did not take the broad, beaten road which led to the far-off plantation of Valmondé. She walked across a deserted field, where the stubble bruised her tender feet, so delicately shod, and tore her thin gown to shreds.

She disappeared among the reeds and willows that grew thick along the banks of the deep, sluggish bayou; and she did not come back again.

Some weeks later there was a curious scene enacted at L'Abri. In the center of the smoothly swept back yard was a great bonfire. Armand Aubigny sat in the wide hallway that commanded a view of the spectacle; and it was he who dealt out to a half dozen negroes the material which kept this fire ablaze.

A graceful cradle of willow, with all its dainty furbishings, was laid upon the pyre, which had already been fed with the richness of a priceless layette. Then there were silk gowns, and velvet and satin ones added to these; laces, too, and embroideries; bonnets and gloves; for the corbeille had been of rare quality.

The last thing to go was a tiny bundle of letters; innocent little scribblings that Désirée had sent to him during the days of their espousal. There was the remnant of one back in the drawer from which he took them. But it was not Désirée's; it was part of an old letter from his mother to his father. He read it. She was thanking God for the blessing of her husband's love: —

"But above all," she wrote, "night and day, I thank the good God for having so arranged our lives that our dear Armand will never know that his mother, who adores him, belongs to the race that is cursed with the brand of slavery."

THE REVOLT OF "MOTHER"

Mary Eleanor Wilkins Freeman (1852-1930)

"Father!"

"What is it?"

"What are them men diggin' over there in the field for?"

There was a sudden dropping and enlarging of the lower part of the old man's face, as if some heavy weight had settled therein; he shut his mouth tight, and went on harnessing the great bay mare. He hustled the collar on to her neck with a jerk.

"Father!"

The old man slapped the saddle upon the mare's back.

"Look here, father, I want to know what them men are diggin' over in the field for, an' I'm goin' to know."

"I wish you'd go into the house, mother, an' 'tend to your own affairs," the old man said then. He ran his words together, and his speech was almost as inarticulate as a growl.

But the woman understood; it was her most native tongue. "I ain't goin' into the house till you tell me what them men are doin' over there in the field," said she.

Then she stood waiting. She was a small woman, short and straight-waisted like a child in her brown cotton gown. Her forehead was mild and benevolent between the smooth curves of gray hair; there were meek downward lines about her nose and mouth; but her eyes, fixed upon the old man, looked as if the meekness had been the result of her own will, never of the will of another.

They were in the barn, standing before the wide open doors. The spring air, full of the smell of growing grass and unseen blossoms, came in their faces. The deep yard in front was littered with farm wagons and piles of wood; on the edges, close to the fence and the house, the grass was a vivid green, and there were some dandelions.

The old man glanced doggedly at his wife as he tightened the last buckles on the harness. She looked as immovable to him as one of the rocks in his pastureland, bound to the earth with generations of blackberry vines. He slapped the reins over the horse, and started forth from the barn.

"*Father!* said she.

The old man pulled up. "What is it?"

"I want to know what them men are diggin' over there in that field for."

"They're diggin' a cellar, I s'pose, if you've got to know."

"A cellar for what?"

"A barn."

"A barn? You ain't goin' to build a barn over there where we was goin' to have a house, father?"

The old man said not another word. He hurried the horse into the farm wagon, and clattered out of the yard, jouncing as sturdily on his seat as a boy.

The woman stood a moment looking after him, then she went out of the barn across a corner of the yard to the house. The house, standing at right angles with the great barn and a long reach of sheds and out-buildings, was infinitesimal compared with them. It was scarcely as commodious for people as the little boxes under the barn eaves were for doves.

A pretty girl's face, pink and delicate as a flower, was looking out of one of the house windows. She was watching three men who were digging over in the field which bounded the yard near the road line. She turned quietly when the woman entered.

"What are they diggin' for, mother?" said she. "Did he tell you?"

"They're diggin' for — a cellar for a new barn."

"Oh, mother, he ain't goin' to build another barn?"

"That's what he says."

A boy stood before the kitchen glass combing his hair. He combed slowly and painstakingly, arranging his brown hair in a smooth hillock over his forehead. He did not seem to pay any attention to the conversation.

"Sammy, did you know father was goin' to build a new barn?" asked the girl.

The boy combed assiduously.

"Sammy!"

He turned, and showed a face like his father's under his smooth crest of hair. "Yes, I s'pose I did," he said, reluctantly.

"How long have you known it?" asked his mother.

"'Bout three months, I guess."

"Why didn't you tell of it?"

"Didn't think 'twould do no good."

"I don't see what father wants another barn for," said the girl, in her sweet slow voice. She turned again to the window, and stared out at the digging men in the field. Her tender sweet face was full of a gentle distress. Her forehead was as bald and innocent as a baby's, with the light hair strained back from it in a row of curl-papers. She was quite large, but her soft curves did not look as if they covered muscles.

Her mother looked sternly at the boy. "Is he goin' to buy more cows?" said she.

The boy did not reply; he was tying his shoes.

"Sammy, I want you to tell me if he's goin' to buy more cows."

"I s'pose he is."

"How many?"

"Four, I guess."

His mother said nothing more. She went into the pantry, and there was a clatter of dishes. The boy got his cap from a nail behind the door, took an old arithmetic from the shelf, and started for school. He was lightly built, but clumsy. He went out of the yard with a curious spring in the hips, that made his loose home-made jacket tilt up in the rear.

The girl went to the sink, and began to wash the dishes that were piled up there. Her mother came promptly out of the pantry, and shoved her aside. "You wipe 'em," said she; "I'll wash. There's a good many this mornin'."

The mother plunged her hands vigorously into the water, the girl wiped the plates slowly and dreamily. "Mother," said she, "don't you think it's too bad father's goin' to build that new barn, much as we need a decent house to live in?"

Her mother scrubbed a dish fiercely. "You 'ain't found out yet we're women-folks, Nanny Penn," said she. "You 'ain't seen enough of men-folks yet to. One of these days you'll find it out, an' then you'll know that we know only what men-folks think we do, so far as any use of it goes, an' how we'd ought to reckon men-folks in with Providence an' not complain of what they do any more than we do of the weather."

"I don't care; I don't believe George is anything like that, anyhow," said Nanny. Her delicate face flushed pink, her lips pouted softly, as if she were going to cry.

"You wait an' see. I guess George Eastman ain't no better than other men. You hadn't ought to judge father, though. He can't help it, 'cause he don't look at things jest the way we do. An' we've been pretty comfortable here, after all. The roof don't leak — 'ain't never but once — that's one thing. Father kept it shingled right up."

"I do wish we had a parlor."

"I guess it won't hurt George Eastman any to come to see you in a nice clean kitchen. I guess a good many girls don't have as good a place as this. Nobody's ever heard me complain."

"I 'ain't complained either, mother."

"Well, I don't think you'd better, a good father an' a good home as you've got. S'pose your father made you go out an' work for your livin'? Lots of girls have to that ain't no stronger an' better able to than you be."

Sarah Penn washed the frying-pan with a conclusive air. She scrubbed the outside of it as faithfully as the inside. She was a masterly keeper of her box of a house. Her one livingroom never seemed to have in it any of the dust which the friction of life with inanimate matter produces. She swept, and there seemed to be no dirt to go before the broom; she cleaned, and one could see no difference.

She was like an artist so perfect that he has apparently no art. To-day she got out a mixing bowl and a board, and rolled some pies, and there was no more flour upon her than upon her daughter who was doing finer work. Nanny was to be married in the fall, and she was sewing on some white cambric and embroidery. She sewed industriously while her mother cooked, her soft milk-white hands and wrists showed whiter than her delicate work.

"We must have the stove moved out in the shed before long," said Mrs. Penn. "Talk about not havin' things, it's been a real blessin' to be able to put a stove up in that shed in hot weather. Father did one good thing when he fixed that stove-pipe out there."

Sarah Penn's face as she rolled her pies had that expression of meek vigor which might have characterized one of the New Testament saints. She was making mince-pies. Her husband, Adoniram Penn, liked them better than any other kind. She baked twice a week. Adoniram often liked a piece of pie between meals. She hurried this morning. It had been later than usual when she began, and she wanted to have a pie baked for dinner. However deep a resentment she might be forced to hold against her husband, she would never fail in sedulous attention to his wants.

Nobility of character manifests itself at loop-holes when it is not provided with large doors. Sarah Penn's showed itself today in flaky dishes of pastry. So she made the pies faithfully, while across the table she could see, when she glanced up from her work, the sight that rankled in her patient and steadfast soul — the digging of the cellar of the new barn in the place where Adoniram forty years ago had promised her their new house should stand.

The pies were done for dinner. Adoniram and Sammy were home a few minutes after twelve o'clock. The dinner was eaten with serious haste. There was never much conversation at the table in the Penn family. Adoniram asked a blessing, and they ate promptly, then rose up and went about their work.

Sammy went back to school, taking soft sly lopes out of the yard like a rabbit. He wanted a game of marbles before school, and feared his father would give him some chores to do. Adoniram hastened to the door and called after him, but he was out of sight.

"I don't see what you let him go for, mother," said he. "I wanted him to help me unload that wood."

Adoniram went to work out in the yard unloading wood from the wagon. Sarah put away the dinner dishes, while Nanny took down her curl-papers and changed her dress. She was going down to the store to buy some more embroidery and thread.

When Nanny was gone, Mrs. Penn went to the door. "Father!" she called.

"Well, what is it?"

"I want to see you jest a minute, father."

"I can't leave this wood nohow. I've got to git it unloaded an' go for a load of gravel afore two o'clock. Sammy had ought to helped me. You hadn't ought to let him go to school so early."

"I want to see you jest a minute."

"I tell ye I can't, nohow, mother."

"Father, you come here." Sarah Penn stood in the door like a queen; she held her head as if it bore a crown; there was that patience which makes authority royal in her voice. Adoniram went.

Mrs. Penn led the way into the kitchen, and pointed to a chair. "Sit down, father," said she; "I've got somethin' I want to say to you."

He sat down heavily; his face was quite stolid, but he looked at her with restive eyes. "Well, what is it, mother?"

"I want to know what you're buildin' that new barn for, father?"

"I 'ain't got nothin' to say about it."

"It can't be you think you need another barn?"

"I tell ye I 'ain't got nothin' to say about it, mother; an' I ain't goin' to say nothin'."

"Be you goin' to buy more cows?"

Adoniram did not reply; he shut his mouth tight.

"I know you be, as well as I want to. Now, father, look here" — Sarah Penn had not sat down; she stood before her husband in the humble fashion of a Scripture woman — "I'm goin' to talk real plain to you: I never have sence I married you, but I'm goin' to now. I 'ain't never complained, an' I ain't goin' to complain now, but I'm goin' to talk plain. You see this room here, father; you look at it well. You see there ain't no carpet on the floor, an' you see the paper is all dirty, an' droppin' off the walls. We 'ain't had no new paper on it for ten year, an' then I put it on myself, an' it didn't cost but nine-pence a roll. You see this room, father; it's all the one I've had to work in an' eat in an' sit in sence we was married. There ain't another woman in the whole town whose husband 'ain't got half the means you have but what's got better. It's all the room Nanny's got to have her company in; an' there ain't one of her mates but what's got better, an' their fathers not so able as hers is. It's all the room she'll have to be married in. What would you have thought, father, if we had had our weddin' in a room no better than this? I was married in my mother's parlor, with a carpet on the floor, an' stuffed furniture, an' a mahogany card-table. An' this is all the room my daughter will have to be married in. Look here, father!"

Sarah Penn went across the room as though it were a tragic stage. She flung open a door and disclosed a tiny bedroom, only large enough for a bed and bureau, with a path between. "There, father," said she — "there's all the room I've had to sleep in for forty year. All my children were born there — the two that died, an' the two that's livin'. I was sick with a fever there."

She stepped to another door and opened it. It led into the small, ill-lighted pantry. "Here," said she, "is all the buttery I've got — every place I've got for my dishes to set away my victuals in, an' to keep my milk-pans in. Father, I've been takin' care of the milk of six cows in this place, an' now you're goin' to build a new barn, an' keep more cows, an' give me more to do in it."

She threw open another door. A narrow crooked flight of stairs wound upward from it. "There, father!" said she; "I want you to look at the stairs that go up to them two unfinished chambers that are all the places our son an' daughter have had to sleep in all their lives. There ain't a prettier girl in town nor a more ladylike one than Nanny, an' that's the place she has to sleep in. It ain't so good as your horse's stall; it ain't so warm an' tight."

Sarah Penn went back and stood before her husband. "Now, father," said she, "I want to know if you think you're doin' right an' accordin' to what you profess. Here, when we was married, forty year ago, you promised me faithful that we should have a new house built in that lot over in the field before the year was out. You said you had money enough, an' you wouldn't ask me to live in no such place as this. It is forty year now, an' you've been makin' more money, an' I've been savin' of it for you ever since, an' you 'ain't built no house yet. You've built sheds, an' cow-houses an' one new barn, an' now you're goin' to build another. Father, I want to know if you think it's right. You're lodgin' your dumb beasts better than you are your own flesh an' blood. I want to know if you think it's right."

"I 'ain't got nothin' to say."

"You can't say nothin' without ownin' it ain't right, father. An' there's another thing — I ain't complained; I've got along forty year, an' I s'pose I should forty more, if it wa'n't for that — if we don't have another house, Nanny she can't live with us after she's married. She'll have to go somewheres else to live away from us, an' it don't seem as if I could have it so, noways, father. She wa'n't ever strong. She's got considerable color, but there wa'n't never any backbone to her. I've always took the heft of everything off her, an' she ain't fit to keep house an' do everything herself. She'll be all worn out inside of a year. Think of her doin' all the washin' an' ironin' an' bakin' with them soft white hands an' arms, an' sweepin'! I can't have it so, noways, father."

Mrs. Penn's face was burning; her mild eyes gleamed. She had pleaded her little cause like a Webster; she had ranged from severity to pathos; but her opponent employed that obstinate silence which makes eloquence futile with mocking echoes. Adoniram arose clumsily.

"Father, 'ain't you got nothin' to say?" said Mrs. Penn.

"I've got to go off after that load of gravel. I can't stan' here talkin' all day."

"Father, won't you think it over, an' have a house built there instead of a barn?"

"I 'ain't got nothin' to say."

Adoniram shuffled out. Mrs. Penn went into her bedroom. When she came out, her eyes were red. She had a roll of unbleached cotton cloth. She spread it out on the kitchen table, and began cutting out some shirts for her husband. The men over in the field had a team to help them this afternoon; she could hear their halloos. She had a scanty pattern for the shirts; she had to plan and piece the sleeves.

Nanny came home with her embroidery, and sat down with her needle-work. She had taken down her curl-papers, and there was a soft roll of fair hair like an aureole over her forehead; her face was as delicately fine and clear as porcelain. Suddenly she looked up, and the tender red flamed all over her face and neck. "Mother," said she.

"What say?"

"I've been thinkin' — I don't see how we're goin' to have any — weddin' in this room. I'd be ashamed to have his folks come if we didn't have anybody else."

"Mebbe we can have some new paper before then; I can put it on. I guess you won't have no call to be ashamed of your belongin's."

"We might have the weddin' in the new barn," said Nanny, with gentle pettishness. "Why, mother, what makes you look so?"

Mrs. Penn had started, and was staring at her with a curious expression. She turned again to her work, and spread out a pattern carefully on the cloth. "Nothin'," said she.

Presently Adoniram clattered out of the yard in his two-wheeled dump cart, standing as proudly upright as a Roman charioteer. Mrs. Penn opened the door and stood there a minute looking out; the halloos of the men sounded louder.

It seemed to her all through the spring months that she heard nothing but the halloos and the noises of saws and hammers. The new barn grew fast. It was a fine edifice for this little village. Men came on pleasant Sundays, in their meeting suits and clean shirt bosoms, and stood around it admiringly. Mrs. Penn did not speak of it, and Adoniram did not mention it to her, although sometimes, upon a return from inspecting it, he bore himself with injured dignity.

"It's a strange thing how your mother feels about the new barn," he said, confidentially, to Sammy one day.

Sammy only grunted after an odd fashion for a boy: he had learned it from his father.

The barn was all completed ready for use by the third week in July. Adoniram had planned to move his stock in on Wednesday; on Tuesday he received a letter which changed his plans. He came in with it early in the morning. "Sammy's been to the post-office," said he, "an' I've got a letter from Hiram." Hiram was Mrs. Penn's brother, who lived in Vermont.

"Well," said Mrs. Penn, "what does he say about the folks?"

"I guess they're all right. He says he thinks if I come up country right off there's a chance to buy jest the kind of a horse I want." He stared reflectively out of the window at the new barn.

Mrs. Penn was making pies. She went on clapping the rolling-pin into the crust, although she was very pale, and her heart beat loudly.

"I dunno' but what I'd better go," said Adoniram. "I hate to go off jest now, right in the midst of hayin', but the ten-acre lot's cut, an' I guess Rufus an' the others can git along without me three or four days. I can't get a horse round here to suit me, nohow, an' I've got to have another for all that wood-haulin' in the fall. I told Hiram to watch out, an' if he got wind of a good horse to let me know. I guess I'd better go."

"I'll get out your clean shirt an' collar," said Mrs. Penn, calmly.

She laid out Adoniram's Sunday suit and his clean clothes on the bed in the little bedroom. She got his shaving water and razor ready. At last she buttoned on his collar and fastened his black cravat.

Adoniram never wore his collar and cravat except on extra occasions. He held his head high, with a rasped dignity. When he was all ready, with his coat and hat brushed, and a lunch of pie and cheese in a paper bag, he hesitated on the threshold of the door. He looked at his wife, and his manner was defiantly apologetic. "*If* them cows come to-day, Sammy can drive 'em into the new barn," said he; "an' when they bring the hay up, they can pitch it in there."

"Well," replied Mrs. Penn.

Adoniram set his shaven face ahead and started. When he had cleared the door-step, he turned and looked back with a kind of nervous solemnity. "I shall be back by Saturday if nothin' happens," said he.

"Do be careful, father," returned his wife.

She stood in the door with Nanny at her elbow and watched him out of sight. Her eyes had a strange, doubtful expression in them; her peaceful forehead was contracted. She went in, and about her baking again. Nanny sat sewing. Her wedding day was drawing nearer, and she was getting pale and thin with her steady sewing. Her mother kept glancing at her.

"Have you got that pain in your side this mornin'?" she asked.

"A little."

Mrs. Penn's face, as she worked, changed, her perplexed forehead smoothed, her eyes were steady, her lips firmly set. She formed a maxim for herself, although incoherently with her unlettered thoughts. "Unsolicited opportunities are the guideposts of the Lord to the new roads of life," she repeated in effect, and she made up her mind to her course of action.

"S'posin' I *had* wrote to Hiram," she muttered once, when she was in the pantry — "s'posin' I had wrote, an' asked him if he knew of any horse? But I didn't, an' father's goin' wa'n't none of my doin'. It looks like a Providence." Her voice rang out quite loud at the last.

"What you talkin' about, mother?" called Nanny.

"Nothin'."

Mrs. Penn hurried her baking; at eleven o'clock it was all done. The load of hay from the west field came slowly down the cart track, and drew up at the new barn. Mrs. Penn ran out. "Stop!" she screamed — "stop!"

The men stopped and looked; Sammy upreared from the top of the load, and stared at his mother.

"Stop!" she cried out again. "Don't you put the hay in that barn; put it in the old one."

"Why, he said to put it in here," returned one of the haymakers, wonderingly. He was a young man, a neighbor's son, whom Adoniram hired by the year to help on the farm.

"Don't you put the hay in the new barn; there's room enough in the old one, ain't there?" said Mrs. Penn.

"Room enough," returned the hired man, in his thick, rustic tones. "Didn't need the new barn, nohow, far as room's concerned. Well, I s'pose he changed his mind." He took hold of the horses' bridles.

Mrs. Penn went back to the house. Soon the kitchen windows were darkened, and a fragrance like warm honey came into the room.

Nanny laid down her work. "I thought father wanted them to put the hay into the new barn?" she said, wonderingly.

"It's all right," replied her mother.

Sammy slid down from the load of hay and came in to see if dinner was ready.

"I ain't goin' to get a regular dinner to-day, as long as father's gone," said his mother. "I've let the fire go out. You can have some bread an' milk an' pie. I thought we could get along." She set out some bowls of milk, some bread, and a pie on the kitchen table. "You'd better eat your dinner now," said she. "You might jest as well get through with it. I want you to help me afterward."

Nanny and Sammy stared at each other. There was something strange in their mother's manner. Mrs. Penn did not eat anything herself. She went into the pantry, and they heard her moving dishes while they ate. Presently she came out with a pile of plates. She got the clothes-basket out of the shed, and packed them in it. Nanny and Sammy watched. She brought out cups and saucers, and put them in with the plates.

"What you goin' to do, mother?" inquired Nanny, in a timid voice. A sense of something unusual made her tremble, as if it were a ghost. Sammy rolled his eyes over his pie.

"You'll see what I'm goin' to do," replied Mrs. Penn. "If you're through, Nanny, I want you to go up stairs an' pack up your things; an' I want you, Sammy, to help me take down the bed in the bed-room."

"Oh, mother, what for?" gasped Nanny.

"You'll see."

During the next few hours a feat was performed by this simple, pious New England mother which was equal in its way to Wolfe's storming of the Heights of Abraham. It took no more genius and audacity of bravery for Wolfe to cheer his wondering soldiers up those steep precipices, under the sleeping eyes of the enemy, than for Sarah Penn, at the head of her children, to move all her little household goods into the new barn while her husband was away.

Nanny and Sammy followed their mother's instructions without a murmur; indeed, they were overawed. There is a certain uncanny and superhuman quality about all such purely original undertakings as their mother's was to them. Nanny went back and forth with her light loads, and Sammy tugged with sober energy.

At five o'clock in the afternoon the little house in which the Penns had lived for forty years had emptied itself into the new barn.

Every builder builds somewhat for unknown purposes, and is in a measure a prophet. The architect of Adoniram Penn's barn, while he designed it for the comfort of four-footed animals, had planned better than he knew for the comfort of humans. Sarah Penn saw at a glance its possibilities. Those great box-stalls, with quilts hung before them, would make better bedrooms than the one she had occupied for forty years, and there was a tight carriage-room. The harness-room, with its chimney and shelves, would make a kitchen of her dreams. The great middle space would make a parlor, by-and-by, fit for a palace. Up stairs there was as much room as down. With partitions and windows, what a house would there be! Sarah looked at the row of stanchions before the allotted space for cows, and reflected that she would have her front entry there.

At six o'clock the stove was up in the harness-room, the kettle was boiling, and the table set for tea. It looked almost as home-like as the abandoned house across the yard had ever done. The young hired man milked, and Sarah directed him calmly to bring the milk to the new barn. He came gaping, dropping little blots of foam from the brimming pails on the grass. Before the next morning he had spread the story of Adoniram Penn's wife moving into the new barn all over the little village. Men assembled in the store and talked it over, women with shawls over their heads scuttled into each other's houses before their work was done. Any deviation from the ordinary course of life in this quiet town was enough to stop all progress in it. Everybody paused to look at the staid, independent figure on the side track. There was a difference of opinion with regard to her. Some held her to be insane; some, of a lawless and rebellious spirit.

Friday the minister went to see her. It was in the forenoon, and she was at the barn door shelling peas for dinner. She looked up and returned his salutation with dignity, then she went on with her work. She did not invite him in. The saintly expression of her face remained fixed, but there was an angry flush over it.

The minister stood awkwardly before her and talked. She handled the peas as if they were bullets. At last she looked up, and her eyes showed the spirit that her meek front had covered for a lifetime.

"There ain't no use talkin', Mr. Hersey," said she. "I've thought it all over an' over, an' I believe I'm doin' what's right. I've made it the subject of prayer, an' it's betwixt me an' the Lord an' Adoniram. There ain't no call for nobody else to worry about it."

"Well, of course if you have brought it to the Lord in prayer, and feel satisfied that you are doing right, Mrs. Penn," said the minister, helplessly. His thin gray-bearded face was pathetic. He was a sickly man; his youthful confidence had cooled; he had to scourge himself up to some of his pastoral duties as relentlessly as a Catholic ascetic, and then he was prostrated by the smart.

"I think it's right jest as much as I think it was right for our forefathers to come over from the old country 'cause they didn't have what belonged to 'em," said Mrs. Penn. She arose. The barn threshold might have been Plymouth Rock from her bearing. "I don't doubt you mean well, Mr. Hersey," said she, "but there are things people hadn't ought to interfere with. I've been a member of the church for over forty year. I've got my own mind an' my own feet, an' I'm goin' to think my own thoughts an' go my own ways, an' nobody but the Lord is goin' to dictate to me unless I've a mind to have him. Won't you come in an' set down? How is Mis' Hersey?"

"She is well, I thank you," replied the minister. He added some more perplexed apologetic remarks; then he retreated.

He could expound the intricacies of every character study in the Scriptures, he was competent to grasp the Pilgrim Fathers and all historical innovators, but Sarah Penn was beyond him. He could deal with primal cases, but parallel ones worsted him. But, after all, although it was aside from his province, he wondered more how Adoniram Penn would deal with his wife than how the Lord would. Everybody shared the wonder. When Adoniram's four new cows arrived, Sarah ordered three to be put in the old barn, the other in the house shed where the cooking-stove had stood. That added to the excitement. It was whispered that all four cows were domiciled in the house.

Toward sunset on Saturday, when Adoniram was expected home, there was a knot of men in the road near the new barn. The hired man had milked, but he still hung around the premises. Sarah Penn had supper all ready. There were brown-bread and baked beans and a custard pie; it was the supper that Adoniram loved on a Saturday night. She had on a clean calico, and she bore herself imperturbably. Nanny and Sammy kept close at her heels. Their eyes were large, and Nanny was full of nervous tremors. Still there was to them more pleasant excitement than anything else. An inborn confidence in their mother over their father asserted itself.

Sammy looked out of the harness-room window. "There he is," he announced, in an awed whisper. He and Nanny peeped around the casing. Mrs. Penn kept on about her work. The children watched Adoniram leave the new horse standing in the drive while he went to the house door. It was fastened. Then he went around to the shed. That door was seldom locked, even when the family was away. The thought how her father would be confronted by the cow flashed upon Nanny. There was a hysterical sob in her throat. Adoniram emerged from the shed and stood looking about in a dazed fashion. His lips moved; he was saying something, but they could not hear what it was. The hired man was peeping around a corner of the old barn, but nobody saw him.

Adoniram took the new horse by the bridle and led him across the yard to the new barn. Nanny and Sammy slunk close to their mother. The barn doors rolled back, and there stood Adoniram, with the long mild face of the great Canadian farm horse looking over his shoulder.

Nanny kept behind her mother, but Sammy stepped suddenly forward, and stood in front of her.

Adoniram stared at the group. "What on airth you all down here for?" said he. "What's the matter over to the house?"

"We've come here to live, father," said Sammy. His shrill voice quavered out bravely.

"What" — Adoniram sniffed — "what is it smells like cookin'?" said he. He stepped forward and looked in the open door of the harness-room. Then he turned to his wife. His old bristling face was pale and frightened. "What on airth does this mean, mother?" he gasped.

"You come in here, father," said Sarah. She led the way into the harness-room and shut the door. "Now, father," said she, "you needn't be scared. I ain't crazy. There ain't nothin' to be upset over. But we've come here to live, an' we're goin' to live here. We've got jest as good a right here as new horses an' cows. The house wa'n't fit for us to live in any longer, an' I made up my mind I wa'n't goin' to stay there. I've done my duty by you forty year, an' I'm goin' to do it now; but I'm goin' to live here. You've got to put in some windows and partitions; an' you'll have to buy some furniture."

"Why, mother!" the old man gasped.

"You'd better take your coat off an' get washed — there's the wash-basin — an' then we'll have supper."

"Why, mother!"

Sammy went past the window, leading the new horse to the old barn. The old man saw him, and shook his head speechlessly. He tried to take off his coat, but his arms seemed to lack the power. His wife helped him. She poured some water into the tin basin, and put in a piece of soap. She got the comb and brush, and smoothed his thin gray hair after he had washed. Then she put the beans, hot bread, and tea on the table. Sammy came in, and the family drew up. Adoniram sat looking dazedly at his plate, and they waited.

"Ain't you goin' to ask a blessin', father?" said Sarah.

And the old man bent his head and mumbled.

All through the meal he stopped eating at intervals, and stared furtively at his wife; but he ate well. The home food tasted good to him, and his old frame was too sturdily healthy to be affected by his mind. But after supper he went out and sat down on the step of the smaller door at the right of the barn, through which he had meant his Jerseys to pass in stately file, but which Sarah designed for her front house door, and he leaned his head on his hands.

After the supper dishes were cleared away and the milk-pans washed, Sarah came out to him. The twilight was deepening. There was a clear green glow in the sky. Before them stretched the smooth level of field; in the distance was a cluster of hay-stacks like the huts of a village; the air was very cool and calm and sweet. The landscape might have been an ideal one of peace.

Sarah bent over and touched her husband on one of his thin, sinewy shoulders. "Father!"

The old man's shoulders heaved: he was weeping.

"Why, don't do so, father," said Sarah.

"I'll — put up the — partitions, an' — everything you — want, mother."

Sarah put her apron up to her face; she was overcome by her own triumph.

Adoniram was like a fortress whose walls had no active resistance, and went down the instant the right besieging tools were used. "Why, mother," he said, hoarsely, "I hadn't no idee you was so set on't as all this comes to."

THE WIFE OF HIS YOUTH

Charles W. Chesnutt (1858-1932)

I

Mr. Ryder was going to give a ball. There were several reasons why this was an opportune time for such an event.

Mr. Ryder might aptly be called the dean of the Blue Veins. The original Blue Veins were a little society of colored persons organized in a certain Northern city shortly after the war. Its purpose was to establish and maintain correct social standards among a people whose social condition presented almost unlimited room for improvement. By accident, combined perhaps with some natural affinity, the society consisted of individuals who were, generally speaking, more white than black. Some envious outsider made the suggestion that no one was eligible for membership who was not white enough to show blue veins. The suggestion was readily adopted by those who were not of the favored few, and since that time the society, though possessing a longer and more pretentious name, had been known far and wide as the "Blue Vein Society," and its members as the "Blue Veins."

The Blue Veins did not allow that any such requirement existed for admission to their circle, but, on the contrary, declared that character and culture were the only things considered; and that if most of their members were light-colored, it was because such persons, as a rule, had had better opportunities to qualify themselves for membership. Opinions differed, too, as to the usefulness of the society. There were those who had been known to assail it violently as a glaring example of the very prejudice from which the colored race had suffered most; and later, when such critics had succeeded in getting on the inside, they had been heard to maintain with zeal and earnestness that the society was a life-boat, an anchor, a bulwark and a shield, a pillar of cloud by day and of fire by night, to guide their people through the social wilderness. Another alleged prerequisite for Blue Vein membership was that of free birth; and while there was really no such requirement, it is doubtless true that very few of the members would have been unable to meet it if there had been. If there were one or two of the older members who had come up from the South and from slavery, their history presented enough romantic circumstances to rob their servile origin of its grosser aspects. While there were no such tests of eligibility, it is true that the Blue Veins had their notions on these subjects, and that not all of them were equally liberal in regard to the things they collectively disclaimed. Mr. Ryder was one of the most conservative. Though he had not been among the founders of the society, but had come in some years later, his genius for social leadership was such that he had speedily become its recognized adviser and head, the custodian of its standards, and the preserver of its traditions. He shaped its social policy, was active in providing for its entertainment, and when the interest fell off, as it sometimes did, he fanned the embers until they burst again into a cheerful flame. There were still other reasons for his popularity. While he was not as white as some of the Blue Veins, his appearance was such as to confer distinction upon them. His features were of a refined type, his hair was almost straight; he was always neatly dressed; his manners were irreproachable, and his morals above suspicion. He had come to Groveland a young man, and obtaining employment in the office of a railroad company as messenger had in time worked himself up to the position of stationery clerk, having charge of the distribution of the office supplies for the whole company. Although the lack of early training had hindered the orderly development of a naturally fine mind, it had not prevented him from doing a great deal of reading or from forming decidedly literary tastes. Poetry was his passion. He could repeat whole pages of the great English poets ; and if his pronunciation was sometimes faulty, his eye, his voice, his gestures, would respond to the changing sentiment with a precision that revealed a poetic soul, and disarm criticism. He was economical, and had saved money; he owned and occupied a very comfortable house on a respectable street. His residence was handsomely furnished, containing among other things a good library, especially rich in poetry, a piano, and some choice engravings. He generally shared his house with some young couple, who looked after his wants and were company for him; for Mr. Ryder was a single man. In the early days of his connection with the Blue Veins he had been regarded as quite a catch, and ladies and their mothers had manoeuvred with much ingenuity to capture him. Not, however, until Mrs. Molly Dixon visited Groveland had any woman ever made him wish to change his condition to that of a married man.

Mrs. Dixon had come to Groveland from Washington in the spring, and before the summer was over she had won Mr. Ryder's heart. She possessed many attractive qualities. She was much younger than he; in fact, he was old enough to have been her father, though no one knew exactly how old he was. She was whiter than he, and better educated. She had moved in the best colored society of the country, at Washington, and had taught in the schools of that city. Such a superior person had been eagerly welcomed to the Blue Vein Society, and had taken a leading part in its activities. Mr. Ryder had at first been attracted by her charms of person, for she was very good looking and not over twenty-five; then by her refined manners and by the vivacity of her wit. Her husband had been a government clerk, and at his death had left a considerable life insurance. She was visiting friends in Groveland, and, finding the town and the people to her liking, had prolonged her stay indefinitely. She had not seemed displeased at Mr. Ryder's attentions, but on the contrary had given him every proper encouragement; indeed, a younger and less cautious man would long since have spoken. But he had made up his mind, and had only to determine the time when he would ask her to be his wife. He decided to give a ball in her honor, and at some time during the evening of the ball to offer her his heart and hand. He had no special fears about the outcotme, but, with a little touch of romance, he wanted the surroundings to be in harmony with his own feelings when he should have received the answer he expected.

Mr. Ryder resolved that this ball should mark an epoch in the social history of Groveland. He knew, of course, — no one could know better, — the entertainments that had taken place in past years, and what must be done to surpass them. His ball must be worthy of the lady in whose honor it was to be given, and must, by the quality of its guests, set an example for the future. He had observed of late a growing liberality, almost a laxity, in social matters, even among members of his own set, and had several times been forced to meet in a social way persons whose complexions and callings in life were hardly up to the standard which he considered proper for the society to maintain. He had a theory of his own.

"I have no race prejudice," he would say, "but we people of mixed blood are ground between the upper and the nether millstone. Our fate lies between absorption by the white race and extinction in the black. The one doesn't want us yet, but may take us in time. The other would welcome us, but it would be for us a backward step. 'With malice towards none, with charity for all,' we must do the best we can for ourselves and those who are to follow us. Self-preservation is the first law of nature."

His ball would serve by its exclusiveness to counteract leveling tendencies, and his marriage with Mrs. Dixon would help to further the upward process of absorption he had been wishing and waiting for.

II

The ball was to take place on Friday night. The house had been put in order, the carpets covered with canvas, the halls and stairs decorated with palms and potted plants; and in the afternoon Mr. Ryder sat on his front porch, which the shade of a vine running up over a wire netting made a cool and pleasant lounging-place. He expected to respond to the toast "The Ladies," at the supper, and from a volume of Tennyson — his favorite poet — was fortifying himself with apt quotations. The volume was open at "A Dream of Fair Women." His eyes fell on these lines, and he read them aloud to judge better of their effect: —

"At length I saw a lady within call.
  Stiller than chisell'd marble, standing there;
 A daughter of the gods, divinely tall,
  And most divinely fair."

He marked the verse, and turning the page read the stanza beginning, —

"O sweet pale Margaret,
  O rare pale Margaret."

He weighed the passage a moment, and decided that it would not do. Mrs. Dixon was the palest lady he expected at the ball, and she was of a rather ruddy complexion, and of lively disposition and buxom build. So he ran over the leaves until his eye rested on the description of Queen Guinevere: —

"She seem'd a part of joyous Spring:
 A gown of grass-green silk she wore,
 Buckled with golden clasps before;
 A light-green tuft of plumes she bore
 Closed in a golden ring.

* * *

"She look'd so lovely, as she sway'd
 The rein with dainty finger-tips,
 A man had given all other bliss,
 And all his worldly worth for this,
 To waste his whole heart in one kiss
 Upon her perfect lips."

As Mr. Ryder murmured these words audibly, with an appreciative thrill, he heard the latch of his gate click, and a light footfall sounding on the steps. He turned his head, and saw a woman standing before the door.

She was a little woman, not five feet tall, and proportioned to her height. Although she stood erect, and looked around her with very bright and restless eyes, she seemed quite old; for her face was crossed and recrossed with a hundred wrinkles, and around the edges of her bonnet could be seen protruding here and there a tuft of short gray wool. She wore a blue calico gown of ancient cut, a little red shawl fastened around her shoulders with an old-fashioned brass brooch, and a large bonnet profusely ornamented with faded red and yellow artificial flowers. And she was very black — so black that her toothless gums, revealed when she opened her mouth to speak, were not red, but blue. She looked like a bit of the old plantation life, summoned up from the past by the wave of a magician's wand, as the poet's fancy had called into being the gracious shapes of which Mr. Ryder had just been reading.

He rose from his chair and came over to where she stood.

"Good-afternoon, madam," he said.

"Good-evenin', suh," she answered, ducking suddenly with a quaint curtsy. Her voice was shrill and piping, but softened somewhat by age. "Is dis yere whar Mistuh Ryduh lib, suh?" she asked, looking around her doubtfully, and glancing into the open windows, through which some of the preparations for the evening were visible.

"Yes," he replied, with an air of kindly patronage, unconsciously flattered by her manner, "I am Mr. Ryder. Did you want to see me?"

"Yas, suh, ef I ain't 'sturbin' of you too much."

"Not at all. Have a seat over here behind the vine, where it is cool. What can I do for you?"

" 'Scuse me, suh," she continued, when she had sat down on the edge of a chair, " 'scuse me, suh, I's lookin' for my husban'. I heerd you wuz a big man an' had libbed heah a long time, an' I 'lowed you wouldn't min' ef I'd come roun' an' ax you ef you'd eber heerd of a merlatter man by de name er Sam Taylor 'quirin' roun' in de chu'ches ermongs' de people fer his wife 'Liza Jane?"

Mr. Ryder seemed to think for a moment.

"There used to be many such cases right after the war," he said, "but it has been so long that I have forgotten them. There are very few now. But tell me your story, and it may refresh my memory."

She sat back farther in her chair so as to be more comfortable, and folded her withered hands in her lap.

"My name's 'Liza," she began, " 'Liza Jane. Wen I wuz young I us'ter b'long ter Marse Bob Smif, down in old Missourn. I wuz bawn down dere. W'en I wuz a gal I wuz married ter a man named Jim. But Jim died, an' after dat I married a merlatter man named Sam Taylor. Sam wuz free-bawn, but his mammy and daddy died, an' de w'ite folks 'prenticed him ter my marster fer ter work fer 'im 'tel he wuz growed up. Sam worked in de fiel', an' I wuz de cook. One day Ma'y Ann, ole miss's maid, come rushin' out ter de kitchen, an' says she, ' 'Liza Jane, ole marse gwine sell yo' Sam down de ribber.'

" 'Go way f'm yere,' says I; 'my husban' 's free!'

" 'Don' make no diff'ence. I heerd ole marse tell ole miss he wuz gwine take yo' Sam 'way wid 'im ter-morrow, fer he needed money, an' he knowed whar he could git a t'ousan' dollars fer Sam an' no questions axed.'

"W'en Sam come home f'm de fiel', dat night, I tole him 'bout ole marse gwine steal 'im, an' Sam run erway. His time wuz mos' up, an' he swo' dat w'en he wuz twenty-one he would come back an' he'p me run erway, er else save up de money ter buy my freedom. An' I know he'd 'a' done it, fer he thought a heap er me, Sam did. But w'en he come back he didn' fin' me, fer I wuzn' dere. Ole marse had heerd dat I warned Sam, so he had me whip' an' sol' down de ribber.

"Den de wah broke out, an' w'en it wuz ober de cullud folks wuz scattered. I went back ter de ole home; but Sam wuzn' dere, an' I couldn' l'arn nuffin' 'bout 'im. But I knowed he'd be'n dere to look fer me an' hadn' foun' me, an' had gone erway ter hunt fer me.

"I's be'n lookin' fer 'im eber sence," she added simply, as though twenty-five years were but a couple of weeks, "an' I knows he's be'n lookin' fer me. Fer he sot a heap er sto' by me, Sam did, an' I know he's be'n huntin' fer me all dese years, — 'less'n he's be'n sick er sump'n, so he couldn' work, er out'n his head, so he couldn' 'member his promise. I went back down de ribber, fer I 'lowed he'd gone down dere lookin' fer me. I's be'n ter Noo Orleens, an' Atlanty, an' Charleston, an' Richmon'; an' w'en I'd be'n all ober de Souf I come ter de Norf. Fer I knows I'll fin' 'im some er dese days," she added softly, "er he'll fin' me, an' den we'll bofe be as happy in freedom as we wuz in de ole days befo' de wah." A smile stole over her withered countenance as she paused a moment, and her bright eyes softened into a far-away look.

This was the substance of the old woman's story. She had wandered a little here and there. Mr. Ryder was looking at her curiously when she finished.

"How have you lived all these years?" he asked.

"Cookin', suh. I's a good cook. Does you know anybody w'at needs a good cook, suh? I's stoppin' wid a cullud fam'ly roun' de corner yonder 'tel I kin fin' a place."

"Do you really expect to find your husband? He may be dead long ago."

She shook her head emphatically. "Oh no, he ain' dead. De signs an' de tokens tells me. I dremp three nights runnin' on'y dis las' week dat I foun' him."

"He may have married another woman. Your slave marriage would not have prevented him, for you never lived with him after the war, and without that your marriage doesn't count."

"Wouldn' make no diff'ence wid Sam. He wouldn' marry no yuther 'ooman 'tel he foun' out 'bout me. I knows it," she added. "Sump'n's be'n tellin' me all dese years dat I's gwine fin' Sam 'fo I dies."

"Perhaps he's outgrown you, and climbed up in the world where he wouldn't care to have you find him."

"No, indeed, suh," she replied, "Sam ain' dat kin' er man. He wuz good ter me, Sam wuz, but he wuzn' much good ter nobody e'se, fer he wuz one er de triflin'es' han's on de plantation. I 'spec's ter haf ter suppo't 'im w'en I fin' 'im, fer he nebber would work 'less'n he had ter. But den he wuz free, an' he didn' git no pay fer his work, an' I don' blame 'im much. Mebbe he's done better sence he run erway, but I ain' 'spectin' much."

"You may have passed him on the street a hundred times during the twenty-five years, and not have known him; time works great changes."

She smiled incredulously. "I'd know 'im 'mongs' a hund'ed men. Fer dey wuzn' no yuther merlatter man like my man Sam, an' I couldn' be mistook. I's toted his picture roun' wid me twenty-five years."

"May I see it?" asked Mr. Ryder. "It might help me to remember whether I have seen the original."

As she drew a small parcel from her bosom, he saw that it was fastened to a string that went around her neck. Removing several wrappers, she brought to light an old-fashioned daguerreotype in a black case. He looked long and intently at the portrait. It was faded with time, but the features were still distinct, and it was easy to see what manner of man it had represented.

He closed the case, and with a slow movement handed it back to her.

"I don't know of any man in town who goes by that name," he said, "nor have I heard of any one making such inquiries. But if you will leave me your address, I will give the matter some attention, and if I find out anything I will let you know."

She gave him the number of a house in the neighborhood, and went away, after thanking him warmly.

He wrote down the address on the flyleaf of the volume of Tennyson, and, when she had gone, rose to his feet and stood looking after her curiously. As she walked down the street with mincing step, he saw several persons whom she passed turn and look back at her with a smile of kindly amusement. When she had turned the corner, he went upstairs to his bedroom, and stood for a long time before the mirror of his dressing-case, gazing thoughtfully at the reflection of his own face.

III

At eight o'clock the ballroom was a blaze of light and the guests had begun to assemble; for there was a literary programme and some routine business of the society to be gone through with before the dancing. A black servant in evening dress waited at the door and directed the guests to the dressing-rooms.

The occasion was long memorable among the colored people of the city; not alone for the dress and display, but for the high average of intelligence and culture that distinguished the gathering as a whole. There were a number of schoolteachers, several young doctors, three or four lawyers, some professional singers, an editor, a lieutenant in the United States army spending his furlough in the city, and others in various polite callings; these were colored, though most of them would not have attracted even a casual glance because of any marked difference from white people. Most of the ladies were in evening costume, and dress coats and dancing-pumps were the rule among the men. A band of string music, stationed in an alcove behind a row of palms, played popular airs while the guests were gathering.

The dancing began at half past nine. At eleven o'clock supper was served. Mr. Ryder had left the ballroom some little time before the intermission, but reappeared at the supper-table. The spread was worthy of the occasion, and the guests did full justice to it. When the coffee had been served, the toastmaster, Mr. Solomon Sadler, rapped for order. He made a brief introductory speech, complimenting host and guests, and then presented in their order the toasts of the evening. They were responded to with a very fair display of after-dinner wit.

"The last toast," said the toast-master, when he reached the end of the list, "is one which must appeal to us all. There is no one of us of the sterner sex who is not at some time dependent upon woman, — in infancy for protection, in manhood for companionship, in old age for care and comforting. Our good host has been trying to live alone, but the fair faces I see around me to-night prove that he too is largely dependent upon the gentler sex for most that makes life worth living, — the society and love of friends, — and rumor is at fault if he does not soon yield entire subjection to one of them. Mr. Ryder will now respond to the toast, — The Ladies."

There was a pensive look in Mr. Ryder's eyes as he took the floor and adjusted his eyeglasses. He began by speaking of woman as the gift of Heaven to man, and after some general observations on the relations of the sexes he said: "But perhaps the quality which most distinguishes woman is her fidelity and devotion to those she loves. History is full of examples, but has recorded none more striking than one which only to-day came under my notice."

He then related, simply but effectively, the story told by his visitor of the afternoon. He told it in the same soft dialect, which came readily to his lips, while the company listened attentively and sympathetically. For the story had awakened a responsive thrill in many hearts. There were some present who had seen, and others who had heard their fathers and grandfathers tell, the wrongs and sufferings of this past generation, and all of them still felt, in their darker moments, the shadow hanging over them. Mr. Ryder went on: —

"Such devotion and such confidence are rare even among women. There are many who would have searched a year, some who would have waited five years, a few who might have hoped ten years; but for twenty-five years this woman has retained her affection for and her faith in a man she has not seen or heard of in all that time.

"She came to me to-day in the hope that I might be able to help her find this long-lost husband. And when she was gone I gave my fancy rein, and imagined a case I will put to you.

"Suppose that this husband, soon after his escape, had learned that his wife had been sold away, and that such inquiries as he could make brought no information of her whereabouts. Suppose that he was young, and she much older than he; that he was light, and she was black; that their marriage was a slave marriage, and legally binding only if they chose to make it so after the war. Suppose, too, that he made his way to the North, as some of us have done, and there, where he had larger opportunities, had improved them, and had in the course of all these years grown to be as different from the ignorant boy who ran away from fear of slavery as the day is from the night. Suppose, even, that he had qualified himself, by industry, by thrift, and by study, to win the friendship and be considered worthy the society of such people as these I see around me to-night, gracing my board and filling my heart with gladness; for I am old enough to remember the day when such a gathering would not have been possible in this land. Suppose, too, that, as the years went by, this man's memory of the past grew more and more indistinct, until at last it was rarely, except in his dreams, that any image of this bygone period rose before his mind. And then suppose that accident should bring to his knowledge the fact that the wife of his youth, the wife he had left behind him, — not one who had walked by his side and kept pace with him in his upward struggle, but one upon whom advancing years and a laborious life had set their mark, — was alive and seeking him, but that he was absolutely safe from recognition or discovery, unless he chose to reveal himself. My friends, what would the man do? I will suppose that he was one who loved honor, and tried to deal justly with all men. I will even carry the case further, and suppose that perhaps he had set his heart upon another, whom he had hoped to call his own. What would he do, or rather what ought he to do, in such a crisis of a lifetime?

"It seemed to me that he might hesitate, and I imagined that I was an old friend, a near friend, and that he had come to me for advice; and I argued the case with him. I tried to discuss it impartially. After we had looked upon the matter from every point of view, I said to him, in words that we all know:

> 'This above all: to thine own self be true,
> And it must follow, as the night the day,
> Thou canst not then be false to any man.'

Then, finally, I put the question to him, 'Shall you acknowledge her?'

"And now, ladies and gentlemen, friends and companions, I ask you, what should he have done?"

There was something in Mr. Ryder's voice that stirred the hearts of those who sat around him. It suggested more than mere sympathy with an imaginary situation; it seemed rather in the nature of a personal appeal. It was observed, too, that his look rested more especially upon Mrs. Dixon, with a mingled expression of renunciation and inquiry.

She had listened, with parted lips and streaming eyes. She was the first to speak: "He should have acknowledged her."

"Yes," they all echoed, "he should have acknowledged her."

"My friends and companions," responded Mr. Ryder, "I thank you, one and all. It is the answer I expected, for I knew your hearts."

He turned and walked toward the closed door of an adjoining room, while every eye followed him in wondering curiosity. He came back in a moment, leading by the hand his visitor of the afternoon, who stood startled and trembling at the sudden plunge into this scene of brilliant gayety. She was neatly dressed in gray, and wore the white cap of an elderly woman.

"Ladies and gentlemen," he said, "this is the woman, and I am the man, whose story I have told you. Permit me to introduce to you the wife of my youth."

UP THE COOLLY

Hamlin Garland (1860-1940)

"Keep the main-travelled road up the coulee — it's the second house after crossin' the crick."

The ride from Milwaukee to the Mississippi is a fine ride at any time, superb in summer. To lean back in a reclining chair and whirl away in a breezy July day, past lakes, groves of oak, past fields of barley being reaped, past hayfields, where the heavy grass is toppling before the swift sickle, is a panorama of delight, a road full of delicious surprises, where down a sudden vista lakes open, or a distant wooded hill looms darkly blue, or swift streams, foaming deep down the solid rock, send whiffs of cool breezes in at the window.

It has majesty, breadth. The farming has nothing apparently petty about it. All seems vigorous, youthful, and prosperous. Mr. Howard McLane in his chair let his newspaper fall on his lap and gazed out upon it with dreaming eyes. It had a certain mysterious glamour to him; the lakes were cooler and brighter to his eye, the greens fresher, and the grain more golden than to anyone else, for he was coming back to it all after an absence of ten years. It was, besides, his West. He still took pride in being a Western man.

His mind all day flew ahead of the train to the little town far on toward the Mississippi, where he had spent his boyhood and youth. As the train passed the Wisconsin River, with its curiously carved cliffs, its cold, dark, swift-swirling water eating slowly under cedar-clothed banks, Howard began to feel curious little movements of the heart, like a lover as he nears his sweetheart.

The hills changed in character, growing more intimately recognizable. They rose higher as the train left the ridge and passed down into the Black River valley, and specifically into the La Crosse valley. They ceased to have any hint of upheavals of rock, and became simply parts of the ancient level left standing after the water had practically given up its postglacial, scooping action.

It was about six o'clock as he caught sight of the dear broken line of hills on which his baby eyes had looked thirty-five years ago. A few minutes later and the train drew up at the grimy little station set in at the hillside, and, giving him just time to leap off, plunged on again toward the West. Howard felt a ridiculous weakness in his legs as he stepped out upon the broiling hot splintery planks of the station and faced the few idlers lounging about. He simply stood and gazed with the same intensity and absorption one of the idlers might show standing before the Brooklyn Bridge.

The town caught and held his eyes first. How poor and dull and sleepy and squalid it seemed! The one main street ended at the hillside at his left and stretched away to the north, between two rows of the usual village stores, unrelieved by a tree or a touch of beauty. An unpaved street, drab-colored, miserable, rotting wooden buildings, with the inevitable battlements — the same, only worse, was the town.

The same, only more beautiful still, was the majestic amphitheater of green wooded hills that circled the horizon, and toward which he lifted his eyes. He thrilled at the sight.

"Glorious!" he cried involuntarily.

Accustomed to the White Mountains, to the Allghenies, he had wondered if these hills would retain their old-time charm. They did. He took off his hat to them as he stood there. Richly wooded, with gently sloping green sides, rising to massive square or rounded tops with dim vistas, they glowed down upon the squalid town, gracious, lofty in their greeting, immortal in their vivid and delicate beauty.

He was a goodly figure of a man as he stood there beside his valise. Portly, erect, handsomely dressed, and with something unusually winning in his brown mustache and blue eyes, something scholarly suggested by the pinch-nose glasses, something strong in the repose of the head. He smiled as he saw how unchanged was the grouping of the old loafers on the salt barrels and nail kegs. He recognized most of them — a little dirtier, a little more bent, and a little grayer.

They sat in the same attitudes, spat tobacco with the same calm delight, and joked each other, breaking into short and sudden fits of laughter, and pounded each other on the back, just as when he was a student at the La Crosse Seminary and going to and fro daily on the train.

They ruminated on him as he passed, speculating in a perfectly audible way upon his business.

"Looks like a drummer."

"No, he ain't no drummer. See them Boston glasses?"

"That's so. Guess he's a teacher."

"Looks like a moneyed cuss."

"Bos'n, I *guess*."

He knew the one who spoke last — Freeme Cole, a man who was the fighting wonder of Howard's boyhood, now degenerated into a stoop-shouldered, faded, garrulous, and quarrelsome old man. Yet there was something epic in the old man's stories, something enthralling in the dramatic power of recital.

Over by the blacksmith shop the usual game of "quaits" was in progress, and the drug clerk on the corner was chasing a crony with the squirt pump, with which he was about to wash the windows. A few teams stood ankle-deep in the mud, tied to the fantastically gnawed pine pillars of the wooden awnings. A man on a load of hay was "jawing" with the attendant of the platform scales, who stood below, pad and pencil in hand.

"Hit 'im! hit 'im! Jump off and knock 'im!" suggested a bystander, jovially.

Howard knew the voice.

"Talk's cheap. Takes money t' buy whiskey," he said when the man on the load repeated his threat of getting off and whipping the scalesman.

"You're William McTurg," Howard said, coming up to him.

"I am, sir," replied the soft-voiced giant turning and looking down on the stranger with an amused twinkle in his deep brown eyes. He stood as erect as an Indian, though his hair and beard were white.

"I'm Howard McLane."

"Ye begin t' look it," said McTurg, removing his right hand from his pocket. "How are yeh?"

"I'm first-rate. How's Mother and Grant?"

"Saw 'im plowing corn as I came down. Guess he's all right. Want a boost?"

"Well, yes. Are you down with a team?"

"Yep. 'Bout goin' home. Climb right in. That's my rig, right there," nodding at a sleek bay colt hitched in a covered buggy. "Heave y'r grip under the seat."

They climbed into the seat after William had lowered the buggy top and unhitched the horse from the post. The loafers were mildly curious. Guessed Bill had got hooked onto by a lightnin'-rod peddler, or somethin' o' that kind.

"Want to go by river, or 'round by the hills?"

"Hills, I guess."

The whole matter began to seem trivial, as if he had only been away for a month or two.

William McTurg was a man little given to talk. Even the coming back of a nephew did not cause any flow of questions or reminiscences. They rode in silence. He sat a little bent forward, the lines held carelessly in his hands, his great leonine head swaying to and fro with the movement of the buggy.

As they passed familiar spots, the younger man broke the silence with a question.

"That's old man McElvaine's place, ain't it?"

"Old man living?"

"I guess he is. Husk more corn 'n any man he c'n hire."

On the edge of the village they passed an open lot on the left, marked with circus rings of different eras.

"There's the old ball ground. Do they have circuses on it just the same as ever?"

"Just the same."

"What fun that field calls up! The games of ball we used to have! Do you play yet?"

"Sometimes. Can't stoop so well as I used to." He smiled a little. "Too much fat."

It all swept back upon Howard in a flood of names and faces and sights and sounds; something sweet and stirring somehow, though it had little of esthetic charm at the time. They were passing along lanes now, between superb fields of corn, wherein plowmen were at work. Kingbirds flew from post to post ahead of them; the insects called from the grass. The valley slowly outspread below them. The workmen in the fields were "turning out" for the night; they all had a word of chaff with McTurg.

Over the western wall of the circling amphitheater the sun was setting. A few scattering clouds were drifting on the west wind, their shadows sliding down the green and purple slopes. The dazzling sunlight flamed along the luscious velvety grass, and shot amid the rounded, distant purple peaks, and streamed in bars of gold and crimson across the blue mist of the narrower upper coulee.

The heart of the young man swelled with pleasure almost like pain, and the eyes of the silent older man took on a far-off, dreaming look, as he gazed at the scene which had repeated itself a thousand times in his life, but of whose beauty he never spoke.

Far down to the left was the break in the wall through which the river ran on its way to join the Mississippi. As they climbed slowly among the hills, the valley they had left grew still more beautiful, as the squalor of the little town was hid by the dusk of distance. Both men were silent for a long time. Howard knew the peculiarities of his companion too well to make any remarks or ask any questions, and besides it was a genuine pleasure to ride with one who could feel that silence was the only speech amid such splendors.

Once they passed a little brook singing in a mournfully sweet way its eternal song over its pebbles. It called back to Howard the days when he and Grant, his younger brother, had fished in this little brook for trout, with trousers rolled above the knee and wrecks of hats upon their heads.

"Any trout left?" he asked.

"Not many. Little fellers." Finding the silence broken, William asked the first question since he met Howard. "Le's see: you're a show feller now? B'long to a troupe?"

"Yes, yes; I'm an actor."

"Pay much?"

"Pretty well."

That seemed to end William's curiosity about the matter.

"Ah, there's our old house, ain't it?" Howard broke out, pointing to one of the houses farther up the coulee. "It'll be a surprise to them, won't it?"

"Yep; only they don't live there."

"What! They don't!"

"Who does?"

"Dutchman."

Howard was silent for some moments. "Who lives on the Dunlap place?"

" 'Nother Dutchman."

"Where's Grant living, anyhow?"

"Farther up the Coolly."

"Well, then I'd better get out here, hadn't I?"

"Oh, I'll drive yeh up."

"No, I'd rather walk."

The sun had set, and the coulee was getting dusk when Howard got out of McTurg's carriage and set off up the winding lane toward his brother's house. He walked slowly to absorb the coolness and fragrance and color of the hour. The katydids sang a rhythmic song of welcome to him. Fireflies were in the grass. A whippoorwill in the deep of the wood was calling weirdly, and an occasional night hawk, flying high, gave his grating shriek, or hollow boom, suggestive and resounding.

He had been wonderfully successful, and yet had carried into his success as a dramatic author as well as actor a certain puritanism that made him a paradox to his fellows. He was one of those actors who are always in luck, and the best of it was he kept and made use of his luck. Jovial as he appeared, he was inflexible as granite against drink and tobacco. He retained through it all a certain freshness of enjoyment that made him one of the best companions in the profession; and now as he walked on, the hour and the place appealed to him with great power. It seemed to sweep away the life that came between.

How close it all was to him, after all! In his restless life, surrounded by the glare of electric lights, painted canvas, hot colors, creak of machinery, mock trees, stones, and brooks, he had not lost but gained appreciation for the coolness, quiet and low tones, the shyness of the wood and field.

In the farmhouse ahead of him a light was shining as he peered ahead, and his heart gave another painful movement. His brother was awaiting him there, and his mother, whom he had not seen for ten years and who had grown unable to write. And when Grant wrote, which had been more and more seldom of late, his letters had been cold and curt.

He began to feel that in the pleasure and excitement of his life he had grown away from his mother and brother. Each summer he had said, "Well, now I'll go home *this* year sure." But a new play to be produced, or a yachting trip, or a tour of Europe, had put the homecoming off; and now it was with a distinct consciousness of neglect of duty that he walked up to the fence and looked into the yard, where William had told him his brother lived.

It was humble enough — a small white house, story-and-a-half structure, with a wing, set in the midst of a few locust trees; a small drab-colored barn, with a sagging ridge pole; a barnyard full of mud, in which a few cows were standing, fighting the flies and waiting to be milked. An old man was pumping water at the well; the pigs were squealing from a pen nearby; a child was crying.

Instantly the beautiful, peaceful valley was forgotten. A sickening chill struck into Howard's soul as he looked at it all. In the dim light he could see a figure milking a cow. Leaving his valise at the gate, he entered and walked up to the old man, who had finished pumping and was about to go to feed the hogs.

"Good evening," Howard began. "Does Mr. Grant McLane live here?"

"Yes, sir, he does. He's right over there milkin'."

"I'll go over there an — "

"Don't b'lieve I would. It's darn muddy over there. It's been turrible rainy. He'll be done in a minute, anyway."

"Very well; I'll wait."

As he waited, he could hear a woman's fretful voice, and the impatient jerk and jar of kitchen things, indicative of ill temper or worry. The longer he stood absorbing this farm scene, with all its sordidness, dullness, triviality, and its endless drudgeries, the lower his heart sank. All the joy of the homecoming was gone, when the figure arose from the cow and approached the gate, and put the pail of milk down on the platform by the pump.

"Good evening," said Howard out of the dusk.

Grant stared a moment. "Good evening."

Howard knew the voice, though it was older and deeper and more sullen. "Don't you know me, Grant? I am Howard.

The man approached him, gazing intently at his face. "You are?" after a pause. "Well, I'm glad to see yeh, but I can't shake hands. That damned cow had laid down in the mud."

They stood and looked at each other. Howard's cuffs, collar, and shirt, alien in their elegance, showed through the dusk, and a glint of light shot out from the jewel of his necktie, as the light from the house caught it at the right angle. As they gazed in silence at each other, Howard divined something of the hard, bitter feeling which came into Grant's heart as he stood there, ragged, ankle-deep in muck, his sleeves rolled up, a shapeless old straw hat on his head.

The gleam of Howard's white hands angered him. When he spoke, it was in a hard, gruff tone, full of rebellion.

"Well, go in the house and set down. I'll be in soon's I strain the milk and wash the dirt off my hands."

"But Mother — "

"She's 'round somewhere. Just knock on the door under the porch 'round there."

Howard went slowly around the corner of the house, past a vilely smelling rain barrel, toward the west. A gray-haired woman was sitting in a rocking chair on the porch, her hands in her lap, her eyes fixed on the faintly yellow sky, against which the hills stood dim purple silhouettes and the locust trees were etched as fine as lace. There was sorrow, resignation, and a sort of dumb despair in her attitude.

Howard stood, his throat swelling till it seemed as if he would suffocate. This was his mother — the woman who bore him, the being who had taken her life in her hand for him; and he, in his excited and pleasurable life, had neglected her!

He stepped into the faint light before her. She turned and looked at him without fear. "Mother!" he said. She uttered one little, breathing, gasping cry, called his name, rose, and stood still. He bounded up the steps and took her in his arms.

"Mother! Dear old Mother!"

In the silence, almost painful, which followed, an angry woman's voice could be heard inside: "I don't care. I am't goin' to wear myself out fer him. He c'n eat out here with us, or else — "

Mrs. McLane began speaking. "Oh, I've longed to see yeh, Howard. I was afraid you wouldn't come till — too late."

"What do you mean, Mother? Ain't you well?"

"I don't seem to be able to do much now 'cept sit around and knit a little. I tried to pick some berries the other day, and I got so dizzy I had to give it up."

"You mustn't work. You *needn't* work. Why didn't you write to me how you were?" Howard asked in an agony of remorse.

"Well, we felt as if you probably had all you could do to take care of yourself."

"Are you married, Howard?"

"No, Mother; and there ain't any excuse for me — not a bit," he said, dropping back into her colloquialisms." I'm ashamed when I think of how long it's been since I saw you. I could have come."

"It don't matter now," she interrupted gently. "It's the way things go. Our boys grow up and leave us."

"Well, come in to supper," said Grant's ungracious voice from the doorway. "Come, Mother."

Mrs. McLane moved with difficulty. Howard sprang to her aid, and leaning on his arm she went through the little sitting room, which was unlighted, out into the kitchen, where the supper table stood near the cookstove.

"How, this is my wife," said Grant in a cold, peculiar tone.

Howard bowed toward a remarkably handsome young woman, on whose forehead was a scowl, which did not change as she looked at him and the old lady.

"Set down, anywhere," was the young woman's cordial invitation.

Howard sat down next to his mother, and facing the wife, who had a small, fretful child in her arms. At Howard's left was the old man, Lewis. The supper was spread upon a gay-colored oilcloth, and consisted of a pan of milk, set in the midst, with bowls at each plate. Beside the pan was a dipper and a large plate of bread, and at one end of the table was a dish of fine honey.

A boy of about fourteen leaned upon the table, his bent shoulders making him look like an old man. His hickory shirt, like that of Grant, was still wet with sweat, and discolored here and there with grease, or green from grass. His hair, freshly wet and combed, was smoothed away from his face, and shone in the light of the kerosene lamp. As he ate, he stared at Howard, as if he would make an inventory of each thread of the visitor's clothing.

"Did I look like that at his age?" thought Howard.

"You see we live jest about the same's ever," said Grant as they began eating, speaking with a grim, almost challenging inflection.

The two brothers studied each other curiously, as they talked of neighborhood scenes. Howard seemed incredibly elegant and handsome to them all, with his rich, soft clothing, his spotless linen, and his exquisite enunciation and ease of speech. He had always been "smooth-spoken," and he had become "elegantly persuasive," as his friends said of him, and it was a large factor in his success.

Every detail of the kitchen, the heat, the flies buzzing aloft, the poor furniture, the dress of the people — all smote him like the lash of a wire whip. His brother was a man of great character. He could see that now. His deep-set, gray eyes and rugged face showed at thirty a man of great natural ability. He had more of the Scotch in his face than Howard, and he looked much older.

He was dressed, like the old man and the boy, in a checked shirt without vest. His suspenders, once gay-colored, had given most of their color to his shirt, and had marked irregular broad bands of pink and brown and green over his shoulders. His hair was uncombed, merely pushed away from his face. He wore a mustache only, though his face was covered with a week's growth of beard. His face was rather gaunt and was brown as leather.

Howard could not eat much. He was disturbed by his mother's strange silence and oppression, and sickened by the long-drawn gasps with which the old man ate his bread and milk, and by the way the boy ate. He had his knife gripped tightly in his fist, knuckles up, and was scooping honey upon his bread.

The baby, having ceased to be afraid, was curious, gazing silently at the stranger.

"Hello, little one! Come and see your uncle. Eh? 'Course 'e will," cooed Howard in the attempt to escape the depressing atmosphere. The little one listened to his inflections as a kitten does, and at last lifted its arms in sign of surrender.

The mother's face cleared up a little. "I declare, she wants to go to you."

" 'Course she does. Dogs and kittens always come to me when I call 'em. Why shouldn't my own niece come?"

He took the little one and began walking up and down the kitchen with her, while she pulled at his beard and nose. "I ought to have you, my lady, in my new comedy. You'd bring down the house."

"You don't mean to say you put babies on the stage, Howard," said his mother in surprise.

"Oh, yes. Domestic comedy must have a baby these days."

"Well, that's another way of makin' a livin', sure," said Grant. The baby had cleared the atmosphere a little. "I s'pose you fellers make a pile of money."

"Sometimes we make a thousand a week; oftener we don't."

"A thousand dollars!" They all stared.

"A thousand dollars sometimes, and then lose it all the next week in another town. The dramatic business is a good deal like gambling — you take your chances."

"I wish you weren't in it, Howard. I don't like to have my son — "

"I wish I was in somethin' that paid better'n farmin'. Anything under God's heavens is better'n farmin'," said Grant.

"No, I ain't laid up much," Howard went on, as if explaining why he hadn't helped them. "Costs me a good deal to live, and I need about ten thousand dollars leeway to work on. I've made a good living, but I — I ain't made any money."

Grant looked at him, darkly meditative.

Howard went on:

"How'd ye come to sell the old farm? I was in hopes — "

"How'd we come to sell it?" said Grant with terrible bitterness. "We had something on it that didn't leave anything to sell. You probably don't remember anything about it, but there was a mortgage on it that eat us up in just four years by the almanac. "Most killed Mother to leave it. We wrote to you for money, but I don't s'pose you remember that."

"No, you didn't."

"Yes, I did."

"When was it? I don't — why, it's — I never received it. It must have been that summer I went with Rob Mannmg to Europe." Howard put the baby down and faced his brother. "Why, Grant, you didn't think I refused to help?"

"Well, it looked that way. We never heard a word from yeh all summer, and when y' did write, it was all about yerself 'n plays 'n things we didn't know anything about. I swore to God I'd never write to you again, and I won't."

"But, good heavens! I never got it."

"Suppose you didn't. You might of known we were poor as Job's off-ox. Everybody is that earns a living. We fellers on the farm have to earn a livin' for ourselves and you fellers that don't work. I don't blame yeh. I'd do it if I could."

"Grant, don't talk so! Howard didn't realize — "

"I tell yeh I don't blame 'im. Only I don't want him to come the brotherly business over me, after livin' as he has — that's all." There was a bitter accusation in the man's voice.

Howard leaped to his feet, his face twitching. "By God, I'll go back tomorrow morning!" he threatened.

"Go, an' be damned! I don't care what yeh do," Grant growled, rising and going out.

"Boys," called the mother, piteously, "it's terrible to see you quarrel."

"But I'm not to blame, Mother," cried Howard in a sickness that made him white as chalk. "The man is a savage. I came home to help you all, not to quarrel."

"Grant's got one o' his fits on," said the young wife, speaking for the first time. "Don't pay any attention to him. He'll be all right in the morning."

"If it wasn't for you, Mother, I'd leave now and never see that savage again."

He lashed himself up and down in the room, in horrible disgust and hate of his brother and of this home in his heart. He remembered his tender anticipations of the homecoming with a kind of self-pity and disgust. This was his greeting!

He went to bed, to toss about on the hard, straw-filled mattress in the stuffy little best room. Tossing, writhing under the bludgeoning of his brother's accusing inflections, a dozen times he said, with a half-articulate snarl:

"He can go to hell! I'll not try to do anything more for him. I don't care if he *is* my brother; he has no right to jump on me like that. On the night of my return, too. My God! he is a brute, a savage!"

He thought of the presents in his trunk and valise which he couldn't show to him that night, after what had been said. He had intended to have such a happy evening of it, such a tender reunion! It was to be so bright and cheery!

In the midst of his cursings, his hot indignation, would come visions of himself in his own modest rooms. He seemed to be yawning and stretching in his beautiful bed, the sun shining in, his books, foils, pictures around him, to say good morning and tempt him to rise, while the squat little clock on the mantel struck eleven warningly.

He could see the olive walls, the unique copper-and-crimson arabesque frieze (his own selection), and the delicate draperies; an open grate full of glowing coals, to temper the sea winds; and in the midst of it, between a landscape by Enneking and an Indian in a canoe in a canyon, by Brush, he saw a somber landscape by a master greater than Millet, a melancholy subject, treated with pitiless fidelity.

A farm in the valley! Over the mountains swept jagged, gray, angry, sprawling clouds, sending a freezing, thin drizzle of rain, as they passed, upon a man following a plow. The horses had a sullen and weary look, and their manes and tails streamed sidewise in the blast. The plowman clad in a ragged gray coat, with uncouth, muddy boots upon his feet, walked with his head inclined toward the sleet, to shield his face from the cold and sting of it. The soil rolled away, black and sticky and with a dull sheen upon it. Nearby, a boy with tears on his cheeks was watching cattle, a dog seated near, his back to the gale.

As he looked at this picture, his heart softened. He looked down at the sleeve of his soft and fleecy nightshirt, at his white, rounded arm, muscular yet fine as a woman's, and when he looked for the picture it was gone. Then came again the assertive odor of stagnant air, laden with camphor; he felt the springless bed under him, and caught dimly a few soap-advertising lithographs on the walls. He thought of his brother, in his still more inhospitable bedroom, disturbed by the child, condemned to rise at five o'clock and begin another day's pitiless labor. His heart shrank and quivered, and the tears started to his eyes.

"I forgive him, poor fellow! He's not to blame."

II

He woke, however, with a dull, languid pulse and an oppressive melancholy on his heart. He looked around the little room, clean enough, but oh, how poor! how barren! Cold plaster walls, a cheap washstand, a wash set of three pieces, with a blue band around each; the windows, rectangular, and fitted with fantastic green shades.

Outside he could hear the bees humming. Chickens were merrily moving about. Cowbells far up the road were sounding irregularly. A jay came by and yelled an insolent reveille, and Howard sat up. He could hear nothing in the house but the rattle of pans on the back side of the kitchen. He looked at his watch and saw it was half-past seven. His brother was in the field by this time, after milking, currying the horses, and eating breakfast — had been at work two hours and a half.

He dressed himself hurriedly in a neglige shirt with a windsor scad, light-colored, serviceable trousers with a belt, russet shoes, and a tennis hat — a knockabout costume, he considered. His mother, good soul, thought it a special suit put on for her benefit and admired it through her glasses.

He kissed her with a bright smile, nodded at Laura the young wife, and tossed the baby, all in a breath, and with the manner, as he himself saw, of the returned captain in the war dramas of the day.

"Been to breakfast?" He frowned reproachfully. "Why didn't you call me? I wanted to get up, just as I used to, at sunrise."

"We thought you was tired, and so we didn't — "

"Tired! Just wait till you see me help Grant pitch hay or something. Hasn't finished his haying, has he?"

'No, I guess not. He will today if it don't rain again."

"Well, breakfast is all ready — Howard," said Laura, hesitating a little on his name.

"Good! I am ready for it. Bacon and eggs, as I'm a jay! Just what I was wanting. I was saying to myself. 'Now if they'll only get bacon and eggs and hot biscuits and honey — ' Oh, say, mother, I heard the bees humming this morning; same noise they used to make when I was a boy, exactly. Must be the same bees. — Hey, you young rascal! come here and have some breakfast with your uncle."

"I never saw her take to anyone so quick," Laura smiled. Howard noticed her in particular for the first time. She had on a clean calico dress and a gingham apron, and she looked strong and fresh and handsome. Her head was intellectual, her eyes full of power. She seemed anxious to remove the impression of her unpleasant looks and words the night before. Indeed, it would have been hard to resist Howard's sunny good nature.

The baby laughed and crowed. The old mother could not take her dim eyes off the face of her son, but sat smiling at him as he ate and rattled on. When he rose from the table at last, after eating heartily and praising it all, he said with a smile:

"Well, now I'll just telephone down to the express and have my trunk brought up. I've got a few little things in there you'll enjoy seeing. But this fellow," indicating the baby, "I didn't take into account. But never mind; Uncle Howard make that all right."

"You ain't goin' to lay it up agin Grant, be you, my son?" Mrs. McLane faltered as they went out into the best room.

"Of course not! He didn't mean it. Now, can't you send word down and have my trunk brought up? Or shall I have to walk down?"

"I guess I'll see somebody goin' down," said Laura.

"All right. Now for the hayfield," he smiled and went out into the glorious morning.

The circling hills the same, yet not the same as at night. A cooler, tenderer, more subdued cloak of color up on them. Far down the valley a cool, deep, impalpable, blue mist lay, under which one divined the river Ian, under its elms and basswoods and wild grapevines. On the shaven slopes of the hills cattle and sheep were feeding, their cries and bells coming to the ear with a sweet suggestiveness. There was something immemorial in the sunny slopes dotted with red and brown and gray cattle.

Walking toward the haymakers, Howard felt a twinge of pain and distrust. Would he ignore it all and smile?

He stopped short. He had not seen Grant smile in so long — he couldn't quite see him smiling. He had been cold and bitter for years. When he came up to them, Grant was pitching on; the old man was loading, and the boy was raking after.

"Good morning," Howard cried cheerily. The old man nodded, the boy stared. Grant growled something, without looking up. These "finical" things of saying good morning and good night are not much practiced in such homes as Grant McLane's.

"Need some help? I'm ready to take a hand. Got on my regimentals this morning."

Grant looked at him a moment.

"You look like it."

"Gimme a hold on that fork, and I'll show you. I'm not so soft as I look, now you bet."

He laid hold upon the fork in Grant's hands, who released it sullenly and stood back sneering. Howard struck the fork into the pile in the old way, threw his left hand to the end of the polished handle, brought it down into the hollow of his thigh, and laid out his strength till the handle bent like a bow. "Oop she rises!" he called laughingly, as the whole pile began slowly to rise, and finally rolled upon the high load.

"Oh, I ain't forgot how to do it," he laughed as he looked around at the boy, who was studying the jacket and hat with a devouring gaze.

Grant was studying him too, but not in admiration.

"I shouldn't say you had," said the old man, tugging at the forkful.

'Mighty funny to come out here and do a little of this. But if you had to come here and do it all the while, you wouldn't look so white and soft in the hands," Grant said as they moved on to another pile. "Give me that fork. You'll be spoiling your fine clothes."

"Oh, these don't matter. They're made for this kind of thing."

"Oh, are they? I guess I'll dress in that kind of a rig. What did that shirt cost? I need one."

"Six dollars a pair; but then it's old."

"And them pants," he pursued; "they cost six dollars, too, didn't they?"

Howard's face darkened. He saw his brother's purpose. He resented it. "They cost fifteen dollars, if you want to know, and the shoes cost six-fifty. This ring on my cravat cost sixty dollars, and the suit I had on last night cost eighty-five. My suits are made by Breckstein, on Fifth Avenue and Twentieth Street, if you want to patronize him," he ended brutally, spurred on by the sneer in his brother's eyes. "I'll introduce you."

"Good idea," said Grant with a forced, mocking smile. "I need just such a get up for haying and corn plowing. Singular I never thought of it. Now my pants cost eighty-five cents, s'penders fifteen, hat twenty, shoes one-fifty; stockin's I don't bother about."

He had his brother at a disadvantage, and he grew fluent and caustic as he went on, almost changing places with Howard, who took the rake out of the boy's hands and followed, raking up the scatterings.

"Singular we fellers here are discontented and mulish, am't it? Singular we don't believe your letters when you write, sayin', 'I just about make a live of it'? Singular we think the country's goin' to hell, we fellers, in a two dollar suit, wadin' around in the mud or sweatin' around in the hayfield, while you fellers lay around New York and smoke and wear good clothes and toady to millionaires?"

Howard threw down the rake and folded his arms. 'My God! you're enough to make a man forget the same mother bore us!"

"I guess it wouldn't take much to make you forget that. You ain't put much thought on me nor her for ten years."

The old man cackled, the boy grinned, and Howard, sick and weak with anger and sorrow, turned away and walked down toward the brook. He had tried once more to get near his brother and had failed. O God! how miserably, pitiably! The hot blood gushed all over him as he thought of the shame and disgrace of it.

He, a man associating with poets, artists, sought after by brilliant women, accustomed to deference even from such people, to be sneered at, outfaced, shamed, shoved aside, by a man in a stained hickory shirt and patched overalls, and that man his brother! He lay down on the bright grass, with the sheep all around him, and writhed and groaned with the agony and despair of it.

And worst of all, underneath it was a consciousness that Grant was right in distrusting him. He *had* neglected him; he *had* said, "I guess they're getting along all right." He had put them behind him when the invitation to spend summer on the Mediterranean or in the Adirondacks came.

"What can I do? What can I do?" he groaned.

The sheep nibbled the grass near him, the jays called pertly, "Shame, shame," a quail piped somewhere on the hillside, and the brook sung a soft, soothing melody that took away at last the sharp edge of his pain, and he sat up and gazed down the valley, bright with the sun and apparently filled with happy and prosperous people.

Suddenly a thought seized him. He stood up so suddenly the sheep fled in affright. He leaped the brook, crossed the flat, and began searching in the bushes on the hillside. "Hurrah!" he said with a smile.

He had found an old road which he used to travel when a boy — a road that skirted the edge of the valley, now grown up to brush, but still passable for footmen. As he ran lightly along down the beautiful path, under oaks and hickories, past masses of poison ivy, under hanging grapevines, through clumps of splendid hazelnut bushes loaded with great sticky, rough, green burrs, his heart threw off part of its load.

How it all came back to him! How many days, when the autumn sun burned the frost off the bushes, had he gathered hazelnuts here with his boy and girl friends — Hugh and Shelley McTurg, Rome Sawyer, Orrin McIlvaine, and the rest! What had become of them all? How he had forgotten them!

This thought stopped him again, and he fell into a deep muse, leaning against an oak tree and gazing into the vast fleckless space above. The thrilling, inscrutable mystery of life fell upon him like a blinding light. Why was he living in the crush and thunder and mental unrest of a great city, while his companions, seemingly his equal, in powers, were milking cows, making butter, and growing corn and wheat in the silence and drear monotony of the farm?

His boyish sweethearts! Their names came back to his ear now with a dull, sweet sound as of faint bells. He saw their faces, their pink sunbonnets tipped back upon their necks, their brown ankles flying with the swift action of the scurrying partridge. His eyes softened; he took off his hat. The sound of the wind and the leaves moved him almost to tears.

A woodpecker gave a shrill, high-keyed, sustained cry, "Ki, ki, ki!" and he started from his reverie, the dapples of sun and shade falling upon his lithe figure as he hurried on down the path.

He came at last to a field of corn that ran to the very wall of a large weather-beaten house, the sight of which made his breathing quicker. It was the place where he was born. The mystery of his life began there. In the branches of those poplar and hickory trees he had swung and sung in the rushing breeze, fearless as a squirrel. Here was the brook where, like a larger Kildee, he with Grant had waded after crawfish, or had stolen upon some wary trout, rough-cut pole in hand.

Seeing someone in the garden, he went down along the corn row through the rustling ranks of green leaves. An old woman was picking berries, a squat and shapeless figure.

"Good morning," he called cheerily.

"Morgen," she said, looklng up at him with a startled and very red face. She was German in every line of her body.

"Ich bin Herr McLane," he said after a pause.

"So?" she replied with a questioning inflection.

"Yah; ich bin Herr Grant's bruder."

"Ach, So!" she said with a downward inflection. "Ich no spick Inglish. No spick Inglis."

"Ich bin durstig," he said. Leaving her pans, she went with him to the house, which was what he wanted to see.

"Ich bin hier geboren."

"Ach, so!" She recognized the little bit of sentiment, and said some sentences in German whose general meaning was sympathy. She took him to the cool cellar where the spring had been trained to run into a tank containing pans of cream and milk, she gave him a cool draught from a large tin cup, and then at his request they went upstairs. The house was the same, but somehow seemed cold and empty. It was clean and sweet, but it had so little evidence of being lived in. The old part, which was built of logs, was used as best room, and modeled after the best rooms of the neighboring Yankee homes, only it was emptier, without the cabinet organ and the rag carpet and the chromos.

The old fireplace was bricked up and plastered — the fireplace beside which in the far-off days he had lain on winter nights, to hear his uncles tell tales of hunting, or to hear them play the violin, great dreaming giants that they were.

The old woman went out and left him sitting there, the center of a swarm of memories coming and going like so many ghostly birds and butterflies.

A curious heartache and listlessness, a nerveless mood came on him. What was it worth, anyhow — success? Struggle, strife, trampling on someone else. His play crowding out some other poor fellow's hope. The hawk eats the partridge, the partridge eats the flies and bugs, the bugs eat each other, and the hawk, when he in his turn is shot by man. So, in the world of business, the life of one man seemed to him to be drawn from the life of another man, each success to spring from other failures.

He was like a man from whom all motives had been withdrawn. He was sick, sick to the heart. Oh, to be a boy again! An ignorant baby, pleased with a block and string, with no knowledge and no care of the great unknown! To lay his head again on his mother's bosom and rest! To watch the flames on the hearth!

Why not? Was not that the very thing to do? To buy back the old farm? It would cripple him a little for the next season, but he could do it. Think of it! To see his mother back in the old home, with the fireplace restored, the old furniture in the sitting room around her, and fine new things in the parlor!

His spirits rose again. Grant couldn't stand out when he brought to him a deed of the farm. Surely his debt would be canceled when he had seen them all back in the wide old kitchen. He began to plan and to dream. He went to the windows and looked out on the yard to see how much it had changed.

He'd build a new barn and buy them a new carriage. His heart glowed again, and his lips softened into their usual feminine grace — lips a little full and falling easily into curves.

The old German woman came in at length, bringing some cakes and a bowl of milk, smiling broadly and hospitably as she waddled forward.

"Ach! Goot!" he said, smacking his lips over the pleasant draught.

"Wo ist ihre goot mann?" he inquired, ready for business.

III

When Grant came in at noon, Mrs. McLane met him at the door with a tender smile on her face.

"Where's Howard, Grant?"

"I don't know," he replied in a tone that implied "I don't care."

The dim eyes clouded with quick tears.

"Ain't you seen him?"

"Not since nine o'clock."

"Where d'you think he is?"

"I tell yeh I don't know. He'll take care of himself; don't worry."

He flung off his hat and plunged into the wash basin. His shirt was wet with sweat and covered with dust of the hay and fragments of leaves. He splashed his burning face with the water, paying no further attention to his mother. She spoke again, very gently, in reproof:

"Grant, why do you stand out against Howard so?"

"I don't stand out against him," he replied harshly, pausing with the towel in his hands. His eyes were hard and piercing. "But if he expects me to gush over his coming back, he's fooled, that's all. He's left us to paddle our own canoe all this while, and, so far as I'm concerned, he can leave us alone hereafter. He looked out for his precious hide mighty well, and now he comes back here to play big gun and pat us on the head. I don't propose to let him come that over me."

Mrs. McLane knew too well the temper of her son to say any more, but she inquired about Howard of the old hired man.

"He went off down the valley. He 'n' Grant had s'm words, and he pulled out down toward the old farm. That's the last I see of 'im."

Laura took Howard's part at the table. "Pity you can't be decent," she said, brutally direct as usual. "You treat Howard as if he was a-a-I do' know what."

"Will you let me alone?"

"No, I won't. If you think I'm going to set by an' agree to your bullyraggin' him, you're mistaken. It's a shame! You're mad 'cause he's succeeded and you ain't. He ain't to blame for his brains. If you and I'd had any, we'd 'a' succeeded, too. It ain't our fault and it ain't his; so what's the use?"

There was a look came into Grant's face that the wife knew. It meant bitter and terrible silence. He ate his dinner without another word.

It was beginning to cloud up. A thin, whitish, all-pervasive vapor which meant rain was dimming the sky, and he forced his hands to their utmost during the afternoon in order to get most of the down hay in before the rain came. He was pitching hay up into the barn when Howard came by just before one o'clock.

It was windless there. The sun fell through the white mist with undiminished fury, and the fragrant hay sent up a breath that was hot as an oven draught. Grant was a powerful man, and there was something majestic in his action as he rolled the huge flakes of hay through the door. The sweat poured from his face like rain, and he was forced to draw his dripping sleeve across his face to clear away the blinding sweat that poured into his eyes.

Howard stood and looked at him in silence, remembering how often he had worked there in that furnace heat, his muscles quivering, cold chills running over his flesh, red shadows dancing before his eyes.

His mother met him at the door anxiously, but smiled as she saw his pleasant face and cheerful eyes.

"You're a little late, m' son."

Howard spent most of the afternoon sitting with his mother on the porch, or under the trees, lying sprawled out like a boy, resting at times with sweet forgetfulness of the whole world, but feeling a dull pain whenever he remembered the stern, silent man pitching hay in the hot sun on the torrid side of the barn.

His mother did not say anything about the quarrel; she feared to reopen it.

She talked mainly of old times in a gentle monotone of reminiscence, while he listened, looking up into her patient face.

The heat slowly lessened as the sun sank down toward the dun clouds rising like a more distant and majestic line of mountains beyond the western hills. The sound of cowbells came irregularly to the ear, and the voices and sounds of the haying fields had a jocund, thrilling effect on the ear of the city dweller.

He was very tender. Everything conspired to make him simple, direct, and honest.

"Mother, if you'll only forgive me for staying away so long, I'll surely come to see you every summer."

She had nothing to forgive. She was so glad to have him there at her feet — her great, handsome, successful boy! She could only love him and enjoy him every moment of the precious days. If Grant would only reconcile himself to Howard! That was the great thorn in her flesh.

Howard told her how he had succeeded.

"It was luck, Mother. First I met Cooke, and he introduced me to Jake Saulsman of Chicago. Jake asked me to go to New York with him, and — I don't know why — took a fancy to me some way. He introduced me to a lot of the fellows in New York, and they all helped me along. I did nothing to merit it. Everybody helps me. Anybody can succeed in that way."

The doting mother thought it not at all strange that they all helped him.

At the supper table Grant was gloomily silent, ignoring Howard completely. Mrs. McLane sat and grieved silently, not daring to say a word in protest. Laura and the baby tried to amuse Howard, and under cover of their talk the meal was eaten.

The boy fascinated Howard. He "sawed wood" with a rapidity and uninterruptedness which gave alarm. He had the air of coaling up for a long voyage.

"At that age," Howard thought, "I must have gripped my knife in my right hand so, and poured my tea into my saucer so. I must have buttered and bit into a huge slice of bread just so, and chewed at it with a smacking sound in just that way. I must have gone to the length of scooping up honey with my knife blade."

It was magically, mystically beautiful over all this squalor and toil and bitterness, from five till seven — a moving hour. Again the falling sun streamed in broad banners across the valleys; again the blue mist lay far down the coulee over the river; the cattle called from the hills in the moistening, sonorous air; the bells came in a pleasant tangle of sound; the air pulsed with the deepening chorus of katydids and other nocturnal singers.

Sweet and deep as the very springs of his life was all this to the soul of the elder brother; but in the midst of it, the younger man, in ill-smelling clothes and great boots that chafed his feet, went out to milk the cows — on whose legs the flies and mosquitoes swarmed, bloated with blood — to sit by the hot side of the cow and be lashed with her tall as she tried frantically to keep the savage insects from eating her raw.

"The poet who writes of milking the cows does it from the hammock, looking on," Howard soliloquized as he watched the old man Lewis racing around the filthy yard after one of the young heifers that had kicked over the pail in her agony with the flies and was unwilling to stand still and be eaten alive.

"So, so! you beast!" roared the old man as he finally cornered the shrinking, nearly frantic creature.

"Don't you want to look at the garden?" asked Mrs. McLane of Howard; and they went out among the vegetables and berries.

The bees were coming home heavily laden and crawling slowly into the hives. The level, red light streamed through the trees, blazed along the grass, and lighted a few old-fashioned flowers into red and gold flame. It was beautiful, and Howard looked at it through his half-shut eyes as the painters do, and turned away with a sigh at the sound of blows where the wet and grimy men were assailing the frantic cows.

"There's Wesley with your trunk," Mrs. McLane said, recalling him to himself.

Wesley helped him carry the trunk in and waved off thanks.

"Oh, that's all right," he said; and Howard knew the Western man too well to press the matter of pay.

As he went in an hour later and stood by the trunk, the dull ache came back into his heart. How he had failed! It seemed like a bitter mockery now to show his gifts.

Grant had come in from his work, and with his feet released from his chafing boots, in his wet shirt and milk-splashed overalls, sat at the kitchen table reading a newspaper which he held close to a small kerosene lamp. He paid no attention to anyone. His attitude, curiously like his father's, was perfectly definite to Howard. It meant that from that time forward there were to be no words of any sort between them. It meant that they were no longer brothers, not even acquaintances. "How inexorable that face!" thought Howard.

He turned sick with disgust and despair, and would have closed his trunk without showing any of the presents, only for the childish expectancy of his mother and Laura.

"Here's something for you, Mother," he said, assuming a cheerful voice as he took a fold of fine silk from the trunk and held it up. "All the way from Paris."

He laid it on his mother's lap and stooped and kissed her, and then turned hastily away to hide the tears that came to his own eyes as he saw her keen pleasure.

"And here's a parasol for Laura. I don't know how I came to have that in here. And here's General Grant's autobiography for his namesake," he said with an effort at carelessness, and waited to hear Grant rise.

"Grant, won't you come in?" asked his mother quiveringly.

Grant did not reply nor move. Laura took the handsome volumes out and laid them beside him on the table. He simply pushed them to one side and went on with his reading.

Again that horrible anger swept hot as flame over Howard. He could have cursed him. His hands shook as he handed out other presents to his mother and Laura and the baby. He tried to joke.

"I didn't know how old the baby was, so she'll have to grow to some of these things."

But the pleasure was all gone for him and for the rest. His heart swelled almost to a feeling of pain as he looked at his mother. There she sat with the presents in her lap. The shining silk came too late for her. It threw into appalling relief her age, her poverty, her work-weary frame. "My God!" he almost cried aloud, "how little it would have taken to lighten her life!"

Upon this moment, when it seemed as if he could endure no more, came the smooth voice of William McTurg:

"Hello, folkses!"

"Hello, Uncle Bill! Come in."

"That's what we came for," laughed a woman's voice.

"Is that you, Rose?" asked Laura.

"It's me — Rose," replied the laughing girl as she bounced into the room and greeted everybody in a breathless sort of way.

"You don't mean little Rosy?"

"Big Rosy now," said William.

Howard looked at the handsome girl and smiled, saying in a nasal sort of tone, "Wal, wal! Rosy, how you've growed since I saw yeh!"

"Oh, look at all this purple and fine linen! Am I left out?"

Rose was a large girl of twenty-five or thereabouts, and was called an old maid. She radiated good nature from every line of her buxom self. Her black eyes were full of drollery, and she was on the best of terms with Howard at once. She had been a teacher, but that did not prevent her from assuming a peculiar directness of speech. Of course they talked about old friends.

"Where's Rachel?" Howard inquired. Her smile faded away.

"Shellie married Orrin McIlvaine. They're way out in Dakota. Shellie's havin' a hard row of stumps."

There was a little silence.

"And Tommy?"

"Gone West. Most all the boys have gone West. That's the reason there's so many old maids."

"You don't mean to say — "

"I don't *need* to say-I'm an old maid. Lots of the girls are."

"It don't pay to marry these days."

"Are you married?"

"Not yet." His eyes lighted up again in a humorous way.

"Not yet! That's good! That's the way old maids all talk."

"You don't mean to tell me that no young fellow comes prowling around — "

"Oh, a young Dutchman or Norwegian once in a while. Nobody that counts. Fact is, we're getting like Boston — four women to one man; and when you consider that we're getting more particular each year, the outlook is — well, it's dreadful!"

"It certainly is."

"Marriage is a failure these days for most of us. We can't live on the farm, and can't get a living in the city, and there we are." She laid her hand on his arm. "I declare, Howard, you're the same boy you used to be. I ain't a bit afraid of you, for all your success."

"And you're the same girl? No, I can't say that. It seems to me you've grown more than I have — I don't mean physically, I mean mentally," he explained as he saw her smile in the defensive way a fleshy girl has, alert to ward off a joke.

They were in the midst of talk, Howard telling one of his funny stories, when a wagon clattered up to the door and merry voices called loudly:

"Whoa, there, Sampson!"

"Hullo, the house!"

Rose looked at her father with a smile in her black eyes exactly like his. They went to the door.

"Hullo! What's wanted?"

"Grant McLane live here?"

"Yup. Right here."

A moment later there came a laughing, chatting squad of women to the door. Mrs. McLane and Laura stared at each other in amazement. Grant went outdoors.

Rose stood at the door as if she were hostess.

"Come in, Nettie. Glad to see yeh — glad to see yeh! Mrs. McIlvaine, come right in! Take a seat. Make yerself to home, *do!* And Mrs. Peavey! Wal, I never! This must be a surprise party. Well, I swan! How many more o' ye air they?"

All was confusion, merriment, handshakings as Rose introduced them in her roguish way.

"Folks, this is Mr. Howard McLane of New York. He's an actor, but it hain't spoiled him a bit as I can see. How, this is Nettie McIlvaine — Wilson that was."

Howard shook hands with Nettie, a tall, plain girl with prominent teeth.

"This is Ma McIlvaine."

"She looks just the same," said Howard, shaking her hand and feeling how hard and work-worn it was.

And so amid bustle, chatter, and invitations "to lay off y'r things an' stay awhile," the women got disposed about the room at last. Those that had rocking chairs rocked vigorously to and fro to hide their embarrassment. They all talked in loud voices.

Howard felt nervous under this furtive scrutiny. He wished his clothes didn't look so confoundedly dressy. Why didn't he have sense enough to go and buy a fifteen-dollar suit of diagonals for everyday wear.

Rose was the life of the party. Her tongue rattled on in the most delightful way.

"It's all Rose an' Bill's doin's," Mrs. McIlvaine explained. "They told us to come over an' pick up anybody we see on the road. So we did."

Howard winced a little at her familiarity of tone. He couldn't help it for the life of him.

"Well, I wanted to come tonight because I'm going away next week, and I wanted to see how he'd act at a surprise party again," Rose explained.

"Married, I s'pose," said Mrs. McIlvaine abruptly.

"No, not yet."

"Good land! Why, y' mus' be thirty-five, How. Must a dis'p'inted y'r mam not to have a young 'un to call 'er granny."

The men came clumping in, talking about haying and horses. Some of the older ones Howard knew and greeted, but the younger ones were mainly too much changed. They were all very ill at ease. Most of them were in compromise dress — something lying between working "rig" and Sunday dress. Most of them had on clean shirts and paper collars, and wore their Sunday coats (thick woolen garments) over rough trousers. All of them crossed their legs at once, and most of them sought the wall and leaned back perilously upon the hind legs of their chairs, eyeing Howard slowly.

For the first few minutes the presents were the subjects of conversation. The women especially spent a good deal of talk upon them.

Howard found himself forced to taking the initiative, so he inquired about the crops and about the farms.

"I see you don't plow the hills as we used to. And reap! *What* a job it ust to be. It makes the hills more beautiful to have them covered with smooth grass and cattle."

There was only dead silence to this touching upon the idea of beauty.

"I s'pose it pays reasonably."

"Not enough to kill," said one of the younger men. "You c'n see that by the houses we live in — that is, most of us. A few that came in early an' got land cheap, like McIlvaine, here — he got a lift that the rest of us can't get."

"I'm a free trader, myself," said one young fellow, blushing and looking away as Howard turned and said cheerily:

"So'm I."

The rest semed to feel that this was a tabooed subject — a subject to be talked out of doors, where one could prance about and yell and do justice to it.

Grant sat silently in the kitchen doorway, not saying a word, not looking at his. brother.

"Well, I don't never use hot vinegar for mine," Mrs. McIlvaine was heard to say. "I jest use hot water, an' I rinse 'em out good, and set 'em bottom-side up in the sun. I do' know but what hot vinegar would be more cleansin'."

Rose had the younger folks in a giggle with a droll telling of a joke on herself.

"How'd y' stop 'em from laffin'?"

"I let 'em laugh. Oh, my school is a disgrace — so one director says. But I like to see children laugh. It broadens their cheeks."

"Yes, that's all handwork." Laura was showing the baby's Sunday clothes.

"Goodness Peter! How do you find time to do so much?"

"I take time."

Howard, being the lion of the evening, tried his best to be agreeable. He kept near his mother, because it afforded her so much pride and satisfaction, and because he was obliged to keep away from Grant, who had begun to talk to the men. Howard talked mainly about their affairs, but still was forced more and more into talking of life in the city. As he told of the theater and the concerts, a sudden change fell upon them; they grew sober, and he felt deep down in the hearts of these people a melancholy which was expressed only elusively with little tones or sighs. Their gaiety was fitful.

They were hungry for the world, for art — these young people. Discontented and yet hardly daring to acknowledge it; indeed, few of them could have made definite statement of their dissatisfaction. The older people felt it less. They practically said, with a sigh of pathetic resignation:

"Well, I don't expect ever to see these things *now*."

A casual observer would have said, "What a pleasant bucolic — this little surprise party of welcome!" But Howard with his native ear and eye had no such pleasing illusion. He knew too well these suggestions of despair and bitterness. He knew that, like the smile of the slave, this cheerfulness was self-defense; deep down was another self.

Seeing Grant talking with a group of men over by the kitchen door, he crossed over slowly and stood listening. Wesley Cosgrove — a tall, rawboned young fellow with a grave, almost tragic face — was saying:

"Of course I ain't. Who is? A man that's satisfied to live as we do is a fool."

"The worst of it is," said Grant without seeing Howard, a man can't get out of it during his lifetime, and *I* don't know that he'll have any chance in the next-the speculator'll be there ahead of us."

The rest laughed, but Grant went on grimly:

"Ten years ago Wes, here, could have got land in Dakota pretty easy, but now it's about all a feller's life's worth to try it. I tell you things seem shuttin' down on us fellers."

"Plenty o' land to rent?" suggested someone.

"Yes, in terms that skin a man alive. More than that, farmin' ain't so free a life as it used to be. This cattle-raisin' and butter-makin' makes a nigger of a man. Binds him right down to the grindstone, and he gets nothin' out of it — that's what rubs it in. He simply wallers around in the manure for somebody else. I'd like to know what a man's life is worth who lives as we do? How much higher is it than the lives the niggers used to live?"

These brutally bald words made Howard thrill with emotion like some great tragic poem. A silence fell on the group.

"That's the God's truth, Grant," said young Cosgrove after a pause.

"A man like me is helpless," Grant was saying. "Just like a fly in a pan of molasses. There ain't any escape for him. The more he tears around, the more liable he is to rip his legs off."

"What can he do?"

The men listened in silence.

"Oh, come, don't talk politics all night!" cried Rose, breaking in. "Come, let's have a dance. Where's that fiddle?"

"Fiddle!" cried Howard, glad of a chance to laugh. "Well, now! Bring out that fiddle. Is it William's?"

"Yes, Pap's old fiddle."

"Oh, gosh! he don't want to hear me play," protested William. "He's heard s' many fiddlers."

"Fiddlers! I've heard a thousand violinists, but not fiddlers. Come, give us 'Honest John.' "

William took the fiddle in his work-calloused and crooked hands and began tuning it. The group at the kitchen door turned to listen, their faces lighting up a little. Rose tried to get a set on the floor.

"Oh, good land!" said some. "We're all tuckered out. What makes you so anxious?"

"She wants a chance to dance with the New Yorker."

"That's it exactly," Rose admitted.

"Wal, if you'd churned and mopped and cooked for hayin' hands as I have today, you wouldn't be so full o' nonsense."

"Oh, bother! Life's short. Come quick, get Bettie out. Come, Wes, never mind your hobbyhorse."

By incredible exertion she got a set on the floor, and William got the fiddle in tune. Howard looked across at Wesley, and thought the change in him splendidly dramatic. His face had lighted up into a kind of deprecating, boyish smile. Rose could do anything with him.

William played some of the old tunes that had a thousand associated memories in Howard's brain, memories of harvest moons, of melon feasts, and of clear, cold winter nights. As he danced, his eyes filled with a tender, luminous light. He came closer to them all than he had been able to do before. Grant had gone out into the kitchen.

After two or three sets had been danced, the company took seats and could not be stirred again. So Laura and Rose disappeared for a few moments, and returning, served strawberries and cream, which she "just happened to have in the house."

And then William played again. His fingers, now grown more supple, brought out clearer, firmer tones. As he played, silence fell on these people. The magic of music sobered every face; the women looked older and more careworn, the men slouched sullenly in their chairs or leaned back against the wall.

It seemed to Howard as if the spirit of tragedy had entered this house. Music had always been William's unconscious expression of his unsatisfied desires. He was never melancholy except when he played. Then his eyes grew somber, his drooping face full of shadows.

He played on slowly, softly, wailing Scotch tunes and mournful Irish songs. He seemed to find in the songs of these people, and especially in a wild, sweet, low-keyed Negro song, some expression for his indefinable inner melancholy.

He played on, forgetful of everybody, his long beard sweeping the violin, his toilworn hands marvelously obedient to his will.

At last he stopped, looked up with a faint, deprecating smile, and said with a sigh:

"Well, folkses, time to go home."

The going was quiet. Not much laughing. Howard stood at the door and said good night to them all, his heart very tender.

"Come and see us," they said.

"I will," he replied cordially. "I'll try and get around to see everybody, and talk over old times, before I go back."

After the wagons had driven out of the yard, Howard turned and put his arm about his mother's neck.

"Tired?"

"A little."

"Well, now, good night. I'm going for a little stroll." His brain was too active to sleep. He kissed his mother good night and went out into the road, his hat in his hand, the cool, moist wind on his hair.

It was very dark, the stars being partly hidden by a thin vapor. On each side the hills rose, every line familiar as the face of an old friend. A whippoorwill called occasionally from the hillside, and the spasmodic jangle of a bell now and then told of some cow's battle with the mosquitoes.

As he walked, he pondered upon the tragedy he had rediscovered in these people's lives. Out here under the inexorable spaces of the sky, a deep distaste of his own life took possession of him. He felt like giving it all up. He thought of the infinite tragedy of these lives which the world loves to call "peaceful and pastoral." His mind went out in the aim to help them. What could he do to make life better worth living? Nothing.

They must live and die practically as he saw them tonight.

And yet he knew this was a mood, and that in a few hours the love and the habit of life would come back upon him and upon them; that he would go back to the city in a few days; that these people would live on and make the best of it.

"*I'll* make the best of it," he said at last, and his thought came back to his mother and Grant.

IV

The next day was a rainy day; not a shower, but a steady rain — an unusual thing in midsummer in the West. A cold, dismal day in the fireless, colorless farmhouses. It came to Howard in that peculiar reaction which surely comes during a visit of this character, when thought is a weariness, when the visitor longs for his own familiar walls and pictures and books, and longs to meet his friends, feeling at the same time the tragedy of life which makes friends nearer and more congenial than blood relations.

Howard ate his breakfast alone, save Baby and Laura, its mother, going about the room. Baby and mother alike insisted on feeding him to death. Already dyspeptic pangs were setting in.

"Now ain't there something more I can — "

"Good heavens! No!" he cried in dismay. "I'm likely to die of dyspepsia now. This honey and milk, and these delicious hot biscuits — "

"I'm afraid it ain't much like the breakfasts you have in the city."

"Well, no, it ain't," he confessed. "But this is the kind a man needs when he lives in the open air."

She sat down opposite him, with her elbows on the table, her chin in her palm, her eyes full of shadows.

"I'd like to go to a city once. I never saw a town bigger'n Lumberville. I've never seen a play, but I've read of 'em in the magazines. It must be wonderful; they say they have wharves and real ships coming up to the wharf, and people getting off and on. How do they do it?"

"Oh, that's too long a story to tell. It's a lot of machinery and paint and canvas. If I told you how it was done, you wouldn't enjoy it so well when you come on and see it."

"Do you ever expect to see me in New York?"

"Why, yes. Why not? I expect Grant to come on and bring you all some day, especially Tonikins here. Tonikins, you hear, sir? I expect you to come on you' forf birfday, sure." He tried thus to stop the woman's gloomy confidence.

"I hate farm life," she went on with a bitter inflection. "It's nothing but fret, fret and work the whole time, never going any place, never seeing anybody but a lot of neighbors just as big fools as you are. I spend my time fighting flies and washing dishes and churning. I'm sick of it all."

Howard was silent. What could he say to such an indictment? The ceiling swarmed with flies which the cold rain had driven to seek the warmth of the kitchen. The gray rain was falling with a dreary sound outside, and down the kitchen stovepipe an occasional drop fell on the stove with a hissing, angry sound.

The young wife went on with a deeper note:

"I lived in Lumberville two years, going to school, and I know a little something of what city life is. If I was a man, I bet I wouldn't wear my life out on a farm, as Grant does. I'd get away and I'd do something. I wouldn't care what, but I'd get away."

There was a certain volcanic energy back of all the woman said that made Howard feel she'd make the attempt. She didn't know that the struggle for a place to stand on this planet was eating the heart and soul out of men and women in the city, just as in the country. But he could say nothing. If he had said in conventional phrase, sitting there in his soft clothing, "We must make the best of it all," the woman could justly have thrown the dishcloth in his face. He could say nothing.

"I was a fool for ever marrying," she went on, while the baby pushed a chair across the room. "I made a decent living teaching, I was free to come and go, my money was my own. Now I'm fled right down to a churn or a dishpan, I never have a cent of my own. *He's* growlin' round half the time, and there's no chance of his ever being different."

She stopped with a bitter sob in her throat. She forgot she was talking to her husband's brother. She was conscious only of his sympathy.

As if a great black cloud had settled down upon him, Howard felt it all — the horror, hopelessness, immanent tragedy of it all. The glory of nature, the bounty and splendor of the sky, only made it the more benumbing. He thought of a sentence Millet once wrote:

"I see very well the aureole of the dandelions, and the sun also, far down there behind the hills, flinging his glory upon the clouds. But not alone that — I see in the plains the smoke of the tired horses at the plough, or, on a stony-hearted spot of ground, a back-broken man trying to raise himself upright for a moment to breathe. The tragedy is surrounded by glories — that is no invention of mine."

Howard arose abruptly and went back to his little bedroom, where he walked up and down the floor till he was calm enough to write, and then he sat down and poured it all out to "Dearest Margaret," and his first sentence was this:

"If it were not *for* you (just to let you know the mood I'm in) — if it were not for you, and I had the world in my hands, I'd crush it like a puff-ball; evil so predominates, suffering is so universal and persistent, happiness so fleeting and so infrequent."

He wrote on for two hours, and by the time he had sealed and directed several letters he felt calmer, but still terribly depressed. The rain was still falling, sweeping down from the half-seen hills, wreathing the wooded peaks with a gray garment of mist and filling the valley with a whitish cloud.

It fell around the house drearily. It ran down into the tubs placed to catch it, dripped from the mossy pump, and drummed on the upturned milk pails, and upon the brown and yellow beehives under the maple trees. The chickens seemed depressed, but the irrepressible bluejay screamed amid it all, with the same insolent spirit, his plumage untarnished by the wet. The barnyard showed a horrible mixture of mud and mire, through which Howard caught glimpses of the men, slumping to and fro without more additional protection than a ragged coat and a shapeless felt hat.

In the sitting room where his mother sat sewing there was not an ornament, save the etching he had brought. The clock stood on a small shell, its dial so much defaced that one could not tell the time of day; and when it struck, it was with noticeably disproportionate deliberation, as if it wished to correct any mistake into which the family might have fallen by reason of its illegible dial.

The paper on the walls showed the first concession of the Puritans to the Spirit of Beauty, and was made up of a heterogeneous mixture of flowers of unheard-of shapes and colors, arranged in four different ways along the wall. There were no books, no music, and only a few newspapers in sight — a bare, blank, cold, drab-colored shelter from the rain, not a home. Nothing cozy, nothing heart-warming; a grim and horrible shed.

"What are they doing? It can't be they're at work such a day as this," Howard said, standing at the window.

"They find plenty to do, even on rainy days," answered his mother. "Grant always has some job to set the men at. It's the only way to live."

"I'll go out and see them." He turned suddenly. "Mother, why should Grant treat me so? Have I deserved it?"

Mrs. McLane sighed in pathetic hopelessness. "I don't know, Howard. I'm worried about Grant. He gets more an' more downhearted an' gloomy every day. Seem's if he'd go crazy. He don't care how he looks anymore, won't dress up on

Sunday. Days an' days he'll go aroun' not sayin' a word. I was in hopes you could help him, Howard."

"My coming seems to have had an opposite effect. He hasn't spoken a word to me, except when he had to, since I came. Mother, what do you say to going home with me to New York?"

"Oh, I couldn't do that!" she cried in terror. "I couldn't live in a big city — never!"

"There speaks the truly rural mind," smiled Howard at his mother, who was looking up at him through her glasses with a pathetic forlornness which sobered him again. "Why, Mother, you could live in Orange, New Jersey, or out in Connecticut, and be just as lonesome as you are here. You wouldn't need to live in the city. I could see you then every day or two."

"Well, I couldn't leave Grant an' the baby, anyway," she replied, not realizing how one could live in New Jersey and do business daily in New York.

"Well, then, how would you like to go back into the old house?" he said, facing her.

The patient hands fell to the lap, the dim eyes fixed in searching glance on his face. There was a wistful cry in the voice.

"Oh, Howard! Do you mean — "

He came and sat down by her, and put his arm about her and hugged her hard. "I mean, you dear, good, patient, work-weary old Mother, I'm going to buy back the old farm and put you in it."

There was no refuge for her now except in tears, and she put up her thin, trembling old hands about his neck and cried in that easy, placid, restful way age has.

Howard could not speak. His throat ached with remorse and pity. He saw his forgetfulness of them all once more without relief — the black thing it was!

"There, there, Mother, don't cry!" he said, torn with anguish by her tears. Measured by man's tearlessness, her weeping seemed terrible to him. "I didn't realize how things were going here. It was all my fault — or, at least, most of it. Grant's letter didn't reach me. I thought you were still on the old farm. But no matter; it's all over now. Come, don't cry anymore, Mother dear. I'm going to take care of you now."

It had been years since the poor, lonely woman had felt such warmth of love. Her sons had been like her husband, chary of expressing their affection; and like most Puritan families, there was little of caressing among them. Sitting there with the rain on the roof and driving through the trees, they planned getting back into the old house. Howard's plan seemed to her full of splendor and audacity. She began to understand his power and wealth now, as he put it into concrete form before her.

"I wish I could eat Thanksgiving dinner there with you," he said at last, "but it can't be thought of. However, I'll have you all in there before I go home. I'm going out now and tell Grant. Now don't worry any more; I'm going to fix it all up with him, sure." He gave her a parting hug.

Laura advised him not to attempt to get to the barn; but as he persisted in going, she hunted up an old rubber coat for him. "You'll mire down and spoil your shoes," she said, glancing at his neat calf gaiters.

"Darn the difference!" he laughed in his old way. "Besides, I've got rubbers."

"Better go round by the fence," she advised as he stepped out into the pouring rain.

How wretchedly familiar it all was! The miry cow yard, with the hollow trampled out around the horse trough, the disconsolate hens standing under the wagons and sheds, a pig wallowing across its sty, and for atmosphere the desolate, falling rain. It was so familiar he felt a pang of the old rebellious despair which seized him on such days in his boyhood.

Catching up courage, he stepped out on the grass, opened the gate, and entered the barnyard. A narrow ribbon of turf ran around the fence, on which he could walk by clinging with one hand to the rough boards. In this way he slowly made his way around the periphery, and came at last to the open barn door without much harm.

It was a desolate interior. In the open floorway Grant, seated upon a half-bushel, was mending a harness. The old man was holding the trace in his hard brown hands; the boy was lying on a wisp of hay. It was a small barn, and poor at that. There was a bad smell, as of dead rats, about it, and the rain fell through the shingles here and there. To the right, and below, the horses stood, looking up with their calm and beautiful eyes, in which the whole scene was idealized.

Grant looked up an instant and then went on with his work.

"Did yeh wade through?" grinned Lewis, exposing his broken teeth.

"No, I kinder circumambiated the pond." He sat down on the little toolbox near Grant. "Your barn is good deal like that in 'The Arkansas Traveller.' Needs a new roof, Grant." His voice had a pleasant sound, full of the tenderness of the scene through which he had just been. "In fact, you need a new barn."

"I need a good many things more'n I'll ever get," Grant replied shortly.

"How long did you say you'd been on this farm?"

"Three years this fall."

"I don't s'pose you've been able to think of buying — Now hold on, Grant," he cried, as Grant threw his head back. "For God's sake, don't get mad again! Wait till you see what I'm driving at."

"I don't see what you're drivin' at, and I don't care. All I want you to do is to let us alone. That ought to be easy enough for you."

"I tell you, I didn't get your letter. I didn't know you'd lost the old farm." Howard was determined not to quarrel. "I didn't suppose — "

"You might 'a' come to see."

"Well, I'll admit that. All I can say in excuse is that since I got to managing plays I've kept looking ahead to making a big hit and getting a barrel of money — just as the old miners used to hope and watch. Besides, you don't understand how much pressure there is on me. A hundred different people pulling and hauling to have me go here or go there, or do this or do that. When it isn't yachting, it's canoeing, or — "

He stopped. His heart gave a painful throb, and a shiver ran through him. Again he saw his life, so rich, so bright, so free, set over against the routine life in the little low kitchen, the barren sitting room, and this still more horrible barn. Why should his brother sit there in wet and grimy clothing mending a broken trace, while he enjoyed all the light and civilization of the age?

He looked at Grant's fine figure, his great strong face; recalled his deep, stern, masterful voice. "Am I so much superior to him? Have not circumstances made me and destroyed him?"

"Grant, for God's sake, don't sit there like that! I'll admit I've been negligent and careless. I can't understand it all myself. But let me do something for you now. I've sent to New York for five thousand dollars. I've got terms on the old farm. Let me see you all back there once more before I return."

"I don't want any of your charity."

"It ain't charity. It's only justice to you." He rose. "Come now, let's get at an understanding, Grant. I can't go on this way. I can't go back to New York and leave you here like this."

Grant rose, too. "I tell you, I don't ask your help. You can't fix this thing up with money. If you've got more brains 'n I have, why it's all right. I ain't got any right to take anything that I don't earn."

"But you don't get what you do earn. It ain't your fault. I begin te see it now. Being the oldest, I had the best chance. I was going to town to school while you were plowing and husking corn. Of course I thought you'd be going soon, yourself. I had three years the start of you. If you'd been in my place, you might have met a man like Cooke, you might have gone to New York and have been where I am'.

"Well, it can't be helped now. So drop it."

"But it must be!" Howard said, pacing about, his hands in his coat pockets. Grant had stopped work, and was gloomily looking out of the door at a pig nosing in the mud for stray grains of wheat at the granary door:

"Good God! I see it all now," Howard burst out in an impassioned tone. "I went ahead with my education, got my start in life, then Father died, and you took up his burdens. Circumstances made me and crushed you. That's all there is about that. Luck made me and cheated you. It ain't right."

His voice faltered. Both men were now oblivious of their companions and of the scene. Both were thinking of the days when they both planned great things in the way of an education, two ambitious, dreamful boys.

"I used to think of you, Grant, when I pulled out Monday morning in my best suit — cost fifteen dollars in those days." He smiled a little at the recollection. "While you in overalls and an old 'wammus' was going out into the field to plow, or husk corn in the mud. It made me feel uneasy, but, as I said, I kept saying to myself, 'His turn'll come in a year or two.' But it didn't."

His voice choked. He walked to the door, stood a moment, came back. His eyes were full of tears.

"I tell you, old man, many a time in my boardinghouse down to the city, when I thought of the jolly times I was having, my heart hurt me. But I said: 'It's no use to cry. Better go on and do the best you can, and then help them afterward. There'll only be one more miserable member of the family if you stay at home.'

Besides, it seemed right to me to have first chance. But I never thought you'd be shut off, Grant. If I had, I never would have gone on. Come, old man, I want you to believe that." His voice was very tender now and almost humble.

"I don't know as I blame yeh for that, How," said Grant slowly. It was the first time he had called Howard by his boyish nickname. His voice was softer, too, and higher in key. But he looked steadily away.

"I went to New York. People liked my work. I was very successful, Grant; more successful than you realize. I could have helped you at any time. There's no use lying about it. And I ought to have done it; but some way — it's no excuse, I don't mean it for an excuse, only an explanation — some way I got in with the boys. I don't mean I was a drinker and all that. But I bought pictures and kept a horse and a yacht, and of course I had to pay my share of all expeditions, and — oh, what's the use!"

He broke off, turned, and threw his open palms out toward his brother, as if throwing aside the last attempt at an excuse.

"I *did* neglect you, and it's a damned shame! and I ask your forgiveness. Come, old man!"

He held out his hand, and Grant slowly approached and took it. There was a little silence. Then Howard went on, his voice trembling, the tears on his face.

"I want you to let me help you, old man. That's the way to forgive me. Will you?"

"Yes, if you can help me."

Howard squeezed his hand. "That's right, old man. Now you make me a boy again. Course I can help you. I've got ten — "

"I don't mean that, How." Grant's voice was very grave. "Money can't give me a chance now."

"What do you mean?"

"I mean life ain't worth very much to me. I'm too old to take a new start. I'm a dead failure. I've come to the conclusion that life's a failure for ninety-nine per cent of us. You can't help me now. It's too late."

The two men stood there, face to face, hands clasped, the one fair-skinned, full-lipped, handsome in his neat sult; the other tragic, somber in his softened mood, his large, long, rugged Scotch face bronzed with sun and scarred with wrinkles that had histories, like saber cuts on a veteran, the record of his battles.

THE YELLOW WALLPAPER

Charlotte Perkins Gilman (1860-1935)

It is very seldom that mere ordinary people like John and myself secure ancestral halls for the summer.

A colonial mansion, a hereditary estate, I would say a haunted house, and reach the height of romantic felicity — but that would be asking too much of fate!

Still I will proudly declare that there is something queer about it.

Else, why should it be let so cheaply? And why have stood so long untenanted?

John laughs at me, of course, but one expects that in marriage.

John is practical in the extreme. He has no patience with faith, an intense horror of superstition, and he scoffs openly at any talk of things not to be felt and seen and put down in figures.

John is a physician, and *perhaps* — (I would not say it to a living soul, of course, but this is dead paper and a great relief to my mind) — *perhaps* that is one reason I do not get well faster.

You see he does not believe I am sick!

And what can one do?

If a physician of high standing, and one's own husband, assures friends and relatives that there is really nothing the matter with one but temporary nervous depression — a slight hysterical tendency — what is one to do?

My brother is also a physician, and also of high standing, and he says the same thing.

So I take phosphates or phosphites — whichever it is, and tonics, and journeys, and air, and exercise, and am absolutely forbidden to "work" until I am well again.

Personally, I disagree with their ideas.

Personally, I believe that congenial work, with excitement and change, would do me good.

But what is one to do?

I did write for a while in spite of them; but it *does* exhaust me a good deal — having to be so sly about it, or else meet with heavy opposition.

I sometimes fancy that in my condition if I had less opposition and more society and stimulus — but John says the very worst thing I can do is to think about my condition, and I confess it always makes me feel bad.

So I will let it alone and talk about the house.

The most beautiful place! It is quite alone standing well back from the road, quite three miles from the village. It makes me think of English places that you read about, for there are hedges and walls and gates that lock, and lots of separate little houses for the gardeners and people.

There is a *delicious* garden! I never saw such a garden — large and shady, full of box-bordered paths, and lined with long grape-covered arbors with seats under them.

There were greenhouses, too, but they are all broken now.

There was some legal trouble, I believe, something about the heirs and coheirs; anyhow, the place has been empty for years.

That spoils my ghostliness, I am afraid, but I don't care — there is something strange about the house — I can feel it.

I even said so to John one moonlight evening but he said what I felt was a draught, and shut the window.

I get unreasonably angry with John sometimes. I'm sure I never used to be so sensitive. I think it is due to this nervous condition.

But John says if I feel so, I shall neglect proper self-control; so I take pains to control myself — before him, at least, and that makes me very tired.

I don't like our room a bit. I wanted one downstairs that opened on the piazza and had roses all over the window, and such pretty old-fashioned chintz hangings! but John would not hear of it.

He said there was only one window and not room for two beds, and no near room for him if he took another.

He is very careful and loving, and hardly lets me stir without special direction.

I have a schedule prescription for each hour in the day; he takes all care from me, and so I feel basely ungrateful not to value it more.

He said we came here solely on my account, that I was to have perfect rest and all the air I could get. "Your exercise depends on your strength, my dear," said he, "and your food somewhat on your appetite; but air you can absorb all the time. ' So we took the nursery at the top of the house.

It is a big, airy room, the whole floor nearly, with windows that look all ways, and air and sunshine galore. It was nursery first and then playroom and gymnasium, I should judge; for the windows are barred for little children, and there are rings and things in the walls.

The paint and paper look as if a boys' school had used it. It is stripped off — the paper in great patches all around the head of my bed, about as far as I can reach, and in a great place on the other side of the room low down. I never saw a worse paper in my life.

One of those sprawling flamboyant patterns committing every artistic sin.

It is dull enough to confuse the eye in following, pronounced enough to constantly irritate and provoke study, and when you follow the lame uncertain curves for a little distance they suddenly commit suicide — plunge off at outrageous angles, destroy themselves in unheard of contradictions.

The color is repellent, almost revolting; a smouldering unclean yellow, strangely faded by the slow-turning sunlight.

It is a dull yet lurid orange in some places, a sickly sulphur tint in others.

No wonder the children hated it! I should hate it myself if I had to live in this room long.

There comes John, and I must put this away, — he hates to have me write a word.

We have been here two weeks, and I haven't felt like writing before, since that first day.

I am sitting by the window now, up in this atrocious nursery, and there is nothing to hinder my writing as much as I please, save lack of strength.

John is away all day, and even some nights when his cases are serious.

I am glad my case is not serious!

But these nervous troubles are dreadfully depressing.

John does not know how much I really suffer. He knows there is no *reason* to suffer, and that satisfies him.

Of course it is only nervousness. It does weigh on me so not to do my duty in any way!

I meant to be such a help to John, such a real rest and comfort, and here I am a comparative burden already!

Nobody would believe what an effort it is to do what little I am able, — to dress and entertain, and order things.

It is fortunate Mary is so good with the baby. Such a dear baby!

And yet I *cannot* be with him, it makes me so nervous.

I suppose John never was nervous in his life. He laughs at me so about this wall-paper!

At first he meant to repaper the room, but afterwards he said that I was letting it get the better of me, and that nothing was worse for a nervous patient than to give way to such fancies.

He said that after the wall-paper was changed it would be the heavy bedstead, and then the barred windows, and then that gate at the head of the stairs, and so on.

"You know the place is doing you good," he said, "and really, dear, I don't care to renovate the house just for a three months' rental."

"Then do let us go downstairs," I said, "there are such pretty rooms there."

Then he took me in his arms and called me a blessed little goose, and said he would go down to the cellar, if I wished, and have it whitewashed into the bargain.

But he is right enough about the beds and windows and things.

It is an airy and comfortable room as any one need wish, and, of course, I would not be so silly as to make him uncomfortable just for a whim.

I'm really getting quite fond of the big room, all but that horrid paper.

Out of one window I can see the garden, those mysterious deepshaded arbors, the riotous old-fashioned flowers, and bushes and gnarly trees.

Out of another I get a lovely view of the bay and a little private wharf belonging to the estate. There is a beautiful shaded lane that runs down there from the house. I always fancy I see people walking in these numerous paths and arbors, but John has cautioned me not to give way to fancy in the least. He says that with my imaginative power and habit of story-making, a nervous weakness like mine is sure to lead to all manner of excited fancies, and that I ought to use my will and good sense to check the tendency. So I try.

I think sometimes that if I were only well enough to write a little it would relieve the press of ideas and rest me.

But I find I get pretty tired when I try.

It is so discouraging not to have any advice and companionship about my work. When I get really well, John says we will ask Cousin Henry and Julia down for a long visit; but he says he would as soon put fireworks in my pillow-case as to let me have those stimulating people about now.

I wish I could get well faster.

But I must not think about that. This paper looks to me as if it *knew* what a vicious influence it had!

There is a recurrent spot where the pattern lolls like a broken neck and two bulbous eyes stare at you upside down.

I get positively angry with the impertinence of it and the everlastingness. Up and down and sideways they crawl, and those absurd, unblinking eyes are everywhere There is one place where two breaths didn't match, and the eyes go all up and down the line, one a little higher than the other.

I never saw so much expression in an inanimate thing before, and we all know how much expression they have! I used to lie awake as a child and get more entertainment and terror out of blank walls and plain furniture than most children could find in a toy-store.

I remember what a kindly wink the knobs of our big, old bureau used to have, and there was one chair that always seemed like a strong friend.

I used to feel that if any of the other things looked too fierce I could always hop into that chair and be safe.

The furniture in this room is no worse than inharmonious, however, for we had to bring it all from downstairs. I suppose when this was used as a playroom they had to take the nursery things out, and no wonder! I never saw such ravages as the children have made here.

The wall-paper, as I said before, is torn off in spots, and it sticketh closer than a brother — they must have had perseverance as well as hatred.

Then the floor is scratched and gouged and splintered, the plaster itself is dug out here and there, and this great heavy bed which is all we found in the room, looks as if it had been through the wars.

But I don't mind it a bit — only the paper.

There comes John's sister. Such a dear girl as she is, and so careful of me! I must not let her find me writing.

She is a perfect and enthusiastic housekeeper, and hopes for no better profession. I verily believe she thinks it is the writing which made me sick!

But I can write when she is out, and see her a long way off from these windows.

There is one that commands the road, a lovely shaded winding road, and one that just looks off over the country. A lovely country, too, full of great elms and velvet meadows.

This wall-paper has a kind of sub-pattern in a different shade, a particularly irritating one, for you can only see it in certain lights, and not clearly then.

But in the places where it isn't faded and where the sun is just so — I can see a strange, provoking, formless sort of figure, that seems to skulk about behind that silly and conspicuous front design.

There's sister on the stairs!

Well, the Fourth of July is over! The people are all gone and I am tired out. John thought it might do me good to see a little company, so we just had mother and Nellie and the children down for a week.

Of course I didn't do a thing. Jennie sees to everything now.

But it tired me all the same.

John says if I don't pick up faster he shall send me to Weir Mitchell in the fall.

But I don't want to go there at all. I had a friend who was in his hands once, and she says he is just like John and my brother, only more so!

Besides, it is such an undertaking to go so far.

I don't feel as if it was worth while to turn my hand over for anything, and I'm getting dreadfully fretful and querulous.

I cry at nothing, and cry most of the time.

Of course I don't when John is here, or anybody else, but when I am alone.

And I am alone a good deal just now. John is kept in town very often by serious cases, and Jennie is good and lets me alone when I want her to.

So I walk a little in the garden or down that lovely lane, sit on the porch under the roses, and lie down up here a good deal.

I'm getting really fond of the room in spite of the wall-paper. Perhaps *because* of the wall-paper.

It dwells in my mind so!

I lie here on this great immovable bed — it is nailed down, I believe — and follow that pattern about by the hour. It is as good as gymnastics, I assure you. I start, we'll say, at the bottom, down in the corner over there where it has not been touched, and I determine for the thousandth time that I *will* follow that pointless pattern to some sort of a conclusion.

I know a little of the principle of design, and I know this thing was not arranged on any laws of radiation, or alternation, or repetition, or symmetry, or anything else that I ever heard of.

It is repeated, of course, by the breadths, but not otherwise.

Looked at in one way each breadth stands alone, the bloated curves and flourishes — a kind of "debased Romanesque" with delirium tremens — go waddling up and down in isolated columns of fatuity.

But, on the other hand, they connect diagonally, and the sprawling outlines run off in great slanting waves of optic horror, like a lot of wallowing seaweeds in full chase.

The whole thing goes horizontally, too, at least it seems so, and I exhaust myself in trying to distinguish the order of its going in that direction.

They have used a horizontal breadth for a frieze, and that adds wonderfully to the confusion.

There is one end of the room where it is almost intact, and there, when the crosslights fade and the low sun shines directly upon it, I can almost fancy radiation after all, — the interminable grotesques seem to form around a common center and rush off in headlong plunges of equal distraction.

It makes me tired to follow it. I will take a nap I guess.

I don't know why I should write this.

I don't want to.

I don't feel able. And I know John would think it absurd. But I must say what I feel and think in some way — it is such a relief!

But the effort is getting to be greater than the relief.

Half the time now I am awfully lazy, and lie down ever so much.

John says I mustn't lose my strength, and has me take cod liver oil and lots of tonics and things, to say nothing of ale and wine and rare meat.

Dear John! He loves me very dearly, and hates to have me sick. I tried to have a real earnest reasonable talk with him the other day, and tell him how I wish he would let me go and make a visit to Cousin Henry and Julia.

But he said I wasn't able to go, nor able to stand it after I got there; and I did not make out a very good case for myself, for I was crying before I had finished

It is getting to be a great effort for me to think straight. Just this nervous weakness I suppose.

And dear John gathered me up in his arms, and just carried me upstairs and laid me on the bed, and sat by me and read to me till it tired my head.

He said I was his darling and his comfort and all he had, and that I must take care of myself for his sake, and keep well.

He says no one but myself can help me out of it, that I must use my will and self-control and not let any silly fancies run away with me.

There's one comfort, the baby is well and happy, and does not have to occupy this nursery with the horrid wall-paper.

If we had not used it, that blessed child would have! What a fortunate escape!

Why, I wouldn't have a child of mine, an impressionable little thing, live in such a room for worlds.

I never thought of it before, but it is lucky that John kept me here after all, I can stand it so much easier than a baby, you see.

Of course I never mention it to them any more — I am too wise, — but I keep watch of it all the same.

There are things in that paper that nobody knows but me, or ever will.

Behind that outside pattern the dim shapes get clearer every day.

It is always the same shape, only very numerous.

And it is like a woman stooping down and creeping about behind that pattern. I don't like it a bit. I wonder — I begin to think — I wish John would take me away from here!

It is so hard to talk with John about my case, because he is so wise, and because he loves me so.

But I tried it last night.

It was moonlight. The moon shines in all around just as the sun does.

I hate to see it sometimes, it creeps so slowly, and always comes in by one window or another.

John was asleep and I hated to waken him, so I kept still and watched the moonlight on that undulating wall-paper till I felt creepy.

The faint figure behind seemed to shake the pattern, just as if she wanted to get out.

I got up softly and went to feel and see if the paper *did* move, and when I came back John was awake.

"What is it, little girl?" he said. "Don't go walking about like that — you'll get cold."

I thought it was a good time to talk, so I told him that I really was not gaining here, and that I wished he would take me away.

"Why darling!" said he, "our lease will be up in three weeks, and I can't see how to leave before.

"The repairs are not done at home, and I cannot possibly leave town just now. Of course if you were in any danger, I could and would, but you really are better, dear, whether you can see it or not. I am a doctor, dear, and I know. You are gaining flesh and color, your appetite is better, I feel really much easier about you."

"I don't weigh a bit more," said I, "nor as much; and my appetite may be better in the evening when you are here, but it is worse in the morning when you are away!"

"Bless her little heart!" said he with a big hug, "she shall be as sick as she pleases! But now let's improve the shining hours by going to sleep, and talk about it in the morning!"

"And you won't go away?" I asked gloomily.

"Why, how can I, dear? It is only three weeks more and then we will take a nice little trip of a few days while Jennie is getting the house ready. Really dear you are better!"

"Better in body perhaps — " I began, and stopped short, for he sat up straight and looked at me with such a stern, reproachful look that I could not say another word.

"My darling," said he, "I beg of you, for my sake and for our child's sake, as well as for your own, that you will never for one instant let that idea enter your mind! There is nothing so dangerous, so fascinating, to a temperament like yours. It is a false and foolish fancy. Can you not trust me as a physician when I tell you so?"

So of course I said no more on that score, and we went to sleep before long. He thought I was asleep first, but I wasn't, and lay there for hours trying to decide whether that front pattern and the back pattern really did move together or separately.

On a pattern like this, by daylight, there is a lack of sequence, a defiance of law, that is a constant irritant to a normal mind.

The color is hideous enough, and unreliable enough, and infuriating enough, but the pattern is torturing.

You think you have mastered it, but just as you get well underway in following, it turns a back somersault and there you are. It slaps you in the face, knocks you down, and tramples upon you. It is like a bad dream.

The outside pattern is a florid arabesque, reminding one of a fungus. If you can imagine a toadstool in joints, an interminable string of toadstools, budding and sprouting in endless convolutions — why, that is something like it.

That is, sometimes!

There is one marked peculiarity about this paper, a thing nobody seems to notice but myself, and that is that it changes as the light changes.

When the sun shoots in through the east window — I always watch for that first long, straight ray — it changes so quickly that I never can quite believe it.

That is why I watch it always.

By moonlight — the moon shines in all night when there is a moon — I wouldn't know it was the same paper.

At night in any kind of light, in twilight, candlelight, lamplight, and worst of all by moonlight, it becomes bars! The outside pattern I mean, and the woman behind it is as plain as can be.

I didn't realize for a long time what the thing was that showed behind, that dim sub-pattern, but now I am quite sure it is a woman.

By daylight she is subdued, quiet. I fancy it is the pattern that keeps her so still. It is so puzzling. It keeps me quiet by the hour.

I lie down ever so much now. John says it is good for me, and to sleep all I can.

Indeed he started the habit by making me lie down for an hour after each meal.

It is a very bad habit I am convinced, for you see I don't sleep.

And that cultivates deceit, for I don't tell them I'm awake — O no!

The fact is I am getting a little afraid of John.

He seems very queer sometimes, and even Jennie has an inexplicable look.

It strikes me occasionally, just as a scientific hypothesis, — that perhaps it is the paper!

I have watched John when he did not know I was looking, and come into the room suddenly on the most innocent excuses, and I've caught him several times *looking at the paper!* And Jennie too. I caught Jennie with her hand on it once.

She didn't know I was in the room, and when I asked her in a quiet, a very quiet voice, with the most restrained manner possible, what she was doing with the paper — she turned around as if she had been caught stealing, and looked quite angry — asked me why I should frighten her so!

Then she said that the paper stained everything it touched, that she had found yellow smooches on all my clothes and John's, and she wished we would be more careful!

Did not that sound innocent? But I know she was studying that pattern, and I am determined that nobody shall find it out but myself!

Life is very much more exciting now than it used to be. You see I have something more to expect, to look forward to, to watch. I really do eat better, and am more quiet than I was.

John is so pleased to see me improve ! He laughed a little the other day, and said I seemed to be flourishing in spite of my wall-paper.

I turned it off with a laugh. I had no intention of telling him it was *because* of the wall-paper — he would make fun of me. He might even want to take me away.

I don't want to leave now until I have found it out. There is a week more, and I think that will be enough.

I'm feeling ever so much better! I don't sleep much at night, for it is so interesting to watch developments; but I sleep a good deal in the daytime.

In the daytime it is tiresome and perplexing.

There are always new shoots on the fungus, and new shades of yellow all over it. I cannot keep count of them, though I have tried conscientiously.

It is the strangest yellow, that wall-paper! It makes me think of all the yellow things I ever saw — not beautiful ones like buttercups, but old foul, bad yellow things.

But there is something else about that paper — the smell! I noticed it the moment we came into the room, but with so much air and sun it was not bad. Now we have had a week of fog and rain, and whether the windows are open or not, the smell is here.

It creeps all over the house.

I find it hovering in the dining-room, skulking in the parlor, hiding in the hall, lying in wait for me on the stairs.

It gets into my hair.

Even when I go to ride, if I turn my head suddenly and surprise it — there is that smell!

Such a peculiar odor, too! I have spent hours in trying to analyze it, to find what it smelled like.

It is not bad — at first, and very gentle, but quite the subtlest, most enduring odor I ever met.

In this damp weather it is awful, I wake up in the night and find it hanging over me.

It used to disturb me at first. I thought seriously of burning the house — to reach the smell.

But now I am used to it. The only thing I can think of that it is like is the *color* of the paper! A yellow smell.

There is a very funny mark on this wall, low down, near the mopboard. A streak that runs round the room. It goes behind every piece of furniture, except the bed, a long, straight, even smooch, as if it had been rubbed over and over.

I wonder how it was done and who did it, and what they did it for. Round and round and round — round and round and round — it makes me dizzy!

I really have discovered something at last.

Through watching so much at night, when it changes so, I have finally found out.

The front pattern *does* move — and no wonder! The woman behind shakes it!

Sometimes I think there are a great many women behind, and sometimes only one, and she crawls around fast, and her crawling shakes it all over.

Then in the very bright spots she keeps still, and in the very shady spots she just takes hold of the bars and shakes them hard.

And she is all the time trying to climb through. But nobody could climb through that pattern — it strangles so; I think that is why it has so many heads.

They get through, and then the pattern strangles them off and turns them upside down, and makes their eyes white!

If those heads were covered or taken off it would not be half so bad.

I think that woman gets out in the daytime!

And I'll tell you why — privately — I've seen her!

I can see her out of every one of my windows!

It is the same woman, I know, for she is always creeping, and most women do not creep by daylight.

I see her on that long road under the trees, creeping along, and when a carriage comes she hides under the blackberry vines.

I don't blame her a bit. It must be very humiliating to be caught creeping by daylight!

I always lock the door when I creep by daylight. I can't do it at night, for I know John would suspect something at once.

And John is so queer now, that I don't want to irritate him. I wish he would take another room! Besides, I don't want anybody to get that woman out at night but myself.

I often wonder if I could see her out of all the windows at once.

But, turn as fast as I can, I can only see out of one at one time.

And though I always see her, she may be able to creep faster than I can turn!

I have watched her sometimes away off in the open country, creeping as fast as a cloud shadow in a high wind.

If only that top pattern could be gotten off from the under one! I mean to try it, little by little.

I have found out another funny thing, but I shan't tell it this time! It does not do to trust people too much.

There are only two more days to get this paper off, and I believe John is beginning to notice. I don't like the look in his eyes.

And I heard him ask Jennie a lot of professional questions about me. She had a very good report to give.

She said I slept a good deal in the daytime.

John knows I don't sleep very well at night, for all I'm so quiet!

He asked me all sorts of questions, too, and pretended to be very loving and kind.

As if I couldn't see through him!

Still, I don't wonder he acts so, sleeping under this paper for three months.

It only interests me, but I feel sure John and Jennie are secretly affected by it.

Hurrah! This is the last day, but it is enough. John to stay in town over night, and won't be out until this evening.

Jennie wanted to sleep with me — the sly thing! but I told her I should undoubtedly rest better for a night all alone.

That was clever, for really I wasn't alone a bit! As soon as it was moonlight and that poor thing began to crawl and shake the pattern, I got up and ran to help her.

I pulled and she shook, I shook and she pulled, and before morning we had peeled off yards of that paper.

A strip about as high as my head and half around the room.

And then when the sun came and that awful pattern began to laugh at me, I declared I would finish it to-day!

We go away to-morrow, and they are moving all my furniture down again to leave things as they were before.

Jennie looked at the wall in amazement, but I told her merrily that I did it out of pure spite at the vicious thing.

She laughed and said she wouldn't mind doing it herself, but I must not get tired.

How she betrayed herself that time!

But I am here, and no person touches this paper but me, — not *alive!*

She tried to get me out of the room — it was too patent! But I said it was so quiet and empty and clean now that I believed I would lie down again and sleep all I could; and not to wake me even for dinner — I would call when I woke.

So now she is gone, and the servants are gone, and the things are gone, and there is nothing left but that great bedstead nailed down, with the canvas mattress we found on it.

We shall sleep downstairs to-night, and take the boat home to-morrow.

I quite enjoy the room, now it is bare again.

How those children did tear about here!

This bedstead is fairly gnawed!

But I must get to work.

I have locked the door and thrown the key down into the front path.

I don't want to go out, and I don't want to have anybody come in, till John comes.

I want to astonish him.

I've got a rope up here that even Jennie did not find. If that woman does get out, and tries to get away, I can tie her!

But I forgot I could not reach far without anything to stand on!

This bed will *not* move!

I tried to lift and push it until I was lame, and then I got so angry I bit off a little piece at one corner — but it hurt my teeth.

Then I peeled off all the paper I could reach standing on the floor. It sticks horribly and the pattern just enjoys it! All those strangled heads and bulbous eyes and waddling fungus growths just shriek with derision!

I am getting angry enough to do something desperate. To jump out of the window would be admirable exercise, but the bars are too strong even to try.

Besides I wouldn't do it. Of course not. I know well enough that a step like that is improper and might be misconstrued.

I don't like to *look* out of the windows even — there are so many of those creeping women, and they creep so fast.

I wonder if they all come out of that wall-paper as I did?

But I am securely fastened now by my well-hidden rope — you don't get *me* out in the road there!

I suppose I shall have to get back behind the pattern when it comes night, and that is hard!

It is so pleasant to be out in this great room and creep around as I please!

I don't want to go outside. I won't, even if Jennie asks me to.

For outside you have to creep on the ground, and everything is green instead of yellow.

But here I can creep smoothly on the floor, and my shoulder just fits in that long smooch around the wall, so I cannot lose my way.

Why there's John at the door!

It is no use, young man, you can't open it!

How he does call and pound!

Now he's crying for an axe.

It would be a shame to break down that beautiful door!

"John dear!" said I in the gentlest voice, "the key is down by the front steps, under a plantain leaf!"

That silenced him for a few moments.

Then he said — very quietly indeed, "Open the door, my darling!"

"I can't," said I. "The key is down by the front door under a plantain leaf!"

And then I said it again, several times, very gently and slowly, and said it so often that he had to go and see, and he got it of course, and came in. He stopped short by the door.

"What is the matter?" he cried. "For God's sake, what are you doing!"

I kept on creeping just the same, but I looked at him over my shoulder.

"I've got out at last," said I, "in spite of you and Jane. And I've pulled off most of the paper, so you can't put me back!"

Now why should that man have fainted? But he did, and right across my path by the wall, so that I had to creep over him every time!

A JOURNEY

Edith Wharton (1862-1937)

As she lay in her berth, staring at the shadows overhead, the rush of the wheels was in her brain, driving her deeper and deeper into circles of wakeful lucidity. The sleeping-car had sunk into its night-silence. Through the wet window-pane she watched the sudden lights, the long stretches of hurrying blackness. Now and then she turned her head and looked through the opening in the hangings at her husband's curtains across the aisle. . . .

She wondered restlessly if he wanted anything and if she could hear him if he called. His voice had grown very weak within the last months and it irritated him when she did not hear. This irritability, this increasing childish petulance seemed to give expression to their imperceptible estrangement. Like two faces looking at one another through a sheet of glass they were close together, almost touching, but they could not hear or feel each other: the conductivity between them was broken. She, at least, had this sense of separation, and she fancied sometimes that she saw it reflected in the look with which he supplemented his failing words. Doubtless the fault was hers. She was too impenetrably healthy to be touched by the irrelevancies of disease. Her self-reproachful tenderness was tinged with the sense of his irrationality: she had a vague feeling that there was a purpose in his helpless tyrannies. The suddenness of the change had found her so unprepared. A year ago their pulses had beat to one robust measure; both had the same prodigal confidence in an exhaustless future. Now their energies no longer kept step: hers still bounded ahead of life, preempting unclaimed regions of hope and activity, while his lagged behind, vainly struggling to overtake her.

When they married, she had such arrears of living to make up: her days had been as bare as the whitewashed school-room where she forced innutritious facts upon reluctant children. His coming had broken in on the slumber of circumstance, widening the present till it became the encloser of remotest chances. But imperceptibly the horizon narrowed. Life had a grudge against her: she was never to be allowed to spread her wings.

At first the doctors had said that six weeks of mild air would set him right; but when he came back this assurance was explained as having of course included a winter in a dry climate. They gave up their pretty house, storing the wedding presents and new furniture, and went to Colorado. She had hated it there from the first. Nobody knew her or cared about her; there was no one to wonder at the good match she had made, or to envy her the new dresses and the visiting-cards which were still a surprise to her. And he kept growing worse. She felt herself beset with difficulties too evasive to be fought by so direct a temperament. She still loved him, of course; but he was gradually, undefinably ceasing to be himself. The man she had married had been strong, active, gently masterful: the male whose pleasure it is to clear a way through the material obstructions of life; but now it was she who was the protector, he who must be shielded from importunities and given his drops or his beef-juice though the skies were falling. The routine of the sick-room bewildered her; this punctual administering of medicine seemed as idle as some uncomprehended religious mummery.

There were moments, indeed, when warm gushes of pity swept away her instinctive resentment of his condition, when she still found his old self in his eyes as they groped for each other through the dense medium of his weakness. But these moments had grown rare. Sometimes he frightened her: his sunken expressionless face seemed that of a stranger; his voice was weak and hoarse; his thin-lipped smile a mere muscular contraction. Her hand avoided his damp soft skin, which had lost the familiar roughness of health: she caught herself furtively watching him as she might have watched a strange animal. It frightened her to feel that this was the man she loved; there were hours when to tell him what she suffered seemed the one escape from her fears. But in general she judged herself more leniently, reflecting that she had perhaps been too long alone with him, and that she would feel differently when they were at home again, surrounded by her robust and buoyant family. How she had rejoiced when the doctors at last gave their consent to his going home! She knew, of course, what the decision meant; they both knew. It meant that he was to die; but they dressed the truth in hopeful euphuisms, and at times, in the joy of preparation, she really forgot the purpose of their journey, and slipped into an eager allusion to next year's plans.

At last the day of leaving came. She had a dreadful fear that they would never get away; that somehow at the last moment he would fail her; that the doctors held one of their accustomed treacheries in reserve; but nothing happened. They drove to the station, he was installed in a seat with a rug over his knees and a cushion at his back, and she hung out of the window waving unregretful farewells to the acquaintances she had really never liked till then.

The first twenty-four hours had passed off well. He revived a little and it amused him to look out of the window and to observe the humours of the car. The second day he began to grow weary and to chafe under the dispassionate stare of the freckled child with the lump of chewing-gum. She had to explain to the child's mother that her husband was too ill to be disturbed: a statement received by that lady with a resentment visibly supported by the maternal sentiment of the whole car. . . .

That night he slept badly and the next morning his temperature frightened her: she was sure he was growing worse. The day passed slowly, punctuated by the small irritations of travel. Watching his tired face, she traced in its contractions every rattle and jolt of the tram, till her own body vibrated with sympathetic fatigue. She felt the others observing him too, and hovered restlessly between him and the line of interrogative eyes. The freckled child hung about him like a fly; offers of candy and picture-books failed to dislodge her: she twisted one leg around the other and watched him imperturbably. The porter, as he passed, lingered with vague proffers of help, probably inspired by philanthropic passengers swelling with the sense that "something ought to be done"; and one nervous man in a skull-cap was audibly concerned as to the possible effect on his wife's health.

The hours dragged on in a dreary inoccupation. Towards dusk she sat down beside him and he laid his hand on hers. The touch startled her. He seemed to be calling her from far off. She looked at him helplessly and his smile went through her like a physical pang.

"Are you very tired?" she asked.

"No, not very."

"We'll be there soon now."

"Yes, very soon."

"This time to-morrow — "

He nodded and they sat silent. When she had put him to bed and crawled into her own berth she tried to cheer herself with the thought that in less than twenty-four hours they would be in New York. Her people would all be at the station to meet her — she pictured their round unanxious faces pressing through the crowd. She only hoped they would not tell him too loudly that he was looking splendidly and would be all right in no time: the subtler sympathies developed by long contact with suffering were making her aware of a certain coarseness of texture in the family sensibilities.

Suddenly she thought she heard him call. She parted the curtains and listened. No, it was only a man snoring at the other end of the car. His snores had a greasy sound, as though they passed through tallow. She lay down and tried to sleep. . . . Had she not heard him move? She started up trembling. . . . The silence frightened her more than any sound. He might not be able to make her hear — he might be calling her now. . . . What made her think of such things? It was merely the familiar tendency of an over-tired mind to fasten itself on the most intolerable chance within the range of its forebodings. . . . Putting her head out, she listened; but she could not distinguish his breathing from that of the other pairs of lungs about her. She longed to get up and look at him, but she knew the impulse was a mere vent for her restlessness, and the fear of disturbing him restrained her. . . . The regular movement of his curtain reassured her, she knew not why; she remembered that he had wished her a cheerful good-night; and the sheer inability to endure her fears a moment longer made her put them from her with an effort of her whole sound tired body. She turned on her side and slept.

She sat up stiffly, staring out at the dawn. The train was rushing through a region of bare hillocks huddled against a lifeless sky. It looked like the first day of creation. The air of the car was close, and she pushed up her window to let in the keen wind. Then she looked at her watch: it was seven o'clock, and soon the people about her would be stirring. She slipped into her clothes, smoothed her dishevelled hair and crept to the dressing-room. When she had washed her face and adjusted her dress she felt more hopeful. It was always a struggle for her not to be cheerful in the morning. Her cheeks burned deliciously under the coarse towel and the wet hair about her temples broke into strong upward tendrils. Every inch of her was full of life and elasticity. And in ten hours they would be at home!

She stepped to her husband's berth: it was time for him to take his early glass of milk. The window-shade was down, and in the dusk of the curtained enclosure she could just see that he lay sideways, with his face away from her. She leaned over him and drew up the shade. As she did so she touched one of his hands. It felt cold. . . .

She bent closer, laying her hand on his arm and calling him by name. He did not move. She spoke again more loudly; she grasped his shoulder and gently shook it. He lay motionless. She caught hold of his hand again: it slipped from her limply, like a dead thing. A dead thing?

Her breath caught. She must see his face. She leaned forward, and hurriedly, shrinkingly, with a sickening reluctance of the flesh, laid her hands on his shoulders and turned him over. His head fell back; his face looked small and smooth; he gazed at her with steady eyes.

She remained motionless for a long time, holding him thus; and they looked at each other. Suddenly she shrank back: the longing to scream, to call out, to fly from him, had almost overpowered her. But a strong hand arrested her. Good God! If it were known that he was dead they would be put off the train at the next station —

In a terrifying flash of remembrance there arose before her a scene she had once witnessed in travelling, when a husband and wife, whose child had died in the train, had been thrust out at some chance station. She saw them standing on the platform with the child's body between them; she had never forgotten the dazed look with which they followed the receding train. And this was what would happen to her. Within the next hour she might find herself on the platform of some strange station, alone with her husband's body. . . . Anything but that! It was too horrible — She quivered like a creature at bay.

As she cowered there, she felt the train moving more slowly. It was coming then — they were approaching a station! She saw again the husband and wife standing on the lonely platform; and with a violent gesture she drew down the shade to hide her husband's face.

Feeling dizzy, she sank down on the edge of the berth, keeping away from his outstretched body, and pulling the curtains close, so that he and she were shut into a kind of sepulchral twilight. She tried to think. At all costs she must conceal the fact that he was dead. But how? Her mind refused to act: she could not plan, combine. She could think of no way but to sit there, clutching the curtains, all day long. . . .

She heard the porter making up her bed; people were beginning to move about the car; the dressing-room door was being opened and shut. She tried to rouse herself. At length with a supreme effort she rose to her feet, stepping into the aisle of the car and drawing the curtains tight behind her. She noticed that they still parted slightly with the motion of the car, and finding a pin in her dress she fastened them together. Now she was safe. She looked round and saw the porter. She fancied he was watching her.

"Ain't he awake yet?" he enquired.

"No," she faltered.

"I got his milk all ready when he wants it. You know you told me to have it for him by seven."

She nodded silently and crept into her seat.

At half-past eight the train reached Buffalo. By this time the other passengers were dressed and the berths had been folded back for the day. The porter, moving to and fro under his burden of sheets and pillows, glanced at her as he passed. At length he said: "Ain't he going to get up? You know we're ordered to make up the berths as early as we can."

She turned cold with fear. They were just entering the station.

"Oh, not yet," she stammered. "Not till he's had his milk. Won't you get it, please?"

"All right. Soon as we start again."

When the train moved on he reappeared with the milk. She took it from him and sat vaguely looking at it: her brain moved slowly from one idea to another, as though they were stepping-stones set far apart across a whirling flood. At length she became aware that the porter still hovered expectantly.

"Will I give it to him?" he suggested.

"Oh, no," she cried, rising. "He — he's asleep yet, I think — "

She waited till the porter had passed on; then she unpinned the curtains and slipped behind them. In the semi-obscurity her husband's face stared up at her like a marble mask with agate eyes. The eyes were dreadful. She put out her hand and drew down the lids. Then she remembered the glass of milk in her other hand: what was she to do with it? She thought of raising the window and throwing it out; but to do so she would have to lean across his body and bring her face close to his. She decided to drink the milk.

She returned to her seat with the empty glass and after a while the porter came back to get it.

"When'll I fold up his bed?" he asked.

"Oh, not now — not yet; he's ill — he's very ill. Can't you let him stay as he is? The doctor wants him to lie down as much as possible."

He scratched his head. "Well, if he's *really* sick — "

He took the empty glass and walked away, explaining to the passengers that the party behind the curtains was too sick to get up just yet.

She found herself the center of sympathetic eyes. A motherly woman with an intimate smile sat down beside her.

"I'm real sorry to hear your husband's sick. I've had a remarkable amount of sickness in my family and maybe I could assist you. Can I take a look at him?"

"Oh, no — no, please! He mustn't be disturbed."

The lady accepted the rebuff indulgently.

"Well, it's just as you say, of course, but you don't look to me as if you'd had much experience in sickness and I'd have been glad to assist you. What do you generally do when your husband's taken this way?"

"I — I let him sleep."

"Too much sleep ain't any too healthful either. Don't you give him any medicine?"

"Y — yes."

"Don't you wake him to take it?"

"Yes."

"When does he take the next dose?"

"Not for — two hours — "

The lady looked disappointed. "Well, if I was you I'd try giving it oftener. That's what I do with my folks."

After that many faces seemed to press upon her. The passengers were on their way to the dining-car, and she was conscious that as they passed down the aisle they glanced curiously at the closed curtains. One lantern-jawed man with prominent eyes stood still and tried to shoot his projecting glance through the division between the folds. The freckled child, returning from breakfast, waylaid the passers with a buttery clutch, saying in a loud whisper, "He's sick"; and once the conductor came by, asking for tickets. She shrank into her corner and looked out of the window at the flying trees and houses, meaningless hieroglyphs of an endlessly unrolled papyrus.

Now and then the train stopped, and the newcomers on entering the car stared in turn at the closed curtains. More and more people seemed to pass — their faces began to blend fantastically with the images surging in her brain. . . .

Later in the day a fat man detached himself from the mist of faces. He had a creased stomach and soft pale lips. As he pressed himself into the seat facing her she noticed that he was dressed in black broadcloth, with a soiled white tie.

"Husband's pretty bad this morning, is he?"

"Yes."

"Dear, dear! Now that's terribly distressing, ain't it?" An apostolic smile revealed his gold-filled teeth.

"Of course you know there's no sech thing as sickness. Ain't that a lovely thought? Death itself is but a deloosion of our grosser senses. On'y lay yourself open to the influx of the sperrit, submit yourself passively to the action of the divine force, and disease and dissolution will cease to exist for you. If you could indooce your husband to read this little pamphlet — "

The faces about her again grew indistinct. She had a vague recollection of hearing the motherly lady and the parent of the freckled child ardently disputing the relative advantages of trying several medicines at once, or of taking each in turn; the motherly lady maintaining that the competitive system saved time; the other objecting that you couldn't tell which remedy had effected the cure; their voices went on and on, like bell-buoys droning through a fog. . . . The porter came up now and then with questions that she did not understand, but that somehow she must have answered since he went away again without repeating them; every two hours the motherly lady reminded her that her husband ought to have his drops; people left the car and others replaced them . . .

Her head was spinning and she tried to steady herself by clutching at her thoughts as they swept by, but they slipped away from her like bushes on the side of a sheer precipice down which she seemed to be falling. Suddenly her mind grew clear again and she found herself vividly picturing what would happen when the train reached New York. She shuddered as it occurred to her that he would be quite cold and that some one might perceive he had been dead since morning.

She thought hurriedly: — "If they see I am not surprised they will suspect something. They will ask questions, and if I tell them the truth they won't believe me — no one would believe me! It will be terrible" — and she kept repeating to herself: — "I must pretend I don't know. I must pretend I don't know. When they open the curtains I must go up to him quite naturally — and then I must scream!" She had an idea that the scream would be very hard to do.

Gradually new thoughts crowded upon her, vivid and urgent: she tried to separate and restrain them, but they beset her clamorously, like her school-children at the end of a hot day, when she was too tired to silence them. Her head grew confused, and she felt a sick fear of forgetting her part, of betraying herself by some unguarded word or look.

"I must pretend I don't know," she went on murmuring. The words had lost their significance, but she repeated them mechanically, as though they had been a magic formula, until suddenly she heard herself saying: "I can't remember, I can't remember!"

Her voice sounded very loud, and she looked about her in terror; but no one seemed to notice that she had spoken.

As she glanced down the car her eye caught the curtains of her husband's berth, and she began to examine the monotonous arabesques woven through their heavy folds. The pattern was intricate and difficult to trace; she gazed fixedly at the curtains and as she did so the thick stuff grew transparent and through it she saw her husband's face — his dead face. She struggled to avert her look, but her eyes refused to move and her head seemed to be held in a vice. At last, with an effort that left her weak and shaking, she turned away; but it was of no use; close in front of her, small and smooth, was her husband's face. It seemed to be suspended in the air between her and the false braids of the woman who sat in front of her. With an uncontrollable gesture she stretched out her hand to push the face away, and suddenly she felt the touch of his smooth skin. She repressed a cry and half started from her seat. The woman with the false braids looked around, and feeling that she must justify her movement in some way she rose and lifted her travelling-bag from the opposite seat. She unlocked the bag and looked into it; but the first object her hand met was a small flask of her husband's, thrust there at the last moment, in the haste of departure. She locked the bag and closed her eyes. . . . his face was there again, hanging between her eye-balls and lids like a waxen mask against a red curtain. . . .

She roused herself with a shiver. Had she fainted or slept? Hours seemed to have elapsed; but it was still broad day, and the people about her were sitting in the same attitudes as before.

A sudden sense of hunger made her aware that she had eaten nothing since morning. The thought of food filled her with disgust, but she dreaded a return of faintness, and remembering that she had some biscuits in her bag she took one out and ate it. The dry crumbs choked her, and she hastily swallowed a little brandy from her husband's flask. The burning sensation in her throat acted as a counter-irritant, momentarily relieving the dull ache of her nerves. Then she felt a gently-stealing warmth, as though a soft air fanned her, and the swarming fears relaxed their clutch, receding through the stillness that enclosed her, a stillness soothing as the spacious quietude of a summer day. She slept.

Through her sleep she felt the impetuous rush of the train. It seemed to be life itself that was sweeping her on with headlong inexorable force — sweeping her into darkness and terror, and the awe of unknown days. — Now all at once everything was still — not a sound, not a pulsation. . . . She was dead in her turn, and lay beside him with smooth upstaring face. How quiet it was! — and yet she heard feet coming, the feet of the men who were to carry them away... She could feel too — she felt a sudden prolonged vibration, a series of hard shocks, and then another plunge into darkness: the darkness of death this time — a black whirlwind on which they were both spinning like leaves, in wild uncoiling spirals, with millions and millions of the dead. . . .

She sprang up in terror. Her sleep must have lasted a long time, for the winter day had paled and the lights had been lit. The car was in confusion, and as she regained her self-possession she saw that the passengers were gathering up their wraps and bags. The woman with the false braids had brought from the dressing-room a sickly ivy-plant in a bottle, and the Christian Scientist was reversing his cuffs. The porter passed down the aisle with his impartial brush. An impersonal figure with a gold-banded cap asked for her husband's ticket. A voice shouted "Baig-gage express!" and she heard the clicking of metal as the passengers handed over their checks.

Presently her window was blocked by an expanse of sooty wall, and the train passed into the Harlem tunnel. The journey was over; in a few minutes she would see her family pushing their joyous way through the throng at the station. Her heart dilated. The worst terror was past. . . .

"We'd better get him up now, hadn't we?" asked the porter, touching her arm.

He had her husband's hat in his hand and was meditatively revolving it under his brush.

She looked at the hat and tried to speak; but suddenly the car grew dark. She flung up her arms, struggling to catch at something, and fell face downward, striking her head against the dead man's berth.

THE TRIMMED LAMP

O. Henry (1862-1910)

Of course there are two sides to the question. Let us look at the other. We often hear "shop-girls" spoken of. No such persons exist. There are girls who work in shops. They make their living that way. But why turn their occupation into an adjective? Let us be fair. We do not refer to the girls who live on Fifth Avenue as "marriage-girls."

Lou and Nancy were chums. They came to the big city to find work because there was not enough to eat at their homes to go around. Nancy was nineteen; Lou was twenty. Both were pretty, active, country girls who had no ambition to go on the stage.

The little cherub that sits up aloft guided them to a cheap and respectable boarding-house. Both found positions and became wage-earners. They remained chums. It is at the end of six months that I would beg you to step forward and be introduced to them. Meddlesome Reader: My Lady friends, Miss Nancy and Miss Lou. While you are shaking hands please take notice — cautiously — of their attire. Yes, cautiously; for they are as quick to resent a stare as a lady in a box at the horse show is.

Lou is a piece-work ironer in a hand laundry. She is clothed in a badly-fitting purple dress, and her hat plume is four inches too long; but her ermine muff and scarf cost $25, and its fellow beasts will be ticketed in the windows at $7.98 before the season is over. Her cheeks are pink, and her light blue eyes bright. Contentment radiates from her.

Nancy you would call a shop-girl — because you have the habit. There is no type; but a perverse generation is always seeking a type; so this is what the type should be. She has the high-ratted pompadour, and the exaggerated straight-front. Her skirt is shoddy, but has the correct flare. No furs protect her against the bitter spring air, but she wears her short broadcloth jacket as jauntily as though it were

Persian lamb! On her face and in her eyes, remorseless type-seeker, is the typical shop-girl expression. It is a look of silent but contemptuous revolt against cheated womanhood; of sad prophecy of the vengeance to come. When she laughs her loudest the look is still there. The same look can be seen in the eyes of Russian peasants; and those of us left will see it some day on Gabriel's face when he comes to blow us up. It is a look that should wither and abash man; but he has been known to smirk at it and offer flowers — with a string tied to them.

Now lift your hat and come away, while you receive Lou's cheery "See you again," and the sardonic, sweet smile of Nancy that seems, somehow, to miss you and go fluttering like a white moth up over the housetops to the stars.

The two waited on the corner for Dan. Dan was Lou's steady company. Faithful? Well, he was on hand when Mary would have had to hire a dozen subpoena servers to find her lamb.

"Ain't you cold, Nance?" said Lou. "Say, what a chump you are for working in that old store for $8 a week! I made $18.50 last week. Of course ironing ain't as swell work as selling lace behind a counter, but it pays. None of us ironers make less than $10. And I don't know that it's any less respectful work, either."

"You can have it," said Nancy, with uplifted nose. "I'll take my eight a week and hall bedroom. I like to be among nice things and swell people. And look what a chance I've got! Why, one of our glove girls married a Pittsburg — steel maker, or blacksmith or something — the other day worth a million dollars. I'll catch a swell myself some time. I ain't bragging on my looks or anything; but I'll take my chances where there's big prizes offered. What show would a girl have in a laundry?"

"Why, that's where I met Dan," said Lou, triumphantly. "He came in for his Sunday shirt and collars and saw me at the first board, ironing. We all try to get to work at the first board. Ella Maginnis was sick that day, and I had her place. He said he noticed my arms first, how round and white they was. I had my sleeves rolled up. Some nice fellows come into laundries. You can tell 'em by their bringing their clothes in suit cases; and turning in the door sharp and sudden."

"How can you wear a waist like that, Lou?" said Nancy, gazing down at the offending article with sweet scorn in her heavy-lidded eyes. "It shows fierce taste."

"This waist?" cried Lou, with wide-eyed indignation. "Why, I paid $16 for this waist. It's worth twenty-five. A woman left it to be laundered, and never called for it. The boss sold it to me. It's got yards and yards of hand embroidery on it. Better talk about that ugly, plain thing you've got on."

"This ugly, plain thing," said Nancy, calmly, "was copied from one that Mrs. Van Alstyne Fisher was wearing. The girls say her bill in the store last year was $12,000. I made mine, myself. It cost me $1.50. Ten feet away you couldn't tell it from hers."

"Oh, well," said Lou, good-naturedly, "if you want to starve and put on airs, go ahead. But I'll take my job and good wages; and after hours give me something as fancy and attractive to wear as I am able to buy."

But just then Dan came — a serious young man with a ready-made necktie, who had escaped the city's brand of frivolity — an electrician earning 30 dollars per week who looked upon Lou with the sad eyes of Romeo, and thought her embroidered waist a web in which any fly should delight to be caught.

"My friend, Mr. Owens — shake hands with Miss Danforth," said Lou.

"I'm mighty glad to know you, Miss Danforth," said Dan, with outstretched hand. "I've heard Lou speak of you so often."

"Thanks," said Nancy, touching his fingers with the tips of her cool ones, "I've heard her mention you — a few times."

Lou giggled.

"Did you get that handshake from Mrs. Van Alstyne Fisher, Nance?" she asked.

"If I did, you can feel safe in copying it," said Nancy.

"Oh, I couldn't use it, at all. It's too stylish for me. It's intended to set off diamond rings, that high shake is. Wait till I get a few and then I'll try it."

"Learn it first," said Nancy wisely, "and you'll be more likely to get the rings."

"Now, to settle this argument," said Dan, with his ready, cheerful smile, "let me make a proposition. As I can't take both of you up to Tiffany's and do the right thing, what do you say to a little vaudeville? I've got the tickets. How about looking at stage diamonds since we can't shake hands with the real sparklers?"

The faithful squire took his place close to the curb; Lou next, a little peacocky in her bright and pretty clothes; Nancy on the inside, slender, and soberly clothed as the sparrow, but with the true Van Alstyne Fisher walk — thus they set out for their evening's moderate diversion.

I do not suppose that many look upon a great department store as an educational institution. But the one in which Nancy worked was something like that to her. She was surrounded by beautiful things that breathed of taste and refinement. If you live in an atmosphere of luxury, luxury is yours whether your money pays for it, or another's.

The people she served were mostly women whose dress, manners, and position in the social world were quoted as criterions. From them Nancy began to take toll — the best from each according to her view.

From one she would copy and practice a gesture, from another an eloquent lifting of an eyebrow, from others, a manner of walking, of carrying a purse, of smiling, of greeting a friend, of addressing "inferiors in station." From her best beloved model, Mrs. Van Alstyne Fisher, she made requisition for that excellent thing, a soft, low voice as clear as silver and as perfect in articulation as the notes of a thrush. Suffused in the aura of this high social refinement and good breeding, it was impossible for her to escape a deeper effect of it. As good habits are said to be better than good principles, so, perhaps, good manners are better than good habits. The teachings of your parents may not keep alive your New England conscience; but if you sit on a straight-back chair and repeat the words "prisms and pilgrims" forty times the devil will flee from you. And when Nancy spoke in the Van Alstyne Fisher tones she felt the thrill of noblesse oblige to her very bones.

There was another source of learning in the great departmental school. Whenever you see three or four shop-girls gather in a bunch and jingle their wire bracelets as an accompaniment to apparently frivolous conversation, do not think that they are there for the purpose of criticizing the way Ethel does her back hair. The meeting may lack the dignity of the deliberative bodies of man; but it has all the importance of the occasion on which Eve and her first daughter first put their heads together to make Adam understand his proper place in the household. It is Woman's Conference for Common Defense and Exchange of Strategical Theories of Attack and Repulse upon and against the World, which is a Stage, and Man, its Audience who Persists in Throwing Bouquets Thereupon. Woman, the most helpless of the young of any animal — with the fawn's grace but without its fleetness; with the bird's beauty but without its power of flight; with the honey-bee's burden of sweetness but without its — Oh, let's drop that simile — some of us may have been stung.

During this council of war they pass weapons one to another, and exchange stratagems that each has devised and formulated out of the tactics of life.

"I says to 'im," says Sadie, "ain't you the fresh thing! Who do you suppose I am, to be addressing such a remark to me? And what do you think he says back to me?"

The heads, brown, black, flaxen, red, and yellow bob together; the answer is given; and the parry to the thrust is decided upon, to be used by each thereafter in passages-at-arms with the common enemy, man.

Thus Nancy learned the art of defense; and to women successful defense means victory.

The curriculum of a department store is a wide one. Perhaps no other college could have fitted her as well for her life's ambition — the drawing of a matrimonial prize.

Her station in the store was a favored one. The music room was near enough for her to hear and become familiar with the works of the best composers — at least to acquire the familiarity that passed for appreciation in the social world in which she was vaguely trying to set a tentative and aspiring foot. She absorbed the educating influence of art wares, of costly and dainty fabrics, of adornments that are almost culture to women.

The other girls soon became aware of Nancy's ambition. "Here comes your millionaire, Nancy," they would call to her whenever any man who looked the rôle approached her counter. It got to be a habit of men, who were hanging about while their women folk were shopping, to stroll over to the handkerchief counter and dawdle over the cambric squares. Nancy's imitation high-bred air and genuine dainty beauty was what attracted. Many men thus came to display their graces before her. Some of them may have been millionaires; others were certainly no more than their sedulous apes. Nancy learned to discriminate. There was a window at the end of the handkerchief counter; and she could see the rows of vehicles waiting for the shoppers in the street below. She looked and perceived that automobiles differ as well as do their owners.

Once a fascinating gentleman bought four dozen handkerchiefs, and wooed her across the counter with a King Cophetua air. When he had gone one of the girls said:

"What's wrong, Nance, that you didn't warm up to that fellow. He looks the swell article, all right, to me."

"Him?" said Nancy, with her coolest, sweetest, most impersonal, Van Alstyne Fisher smile; "not for mine. I saw him drive up outside. A 12 H. P. machine and an Irish chauffeur! And you saw what kind of handkerchiefs he bought — silk! And he's got dactylis on him. Give me the real thing or nothing, if you please."

Two of the most "refined" women in the store — a forelady and a cashier — had a few "swell gentlemen friends" with whom they now and then dined. Once they included Nancy in an invitation. The dinner took place in a spectacular café whose tables are engaged for New Year's eve a year in advance. There were two "gentlemen friends" — one without any hair on his head — high living ungrew it; and we can prove it — the other a young man whose worth and sophistication he impressed upon you in two convincing ways — he swore that all the wine was corked; and he wore diamond cuff buttons. This young man perceived irresistible excellencies in Nancy. His taste ran to shop-girls; and here was one that added the voice and manners of his high social world to the franker charms of her own caste. So, on the following day, he appeared in the store and made her a serious proposal of marriage over a box of hem-stitched, grass-bleached Irish linens. Nancy declined. A brown pompadour ten feet away had been using her eyes and ears. When the rejected suitor had gone she heaped carboys of upbraidings and horror upon Nancy's head.

"What a terrible little fool you are! That fellow's a millionaire — he's a nephew of old Van Skittles himself. And he was talking on the level, too. Have you gone crazy, Nance?"

"Have I?" said Nancy. "I didn't take him, did I? He isn't a millionaire so hard that you could notice it, anyhow. His family only allows him $20,000 a year to spend. The bald-headed fellow was guying him about it the other night at supper."

The brown pompadour came nearer and narrowed her eyes.

"Say, what do you want?" she inquired, in a voice hoarse for lack of chewing-gum. "Ain't that enough for you? Do you want to be a Mormon, and marry Rockefeller and Gladstone Dowie and the King of Spain and the whole bunch? Ain't $20,000 a year good enough for you?"

Nancy flushed a little under the level gaze of the black, shallow eyes.

"It wasn't altogether the money, Carrie," she explained. "His friend caught him in a rank lie the other night at dinner. It was about some girl he said he hadn't been to the theater with. Well, I can't stand a liar. Put everything together — I don't like him; and that settles it. When I sell out it's not going to be on any bargain day. I've got to have something that sits up in a chair like a man, anyhow. Yes, I'm looking out for a catch; but it's got to be able to do something more than make a noise like a toy bank."

"The physiopathic ward for yours!" said the brown pompadour, walking away.

These high ideas, if not ideals — Nancy continued to cultivate on $8 per week. She bivouacked on the trail of the great unknown "catch," eating her dry bread and tightening her belt day by day. On her face was the faint, soldierly, sweet, grim smile of the preordained man-hunter. The store was her forest; and many times she raised her rifle at game that seemed broad-antlered and big; but always some deep unerring instinct — perhaps of the huntress, perhaps of the woman — made her hold her fire and take up the trail again.

Lou flourished in the laundry. Out of her $18.50 per week she paid $6 for her room and board. The rest went mainly for clothes. Her opportunities for bettering her taste and manners were few compared with Nancy's. In the steaming laundry there was nothing but work, work and her thoughts of the evening pleasures to come. Many costly and showy fabrics passed under her iron; and it may be that her growing fondness for dress was thus transmitted to her through the conducting metal.

When the day's work was over Dan awaited her outside, her faithful shadow in whatever light she stood.

Sometimes he cast an honest and troubled glance at Lou's clothes that increased in conspicuity rather than in style; but this was no disloyalty; he deprecated the attention they called to her in the streets.

And Lou was no less faithful to her chum. There was a law that Nancy should go with them on whatsoever outings they might take. Dan bore the extra burden heartily and in good cheer. It might be said that Lou furnished the color, Nancy the tone, and Dan the weight of the distraction-seeking trio. The escort, in his neat but obviously ready-made suit, his ready-made tie and unfailing, genial, ready-made wit never startled or clashed. He was of that good kind that you are likely to forget while they are present, but remember distinctly after they are gone.

To Nancy's superior taste the flavor of these ready-made pleasures was sometimes a little bitter: but she was young; and youth is a gourmand, when it cannot be a gourmet.

"Dan is always wanting me to marry him right away," Lou told her once. "But why should I? I'm independent. I can do as I please with the money I earn; and he never would agree for me to keep on working afterward. And say, Nance, what do you want to stick to that old store for, and half starve and half dress yourself? I could get you a place in the laundry right now if you'd come. It seems to me that you could afford to be a little less stuck-up if you could make a good deal more money."

"I don't think I'm stuck-up, Lou," said Nancy, "but I'd rather live on half rations and stay where I am. I suppose I've got the habit. It's the chance that I want. I don't expect to be always behind a counter. I'm learning something new every day. I'm right up against refined and rich people all the time — even if I do only wait on them; and I'm not missing any pointers that I see passing around."

"Caught your millionaire yet?" asked Lou with her teasing laugh.

"I haven't selected one yet," answered Nancy. "I've been looking them over."

"Goodness! the idea of picking over 'em! Don't you ever let one get by you Nance — even if he's a few dollars shy. But of course you're joking — millionaires don't think about working girls like us."

"It might be better for them if they did," said Nancy, with cool wisdom. "Some of us could teach them how to take care of their money."

"If one was to speak to me," laughed Lou, "I know I'd have a duck-fit."

"That's because you don't know any. The only difference between swells and other people is you have to watch 'em closer. Don't you think that red silk lining is just a little bit too bright for that coat, Lou?"

Lou looked at the plain, dull olive jacket of her friend.

"Well, no I don't — but it may seem so beside that faded-looking thing you've got on."

"This jacket," said Nancy, complacently, "has exactly the cut and fit of one that Mrs. Van Alstyne Fisher was wearing the other day. The material cost me $3.98. I suppose hers cost about $100 more."

"Oh, well," said Lou lightly, "it don't strike me as millionaire bait. Shouldn't wonder if I catch one before you do, anyway."

Truly it would have taken a philosopher to decide upon the values of the theories held by the two friends. Lou, lacking that certain pride and fastidiousness that keeps stores and desks filled with girls working for the barest living, thumped away gaily with her iron in the noisy and stifling laundry. Her wages supported her even beyond the point of comfort; so that her dress profited until sometimes she cast a sidelong glance of impatience at the neat but inelegant apparel of Dan — Dan the constant, the immutable, the undeviating.

As for Nancy, her case was one of tens of thousands. Silk and jewels and laces and ornaments and the perfume and music of the fine world of good-breeding and taste — these were made for woman; they are her equitable portion. Let her keep near them if they are a part of life to her, and if she will. She is no traitor to herself, as Esau was; for she keeps he birthright and the pottage she earns is often very scant.

In this atmosphere Nancy belonged; and she throve in it and ate her frugal meals and schemed over her cheap dresses with a determined and contented mind. She already knew woman; and she was studying man, the animal, both as to his habits and eligibility. Some day she would bring down the game that she wanted; but she promised herself it would be what seemed to her the biggest and the best, and nothing smaller.

Thus she kept her lamp trimmed and burning to receive the bridegroom when he should come.

But, another lesson she learned, perhaps unconsciously. Her standard of values began to shift and change. Sometimes the dollar-mark grew blurred in her mind's eye, and shaped itself into letters that spelled such words as "truth" and "honor" and now and then just "kindness." Let us make a likeness of one who hunts the moose or elk in some mighty wood. He sees a little dell, mossy and embowered, where a rill trickles, babbling to him of rest and comfort. At these times the spear of Nimrod himself grows blunt.

So, Nancy wondered sometimes if Persian lamb was always quoted at its market value by the hearts that it covered.

One Thursday evening Nancy left the store and turned across Sixth Avenue westward to the laundry. She was expected to go with Lou and Dan to a musical comedy.

Dan was just coming out of the laundry when she arrived. There was a queer, strained look on his face.

"I thought I would drop around to see if they had heard from her," he said.

"Heard from who?" asked Nancy. "Isn't Lou there?"

"I thought you knew," said Dan. "She hasn't been here or at the house where she lived since Monday. She moved all her things from there. She told one of the girls in the laundry she might be going to Europe."

"Hasn't anybody seen her anywhere?" asked Nancy.

Dan looked at her with his jaws set grimly, and a steely gleam in his steady gray eyes.

"They told me in the laundry," he said, harshly, "that they saw her pass yesterday — in an automobile. With one of the millionaires, I suppose, that you and Lou were forever busying your brains about."

For the first time Nancy quailed before a man. She laid her hand that trembled slightly on Dan's sleeve.

"You've no right to say such a thing to me, Dan — as if I had anything to do with it!"

"I didn't mean it that way," said Dan, softening. He fumbled in his vest pocket.

"I've got the tickets for the show to-night," he said, with a gallant show of lightness. "If you — "

Nancy admired pluck whenever she saw it.

"I'll go with you, Dan," she said.

Three months went by before Nancy saw Lou again.

At twilight one evening the shop-girl was hurrying home along the border of a little quiet park. She heard her name called, and wheeled about in time to catch Lou rushing into her arms.

After the first embrace they drew their heads back as serpents do, ready to attack or to charm, with a thousand questions trembling on their swift tongues. And then Nancy noticed that prosperity had descended upon Lou, manifesting itself in costly furs, flashing gems, and creations of the tailors' art.

"You little fool!" cried Lou, loudly and affectionately. "I see you are still working in that store, and as shabby as ever. And how about that big catch you were going to make — nothing doing yet, I suppose?"

And then Lou looked, and saw that something better than prosperity had descended upon Nancy — something that shone brighter than gems in her eyes and redder than a rose in her cheeks, and that danced like electricity anxious to be loosed from the tip of her tongue.

"Yes, I'm still in the store," said Nancy, "but I'm going to leave it next week. I've made my catch — the biggest catch in the world. You won't mind now Lou, will you? — I'm going to be married to Dan — to Dan! — he's my Dan now — why, Lou!"

Around the corner of the park strolled one of those new-crop, smooth-faced young policemen that are making the force more endurable — at least to the eye. He saw a woman with an expensive fur coat, and diamond-ringed hands crouching down against the iron fence of the park sobbing turbulently, while a slender, plainly-dressed working girl leaned close, trying to console her. But the Gibsonian cop, being of the new order, passed on, pretending not to notice, for he was wise enough to know that these matters are beyond help so far as the power he represents is concerned, though he rap the pavement with his nightstick till the sound goes up to the furthermost stars.

A DEAL IN WHEAT

Frank Norris (1870-1902)

I. The Bear — Wheat at Sixty-Two

As Sam Lewiston backed the horse into the shafts of his backboard and began hitching the tugs to the whiffletree, his wife came out from the kitchen door of the house and drew near, and stood for some time at the horse's head, her arms folded and her apron rolled around them. For a long moment neither spoke. They had talked over the situation so long and so comprehensively the night before that there seemed to be nothing more to say.

The time was late in the summer, the place a ranch in southwestern Kansas, and Lewiston and his wife were two of a vast population of farmers, wheat growers, who at that moment were passing through a crisis — a crisis that at any moment might culminate in tragedy. Wheat was down to sixty-six.

At length Emma Lewiston spoke.

"Well," she hazarded, looking vaguely out across the ranch toward the horizon, leagues distant; "well, Sam, there's always that offer of brother Joe's. We can quit — and go to Chicago — if the worst comes."

"And give up!" exclaimed Lewiston, running the lines through the torets.

"Leave the ranch! Give up! After all these years!"

His wife made no reply for the moment. Lewiston climbed into the buckboard and gathered up the lines. "Well, here goes for the last try, Emmie," he said. "Good-by, girl. Maybe things will look better in town to-day."

"Maybe," she said gravely. She kissed her husband good-by and stood for some time looking after the buckboard traveling toward the town in a moving pillar of dust.

"I don't know," she murmured at length; "I don't know just how we're going to make out."

When he reached town, Lewiston tied the horse to the iron railing in front of the Odd Fellows' Hall, the ground floor of which was occupied by the post-office, and went across the street and up the stairway of a building of brick and granite — quite the most pretentious structure of the town — and knocked at a door upon the first landing. The door was furnished with a pane of frosted glass, on which, in gold letters, was inscribed, "Bridges & Co., Grain Dealers."

Bridges himself, a middle-aged man who wore a velvet skull-cap and who was smoking a Pittsburg stogie, met the farmer at the counter and the two exchanged perfunctory greetings.

"Well," said Lewiston, tentatively, after awhile.

"Well, Lewiston," said the other, "I *can't* take that wheat of yours at any better than sixty-two."

"Sixty-two."

"It's the Chicago price that does it, Lewiston. Truslow is bearing the stuff for all he's worth. It's Truslow and the bear clique that stick the knife into us. The price broke again this morning. We've just got a wire."

"Good heavens," murmured Lewiston, looking vaguely from side to side. "That — that ruins me. I can't carry my grain any longer — what with storage charges and — and — Bridges, I don't see just how I'm going to make out. Sixty-two cents a bushel! Why, man, what with this and with that it's cost me nearly a dollar a bushel to raise that wheat, and now Truslow ——"

He turned away abruptly with a quick gesture of infinite discouragement.

He went down the stairs, and making his way to where his buckboard was hitched, got in, and, with eyes vacant, the reins slipping and sliding in his limp, half-open hands, drove slowly back to the ranch. His wife had seen him coming, and met him as he drew up before the barn.

"Well?" she demanded.

"Emmie," he said as he got out of the buckboard, laying his arm across her shoulder, "Emmie, I guess we'll take up with Joe's offer. We'll go to Chicago. We're cleaned out!"

II. The Bull — Wheat at a Dollar-Ten

> . . . —— and said Party of the Second Part further covenants and agrees to merchandise such wheat in foreign ports, it being understood and agreed between the Party of the First Part and the Party of the Second Part that the wheat hereinbefore mentioned is released and sold to the Party of the Second Part for export purposes only, and not for consumption or distribution within the boundaries of the United States of America or of Canada.

"Now, Mr. Gates, if you will sign for Mr. Truslow I guess that'll be all," remarked Hornung when he had finished reading.

Hornung affixed his signature to the two documents and passed them over to Gates, who signed for his principal and client, Truslow — or, as he had been called ever since he had gone into the fight against Hornung's corner — the Great

Bear. Hornung's secretary was called in and witnessed the signatures, and Gates thrust the contract into his Gladstone bag and stood up, smoothing his hat.

"You will deliver the warehouse receipts for the grain," began Gates.

"I'll send a messenger to Truslow's office before noon," interrupted Hornung. "You can pay by certified check through the Illinois Trust people."

When the other had taken himself off, Hornung sat for some moments gazing abstractedly toward his office windows, thinking over the whole matter. He had just agreed to release to Truslow, at the rate of one dollar and ten cents per bushel, one hundred thousand out of the two million and odd bushels of wheat that he, Hornung, controlled, or actually owned. And for the moment he was wondering if, after all, he had done wisely in not goring the Great Bear to actual financial death. He had made him pay one hundred thousand dollars. Truslow was good for this amount. Would it not have been better to have put a prohibitive figure on the grain and forced the Bear into bankruptcy? True, Hornung would then be without his enemy's money, but Truslow would have been eliminated from the situation, and that — so Hornung told himself — was always a consummation most devoutly, strenuously and diligently to be striven for. Truslow once dead was dead, but the Bear was never more dangerous than when desperate.

"But so long as he can't get *wheat*," muttered Hornung at the end of his reflections, "he can't hurt me. And he can't get it. That I *know*."

For Hornung controlled the situation. So far back as the February of that year an "unknown bull" had been making his presence felt on the floor of the Board of Trade. By the middle of March the commercial reports of the daily press had begun to speak of "the powerful bull clique"; a few weeks later that legendary condition of affairs implied and epitomized in the magic words "Dollar Wheat" had been attained, and by the first of April, when the price had been boosted to one dollar and ten cents a bushel, Hornung had disclosed his hand, and in place of mere rumours, the definite and authoritative news that May wheat had been cornered in the Chicago pit went flashing around the world from Liverpool to Odessa and from Duluth to Buenos Ayres.

It was — so the veteran operators were persuaded — Truslow himself who had made Hornung's corner possible. The Great Bear had for once over-reached himself, and, believing himself all-powerful, had hammered the price just the fatal fraction too far down. Wheat had gone to sixty-two — for the time, and under the circumstances, an abnormal price.

When the reaction came it was tremendous. Hornung saw his chance, seized it, and in a few months had turned the tables, had cornered the product, and virtually driven the bear clique out of the pit.

On the same day that the delivery of the hundred thousand bushels was made to Truslow, Hornung met his broker at his lunch club.

"Well," said the latter, "I see you let go that line of stuff to Truslow."

Hornung nodded; but the broker added:

"Remember, I was against it from the very beginning. I know we've cleared up over a hundred thou'. I would have fifty times preferred to have lost twice that and *smashed Truslow dead*. Bet you what you like he makes us pay for it somehow."

"Huh!" grunted his principal. "How about insurance, and warehouse charges, and carrying expenses on that lot? Guess we'd have had to pay those, too, if we'd held on."

But the other put up his chin, unwilling to be persuaded. "I won't sleep easy," he declared, "till Truslow is busted."

III. The Pit

Just as Going mounted the steps on the edge of the pit the great gong struck, a roar of a hundred voices developed with the swiftness of successive explosions, the rush of a hundred men surging downward to the center of the pit filled the air with the stamp and grind of feet, a hundred hands in eager strenuous gestures tossed upward from out the brown of the crowd, the official reporter in his cage on the margin of the pit leaned far forward with straining ear to catch the opening bid, and another day of battle was begun.

Since the sale of the hundred thousand bushels of wheat to Truslow the "Hornung crowd" had steadily shouldered the price higher until on this particular morning it stood at one dollar and a half. That was Hornung's price. No one else had any grain to sell.

But not ten minutes after the opening, Going was surprised out of all countenance to hear shouted from the other side of the pit these words:

"Sell May at one-fifty."

Going was for the moment touching elbows with Kimbark on one side and with Merriam on the other, all three belonging to the "Hornung crowd." Their answering challenge of "*Sold*" was as the voice of one man. They did not pause to reflect upon the strangeness of the circumstance. (That was for afterward.) Their response to the offer was as unconscious, as reflex action and almost as rapid, and before the pit was well aware of what had happened the transaction of one thousand bushels was down upon Going's trading-card and fifteen hundred dollars had changed hands. But here was a marvel — the whole available supply of wheat cornered, Hornung master of the situation, invincible, unassailable; yet behold a man willing to sell, a Bear bold enough to raise his head.

"That was Kennedy, wasn't it, who made that offer?" asked Kimbark, as Going noted down the trade — "Kennedy, that new man?"

"Yes; who do you suppose he's selling for; who's willing to go short at this stage of the game?"

"Maybe he ain't short."

"Short! Great heavens, man; where'd he get the stuff?"

"Blamed if I know. We can account for every handful of May. Steady! Oh, there he goes again."

"Sell a thousand May at one-fifty," vociferated the bear-broker, throwing out his hand, one finger raised to indicate the number of "contracts" offered. This time it was evident that he was attacking the Hornung crowd deliberately, for, ignoring the jam of traders that swept toward him, he looked across the pit to where Going and Kimbark were shouting "*Sold! Sold!*" and nodded his head.

A second time Going made memoranda of the trade, and either the Hornung holdings were increased by two thousand bushels of May wheat or the Hornung bank account swelled by at least three thousand dollars of some unknown short's money.

Of late — so sure was the bull crowd of its position — no one had even thought of glancing at the inspection sheet on the bulletin board. But now one of Going's messengers hurried up to him with the announcement that this sheet showed receipts at Chicago for that morning of twenty-five thousand bushels, and not credited to Hornung. Some one had got hold of a line of wheat overlooked by the "clique" and was dumping it upon them.

"Wire the Chief," said Going over his shoulder to Merriam. This one struggled out of the crowd, and on a telegraph blank scribbled:

> Strong bear movement — New man — Kennedy — Selling in lots of five contracts — Chicago receipts twenty-five thousand.

The message was despatched, and in a few moments the answer came back, laconic, of military terseness:

> Support the market.

And Going obeyed, Merriam and Kimbark following, the new broker fairly throwing the wheat at them in thousand-bushel lots.

"Sell May at 'fifty; sell May; sell May." A moment's indecision, an instant's hesitation, the first faint suggestion of weakness, and the market would have broken under them. But for the better part of four hours they stood their ground, taking all that was offered, in constant communication with the Chief, and from time to time stimulated and steadied by his brief, unvarying command:

"Support the market."

At the close of the session they had bought in the twenty-five thousand bushels of May. Hornung's position was as stable as a rock, and the price closed even with the opening figure — one dollar and a half.

But the morning's work was the talk of all La Salle Street. Who was back of the raid?

What was the meaning of this unexpected selling? For weeks the pit trading had been merely nominal. Truslow, the Great Bear, from whom the most serious attack might have been expected, had gone to his country seat at Geneva Lake, in Wisconsin, declaring himself to be out of the market entirely. He went bass-fishing every day.

IV. The Belt Line

On a certain day toward the middle of the month, at a time when the mysterious Bear had unloaded some eighty thousand bushels upon Hornung, a conference was held in the library of Hornung's home. His broker attended it, and also a clean-faced, bright-eyed individual whose name of Cyrus Ryder might have been found upon the pay-roll of a rather well-known detective agency. For upward of half an hour after the conference began the detective spoke, the other two listening attentively, gravely.

"Then, last of all," concluded Ryder, "I made out I was a hobo, and began stealing rides on the Belt Line Railroad. Know the road? It just circles Chicago. Truslow owns it. Yes? Well, then I began to catch on. I noticed that cars of certain numbers — thirty-one nought thirty-four, thirty-two one ninety — well, the numbers don't matter, but anyhow, these cars were always switched onto the sidings by Mr. Truslow's main elevator D soon as they came in. The wheat was shunted in, and they were pulled out again. Well, I spotted one car and stole a ride on her. Say, look here, *that car went right around the city on the Belt, and came back to D again, and the same wheat in her all the time.* The grain was reinspected — it was raw, I tell you — and the warehouse receipts made out just as though the stuff had come in from Kansas or Iowa."

"The same wheat all the time!" interrupted Hornung.

"The same wheat — your wheat, that you sold to Truslow."

"Great snakes!" ejaculated Hornung's broker. "Truslow never took it abroad at all."

"Took it abroad! Say, he's just been running it around Chicago, like the supers in 'Shenandoah,' round an' round, so you'd think it was a new lot, an' selling it back to you again."

"No wonder we couldn't account for so much wheat."

"Bought it from us at one-ten, and made us buy it back — our own wheat — at one-fifty."

Hornung and his broker looked at each other in silence for a moment. Then all at once Hornung struck the arm of his chair with his fist and exploded in a roar of laughter. The broker stared for one bewildered moment, then followed his example.

"Sold! Sold!" shouted Hornung almost gleefully. "Upon my soul it's as good as a Gilbert and Sullivan show. And we — Oh, Lord! Billy, shake on it, and hats off to my distinguished friend, Truslow. He'll be President some day. Hey! What? Prosecute him? Not I."

"He's done us out of a neat hatful of dollars for all that," observed the broker, suddenly grave.

"Billy, it's worth the price."

"We've got to make it up somehow."

"Well, tell you what. We were going to boost the price to one seventy-five next week, and make that our settlement figure."

"Can't do it now. Can't afford it."

"No. Here; we'll let out a big link; we'll put wheat at two dollars, and let it go at that."

"Two it is, then," said the broker.

V. The Bread Line

The street was very dark and absolutely deserted. It was a district on the "South Side," not far from the Chicago River, given up largely to wholesale stores, and after nightfall was empty of all life. The echoes slept but lightly hereabouts, and the slightest footfall, the faintest noise, woke them upon the instant and sent them clamouring up and down the length of the pavement between the iron shuttered fronts. The only light visible came from the side door of a certain "Vienna" bakery, where at one o'clock in the morning loaves of bread were given away to any who should ask. Every evening about nine o'clock the outcasts began to gather about the side door. The stragglers came in rapidly, and the line — the "bread line," as it was called — began to form. By midnight it was usually some hundred yards in length, stretching almost the entire length of the block.

Toward ten in the evening, his coat collar turned up against the fine drizzle that pervaded the air, his hands in his pockets, his elbows gripping his sides, Sam Lewiston came up and silently took his place at the end of the line.

Unable to conduct his farm upon a paying basis at the time when Truslow, the "Great Bear," had sent the price of grain down to sixty-two cents a bushel, Lewiston had turned over his entire property to his creditors, and, leaving Kansas for good, had abandoned farming, and had left his wife at her sister's boarding-house in Topeka with the understanding that she was to join him in Chicago so soon as he had found a steady job. Then he had come to Chicago and had turned workman. His brother Joe conducted a small hat factory on Archer Avenue, and for a time he found there a meager employment. But difficulties had occurred, times were bad, the hat factory was involved in debts, the repealing of a certain import duty on manufactured felt overcrowded the home market with cheap Belgian and French products, and in the end his brother had assigned and gone to Milwaukee.

Thrown out of work, Lewiston drifted aimlessly about Chicago, from pillar to post, working a little, earning here a dollar, there a dime, but always sinking, sinking, till at last the ooze of the lowest bottom dragged at his feet and the rush of the great ebb went over him and engulfed him and shut him out from the light, and a park bench became his home and the "bread line" his chief makeshift of subsistence.

He stood now in the enfolding drizzle, sodden, stupefied with fatigue. Before and behind stretched the line. There was no talking. There was no sound. The street was empty. It was so still that the passing of a cable-car in the adjoining thoroughfare grated like prolonged rolling explosions, beginning and ending at immeasurable distances. The drizzle descended incessantly. After a long time midnight struck.

There was something ominous and gravely impressive in this interminable line of dark figures, close-pressed, soundless; a crowd, yet absolutely still; a close-packed, silent file, waiting, waiting in the vast deserted night-ridden street; waiting without a word, without a movement, there under the night and under the slow-moving mists of rain.

Few in the crowd were professional beggars. Most of them were workmen, long since out of work, forced into idleness by long-continued "hard times," by ill luck, by sickness. To them the "bread line" was a godsend. At least they could not starve. Between jobs here in the end was something to hold them up — a small platform, as it were, above the sweep of black water, where for a moment they might pause and take breath before the plunge.

The period of waiting on this night of rain seemed endless to those silent, hungry men; but at length there was a stir. The line moved. The side door opened. Ah, at last! They were going to hand out the bread.

But instead of the usual white-aproned under-cook with his crowded hampers there now appeared in the doorway a new man — a young fellow who looked like a bookkeeper's assistant. He bore in his hand a placard, which he tacked to the outside of the door. Then he disappeared within the bakery, locking the door after him.

A shudder of poignant despair, an unformed, inarticulate sense of calamity, seemed to run from end to end of the line. What had happened? Those in the rear, unable to read the placard, surged forward, a sense of bitter disappointment clutching at their hearts.

The line broke up, disintegrated into a shapeless throng — a throng that crowded forward and collected in front of the shut door whereon the placard was affixed. Lewiston, with the others, pushed forward. On the placard he read these words:

> Owing to the fact that the price of grain has been increased to two dollars a bushel, there will be no distribution of bread from this bakery until further notice.

Lewiston turned away, dumb, bewildered. Till morning he walked the streets, going on without purpose, without direction. But now at last his luck had turned. Overnight the wheel of his fortunes had creaked and swung upon its axis, and before noon he had found a job in the street-cleaning brigade. In the course of time he rose to be first shift-boss, then deputy inspector, then inspector, promoted to the dignity of driving in a red wagon with rubber tires and drawing a salary instead of mere wages. The wife was sent for and a new start made.

But Lewiston never forgot. Dimly he began to see the significance of things. Caught once in the cogs and wheels of a great and terrible engine, he had seen — none better — its workings. Of all the men who had vainly stood in the "bread line" on that rainy night in early summer, he, perhaps, had been the only one who had struggled up to the surface again. How many others had gone down in the great ebb? Grim question; he dared not think how many.

He had seen the two ends of a great wheat operation — a battle between Bear and Bull. The stories (subsequently published in the city's press) of Truslow's countermove in selling Hornung his own wheat, supplied the unseen section. The farmer — he who raised the wheat — was ruined upon one hand; the workingman — he who consumed it — was ruined upon the other. But between the two, the great operators, who never saw the wheat they traded in, bought and sold the world's food, gambled in the nourishment of entire nations, practised their tricks, their chicanery and oblique shifty "deals," were reconciled in their differences, and went on through their appointed way, jovial, contented, enthroned, and unassailable.

THE LOST PHOEBE

Theodore Dreiser (1871-1945)

THEY lived together in a part of the country which was not so prosperous as it had once been, about three miles from one of those small towns that, instead of increasing in population, is steadily decreasing. The territory was not very thickly settled; perhaps a house every other mile or so, with large areas of corn- and wheat-land and fallow fields that at odd seasons had been sown to timothy and clover. Their particular house was part log and part frame, the log portion being the old original home of Henry's grandfather. The new portion, of now rain- beaten, time-worn slabs, through which the wind squeaked in the chinks at times, and which several overshadowing elms and a butternut-tree made picturesque and reminiscently pathetic, but a little damp, was erected by Henry when he was twenty-one and just married.

That was forty-eight years before. The furniture inside, like the house outside, was old and mildewy and reminiscent of an earlier day. You have seen the what-not of cherry wood, perhaps, with spiral legs and fluted top. It was there. The old-fashioned four poster bed, with its ball-like protuberances and deep curving incisions, was there also, a sadly alienated descendant of an early Jacobean ancestor. The bureau of cherry was also high and wide and solidly built, but faded-looking, and with a musty odor. The rag carpet that underlay all these sturdy examples of enduring furniture was a weak, faded, lead-and-pink-colored affair woven by Phoebe Ann's own hands, when she was fifteen years younger than she was when she died. The creaky wooden loom on which it had been done now stood like a dusty, bony skeleton, along a broken rocking-chair, a worm-eaten clothes-press — Heaven knows how old — a lime-stained bench that had once been used to keep flowers on outside the door, and other decrepit factors of household utility, in an east room that was a lean-to against this so-called main portion. All sorts of other broken-down furniture were about this place; an antiquated clothes-horse, cracked in two of its ribs; a broken mirror in an old cherry frame, which had fallen from a nail and cracked itself three days before their youngest son, Jerry, died; an extension hat-rack, which once had had porceline knobs on the ends of its pegs; and a sewing-machine, long since outdone in its clumsy mechanism by rivals of a newer generation.

The orchard to the east of the house was full of gnarled old apple-trees, worm-eaten as to trunks and branches, and fully ornamented with green and white lichens, so that it had a sad, greenish-white, silvery effect in moonlight. The low outhouses, which had once housed chickens, a horse or two, a cow, and several pigs, were coveted with patches of moss as their roof, and the sides had been free of paint for so long that they, were blackish gray as to color, and a little spongy. The picket-fence in front, with its gate squeaky and askew, and the side fences of the stake-and-rider type were in an equally run-down condition. As a matter of fact, they had aged synchronously with the persons who lived here, old Henry Reifsneider and his wife Phoebe Ann.

They had lived here, these two, ever since their marriage, forty-eight years before, and Henry had lived here before that from his childhood up. His father and mother, well along in years when he was a boy, had invited him to bring his wife here when he had first fallen in love and decided to marry; and he had done so. His father and mother were the companions of himself and his wife for ten years after they were married, when both died; and then Henry and Phoebe were left with their five children growing lustily apace. But all sorts of things had happened since then. Of the seven children, all told, that had been born to them, three had died; one girl had gone to Kansas; one boy had gone to Sioux Falls, never even to be heard of after; another boy had gone to Washington; and the last girl lived five counties away in the same state, but was so burdened with cares of her own that she rarely gave them a thought. Time and a commonplace home life that had never been attractive had weaned them thoroughly, so that, wherever they were, they gave little thought as to how it might be with their father and mother.

Old Henry Reifsneider and his wife Phoebe were a loving couple. You perhaps know how it is with simple natures that fasten themselves like lichens on the stones of circumstance and weather their days to a crumbling conclusion. The great world sounds widely, but it has no call for them. They have no soaring intellect. The orchard, the meadow, the cornfield, the pig-pen, and the chicken-lot measure the range of their human activities. When the wheat is headed it is reaped and threshed; when the corn is browned and frosted it is cut and shocked; when the timothy is in full head it is cut, and the hay-cock erected. After that comes winter, with the hauling of grain to market, the sawing and splitting of wood, the simple chores of fire-building, meal-getting, occasional repairing, and visiting. Beyond these and the changes of weather — the snows, the rains, and the fair days — there are no immediate, significant things. All the rest of life is a far-off, clamorous phantasmagoria flickering like Northern lights in the night, and sounding as faintly as cow-bells tinkling in the distance.

Old Henry and his wife Phoebe were as fond of each other as it is possible for two old people to be who have nothing else in this life to be fond of. He was a thin old man, seventy when she died, a queer, crotchety person with coarse gray-black hair and beard, quite straggly and unkempt. He looked at you out of dull, fishy, watery eyes that had deep-brown crow's-feet at the sides. His clothes, like the clothes of many farmers, were aged and angular and baggy, standing out at the pockets, not fitting about the neck, protuberant and worn at elbow and knee. Phoebe Ann was thin and shapeless, a very umbrella of a woman, clad in shabby black, and with a black bonnet for her best wear. As time had passed, and they had only themselves to look after, their movements had come slower and slower, their activities fewer and fewer. The annual keep of pigs had been reduced from five to one grunting porker, and the single horse which Henry now retained was a sleepy animal, not over-nourished and not very clean. The chickens, of which formerly there was a large flock, had almost disappeared, owing to ferrets, foxes, and the lack of proper care, which produces disease. The former healthy garden was now a straggling memory of itself, and the vines and flower-beds that formerly ornamented the windows and dooryard had now become choking thickets. A will had been made which divided the small tax-eaten property equally among the remaining four, so that it was really of no interest to any of them. Yet these two lived together in peace and sympathy, only that now and then old Henry would become unduly cranky, complaining almost invariably that something had been neglected or mislaid which was of no importance at all.

"Phoebe, where's my corn-knife? You ain't never minded to let my things alone no more."

"Now you hush, Henry," his wife would caution him in a cracked and squeaky voice. "If you don't, I'll leave yuh. I'll git up and walk out of here some day, and then where would y' be? Y' ain't got anybody but me to look after yuh, so yuh just behave yourself. Your corn knife's on the mantel where it's allus been unless you've gone an' put it summers else."

Old Henry, who knew his wife would never leave him in any circumstances, used to speculate at times as to what he would do if she were to die. That was the one leaving that he really feared. As he climbed on the chair at night to wind the old, long-pendulumed, double-weighted clock, or went finally to the front and the back door to see that they were safely shut in, it was a comfort to know that Phoebe was there, properly ensconced on her side of the bed, and that if he stirred restlessly in the night, she would be there to ask what he wanted.

"Now, Henry, do lie still! You're as restless as a chicken."

"Well, I can't sleep, Phoebe."

"Well, yuh needn't roll so, anyhow. Yuh kin let me sleep."

This usually reduced him to a state of somnolent ease. If she wanted a pail of water, it was a grumbling pleasure for him to get it; and if she did rise first to build the fires, he saw that the wood was cut and placed within easy reach. They divided this simple world nicely between them.

As the years had gone on, however, fewer and fewer people had called. They were well-known for a distance of as much as ten square miles as old Mr. and Mrs. Reifsneider, honest, moderately Christian, but too old to be really interesting any longer. The writing of letters had become an almost impossible burden too difficult to continue or even negotiate via others, although an occasional letter still did arrive from the daughter in Pemberton County. Now and then some old friend stopped with a pie or cake or a roasted chicken or duck, or merely to see that they were well; but even these kindly reminded visits were no longer frequent.

One day in the early spring of her sixty-fourth year Mrs. Reifsneider took sick, and from a low fever passed into some indefinable ailment which, because of her age, was no longer curable. Old Henry drove to Swinnerton, the neighboring town, and procured a doctor. Some friends called, and the immediate care of her was taken off his hands. Then one chill spring night she died, and old Henry, in a fog of sorrow and uncertainty, followed her body to the nearest graveyard, an unattractive space with a few pines growing in it. Although he might have gone to the daughter in Pemberton or sent for her, it was really too much trouble and he was too weary and fixed. It was suggested to him at once by one friend and another that he come to stay with them awhile, but he did not see fit. He was so old and so fixed in his notions and so accustomed to the exact surroundings he had known all his days, that he could not think of leaving. He wanted to remain near where they had put his Phoebe; and the fact that he would have to live alone did not trouble him in the least. The living children were notified and the care of him offered if he would leave, but he would not.

"I kin make a shift for myself," he continually announced to old Dr. Morrow, who had attended his wife in this case. "I kin cook a little, and, besides, it don't take much more'n coffee and bread in the mornin's to satisfy me. I'll get along now well enough. Yuh just let me be." And after many pleadings and proffers of advice, with supplies of coffee and bacon and baked bread duly offered and accepted, he was left to himself. For a while he sat idly outside his door brooding in the spring sun. He tried to revive his interest in farming, and to keep himself busy and free from thought by looking after the fields, which of late had been much neglected. It was a gloomy thing to come in of an evening, however, or in the afternoon and find no shadow of Phoebe where everything suggested her. By degrees he put a few of her things away. At night he sat beside his lamp and read in the papers that were left him occasionally or in a Bible that he had neglected for years, but he could get little solace from these things. Mostly he held his hand over his mouth and looked at the floor as he sat and thought of what had become of her, and how soon he himself would die. He made a great business of making his coffee in the morning and frying himself another a little bacon at night; but his appetite was gone. The shell in which he had been housed so long seemed vacant, and its shadows were suggestive of immedicable griefs. So he lived quite dolefully for five long months, and then a change began.

It was one night, after he had looked after the front and the back door, wound the clock, blown out the light, and gone through all the selfsame, notions that he had indulged in for years, that he went to bed not so much to sleep as to think. It was a moonlight night. The green-lichen-covered orchard just outside and to be seen from his bed where he now lay was a silvery affair, sweetly spectral. The moon shone through the east windows, throwing the pattern of the panes on the wooden floor, and making the old furniture, to which he was accustomed, stand out dimly in the room. As usual he had been thinking of Phoebe and the years when they had been young together, and of the children who had gone, and the poor shift he was making of his present days. The house was coming to be in a very bad state indeed. The bedclothes were in disorder and not clean, for he made a wretched shift of washing. It was a terror to him. The roof leaked, causing things, some of them, to remain damp for weeks at a time, but he was getting into that brooding state where he would accept anything rather than exert himself. He preferred to pace slowly to and fro or to sit and think.

By twelve o'clock of this particular night he was asleep, however, and by two had waked again. The moon by this time had shifted to a position on the western side of the house, and it now shone in through the windows of the living-room and those of the kitchen beyond. A certain combination of furniture — a chair near a table, with his coat on it, the half-open kitchen door casting a shadow, and the position of a lamp near a paper — gave him an exact representation of Phoebe leaning over the table as he had often seen her do in life. It gave him a great start. Could it be she — or her ghost? He had scarcely ever believed in spirits; and still — He looked at her fixedly in the feeble half-light, his old hair tingling odd at the roots, and then sat up. The figure did not move. He put his thin legs out of the bed and sat looking at her, wondering if this could really be Phoebe. They had talked of ghosts often in their lifetime, of apparitions and omens; but they had never agreed that such things could be. It had never been a part of his wife's creed that she could have a spirit that could return to walk the earth. Her after-world was quite a different affair, a vague heaven, no less, from which the righteous did not trouble to return. Yet here she was now, bending over the table in her black skirt and gray shawl, her pale profile outlined against the moonlight.

"Phoebe," he called, thrilling from head to toe and putting out one bony hand, "have yuh come back?"

The figure did not stir, and he arose and walked uncertainly to the door, looking at it fixedly the while. As he drew near, however, the apparition resolved itself into its primal content — his old coat over the backed chair, the lamp by the paper, the half-open door.

"Well," he said to himself, his mouth open, "I thought shore I saw her." And he ran his hand strangely and vaguely through his hair, the nervous tension relaxed. Vanished as it had, it gave him the idea that she might return.

Another night, because of this first illusion, and because his mind was now constantly on her and he was old, he looked out of the window that was nearest his bed and commanded a hen-coop and pig-pen and a part of the wagon-shed, and there, a faint mist exuding from the damp of the ground, he thought he saw her again. It was one of those little wisps of mist, one of those faint exhalations of the earth that rise in a cool night after a warm day, and flicker like small white cypresses of fog before they disappear. In life it had been a custom of hers to cross this lot from her kitchen door to the pig-pen to throw in any scrap that was left from her cooking, and here she was again. He sat up and watched it strangely, doubtfully, because of his previous experience, but inclined, because of the nervous titillation that passed over his body, to believe that spirits really were, and that Phoebe, who would be concerned because of his lonely state, must be thinking about him, and hence returning. What other way would she have? How otherwise could she express herself? It would be within the province of her charity so to do, and like her loving interest in him. He quivered and watched it eagerly; but, a faint breath of air stirring, it wound away toward the fence and disappeared.

A third night, as he was actually dreaming, some ten days later, she came to his bedside and put her hand on his head.

"Poor Henry!" she said. "It's too bad."

He roused out of his sleep, actually to see her, he thought, moving from his bed-room into the one living-room, her figure a shadowy mass of black. The weak straining of his eyes caused little points of light to flicker about the outlines of her form. He arose greatly astonished, walked the floor in the cool room, convinced that Phoebe was coming back to him. If he only thought sufficiently, if he made it perfectly clear by his feeling that he needed her greatly, she would come back, this kindly wife, and tell him what to do. She would perhaps be with him much of the time, in the night, anyhow; and that would make him less lonely, this state more endurable.

In age and with the feeble it is not such a far cry from the subtleties of illusion to actual hallucination, and in due time this transition was made for Henry. Night after night he waited, expecting her return. Once in his weird mood he thought he saw a pale light moving about the room, and another time he thought he saw her walking in the orchard after dark. It was virtually unendurable that he woke with the thought that she was not dead. How he had arrived at this conclusion it is hard to say. His mind had gone. In its place was a fixed illusion. He and Phoebe had had a senseless quarrel. He had reproached her for not leaving his pipe where he was accustomed to find it, and she had left. It was an aberrated fulfillment of her old jesting threat that if he did not behave himself she would leave him.

"I guess I could find yuh ag'in," he had always said. But her cackling threat had always been:

"Yuh'll not find me if I ever leave yuh. I guess I kin git some place where yuh can't find me."

This morning when he arose he did not think to build the fire in the customary way or to grind his coffee and cut his bread, as was his wont, but solely meditate as to where he should search for her and should induce her to come back. Recently the one horse had been dispensed with because he found it cumbersome and beyond his needs. He took down his soft crush hat after he had dressed himself, a new glint of interest and determination in his eye, and taking his black crook cane from behind the door, where he had always placed it, started out briskly to look for her among the nearest neighbors. His old shoes clumped soundly in the dust as he walked, and his gray-black locks, now grown rather long, straggled out in a dramatic fringe or halo from under his hat. His short coat stirred busily as he walked, and his hands and face were peaked and pale.

"Why, hello, Henry! Where're yuh goin' this mornin'?" inquired Farmer Dodge, who, hauling a load of wheat to market, encountered him on the public road. He had not seen the aged farmer in months, not since his wife's death, and he wondered now, seeing him looking so spry.

"Yuh ain't seen Phoebe, have yuh?" inquired the old man, looking up quizzically.

"Phoebe who?" inquired Farmer Dodge, not for the moment connecting the name with Henry's dead wife.

"Why, my wife Phoebe, o' course. Who do yuh s'pose I mean?" He stared up with a pathetic sharpness of glance from under his shaggy, gray eyebrows.

"Wall, I'll swan, Henry, yuh ain't jokin', are yuh?" said the solid Dodge, a pursy man, with a smooth, hard, red face. "It can't be your wife yuh're talkin' about. She's dead."

"Dead! Shucks!" retorted the demented Reifsneider. "She left me early this mornin', while I was sleepin'. She allus got up to build the fire, but she's gone now. We had a little spat last night, an' I guess that's the reason. But I guess I kin find her. She's gone over to Matilda Race's; that's where she's gone."

He started briskly up the road, leaving the amazed Dodge to stare in wonder after him.

"Well, I'll be switched!" he said aloud to himself, "He's clean out'n his head. That poor old feller's been livin' down there till he's gone outen his mind. I'll have to notify the authorities." And he flicked his whip with great enthusiasm. "Geddapi" he said, and was off.

Reifsneider met no one else in this poorly populated region until he reached the whitewashed fence of Matilda Race and her husband three miles away. He had passed several other houses en route, but these not being within the range of his illusion were not considered. His wife, who had known Matilda well, must be here. He opened the picket-gate which guarded the walk, and stamped briskly up to the door.

"Why, Mr. Reifsneider," exclaimed old Matilda herself, a stout woman, looking out of the door in answer to his knock, "what brings yuh here this mornin'?"

"Is Phoebe here?" he demanded eagerly.

"Phoebe who? What Phoebe?" replied Mrs. Race, curious as to this sudden development of energy on his part.

"Why, my Phoebe, o' course. My wife Phoebe. Who do yuh s'pose? Ain't she here now?"

"Lawsy me!' exclaimed Mrs. Race, opening her mouth. "Yuh pore man! So you're clean out'n your mind now. Yuh come right in and sit down. I'll git yuh a cup o' coffee. O' course your wife ain't here; but yuh come in an' sit down. I'll find her fer yuh after a while. I know where she is."

The old farmer's eyes softened, and he entered. He was so thin and pale a specimen, pantalooned and patriarchal, that he aroused Mrs. Race's extremest sympathy as he took off his hat and laid it on his knees quite softly and mildly.

"We had a quarrel last night, an' she left me," he volunteered.

"Laws! laws!" sighed Mrs. Race, there being no one present with whom to share her astonishment as she went to her kitchen. "The pore man! Now somebody's just got to look after him. He can't be allowed to run around the country this way lookin' for his dead wife. It's turrible."

She boiled him a pot of coffee and brought in some of her new-baked bread and fresh butter. She set out some of her best jam and put a couple of eggs to boil, lying wholeheartedly the while.

"Now yuh stay right there, Uncle Henry, till Jake comes in, an' I'll send him to look for Phoebe. I think it's more'n likely she's over to Swinnerton with some of her friends. Anyhow, we'll find out. Now yuh just drink this coffee an' eat this bread. Yuh must be tired. Yuh've had a long walk this mornin'." Her idea was to take counsel with Jake, "her man," and perhaps have him notify the authorities.

She bustled about, meditating on the uncertainties of life, while old Reifsneider thrummed on the rim of his hat with his pale fingers and later ate abstractedly of what she offered. His mind was on his wife, however, and since she was not here, or did not appear, it wandered vaguely away to a family by the name of Murray, miles away in another direction. He decided after a time that he would not wait for Jake Race to hunt his wife but would seek her for himself. He must be on, and urge her to come back.

"Well, I'll be goin'," he said, getting up and looking strangely about him. "I guess she didn't come here after all. She went over to the Murrays', I guess. I'll not wait any longer, Mis' Race. There's a lot to do over to the house to-day." And out he marched in the face of her protests taking to the dusty road again in the warm spring sun, his cane striking the earth as he went.

It was two hours later that this pale figure of a man appeared in the Murrays' doorway, dusty, perspiring, eager. He had tramped all of five miles, and it was noon. An amazed husband and wife of sixty heard his strange query, and realized also that he was mad. They begged him to stay to dinner, intending to notify the authorities later and see what could be done; but though he stayed to partake of a little something, he did not stay long, and was off again to another distant farmhouse, his idea of many things to do and his need of Phoebe impelling him. So it went for that day and the next and the next, the circle of his inquiry ever widening.

The process by which a character assumes the significance of being peculiar, his antics weird, yet harmless, in such a community is often involute and pathetic. This day, as has been said, saw Reifsneider at other doors, eagerly asking his unnatural question, and leaving a trail of amazement, sympathy, and pity in his wake. Although the authorities were informed — the county sheriff, no less — it was not deemed advisable to take him into custody; for when those who knew old Henry, and had for so long, reflected on the condition of the county insane asylum, a place which, because of the poverty of the district, was of staggering aberration and sickening environment, it was decided to let him remain at large; for, strange to relate, it was found on investigation that at night he returned peaceably enough to his lonesome domicile there to discover whether his wife had returned, and to brood in loneliness until the morning. Who would lock up a thin, eager, seeking old man with iron-gray hair and an attitude of kindly, innocent inquiry, particularly when he was well known for a past of only kindly servitude and reliability? Those who had known him best rather agreed that he should be allowed to roain at large. He could do no harm. There were many who were willing to help him as to food, old clothes, the odds and ends of his daily life — at least at first. His figure after a time became not so much a common-place as an accepted curiosity, and the replies, "Why, no, Henry; I ain't see her," or "No, Henry; she ain't been here to-day," more customary.

For several years thereafter then he was an odd figure in the sun and rain, on dusty roads and muddy ones, encountered occasionally in strange and unexpected places, pursuing his endless search. Undernourishment, after a time, although the neighbors and those who knew his history gladly contributed from their store, affected his body; for he walked much and ate little. The longer he roamed the public highway in this manner, the deeper became his strange hallucination; and finding it harder and harder to return from his more and more distant pilgrimages he finally began taking a few utensils with him from his home, making a small package of them, in order that he might not be compelled to return, in an old tin coffee-pot of large size he placed a small tin cup, a knife, fork, and spoon, some salt and pepper and to the outside of it, by a string forced through a pierced hole, he fastened a plate, which could be released, and which was his woodland table. It was no trouble for him to secure the little food that he needed and with a strange, almost religious dignity, he had hesitation in asking for that much. By degrees his hair became longer and longer, his once black hat became an earthen brown, and his clothes threadbare and dusty.

For all of three years he walked, and none knew how wide were his perambulations, nor how he survived the storms and cold. They could not see him, with homely rural understanding and forethought, sheltering himself in hay-cocks, or by the sides of cattle, whose warm bodies protected him from the cold, and whose dull understandings were not opposed to his harmless presence. Overhanging rocks and trees kept him at times from the rain, and a friendly hay-loft or corn-crib was not above his humble consideration.

The involute progression of hallucination is strange. From asking at doors and being constantly rebuffed or denied, he finally came to the conclusion that although his Phoebe might not be in any of the houses at the doors of which he inquired, she might nevertheless be within the sound of his voice. And so, from patient inquiry, he began to call sad, occasional cries, that ever and anon waked the quiet landscapes and ragged hill regions, and set to echoing his thin "O-o-o Phoebe! O-o-o Phoebe!" It had a pathetic, albeit insane, ring, and many a farmer or plowboy came to know it even from afar and say, "There goes old Reifsneider."

Another thing that puzzled him greatly after a time and after many hundreds of inquiries was, when he no longer had any particular dooryard in view and no special inquiry to make, which way to go. These cross-roads, which occasionally led in four or even six directions, came after a time to puzzle him. But to solve this knotty problem, which became more and more of a puzzle, there came to his aid another hallucination. Phoebe's spirit or some power of the air or wind or nature would tell him. If he stood at the center of the parting of the ways, closed his eyes, turned thrice about, and called "O-o-o Phoebe!" twice, and then threw his cane straight before him, that would surely indicate which way to go for Phoebe, or one of these mystic powers would surely govern its direction and fall! In whichever direction it went, even though, as was not infrequently the case, it took him back along the path he had already come, or across fields, he was not so far gone in his mind but that he gave himself ample time to search before he called again. Also the hallucination seemed to persist that at some time he would surely find her. There were hours when his feet were sore, and his limbs weary, when he would stop in the heat to wipe his seamed brow, or in the cold to beat his arms. Sometimes, after throwing away his cane, and finding it indicating the direction from which he had just come, he would shake his head wearily and philosophically, as if contemplating the unbelievable or an untoward fate, and then start briskly off. His strange figure came finally to be known in the farthest reaches of three or four counties. Old Reifsneider was a pathetic character. His fame was wide.

Near a little town called Watersville, in Green County, perhaps four miles from that minor center of human activity, there was a place or precipice locally known as the Red Cliff, a sheer wall of red sandstone, perhaps a hundred feet high, which raised its sharp face for half a mile or more above the fruitful cornfields and orchards that lay beneath, and which was surmounted by a thick grove of trees. The slope that slowly led up to it from the opposite side was covered by a rank growth of beech, hickory, and ash, through which threaded a number of wagon-tracks crossing various angles. In fair weather it had become old Reifsneider's habit, so inured was he by now to the open, to make his bed in some such patch of trees as this to fry his bacon or boil his eggs at the foot of some tree before laying himself down for the night. Occasionally, so light and inconsequential was his sleep, he would walk at night. More often, the moonlight or some sudden wind stirring in the trees or a reconroitering animal arousing him, he would sit up and think, or pursue his quest in the moonlight or the dark, a strange, unnatural, half wild, half savage-looking but utterly harmless creature, calling at lonely road crossings, staring at dark and shuttered houses, and wondering where, where Phoebe could really be.

That particular full that comes in the systole-diastole of this earthly ball at two o'clock in the morning invariably aroused him, and though he might not go any farther he would sit up and contemplate the darkness or the stars, wondering. Sometimes in the strange processes of his mind he would fancy that he saw moving among the trees the figure of his lost wife, and then he would get up to follow, taking his utensils, always on a string, and his cane. If she seemed to evade him too easily he would run, or plead, or, suddenly losing track of the fancied figure, stand awed or disappointed, grieving for the moment over the almost insurmountable difficulties of his search.

It was in the seventh year of these hopeless peregrinations, in the dawn of a similar springtime to that in which his wife had died, that he came at last one night to the vicinity of this self-same patch that crowned the rise to the Red Cliff. His far-flung cane, used as a divining-rod at the last cross-roads, had brought him hither. He had walked many, many miles. It was after ten o'clock at night, and he was very weary. Long wandering and little eating had left him but a shadow of his former self. It was a question now not so much of physical strength but of spiritual endurance which kept him up. He had scarcely eaten this day, and now exhausted he set himself down in the dark to rest and possibly to sleep.

Curiously on this occasion a strange suggestion of the presence of his wife surrounded him. It would not be long now, he counseled with himself, although the long months had brought him nothing, until he should see her, talk to her. He fell asleep after a time, his head on his knees. At midnight the moon began to rise, and at two in the morning, his wakeful hour, was a large silver disk shining through the trees to the east. He opened his eyes when the radiance came strong, making a silver pattern at his feet and lighting the woods with strange lusters and silvery, shadowy forms. As usual, his old notion that his wife must be near occurred to him on this occasion and he looked about him with a speculative, anticipatory eye. What was it that moved in the distant shadows along the path by which he had entered — a pale, flickering will-o'-the-wisp that bobbed gracefully among the trees and riveted his expectant gaze? Moonlight and shadows combined to give it a strange form and a stranger reality, this fluttering of bog-fire or dancing of wandering fire-flies. Was it truly his lost Phoebe? By a circuitous route it passed about him, and in his fevered state he fancied that he could see the very eyes of her, not as she was when he last saw her in the black dress and shawl but now a strangely younger Phoebe, gayer, sweeter, the one whom he had known years before as a girl. Old Reifsneider got up. He had been expecting and dreaming of this hour all these years, and now as he saw the feeble light dancing lightly before him he peered at it questioningly, one thin hand in his gray hair.

Of a sudden there came to him now for the first time in many years the full charm of her girlish figure as he had known it in boyhood, the pleasing, sympathetic smile, the brown hair, the blue sash she had once worn about her waist at a picnic, her gay, graceful movements. He walked around the base of the tree, straining with his eyes, forgetting for once his cane and utensils, and following eagerly after. On she moved before him, a will-o'-the-wisp of the spring, a little flame above her head, and it seemed as though among the small saplings of ash and beech and the thick trunks of hickory and elm that she signaled with a young, a lightsome hand.

"O Phoebe! Phoebe!" he called. "Have yuh really come? Have yuh really answered me?" And hurrying faster, he fell once, scrambling lamely to his feet, only to see the light in the distance dancing illusively on. On and on he hurried until he was fairly running, brushing his ragged arms against the trees, striking his hands and face against impeding twigs. His hat was gone, his lungs were breathless, his reason quite astray, when coming to the edge of the cliff he saw her below among a silvery bed of apple-trees now blooming in the spring.

"O Phoebe!" he called. "O Phoebe! Oh, no, don't leave me!" And feeling the lure of a world where love was young and Phoebe as this vision presented her, a delightful epitome of their quondam youth, he gave a gay cry of "Oh, wait, Phoebe!" and leaped.

Some farmer-boys, reconnoitering this region of bounty and prospect some few days afterward, found first the tin utensils tied together under the tree where he had left them, and then later at the foot of the cliff, pale, broken, but elate, a molded smile of peace and delight upon his lips, his body. His old hat was discovered lying under some low-growing saplings the twigs of which had held it back. No one of all the simple population knew how eagerly and joyously he had found his lost mate.

THE BLUE HOTEL

Stephen Crane (1871-1900)

I

The Palace Hotel at Fort Romper was painted a light blue, a shade that is on the legs of a kind of heron, causing the bird to declare its position against any background. The Palace Hotel, then, was always screaming and howling in a way that made the dazzling winter landscape of Nebraska seem only a gray swampish hush. It stood alone on the prairie, and when the snow was falling the town two hundred yards away was not visible. But when the traveller alighted at the railway station he was obliged to pass the Palace Hotel before he could come upon the company of low clapboard houses which composed Fort Romper, and it was not to be thought that any traveller could pass the Palace Hotel without looking at it. Pat Scully, the proprietor, had proved himself a master of strategy when he chose his paints. It is true that on clear days, when the great trans-continental expresses, long lines of swaying Pullmans, swept through Fort Romper, passengers were overcome at the sight, and the cult that knows the brown-reds and the subdivisions of the dark greens of the East expressed shame, pity, horror, in a laugh. But to the citizens of this prairie town and to the people who would naturally stop there, Pat Scully had performed a feat. With this opulence and splendor, these creeds, classes, egotisms, that streamed through Romper on the rails day after day, they had no color in common.

As if the displayed delights of such a blue hotel were not sufficiently enticing, it was Scully's habit to go every morning and evening to meet the leisurely trains that stopped at Romper and work his seductions upon any man that he might see wavering, gripsack in hand.

One morning, when a snow-crusted engine dragged its long string of freight cars and its one passenger coach to the station, Scully performed the marvel of catching three men. One was a shaky and quick-eyed Swede, with a great shining cheap valise; one was a tall bronzed cowboy, who was on his way to a ranch near the Dakota line; one was a little silent man from the East, who didn't look it, and didn't announce it. Scully practically made them prisoners. He was so nimble and merry and kindly that each probably felt it would be the height of brutality to try to escape. They trudged off over the creaking board sidewalks in the wake of the eager little Irishman. He wore a heavy fur cap squeezed tightly down on his head. It caused his two red ears to stick out stiffly, as if they were made of tin.

At last, Scully, elaborately, with boisterous hospitality, conducted them through the portals of the blue hotel. The room which they entered was small. It seemed to be merely a proper temple for an enormous stove, which, in the center, was humming with godlike violence. At various points on its surface the iron had become luminous and glowed yellow from the heat. Beside the stove Scully's son Johnnie was playing High-Five with an old farmer who had whiskers both gray and sandy. They were quarrelling. Frequently the old farmer turned his face towards a box of sawdust — colored brown from tobacco juice — that was behind the stove, and spat with an air of great impatience and irritation. With a loud flourish of words Scully destroyed the game of cards, and bustled his son up-stairs with part of the baggage of the new guests. He himself conducted them to three basins of the coldest water in the world. The cowboy and the Easterner burnished themselves fiery-red with this water, until it seemed to be some kind of a metal polish. The Swede, however, merely dipped his fingers gingerly and with trepidation. It was notable that throughout this series of small ceremonies the three travellers were made to feel that Scully was very benevolent. He was conferring great favors upon them. He handed the towel from one to the other with an air of philanthropic impulse.

Afterwards they went to the first room, and, sitting about the stove, listened to Scully's officious clamor at his daughters, who were preparing the mid-day meal. They reflected in the silence of experienced men who tread carefully amid new people. Nevertheless, the old farmer, stationary, invincible in his chair near the warmest part of the stove, turned his face from the sawdust box frequently and addressed a glowing commonplace to the strangers. Usually he was answered in short but adequate sentences by either the cowboy or the Easterner. The Swede said nothing. He seemed to be occupied in making furtive estimates of each man in the room. One might have thought that he had the sense of silly suspicion which comes to guilt. He resembled a badly frightened man.

Later, at dinner, he spoke a little, addressing his conversation entirely to Scully. He volunteered that he had come from New York, where for ten years he had worked as a tailor. These facts seemed to strike Scully as fascinating, and afterwards he volunteered that he had lived at Romper for fourteen years. The Swede asked about the crops and the price of labor. He seemed barely to listen to Scully's extended replies. His eyes continued to rove from man to man.

Finally, with a laugh and a wink, he said that some of these Western communities were very dangerous; and after his statement he straightened his legs under the table, tilted his head, and laughed again, loudly. It was plain that the demonstration had no meaning to the others. They looked at him wondering and in silence.

II

As the men trooped heavily back into the front-room, the two little windows presented views of a turmoiling sea of snow. The huge arms of the wind were making attempts — mighty, circular, futile — to embrace the flakes as they sped. A gate-post like a still man with a blanched face stood aghast amid this profligate fury. In a hearty voice Scully announced the presence of a blizzard. The guests of the blue hotel, lighting their pipes, assented with grunts of lazy masculine contentment. No island of the sea could be exempt in the degree of this little room with its humming stove. Johnnie, son of Scully, in a tone which defined his opinion of his ability as a card-player, challenged the old farmer of both gray and sandy whiskers to a game of High-Five. The farmer agreed with a contemptuous and bitter scoff. They sat close to the stove, and squared their knees under a wide board. The cowboy and the Easterner watched the game with interest. The Swede remained near the window, aloof, but with a countenance that showed signs of an inexplicable excitement.

The play of Johnnie and the gray-beard was suddenly ended by another quarrel. The old man arose while casting a look of heated scorn at his adversary. He slowly buttoned his coat, and then stalked with fabulous dignity from the room. In the discreet silence of all other men the Swede laughed. His laughter rang somehow childish. Men by this time had begun to look at him askance, as if they wished to inquire what ailed him.

A new game was formed jocosely. The cowboy volunteered to become the partner of Johnnie, and they all then turned to ask the Swede to throw in his lot with the little Easterner. He asked some questions about the game, and, learning that it wore many names, and that he had played it when it was under an alias, he accepted the invitation. He strode towards the men nervously, as if he expected to be assaulted. Finally, seated, he gazed from face to face and laughed shrilly. This laugh was so strange that the Easterner looked up quickly, the cowboy sat intent and with his mouth open, and Johnnie paused, holding the cards with still fingers.

Afterwards there was a short silence. Then Johnnie said, "Well, let's get at it. Come on now!" They pulled their chairs forward until their knees were bunched under the board. They began to play, and their interest in the game caused the others to forget the manner of the Swede.

The cowboy was a board-whacker. Each time that he held superior cards he whanged them, one by one, with exceeding force, down upon the improvised table, and took the tricks with a glowing air of prowess and pride that sent thrills of indignation into the hearts of his opponents. A game with a board-whacker in it is sure to become intense. The countenances of the Easterner and the Swede were miserable whenever the cowboy thundered down his aces and kings, while Johnnie, his eyes gleaming with joy, chuckled and chuckled.

Because of the absorbing play none considered the strange ways of the Swede. They paid strict heed to the game. Finally, during a lull caused by a new deal, the Swede suddenly addressed Johnnie: "I suppose there have been a good many men killed in this room." The jaws of the others dropped and they looked at him.

"What in hell are you talking about?" said Johnnie.

The Swede laughed again his blatant laugh, full of a kind of false courage and defiance. "Oh, you know what I mean all right," he answered.

"I'm a liar if I do!" Johnnie protested. The card was halted, and the men stared at the Swede. Johnnie evidently felt that as the son of the proprietor he should make a direct inquiry. "Now, what might you be drivin' at, mister?" he asked. The Swede winked at him. It was a wink full of cunning. His fingers shook on the edge of the board. "Oh, maybe you think I have been to nowheres. Maybe you think I'm a tenderfoot?"

"I don't know nothin' about you," answered Johnnie, "and I don't give a damn where you've been. All I got to say is that I don't know what you're driving at. There hain't never been nobody killed in this room."

The cowboy, who had been steadily gazing at the Swede, then spoke: "What's wrong with you, mister?"

Apparently it seemed to the Swede that he was formidably menaced. He shivered and turned white near the corners of his mouth. He sent an appealing glance in the direction of the little Easterner. During these moments he did not forget to wear his air of advanced pot-valor. "They say they don't know what I mean," he remarked mockingly to the Easterner.

The latter answered after prolonged and cautious reflection. "I don't understand you," he said, impassively.

The Swede made a movement then which announced that he thought he had encountered treachery from the only quarter where he had expected sympathy, if not help. "Oh, I see you are all against me. I see — "

The cowboy was in a state of deep stupefaction. "Say," he cried, as he tumbled the deck violently down upon the board "— say, what are you gittin' at, hey?"

The Swede sprang up with the celerity of a man escaping from a snake on the floor. "I don't want to fight!" he shouted. "I don't want to fight!"

The cowboy stretched his long legs indolently and deliberately. His hands were in his pockets. He spat into the sawdust box. "Well, who the hell thought you did?" he inquired.

The Swede backed rapidly towards a corner of the room. His hands were out protectingly in front of his chest, but he was making an obvious struggle to control his fright. "Gentlemen," he quavered, "I suppose I am going to be killed before I can leave this house! I suppose I am going to be killed before I can leave this house!" In his eyes was the dying-swan look. Through the windows could be seen the snow turning blue in the shadow of dusk. The wind tore at the house and some loose thing beat regularly against the clap-boards like a spirit tapping.

A door opened, and Scully himself entered. He paused in surprise as he noted the tragic attitude of the Swede. Then he said, "What's the matter here?"

The Swede answered him swiftly and eagerly: "These men are going to kill me."

"Kill you!" ejaculated Scully. "Kill you! What are you talkin'?"

The Swede made the gesture of a martyr.

Scully wheeled sternly upon his son. "What is this, Johnnie?"

The lad had grown sullen. "Damned if I know," he answered. "I can't make no sense to it." He began to shuffle the cards, fluttering them together with an angry snap. "He says a good many men have been killed in this room, or something like that. And he says he's goin' to be killed here too. I don't know what ails him. He's crazy, I shouldn't wonder."

Scully then looked for explanation to the cowboy, but the cowboy simply shrugged his shoulders.

"Kill you?" said Scully again to the Swede. "Kill you? Man, you're off your nut."

"Oh, I know," burst out the Swede. "I know what will happen. Yes, I'm crazy — yes. Yes, of course, I'm crazy — yes. But I know one thing — " There was a sort of sweat of misery and terror upon his face. "I know I won't get out of here alive."

The cowboy drew a deep breath, as if his mind was passing into the last stages of dissolution. "Well, I'm dog-goned," he whispered to himself.

Scully wheeled suddenly and faced his son. "You've been troublin' this man!"

Johnnie's voice was loud with its burden of grievance. "Why, good Gawd, I ain't done nothin' to 'im."

The Swede broke in. "Gentlemen, do not disturb yourselves. I will leave this house. I will go away because" — he accused them dramatically with his glance — "because I do not want to be killed."

Scully was furious with his son. "Will you tell me what is the matter, you young divil? What's the matter, anyhow? Speak out!"

"Blame it!" cried Johnnie in despair, "don't I tell you I don't know. He — he says we want to kill him, and that's all I know. I can't tell what ails him."

The Swede continued to repeat: "Never mind, Mr. Scully; nevermind. I will leave this house. I will go away, because I do not wish to be killed. Yes, of course, I am crazy — yes. But I know one thing! I will go away. I will leave this house. Never mind, Mr. Scully; never mind. I will go away."

"You will not go 'way," said Scully. "You will not go 'way until I hear the reason of this business. If anybody has troubled you I will take care of him. This is my house. You are under my roof, and I will not allow any peaceable man to be troubled here." He cast a terrible eye upon Johnnie, the cowboy, and the Easterner.

"Never mind, Mr. Scully; never mind. I will go away. I do not wish to be killed." The Swede moved towards the door, which opened upon the stairs. It was evidently his intention to go at once for his baggage.

"No, no," shouted Scully peremptorily; but the white-faced man slid by him and disappeared. "Now," said Scully severely, "what does this mane?"

Johnnie and the cowboy cried together: "Why, we didn't do nothin' to 'im!"

Scully's eyes were cold. "No," he said, "you didn't?"

Johnnie swore a deep oath. "Why this is the wildest loon I ever see. We didn't do nothin' at all. We were jest sittin' here playin' cards, and he — "

The father suddenly spoke to the Easterner. "Mr. Blanc," he asked, "what has these boys been doin'?"

The Easterner reflected again. "I didn't see anything wrong at all," he said at last, slowly.

Scully began to howl. "But what does it mane?" He stared ferociously at his son. "I have a mind to lather you for this, me boy."

Johnnie was frantic. "Well, what have I done?" he bawled at his father.

III

"I think you are tongue-tied," said Scully finally to his son, the cowboy, and the Easterner; and at the end of this scornful sentence he left the room.

Up-stairs the Swede was swiftly fastening the straps of his great valise. Once his back happened to be half turned towards the door, and, hearing a noise there, he wheeled and sprang up, uttering a loud cry. Scully's wrinkled visage showed grimly in the light of the small lamp he carried. This yellow effulgence, streaming upward, colored only his prominent features, and left his eyes, for instance, in mysterious shadow. He resembled a murderer.

"Man! man!" he exclaimed, "have you gone daffy?"

"Oh, no! Oh, no!" rejoined the other. "There are people in this world who know pretty nearly as much as you do — understand?"

For a moment they stood gazing at each other. Upon the Swede's deathly pale cheeks were two spots brightly crimson and sharply edged, as if they had been carefully painted. Scully placed the light on the table and sat himself on the edge of the bed. He spoke ruminatively. "By cracky, I never heard of such a thing in my life. It's a complete muddle. I can't, for the soul of me, think how you ever got this idea into your head." Presently he lifted his eyes and asked: "And did you sure think they were going to kill you?"

The Swede scanned the old man as if he wished to see into his mind. "I did," he said at last. He obviously suspected that this answer might precipitate an outbreak. As he pulled on a strap his whole arm shook, the elbow wavering like a bit of paper.

Scully banged his hand impressively on the foot-board of the bed. "Why, man, we're goin' to have a line of ilictric street-cars in this town next spring."

" 'A line of electric street-cars,' " repeated the Swede, stupidly.

"And," said Scully, "there's a new railroad goin' to be built down from Broken Arm to here. Not to mintion the four churches and the smashin' big brick school-house. Then there's the big factory, too. Why, in two years Romper 'll be a met-tro-*pol*-is."

Having finished the preparation of his baggage, the Swede straightened himself. "Mr. Scully," he said, with sudden hardihood, "how much do I owe you?"

"You don't owe me anythin'," said the old man, angrily.

"Yes, I do," retorted the Swede. He took seventy-five cents from his pocket and tendered it to Scully; but the latter snapped his fingers in disdainful refusal. However, it happened that they both stood gazing in a strange fashion at three silver pieces on the Swede's open palm.

"I'll not take your money," said Scully at last. "Not after what's been goin' on here." Then a plan seemed to strike him. "Here," he cried, picking up his lamp and moving towards the door. "Here! Come with me a minute."

"No," said the Swede, in overwhelming alarm.

"Yes," urged the old man. "Come on! I want you to come and see a picter — just across the hall — in my room."

The Swede must have concluded that his hour was come. His jaw dropped and his teeth showed like a dead man's. He ultimately followed Scully across the corridor, but he had the step of one hung in chains.

Scully flashed the light high on the wall of his own chamber. There was revealed a ridiculous photograph of a little girl. She was leaning against a balustrade of gorgeous decoration, and the formidable bang to her hair was prominent. The figure was as graceful as an upright sled-stake, and, withal, it was of the hue of lead. "There," said Scully, tenderly, "that's the picter of my little girl that died. Her name was Carrie. She had the purtiest hair you ever saw! I was that fond of her, she — "

Turning then, he saw that the Swede was not contemplating the picture at all, but, instead, was keeping keen watch on the gloom in the rear.

"Look, man!" cried Scully, heartily. "That's the picter of my little gal that died. Her name was Carrie. And then here's the picter of my oldest boy, Michael. He's a lawyer in Lincoln, an' doin' well. I gave that boy a grand eddycation, and I'm glad for it now. He's a fine boy. Look at 'im now. Ain't he bold as blazes, him there in Lincoln, an honored an' respicted gintleman. An honored an' respicted gintleman," concluded Scully with a flourish. And, so saying, he smote the Swede jovially on the back.

The Swede faintly smiled.

"Now," said the old man, "there's only one more thing." He dropped suddenly to the floor and thrust his head beneath the bed. The Swede could hear his muffled voice. "I'd keep it under me piller if it wasn't for that boy Johnnie. Then there's the old woman — Where is it now? I never put it twice in the same place. Ah, now come out with you!"

Presently he backed clumsily from under the bed, dragging with him an old coat rolled into a bundle. "I've fetched him," he muttered. Kneeling on the floor, he unrolled the coat and extracted from its heart a large yellow-brown whiskey bottle.

His first maneuver was to hold the bottle up to the light. Reassured, apparently, that nobody had been tampering with it, he thrust it with a generous movement towards the Swede.

The weak-kneed Swede was about to eagerly clutch this element of strength, but he suddenly jerked his hand away and cast a look of horror upon Scully.

"Drink," said the old man affectionately. He had risen to his feet, and now stood facing the Swede.

There was a silence. Then again Scully said: "Drink!"

The Swede laughed wildly. He grabbed the bottle, put it to his mouth, and as his lips curled absurdly around the opening and his throat worked, he kept his glance, burning with hatred, upon the old man's face.

IV

After the departure of Scully the three men, with the card-board still upon their knees, preserved for a long time an astounded silence. Then Johnnie said: "That's the dod-dangest Swede I ever see."

"He ain't no Swede," said the cowboy, scornfully.

"Well, what is he then?" cried Johnnie. "What is he then?"

"It's my opinion," replied the cowboy deliberately, "he's some kind of a Dutchman." It was a venerable custom of the country to entitle as Swedes all light-haired men who spoke with a heavy tongue. In consequence the idea of the cowboy was not without its daring. "Yes, sir," he repeated. "It's my opinion this feller is some kind of a Dutchman."

"Well, he says he's a Swede, anyhow," muttered Johnnie, sulkily. He turned to the Easterner: "What do you think, Mr. Blanc?"

"Oh, I don't know," replied the Easterner.

"Well, what do you think makes him act that way?" asked the cowboy.

"Why, he's frightened." The Easterner knocked his pipe against a rim of the stove. "He's clear frightened out of his boots."

"What at?" cried Johnnie and cowboy together.

The Easterner reflected over his answer.

"What at?" cried the others again.

"Oh, I don't know, but it seems to me this man has been reading dime-novels, and he thinks he's right out in the middle of it — the shootin' and stabbin' and all."

"But," said the cowboy, deeply scandalized, "this ain't Wyoming, ner none of them places. This is Nebrasker."

"Yes," added Johnnie, "an' why don't he wait till he gits *out West?*"

The travelled Easterner laughed. "It isn't different there even — not in these days. But he thinks he's right in the middle of hell."

Johnnie and the cowboy mused long.

"It's awful funny," remarked Johnnie at last.

"Yes," said the cowboy. "This is a queer game. I hope we don't git snowed in, because then we'd have to stand this here man bein' around with us all the time. That wouldn't be no good."

"I wish pop would throw him out," said Johnnie.

Presently they heard a loud stamping on the stairs, accompanied by ringing jokes in the voice of old Scully, and laughter, evidently from the Swede. The men around the stove stared vacantly at each other. "Gosh!" said the cowboy. The door flew open, and old Scully, flushed and anecdotal, came into the room. He was jabbering at the Swede, who followed him, laughing bravely. It was the entry of two roisterers from a banquet-hall.

"Come now," said Scully sharply to the three seated men, "move up and give us a chance at the stove." The cowboy and the Easterner obediently sidled their chairs to make room for the new-comers. Johnnie, however, simply arranged himself in a more indolent attitude, and then remained motionless.

"Come! Git over, there," said Scully.

"Plenty of room on the other side of the stove," said Johnnie.

"Do you think we want to sit in the draught?" roared the father.

But the Swede here interposed with a grandeur of confidence. "No, no. Let the boy sit where he likes," he cried in a bullying voice to the father.

"All right! All right!" said Scully, deferentially. The cowboy and the Easterner exchanged glances of wonder.

The five chairs were formed in a crescent about one side of the stove. The Swede began to talk; he talked arrogantly, profanely, angrily. Johnnie, the cowboy, and the Easterner maintained a morose silence, while old Scully appeared to be receptive and eager, breaking in constantly with sympathetic ejaculations.

Finally the Swede announced that he was thirsty. He moved in his chair, and said that he would go for a drink of water.

"I'll git it for you," cried Scully at once.

"No," said the Swede, contemptuously. "I'll get it for myself." He arose and stalked with the air of an owner off into the executive parts of the hotel.

As soon as the Swede was out of hearing Scully sprang to his feet and whispered intensely to the others: "Up-stairs he thought I was tryin' to poison 'im."

"Say," said Johnnie, "this makes me sick. Why don't you throw 'im out in the snow?"

"Why, he's all right now," declared Scully. "It was only that he was from the East, and he thought this was a tough place. That's all. He's all right now."

The cowboy looked with admiration upon the Easterner. "You were straight," he said. "You were on to that there Dutchman."

"Well," said Johnnie to his father, "he may be all right now, but I don't see it. Other time he was scared, but now he's too fresh."

Scully's speech was always a combination of Irish brogue and idiom, Western twang and idiom, and scraps of curiously formal diction taken from the story-books and newspapers. He now hurled a strange mass of language at the head of his son. "What do I keep? What do I keep? What do I keep?" he demanded, in a voice of thunder. He slapped his knee impressively, to indicate that he himself was going to make reply, and that all should heed. "I keep a hotel," he shouted. "A hotel, do you mind? A guest under my roof has sacred privileges. He is to be intimidated by none. Not one word shall he hear that would prejudice him in favor of goin' away. I'll not have it. There's no place in this here town where they can say they iver took in a guest of mine because he was afraid to stay here." He wheeled suddenly upon the cowboy and the Easterner. "Am I right?"

"Yes, Mr. Scully," said the cowboy, "I think you're right."

"Yes, Mr. Scully," said the Easterner, "I think you're right."

V

At six-o'clock supper, the Swede fizzed like a fire-wheel. He sometimes seemed on the point of bursting into riotous song, and in all his madness he was encouraged by old Scully. The Easterner was incased in reserve; the cowboy sat in wide-mouthed amazement, forgetting to eat, while Johnnie wrathily demolished great plates of food. The daughters of the house, when they were obliged to replenish the biscuits, approached as warily as Indians, and, having succeeded in their purpose, fled with ill-concealed trepidation. The Swede domineered the whole feast, and he gave it the appearance of a cruel bacchanal. He seemed to have grown suddenly taller; he gazed, brutally disdainful, into every face. His voice rang through the room. Once when he jabbed out harpoon-fashion with his fork to pinion a biscuit, the weapon nearly impaled the hand of the Easterner which had been stretched quietly out for the same biscuit.

After supper, as the men filed towards the other room, the Swede smote Scully ruthlessly on the shoulder. "Well, old boy, that was a good, square meal." Johnnie looked hopefully at his father; he knew that shoulder was tender from an old fall; and, indeed, it appeared for a moment as if Scully was going to flame out over the matter, but in the end he smiled a sickly smile and remained silent. The others understood from his manner that he was admitting his responsibility for the Swede's new view-point.

Johnnie, however, addressed his parent in an aside. "Why don't you license somebody to kick you down-stairs?" Scully scowled darkly by way of reply.

When they were gathered about the stove, the Swede insisted on another game of High Five. Scully gently deprecated the plan at first, but the Swede turned a wolfish glare upon him. The old man subsided, and the Swede canvassed the others. In his tone there was always a great threat. The cowboy and the Easterner both remarked indifferently that they would play. Scully said that he would presently have to go to meet the 6.58 train, and so the Swede turned menacingly upon Johnnie. For a moment their glances crossed like blades, and then Johnnie smiled and said, "Yes, I'll play."

They formed a square, with the little board on their knees. The Easterner and the Swede were again partners. As the play went on, it was noticeable that the cowboy was not board-whacking as usual. Meanwhile, Scully, near the lamp, had put on his spectacles and, with an appearance curiously like an old priest, was reading a newspaper. In time he went out to meet the 6.58 train, and, despite his precautions, a gust of polar wind whirled into the room as he opened the door. Besides scattering the cards, it dulled the players to the marrow. The Swede cursed frightfully. When Scully returned, his entrance disturbed a cosey and friendly scene. The Swede again cursed. But presently they were once more intent, their heads bent forward and their hands moving swiftly. The Swede had adopted the fashion of board-whacking.

Scully took up his paper and for a long time remained immersed in matters which were extraordinarily remote from him. The lamp burned badly, and once he stopped to adjust the wick. The newspaper, as he turned from page to page, rustled with a slow and comfortable sound. Then suddenly he heard three terrible words: "You are cheatin'!"

Such scenes often prove that there can be little of dramatic import in environment. Any room can present a tragic front; any room can be comic. This little den was now hideous as a torture-chamber. The new faces of the men themselves had changed it upon the instant. The Swede held a huge fist in front of Johnnie's face, while the latter looked steadily over it into the blazing orbs of his accuser. The Easterner had grown pallid; the cowboy's jaw had dropped in that expression of bovine amazement which was one of his important mannerisms. After the three words, the first sound in the room was made by Scully's paper as it floated forgotten to his feet. His spectacles had also fallen from his nose, but by a clutch he had saved them in air. His hand, grasping the spectacles, now remained poised awkwardly and near his shoulder. He stared at the card-players.

Probably the silence was while a second elapsed. Then, if the floor had been suddenly twitched out from under the men they could not have moved quicker. The five had projected themselves headlong towards a common point. It happened that Johnnie, in rising to hurl himself upon the Swede, had stumbled slightly because of his curiously instinctive care for the cards and the board. The loss of the moment allowed time for the arrival of Scully, and also allowed the cowboy time to give the Swede a great push which sent him staggering back. The men found tongue together, and hoarse shouts of rage, appeal, or fear burst from every throat. The cowboy pushed and jostled feverishly at the Swede, and the Easterner and Scully clung wildly to Johnnie; but, through the smoky air, above the swaying bodies of the peace-compellers, the eyes of the two warriors ever sought each other in glances of challenge that were at once hot and steely.

Of course the board had been overturned, and now the whole company of cards was scattered over the floor, where the boots of the men trampled the fat and painted kings and queens as they gazed with their silly eyes at the war that was waging above them.

Scully's voice was dominating the yells. "Stop now? Stop, I say! Stop, now —"

Johnnie, as he struggled to burst through the rank formed by Scully and the Easterner, was crying, "Well, he says I cheated! He says I cheated! I won't allow no man to say I cheated! If he says I cheated, he's a —— ——!"

The cowboy was telling the Swede, "Quit, now! Quit, d'ye hear — "

The screams of the Swede never ceased: "He did cheat! I saw him! I saw him — "

As for the Easterner, he was importuning in a voice that was not heeded: "Wait a moment, can't you? Oh, wait a moment. What's the good of a fight over a game of cards? Wait a moment — "

In this tumult no complete sentences were clear. "Cheat" — "Quit" — "He says" — these fragments pierced the uproar and rang out sharply. It was remarkable that, whereas Scully undoubtedly made the most noise, he was the least heard of any of the riotous band.

Then suddenly there was a great cessation. It was as if each man had paused for breath; and although the room was still lighted with the anger of men, it could be seen that there was no danger of immediate conflict, and at once Johnnie, shouldering his way forward, almost succeeded in confronting the Swede. "What did you say I cheated for? What did you say I cheated for? I don't cheat, and I won't let no man say I do!"

The Swede said, "I saw you! I saw you!"

"Well," cried Johnnie, "I'll fight any man what says I cheat!"

"No, you won't," said the cowboy. "Not here."

"Ah, be still, can't you?" said Scully, coming between them.

The quiet was sufficient to allow the Easterner's voice to be heard. He was repealing, "Oh, wait a moment, can't you? What's the good of a fight over a game of cards? Wait a moment!"

Johnnie, his red face appearing above his father's shoulder, hailed the Swede again. "Did you say I cheated?"

The Swede showed his teeth. "Yes."

"Then," said Johnnie, "we must fight."

"Yes, fight," roared the Swede. He was like a demoniac. "Yes, fight! I'll show you what kind of a man I am! I'll show you who you want to fight! Maybe you think I can't fight! Maybe you think I can't! I'll show you, you skin, you card-sharp! Yes, you cheated! You cheated! You cheated!"

"Well, let's go at it, then, mister," said Johnnie, coolly.

The cowboy's brow was beaded with sweat from his efforts in intercepting all sorts of raids. He turned in despair to Scully. "What are you goin' to do now?"

A change had come over the Celtic visage of the old man. He now seemed all eagerness; his eyes glowed.

"We'll let them fight," he answered, stalwartly. "I can't put up with it any longer. I've stood this damned Swede till I'm sick. We'll let them fight."

VI

The men prepared to go out-of-doors. The Easterner was so nervous that he had great difficulty in getting his arms into the sleeves of his new leather coat. As the cowboy drew his fur cap down over his ears his hands trembled. In fact, Johnnie and old Scully were the only ones who displayed no agitation. These preliminaries were conducted without words.

Scully threw open the door. "Well, come on," he said. Instantly a terrific wind caused the flame of the lamp to struggle at its wick, while a puff of black smoke sprang from the chimney-top. The stove was in mid-current of the blast, and its voice swelled to equal the roar of the storm. Some of the scarred and bedabbled cards were caught up from the floor and dashed helplessly against the farther wall. The men lowered their heads and plunged into the tempest as into a sea.

No snow was falling, but great whirls and clouds of flakes, swept up from the ground by the frantic winds, were streaming southward with the speed of bullets. The covered land was blue with the sheen of an unearthly satin, and there was no other hue save where, at the low, black railway station — which seemed incredibly distant — one light gleamed like a tiny jewel. As the men floundered into a thigh deep drift, it was known that the Swede was bawling out something. Scully went to him, put a hand on his shoulder and projected an ear. "What's that you say?" he shouted.

"I say," bawled the Swede again, "I won't stand much show against this gang. I know you'll all pitch on me."

Scully smote him reproachfully on the arm. "Tut, man!" he yelled. The wind tore the words from Scully's lips and scattered them far alee.

"You are all a gang of — " boomed the Swede, but the storm also seized the remainder of this sentence.

Immediately turning their backs upon the wind, the men had swung around a corner to the sheltered side of the hotel. It was the function of the little house to preserve here, amid this great devastation of snow, an irregular V-shape of heavily incrusted grass, which crackled beneath the feet. One could imagine the great drifts piled against the windward side. When the party reached the comparative peace of this spot it was found that the Swede was still bellowing.

"Oh, I know what kind of a thing this is! I know you'll all pitch on me. I can't lick you all!"

Scully turned upon him panther fashion. "You'll not have to whip all of us. You'll have to whip my son Johnnie. An' the man what troubles you durin' that time will have me to dale with."

The arrangements were swiftly made. The two men faced each other, obedient to the harsh commands of Scully, whose face, in the subtly luminous gloom, could be seen set in the austere impersonal lines that are pictured on the countenances of the Roman veterans. The Easterner's teeth were chattering, and he was hopping up and down like a mechanical toy. The cowboy stood rock-like.

The contestants had not stripped off any clothing. Each was in his ordinary attire. Their fists were up, and they eyed each other in a calm that had the elements of leonine cruelty in it.

During this pause, the Easterner's mind, like a film, took lasting impressions of three men — the iron-nerved master of the ceremony; the Swede, pale, motionless, terrible; and Johnnie, serene yet ferocious, brutish yet heroic. The entire prelude had in it a tragedy greater than the tragedy of action, and this aspect was accentuated by the long, mellow cry of the blizzard, as it sped the tumbling and wailing flakes into the black abyss of the south.

"Now!" said Scully.

The two combatants leaped forward and crashed together like bullocks. There was heard the cushioned sound of blows, and of a curse squeezing out from between the tight teeth of one.

As for the spectators, the Easterner's pent-up breath exploded from him with a pop of relief, absolute relief from the tension of the preliminaries. The cowboy bounded into the air with a yowl. Scully was immovable as from supreme amazement and fear at the fury of the fight which he himself had permitted and arranged.

For a time the encounter in the darkness was such a perplexity of flying arms that it presented no more detail than would a swiftly revolving wheel. Occasionally a face, as if illumined by a flash of light, would shine out, ghastly and marked with pink spots. A moment later, the men might have been known as shadows, if it were not for the involuntary utterance of oaths that came from them in whispers.

Suddenly a holocaust of warlike desire caught the cowboy, and he bolted forward with the speed of a broncho. "Go it, Johnnie! go it! Kill him! Kill him!"

Scully confronted him. "Kape back," he said; and by his glance the cowboy could tell that this man was Johnnie's father.

To the Easterner there was a monotony of unchangeable fighting that was an abomination. This confused mingling was eternal to his sense, which was concentrated in a longing for the end, the priceless end. Once the fighters lurched near him, and as he scrambled hastily backward he heard them breathe like men on the rack.

"Kill him, Johnnie! Kill him! Kill him! Kill him!" The cowboy's face was contorted like one of those agony masks in museums.

"Keep still," said Scully, icily.

Then there was a sudden loud grunt, incomplete, cut short, and Johnnie's body swung away from the Swede and fell with sickening heaviness to the grass. The cowboy was barely in time to prevent the mad Swede from flinging himself upon his prone adversary. "No, you don't," said the cowboy, interposing an arm. "Wait a second."

Scully was at his son's side. "Johnnie! Johnnie, me boy!" His voice had a quality of melancholy tenderness. "Johnnie! Can you go on with it?" He looked anxiously down into the bloody, pulpy face of his son.

There was a moment of silence, and then Johnnie answered in his ordinary voice, "Yes, I — it — yes."

Assisted by his father he struggled to his feet. "Wait a bit now till you git your wind," said the old man.

A few paces away the cowboy was lecturing the Swede. "No, you don't! Wait a second!"

The Easterner was plucking at Scully's sleeve. "Oh, this is enough," he pleaded. "This is enough! Let it go as it stands. This is enough!"

"Bill," said Scully, "git out of the road." The cowboy stepped aside. "Now." The combatants were actuated by a new caution as they advanced towards collision. They glared at each other, and then the Swede aimed a lightning blow that carried with it his entire weight. Johnnie was evidently half stupid from weakness, but he miraculously dodged, and his fist sent the over-balanced Swede sprawling.

The cowboy, Scully, and the Easterner burst into a cheer that was like a chorus of triumphant soldiery, but before its conclusion the Swede had scuffled agilely to his feet and come in berserk abandon at his foe. There was another perplexity of flying arms, and Johnnie's body again swung away and fell, even as a bundle might fall from a roof. The Swede instantly staggered to a little wind-waved tree and leaned upon it, breathing like an engine, while his savage and flame-lit eyes roamed from face to face as the men bent over Johnnie. There was a splendor of isolation in his situation at this time which the Easterner felt once when, lifting his eyes from the man on the ground, he beheld that mysterious and lonely figure, waiting.

"Are you any good yet, Johnnie?" asked Scully in a broken voice.

The son gasped and opened his eyes languidly. After a moment he answered, "No — I ain't — any good — any — more." Then, from shame and bodily ill he began to weep, the tears furrowing down through the blood-stains on his face. "He was too — too — too heavy for me."

Scully straightened and addressed the waiting figure. "Stranger," he said, evenly, "it's all up with our side." Then his voice changed into that vibrant huskiness which is commonly the tone of the most simple and deadly announcements. "Johnnie is whipped."

Without replying, the victor moved off on the route to the front door of the hotel.

The cowboy was formulating new and un-spellable blasphemies. The Easterner was startled to find that they were out in a wind that seemed to come direct from the shadowed arctic floes. He heard again the wail of the snow as it was flung to its grave in the south. He knew now that all this time the cold had been sinking into him deeper and deeper, and he wondered that he had not perished. He felt indifferent to the condition of the vanquished man.

"Johnnie, can you walk?" asked Scully.

"Did I hurt — hurt him any?" asked the son.

"Can you walk, boy? Can you walk?"

Johnnie's voice was suddenly strong. There was a robust impatience in it. "I asked you whether I hurt him any!"

"Yes, yes, Johnnie," answered the cowboy, consolingly; "he's hurt a good deal."

They raised him from the ground, and as soon as he was on his feet he went tottering off, rebuffing all attempts at assistance. When the party rounded the corner they were fairly blinded by the pelting of the snow. It burned their faces like fire. The cowboy carried Johnnie through the drift to the door. As they entered some cards again rose from the floor and beat against the wall.

The Easterner rushed to the stove. He was so profoundly chilled that he almost dared to embrace the glowing iron. The Swede was not in the room. Johnnie sank into a chair, and, folding his arms on his knees, buried his face in them. Scully, warming one foot and then the other at a rim of the stove, muttered to himself with Celtic mournfulness. The cowboy had removed his fur cap, and with a dazed and rueful air he was running one hand through his tousled locks. From overhead they could hear the creaking of boards, as the Swede tramped here and there in his room.

The sad quiet was broken by the sudden flinging open of a door that led towards the kitchen. It was instantly followed by an inrush of women. They precipitated themselves upon Johnnie amid a chorus of lamentation. Before they carried their prey off to the kitchen, there to be bathed and harangued with that mixture of sympathy and abuse which is a feat of their sex, the mother straightened herself and fixed old Scully with an eye of stern reproach. "Shame be upon you, Patrick Scully!" she cried. "Your own son, too. Shame be upon you!"

"There, now! Be quiet, now!" said the old man, weakly.

"Shame be upon you, Patrick Scully!" The girls, rallying to this slogan, sniffed disdainfully in the direction of those trembling accomplices, the cowboy and the Easterner. Presently they bore Johnnie away, and left the three men to dismal reflection.

VII

"I'd like to fight this here Dutchman myself," said the cowboy, breaking a long silence.

Scully wagged his head sadly. "No, that wouldn't do. It wouldn't be right. It wouldn't be right."

"Well, why wouldn't it?" argued the cowboy. "I don't see no harm in it."

"No," answered Scully, with mournful heroism. "It wouldn't be right. It was Johnnie's fight, and now we mustn't whip the man just because he whipped Johnnie."

"Yes, that's true enough," said the cowboy; "but — he better not get fresh with me, because I couldn't stand no more of it."

"You'll not say a word to him," commanded Scully, and even then they heard the tread of the Swede on the stairs. His entrance was made theatric. He swept the door back with a bang and swaggered to the middle of the room. No one looked at him. "Well," he cried, insolently, at Scully, "I s'pose you'll tell me now how much I owe you?"

The old man remained stolid. "You don't owe me nothin'."

"Huh!" said the Swede, "huh! Don't owe 'im nothin'."

The cowboy addressed the Swede. "Stranger, I don't see how you come to be so gay around here."

Old Scully was instantly alert. "Stop!" he shouted, holding his hand forth, fingers upward. "Bill, you shut up!"

The cowboy spat carelessly into the sawdust box. "I didn't say a word, did I?" he asked.

"Mr. Scully," called the Swede, "how much do I owe you?" It was seen that he was attired for departure, and that he had his valise in his hand.

"You don't owe me nothin'," repeated Scully in his same imperturbable way.

"Huh!" said the Swede. "I guess you're right. I guess if it was any way at all, you'd owe me somethin'. That's what I guess." He turned to the cowboy. "'Kill him! Kill him! Kill him!'" he mimicked, and then guffawed victoriously. "'Kill him!'" He was convulsed with ironical humor.

But he might have been jeering the dead. The three men were immovable and silent, staring with glassy eyes at the stove.

The Swede opened the door and passed into the storm, giving one derisive glance backward at the still group.

As soon as the door was closed, Scully and the cowboy leaped to their feet and began to curse. They trampled to and fro, waving their arms and smashing into the air with their fists. "Oh, but that was a hard minute!" wailed Scully. "That was a hard minute! Him there leerin' and scoffin'! One bang at his nose was worth forty dollars to me that minute! How did you stand it, Bill?"

"How did I stand it?" cried the cowboy in a quivering voice. "How did I stand it? Oh!"

The old man burst into sudden brogue. "I'd loike to take that Swade," he wailed, "and hould 'im down on a shtone flure and bate 'im to a jelly wid a shtick!"

The cowboy groaned in sympathy. "I'd like to git him by the neck and ha-ammer him " — he brought his hand down on a chair with a noise like a pistol-shot — "hammer that there Dutchman until he couldn't tell himself from a dead coyote!"

"I'd bate 'im until he — "

"I'd show *him* some things — "

And then together they raised a yearning, fanatic cry — "Oh-o-oh! if we only could — "

"Yes!"

"Yes!"

"And then I'd — "

"O-o-oh!"

VIII

The Swede, tightly gripping his valise, tacked across the face of the storm as if he carried sails. He was following a line of little naked, gasping trees, which he knew must mark the way of the road. His face, fresh from the pounding of Johnnie's fists, felt more pleasure than pain in the wind and the driving snow. A number of square shapes loomed upon him finally, and he knew them as the houses of the main body of the town. He found a street and made travel along it, leaning heavily upon the wind whenever, at a corner, a terrific blast caught him.

He might have been in a deserted village. We picture the world as thick with conquering and elate humanity, but here, with the bugles of the tempest pealing, it was hard to imagine a peopled earth. One viewed the existence of man then as a marvel, and conceded a glamour of wonder to these lice which were caused to cling to a whirling, fire-smote, ice-locked, disease-stricken, space-lost bulb. The conceit of man was explained by this storm to be the very engine of life. One was a coxcomb not to die in it. However, the Swede found a saloon.

In front of it an indomitable red light was burning, and the snow-flakes were made blood color as they flew through the circumscribed territory of the lamp's shining. The Swede pushed open the door of the saloon and entered. A sanded expanse was before him, and at the end of it four men sat about a table drinking. Down one side of the room extended a radiant bar, and its guardian was leaning upon his elbows listening to the talk of the men at the table. The Swede dropped his valise upon the floor, and, smiling fraternally upon the barkeeper, said, "Gimme some whiskey, will you?" The man placed a bottle, a whiskey-glass, and a glass of ice-thick water upon the bar. The Swede poured himself an abnormal portion of whiskey and drank it in three gulps. "Pretty bad night," remarked the bartender, indifferently. He was making the pretension of blindness which is usually a distinction of his class; but it could have been seen that he was furtively studying the half-erased blood-stains on the face of the Swede. "Bad night," he said again.

"Oh, it's good enough for me," replied the Swede, hardily, as he poured himself some more whiskey. The barkeeper took his coin and maneuvered it through its reception by the highly nickelled cash-machine. A bell rang; a card labelled "20 cts." had appeared.

"No," continued the Swede, "this isn't too bad weather. It's good enough for me."

"So?" murmured the barkeeper, languidly.

The copious drams made the Swede's eyes swim, and he breathed a trifle heavier. "Yes, I like this weather. I like it. It suits me." It was apparently his design to impart a deep significance to these words.

"So?" murmured the bartender again. He turned to gaze dreamily at the scroll-like birds and bird-like scrolls which had been drawn with soap upon the mirrors back of the bar.

"Well, I guess I'll take another drink," said the Swede, presently. "Have something?"

"No, thanks; I'm not drinkin'," answered the bartender. Afterwards he asked, "How did you hurt your face?"

The Swede immediately began to boast loudly. "Why, in a fight. I thumped the soul out of a man down here at Scully's hotel."

The interest of the four men at the table was at last aroused.

"Who was it?" said one.

"Johnnie Scully," blustered the Swede. "Son of the man what runs it. He will be pretty near dead for some weeks, I can tell you. I made a nice thing of him, I did. He couldn't get up. They carried him in the house. Have a drink?"

Instantly the men in some subtle way incased themselves in reserve. "No, thanks," said one. The group was of curious formation. Two were prominent local business men; one was the district-attorney; and one was a professional gambler of the kind known as "square." But a scrutiny of the group would not have enabled an observer to pick the gambler from the men of more reputable pursuits. He was, in fact, a man so delicate in manner, when among people of fair class, and so judicious in his choice of victims, that in the strictly masculine part of the town's life he had come to be explicitly trusted and admired. People called him a thoroughbred. The fear and contempt with which his craft was regarded was undoubtedly the reason that his quiet dignity shone conspicuous above the quiet dignity of men who might be merely hatters, billiard markers, or grocery-clerks. Beyond an occasional unwary traveller, who came by rail, this gambler was supposed to prey solely upon reckless and senile farmers, who, when flush with good crops, drove into town in all the pride and confidence of an absolutely invulnerable stupidity. Hearing at times in circuitous fashion of the despoilment of such a farmer, the important men of Romper invariably laughed in contempt of the victim, and, if they thought of the wolf at all, it was with a kind of pride at the knowledge that he would never dare think of attacking their wisdom and courage. Besides, it was popular that this gambler had a real wife and two real children in a neat cottage in a suburb, where he led an exemplary home life; and when any one even suggested a discrepancy in his character, the crowd immediately vociferated descriptions of this virtuous family circle. Then men who led exemplary home lives, and men who did not lead exemplary home lives, all subsided in a bunch, remarking that there was nothing more to be said.

However, when a restriction was placed upon him — as, for instance, when a strong clique of members of the new Pollywog Club refused to permit him, even as a spectator, to appear in the rooms of the organization — the candor and gentleness with which he accepted the judgment disarmed many of his foes and made his friends more desperately partisan. He invariably distinguished between himself and a respectable Romper man so quickly and frankly that his manner actually appeared to be a continual broadcast compliment.

And one must not forget to declare the fundamental fact of his entire position in Romper. It is irrefutable that in all affairs outside of his business, in all matters that occur eternally and commonly between man and man, this thieving card-player was so generous, so just, so moral, that, in a contest, he could have put to flight the consciences of nine-tenths of the citizens of Romper.

And so it happened that he was seated in this saloon with the two prominent local merchants and the district-attorney.

The Swede continued to drink raw whiskey, meanwhile babbling at the barkeeper and trying to induce him to indulge in potations. "Come on. Have a drink. Come on. What — no? Well, have a little one, then. By gawd, I've whipped a man to-night, and I want to celebrate. I whipped him good, too. Gentlemen," the Swede cried to the men at the table, "have a drink?"

"Ssh!" said the barkeeper.

The group at the table, although furtively attentive, had been pretending to be deep in talk, but now a man lifted his eyes towards the Swede and said, shortly, "Thanks. We don't want any more."

At this reply the Swede ruffled out his chest like a rooster. "Well," he exploded, "it seems I can't get anybody to drink with me in this town. Seems so, don't it? Well!"

"Ssh!" said the barkeeper.

"Say," snarled the Swede, "don't you try to shut me up. I won't have it. I'm a gentleman, and I want people to drink with me. And I want 'em to drink with me now. *Now* — do you understand?" He rapped the bar with his knuckles.

Years of experience had calloused the bartender. He merely grew sulky. "I hear you," he answered.

"Well," cried the Swede, "listen hard then. See those men over there? Well, they're going to drink with me, and don't you forget it. Now you watch."

"Hi!" yelled the barkeeper, "this won't do!"

"Why won't it?" demanded the Swede. He stalked over to the table, and by chance laid his hand upon the shoulder of the gambler. "How about this?" he asked, wrathfully. "I asked you to drink with me."

The gambler simply twisted his head and spoke over his shoulder. "My friend, I don't know you."

"Oh, hell!" answered the Swede, "come and have a drink."

"Now, my boy," advised the gambler, kindly, "take your hand off my shoulder and go 'way and mind your own business." He was a little, slim man, and it seemed strange to hear him use this tone of heroic patronage to the burly Swede. The other men at the table said nothing.

"What! You won't drink with me, you little dude? I'll make you then! I'll make you!" The Swede had grasped the gambler frenziedly at the throat, and was dragging him from his chair. The other men sprang up. The barkeeper dashed around the corner of his bar. There was a great tumult, and then was seen a long blade in the hand of the gambler. It shot forward, and a human body, this citadel of virtue, wisdom, power, was pierced as easily as if it had been a melon. The Swede fell with a cry of supreme astonishment.

The prominent merchants and the district attorney must have at once tumbled out of the place backward. The bartender found himself hanging limply to the arm of a chair and gazing into the eyes of a murderer.

"Henry," said the latter, as he wiped his knife on one of the towels that hung beneath the bar-rail, "you tell 'em where to find me. I'll be home, waiting for 'em." Then he vanished. A moment afterwards the barkeeper was in the street dinning through the storm for help, and, moreover, companionship.

The corpse of the Swede, alone in the saloon, had its eyes fixed upon a dreadful legend that dwelt atop of the cash-machine: "This registers the amount of your purchase."

IX

Months later, the cowboy was frying pork over the stove of a little ranch near the Dakota line, when there was a quick thud of hoofs outside, and presently the Easterner entered with the letters and the papers.

"Well," said the Easterner at once, "the chap that killed the Swede has got three years. Wasn't much, was it?"

"He has? Three years?" The cowboy poised his pan of pork, while he ruminated upon the news. "Three years. That ain't much."

"No. It was a light sentence," replied the Easterner as he unbuckled his spurs. "Seems there was a good deal of sympathy for him in Romper."

"If the bartender had been any good," observed the cowboy, thoughtfully, "he would have gone in and cracked that there Dutchman on the head with a bottle in the beginnin' of it and stopped all this here murderin'."

"Yes, a thousand things might have happened," said the Easterner, tartly.

The cowboy returned his pan of pork to the fire, but his philosophy continued. "It's funny, ain't it? If he hadn't said Johnnie was cheatin' he'd be alive this minute. He was an awful fool. Game played for fun, too. Not for money. I believe he was crazy."

"I feel sorry for that gambler," said the Easterner.

"Oh, so do I," said the cowboy. "He don't deserve none of it for killin' who he did."

"The Swede might not have been killed if everything had been square."

"Might not have been killed?" exclaimed the cowboy. "Everythin' square? Why, when he said that Johnnie was cheatin' and acted like such a jackass? And then in the saloon he fairly walked up to git hurt?" With these arguments the cowboy browbeat the Easterner and reduced him to rage.

"You're a fool!" cried the Easterner, viciously. "You're a bigger jackass than the Swede by a million majority. Now let me tell you one thing. Let me tell you something. Listen! Johnnie *was* cheating!"

" 'Johnnie,' " said the cowboy, blankly. There was a minute of silence, and then he said, robustly, "Why, no. The game was only for fun."

"Fun or not," said the Easterner, "Johnnie was cheating. I saw him. I know it. I saw him. And I refused to stand up and be a man. I let the Swede fight it out alone. And you — you were simply puffing around the place and wanting to fight. And then old Scully himself! We are all in it! This poor gambler isn't even a noun. He is kind of an adverb. Every sin is the result of a collaboration. We, five of us, have collaborated in the murder of this Swede. Usually there are from a dozen to forty women really involved in every murder, but in this case it seems to be only five men — you, I, Johnnie, old Scully, and that fool of an unfortunate gambler came merely as a culmination, the apex of a human movement, and gets all the punishment."

The cowboy, injured and rebellious, cried out blindly into this fog of mysterious theory: "Well, I didn't do anythin', did I?"

THE LYNCHING OF JUBE BENSON

Paul Laurence Dunbar (1872-1906)

Gordon Fairfax's library held but three men, but the air was dense with clouds of smoke. The talk had drifted from one topic to another much as the smoke wreaths had puffed, floated, and thinned away. Then Handon Gay, who was an ambitious young reporter, spoke of a lynching story in a recent magazine, and the matter of punishment without trial put new life into the conversation.

"I should like to see a real lynching," said Gay rather callously.

"Well, I should hardly express it that way," said Fairfax, "but if a real, live lynching were to come my way, I should not avoid it."

"I should," spoke the other from the depths of his chair, where he had been puffing in moody silence. Judged by his hair, which was freely sprinkled with gray, the speaker might have been a man of forty-five or fifty, but his face, though lined and serious, was youthful, the face of a man hardly past thirty.

"What, you, Dr. Melville? Why, I thought that you physicians wouldn't weaken at anything."

"I have seen one such affair," said the doctor gravely, "in fact, I took a prominent part in it."

"Tell us about it," said the reporter, feeling for his pencil and notebook, which he was, nevertheless, careful to hide from the speaker.

The men drew their chairs eagerly up to the doctor's, but for a minute he did not seem to see them, but sat gazing abstractedly into the fire, then he took a long draw upon his cigar and began:

"I can see it all very vividly now. It was in the summer time and about seven years ago. I was practising at the time down in the little town of Bradford. It was a small and primitive place, just the location for an impecunious medical man, recently out of college.

"In lieu of a regular office, I attended to business in the first of two rooms which I rented from Hiram Daly, one of the more prosperous of the townsmen. Here I boarded and here also came my patients — white and black — whites from every section, and blacks from 'nigger town,' as the west portion of the place was called.

"The people about me were most of them coarse and rough, but they were simple and generous, and as time passed on I had about abandoned my intention of seeking distinction in wider fields and determined to settle into the place of a modest country doctor. This was rather a strange conclusion for a young man to arrive at, and I will not deny that the presence in the house of my host's beautiful young daughter, Annie, had something to do with my decision. She was a beautiful young girl of seventeen or eighteen, and very far superior to her surroundings. She had a native grace and a pleasing way about her that made everybody that came under her spell her abject slave. White and black who knew her loved her, and none, I thought, more deeply and respectfully than Jube Benson, the black man of all work about the place.

"He was a fellow whom everybody trusted; an apparently steady-going, grinning sort, as we used to call him. Well, he was completely under Miss Annie's thumb, and would fetch and carry for her like a faithful dog. As soon as he saw that I began to care for Annie, and anybody could see that, he transferred some of his allegiance to me and became my faithful servitor also. Never did a man have a more devoted adherent in his wooing than did I, and many a one of Annie's tasks which he volunteered to do gave her an extra hour with me. You can imagine that I liked the boy and you need not wonder any more that as both wooing and my practice waxed apace, I was content to give up my great ambitions and stay just where I was.

"It wasn't a very pleasant thing, then, to have an epidemic of typhoid break out in the town that kept me going so that I hardly had time for the courting that a fellow wants to carry on with his sweetheart while he is still young enough to call her his girl. I fumed, but duty was duty, and I kept to my work night and day. It was now that Jube proved how invaluable he was as a coadjutor. He not only took messages to Annie, but brought sometimes little ones from her to me, and he would tell me little secret things that he had overheard her say that made me throb with joy and swear at him for repeating his mistress' conversation. But best of all, Jube was a perfect Cerberus, and no one on earth could have been more effective in keeping away or deluding the other young fellows who visited the Dalys. He would tell me of it afterwards, chuckling softly to himself. 'An', Doctah, I say to Mistah Hemp Stevens, "'Scuse us, Mistah Stevens, but Miss Annie, she des gone out," an' den he go outer de gate lookin' moughty lonesome. When Sam Elkins come, I say, "Sh, Mistah Elkins, Miss Annie, she done tuk down," an' he say, "What, Jube, you don' reckon hit de ——" Den he stop an' look skeert, an' I say, "I feared hit is, Mistah Elkins," an' sheks my haid ez solemn. He goes outer de gate lookin' lak his bes' frien' done daid, an' all de time Miss Annie behine de cu'tain ovah de po'ch des' a laffin' fit to kill.'

"Jube was a most admirable liar, but what could I do? He knew that I was a young fool of a hypocrite, and when I would rebuke him for these deceptions, he would give way and roll on the floor in an excess of delighted laughter until from very contagion I had to join him — and, well, there was no need of my preaching when there had been no beginning to his repentance and when there must ensue a continuance of his wrong-doing.

"This thing went on for over three months, and then, pouf! I was down like a shot. My patients were nearly all up, but the reaction from overwork made me an easy victim of the lurking germs. Then Jube loomed up as a nurse. He put everyone else aside, and with the doctor, a friend of mine from a neighbouring town, took entire charge of me. Even Annie herself was put aside, and I was cared for as tenderly as a baby. Tom, that was my physician and friend, told me all about it afterward with tears in his eyes. Only he was a big, blunt man and his expressions did not convey all that he meant. He told me how my nigger had nursed me as if I were a sick kitten and he my mother. Of how fiercely he guarded his right to be the sole one to 'do' for me, as he called it, and how, when the crisis came, he hovered, weeping, but hopeful, at my bedside, until it was safely passed, when they drove him, weak and exhausted, from the room. As for me, I knew little about it at the time, and cared less. I was too busy in my fight with death. To my chimerical vision there was only a black but gentle demon that came and went, alternating with a white fairy, who would insist on coming in on her head, growing larger and larger and then dissolving. But the pathos and devotion in the story lost nothing in my blunt friend's telling.

"It was during the period of a long convalescence, however, that I came to know my humble ally as he really was, devoted to the point of abjectness. There were times when for very shame at his goodness to me, I would beg him to go away, to do something else. He would go, but before I had time to realise that I was not being ministered to, he would be back at my side, grinning and pottering just the same. He manufactured duties for the joy of performing them. He pretended to see desires in me that I never had, because he liked to pander to them, and when I became entirely exasperated, and ripped out a good round oath, he chuckled with the remark, 'Dah, now, you sholy is gittin' well. Nevah did hyeah a man anywhaih nigh Jo'dan's sho' cuss lak dat.'

"Why, I grew to love him, love him, oh, yes, I loved him as well — oh, what am I saying? All human love and gratitude are damned poor things; excuse me, gentlemen, this isn't a pleasant story. The truth is usually a nasty thing to stand.

"It was not six months after that that my friendship to Jube, which he had been at such great pains to win, was put to too severe a test.

"It was in the summer time again, and as business was slack, I had ridden over to see my friend, Dr. Tom. I had spent a good part of the day there, and it was past four o'clock when I rode leisurely into Bradford. I was in a particularly joyous mood and no premonition of the impending catastrophe oppressed me. No sense of sorrow, present or to come, forced itself upon me, even when I saw men hurrying through the almost deserted streets. When I got within sight of my home and saw a crowd surrounding it, I was only interested sufficiently to spur my horse into a jog trot, which brought me up to the throng, when something in the sullen, settled horror in the men's faces gave me a sudden, sick thrill. They whispered a word to me, and without a thought, save for Annie, the girl who had been so surely growing into my heart, I leaped from the saddle and tore my way through the people to the house.

"It was Annie, poor girl, bruised and bleeding, her face and dress torn from struggling. They were gathered round her with white faces, and, oh, with what terrible patience they were trying to gain from her fluttering lips the name of her murderer. They made way for me and I knelt at her side. She was beyond my skill, and my will merged with theirs. One thought was in our minds.

"'Who?' I asked.

"Her eyes half opened, 'That black ——' She fell back into my arms dead.

"We turned and looked at each other. The mother had broken down and was weeping, but the face of the father was like iron.

"'It is enough,' he said; 'Jube has disappeared.' He went to the door and said to the expectant crowd, 'She is dead.'

"I heard the angry roar without swelling up like the noise of a flood, and then I heard the sudden movement of many feet as the men separated into searching parties, and laying the dead girl back upon her couch, I took my rifle and went out to join them.

"As if by intuition the knowledge had passed among the men that Jube Benson had disappeared, and he, by common consent, was to be the object of our search. Fully a dozen of the citizens had seen him hastening toward the woods and noted his skulking air, but as he had grinned in his old good-natured way they had, at the time, thought nothing of it. Now, however, the diabolical reason of his slyness was apparent. He had been shrewd enough to disarm suspicion, and by now was far away. Even Mrs. Daly, who was visiting with a neighbour, had seen him stepping out by a back way, and had said with a laugh, 'I reckon that black rascal's a-running off somewhere.' Oh, if she had only known.

"'To the woods! To the woods!' that was the cry, and away we went, each with the determination not to shoot, but to bring the culprit alive into town, and then to deal with him as his crime deserved.

"I cannot describe the feelings I experienced as I went out that night to beat the woods for this human tiger. My heart smouldered within me like a coal, and I went forward under the impulse of a will that was half my own, half some more malignant power's. My throat throbbed drily, but water nor whiskey would not have quenched my thirst. The thought has come to me since that now I could interpret the panther's desire for blood and sympathise with it, but then I thought nothing. I simply went forward, and watched, watched with burning eyes for a familiar form that I had looked for as often before with such different emotions.

"Luck or ill-luck, which you will, was with our party, and just as dawn was graying the sky, we came upon our quarry crouched in the corner of a fence. It was only half light, and we might have passed, but my eyes had caught sight of him, and I raised the cry. We levelled our guns and he rose and came toward us.

"'I t'ought you wa'n't gwine see me,' he said sullenly, 'I didn't mean no harm.'

" 'Harm!'

"Some of the men took the word up with oaths, others were ominously silent.

"We gathered around him like hungry beasts, and I began to see terror dawning in his eyes. He turned to me, 'I's moughty glad you's hyeah, doc,' he said, 'you ain't gwine let 'em whup me.'

" 'Whip you, you hound,' I said, 'I'm going to see you hanged,' and in the excess of my passion I struck him full on the mouth. He made a motion as if to resent the blow against even such great odds, but controlled himself.

" 'W'y, doctah,' he exclaimed in the saddest voice I have ever heard, 'w'y, doctah! I ain't stole nuffin' o' yo'n, an' I was comin' back. I only run off to see my gal, Lucy, ovah to de Centah.'

" 'You lie!' I said, and my hands were busy helping the others bind him upon a horse. Why did I do it? I don't know. A false education, I reckon, one false from the beginning. I saw his black face glooming there in the half light, and I could only think of him as a monster. It's tradition. At first I was told that the black man would catch me, and when I got over that, they taught me that the devil was black, and when I had recovered from the sickness of that belief, here were Jube and his fellows with faces of menacing blackness. There was only one conclusion: This black man stood for all the powers of evil, the result of whose machinations had been gathering in my mind from childhood up. But this has nothing to do with what happened.

"After firing a few shots to announce our capture, we rode back into town with Jube. The ingathering parties from all directions met us as we made our way up to the house. All was very quiet and orderly. There was no doubt that it was as the papers would have said, a gathering of the best citizens. It was a gathering of stern, determined men, bent on a terrible vengeance.

"We took Jube into the house, into the room where the corpse lay. At sight of it, he gave a scream like an animal's and his face went the colour of storm-blown water. This was enough to condemn him. We divined, rather than heard, his cry of 'Miss Ann, Miss Ann, oh, my God, doc, you don't t'ink I done it?'

"Hungry hands were ready. We hurried him out into the yard. A rope was ready. A tree was at hand. Well, that part was the least of it, save that Hiram Daly stepped aside to let me be the first to pull upon the rope. It was lax at first. Then it tightened, and I felt the quivering soft weight resist my muscles. Other hands joined, and Jube swung off his feet.

"No one was masked. We knew each other. Not even the Culprit's face was covered, and the last I remember of him as he went into the air was a look of sad reproach that will remain with me until I meet him face to face again.

"We were tying the end of the rope to a tree, where the dead man might hang as a warning to his fellows, when a terrible cry chilled us to the marrow.

" 'Cut 'im down, cut 'im down, he ain't guilty. We got de one. Cut him down, fu' Gawd's sake. Here's de man, we foun' him hidin' in de barn!'

"Jube's brother, Ben, and another Negro, came rushing toward us, half dragging, half carrying a miserable-looking wretch between them. Someone cut the rope and Jube dropped lifeless to the ground.

" 'Oh, my Gawd, he's daid, he's daid!' wailed the brother, but with blazing eyes he brought his captive into the centre of the group, and we saw in the full light the scratched face of Tom Skinner — the worst white ruffian in the town — but the face we saw was not as we were accustomed to see it, merely smeared with dirt. It was blackened to imitate a Negro's.

"God forgive me; I could not wait to try to resuscitate Jube. I knew he was already past help, so I rushed into the house and to the dead girl's side. In the excitement they had not yet washed or laid her out. Carefully, carefully, I searched underneath her broken finger nails. There was skin there. I took it out, the little curled pieces, and went with it to my office.

"There, determinedly, I examined it under a powerful glass, and read my own doom. It was the skin of a white man, and in it were embedded strands of short, brown hair or beard.

"How I went out to tell the waiting crowd I do not know, for something kept crying in my ears, 'Blood guilty! Blood guilty!'

"The men went away stricken into silence and awe. The new prisoner attempted neither denial nor plea. When they were gone I would have helped Ben carry his brother in, but he waved me away fiercely, 'You he'ped murder my brothah, you dat was *his* frien', go 'way, go 'way! I'll tek him home myse'f.' I could only respect his wish, and he and his comrade took up the dead man and between them bore him up the street on which the sun was now shining full.

"I saw the few men who had not skulked indoors uncover as they passed, and I — I — stood there between the two murdered ones, while all the while something in my ears kept crying, 'Blood guilty! Blood guilty!'"

The doctor's head dropped into his hands and he sat for some time in silence, which was broken by neither of the men, then he rose, saying, "Gentlemen, that was my last lynching."

PAUL'S CASE

Willa Cather (1873-1947)

It was Paul's afternoon to appear before the faculty of the Pittsburgh High School to account for his various misdemeanors. He had been suspended a week ago, and his father had called at the Principal's office and confessed his perplexity about his son. Paul entered the faculty room suave and smiling. His clothes were a trifle outgrown, and the tan velvet on the collar of his open overcoat was frayed and worn; but for all that there was something of the dandy about him, and he wore an opal pin in his neatly knotted black four-in-hand, and a red carnation in his buttonhole. This latter adornment the faculty somehow felt was not properly significant of the contrite spirit befitting a boy under the ban of suspension.

Paul was tall for his age and very thin, with high, cramped shoulders and a narrow chest. His eyes were remarkable for a certain hysterical brilliancy, and he continually used them in a conscious, theatrical sort of way, peculiarly offensive in a boy. The pupils were abnormally large, as though he were addicted to belladonna, but there was a glassy glitter about them which that drug does not produce.

When questioned by the Principal as to why he was there Paul stated, politely enough, that he wanted to come back to school. This was a lie, but Paul was quite accustomed to lying; found it, indeed, indispensable for overcoming friction. His teachers were asked to state their respective charges against him, which they did with such a rancor and aggrievedness as evinced that this was not a usual case, Disorder and impertinence were among the offenses named, yet each of his instructors felt that it was scarcely possible to put into words the real cause of the trouble, which lay in a sort of hysterically defiant manner of the boy's; in the contempt which they all knew he felt for them, and which he seemingly made not the least effort to conceal. Once, when he had been making a synopsis of a paragraph at the blackboard, his English teacher had stepped to his side and attempted to guide his hand. Paul had started back with a shudder and thrust his hands violently behind him. The astonished woman could scarcely have been more hurt and embarrassed had he struck at her. The insult was so involuntary and definitely personal as to be unforgettable. In one way and another he had made all his teachers, men and women alike, conscious of the same feeling of physical aversion. In one class he habitually sat with his hand shading his eyes; in another he always looked out of the window during the recitation; in another he made a running commentary on the lecture, with humorous intention.

His teachers felt this afternoon that his whole attitude was symbolized by his shrug and his flippantly red carnation flower, and they fell upon him without mercy, his English teacher leading the pack. He stood through it smiling, his pale lips parted over his white teeth. (His lips were continually twitching, and he had a habit of raising his eyebrows that was contemptuous and irritating to the last degree.) Older boys than Paul had broken down and shed tears under that baptism of fire, but his set smile did not once desert him, and his only sign of discomfort was the nervous trembling of the fingers that toyed with the buttons of his overcoat, and an occasional jerking of the other hand that held his hat. Paul was always smiling, always glancing about him, seeming to feel that people might be watching him and trying to detect something. This conscious expression, since it was as far as possible from boyish mirthfulness, was usually attributed to insolence or "smartness."

As the inquisition proceeded one of his instructors repeated an impertinent remark of the boy's, and the Principal asked him whether he thought that a courteous speech to have made a woman. Paul shrugged his shoulders slightly and his eyebrows twitched.

"I don't know," he replied. "I didn't mean to be polite or impolite, either. I guess it's a sort of way I have of saying things regardless."

The Principal, who was a sympathetic man, asked him whether he didn't think that a way it would be well to get rid of. Paul grinned and said he guessed so. When he was told that he could go he bowed gracefully and went out. His bow was but a repetition of the scandalous red carnation.

His teachers were in despair, and his drawing master voiced the feeling of them all when he declared there was something about the boy which none of them understood. He added: "I don't really believe that smile of his comes altogether from insolence; there's something sort of haunted about it. The boy is not strong, for one thing. I happen to know that he was born in Colorado, only a few months before his mother died out there of a long illness. There is something wrong about the fellow."

The drawing master had come to realize that, in looking at Paul, one saw only his white teeth and the forced animation of his eyes. One warm afternoon the boy had gone to sleep at his drawing board, and his master had noted with amazement what a white, blue-veined face it was; drawn and wrinkled like an old man's about the eyes, the lips twitching even in his sleep, and stiff with a nervous tension that drew them back from his teeth.

His teachers left the building dissatisfied and unhappy; humiliated to have felt so vindictive toward a mere boy, to have uttered this feeling in cutting terms, and to have set each other on, as it were, in the gruesome game of intemperate reproach. Some of them remembered having seen a miserable street cat set at bay by a ring of tormentors.

As for Paul, he ran down the hill whistling the "Soldiers' Chorus" from *Faust*, looking wildly behind him now and then to see whether some of his teachers were not there to writhe under his lightheartedness. As it was now late in the afternoon and Paul was on duty that evening as usher at Carnegie Hall, he decided that he would not go home to supper. When he reached the concert hall the doors were not yet open and, as it was chilly outside, he decided to go up into the picture gallery — always deserted at this hour — where there were some of Raffelli's gay studies of Paris streets and an airy blue Venetian scene or two that always exhilarated him. He was delighted to find no one in the gallery but the old guard, who sat in one corner, a newspaper on his knee, a black patch over one eye and the other closed. Paul possessed himself of the peace and walked confidently up and down, whistling under his breath. After a while he sat down before a blue Rico and lost himself. When he bethought him to look at his watch, it was after seven o'clock, and he rose with a start and ran downstairs, making a face at Augustus, peering out from the cast room, and an evil gesture at the Venus de Milo as he passed her on the stairway.

When Paul reached the ushers' dressing room half a dozen boys were there already, and he began excitedly to tumble into his uniform. It was one of the few that at all approached fitting, and Paul thought it very becoming — though he knew that the tight, straight coat accentuated his narrow chest, about which he was exceedingly sensitive. He was always considerably excited while be dressed, twanging all over to the tuning of the strings and the preliminary flourishes of the horns in the music room; but tonight he seemed quite beside himself, and he teased and plagued the boys until, telling him that he was crazy, they put him down on the floor and sat on him.

Somewhat calmed by his suppression, Paul dashed out to the front of the house to seat the early comers. He was a model usher; gracious and smiling he ran up and down the aisles; nothing was too much trouble for him; he carried messages and brought programs as though it were his greatest pleasure in life, and all the people in his section thought him a charming boy, feeling that he remembered and admired them. As the house filled, he grew more and more vivacious and animated, and the color came to his cheeks and lips. It was very much as though this were a great reception and Paul were the host. Just as the musicians came out to take their places, his English teacher arrived with checks for the seats which a prominent manufacturer had taken for the season. She betrayed some embarrassment when she handed Paul the tickets, and a *hauteur* which subsequently made her feel very foolish. Paul was startled for a moment, and had the feeling of wanting to put her out; what business had she here among all these fine people and gay colors? He looked her over and decided that she was not appropriately dressed and must be a fool to sit downstairs in such togs. The tickets had probably been sent her out of kindness, he reflected as he put down a seat for her, and she had about as much right to sit there as he had.

When the symphony began Paul sank into one of the rear seats with a long sigh of relief, and lost himself as he had done before the Rico. It was not that symphonies, as such, meant anything in particular to Paul, but the first sigh of the instruments seemed to free some hilarious and potent spirit within him; something that struggled there like the genie in the bottle found by the Arab fisherman. He felt a sudden zest of life; the lights danced before his eyes and the concert hall blazed into unimaginable splendor. When the soprano soloist came on Paul forgot even the nastiness of his teacher's being there and gave himself up to the peculiar stimulus such personages always had for him. The soloist chanced to be a German woman, by no means in her first youth, and the mother of many children; but she wore an elaborate gown and a tiara, and above all she had that indefinable air of achievement, that world-shine upon her, which, in Paul's eyes, made her a veritable queen of Romance.

After a concert was over Paul was always irritable and wretched until he got to sleep, and tonight he was even more than usually restless. He had the feeling of not being able to let down, of its being impossible to give up this delicious excitement which was the only thing that could be called living at all. During the last number he withdrew and, after hastily changing his clothes in the dressing room, slipped out to the side door where the soprano's carriage stood. Here he began pacing rapidly up and down the walk, waiting to see her come out.

Over yonder, the Schenley, in its vacant stretch, loomed big and square through the fine rain, the windows of its twelve stories glowing like those of a lighted cardboard house under a Christmas tree. All the actors and singers of the better class stayed there when they were in the city, and a number of the big manufacturers of the place lived there in the winter. Paul had often hung about the hotel, watching the people go in and out, longing to enter and leave schoolmasters and dull care behind him forever.

At last the singer came out, accompanied by the conductor, who helped her into her carriage and closed the door with a cordial *auf wiedersehen* which set Paul to wondering whether she were not an old sweetheart of his. Paul followed the carriage over to the hotel, walking so rapidly as not to be far from the entrance when the singer alighted, and disappeared behind the swinging glass doors that were opened by a Negro in a tall hat and a long coat. In the moment that the door was ajar it seemed to Paul that he, too, entered. He seemed to feel himself go after her up the steps, into the warm, lighted building, into an exotic, tropical world of shiny, glistening surfaces and basking ease. He reflected upon the mysterious dishes that were brought into the dining room, the green bottles in buckets of ice, as he had seen them in the supper party pictures of the *Sunday World* supplement. A quick gust of wind brought the rain down with sudden vehemence, and Paul was startled to find that he was still outside in the slush of the gravel driveway; that his boots were letting in the water and his scanty overcoat was clinging wet about him; that the lights in front of the concert hall were out and that the rain was driving in sheets between him and the orange glow of the windows above him. There it was, what he wanted — tangibly before him, like the fairy world of a Christmas pantomime — but mocking spirits stood guard at the doors, and, as the rain beat in his face, Paul wondered whether he were destined always to shiver in the black night outside, looking up at it.

He turned and walked reluctantly toward the car tracks. The end had to come sometime; his father in his nightclothes at the top of the stairs, explanations that did not explain, hastily improvised fictions that were forever tripping him up, his upstairs room and its horrible yellow wallpaper, the creaking bureau with the greasy plush collarbox, and over his painted wooden bed the pictures of George Washington and John Calvin, and the framed motto, "Feed my Lambs," which had been worked in red worsted by his mother.

Half an hour later Paul alighted from his car and went slowly down one of the side streets off the main thoroughfare. It was a highly respectable street, where all the houses were exactly alike, and where businessmen of moderate means begot and reared large families of children, all of whom went to Sabbath school and learned the shorter catechism, and were interested in arithmetic; all of whom were as exactly alike as their homes, and of a piece with the monotony in which they lived. Paul never went up Cordelia Street without a shudder of loathing. His home was next to the house of the Cumberland minister. He approached it tonight with the nerveless sense of defeat, the hopeless feeling of sinking back forever into ugliness and commonness that he had always had when he came home. The moment he turned into Cordelia Street he felt the waters close above his head. After each of these orgies of living he experienced all the physical depression which follows a debauch; the loathing of respectable beds, of common food, of a house penetrated by kitchen odors; a shuddering repulsion for the flavorless, colorless mass of everyday existence; a morbid desire for cool things and soft lights and fresh flowers.

The nearer he approached the house, the more absolutely unequal Paul felt to the sight of it all: his ugly sleeping chamber; the cold bathroom with the grimy zinc tub, the cracked mirror, the dripping spiggots; his father, at the top of the stairs, his hairy legs sticking out from his nightshirt, his feet thrust into carpet slippers. He was so much later than usual that there would certainly be inquiries and reproaches. Paul stopped short before the door. He felt that he could not be accosted by his father tonight; that he could not toss again on that miserable bed. He would not go in. He would tell his father that he had no carfare and it was raining so hard he had gone home with one of the boys and stayed all night.

Meanwhile, he was wet and cold. He went around to the back of the house and tried one of the basement windows, found it open, raised it cautiously, and scrambled down the cellar wall to the floor. There he stood, holding his breath, terrified by the noise he had made, but the floor above him was silent, and there was no creak on the stairs. He found a soapbox, and carried it over to the soft ring of light that streamed from the furnace door, and sat down. He was horribly afraid of rats, so he did not try to sleep, but sat looking distrustfully at the dark, still terrified lest he might have awakened his father. In such reactions, after one of the experiences which made days and nights out of the dreary blanks of the calendar, when his senses were deadened, Paul's head was always singularly clear. Suppose his father had heard him getting in at the window and had come down and shot him for a burglar? Then, again, suppose his father had come down, pistol in hand, and he had cried out in time to save himself, and his father had been horrified to think how nearly he had killed him? Then, again, suppose a day should come when his father would remember that night, and wish there had been no warning cry to stay his hand? With this last supposition Paul entertained himself until daybreak.

The following Sunday was fine; the sodden November chill was broken by the last flash of autumnal summer. In the morning Paul had to go to church and Sabbath school, as always. On seasonable Sunday afternoons the burghers of Cordelia Street always sat out on their front stoops and talked to their neighbors on the next stoop, or called to those across the street in neighborly fashion. The men usually sat on gay cushions placed upon the steps that led down to the sidewalk, while the women, in their Sunday "waists," sat in rockers on the cramped porches, pretending to be greatly at their ease. The children played in the streets; there were so many of them that the place resembled the recreation grounds of a kindergarten. The men on the steps — all in their shirt sleeves, their vests unbuttoned — sat with their legs well apart, their stomachs comfortably protruding, and talked of the prices of things, or told anecdotes of the sagacity of their various chiefs and overlords. They occasionally looked over the multitude of squabbling children, listened affectionately to their high-pitched, nasal voices, smiling to see their own proclivities reproduced in their offspring, and interspersed their legends of the iron kings with remarks about their sons' progress at school, their grades in arithmetic, and the amounts they had saved in their toy banks.

On this last Sunday of November Paul sat all the afternoon on the lowest step of his stoop, staring into the street, while his sisters, in their rockers, were talking to the minister's daughters next door about how many shirtwaists they had made in the last week, and bow many waffles someone had eaten at the last church supper. When the weather was warm, and his father was in a particularly jovial frame of mind, the girls made lemonade, which was always brought out in a red-glass pitcher, ornamented with forget-me-nots in blue enamel. This the girls thought very fine, and the neighbors always joked about the suspicious color of the pitcher.

Today Paul's father sat on the top step, talking to a young man who shifted a restless baby from knee to knee. He happened to be the young man who was daily held up to Paul as a model, and after whom it was his father's dearest hope that he would pattern. This young man was of a ruddy complexion, with a compressed, red mouth, and faded, nearsighted eyes, over which he wore thick spectacles, with gold bows that curved about his ears. He was clerk to one of the magnates of a great steel corporation, and was looked upon in Cordelia Street as a young man with a future. There was a story that, some five years ago — he was now barely twenty-six — he had been a trifle dissipated, but in order to curb his appetites and save the loss of time and strength that a sowing of wild oats might have entailed, he had taken his chief's advice, oft reiterated to his employees, and at twenty-one had married the first woman whom he could persuade to share his fortunes. She happened to be an angular schoolmistress, much older than he, who also wore thick glasses, and who had now borne him four children, all near-sighted, like herself.

The young man was relating how his chief, now cruising in the Mediterranean, kept in touch with all the details of the business, arranging his office hours on his yacht just as though he were at home, and "knocking off work enough to keep two stenographers busy." His father told, in turn, the plan his corporation was considering, of putting in an electric railway plant in Cairo. Paul snapped his teeth; he had an awful apprehension that they might spoil it all before he got there. Yet he rather liked to hear these legends of the iron kings that were told and retold on Sundays and holidays; these stories of palaces in Venice, yachts on the Mediterranean, and high play at Monte Carlo appealed to his fancy, and he was interested in the triumphs of these cash boys who had become famous, though he had no mind for the cash-boy stage.

After supper was over and he had helped to dry the dishes, Paul nervously asked his father whether he could go to George's to get some help in his geometry, and still more nervously asked for carfare. This latter request he had to repeat, as his father, on principle, did not like to hear requests for money, whether much or little. He asked Paul whether he could not go to some boy who lived nearer, and told him that he ought not to leave his schoolwork until Sunday; but he gave him the dime. He was not a poor man, but he had a worthy ambition to come up in the world. His only reason for allowing Paul to usher was that he thought a boy ought to be earning a little.

Paul bounded upstairs, scrubbed the greasy odor of the dishwater from his hands with the ill-smelling soap he hated, and then shook over his fingers a few drops of violet water from the bottle he kept hidden in his drawer. He left the house with his geometry conspicuously under his arm, and the moment he got out of Cordelia Street and boarded a downtown car, he shook off the lethargy of two deadening days and began to live again.

The leading juvenile of the permanent stock company which played at one of the downtown theaters was an acquaintance of Paul's, and the boy had been invited to drop in at the Sunday-night rehearsals whenever he could. For more than a year Paul had spent every available moment loitering about Charley Edwards's dressing room. He had won a place among Edwards's following not only because the young actor, who could not afford to employ a dresser, often found him useful, but because he recognized in Paul something akin to what churchmen term "vocation."

It was at the theater and at Carnegie Hall that Paul really lived; the rest was but a sleep and a forgetting. This was Paul's fairy tale, and it had for him all the allurement of a secret love. The moment he inhaled the gassy, painty, dusty odor behind the scenes, he breathed like a prisoner set free, and felt within him the possibility of doing or saying splendid, brilliant, poetic things. The moment the cracked orchestra beat out the overture from *Martha*, or jerked at the serenade from *Rigoletto*, all stupid and ugly things slid from him, and his senses were deliciously, yet delicately fired.

Perhaps it was because, in Paul's world, the natural nearly always wore the guise of ugliness, that a certain element of artificiality seemed to him necessary in beauty. Perhaps it was because his experience of life elsewhere was so full of Sabbath-school picnics, petty economies, wholesome advice as to how to succeed in life, and the inescapable odors of cooking, that he found this existence so alluring, these smartly clad men and women so attractive, that he was so moved by these starry apple orchards that bloomed perennially under the limelight.

It would be difficult to put it strongly enough how convincingly the stage entrance of that theater was for Paul the actual portal of Romance. Certainly none of the company ever suspected it, least of all Charley Edwards. It was very like the old stories that used to float about London of fabulously rich Jews, who had subterranean halls there, with palms, and fountains, and soft lamps and richly appareled women who never saw the disenchanting light of London day. So, in the midst of that smoke-palled city, enamored of figures and grimy toil, Paul had his secret temple, his wishing carpet, his bit of blue-and-white Mediterranean shore bathed in perpetual sunshine.

Several of Paul's teachers had a theory that his imagination had been perverted by garish fiction, but the truth was that he scarcely ever read at all. The books at home were not such as would either tempt or corrupt a youthful mind, and as for reading the novels that some of his friends urged upon him — well, he got what he wanted much more quickly from music; any sort of music, from an orchestra to a barrel organ. He needed only the spark, the indescribable thrill that made his imagination master of his senses, and he could make plots and pictures enough of his own. It was equally true that he was not stagestruck — not, at any rate, in the usual acceptation of that expression. He had no desire to become an actor, any more than he had to become a musician. He felt no necessity to do any of these things; what he wanted was to see, to be in the atmosphere, float on the wave of it, to be carried out, blue league after blue league, away from everything.

After a night behind the scenes Paul found the schoolroom more than ever repulsive; the bare floors and naked walls; the prosy men who never wore frock coats, or violets in their buttonholes; the women with their dull gowns, shrill voices, and pitiful seriousness about prepositions that govern the dative. He could not bear to have the other pupils think, for a moment, that he took these people seriously; he must convey to them that he considered it all trivial, and was there only by way of a jest, anyway. He had autographed pictures of all the members of the stock company which he showed his classmates, telling them the most incredible stories of his familiarity with these people, of his acquaintance with the soloists who came to Carnegie Hall, his suppers with them and the flowers he sent them. When these stories lost their effect, and his audience grew listless, he became desperate and would bid all the boys good-by, announcing that he was going to travel for a while; going to Naples, to Venice, to Egypt. Then, next Monday, he would slip back, conscious and nervously smiling; his sister was ill, and he should have to defer his voyage until spring.

Matters went steadily worse with Paul at school. In the itch to let his instructors know how heartily he despised them and their homilies, and how thoroughly he was appreciated elsewhere, he mentioned once or twice that he had no time to fool with theorems; adding — with a twitch of the eyebrows and a touch of that nervous bravado which so perplexed them — that he was helping the people down at the stock company; they were old friends of his.

The upshot of the matter was that the Principal went to Paul's father, and Paul was taken out of school and put to work. The manager at Carnegie Hall was told to get another usher in his stead; the doorkeeper at the theater was warned not to admit him to the house; and Charley Edwards remorsefully promised the boy's father not to see him again.

The members of the stock company were vastly amused when some of Paul's stories reached them — especially the women. They were hardworking women, most of them supporting indigent husbands or brothers, and they laughed rather bitterly at having stirred the boy to such fervid and florid inventions. They agreed with the faculty and with his father that Paul's was a bad case.

The eastbound train was plowing through a January snowstorm; the dull dawn was beginning to show gray when the engine whistled a mile out of Newark. Paul started up from the seat where he had lain curled in uneasy slumber, rubbed the breath-misted window glass with his hand, and peered out. The snow was whirling in curling eddies above the white bottom lands, and the drifts lay already deep in the fields and along the fences, while here and there the long dead grass and dried weed stalks protruded black above it. Lights shone from the scattered houses, and a gang of laborers who stood beside the track waved their lanterns.

Paul had slept very little, and he felt grimy and uncomfortable. He had made the all-night journey in a day coach, partly because he was ashamed, dressed as he was, to go into a Pullman, and partly because he was afraid of being seen there by some Pittsburgh businessman, who might have noticed him in Denny & Carson's office. When the whistle awoke him, he clutched quickly at his breast pocket, glancing about him with an uncertain smile. But the little, clay-bespattered Italians were still sleeping, the slatternly women across the aisle were in open-mouthed oblivion, and even the crumby, crying babies were for the nonce stilled. Paul settled back to struggle with his impatience as best he could.

When he arrived at the Jersey City station he hurried through his breakfast, manifestly ill at ease and keeping a sharp eye about him. After he reached the Twenty-third Street station, he consulted a cabman and had himself driven to a men's-furnishings establishment that was just opening for the day. He spent upward of two hours there, buying with endless reconsidering and great care. His new street suit he put on in the fitting room; the frock coat and dress clothes he had bundled into the cab with his linen. Then he drove to a hatter's and a shoe house. His next errand was at Tiffany's, where he selected his silver and a new scarf pin. He would not wait to have his silver marked, he said. Lastly, he stopped at a trunk shop on Broadway and had his purchases packed into various traveling bags.

It was a little after one o'clock when he drove up to the Waldorf, and after settling with the cabman, went into the office. He registered from Washington; said his mother and father had been abroad, and that he had come down to await the arrival of their steamer. He told his story plausibly and had no trouble, since he volunteered to pay for them in advance, in engaging his rooms; a sleeping room, sitting room, and bath.

Not once, but a hundred times, Paul had planned this entry into New York. He had gone over every detail of it with Charley Edwards, and in his scrapbook at home there were pages of description about New York hotels, cut from the Sunday papers. When he was shown to his sitting room on the eighth floor he saw at a glance that everything was as it should be; there was but one detail in his mental picture that the place did not realize, so he rang for the bellboy and sent him down for flowers. He moved about nervously until the boy returned, putting away his new linen and fingering it delightedly as he did so. When the flowers came he put them hastily into water, and then tumbled into a hot bath. Presently he came out of his white bathroom, resplendent in his new silk underwear, and playing with the tassels of his red robe. The snow was whirling so fiercely outside his windows that he could scarcely see across the street, but within the air was deliciously soft and fragrant. He put the violets and jonquils on the taboret beside the couch, and threw himself down, with a long sigh, covering himself with a Roman blanket. He was thoroughly tired; he had been in such haste, he had stood up to such a strain, covered so much ground in the last twenty-four hours, that he wanted to think how it had all come about. Lulled by the sound of the wind, the warm air, and the cool fragrance of the flowers, he sank into deep, drowsy retrospection.

It had been wonderfully simple; when they had shut him out of the theater and concert hall, when they had taken away his bone, the whole thing was virtually determined. The rest was a mere matter of opportunity. The only thing that at all surprised him was his own courage — for he realized well enough that he had always been tormented by fear, a sort of apprehensive dread that, of late years, as the meshes of the lies he had told closed about him, had been pulling the muscles of his body tighter and tighter. Until now he could not remember the time when he had not been dreading something. Even when he was a little boy it was always there — behind him, or before, or on either side. There had always been the shadowed corner, the dark place into which he dared not look, but from which something seemed always to be watching him — and Paul had done things that were not pretty to watch, he knew.

But now he had a curious sense of relief, as though he had at last thrown down the gauntlet to the thing in the corner.

Yet it was but a day since he had been sulking in the traces; but yesterday afternoon that he had been sent to the bank with Denny & Carson's deposit, as usual — but this time he was instructed to leave the book to be balanced. There was above two thousand dollars in checks, and nearly a thousand in the bank notes which he had taken from the book and quietly transferred to his pocket. At the bank he had made out a new deposit slip. His nerves had been steady enough to permit of his returning to the office, where he had finished his work and asked for a full day's holiday tomorrow, Saturday, giving a perfectly reasonable pretext. The bankbook, be knew, would not be returned before Monday or Tuesday, and his father would be out of town for the next week. From the time he slipped the bank notes into his pocket until he boarded the night train for New York, he had not known a moment's hesitation. It was not the first time Paul had steered through treacherous waters.

How astonishingly easy it had all been; here he was, the thing done; and this time there would be no awakening, no figure at the top of the stairs. He watched the snowflakes whirling by his window until he fell asleep.

When he awoke, it was three o'clock in the afternoon. He bounded up with a start; half of one of his precious days gone already! He spent more than an hour in dressing, watching every stage of his toilet carefully in the mirror. Everything was quite perfect; he was exactly the kind of boy he had always wanted to be.

When he went downstairs Paul took a carriage and drove up Fifth Avenue toward the Park. The snow had somewhat abated; carriages and tradesmen's wagons were hurrying soundlessly to and fro in the winter twilight; boys in woolen mufflers were shoveling off the doorsteps; the avenue stages made fine spots of color against the white street. Here and there on the corners were stands, with whole flower gardens blooming under glass cases, against the sides of which the snowflakes stuck and melted; violets, roses, carnations, lilies of the valley — somehow vastly more lovely and alluring that they blossomed thus unnaturally in the snow. The Park itself was a wonderful stage winterpiece.

When he returned, the pause of the twilight had ceased and the tune of the streets had changed. The snow was falling faster, lights streamed from the hotels that reared their dozen stories fearlessly up into the storm, defying the raging Atlantic winds. A long, black stream of carriages poured down the avenue, intersected here and there by other streams, tending horizontally. There were a score of cabs about the entrance of his hotel, and his driver had to wait. Boys in livery were running in and out of the awning stretched across the sidewalk, up and down the red velvet carpet laid from the door to the street. Above, about, within it all was the rumble and roar, the hurry and toss of thousands of human beings as hot for pleasure as himself, and on every side of him towered the glaring affirmation of the omnipotence of wealth.

The boy set his teeth and drew his shoulders together in a spasm of realization; the plot of all dramas, the text of all romances, the nerve-stuff of all sensations was whirling about him like the snowflakes. He burnt like a faggot in a tempest.

When Paul went down to dinner the music of the orchestra came floating up the elevator shaft to greet him. His head whirled as he stepped into the thronged corridor, and he sank back into one of the chairs against the wall to get his breath. The lights, the chatter, the perfumes, the bewildering medley of color — he had, for a moment, the feeling of not being able to stand it. But only for a moment; these were his own people, he told himself. He went slowly about the corridors, through the writing rooms, smoking rooms, reception rooms, as though he were exploring the chambers of an enchanted palace, built and peopled for him alone.

When he reached the dining room he sat down at a table near a window. The flowers, the white linen, the many-colored wineglasses, the gay toilettes of the women, the low popping of corks, the undulating repetitions of the *Blue Danube* from the orchestra, all flooded Paul's dream with bewildering radiance. When the roseate tinge of his champagne was added — that cold, precious, bubbling stuff that creamed and foamed in his glass — Paul wondered that there were honest men in the world at all. This was what all the world was fighting for, he reflected; this was what all the struggle was about. He doubted the reality of his past. Had he ever known a place called Cordelia Street, a place where fagged-looking businessmen got on the early car; mere rivets in a machine they seemed to Paul, — sickening men, with combings of children's hair always hanging to their coats, and the smell of cooking in their clothes. Cordelia Street — Ah, that belonged to another time and country; had he not always been thus, had he not sat here night after night, from as far back as he could remember, looking pensively over just such shimmering textures and slowly twirling the stem of a glass like this one between his thumb and middle finger? He rather thought he had.

He was not in the least abashed or lonely. He had no especial desire to meet or to know any of these people; all he demanded was the right to look on and conjecture, to watch the pageant. The mere stage properties were all he contended for. Nor was he lonely later in the evening, in his lodge at the Metropolitan. He was now entirely rid of his nervous misgivings, of his forced aggressiveness, of the imperative desire to show himself different from his surroundings. He felt now that his surroundings explained him. Nobody questioned the purple; he had only to wear it passively. He had only to glance down at his attire to reassure himself that here it would be impossible for anyone to humiliate him.

He found it hard to leave his beautiful sitting room to go to bed that night, and sat long watching the raging storm from his turret window. When he went to sleep it was with the lights turned on in his bedroom; partly because of his old timidity, and partly so that, if he should wake in the night, there would be no wretched moment of doubt, no horrible suspicion of yellow wallpaper, or of Washington and Calvin above his bed.

Sunday morning the city was practically snowbound. Paul breakfasted late, and in the afternoon he fell in with a wild San Francisco boy, a freshman at Yale, who said he had run down for a "little flyer" over Sunday. The young man offered to show Paul the night side of the town, and the two boys went out together after dinner, not returning to the hotel until seven o'clock the next morning. They had started out in the confiding warmth of a champagne friendship, but their parting in the elevator was singularly cool. The freshman pulled himself together to make his train, and Paul went to bed. He awoke at two o'clock in the afternoon, very thirsty and dizzy, and rang for icewater, coffee, and the Pittsburgh papers.

On the part of the hotel management, Paul excited no suspicion. There was this to be said for him, that he wore his spoils with dignity and in no way made himself conspicuous. Even under the glow of his wine he was never boisterous, though he found the stuff like a magician's wand for wonder-building. His chief greediness lay in his ears and eyes, and his excesses were not offensive ones. His dearest pleasures were the gray winter twilights in his sitting room; his quiet enjoyment of his flowers, his clothes, his wide divan, his cigarette, and his sense of power. He could not remember a time when he had felt so at peace with himself. The mere release from the necessity of petty lying, lying every day and every day, restored his self-respect. He had never lied for pleasure, even at school; but to be noticed and admired, to assert his difference from other Cordelia Street boys; and he felt a good deal more manly, more honest, even, now that he had no need for boastful pretensions, now that he could, as his actor friends used to say, "dress the part." It was characteristic that remorse did not occur to him. His golden days went by without a shadow, and he made each as perfect as he could.

On the eighth day after his arrival in New York he found the whole affair exploited in the Pittsburgh papers, exploited with a wealth of detail which indicated that local news of a sensational nature was at a low ebb. The firm of Denny & Carson announced that the boy's father had refunded the full amount of the theft and that they had no intention of prosecuting. The Cumberland minister had been interviewed, and expressed his hope of yet reclaiming the motherless lad, and his Sabbath-school teacher declared that she would spare no effort to that end. The rumor had reached Pittsburgh that the boy had been seen in a New York hotel, and his father had gone East to find him and bring him home.

Paul had just come in to dress for dinner; he sank into a chair, weak to the knees, and clasped his head in his hands. It was to be worse than jail, even; the tepid waters of Cordelia Street were to close over him finally and forever. The gray monotony stretched before him in hopeless, unrelieved years; Sabbath school, Young People's Meeting, the yellow-papered room, the damp dishtowels; it all rushed back upon him with a sickening vividness. He had the old feeling that the orchestra had suddenly stopped, the sinking sensation that the play was over. The sweat broke out on his face, and he sprang to his feet, looked about him with his white, conscious smile, and winked at himself in the mirror, With something of the old childish belief in miracles with which he had so often gone to class, all his lessons unlearned, Paul dressed and dashed whistling down the corridor to the elevator.

He had no sooner entered the dining room and caught the measure of the music than his remembrance was lightened by his old elastic power of claiming the moment, mounting with it, and finding it all-sufficient. The glare and glitter about him, the mere scenic accessories had again, and for the last time, their old potency. He would show himself that he was game, he would finish the thing splendidly. He doubted, more than ever, the existence of Cordelia Street, and for the first time he drank his wine recklessly. Was he not, after all, one of those fortunate beings born to the purple, was he not still himself and in his own place? He drummed a nervous accompaniment to the Pagliacci music and looked about him, telling himself over and over that it had paid.

He reflected drowsily, to the swell of the music and the chill sweetness of his wine, that he might have done it more wisely. He might have caught an outbound steamer and been well out of their clutches before now. But the other side of the world had seemed too far away and too uncertain then; he could not have waited for it; his need had been too sharp. If he had to choose over again, he would do the same thing tomorrow. He looked affectionately about the dining room, now gilded with a soft mist. Ah, it had paid indeed!

Paul was awakened next morning by a painful throbbing in his head and feet. He had thrown himself across the bed without undressing, and had slept with his shoes on. His limbs and hands were lead heavy, and his tongue and throat were parched and burnt. There came upon him one of those fateful attacks of clear-headedness that never occurred except when he was physically exhausted and his nerves hung loose. He lay still, closed his eyes, and let the tide of things wash over him.

His father was in New York; "stopping at some joint or other," he told himself. The memory of successive summers on the front stoop fell upon him like a weight of black water. He had not a hundred dollars left; and he knew now, more than ever, that money was everything, the wall that stood between all he loathed and all he wanted. The thing was winding itself up; he had thought of that on his first glorious day in New York, and had even provided a way to snap the thread. It lay on his dressing table now; he had got it out last night when he came blindly up from dinner, but the shiny metal hurt his eyes, and he disliked the looks of it.

He rose and moved about with a painful effort, succumbing now and again to attacks of nausea. It was the old depression exaggerated; all the world had become Cordelia Street. Yet somehow he was not afraid of anything, was absolutely calm; perhaps because he had looked into the dark corner at last and knew. It was bad enough, what he saw there, but somehow not so bad as his long fear of it had been. He saw everything clearly now. He had a feeling that he had made the best of it, that he had lived the sort of life he was meant to live, and for half an hour he sat staring at the revolver. But he told himself that was not the way, so he went downstairs and took a cab to the ferry.

When Paul arrived in Newark he got off the train and took another cab, directing the driver to follow the Pennsylvania tracks out of the town. The snow lay heavy on the roadways and had drifted deep in the open fields. Only here and there the dead grass or dried weed stalks projected, singularly black, above it. Once well into the country, Paul dismissed the carriage and walked, floundering along the tracks, his mind a medley of irrelevant things. He seemed to hold in his brain an actual picture of everything he had seen that morning. He remembered every feature of both his drivers, of the toothless old woman from whom he had bought the red flowers in his coat, the agent from whom he had got his ticket, and all of his fellow passengers on the ferry. His mind, unable to cope with vital matters near at hand, worked feverishly and deftly at sorting and grouping these images. They made for him a part of the ugliness of the world, of the ache in his head, and the bitter burning on his tongue. He stooped and put a handful of snow into his mouth as he walked, but that, too, seemed hot. When he reached a little hillside, where the tracks ran through a cut some twenty feet below him, he stopped and sat down.

The carnations in his coat were drooping with the cold, he noticed, their red glory all over. It occurred to him that all the flowers he had seen in the glass cases that first night must have gone the same way, long before this. It was only one splendid breath they had, in spite of their brave mockery at the winter outside the glass; and it was a losing game in the end, it seemed, this revolt against the homilies by which the world is run. Paul took one of the blossoms carefully from his coat and scooped a little hole in the snow, where he covered it up. Then he dozed awhile, from his weak condition, seemingly insensible to the cold.

The sound of an approaching train awoke him, and he started to his feet, remembering only his resolution, and afraid lest he should be too late. He stood watching the approaching locomotive, his teeth chattering, his lips drawn away from them in a frightened smile; once or twice he glanced nervously sidewise, as though he were being watched. When the right moment came, he jumped. As he fell, the folly of his haste occurred to him with merciless clearness, the vastness of what he had left undone. There flashed through his brain, clearer than ever before, the blue of Adriatic water, the yellow of Algerian sands.

He felt something strike his chest, and that his body was being thrown swiftly through the air, on and on, immeasurably far and fast, while his limbs were gently relaxed. Then, because the picture-making mechanism was crushed, the disturbing visions flashed into black, and Paul dropped back into the immense design of things.

TO BUILD A FIRE

Jack London (1876-1916)

Day had broken cold and gray, exceedingly cold and gray, when the man turned aside from the main Yukon trail and climbed the high earth-bank, where a dim and little traveled trail led eastward through the fat spruce timberland. It was a steep bank, and he paused for breath at the top, excusing the act to himself by looking at his watch. It was nine o'clock. There was no sun nor hint of sun, though there was not a cloud in the sky. It was a clear day, and yet there seemed an intangible pall over the face of things, a subtle gloom that made the day dark, and that was due to the absence of sun. This fact did not worry the man. He was used to the lack of sun. It had been days since he had seen the sun, and he knew that a few more days must pass before that cheerful orb, due south, would just peep above the sky-line and dip immediately from view.

The man flung a look back along the way he had come. The Yukon lay a mile wide and hidden under three feet of ice. On top of this ice were as many feet of snow. It was all pure white, rolling in gentle, undulations where the ice jams of the freeze-up had formed. North and south, as far as his eye could see, it was unbroken white, save for a dark hair-line that curved and twisted from around the spruce-covered island to the south, and that curved and twisted away into the north, where it disappeared behind another spruce-covered island. This dark hair-line was the trail — the main trail — that led south five hundred miles to the Chilcoot Pass, Dyea, and salt water; and that led north seventy miles to Dawson, and still on to the north a thousand miles to Nulato, and finally to St. Michael on Bering Sea, a thousand miles and half a thousand more.

But all this — the mysterious, far-reaching hair-line trail, the absence of sun from the sky, the tremendous cold, and the strangeness and weirdness of it all — made no impression on the man. It was not because he was long used to it. He was a newcomer in the land, a *chechaquo*, and this was his first winter. The trouble with him was that he was without imagination. He was quick and alert in the things of life, but only in the things, and not in the significances. Fifty degrees below zero meant eighty-odd degrees of frost. Such fact impressed him as being cold and uncomfortable, and that was all. It did not lead him to meditate upon his frailty as a creature of temperature, and upon man's frailty in general, able only to live within certain narrow limits of heat and cold; and from there on it did not lead him to the conjectural field of immortality and man's place in the universe. Fifty degrees below zero stood for the bite of frost that hurt and that must be guarded against by the use of mittens, ear-flaps, warm moccasins, and thick socks. Fifty degrees below zero was to him just precisely fifty degrees below zero. That there should be anything more to it than that was a thought that never entered his head.

As he turned to go on, he spat speculatively. There was a sharp, explosive crackle that startled him. He spat again. And again, in the air, before it could fall to the snow, the spittle crackled. He knew that at fifty below spittle crackled on the snow, but this spittle had crackled in the air. Undoubtedly it was colder than fifty below — how much colder he did not know. But the temperature did not matter. He was bound for the old claim on the left fork of Henderson Creek, where the boys were already. They had come over across the divide from the Indian Creek country, while he had come the roundabout way to take a look at the possibilities of getting out logs in the spring from the islands in the Yukon. He would be in to camp by six o'clock; a bit after dark, it was true, but the boys would be there, a fire would be going, and a hot supper would be ready. As for lunch, he pressed his hand against the protruding bundle under his jacket. It was also under his shirt, wrapped up in a handkerchief and lying against the naked skin. It was the only way to keep the biscuits from freezing. He smiled agreeably to himself as he thought of those biscuits, each cut open and sopped in bacon grease, and each enclosing a generous slice of fried bacon.

He plunged in among the big spruce trees. The trail was faint. A foot of snow had fallen since the last sled had passed over, and he was glad he was without a sled, traveling light. In fact, he carried nothing but the lunch wrapped in the handkerchief. He was surprised, however, at the cold. It certainly was cold, he concluded as he rubbed his numb nose and cheek-bones with his mittened hand. He was a warm-whiskered man, but the hair on his face did not protect the high cheek-bones and the eager nose that thrust itself aggressively into the frosty air.

At the man's heels trotted a dog, a big native husky, the proper wolfdog, gray-coated and without any visible or temperamental difference from its brother, the wild wolf. The animal was depressed by the tremendous cold. It knew that it was no time for traveling. Its instinct told it a truer tale than was told to the man by the man's judgment. In reality, it was not merely colder than fifty below zero; it was colder than sixty below, than seventy below. It was seventy-five below zero. Since the freezing point is thirty-two above zero, it meant that one hundred and seven degrees of frost obtained. The dog did not know anything about thermometers. Possibly in its brain there was no sharp consciousness of a condition of very cold such as was in the man's brain. But the brute had its instinct. It experienced a vague but menacing apprehension that subdued it and made it slink along at the man's heels, and that made it question eagerly every unwonted movement of the man as if expecting him to go into camp or to seek shelter somewhere and build a fire. The dog had learned fire, and it wanted fire, or else to burrow under the snow and cuddle its warmth away from the air.

The frozen moisture of its breathing had settled on its fur in a fine powder of frost, and especially were its jowls, muzzle, and eyelashes whitened by its crystalled breath. The man's red beard and mustache were likewise frosted, but more solidly, the deposit taking the form of ice and increasing with every warm, moist breath he exhaled. Also, the man was chewing tobacco, and the muzzle of ice held his lips so rigidly that he was unable to clear his chin when he expelled the juice. The result was that a crystal beard of the color and solidity of amber was increasing its length on his chin. If he fell down it would shatter itself, like glass, into brittle fragments. But he did not mind the appendage. It was the penalty all tobacco-chewers paid in that country, and he had been out before in two cold snaps. They had not been so cold as this, he knew, but by the spirit thermometer at Sixty Mile he knew they had been registered at fifty below and at fifty-five.

He held on through the level stretch of woods for several miles, crossed a wide flat of nigger-heads, and dropped down a bank to the frozen bed of a small stream. This was Henderson Creek, and he knew he was ten miles from the forks. He looked at his watch. It was ten o'clock. He was making four miles an hour, and he calculated that he would arrive at the forks at half-past twelve. He decided to celebrate that event by eating his lunch there.

The dog dropped in again at his heels, with a tail drooping discouragement, as the man swung along the creek-bed. The furrow of the old sled-trail was plainly visible, but a dozen inches of snow covered the marks of the last runners. In a month no man had come up or down that silent creek. The man held steadily on. He was not much given to thinking, and just then particularly he had nothing to think about save that he would eat lunch at the forks and that at six o'clock he would be in camp with the boys. There was nobody to talk to; and, had there been, speech would have been impossible because of the ice-muzzle on his mouth. So he continued monotonously to chew tobacco and to increase the length of his amber beard.

Once in a while the thought reiterated itself that it was very cold and that he had never experienced such cold. As he walked along he rubbed his cheek-bones and nose with the back of his mittened hand. He did this automatically, now and again changing hands. But rub as he would, the instant he stopped his cheekbones went numb, and the following instant the end of his nose went numb. He was sure to frost his cheeks; he knew that, and experienced a pang of regret that he had not devised a nose-strap of the sort Bud wore in cold snaps. Such a strap passed across the cheeks, as well, and saved them. But it didn't matter much, after all. What were frosted cheeks? A bit painful, that was all; they were never serious.

Empty as the man's mind was of thoughts, he was keenly observant, and he noticed the changes in the creek, the curves and bends and timber jams, and always he sharply noted where he placed his feet. Once coming around a bend, he shied abruptly, like a startled horse, curved away from the place where he had been walking, and retreated several paces back along the trail. The creek he knew was frozen clear to the bottom, — no creek could contain water in that arctic winter, — but he knew also that there were springs that bubbled out from the hillsides and ran along under the snow and on top the ice of the creek. He knew that the coldest snaps never froze these springs, and he knew likewise their danger. They were traps. They hid pools of water under the snow that might be three inches deep, or three feet. Sometimes a skin of ice half an inch thick covered them, and in turn was covered by the snow. Sometimes there were alternate layers of water and ice-skin, so that when one broke through he kept on breaking through for a while, sometimes wetting himself to the waist.

That was why he had shied in such panic. He had felt the give under his feet and heard the crackle of a snow-hidden ice-skin. And to get his feet wet in such a temperature meant trouble and danger. At the very least it meant delay, for he would be forced to stop and build a fire, and under its protection to bare his feet while he dried his socks and moccasins. He stood and studied the creek-bed and its banks, and decided that the flow of water came from the right. He reflected a while, rubbing his nose and cheeks, then skirted to the left, stepping gingerly and testing the footing for each step. Once clear of the danger, he took a fresh chew of tobacco and swung along at his four-mile gait.

In the course of the next two hours he came upon several similar traps. Usually the snow above the hidden pools had a sunken, candied appearance that advertised the danger. Once again, however, he had a close call; and once, suspecting danger, he compelled the dog to go on in front. The dog did not want to go. It hung back until the man shoved it forward, and then it went quickly across the white, unbroken surface. Suddenly it broke through, floundered to one side, and got away to firmer footing. It had wet its forefeet and legs, and almost immediately the water that clung to it turned to ice. It made quick efforts to lick the ice off its legs, then dropped down in the snow and began to bite out the ice that had formed between the toes. This was a matter of instinct. To permit the ice to remain would mean sore feet. It did not know this. It merely obeyed the mysterious prompting that arose from the deep crypts of its being. But the man knew, having achieved a judgment on the subject, and he removed the mitten from his right hand and helped tear out the ice-particles. He did not expose his fingers more than a minute, and was astonished at the swift numbness that smote them. It certainly was cold. He pulled on the mitten hastily, and beat the hand savagely across his chest.

At twelve o'clock the day was at its brightest. Yet the sun was too far south in its winter journey to clear the horizon. The bulge of the earth intervened between it and Henderson Creek, where the man walked under a clear sky at noon and cast no shadow. At half-past twelve, to the minute, he arrived at the forks of the creek. He was pleased at the speed he had made. If he kept it up, he would certainly be with the boys by six. He unbuttoned his jacket and shirt and drew forth his lunch. The action consumed no more than a quarter of a minute, yet in that brief moment the numbness laid hold of the exposed fingers. He did not put the mitten on, but instead struck the fingers a dozen sharp smashes against his leg. Then he sat down on a snow-covered log to eat. The sting that followed upon the striking of his fingers against his leg ceased so quickly that he was startled. He had had no chance to take a bite of biscuit. He struck the fingers repeatedly and returned them to the mitten, baring the other hand for the purpose of eating. He tried to take a mouthful, but the ice-muzzle prevented. He had forgotten to build a fire and thaw out. He chuckled at his foolishness, and as he chuckled he noted the numbness creeping into the exposed fingers. Also, he noted that the stinging which had first come to his toes when he sat down was already passing away. He wondered whether the toes were warm or numb. He moved them inside the moccasins and decided that they were numb.

He pulled the mitten on hurriedly and stood up. He was a bit frightened. He stamped up and down until the stinging returned into the feet. It certainly was cold, was his thought. That man from Sulphur Creek had spoken the truth when telling how cold it sometimes got in the country. And he had laughed at him at the time! That showed one must not be too sure of things. There was no mistake about it, it was cold. He strode up and down, stamping his feet and threshing his arms, until reassured by the returning warmth. Then he got out matches and proceeded to make a fire. From the undergrowth, where high water of the previous spring had lodged a supply of seasoned twigs, he got his firewood. Working carefully from a small beginning, he soon had a roaring fire, over which he thawed the ice from his face and in the protection of which he ate his biscuits. For the moment the cold of space was outwitted. The dog took satisfaction in the fire, stretching out close enough for warmth and far enough away to escape being singed.

When the man had finished, he filled his pipe and took his comfortable time over a smoke. Then he pulled on his mittens, settled the ear-flaps of his cap firmly about his ears, and took the creek trail up the left fork. The dog was disappointed and yearned back toward the fire. This man did not know cold. Possibly all the generations of his ancestry had been ignorant of cold, of real cold, of cold one hundred and seven degrees below freezing point. But the dog knew; all its ancestry knew, and it had inherited the knowledge. And it knew that it was not good to walk abroad in such fearful cold. It was the time to lie snug in a hole in the snow and wait for a curtain of cloud to be drawn across the face of outer space whence this cold came. On the other hand, there was no keen intimacy between the dog and the man. The one was the toil-slave of the other, and the only caresses it had ever received were the caresses of the whiplash and of harsh and menacing throat-sounds that threatened the whiplash. So, the dog made no effort to communicate its apprehension to the man. It was not concerned in the welfare of the man, it was for its own sake that it yearned back toward the fire. But the man whistled, and spoke to it with the sound of whiplashes and the dog swung in at the man's heel and followed after.

The man took a chew of tobacco and proceeded to start a new amber beard. Also, his moist breath quickly powdered with white his mustache, eyebrows, and lashes. There did not seem to be so many springs on the left fork of the Henderson, and for half an hour the man saw no signs of any. And then it happened. At a place where there were no signs, where the soft, unbroken snow seemed to advertise solidity beneath, the man broke through. It was not deep. He wet himself halfway to the knees before he floundered out to the firm crust.

He was angry, and cursed his luck aloud. He had hoped to get into camp with the boys at six o'clock, and this would delay him an hour, for he would have to build a fire and dry out his foot-gear. This was imperative at that low temperature — he knew that much; and he turned aside to the bank, which he climbed. On top, tangled in the underbrush about the trunks of several small spruce trees, was a high-water deposit of dry firewood — sticks and twigs, principally, but also larger portions of seasoned branches and fine, dry, last-year's grasses. He threw down several large pieces on top of the snow. This served for a foundation and prevented the young flame from drowning itself in the snow it otherwise would melt. The flame he got by touching a match to a small shred of birch bark that he took from his pocket. This burned even more readily than paper. Placing it on the foundation, he fed the young flame with wisps of dry grass and with the tiniest dry twigs.

He worked slowly and carefully, keenly aware of his danger. Gradually, as the flame grew stronger, he increased the size of the twigs with which he fed it. He squatted in the snow, pulling the twigs out from their entanglement in the brush and feeding directly to the flame. He knew there must be no failure. When it is seventy-five below zero, a man must not fail in his first attempt to build a fire — that is, if his feet are wet. If his feet are dry, and he fails, he can run along the trail for half a mile and restore his circulation. But the circulation of wet and freezing feet cannot be restored by running when it is seventy-five below. No matter how fast he runs, the wet feet will freeze the harder.

All this the man knew. The old-timer on Sulphur Creek had told him about it the previous fall, and now he was appreciating the advice. Already all sensation had gone out of his feet. To build the fire he had been forced to remove his mittens, and the fingers had quickly gone numb. His pace of four miles an hour had kept his heart pumping blood to the surface of his body and to all the extremities. But the instant he stopped, the action of the pump eased down. The cold of space smote the unprotected tip of the planet, and he, being on that unprotected tip, received the full force of the blow. The blood of his body recoiled before it. The blood was alive, like the dog, and like the dog it wanted to hide away and cover itself up from the fearful cold. So long as he walked four miles an hour, he pumped that blood, willy-nilly, to the surface; but now it ebbed away and sank down into the recesses of his body. The extremities were the first to feel its absence. His wet feet froze the faster, and his exposed fingers numbed the faster, though they had not yet begun to freeze. Nose and cheeks were already freezing, while the skin of all his body chilled as it lost its blood.

But he was safe. Toes and nose and cheeks would be only touched by the frost, for the fire was beginning to burn with strength. He was feeding it with twigs the size of his finger. In another minute he would be able to feed it with branches the size of his wrist, and then he could remove his wet foot-gear, and, while it dried, he could keep his naked feet warm by the fire, rubbing them at first, of course, with snow. The fire was a success. He was safe. He remembered the advice of the old timer on Sulphur Creek, and smiled. The old-timer had been very serious in laying down the law that no man must travel alone in the Klondike after fifty below. Well, here he was; he had had the accident; he was alone; and he had saved himself. Those old-timers were rather womanish, some of them, he thought. All a man had to do was to keep his head, and he was all right. Any man who was a man could travel alone. But it was surprising, the rapidity with which his cheeks and nose were freezing. And he had not thought his fingers could go lifeless in so short a time. Lifeless they were, for he could scarcely make them move together to grip a twig, and they seemed remote from his body and from him. When he touched a twig, he had to look and see whether or not he had hold of it. The wires were pretty well down between him and his finger-ends.

All of which counted for little. There was the fire, snapping and crackling and promising life with every dancing flame. He started to untie his moccasins. They were coated with ice; the thick German socks were like sheaths of iron halfway to the knees; and the moccasin strings were like rods of steel all twisted and knotted as by some conflagration. For a moment he tugged with his numb fingers, then, realizing the folly of it, he drew his sheath-knife.

But before he could cut the strings, it happened. It was his own fault or, rather, his mistake. He should not have built the fire under the spruce tree. He should have built it in the open. But it had been easier to pull the twigs from the brush and drop them directly on the fire. Now the tree under which he had done this carried a weight of snow on its boughs. No wind had blown for weeks, and each bough was fully freighted. Each time he had pulled a twig he had communicated a slight agitation to the tree — an imperceptible agitation, so far as he was concerned, but an agitation sufficient to bring about the disaster. High up in the tree one bough capsized its load of snow. This fell on the boughs beneath, capsizing them. This process continued, spreading out and involving the whole tree. It grew like an avalanche, and it descended without warning upon the man and the fire, and the fire was blotted out! Where it had burned was a mantle of fresh and disordered snow.

The man was shocked. It was as though he had just heard his own sentence of death. For a moment he sat and stared at the spot where the fire had been. Then he grew very calm. Perhaps the old-timer on Sulphur Creek was right. If he had only had a trail-mate he would have been in no danger now. The trail-mate could have built the fire. Well, it was up to him to build the fire over again, and this second time there must be no failure. Even if he succeeded, he would most likely lose some toes. His feet must be badly frozen by now, and there would be some time before the second fire was ready.

Such were his thoughts, but he did not sit and think them. He was busy all the time they were passing through his mind. He made a new foundation for a fire, this time in the open, where no treacherous tree could blot it out. Next, he gathered dry grasses and tiny twigs from the high-water flotsam. He could not bring his fingers together to pull them out, but he was able to gather them by the handful. In this way he got many rotten twigs and bits of green moss that were undesirable, but it was the best he could do. He worked methodically, even collecting an armful of the larger branches to be used later when the fire gathered strength. And all the while the dog sat and watched him, a certain yearning wistfulness in its eyes, for it looked upon him as the fire-provider, and the fire was slow in coming.

When all was ready, the man reached in his pocket for a second piece of birch bark. He knew the bark was there, and, though he could not feel it with his fingers, he could hear its crisp rustling as he fumbled for it. Try as he would, he could not clutch hold of it. And all the time in his consciousness, was the knowledge that each instant his feet were freezing. This thought tended to put him in a panic, but he fought against it and kept calm. He pulled on his mittens with his teeth, and threshed his arms back and forth, beating his hands with all his might against his sides. He did this sitting down, and he stood up to do it; and all the while the dog sat in the snow, its wolf-brush of a tail curled around warmly over its forefeet, its sharp wolf-ears pricked forward intently as it watched the man. And the man, as he beat and threshed with his arms and hands, felt a great surge of envy as he regarded the creature that was warm and secure in its natural covering.

After a time he was aware of the first far-away signals of sensation in his beaten fingers. The faint tingling grew stronger till it evolved into a stinging ache that was excruciating, but which the man hailed with satisfaction. He stripped the mitten from his right hand and fetched forth the birch bark. The exposed fingers were quickly going numb again. Next he brought out his bunch of sulphur matches. But the tremendous cold had already driven the life out of his fingers. In his effort to separate one match from the others, the whole bunch fell in the snow. He tried to pick it out of the snow, but failed. The dead fingers could neither touch nor clutch. He was very careful. He drove the thought of his freezing feet, and nose, and cheeks, out of his mind, devoting his whole soul to the matches. He watched, using the sense of vision in place of that of touch, and when he saw his fingers on each side the bunch, he closed them — that is, he willed to close them, for the wires were down, and the fingers did not obey. He pulled the mitten on the right hand and beat it fiercely against his knee. Then, with both mittened hands, he scooped the bunch of matches, along with much snow, into his lap. Yet he was no better off.

After some manipulation he managed to get the bunch between the heels of his mittened hands. In this fashion he carried it to his mouth. The ice crackled and snapped when by a violent effort he opened his mouth. He drew the lower jaw in, curled the upper lip out of the way, and scraped the bunch with his upper teeth in order to separate a match. He succeeded in getting one, which he dropped on his lap. He was no better off. He could not pick it up. Then he devised a way. He picked it up in his teeth and scratched it on his leg. Twenty times he scratched before he succeeded in lighting it. As it flamed he held it with his teeth to the birch bark. But the burning brimstone went up his nostrils and into his lungs, causing him to cough spasmodically. The match fell into the snow and went out.

The old-timer on Sulphur Creek was right, he thought in the moment of controlled despair that ensued after fifty below, a man should travel with a partner. He beat his hands, but failed in exciting any sensation. Suddenly he bared both hands, removing the mittens with his teeth. He caught the whole bunch between the heels of his hands. His arm muscles not being frozen enabled him to press the hand-heels tightly against the matches. Then he scratched the bunch along his leg. It flared into flame, seventy sulphur matches at once! There was no wind to blow them out. He kept his head to one side to escape the strangling fumes, and held the blazing bunch to the birth bark. As he so held it, he became aware of sensation in his hand. His flesh was burning. He could smell it. Deep down below the surface he could feel it. The sensation developed into pain that grew acute. And still he endured it, holding the flame of the matches clumsily to the bark that would not light readily because his own burning hands were in the way, absorbing most of the flame.

At last, when he could endure no more, he jerked his hands apart. The blazing matches fell sizzling into the snow, but the birch bark was alight. He began laying dry grasses and the tiniest twigs on the flame. He could not pick and choose, for he had to lift the fuel between the heels of his hands. Small pieces of rotten wood and green moss clung to the twigs, and he bit them off as well as he could with his teeth. He cherished the flame carefully and awkwardly. It meant life, and it must not perish. The withdrawal of blood from the surface of his body now made him begin to shiver, and he grew more awkward. A large piece of green moss fell squarely on the little fire. He tried to poke it out with his fingers, but his shivering frame made him poke too far and he disrupted the nucleus of the little fire, the burning grasses and tiny twigs separating and scattering. He tried to poke them together again, but in spite of the tenseness of the effort, his shivering got away with him, and the twigs were hopelessly scattered. Each twig gushed a puff of smoke and went out. The fire-provider had failed. As he looked apathetically about him, his eyes chanced on the dog, sitting across the ruins of the fire from him, in the snow, making restless, hunching movements, slightly lifting one forefoot and then the other, shifting its weight back and forth on them with wistful eagerness.

The sight of the dog put a wild idea into his head. He remembered the tale of the man, caught in a blizzard, who killed a steer and crawled inside the carcass, and so was saved. He would kill the dog and bury his hands in the warm body until the numbness went out of them. Then he could build another fire. He spoke to the dog, calling it to him; but in his voice was a strange note of fear that frightened the animal, who had never known the man to speak in such way before. Something was the matter, and its suspicious nature sensed danger — it knew not what danger, but somewhere, somehow, in its brain arose an apprehension of the man. It flattened its ears down at the sound of the man's voice, and its restless, hunching movements and the liftings and shiftings of its forefeet became more pronounced; but it would not come to the man. He got on his hands and knees and crawled toward the dog. This unusual posture again excited suspicion, and the animal sidled mincingly away.

The man sat up in the snow for a moment and struggled for calmness. Then he pulled on his mittens, by means of his teeth, and got upon his feet. He glanced down at first in order to assure himself that he was really standing up, for the absence of sensation in his feet left him unrelated to the earth. His erect position in itself started to drive the webs of suspicion from the dog's mind; and when he spoke peremptorily, with the sound of whiplashes in his voice, the dog rendered its customary allegiance and came to him. As it came within reaching distance, the man lost his control. His arms flashed out to the dog, and he experienced genuine surprise when he discovered that his hands could not clutch, that there was neither bend nor feeling in the fingers. He had forgotten for the moment that they were frozen and that they were freezing more and more. All this happened quickly, and before the animal could get away, he encircled its body with his arms. He sat down in the snow, and in this fashion held the dog, while it snarled and whined and struggled.

But it was all he could do, hold its body encircled in his arms and sit there. He realized that he could not kill the dog. There was no way to do it. With his helpless hands he could neither draw nor hold his sheath knife nor throttle the animal. He released it, and it plunged wildly away, with tail between its legs, and still snarling. It halted forty feet away and surveyed him curiously, with ears sharply pricked forward. The man looked down at his hands in order to locate them, and found them hanging on the ends of his arms. It struck him as curious that one should have to use his eyes in order to find out where his hands were. He began threshing his arms back and forth, beating the mittened hands against his sides. He did this for five minutes, violently, and his heart pumped enough blood up to the surface to put a stop to his shivering. But no sensation was aroused in the hands. He had an impression that they hung like weights on the ends of his arms, but when he tried to run the impression down, he could not find it.

A certain fear of death, dull and oppressive, came to him. This fear quickly became poignant as he realized that it was no longer a mere matter of freezing his fingers and toes, or of losing his hands and feet, but that it was a matter of life and death with the chances against him. This threw him into a panic, and he turned and ran up the creek-bed along the old, dim trail. The dog joined in behind and kept up with him. He ran blindly, without intention, in fear such as he had never known in his life. Slowly, as he plowed and floundered through the snow, he began to see things again, the banks of the creek, the old timber-jams, the leafless aspens, and the sky. The running made him feel better. He did not shiver. Maybe, if he ran on, his feet would thaw out; and, anyway, if he ran far enough, he would reach camp and the boys. Without doubt he would lose some fingers and toes and some of his face; but the boys would take care of him, and save the rest of him when he got there. And at the same time there was another thought in his mind that said he would never get to the camp and the boys; that it was too many miles away, that the freezing had too great a start on him, and that he would soon be stiff and dead. This thought he kept in the background and refused to consider. Sometimes it pushed itself forward and demanded to be heard, but he thrust it back and strove to think of other things.

It struck him as curious that he could run at all on feet so frozen that he could not feel them when they struck the earth and took the weight of his body. He seemed to himself to skim along above the surface, and to have no connection with the earth. Somewhere he had once seen a winged Mercury, and he wondered if Mercury felt as he felt when skimming over the earth.

His theory of running until he reached camp and the boys had one flaw in it: he lacked the endurance. Several times he stumbled, and finally he tottered, crumpled up, and fell. When he tried to rise, he failed. He must sit and rest, he decided, and next time he would merely walk and keep on going. As he sat and regained his breath, he noted that he was feeling quite warm and comfortable. He was not shivering, and it even seemed that a warm glow had come to his chest and trunk. And yet, when he touched his nose or cheeks, there was no sensation. Running would not thaw them out. Nor would it thaw out his hands and feet. Then the thought came to him that the frozen portions of his body must be extending. He tried to keep this thought down, to forget it, to think of something else; he was aware of the panicky feeling that it caused, and he was afraid of the panic. But the thought asserted itself, and persisted, until it produced a vision of his body totally frozen. This was too much, and he made another wild run along the trail. Once he slowed down to a walk, but the thought of the freezing extending itself made him run again.

And all the time the dog ran with him, at his heels. When he fell down a second time, it curled its tail over its forefeet and sat in front of him, facing him, curiously eager and intent. The warmth and security of the animal angered him, and he cursed it till it flattened down its ears appealingly. This time the shivering came more quickly upon the man. He was losing in his battle with the frost. It was creeping into his body from all sides. The thought of it drove him on, but he ran no more than a hundred feet, when he staggered and pitched headlong. It was his last panic. When he had recovered his breath and control, he sat up and entertained in his mind the conception of meeting death with dignity. However, the conception did not come to him in such terms. His idea of it was that he had been making a fool of himself, running around like a chicken with its head cut off — such was the simile that occurred to him. Well, he was bound to freeze anyway, and he might as well take it decently. With this new-found peace of mind came the first glimmerings of drowsiness. A good idea, he thought, to sleep off to death. It was like taking an anaesthetic. Freezing was not so bad as people thought. There were lots worse ways to die.

He pictured the boys finding his body next day. Suddenly he found himself with them, coming along the trail and looking for himself. And, still with them, he came around a turn in the trail and found himself lying in the snow. He did not belong with himself any more, for even then he was out of himself, standing with the boys and looking at himself in the snow. It certainly was cold, was his thought. When he got back to the States he could tell the folks what real cold was. He drifted on from this to a vision of the old-timer on Sulphur Creek. He could see him quite clearly, warm and comfortable, and smoking a pipe.

"You were right, old hoss; you were right," the man mumbled to the old-timer of Sulphur Creek.

Then the man drowsed off into what seemed to him the most comfortable and satisfying sleep he had ever known. The dog sat facing him and waiting. The brief day drew to a close in a long, slow twilight. There were no signs of a fire to be made, and, besides, never in the dog's experience had it known a man to sit like that in the snow and make no fire. As the twilight drew on, its eager yearning for the fire mastered it, and with a great lifting and shifting of forefeet, it whined softly, then flattened its ears down in anticipation of being chidden by the man. But the man remained silent. Later, the dog whined loudly. And still later it crept close to the man and caught the scent of death. This made the animal bristle and back away. A little longer it delayed, howling under the stars that leaped and danced and shone brightly in the cold sky. Then it turned and trotted up the trail in the direction of the camp it knew, where were the other food-providers and fire-providers.

I WANT TO KNOW WHY

Sherwood Anderson (1876-1941)

WE got up at four in the morning, that first day in the east. On the evening before we had climbed off a freight train at the edge of town, and with the true instinct of Kentucky boys had found our way across town and to the race track and the stables at once. Then we knew we were all right. Hanley Turner right away found a nigger we knew. It was Bildad Johnson who in the winter works at Ed Becker's livery barn in our home town, Beckersville. Bildad is a good cook as almost all our niggers are and of course he, like everyone in our part of Kentucky who is anyone at all, likes the horses. In the spring Bildad begins to scratch around. A nigger from our country can flatter and wheedle anyone into letting him do most anything he wants. Bildad wheedles the stable men and the trainers from the horse farms in our country around Lexington. The trainers come into town in the evening to stand around and talk and maybe get into a poker game. Bildad gets in with them. He is always doing little favors and telling about things to eat, chicken browned in a pan, and how is the best way to cook sweet potatoes and corn bread. It makes your mouth water to hear him.

When the racing season comes on and the horses go to the races and there is all the talk on the streets in the evenings about the new colts, and everyone says when they are going over to Lexington or to the spring meeting at Churchill Downs or to Latonia, and the horsemen that have been down to New Orleans or maybe at the winter meeting at Havana in Cuba come home to spend a week before they start out again, at such a time when everything talked about in Beckersville is just horses and nothing else and the outfits start out and horse racing is in every breath of air you breathe, Bildad shows up with a job as cook for some outfit. Often when I think about it, his always going all season to the races and working in the livery team in the winter where horses are and where men like to come and talk about being around horses, I wish I was a nigger. It's a foolish thing to say, but that's the way I am about being around horses, just crazy. I can't help it.

Well, I must tell you about what we did and let you in on what I'm talking about. Four of us boys from Beckersville, all whites and sons of men who live in Beckersville regular, made up our minds we were going to the races, not just to Lexington or Louisville, I don't mean, but to the big eastern track we were always hearing our Beckersville men talk about, to Saratoga. We were all pretty young then. I was just turned fifteen and I was the oldest of the four. It was my scheme. I admit that and I talked the others into trying it. There was Hanley Turner and Henry Rieback and Tom Tumberton and myself. I had thirty-seven dollars I had earned during the winter working nights and Saturdays in Enoch Myer's grocery. Henry Rieback had eleven dollars and the others, Hanley and Tom, had only a dollar or two each. We fixed it all up and laid low until the Kentucky spring meetings were over and some of our men, the sportiest ones, the ones we envied the most, had cut out — then we cut out too.

I won't tell you the trouble we had beating our way on freights and all. We went through Cleveland and Buffalo and other cities and saw Niagara Falls. We bought things there, souvenirs and spoons and cards and shells with pictures of the falls on them for our sisters and mothers, but thought we had better not send any of the things home. We didn't want to put the folks on our trail and maybe be nabbed.

We got into Saratoga as I said at night and went to the track. Bildad fed us up. He showed us a place to sleep in hay over a shed and promised to keep still. Niggers are all right about things like that. They won't squeal on you. Often a white man you might meet, when you had run away from home like that, might appear to be all right and give you a quarter or a half dollar or something, and then go right and give you away. White men will do that, but not a nigger. You can trust them. They are squarer with kids. I don't know why.

At the Saratoga meeting that year there were a lot of men from home. Dave Williams and Arthur Mulford and Jerry Myers and others. Then there was a lot from Louisville and Lexington Henry Rieback knew but I didn't. They were professional gamblers and Henry Rieback's father is one too. He is what is called a sheet writer and goes away most of the year to the tracks. In the winter when he is home in Beckersville he don't stay there much but goes away to cities and deals faro. He is a nice man and generous, is always sending Henry presents, a bicycle and a gold watch and a boy scout suit of clothes and things like that.

My own father is a lawyer. He's all right, but don't make much money and can't buy me things and anyway I'm getting so old now I don't expect it. He never said nothing to me against Henry, but Hanley Turner and Tom Tumberton's fathers did. They said to their boys that money so come by is no good and they didn't want their boys brought up to hear gamblers' talk and be thinking about such things and maybe embrace them.

That's all right and I guess the men know what they are talking about, but I don't see what it's got to do with Henry or with horses either. That's what I'm writing this story about. I'm puzzled. I'm getting to be a man and want to think straight and be O.K., and there's something I saw at the race meeting at the eastern track I can't figure out.

I can't help it, I'm crazy about thoroughbred horses. I've always been that way. When I was ten years old and saw I was growing to be big and couldn't be a rider I was so sorry I nearly died. Harry Hellinfinger in Beckersville, whose father is Postmaster, is grown up and too lazy to work, but likes to stand around in the street and get up jokes on boys like sending them to a hardware store for a gimlet to bore square holes and other jokes like that. He played one on me. He told me that if I would eat a half a cigar I would be stunted and not grow any more and maybe could be a rider. I did it. When father wasn't looking I took a cigar out of his pocket and gagged it down some way. It made me awful sick and the doctor had to be sent for, and then it did no good. I kept right on growing. It was a joke. When I told what I had done and why most fathers would have whipped me but mine didn't.

Well, I didn't get stunted and didn't die. It serves Harry Hellinfinger right. Then I made up my mind I would like to be a stable boy, but had to give that up too. Mostly niggers do that work and I knew father wouldn't let me go into it. No use to ask him.

If you've never been crazy about thoroughbreds it's because you've never been around where they are much and don't know any better. They're beautiful. There isn't anything so lovely and clean and full of spunk and honest and everything as some race horses. On the big horse farms that are all around our town Beckersville there are tracks and the horses run in the early morning. More than a thousand times I've got out of bed before daylight and walked two or three miles to the tracks. Mother wouldn't of let me go but father always says, "Let him alone." So I got some bread out of the bread box and some butter and jam, gobbled it and lit out.

At the tracks you sit on the fence with men, whites and niggers, and they chew tobacco and talk, and then the colts are brought out. It's early and the grass is covered with shiny dew and in another field a man is plowing and they are frying things in a shed where the track niggers sleep, and you know how a nigger can giggle and laugh and say things that make you laugh. A white man can't do it and some niggers can't but a track nigger can every time.

And so the colts are brought out and some are just galloped by stable boys, but almost every morning on a big track owned by a rich man who lives maybe in New York, there are always, nearly every morning, a few colts and some of the old race horses and geldings and mares that are cut loose.

It brings a lump up into my throat when a horse runs. I don't mean all horses but some. I can pick them nearly every time. It's in my blood like in the blood of race track niggers and trainers. Even when they just go slop-jogging along with a little nigger on their backs I can tell a winner. If my throat hurts and it's hard for me to swallow, that's him. He'll run like Sam Hill when you let him out. If he don't win every time it'll be a wonder and because they've got him in a pocket behind another or he was pulled or got off bad at the post or something. If I wanted to be a gambler like Henry Roebuck's father I could get rich. I know I could and Henry says so, too. All I would have to do is to wait 'til that hurt comes when I see a horse and then bet every cent. That's what I would do if I wanted to be a gambler, but I don't.

When you're at the tracks in the morning — not the race tracks but the training tracks around Beckersville — you don't see a horse, the kind I've been talking about, very often, but it's nice anyway. Any thoroughbred, that is sired right and out of a good mare and trained by a man that knows how, can run. If he couldn't what would he be there for and not pulling a plow?

Well, out of the stables they come and the boys are on their backs and it's lovely to be there. You hunch down on top of the fence and itch inside you. Over in the sheds the niggers giggle and sing. Bacon is being fried and coffee made. Everything smells lovely. Nothing smells better than coffee and manure and horses and niggers and bacon frying and pipes being smoked out of doors on a morning like that. It just gets you, that's what it does.

But about Saratoga. We was there six days and not a soul from home seen us and everything came off just as we wanted it to, fine weather and horses and races and all. We beat our way home and Bildad gave us a basket with fried chicken and bread and other eatables in, and I had eighteen dollars when we got back to Beckersville. Mother jawed and cried but Pop didn't say much. I told everything we done except one thing. I did and saw that alone. That's what I'm writing about. It got me upset, I think about it at night. Here it is.

At Saratoga we laid up nights in the hay in the shed Bildad had showed us and ate with the niggers early and at night when the race people had all gone away. The men from home stayed mostly in the grandstand and betting field, and didn't come out around the places where the horses are kept except to the paddocks just before a race when the horses are saddled. At Saratoga they don't have paddocks under an open shed as at Lexington and Churchill Downs and other tracks down in our country, but saddle the horses right out in an open place under trees on a lawn as smooth and nice as Banker Bohon's front yard here in Beckersville. It's lovely. The horses are sweaty and nervous and shine and the men come out and smoke cigars and look at them and the trainers are there and the owners, and your heart thumps so you can hardly breathe.

Then the bugle blows for post and the boys that ride come running out with their silk clothes on and you run to get a place by the fence with the niggers.

I always am wanting to be a trainer or owner, and at the risk of being seen and caught and sent home I went to the paddocks before every race. The other boys didn't but I did.

We got to Saratoga on a Friday and on Wednesday the next week the big Mullford Handicap was to be run. Middlestride was in it and Sunstreak. The weather was fine and the track fast. I couldn't sleep the night before.

What had happened was that both these horses are the kind it makes my throat hurt to see. Middlestride is long and looks awkward and is a gelding. He belongs to Joe Thompson, a little owner from home who only has a half-dozen horses. The Mullford Handicap is for a mile and Middlestride can't untrack fast. He goes away slow and is always back at the half, then he begins to run and if the race is a mile and a quarter he'll just eat up everything and get there.

Sunstreak is different. He is a stallion and nervous and belongs on the biggest farm we've got in our country, the Van Riddle place that belongs to Mr. Van Riddle of New York. Sunstreak is like a girl you think about sometimes but never see. He is hard all over and lovely too. When you look at his head you want to kiss him. He is trained by Jerry Tillford who knows me and has been good to me lots of times, lets me walk into a horse's stall to look at him close and other things. There isn't anything as sweet as that horse. He stands at the post quiet and not letting on, but he is just burning up inside. Then when the barrier goes up he is off like his name, Sunstreak. It makes you ache to see him. It hurts you. He just lays down and runs like a bird dog. There can't anything I ever see run like him except Middlestride when he gets untracked and stretches himself.

Gee! I ached to see that race and those two horses run, ached and dreaded it too. I didn't want to see either of our horses beaten. We had never sent a pair like that to the races before. Old men in Beckersville said so and the niggers said so. It was a fact.

Before the race I went over to the paddocks to see. I looked a last look at Middlestride, who isn't such a much standing in a paddock that way, then I went to Sunstreak.

It was his day. I knew when I see him. I forgot all about being seen myself and walked right up. All the men from Beckersville were there and no one noticed me except Jerry Tillford. He saw me and something happened. I'll tell you about that.

I was standing looking at that horse and aching. In some way, I can't tell how, I knew just how Sunstreak felt inside. He was quiet and letting the niggers rub his legs and Mr. Van Riddle himself put the saddle on, but he was just a raging torrent inside. He was like the water in the river at Niagara Falls just before it goes plunk down. That horse wasn't thinking about running. He don't have to think about that. He was just thinking about holding himself back 'til the time for the running came. I knew that. I could just in a way see right inside him. He was going to do some awful running and I knew it. He wasn't bragging or letting on much or prancing or making a fuss, but just waiting. I knew it and Jerry Tillford his trainer knew. I looked up and then that man and I looked into each other's eyes. Something happened to me. I guess I loved the man as much as I did the horse because he knew what I knew. Seemed to me there wasn't anything in the world but that man and the horse and me. I cried and Jerry Tillford had a shine in his eyes. Then I came away to the fence to wait for the race. The horse was better than me, more steadier, and now I know better than Jerry. He was the quietest and he had to do the running.

Sunstreak ran first of course and he busted the world's record for a mile. I've seen that if I never see anything more. Everything came out just as I expected. Middlestride got left at the post and was way back and closed up to be second, just as I knew he would. He'll get a world's record too some day. They can't skin the Beckersville country on horses.

I watched the race calm because I knew what would happen. I was sure. Hanley Turner and Henry Rieback and Tom Tumberton were all more excited than me.

A funny thing had happened to me. I was thinking about Jerry Tillford the trainer and how happy he was all through the race. I liked him that afternoon even more than I ever liked my own father. I almost forgot the horses thinking that way about him. It was because of what I had seen in his eyes as he stood in the paddocks beside Sunstreak before the race started. I knew he had been watching and working with Sunstreak since the horse was a baby colt, had taught him to run and be patient and when to let himself out and not to quit, never. I knew that for him it was like a mother seeing her child do something brave or wonderful. It was the first time I ever felt for a man like that. After the race that night I cut out from Tom and Hanley and Henry. I wanted to be by myself and I wanted to be near Jerry Tillford if I could work it. Here is what happened.

The track in Saratoga is near the edge of town. It is all polished up and trees around, the evergreen kind, and grass and everything painted and nice. If you go past the track you get to a hard road made of asphalt for automobiles, and if you go along this for a few miles there is a road turns off to a little rummy-looking farm house set in a yard.

That night after the race I went along that road because I had seen Jerry and some other men go that way in an automobile. I didn't expect to find them. I walked for a ways and then sat down by a fence to think. It was the direction they went in. I wanted to be as near Jerry as I could. I felt close to him. Pretty soon I went up the side road — I don't know why — and came to the rummy farm house. I was just lonesome to see Jerry, like wanting to see your father at night when you are a young kid. Just then an automobile came along and turned in. Jerry was in it and Henry Rieback's father, and Arthur Bedford from home, and Dave Williams and two other men I didn't know. They got out of the car and went into the house, all but Henry Rieback's father who quarreled with them and said he wouldn't go. It was only about nine o'clock, but they were all drunk and the rummy looking farm house was a place for bad women to stay in. That's what it was. I crept up along a fence and looked through a window and saw.

It's what give me the fantods. I can't make it out. The women in the house were all ugly mean-looking women, not nice to look at or be near. They were homely too, except one who was tall and looked a little like the gelding Middlestride, but not clean like him, but with a hard ugly mouth. She had red hair. I saw everything plain. I got up by an old rose bush by an open window and looked. The women had on loose dresses and sat around in chairs. The men came in and some sat on the women's laps. The place smelled rotten and there was rotten talk, the kind a kid hears around a livery stable in a town like Beckersville in the winter but don't ever expect to hear talked when there are women around. It was rotten. A nigger wouldn't go into such a place.

I looked at Jerry Tillford. I've told you how I had been feeling about him on account of his knowing what was going on inside of Sunstreak in the minute before he went to the post for the race in which he made a world's record.

Jerry bragged in that bad woman house as I know Sunstreak wouldn't never have bragged. He said that he made that horse, that it was him that won the race and made the record. He lied and bragged like a fool. I never heard such silly talk.

And then, what do you suppose he did! He looked at the woman in there, the one that was lean and hard-mouthed and looked a little like the gelding Middlestride, but not clean like him, and his eyes began to shine just as they did when he looked at me and at Sunstreak in the paddocks at the track in the afternoon. I stood there by the window — gee! — but I wished I hadn't gone away from the tracks, but had stayed with the boys and the niggers and the horses. The tall rotten looking woman was between us just as Sunstreak was in the paddocks in the afternoon.

Then, all of a sudden, I began to hate that man. I wanted to scream and rush in the room and kill him. I never had such a feeling before. I was so mad clean through that I cried and my fists were doubled up so my finger nails cut my hands.

And Jerry's eyes kept shining and he waved back and forth, and then he went and kissed that woman and I crept away and went back to the tracks and to bed and didn't sleep hardly any, and then next day I got the other kids to start home with me and never told them anything I seen.

I been thinking about it ever since. I can't make it out. Spring has come again and I'm nearly sixteen and go to the tracks mornings same as always, and I see Sunstreak and Middlestride and a new colt named Strident I'll bet will lay them all out, but no one thinks so but me and two or three niggers.

But things are different. At the tracks the air don't taste as good or smell as good. It's because a man like Jerry Tillford, who knows what he does, could see a horse like Sunstreak run, and kiss a woman like that the same day. I can't make it out. Darn him, what did he want to do like that for? I keep thinking about it and it spoils looking at horses and smelling things and hearing niggers laugh and everything. Sometimes I'm so mad about it I want to fight someone. It gives me the fantods. What did he do it for? I want to know why.

THE GOLDEN HONEYMOON

Ring Lardner (1885-1933)

MOTHER says that when I start talking I never know when to stop. But I tell her the only time I get a chance is when she ain't around, so I have to make the most of it. I guess the fact is neither one of us would be welcome in a Quaker meeting, but as I tell Mother, what did God give us tongues for if He didn't want we should use them? Only she says He didn't give them to us to say the same thing over and over again, like I do, and repeat myself. But I say:

"Well, Mother," I say, "when people is like you and I and been married fifty years, do you expect everything I say will be something you ain't heard me say before? But it may be new to others, as they ain't nobody else lived with me as long as you have."

So she says:

"You can bet they ain't, as they couldn't nobody else stand you that long."

"Well," I tell her, "you look pretty healthy."

"Maybe I do," she will say, "but I looked even healthier before I married you."

You can't get ahead of Mother.

Yes, sir, we was married just fifty years ago the seventeenth day of last December and my daughter and son-in-law was over from Trenton to help us celebrate the Golden Wedding. My son-in-law is John H. Kramer, the real estate man. He made $12,000 one year and is pretty well thought of around Trenton; a good, steady, hard worker. The Rotarians was after him a long time to join, but he kept telling them his home was his club. But Edie fnally made him join. That's my daughter.

Well, anyway, they come over to help us celebrate the Golden Wedding and it was pretty crimpy weather and the furnace don't seem to heat up no more like it used to and Mother made the remark that she hoped this winter wouldn't be as cold as the last, referring to the winter previous. So Edie said if she was us, and nothing to keep us home, she certainly wouldn't spend no more winters up here and why didn't we just shut off the water and close up the house and go down to Tampa, Florida? You know we was there four winters ago and staid five weeks, but it cost us over three hundred and fifty dollars for hotel bill alone. So Mother said we wasn't going no place to be robbed. So my son-in-law spoke up and said that Tampa wasn't the only place in the South, and besides we didn't have to stop at no high price hotel but could rent us a couple rooms and board out somewheres, and he had heard that St. Petersburg, Florida, was *the* spot and if we said the word he would write down there and make inquiries.

Well, to make a long story short, we decided to do it and Edie said it would be our Golden Honeymoon and for a present my son-in-law paid the difference between a section and a compartment so as we could have a compartment and have more privatecy. In a compartment you have an upper and lower berth just like the regular sleeper, but it is a shut in room by itself and got a wash bowl. The car we went in was all compartments and no regular berths at all. It was all compartments.

We went to Trenton the night before and staid at my daughter and son-in-law and we left Trenton the next afternoon at 3.23 P.M.

This was the twelfth day of January. Mother set facing the front of the train, as it makes her giddy to ride backwards. I set facing her, which does not affect me. We reached North Philadelphia at 4.03 P.M. and we reached West Philadelphia at 4.14, but did not go into Broad Street. We reached Baltimore at 6.30 and Washington, D.C., at 7.25. Our train laid over in Washington two hours till another train come along to pick us up and I got out and strolled up the platform and into the Union Station. When I come back, our car had been switched on to another track, but I remembered the name of it, the La Belle, as I had once visited my aunt out in Oconomowoc, Wisconsin, where there was a lake of that name, so I had no difficulty in getting located. But Mother had nearly fretted herself sick for fear I would be left.

"Well," I said, "I would of followed you on the next train."

"You could of," said Mother, and she pointed out that she had the money.

"Well," I said, "we are in Washington and I could of borrowed from the United States Treasury. I would of pretended I was an Englishman."

Mother caught the point and laughed heartily.

Our train pulled out of Washington at 9.40 P.M. and Mother and I turned in early, I taking the upper. During the night we passed through the green fields of old Virginia, though it was too dark to tell if they was green or what color. When we got up in the morning, we was at Fayetteville, North Carolina. We had breakfast in the dining car and after breakfast I got in conversation with the man in the next compartment to ours. He was from Lebanon, New Hampshire, and a man about eighty years of age. His wife was with him, and two unmarried daughters and I made the remark that I should think the four of them would be crowded in one compartment, but he said they had made the trip every winter for fifteen years and knowed how to keep out of each other's way. He said they was bound for Tarpon Springs.

We reached Charleston, South Carolina, at 12.50 P.M. and arrived at Savannah, Georgia, at 4.20. We reached Jacksonville, Florida, at 8.45 P.M. and had an hour and a quarter to lay over there, but Mother made a fuss about me getting off the train, so we had the darky make up our berths and retired before we left Jacksonville. I didn't sleep good as the train done a lot of hemming and hawing, and Mother never sleeps good on a train as she says she is always worrying that I will fall out. She says she would rather have the upper herself, as then she would not have to worry about me, but I tell her I can't take the risk of having it get out that I allowed my wife to sleep in an upper berth. It would make talk.

We was up in the morning in time to see our friends from New Hampshire get off at Tarpon Springs, which we reached at 6.53 A.M.

Several of our fellow passengers got off at Clearwater and some at Belleair, where the train backs right up to the door of the mammoth hotel. Belleair is the winter headquarters for the golf dudes and everybody that got off there had their bag of sticks, as many as ten and twelve in a bag. Women and all. When I was a young man we called it shinny and only needed one club to play with and about one game of it would of been a-plenty for some of these dudes, the way we played it.

The train pulled into St. Petersburg at 8.20 and when we got off the train you would think they was a riot, what with all the darkies barking for the different hotels.

I said to Mother, I said:

"It is a good thing we have got a place picked out to go to and don't have to choose a hotel, as it would be hard to choose amongst them if every one of them is the best."

She laughed.

We found a jitney and I give him the address of the room my son-in-law had got for us and soon we was there and introduced ourselves to the lady that owns the house, a young widow about forty-eight years of age. She showed us our room, which was light and airy with a comfortable bed and bureau and washstand. It was twelve dollars a week, but the location was good, only three blocks from Williams Park.

St. Pete is what folks calls the town, though they also call it the Sunshine City, as they claim they's no other place in the country where they's fewer days when Old Sol don't smile down on Mother Earth, and one of the newspapers gives away all their copies free every day when the sun don't shine. They claim to of only give them away some sixty-odd times in the last eleven years. Another nickname they have got for the town is "the Poor Man's Palm Beach," but I guess they's men that comes there that could borrow as much from the bank as some of the Willie boys over to the other Palm Beach.

During our stay we paid a visit to the Lewis Tent City, which is the headquarters for the Tin Can Tourists. But maybe you ain't heard about them. Well, they are an organization that takes their vacation trips by auto and carries everything with them. That is, they bring along their tents to sleep in and cook in and they don't patronize no hotels or cafeterias, but they have got to be bona fide auto campers or they can't belong to the organization.

They tell me they's over 200,000 members to it and they call themselves the Tin Canners on account of most of their food being put up in tin cans. One couple we seen in the Tent City was a couple from Brady, Texas, named Mr. and Mrs. Pence, which the old man is over eighty years of age and they had come in their auto all the way from home, a distance of 1,641 miles. They took five weeks for the trip, Mr. Pence driving the entire distance.

The Tin Canners hails from every State in the Union and in the summer time they visit places like New England and the Great Lakes region, but in the winter the most of them comes to Florida and scatters all over the State. While we was down there, they was a national convention of them at Gainesville, Florida, and they elected a Fredonia, New York, man as their president. His title is Royal Tin Can Opener of the World. They have got a song wrote up which everybody has got to learn it before they are a member:

"The tin can forever! Hurrah, boys! Hurrah!
Up with the tin can! Down with the foe!
We will rally round the campfire, we'll rally once again,
Shouting, 'We auto camp forever!' "

That is something like it. And the members has also got to have a tin can fastened on to the front of their machine.

I asked Mother how she would like to travel around that way and she said:

"Fine, but not with an old rattle brain like you driving."

"Well," I said, "I am eight years younger than this Mr. Pence who drove here from Texas."

"Yes," she said, "but he is old enough to not be skittish."

You can't get ahead of Mother.

Well, one of the first things we done in St. Petersburg was to go to the Chamber of Commerce and register our names and where we was from as they's great rivalry amongst the different States in regards to the number of their citizens visiting in town and of course our little State don't stand much of a show, but still every little bit helps, as the fella says. All and all, the man told us, they was eleven thousand names registered, Ohio leading with some fifteen hundred-odd and New York State next with twelve hundred. Then come Michigan, Pennsylvania and so on down, with one man each from Cuba and Nevada.

The first night we was there, they was a meeting of the New York-New Jersey Society at the Congregational Church and a man from Ogdensburg, New York State, made the talk. His subject was Rainbow Chasing. He is a Rotarian and a very convicting speaker, though I forget his name.

Our first business, of course, was to find a place to eat and after trying several places we run on to a cafeteria on Central Avenue that suited us up and down. We eat pretty near all our meals there and it averaged about two dollars per day for the two of us, but the food was well cooked and everything nice and clean. A man don't mind paying the price if things is clean and well cooked.

On the third day of February, which is Mother's birthday, we spread ourselves and eat supper at the Poinsettia Hotel and they charged us seventy-five cents for a sirloin steak that wasn't hardly big enough for one.

I said to Mother: "Well," I said, "I guess it's a good thing every day ain't your birthday or we would be in the poorhouse."

"No," says Mother, "because if every day was my birthday, I would be old enough by this time to of been in my grave long ago."

You can't get ahead of Mother.

In the hotel they had a card-room where they was several men and ladies playing five hundred and this new fangled whist bridge. We also seen a place where they was dancing, so I asked Mother would she like to trip the light fantastic toe and she said no, she was too old to squirm like you have got to do now days. We watched some of the young folks at it awhile till Mother got disgusted and said we would have to see a good movie to take the taste out of our mouth. Mother is a great movie heroyne and we go twice a week here at home.

But I want to tell you about the Park. The second day we was there we visited the Park, which is a good deal like the one in Tampa, only bigger, and they's more fun goes on here every day than you could shake a stick at. In the middle they's a big bandstand and chairs for the folks to set and listen to the concerts, which they give you music for all tastes, from Dixie up to classical pieces like Hearts and Flowers.

Then all around they's places marked off for different sports and games — chess and checkers and dominoes for folks that enjoys those kind of games, and roque and horse-shoes for the nimbler ones. I used to pitch a pretty fair shoe myself, but ain't done much of it in the last twenty years.

Well, anyway, we bought a membership ticket in the club which costs one dollar for the season, and they tell me that up to a couple years ago it was fifty cents, but they had to raise it to keep out the riffraff.

Well, Mother and I put in a great day watching the pitchers and she wanted I should get in the game, but I told her I was all out of practice and would make a fool of myself, though I seen several men pitching who I guess I could take their measure without no practice. However, they was some good pitchers, too, and one boy from Akron, Ohio, who could certainly throw a pretty shoe. They told me it looked like he would win them championship of the United States in the February tournament. We come away a few days before they held that and I never did hear if he win. I forget his name, but he was a clean cut young fella and he has got a brother in Cleveland that's a Rotarian.

Well, we just stood around and watched the different games for two or three days and finally I set down in a checker game with a man named Weaver from Danville, Illinois. He was a pretty fair checker player, but he wasn't no match for me, and I hope that don't sound like bragging. But I always could hold my own on a checker-board and the folks around here will tell you the same thing. I played with this Weaver pretty near all morning for two or three mornings and he beat me one game and the only other time it looked like he had a chance, the noon whistle blowed and we had to quit and go to dinner.

While I was playing checkers, Mother would set and listen to the band, as she loves music, classical or no matter what kind, but anyway she was setting there one day and between selections the woman next to her opened up a conversation. She was a woman about Mother's own age, seventy or seventy-one, and finally she asked Mother's name and Mother told her her name and where she was from and Mother asked her the same question, and who do you think the woman was?

Well, sir, it was the wife of Frank M. Hartsell, the man who was engaged to Mother till I stepped in and cut him out, fifty-two years ago!

Yes, sir!

You can imagine Mother's surprise! And Mrs. Hartsell was surprised, too, when Mother told her she had once been friends with her husband, though Mother didn't say how close friends they had been, or that Mother and I was the cause of Hartsell going out West. But that's what we was. Hartsell left his town a month after the engagement was broke off and ain't never been back since. He had went out to Michigan and become a veterinary, and that is where he had settled down, in Hillsdale, Michigan, and finally married his wife.

Well, Mother screwed up her courage to ask if Frank was still living and Mrs. Hartsell took her over to where they was pitching horse-shoes and there was old Frank, waiting his turn. And he knowed Mother as soon as he seen her, though it was over fifty years. He said he knowed her by her eyes.

"Why, it's Lucy Frost!" he says, and he throwed down his shoes and quit the game.

Then they come over and hunted me up and I will confess I wouldn't of knowed him. Him and I is the same age to the month, but he seems to show it more, some way. He is balder for one thing. And his beard is all white, where mine has still got a streak of brown in it. The very first thing I said to him, I said:

"Well, Frank, that beard of yours makes me feel like I was back north. It looks like a regular blizzard."

"Well," he said, "I guess yourn would be just as white if you had it dry cleaned."

But Mother wouldn't stand that.

"Is that so!" she said to Frank. "Well, Chancy ain't had no tobacco in his mouth for over ten years!"

And I ain't!

Well, I excused myself from the checker game and it was pretty close to noon, so we decided to all have dinner together and they was nothing for it only we must try their cafeteria on Third Avenue. It was a little more expensive than ours and not near as good, I thought. I and Mother had about the same dinner we had been having every day and our bill was $1.10. Frank's check was $1.20 for he and his wife. The same meal wouldn't of cost them more than a dollar at our place.

After dinner we made them come up to our house and we all set in the parlor, which the young woman had give us the use of to entertain company. We begun talking over old times and Mother said she was a-scared Mrs. Hartsell would find it tiresome listening to we three talk over old times, but as it turned out they wasn't much chance for nobody else to talk with Mrs. Hartsell in the company. I have heard lots of women that could go it, but Hartsell's wife takes the cake of all the women I ever seen. She told us the family history of everybody in the State of Michigan and bragged for a half hour about her son, who she said is in the drug business in Grand Rapids, and a Rotarian.

When I and Hartsell could get a word in edgeways we joked one another back and forth and I chafed him about being a horse doctor.

"Well, Frank," I said, " you look pretty prosperous, so I suppose they's been plenty of glanders around Hillsdale."

"Well," he said, "I've managed to make more than a fair living. But I've worked pretty hard."

"Yes," I said, "and I suppose you get called out all hours of the night to attend births and so on."

Mother made me shut up.

Well, I thought they wouldn't never go home and I and Mother was in misery trying to keep awake, as the both of us generally always takes a nap after dinner. Finally they went, after we had made an engagement to meet them in the Park the next morning, and Mrs. Hartsell also invited us to come to their place the next night and play five hundred. But she had forgot that they was a meeting of the Michigan Society that evening, so it was not till two evenings later that we had our first card game.

Hartsell and his wife lived in a house on Third Avenue North and had a private setting room besides their bedroom. Mrs. Hartsell couldn't quit talking about their private setting room like it was something wonderful. We played cards with them, with Mother and Hartsell partners against his wife and I. Mrs. Hartsell is a miserable card player and we certainly got the worst of it.

After the game she brought out a dish of oranges and we had to pretend it was just what we wanted, though oranges down there is like a young man's whiskers; you enjoy them at first, but they get to be a pesky nuisance.

We played cards again the next night at our place with the same partners and I and Mrs. Hartsell was beat again. Mother and Hartsell was full of compliments for each other on what a good team they made, but the both of them knowed well enough where the secret of their success laid. I guess all and all we must of played ten different evenings and they was only one night when Mrs. Hartsell and I come out ahead. And that one night wasn't no fault of hern.

When we had been down there about two weeks, we spent one evening as their guest in the Congregational Church, at a social give by the Michigan Society. A talk was made by a man named Bitting of Detroit, Michigan, on How I was Cured of Story Telling. He is a big man in the Rotarians and give a witty talk.

A woman named Mrs. Oxford rendered some selections which Mrs. Hartsell said was grand opera music, but whatever they was my daughter Edie could of give her cards and spades and not made such a hullaballoo about it neither.

Then they was a ventriloquist from Grand Rapids and a young woman about forty-five years of age that mimicked different kinds of birds. I whispered to Mother that they all sounded like a chicken, but she nudged me to shut up.

After the show we stopped in a drug store and I set up the refreshments and it was pretty close to ten o'clock before we finally turned in. Mother and I would of preferred tending the movies, but Mother said we mustn't offend Mrs. Hartsell, though I asked her had we came to Florida to enjoy ourselves or to just not offend an old chatter-box from Michigan.

I felt sorry for Hartsell one morning. The women folks both had an engagement down to the chiropodist's and I run across Hartsell in the Park and he foolishly offered to play me checkers.

It was him that suggested it, not me, and I guess he repented himself before we had played one game. But he was too stubborn to give up and set there while I beat him game after game and the worst part of it was that a crowd of folks had got in the habit of watching me play and there they all was, hooking on, and finally they seen what a fool Frank was making of himself, and they began to chafe him and pass remarks. Like one of them said:

"Who ever told you you was a checker player!"

And:

"You might maybe be good for tiddle-de-winks, but not checkers!

I almost felt like letting him beat me a couple games. But the crowd would of knowed it was a put up job.

Well, the women folks joined us in the Park and I wasn't going to mention our little game, but Hartsell told about it himself and admitted he wasn't no match for me.

"Well," said Mrs. Hartsell, "checkers ain't much of a game anyway, is it?" She said: "It's more of a children's game, ain't it? At least, I know my boy's children used to play it a good deal."

"Yes, ma'am," I said. "It's a children's game the way your husband plays it, too."

Mother wanted to smooth things over, so she said:

"Maybe they's other games where Frank can beat you."

"Yes," said Mrs. Hartsell, "and I bet he could beat you pitching horseshoes."

"Well," I said, "I would give him a chance to try, only I ain't pitched a shoe in over sixteen years."

"Well," said Hartsell, "I ain't played checkers in twenty years."

"You ain't never played it," I said.

"Anyway," says Frank, "Lucy and I is your master at five hundred."

Well, I could of told him why that was, but had decency enough to hold my tongue.

It had got so now that he wanted to play cards every night and when I or Mother wanted to go to a movie, any one of us would have to pretend we had a headache and then trust to goodness that they wouldn't see us sneak into the theater. I don't mind playing cards when my partner keeps their mind on the game, but you take a woman like Hartsell's wife and how can they play cards when they have got to stop every couple seconds and brag about their son in Grand Rapids?

Well, the New York-New Jersey Society announced that they was goin' to give a social evening too and I said to Mother, I said:

"Well, that is one evening when we will have an excuse not to play five hundred."

"Yes," she said, "but we will have to ask Frank and his wife to go to the social with us as they asked us to go to the Michigan social."

"Well," I said, "I had rather stay home than drag that chatterbox everywheres we go."

So Mother said:

"You are getting too cranky. Maybe she does talk a little too much but she is good hearted. And Frank is always good company."

So I said:

"I suppose if he is such good company you wished you had of married him."

Mother laughed and said I sounded like I was jealous. Jealous of a cow doctor!

Anyway we had to drag them along to the social and I will say that we give them a much better entertainment than they had given us.

Judge Lane of Paterson made a fine talk on business conditions and a Mrs. Newell of Westfield imitated birds, only you could really tell what they was the way she done it. Two young women from Red Bank sung a choral selection and we clapped them back and they gave us Home to Our Mountains and Mother and Mrs. Hartsell both had tears in their eyes. And Hartsell, too.

Well, some way or another the chairman got wind that I was there and asked me to make a talk and I wasn't even going to get up, but Mother made me, so I got up and said:

"Ladies and gentlemen," I said. "I didn't expect to be called on for a speech on an occasion like this or no other occasion as I do not set myself up as a speech maker, so will have to do the best I can, which I often say is the best anybody can do."

Then I told them the story about Pat and the motorcycle, using the brogue, and it seemed to tickle them and I told them one or two other stories, but altogether I wasn't on my feet more than twenty or twenty-five minutes and you ought to of heard the clapping and hollering when I set down. Even Mrs. Hartsell admitted that I am quite a speechifier and said if I ever went to Grand Rapids, Michigan, her son would make me talk to the Rotarians.

When it was over, Hartsell wanted we should go to their house and play cards, but his wife reminded him that it was after 9.30 P.M., rather a late hour to start a card game, but he had went crazy on the subject of cards, probably because he didn't have to play partners with his wife. Anyway, we got rid of them and went home to bed.

It was the next morning, when we met over to the Park, that Mrs. Hartsell made the remark that she wasn't getting no exercise so I suggested that why didn't she take part in the roque game.

She said she had not played a game of roque in twenty years, but if Mother would play she would play. Well, at first Mother wouldn't hear of it, but finally consented, more to please Mrs. Hartsell than anything else.

Well, they had a game with a Mrs. Ryan from Eagle, Nebraska, and a young Mrs. Morse from Rutland, Vermont, who Mother had met down to the chiropodist's. Well, Mother couldn't hit a flea and they all laughed at her and I couldn't help from laughing at her myself and finally she quit and said her back was too lame to stoop over. So they got another lady and kept on playing and soon Mrs. Hartsell was the one everybody was laughing at, as she had a long shot to hit the black ball, and as she made the effort her teeth fell out on to the court. I never seen a woman so flustered in my life. And I never heard so much laughing, only Mrs. Hartsell didn't join in and she was madder than a hornet and wouldn't play no more, so the game broke up.

Mrs. Hartsell went home without speaking to nobody, but Hartsell stayed around and finally he said to me, he said:

"Well, I played you checkers the other day and you beat me bad and now what do you say if you and me play a game of horseshoes?"

I told him I hadn't pitched a shoe in sixteen years, but Mother said:

"Go ahead and play. You used to be good at it and maybe it will come back to you."

Well, to make a long story short, I give in. I oughtn't to of never tried it, as I hadn't pitched a shoe in sixteen years, and I only done it to humor Hartsell.

Before we started, Mother patted me on the back and told me to do my best, so we started in and I seen right off that I was in for it, as I hadn't pitched a shoe in sixteen years and didn't have my distance. And besides, the plating had wore off the shoes so that they was points right where they stuck into my thumb and I hadn't throwed more than two or three times when my thumb was raw and it pretty near killed me to hang on to the shoe, let alone pitch it.

Well, Hartsell throws the awkwardest shoe I ever seen pitched and to see him pitch you wouldn't think he would ever come nowheres near, but he is also the luckiest pitcher I ever seen and he made some pitches where the shoe lit five and six feet short and then schoonered up and was a ringer. They's no use trying to beat that kind of luck.

They was a pretty fair size crowd watching us and four or five other ladies besides Mother, and it seems like, when Hartsell pitches, he has got to chew and it kept the ladies on the anxious seat as he don't seem to care which way he is facing when he leaves go.

You would think a man as old as him would of learnt more manners.

Well, to make a long story short, I was just beginning to get my distance when I had to give up on account of my thumb, which I showed it to Hartsell and he seen I couldn't go on, as it was raw and bleeding. Even if I could of stood it to go on myself, Mother wouldn't of allowed it after she seen my thumb. So anyway I quit and Hartsell said the score was nineteen to six, but I don't know what it was. Or don't care, neither.

Well, Mother and I went home and I said I hoped we was through with the Hartsells as I was sick and tired of them, but it seemed like she had promised we would go over to their house that evening for another game of their everlasting cards.

Well, my thumb was giving me considerable pain and I felt kind of out of sorts and I guess maybe I forgot myself, but anyway, when we was about through playing Hartsell made the remark that he wouldn't never lose a game of cards if he could always have Mother for a partner.

So I said:

"Well, you had a chance fifty years ago to always have her for a partner, but you wasn't man enough to keep her."

I was sorry the minute I had said it and Hartsell didn't know what to say and for once his wife couldn't say nothing. Mother tried to smooth things over by making the remark that I must of had something stronger than tea or I wouldn't talk so silly. But Mrs. Hartsell had froze up like an iceberg and hardly said good night to us and I bet her and Frank put in a pleasant hour after we was gone.

As we was leaving, Mother said to him: "Never mind Charley's nonsense, Frank. He is just mad because you beat him all hollow pitching horseshoes and playing cards."

She said that to make up for my slip, but at the same time she certainly riled me. I tried to keep ahold of myself, but as soon as we was out of the house she had to open up the subject and begun to scold me for the break I had made.

Well, I wasn't in no mood to be scolded. So I said:

"I guess he is such a wonderful pitcher and card player that you wished you had married him."

"Well," she said, "at least he ain't a baby to give up pitching because his thumb has got a few scratches."

"And how about you," I said, "making a fool of yourself on the roque court and then pretemiding your back is lame and you can't play no more!"

"Yes," she said, "but when you hurt your thumb I didn't laugh at you, and why did you laugh at me when I sprained my back?"

"Who could help from laughing!" I said.

"Well," she said, "Frank Hartsell didn't laugh."

"Well," I said, "why didn't you marry him?"

"Well," said Mother, "I almost wished I had!"

"And I wished so, too!" I said.

"I'll remember that!" said Mother, and that's the last word she said to me for two days.

We seen the Hartsells the next day in the Park and I was willing to apologize, but they just nodded to us. And a couple days later we heard they had left for Orlando, where they have got relatives.

I wished they had went there in the first place.

Mother and I made it up setting on a bench.

"Listen, Charley," she said. "This is our Golden Honeymoon and we don't want the whole thing spoilt with a silly old quarrel."

"Well," I said, "did you mean that about wishing you had married Hartsell?"

"Of course not," she said, "that is, if you didn't mean that you wished I had, too." So I said:

"I was just tired and all wrought up. I thank God you chose me instead of him as they's no other woman in the world who I could of lived with all these years."

"How about Mrs. Hartsell?" says Mother.

"Good gracious!" I said. "Imagine being married to a woman that plays five hundred like she does and drops her teeth on the roque court!"

"Well," said Mother, "it wouldn't be no worse than being married to a man that expectorates towards ladies and is such a fool in a checker game."

So I put my arm around her shoulder and she stroked my hand and I guess we got kind of spoony.

They was two days left of our stay in St. Petersburg and the next to the last day Mother introduced me to a Mrs. Kendall from Kingston, Rhode Island, who she had met at the chiropodist's.

Mrs. Kendall made us acquainted with her husband, who is in the grocery business. They have got two sons and five grandchildren and one great-grandchild. One of their sons lives in Providence and is way up in the Elks as well as a Rotarian.

We found them very congenial people and we played cards with them the last two nights we was there. They was both experts and I only wished we had met them sooner instead of running into the Hartsells. But the Kendalls will be there again next winter and we will see more of them, that is, if we decide to make the trip again.

We left the Sunshine City on the eleventh day of February, at 11 A.M. This give us a day trip through Florida and we seen all the country we had passed through at night on the way down.

We reached Jacksonville at 7 P.M. and pulled out of there at 8.10 P.M. We reached Fayetteville, North Carolina, at nine o'clock the following morning, and reached Washington, D. C., at 6.30 P.M., laying over there half an hour.

We reached Trenton at 11.01 P.M. and had wired ahead to my daughter and son-in-law and they met us at the train and we went to their house and they put us up for the night. John would of made us stay up all night, telling about our trip, but Edie said we must be tired and made us go to bed. That's my daughter.

The next day we took our train for home and arrived safe and sound, having been gone just one month and a day.

Here comes Mother, so I guess I better shut up.

WINTER DREAMS

F. Scott Fitzgerald (1896-1940)

Some of the caddies were poor as sin and lived in one-room houses with a neurasthenic cow in the front yard, but Dexter Green's father owned the second best grocery store in Dillard — the best one was "The Hub," patronized by the wealthy people from Lake Erminie — and Dexter caddied only for pocket-money.

In the fall when the days became crisp and gray and the long Minnesota winter shut down like the white lid of a box, Dexter's skis moved over the snow that hid the fairways of the golf course. At these times the country gave him a feeling of profound melancholy — it offended him that the links should lie in enforced fallowness, haunted by ragged sparrows for the long season. It was dreary, too, that on the tees where the gay colors fluttered in summer there were now only the desolate sand boxes knee-deep in crusted ice. When he crossed the hills the wind blew cold as misery, and if the sun was out he tramped with his eyes squinted up against the hard dimensionless glare.

In April the winter ceased abruptly. The snow ran down into Lake Erminie scarcely tarrying for the early golfers to brave the season with red and black balls. Without elation, without an interval of moist glory the cold was gone.

Dexter knew that there was something dismal about this northern spring, just as he knew there was something gorgeous about the fall. Fall made him clench his hands and tremble and repeat idiotic sentences to himself and make brisk abrupt gestures of command to imaginary audiences and armies. October filled him with hope which November raised to a sort of ecstatic triumph, and in this mood the fleeting brilliant impressions of the summer at Lake Erminie were ready grist to his mill. He became a golf champion and defeated Mr. T. A. Hedrick in a marvelous match played over a hundred times in the fairways of his imagination, a match each detail of which he changed about untiringly — sometimes winning with almost laughable ease, sometimes coming up magnificently from behind. Again, stepping from a Pierce-Arrow automobile, like Mr. Mortimer Jones, he strolled frigidly into the lounge of the Erminie Golf Club — or perhaps, surrounded by an admiring crowd, he gave an exhibition of fancy diving from the spring board of the Erminie Club raft. . . . Among those most impressed was Mr. Mortimer Jones.

And one day it came to pass that Mr. Jones, himself and not his ghost, came up to Dexter, almost with tears in his eyes and said that Dexter was the —— best caddy in the club and wouldn't he decide not to quit if Mr. Jones made it worth his while, because every other —— caddy in the club lost one ball a hole for him — regularly ——

"No, sir," said Dexter, decisively, "I don't want to caddy any more." Then, after a pause, "I'm too old."

"You're — why, you're not more than fourteen. Why did you decide just this morning that you wanted to quit? You promised that next week you'd go over to the state tournament with me."

"I decided I was too old."

Dexter handed in his "A Class" badge, collected what money was due him from the caddy-master and caught the train for Dillard.

"The best —— caddy I ever saw," shouted Mr. Mortimer Jones over a drink that afternoon. "Never lost a ball! Willing! Intelligent! Quiet! Honest! Grateful! ——"

The little girl who had done this was eleven — beautifully ugly as little girls are apt to be who are destined after a few years to be inexpressibly lovely and bring no end of misery to a great number of men. The spark, however, was perceptible. There was a general ungodliness in the way her lips twisted down at the corners when she smiled and in the — Heaven help us! — in the almost passionate quality of her eyes. Vitality is born early in such women. It was utterly in evidence now, shining through her thin frame in a sort of glow.

She had come eagerly out on to the course at nine o'clock with a white linen nurse and five small new golf clubs in a white canvas bag which the nurse was carrying. When Dexter first saw her she was standing by the caddy house, rather ill-at-ease and trying to conceal the fact by engaging her nurse in an obviously unnatural conversation illumined by startling and irrelevant smiles from herself.

"Well, it's certainly a nice day, Hilda," Dexter heard her say; then she drew down the corners of her mouth, smiled and glanced furtively around, her eyes in transit falling for an instant on Dexter.

Then to the nurse:

"Well, I guess there aren't very many people out here this morning, are there?"

The smile again radiant, blatantly artificial — convincing.

"I don't know what we're supposed to do now," said the nurse, looking nowhere in particular.

"Oh, that's all right" — the smile — "I'll fix it up."

Dexter stood perfectly still, his mouth faintly ajar. He knew that if he moved forward a step his stare would be in her line of vision — if he moved backward he would lose his full view of her face — For a moment he had not realized how young she was. Now he remembered having seen her several times the year before — in bloomers.

Suddenly, involuntarily, he laughed, a short abrupt laugh — then, startled by himself, he turned and began to walk quickly away.

"Boy!"

Dexter stopped.

"Boy —— "

Beyond question he was addressed. Not only that, but he was treated to that absurd smile, that preposterous smile — the memory of which at least half a dozen men were to carry to the grave.

"Boy, do you know where the golf teacher is?"

"He's giving a lesson."

"Well, do you know where the caddy-master is?"

"He's not here yet this morning."

"Oh." For a moment this baffled her. She stood alternately on her right and left foot.

"We'd like to get a caddy," said the nurse. "Mrs. Mortimer Jones sent us out to play golf and we don't know how without we get a caddy."

Here she was stopped by an ominous glance from Miss Jones, followed immediately by the smile.

"There aren't any caddies here except me," said Dexter to the nurse, "and I got to stay here in charge until the caddy-master gets here."

"Oh."

Miss Jones and her retinue now withdrew and at a proper distance from Dexter became involved in a heated conversation. The conversation was concluded by Miss Jones taking one of the clubs and hitting it on the ground with violence. For further emphasis she raised it again and was about to bring it down smartly upon the nurse's bosom, when the nurse seized the club and twisted it from her hands.

"You darn *fool!*" cried Miss Jones wildly.

Another argument ensued. Realizing that the elements of the comedy were implied in the scene, Dexter several times began to smile but each time slew the smile before it reached maturity. He could not resist the monstrous conviction that the little girl was justified in beating the nurse.

The situation was resolved by the fortuitous appearance of the caddy-master who was appealed to immediately by the nurse.

"Miss Jones is to have a little caddy and this one says he can't go."

"Mr. McKenna said I was to wait here till you came," said Dexter quickly.

"Well, he's here now." Miss Jones smiled cheerfully at the caddy-master. Then she dropped her bag and set off at a haughty mince toward the first tee.

"Well?" The caddy-master turned to Dexter. "What you standing there like a dummy for? Go pick up the young lady's clubs."

"I don't think I'll go out today," said Dexter.

"You don't——"

"I think I'll quit."

The enormity of his decision frightened him. He was a favorite caddy and the thirty dollars a month he earned through the summer was not to be made elsewhere in Dillard. But he had received a strong emotional shock and his perturbation required a violent and immediate outlet.

It is not so simple as that, either. As so frequently would be the case in the future, Dexter was unconsciously dictated to by his winter dreams.

Now, of course, the quality and the seasonability of these winter dreams varied, but the stuff of them remained. They persuaded Dexter several years later to pass up a business course at the State University — his father, prospering now, would have paid his way — for the precarious advantage of attending an older and more famous university in the East, where he was bothered by his scanty funds. But do not get the impression, because his winter dreams happened to be concerned at first with musings on the rich, that there was anything shoddy in the boy. He wanted not association with glittering things and glittering people — he wanted the glittering things themselves. Often he reached out for the best without knowing why he wanted it — and sometimes he ran up against the mysterious denials and prohibitions in which life indulges. It is with one of those denials and not with his career as a whole that this story deals.

He made money. It was rather amazing. After college he went to the city from which Lake Erminie draws its wealthy patrons. When he was only twenty-three and had been there not quite two years, there were already people who liked to say, "Now there's a boy — " All about him rich men's sons were peddling bonds precariously, or investing patrimonies precariously, or plodding through the two dozen volumes of canned rubbish in the "George Washington Commercial Course," but Dexter borrowed a thousand dollars on his college degree and his steady eyes, and bought a partnership in a laundry.

It was a small laundry when he went into it. Dexter made a specialty of learning how the English washed fine woolen golf stockings without shrinking them. Inside of a year he was catering to the trade who wore knickerbockers. Men were insisting that their shetland hose and sweaters go to his laundry just as they had insisted on a caddy who could find golf balls. A little later he was doing their wives' lingerie as well — and running five branches in different parts of the city. Before he was twenty-seven he owned the largest string of laundries in his section of the country. It was then that he sold out and went to New York. But the part of his story that concerns us here goes back to when he was making his first big success.

When he was twenty-three Mr. W. L. Hart, one of the gray-haired men who like to say "Now there's a boy" — gave him a guest card to the Lake Erminie Club for over a week-end. So he signed his name one day on the register, and that afternoon played golf in a foursome with Mr. Hart and Mr. Sandwood and Mr. T. A. Hedrick. He did not consider it necessary to remark that he had once carried

Mr. Hart's bag over this same links and that he knew every trap and gully with his eyes shut — but he found himself glancing at the four caddies who trailed them, trying to catch a gleam or gesture that would remind him of himself, that would lessen the gap which lay between his past and his future.

It was a curious day, slashed abruptly with fleeting, familiar impressions. One minute he had the sense of being a trespasser — in the next he was impressed by the tremendous superiority he felt toward Mr. T. A. Hedrick, who was a bore and not even a good golfer any more.

Then, because of a ball Mr. Hart lost near the fifteenth green an enormous thing happened. While they were searching the stiff grasses of the rough there was a clear call of "Fore!" from behind a hill in their rear. And as they all turned abruptly from their search a bright new ball sliced abruptly over the hill and caught Mr. T. A. Hedrick rather neatly in the stomach.

Mr. T. A. Hedrick grunted and cursed.

"By Gad!" cried Mr. Hedrick. "They ought to put some of these crazy women off the course. It's getting to be outrageous."

A head and a voice came up together over the hill:

"Do you mind if we go through?"

"You hit me in the stomach!" thundered Mr. Hedrick.

"Did I?" The girl approached the group of men. "I'm sorry. I yelled 'Fore!' "

Her glance fell casually on each of the men. She nodded to Sandwood and then scanned the fairway for her ball.

"Did I bounce off into the rough?"

It was impossible to determine whether this question was ingenuous or malicious. In a moment, however, she left no doubt, for as her partner came up over the hill she called cheerfully.

"Here I am! I'd have gone on the green except that I hit something."

As she took her stance for a short mashie shot, Dexter looked at her closely. She wore a blue gingham dress, rimmed at throat and shoulders with a white edging that accentuated her tan. The quality of exaggeration, of thinness that had made her passionate eyes and down-turning mouth absurd at eleven was gone now. She was arrestingly beautiful. The color in her cheeks was centered like the color in a picture — it was not a "high" color, but a sort of fluctuating and feverish warmth, so shaded that it seemed at any moment it would recede and disappear. This color and the mobility of her mouth gave a continual impression of flux, of intense life, of passionate vitality — balanced only partially by the sad luxury of her eyes.

She swung her mashie impatiently and without interest, pitching the ball into a sandpit on the other side of the green. With a quick insincere smile and a careless "Thank you!" she went on after it.

"That Judy Jones!" remarked Mr. Hedrick on the next tee, as they waited — some moments — for her to play on ahead. "All she needs is to be turned up and spanked for six months and then to be married off to an old-fashioned cavalry captain."

"Gosh, she's good-looking!" said Mr. Sandwood, who was just over thirty.

"Good-looking!" cried Mr. Hedrick contemptuously. "She always looks as if she wanted to be kissed! Turning those big cow-eyes on every young calf in town!"

It is doubtful if Mr. Hedrick intended a reference to the maternal instinct.

"She'd play pretty good golf if she'd try," said Mr. Sandwood.

"She has no form," said Mr. Hedrick solemnly.

"She has a nice figure," said Mr. Sandwood.

"Better thank the Lord she doesn't drive a swifter ball," said Mr. Hart, winking at Dexter. "Come on. Let's go."

Later in the afternoon the sun went down with a riotous swirl of gold and varying blues and scarlets, and left the dry rustling night of western summer. Dexter watched from the verandah of the Erminie Club, watched the even overlap of the waters in the little wind, silver molasses under the harvest moon. Then the moon held a finger to her lips and the lake became a clear pool, pale and quiet. Dexter put on his bathing suit and swam out to the farthest raft, where he stretched dripping on the wet canvas of the spring board.

There was a fish jumping and a star shining and the lights around the lake were gleaming. Over on a dark peninsula a piano was playing the songs of last summer and of summers before that — songs from "The Pink Lady" and "The Chocolate Soldier" and "Mlle. Modiste" — and because the sound of a piano over a stretch of water had always seemed beautiful to Dexter he lay perfectly quiet and listened.

The tune the piano was playing at that moment had been gay and new five years before when Dexter was a sophomore at college. They had played it at a prom once and because he could not afford the luxury of proms in those days he had stood outside the gymnasium and listened. The sound of the tune and the splash of the fish jumping precipitated in him a sort of ecstasy and it was with that ecstasy he viewed what happened to him now. The ecstasy was a gorgeous appreciation. It was his sense that, for once, he was magnificently atune to life and that everything about him was radiating a brightness and a glamor he might never know again.

A low pale oblong detached itself suddenly from the darkness of the peninsula, spitting forth the reverberate sound of a racing motorboat. Two white streamers of cleft water rolled themselves out behind it and almost immediately the boat was beside him, drowning out the hot tinkle of the piano in the drone of its spray. Dexter, raising himself on his arms, was aware of a figure standing at the wheel, of two dark eyes regarding him over the lengthening space of water — then the boat had gone by and was sweeping in an immense and purposeless circle of spray round and round in the middle of the lake. With equal eccentricity one of the circles flattened out and headed back toward the raft.

"Who's that?" she called, shutting off her motor. She was so near now that Dexter could see her bathing suit, which consisted apparently of pink rompers. "Oh — you're one of the men I hit in the stomach."

The nose of the boat bumped the raft. After an inexpert struggle, Dexter managed to twist the line around a two-by-four. Then the raft tilted rakishly as she sprang on.

"Well, kiddo," she said huskily, "do you" — she broke off. She had sat herself upon the spring board, found it damp and jumped up quickly, — "do you want to go surf-board riding?"

He indicated that he would be delighted.

"The name is Judy Jones. Ghastly reputation but enormously popular." She favored him with an absurd smirk — rather, what tried to be a smirk, for, twist her mouth as she might, it was not grotesque, it was merely beautiful. "See that house over on the peninsula?"

"No."

"Well, there's a house there that I live in only you can't see it because it's too dark. And in that house there is a fella waiting for me. When he drove up by the door I drove out by the dock because he has watery eyes and asks me if I have an ideal."

There was a fish jumping and a star shining and the lights around the lake were gleaming. Dexter sat beside Judy Jones and she explained how her boat was driven. Then she was in the water, swimming to the floating surf-board with an exquisite crawl. Watching her was as without effort to the eye as watching a branch waving or a sea-gull flying. Her arms, burned to butternut, moved sinuously among the dull platinum ripples, elbow appearing first, casting the forearm back with a cadence of falling water, then reaching out and down stabbing a path ahead.

They moved out into the lake and, turning, Dexter saw that she was kneeling on the low rear of the now up-tilted surf-board.

"Go faster," she called, "fast as it'll go."

Obediently he jammed the lever forward and the white spray mounted at the bow. When he looked around again the girl was standing up on the rushing board, her arms spread ecstatically, her eyes lifted toward the moon.

"It's awful cold, kiddo," she shouted. "What's your name anyways."

"The name is Dexter Green. Would it amuse you to know how good you look back there?"

"Yes," she shouted, "it would amuse me. Except that I'm too cold. Come to dinner to-morrow night."

He kept thinking how glad he was that he had never caddied for this girl. The damp gingham clinging made her like a statue and turned her intense mobility to immobility at last.

" — At seven o'clock," she shouted. "Judy Jones, Girl, who hit man in stomach. Better write it down," — and then, "Faster — oh, faster!"

Had he been as calm inwardly as he was in appearance, Dexter would have had time to examine his surroundings in detail. He received, however, an enduring impression that the house was the most elaborate he had ever seen. He had known for a long time that it was the finest on Lake Erminie, with a Pompeiian swimming pool and twelve acres of lawn and garden. But what gave it an air of breathless intensity was the sense that it was inhabited by Judy Jones — that it was as casual a thing to her as the little house in the village had once been to Dexter.

There was a feeling of mystery in it, of bedrooms up-stairs more beautiful and strange than other bedrooms, of gay and radiant activities taking place through these deep corridors and of romances that were not musty and laid already in lavender, but were fresh and breathing and set forth in rich motor cars and in great dances whose flowers were scarcely withered. They were more real because he could feel them all about him, pervading the air with the shades and echoes of still vibrant emotion.

And so while he waited for her to appear he peopled the soft deep summer room and the sun porch that opened from it with the men who had already loved Judy Jones. He knew the sort of men they were — the men who when he first went to college had entered from the great prep-schools with graceful clothes and the deep tan of healthy summer, who did nothing or anything with the same debonair ease.

Dexter had seen that, in one sense, he was better than these men. He was newer and stronger. Yet in acknowledging to himself that he wished his children to be like them he was admitting that he was but the rough, strong stuff from which this graceful aristocracy eternally sprang.

When, a year before, the time had come when he could wear good clothes, he had known who were the best tailors in America, and the best tailor in America had made him the suit he wore this evening. He had acquired that particular reserve peculiar to his university, that set it off from other universities. He recognized the value to him of such a mannerism and he had adopted it; he knew that to be careless in dress and manner required more confidence than to be careful. But carelessness was for his children. His mother's name had been Krimslich. She was a Bohemian of the peasant class and she had talked broken English to the end of her days. Her son must keep to the set patterns.

He waited for Judy Jones in her house, and he saw these other young men around him. It excited him that many men had loved her. It increased her value in his eyes.

At a little after seven Judy Jones came downstairs. She wore a blue silk afternoon dress. He was disappointed at first that she had not put on something more elaborate, and this feeling was accentuated when, after a brief greeting, she went to the door of a butler's pantry and pushing it open called: "You can have dinner, Martha." He had rather expected that a butler would announce dinner, that there would be a cocktail perhaps. It even offended him that she should know the maid's name.

Then he put these thoughts behind him as they sat down together on a chintz-covered lounge.

"Father and mother won't be here," she said.

"Ought I to be sorry?"

"They're really quite nice," she confessed, as if it had just occurred to her. "I think my father's the best looking man of his age I've ever seen. And mother looks about thirty."

He remembered the last time he had seen her father, and found he was glad the parents were not to be here to-night. They would wonder who he was. He had been born in Keeble, a Minnesota village fifty miles farther north, and he always gave Keeble as his home instead of Dillard. Country towns were well enough to come from if they weren't inconveniently in sight and used as foot-stools by fashionable lakes.

Before dinner he found the conversation unsatisfactory. The beautiful Judy seemed faintly irritable — as much so as it was possible to be with a comparative stranger. They discussed Lake Erminie and its golf course, the surf-board riding of the night before and the cold she had caught, which made her voice more husky and charming than ever. They talked of his university which she had visited frequently during the past two years, and of the nearby city which supplied Lake Erminie with its patrons and whither Dexter would return next day to his prospering laundries.

During dinner she slipped into a moody depression which gave Dexter a feeling of guilt. Whatever petulance she uttered in her throaty voice worried him. Whatever she smiled at — at him, at a silver fork, at nothing —, it disturbed him that her smile could have no root in mirth, or even in amusement. When the red corners of her lips curved down, it was less a smile than an invitation to a kiss.

Then, after dinner, she led him out on the dark sun porch and deliberately changed the atmosphere.

"Do I seem gloomy?" she demanded.

"No, but I'm afraid I'm boring you," he answered quickly.

"You're not. I like you. But I've just had rather an unpleasant afternoon. There was a — man I cared about. He told me out of a clear sky that he was poor as a church-mouse. He'd never even hinted it before. Does this sound horribly mundane?"

"Perhaps he was afraid to tell you."

"I suppose he was," she answered thoughtfully. "He didn't start right. You see, if I'd thought of him as poor — well, I've been mad about loads of poor men, and fully intended to marry them all. But in this case, I hadn't thought of him that way and my interest in him wasn't strong enough to survive the shock."

"I know. As if a girl calmly informed her fiancé that she was a widow. He might not object to widows, but —— "

"Let's start right," she suggested suddenly. "Who are you, anyhow?"

For a moment Dexter hesitated. There were two versions of his life that he could tell. There was Dillard and his caddying and his struggle through college, or ——

"I'm nobody," he announced. "My career is largely a matter of futures."

"Are you poor?"

"No," he said frankly. "I'm probably making more money than any man my age in the northwest. I know that's an obnoxious remark, but you advised me to start right."

There was a pause. She smiled, and with a touch of amusement. "You sound like a man in a play."

"It's your fault. You tempted me into being assertive."

Suddenly she turned her dark eyes directly upon him and the corners of her mouth drooped until her face seemed to open like a flower. He dared scarcely to breathe; he had the sense that she was exerting some force upon him, making him overwhelmingly conscious of the youth and mystery that wealth imprisons and preserves, the freshness of many clothes, of cool rooms and gleaming things, safe and proud above the hot struggles of the poor.

The porch was bright with the bought luxury of starshine. The wicker of the settee squeaked fashionably when he put his arm around her, commanded by her eyes. He kissed her curious and lovely mouth and committed himself to the following of a grail.

It began like that — and continued, with varying shades of intensity, on such a note right up to the dénouement. Dexter surrendered a part of himself to the most direct and unprincipled personality with which he had ever come in contact. Whatever the beautiful Judy Jones desired, she went after with the full pressure of her charm. There was no divergence of method, no jockeying for position or premeditation of effects — there was very little mental quality in any of her affairs. She simply made men conscious to the highest degree of her physical loveliness.

Dexter had no desire to change her. Her deficiencies were knit up with a passionate energy that transcended and justified them.

When, as Judy's head lay against his shoulder that first night, she whispered:

"I don't know what's the matter with me. Last night I thought I was in love with a man and tonight I think I'm in love with you —— "

—— it seemed to him a beautiful and romantic thing to say. It was the exquisite excitability that for the moment he controlled and owned. But a week later he was compelled to view this same quality in a different light. She took him in her roadster to a picnic supper and after supper she disappeared, likewise in her roadster, with another man. Dexter became enormously upset and was scarcely able to be decently civil to the other people present. When she assured him that she had not kissed the other man he knew she was lying — yet he was glad that she had taken the trouble to lie to him.

He was, as he found before the summer ended, one of a dozen, a varying dozen, who circulated about her. Each of them had at one time been favored above all others — about half of them still basked in the solace of occasional sentimental revivals. Whenever one showed signs of dropping out through long neglect she granted him a brief honeyed hour which encouraged him to tag along for a year or so longer. Judy made these forays upon the helpless and defeated without malice, indeed half unconscious that there was anything mischievous in what she did.

When a new man came to town everyone dropped out — dates were automatically cancelled.

The helpless part of trying to do anything about it was that she did it all herself. She was not a girl who could be "won" in the kinetic sense — she was proof against cleverness, she was proof against charm. If any of these assailed her too strongly she would immediately resolve the affair to a physical basis and under the magic of her physical splendor the strong as well as the brilliant played her game and not their own. She was entertained only by the gratification of her desires and by the direct exercise of her own charm. Perhaps from so much youthful love, so many youthful lovers, she had come, in self defense, to nourish herself wholly from within.

Succeeding Dexter's first exhilaration came restlessness and dissatisfaction. The helpless ecstasy of losing himself in her charm was a powerful opiate rather than a tonic. It was fortunate for his work during the winter that those moments of ecstasy came infrequently. Early in their acquaintance it had seemed for a while that there was a deep and spontaneous mutual attraction — that first August for example — three days of long evenings on her dusky verandah, of strange wan kisses through the late afternoon, in shadowy alcoves or behind the protecting trellises of the garden arbors, of mornings when she was fresh as a dream and almost shy at meeting him in the clarity of the rising day. There was all the ecstasy of an engagement about it, sharpened by his realization that there was no engagement. It was during those three days that, for the first time, he had asked her to marry him. She said "maybe some day," she said "kiss me," she said "I'd like to marry you," she said "I love you," — she said — nothing.

The three days were interrupted by the arrival of a New York man who visited the Jones' for half September. To Dexter's agony, rumor engaged them. The man was the son of the president of a great trust company. But at the end of a month it was reported that Judy was yawning. At a dance one night she sat all evening in a motor boat with an old beau, while the New Yorker searched the club for her frantically. She told the old beau that she was bored with her visitor and two days later he left. She was seen with him at the station and it was reported that he looked very mournful indeed.

On this note the summer ended. Dexter was twenty-four and he found himself increasingly in a position to do as he wished. He joined two clubs in the city and lived at one of them. Though he was by no means an integral part of the stag-lines at these clubs he managed to be on hand at dances where Judy Jones was likely to appear. He could have gone out socially as much as he liked — he was an eligible young man, now, and popular with downtown fathers. His confessed devotion to Judy Jones had rather solidified his position. But he had no social aspirations and rather despised the dancing men who were always on tap for the Thursday or Saturday parties and who filled in at dinners with the younger married set. Already he was playing with the idea of going east to New York. He wanted to take Judy Jones with him. No disillusion as to the world in which she had grown up could cure his illusion as to her desirability.

Remember that — for only in the light of it can what he did for her be understood.

Eighteen months after he first met Judy Jones he became engaged to another girl. Her name was Irene Scheerer and her father was one of the men who had always believed in Dexter. Irene was light haired and sweet and honorable and a little stout and she had two beaus whom she pleasantly relinquished when Dexter formally asked her to marry him.

Summer, fall, winter, spring, another summer, another fall — so much he had given of his active life to the curved lips of Judy Jones. She had treated him with interest, with encouragement, with malice, with indifference, with contempt. She had inflicted on him the innumerable little slights and indignities possible in such a case — as if in revenge for having ever cared for him at all. She had beckoned him and yawned at him and beckoned him again and he had responded often with bitterness and narrowed eyes. She had brought him ecstatic happiness and intolerable agony of spirit. She had caused him untold inconvenience and not a little trouble. She had insulted him and she had ridden over him and she had played his interest in her against his interest in his work — for fun. She had done everything to him except to criticise him — this she had not done — it seemed to him only because it might have sullied the utter indifference she manifested and sincerely felt toward him.

When autumn had come and gone again it occurred to him that he could not have Judy Jones. He had to beat this into his mind but he convinced himself at last. He lay awake at night for a while and argued it over. He told himself the trouble and the pain she had caused him, he enumerated her glaring deficiencies as a wife. Then he said to himself that he loved her and after a while he fell asleep. For a week, lest he imagine her husky voice over the telephone or her eyes opposite him at lunch, he worked hard and late, and at night he went to his office and plotted out his years.

At the end of a week he went to a dance and cut in on her once. For almost the first time since they had met he did not ask her to sit out with him or tell her that she was lovely. It hurt him that she did not miss these things — that was all. He was not jealous when he saw that there was a new man tonight. He had been hardened against jealousy long before.

He stayed late at the dance. He sat for an hour with Irene Scheerer and talked about books and about music. He knew very little about either. But he was beginning to be master of his own time now and he had a rather priggish notion that he — the young and already fabulously successful Dexter Green — should know more about such things.

That was in October when he was twenty-five. In January Dexter and Irene became engaged. It was to be announced in June and they were to be married three months later.

The Minnesota winter prolonged itself interminably and it was almost May when the winds came soft and the snow ran down into Lake Erminie at last. For the first time in over a year Dexter was enjoying a certain tranquility of spirit. Judy Jones had been in Florida and afterwards in Hot Springs and somewhere she had been engaged and somewhere she had broken it off. At first, when Dexter had definitely given her up, it had made him sad that people still linked them together and asked for news of her, but when he began to be placed at dinner next to Irene

Scheerer people didn't ask him about her any more — they told him about her. He ceased to be an authority on her.

May at last. Dexter walked the streets at night when the darkness was damp as rain, wondering that so soon, with so little done, so much of ecstasy had gone from him. May, one year back had been marked by Judy's poignant, unforgivable, yet forgiven turbulence — it had been one of those rare times when he fancied she had grown to care for him. That old penny's worth of happiness he had spent for this bushel of content. He knew that Irene would be no more than a curtain spread behind him, a hand moving among gleaming tea cups, a voice calling to children . . . fire and loveliness were gone, magic of night and the hushed wonder of the hours and seasons . . . slender lips, down-turning, dropping to his lips like poppy petals, bearing him up into a heaven of eyes . . . a haunting gesture, light of a warm lamp on her hair. The thing was deep in him. He was too strong, too alive for it to die lightly.

In the middle of May when the weather balanced for a few days on the thin bridge that led to deep summer he turned in one night at Irene's house. Their engagement was to be announced in a week now — no one would be surprised at it. And tonight they would sit together on the lounge at the College Club and look on for an hour at the dancers. It gave him a sense of solidity to go with her —— She was so sturdily popular, so intensely a "good egg."

He mounted the steps of the brown stone house and stepped inside.

"Irene," he called.

Mrs. Scheerer came out of the living-room to meet him.

"Dexter," she said, "Irene's gone up-stairs with a splitting headache. She wanted to go with you but I made her go to bed."

"Nothing serious I —— "

"Oh, no. She's going to play golf with you in the morning. You can spare her for just one night, can't you, Dexter?"

Her smile was kind. She and Dexter liked each other. In the living-room he talked for a moment before he said goodnight.

Returning to the College Club, where he had rooms, he stood in the doorway for a moment and watched the dancers. He leaned against the door post, nodded at a man or two — yawned.

"Hello, kiddo."

The familiar voice at his elbow startled him. Judy Jones had left a man and crossed the room to him — Judy Jones, a slender enamelled doll in cloth of gold, gold in a band at her head, gold in two slipper points at her dress's hem. The fragile glow of her face seemed to blossom as she smiled at him. A breeze of warmth and light blew through the room. His hands in the pockets of his dinner jacket tightened spasmodically. He was filled with a sudden excitement.

"When did you get back?" he asked casually.

"Come here and I'll tell you about it."

She turned and he followed her. She had been away — he could have wept at the wonder of her return. She had passed through enchanted streets, doing young things that were like plaintive music. All mysterious happenings, all fresh and quickening hopes, had gone away with her, come back with her now.

She turned in the doorway.

"Have you a car here? If you haven't I have."

"I have a coupé."

In, then, with a rustle of golden cloth. He slammed the door. Into so many cars she had stepped — like this — like that — her back against the leather, so — her elbow resting on the door — waiting. She would have been soiled long since had there been anything to soil her, — except herself — but these things were all her own outpouring.

With an effort he forced himself to start the car and avoiding her surprised glance backed into the street. This was nothing, he must remember. She had done this before and he had put her behind him, as he would have slashed a bad account from his books.

He drove slowly downtown and affecting a disinterested abstraction traversed the deserted streets of the business section, peopled here and there, where a movie was giving out its crowd or where consumptive or pugilistic youth lounged in front of pool halls. The clink of glasses and the slap of hands on the bars issued from saloons, cloisters of glazed glass and dirty yellow light.

She was watching him closely and the silence was embarrassing yet in this crisis he could find no casual word with which to profane the hour. At a convenient turning he began to zig-zag back toward the College Club.

"Have you missed me?" she asked suddenly.

"Everybody missed you."

He wondered if she knew of Irene Scheerer. She had been back only a day — her absence had been almost contemporaneous with his engagement.

"What a remark!" Judy laughed sadly — without sadness. She looked at him searchingly. He became absorbed for a moment in the dashboard.

"You're handsomer than you used to be," she said thoughtfully. "Dexter, you have the most rememberable eyes."

He could have laughed at this, but he did not laugh. It was the sort of thing that was said to sophomores. Yet it stabbed at him.

"I'm awfully tired of everything, kiddo." She called everyone kiddo, endowing the obsolete slang with careless, individual camaraderie. "I wish you'd marry me."

The directness of this confused him. He should have told her now that he was going to marry another girl but he could not tell her. He could as easily have sworn that he had never loved her.

"I think we'd get along," she continued, on the same note, "unless probably you've forgotten me and fallen in love with another girl."

Her confidence was obviously enormous. She had said, in effect, that she found such a thing impossible to believe, that if it were true he had merely committed a childish indiscretion — and probably to show off. She would forgive him, because it was not a matter of any moment but rather something to be brushed aside lightly.

"Of course you could never love anybody but me," she continued. "I like the way you love me. Oh, Dexter, have you forgotten last year?"

"No, I haven't forgotten."

"Neither have I!"

Was she sincerely moved — or was she carried along by the wave of her own acting?

"I wish we could be like that again," she said, and he forced himself to answer:

"I don't think we can."

"I suppose not. . . . I hear you're giving Irene Scheerer a violent rush."

There was not the faintest emphasis on the name, yet Dexter was suddenly ashamed.

"Oh, take me home," cried Judy suddenly, "I don't want to go back to that idiotic dance — with those children."

Then, as he turned up the street that led to the residence district, Judy began to cry quietly to herself. He had never seen her cry before.

The dark street lightened, the dwellings of the rich loomed up around them, he stopped his coupé in front of the great white bulk of the Mortimer Jones' house, somnolent, gorgeous, drenched with the splendor of the damp moonlight. Its solidity startled him. The strong walls, the fine steel of the girders, the breadth and beam and pomp of it were there only to bring out the contrast with the young beauty beside him. It was sturdy to accentuate her slightness — as if to show what a breeze could be generated by a butterfly's wing.

He sat perfectly quiet, his nerves in wild clamor, afraid that if he moved he would find her irresistibly in his arms. Two tears had rolled down her wet face and trembled on her upper lip.

"I'm more beautiful than anybody else," she said brokenly. "Why can't I be happy?" Her moist eyes tore at his stability — mouth turned slowly downward with an exquisite sadness. "I'd like to marry you if you'll have me, Dexter. I suppose you think I'm not worth having but I'll be so beautiful for you, Dexter."

A million phrases of anger, of pride, of passion, of hatred, of tenderness fought on his lips. Then a perfect wave of emotion washed over him, carrying off with it a sediment of wisdom, of convention, of doubt, of honor. This was his girl who was speaking, his own, his beautiful, his pride.

"Won't you come in?" he heard her draw in her breath sharply.

Waiting.

"All right," his voice was trembling, "I'll come in."

It seems strange to say that neither when it was over nor a long time afterward did he regret that night. Looking at it from the perspective of ten years, the fact that Judy's flare for him endured just one month seemed of little importance. Nor did it matter that by his yielding he subjected himself to a deeper agony in the end and gave serious hurt to Irene Scheerer and to Irene's parents who had befriended him. There was nothing sufficiently pictorial about Irene's grief to stamp itself on his mind.

Dexter was at bottom hard-minded. The attitude of the city on his action was of no importance to him, not because he was going to leave the city, but because any outside attitude on the situation seemed superficial. He was completely indifferent to popular opinion. Nor, when he had seen that it was no use, that he did not possess in himself the power to move fundamentally or to hold Judy Jones, did he bear any malice toward her. He loved her and he would love her until the day he was too old for loving — but he could not have her. So he tasted the deep pain that is reserved only for the strong, just as he had tasted for a little while the deep happiness.

Even the ultimate falsity of the grounds upon which Judy terminated the engagement — that she did not want to "take him away" from Irene, that it was on her conscience — did not revolt him. He was beyond any revulsion or any amusement.

He went east in February with the intention of selling out his laundries and settling in New York — but the war came to America in March and changed his plans. He returned to the West, handed over the management of the business to his partner and went into the first officers' training camp in late April. He was one of those young thousands who greeted the war with a certain amount of relief, welcoming the liberation from webs of tangled emotion.

This story is not his biography, remember, although things creep into it which have nothing to do with those dreams he had when he was young. We are almost done with them and with him now. There is only one more incident to be related here and it happens seven years farther on.

It took place in New York, where he had done well — so well that there were no barriers too high for him now. He was thirty-two years old, and, except for one flying trip immediately after the war, he had not been west in seven years. A man named Devlin from Detroit came into his office to see him in a business way, and then and there this incident occurred, and closed out, so to speak, this particular side of his life.

"So you're from the Middle West," said the man Devlin with careless curiosity. "That's funny — I thought men like you were probably born and raised on Wall Street. You know — wife of one of my best friends in Detroit came from your city. I was an usher at the wedding."

Dexter waited with no apprehension of what was coming. There was a magic that his city would never lose for him. Just as Judy's house had always seemed to him more mysterious and gay than other houses, so his dream of the city itself, now that he had gone from it, was pervaded with a melancholy beauty.

"Judy Simms," said Devlin with no particular interest. "Judy Jones she was once."

"Yes, I knew her." A dull impatience spread over him. He had heard, of course, that she was married, — perhaps deliberately he had heard no more.

"Awfully nice girl," brooded Devlin, meaninglessly. "I'm sort of sorry for her."

"Why?" Something in Dexter was alert, receptive, at once.

"Oh, Joe Simms has gone to pieces in a way. I don't mean he beats her, you understand, or anything like that. But he drinks and runs around —— "

"Doesn't she run around?"

"No. Stays at home with her kids."

"Oh."

"She's a little too old for him," said Devlin.

"Too old!" cried Dexter. "Why man, she's only twenty-seven."

He was possessed with a wild notion of rushing out into the streets and taking a train to Detroit. He rose to his feet, spasmodically, involuntarily.

"I guess you're busy," Devlin apologized quickly. "I didn't realize —— "

"No, I'm not busy," said Dexter, steadying his voice, "I'm not busy at all. Not busy at all. Did you say she was — twenty-seven. No, I said she was twenty-seven."

"Yes, you did," agreed Devlin drily.

"Go on, then. Go on."

"What do you mean?"

"About Judy Jones."

Devlin looked at him helplessly.

"Well, that's — I told you all there is to it. He treats her like the devil. Oh, they're not going to get divorced or anything. When he's particularly outrageous she forgives him. In fact, I'm inclined to think she loves him. She was a pretty girl when she first came to Detroit."

A pretty girl! The phrase struck Dexter as ludicrous.

"Isn't she — a pretty girl any more?"

"Oh, she's all right."

"Look here," said Dexter, sitting down suddenly. "I don't understand. You say she was a 'pretty girl' and now you say she's 'all right.' I don't understand what you mean — Judy Jones wasn't a pretty girl, at all. She was a great beauty. Why, I knew her, I knew her. She was —— "

Devlin laughed pleasantly.

"I'm not trying to start a row," he said. "I think Judy's a nice girl and I like her. I can't understand how a man like Joe Simms could fall madly in love with her, but he did." Then he added, "Most of the women like her."

Dexter looked closely at Devlin, thinking wildly that there must be a reason for this, some insensitivity in the man or some private malice.

"Lots of women fade just-like-that," Devlin snapped his fingers. "You must have seen it happen. Perhaps I've forgotten how pretty she was at her wedding. I've seen her so much since then, you see. She has nice eyes."

A sort of dullness settled down upon Dexter. For the first time in his life he felt like getting very drunk. He knew that he was laughing loudly at something Devlin had said but he did not know what it was or why it was funny. When Devlin went, in a few minutes, he lay down on his lounge and looked out the window at the New York skyline into which the sun was sinking in dull lovely shades of pink and gold.

He had thought that having nothing else to lose he was invulnerable at last —

but he knew that he had just lost something more, as surely as if he had married Judy Jones and seen her fade away before his eyes.

The dream was gone. Something had been taken from him. In a sort of panic he pushed the palms of his hands into his eyes and tried to bring up a picture of the waters lapping at Lake Erminie and the moonlit verandah, and gingham on the golf links and the dry sun and the gold color of her neck's soft down. And her mouth damp to his kisses and her eyes plaintive with melancholy and her freshness like new fine linen in the morning. Why, these things were no longer in the world. They had existed and they existed no more.

For the first time in years the tears were streaming down his face. But they were for himself now. He did not care about mouth and eyes and moving hands. He wanted to care and he could not care. For he had gone away and he could never go back any more. The gates were closed, the sun was gone down and there was no beauty but the gray beauty of steel that withstands all time. Even the grief he could have borne was left behind in the country of illusion, of youth, of the richness of life, where his winter dreams had flourished.

"Long ago," he said, "long ago, there was something in me, but now that thing is gone. Now that thing is gone, that thing is gone. I cannot cry. I cannot care. That thing will come back no more."

Also by Coyote Canyon Press

Three Novels by the Brontë Sisters

Jane Eyre, Wuthering Heights, and Agnes Grey

Also by Coyote Canyon Press

Three Soldiers

by John Dos Passos

A gripping exploration of desertion and violence, and the dehumanizing effects of a regimented war machine on ordinary soldiers.

CPSIA information can be obtained
at www.ICGtesting.com
Printed in the USA
LVHW091217081218
599745LV00001B/146/P

9 780982 1